W9-AHF-952

Praise for Jan Kjærstad

"Go on, try something different—this book is witty, savage, elegant and strange—and comes from Norway's leading writer. Hugely entertaining."

—*The Times* (London)

"Whimsically Sterneian, with a dark hint of Paul Auster and a dash of Márquez, breezily narrated by Tom Robbins. . . . Grandly entertaining."

—*Daily Telegraph* (London)

"I read the Norwegian writer Jan Kjærstad's energetic blast of a novel, *The Seducer*. . . . It's an irresistibly playful romp, by turns mischievous, manipulative, intellectual, and bluntly sensual."

—Ali Smith, Books of the Year, *Times Literary Supplement* (London)

"Jan Kjærstad is a Viking of literature."

—Anna Paterson, *Independent* (London)

"Veering from the broadly comic to the beautifully sad, with detours for deadpan meditations on the 'Norwegian national character,' this book is not just big, but big-hearted."

—*New York Times*

"One of the most influential writers of his generation. Say his name, and I think of Milan Kundera, Martin Amis, and Frank Zappa."

—Linn Ullmann

"With more mystery and open questions (from the identity of the woman with all the Wergeland-tales to why Wergeland's wife was murdered), *The Conqueror* eventually also becomes more gripping and rewarding than *The Seducer*. Certainly worthwhile."

—Michael Orthofer, Complete Review

Other Works by Jan Kjærstad

In English Translation

The Seducer
The Discoverer

In Norwegian

FICTION

Kloden dreier stille rundt (The Earth Turns Quietly)
Speil (Mirrors)
Homo Falsus eller det perfekte mord (Homo Falsus or the Perfect Murder)
Det store eventyret (The Great Fairy Tale)
Rand (Brink)
Tegn til kjaerlighet (Signs for Love)
Kongen av Europa (The King of Europe)

ESSAYS

Menneskets matrise (The Matrix of Man)
Menneskets felt (The Human Sphere)

PICTURE BOOKS

Jakten på de skjulte vaffelhjertene (The Hunt for the Hidden Waffle Hearts)
Hos Sheherasad, fantasiens droning (With Sheherazade, Imagination's Queen)

THE CONQUEROR

a novel

JAN KJÆRSTAD

Translated from the Norwegian
by Barbara Haveland

Originally published by H. Aschehoug & Co., Oslo as *Erobreren*, 1996

Published by arrangement with H. Aschehoug & Co. and Arcadia Books

First U.S. edition, 2009

Library of Congress Control Number: 2008926606
ISBN-13: 978-1-934824-03-0 / ISBN-10: 1-934824-03-8

Printed on acid-free paper in the United States of America.

Text set in Bembo, an old-style serif typeface based upon face cuts by Francesco Griffo that were first printed in 1496.

Design by N. J. Furl

Open Letter is the University of Rochester's nonprofit, literary translation press:
Lattimore Hall 411, Box 270082, Rochester, NY 14627

www.openletterbooks.org

THE CONQUEROR

This Is Your Life

"I thought he was going to rape me," the woman said, reporting the incident later. No point beating about the bush: we might as well begin at the end, or the beginning of the end. So, before the bout of erotic vertigo in the chemist's shop, even before the story of the stinking monster in the basement, we have to start with this man, as he sits in the back of a taxi driving through a summery Oslo night; on the surface a perfectly ordinary situation, a situation this man has been in thousands of times before, the rule more than the exception: he is on his way home, late at night in a taxi.

Initially the driver, a woman, an attractive woman, an English undergraduate who did the odd shift, had only caught a glimpse of the man who flagged down her cab in the city center, not far from a bar, and muttered something about Bergen, leading her to think, to begin with, that she had picked up a fare to the west coast—what a fantastic piece of luck—until she realized that of course he meant Bergensveien, in Grorud, because at that same moment she recognized him. The person in the back seat was one of those few Norwegians who did not need to give his address, who could, if they wished, simply say: "Take me home."

She was thrilled, and not a little proud of the fact that, of all the possible cabs for hire on the streets, he should have chosen hers; she sneaked a peek at him in the mirror, noted that he had not bothered to fasten his seatbelt, as if seatbelts were, in his case, unnecessary; he sat there with a happy, almost beatific, smile on his face like he was on a high, had just been presented with a grand award or something. She couldn't wait to tell her friends, her fellow taxi drivers: guess who I drove home the other night, no, honestly, it was *him*. She kept peeking in the mirror, racking her brains for something to say, something about one of his programs, a compliment that wouldn't sound as glib as all the other words of praise that were no doubt heaped on him every day. For, at a time when television turned everything of any importance into entertainment, when television, even Norwegian television, was dominated by mindless game shows and quiz programs, gushing chat shows and primitive debates: confirming, in other words, every misanthrope's assertions that all the people want is bread and circuses—he, her passenger, had restored her faith in television as an art form in its own right. She had something on the tip of her tongue, something she felt was pretty original, something about his program on Sonja Henie, about how suggestive they were, those pirouettes and the ice flying up, how erotic, she had the urge to add, although she didn't know if she dared. It would be like addressing His Majesty the King. Because the man in the back seat was none other than Jonas Wergeland.

They drove along Trondheimsveien, across Carl Berners plass. She hoped he had noticed the paperback copy of D.H. Lawrence's *The Rainbow* lying between the two front seats, a book which she read when she was sitting on the rank. The scent of a restaurant filled the cab: spices, wine, cigars, he had obviously just risen from an excellent dinner. She glanced in the mirror, could no longer make out his features, his face lay in shadow, it looked blank. She remembered with what interest and delight—yes, delight—she had watched *This Is Your Life* not that long ago, on the evening when Jonas Wergeland was the star guest, the youngest ever; what a show that was, a glittering tribute for which everybody had turned out, from an unwontedly animated Minister for the Arts to the legendary writer Axel Stranger; what a life, she had thought, what a man. As if to heighten the thrill she looked in the mirror again, but there was something about the look in his eyes, his whole expression, which did not fit with the face she knew from the television screen, from *This Is Your Life*, the face that had so often held her mesmerized, a face she had even fantasized about, dreamed of, had rude thoughts about.

And just as they are approaching the Sinsen junction, the largest intersection in Norway, it happens. At first all she, the driver, hears are some odd sounds, a kind of gurgling, then she realizes what is happening and pulls to an abrupt halt on the hard shoulder. But it is too late. Jonas Wergeland throws up, a jet of vomit shoots from his mouth, hitting her on the back of the head at the point where the headrest doesn't block the spray, and even then, even as she feels this slimy, foul-smelling substance on her own skin and sees, out of the corner of her eye, how the cover of *The Rainbow* too, has been splattered with sick, she thinks that he must have been taken ill; she has only one thought in her head, she must help him, she is full of concern, tenderness, because she is in his debt, in debt to a man who has caused her to change her views on many things, on the nature of Norway, possibly even on the nature of life itself; she pictures to herself how this dramatic turn of events will only make the story that much better. Just then she catches sight of his face again, two eyes staring at her in the mirror, and she realizes that he is not ill, but drunk, as pissed out of his skull as anybody can be, and not just with alcohol but with hate.

Before she could do a thing, it happened again. Slumped in the back seat, Jonas Wergeland spewed out the contents of his stomach, the stream broken only by short pauses to gasp for breath. He didn't even seem to be aware that he was throwing up. He was like an out-of-hand fire hose, writhing and spraying in all directions. Before she could get out and open the door for him, he had filled the inside of the Mercedes with an unappetizing swill—she could already hear the dressing-down she was going to get from the owner: "Miss Kielland, do you realize that I have just had the inside of this car thoroughly cleaned by Økern Auto Cosmetic?"

But at that moment she was more concerned about Jonas Wergeland, as he fell out of the cab, mumbling and laughing to himself. "My television programs are just as useless as the pyramids," he snorted. "They stay in the desert, jackals piss at their foot and the bourgeoisie climb up on them." Then he raised his head: "Gustave Flaubert," he bawled. "I pinched that from Flaubert, so I bloody did." As if to show that his wits weren't totally befuddled, that there was still something going on up there, he pointed to a sign hanging over the entrance to a restaurant across the street. "Rendezvous," it said. "I met a girl there once," he said, even as he was racked by another violent and painful bout of retching, as if he had toadstools in his stomach and was trying to bring them up. And then, in an unfamiliar, dark, rasping tone: "To hell with all girls."

What was he thinking? What was going on inside Jonas Wergeland's head? I know. I know everything, almost everything. It is a bright summer's night in June. There lies Jonas Wergeland, just down the road from Aker Hospital where he was born, just down the road from the Sinsen junction, Norway's largest interchange, an enormous loop of concrete and tarmac. As a child his heart had always sung when he had driven across here, this point where Oslo spread out beneath him, presented the illusion of itself as a glittering metropolis, rich in possibilities. And now he lay sprawled on that very spot, on high and yet laid low, and felt as if he were spewing over Oslo, over the whole of Norway, in fact.

The taxi driver didn't know which way to turn. She noticed that his jacket was spattered with damp stains, bits of food. It was a slightly old-fashioned jacket and one she recognized: one that, on numerous television chat shows, had lent him the air of an English gentleman. She felt like a witness to an act of blasphemy. "I would honestly never have thought this of you, Mr. Wergeland," she said, for want of anything better, and with a hint of sharpness. "I really did not expect this of you."

In response he discharged a final volley of vomit, a solid mixture of bile and food. There was something about the illusory density of this stream of vomit that put her in mind of films about exorcism, made her think that Jonas Wergeland was acting like a man possessed. "I've been celebrating," he grunted, gazing curiously at the chunks of partially digested lamb and Brussels sprouts in the claret-colored puddle on the ground. "I've been celebrating a great deed," he said as she struggled to haul him into a sitting position, propped up against the wheel of the cab. She looked down at herself. Her clothes were in an awful mess. She was just wondering what she was going to say to the owner of the taxi, what she was going to say to anybody, when Jonas Wergeland keeled over again, to land with his face in his own vomit.

It could have ended there, as a minor—still and all, just a minor—scandal, but then he started shouting, first hurling abuse at the woman who was trying to pick him up. "Get away from me, you fucking whore," he snarled, pulling himself to his feet unaided, as if he had suddenly sobered up. He stood facing her with a menacing look in his eyes—it was at this moment that the thought of rape crossed her mind. And as he stood there he began to hiss something that at first she could not make out, but which gradually became clearer: "I killed a man," he said. "I killed a man, d'you hear? I kicked the balls off him, the bastard."

Then his legs gave way again, he slumped against the wheel. It was a bright summer's night in June, just down the road from the Sinsen junction. A taxi driver stood looking down on Jonas Wergeland, a man who, at a time when television channels had to have a logo up in the corner of the screen so you could tell them apart, at a time when television seemed intent only on satisfying mankind's basest needs, suddenly appeared on the scene and showed her, showed everyone that television could raise their level of cultivation. A young Norwegian woman, a viewer, stood there sadly regarding a man she admired, sitting on the ground in his own vomit, cursing and swearing. "It was as though I was suddenly looking at Dr. Jekyll and Mr. Hyde," she said later. "Or rather, that he was Mr. Hyde, that the Dr. Jekyll bit was just something he had persuaded me to believe in for a long time." She was, as I mentioned earlier, studying English, so this analogy had not been plucked entirely out of thin air.

"I made mincemeat of the son of a bitch," Jonas Wergeland gibbered, laughing all the while—laughing and laughing, roaring with laughter if, that is, he wasn't sobbing. "I'm only sorry I didn't cut off his dick while I was at it!"

The woman had long since called dispatch. She crouched down beside Jonas Wergeland, who now seemed almost out for the count, and she wept. She wept because she had seen something precious, something she truly cared about, shattered. And his last words to her before help arrives, as he opens his eyes and fixes his gaze on the pale-blue, taxi company shirt are: "By Christ, you've got great tits."

The Whole World in His Hand

Jonas and the female breast—it's a long story altogether, that of men and breasts. In Jonas's case, however, it had something to do with his brother. I've given a lot of thought as to who might have been the most important person in Jonas Wergeland's life—a question central to our undertaking—and it would not surprise me to find that it was his brother Daniel, one year his senior. Daniel—dedicated hypocrite that he was—was, after all, the bane of Jonas's life, so to speak. I will have ample opportunity to touch on Daniel's bizarre career later, but first I must address this issue of the breasts.

No matter how different they might have been, throughout their adolescence Daniel and Jonas had one common interest: tits. Boys have different fetishes, but for the brothers, breasts constituted the very crux of life. Scientists have propounded the theory that the female mammary glands got bigger as human beings began to walk more upright, taking over from the backside as the main focus of attraction during the mating season. Daniel and Jonas were living proof that this theory has much to recommend it. The sight of breasts, anytime, anywhere, quite simply set the hormones churning, within Daniel especially; something clicked inside his head. A mere glimpse of the cleavage between two breasts was enough. Newspaper and magazine ads for bras made him positively sick with excitement. Jonas always felt that Daniel's impressive attempts to become Norway's skiing king, the self-inflicted torture of trekking hundreds of miles across the hills around Oslo winter after winter, dated from the day when he saw an old photograph from the Cortina Winter Olympics of 1956, of Hallgeir Brenden, winner of the 15-kilometer cross-country event, with his arms round Sophia Loren's tits. Daniel lived, not in *Sophie's World*, but in Sophia's.

Sophia, Sophia, tits as wisdom.

Every evening for years Daniel would lie in bed and read aloud to Jonas; he read from two books in particular, which he had in some mysterious way got hold of and which he kept hidden inside the air vent in the wall of their room, as if to symbolize that these books represented a sort of safety valve for the pressure that was playing havoc with the boys: these were Agnar Mykle's *Lasso Around the Moon* and *Song of the Red Ruby*. Daniel read certain passages so often, and with such feeling, that Jonas would never forget Mykle's song of praise to breasts of all shapes and sizes, from the modest: "Her small breasts under the white jersey had a lovely shape, like the bowl of a champagne glass," to the more extravagant: "Her breasts were like explosives under her sweater, they looked as if they would blow up were anyone to touch the small, protruding detonator on each one." These uncommonly exalted bedtime readings, all these rousing metaphors, left Jonas, early on, with a suspicion—if not a vision—that, when all is said and done, eroticism and sexuality had to do with imagination and leaps of thought.

Many a time too, Daniel would lie panting in the top bunk, speculating on which material constituted the most provocative wrapping for breasts: what would form the optimum stage curtain for this greatest of all dramas. Silk? Flannel? Soft hide? Gleaming leather? Daniel could spend a whole night enlarging upon the cinematic cliché of "a wet shirt clinging to the skin." Jonas suggested string vests, which would give the breasts the appearance of plump fruit in a net shopping bag. Daniel, for his part—where do they get it from?—was partial to wool. Each time he went to the lavatory, with that characteristic glazed look in his eyes, and turned the key in the lock, Jonas knew that his big brother had seen one of the estate's well-built young mothers go jiggling past in a distractingly tight sweater.

Jonas, too, had his secrets: he daydreamed of how a breast would feel against the palm of the hand, he fantasized about its probable smoothness and warmth and wondered whether it would really be as Daniel said—a thought which prompted a dangerously warm flutter in the pit of the stomach: that a breast grew firm when touched, almost coagulated, to use a word he learned later in chemistry class; and above all perhaps, inspired by Agnar Mykle, he dreamed of nipples, their possible rigidity under the fingertip, like a switch; the mere thought caused his pelvic region to swell with anticipation. So potent was this fantasy that, when the time was ripe, Jonas attempted what could be said to be a pretty reckless marriage by capture.

This happened after Margrete, his first great love, had—as he saw it—"gone to blazes," having dumped him in the most ignominious fashion before moving abroad. You had to pick yourself up. There were other girls. Jonas lived in Grorud, in northeast Oslo, which at that time was developing into an ever more populous satellite town. He had long had his eye on Anne Beate Corneliussen, known among the boys simply as the ABC of Sex. For if Anne Beate was remarkable for anything it was the two gravitational points under her jersey. Apples fell to the ground, and the boys' eyes fell on Anne Beate's breasts. She was, in short, the sort of girl who automatically becomes a drum majorette and marches ahead of the boys' band in a tight uniform, holding that baton—oh, mind-boggling thought—with a firm, acrobatic grip and looking as though she had full control over the entire troop of boys, imperiously decreeing when they should raise their instruments and start to play.

On ordinary days Anne Beate often wore a traditional Setesdal sweater, and maybe it was its beautiful pattern which made Jonas feel that Anne Beate's tits had an ornate look about them, that their swelling contours underneath her jersey were somehow the embodiment of the perfect breast's form, just as the meter rod in Paris was the ur-prototype of a meter. Jonas was devoutly, or perhaps more accurately, hormonally convinced that the greatest joy in the world would be granted to whoever was permitted to lay hands on those breasts. Suddenly he remembered a song from Sunday School: "He's got the whole world in his hands." Jonas knew that that was just how it must feel.

Ironically, two obstacles lay between Jonas and the two objects of his dreams. For one thing, Anne Beate Corneliussen, the ABC of Sex, was alarmingly fickle and unpredictable. On one occasion, when a certain bold lad plucked up the courage to make an impertinent suggestion as they were walking through the front gate of Grorud Elementary School, she calmly removed his glasses, snapped them in two, then stamped on them, leaving the hapless lad to grope his way home, more or less blindly. Secondly, and possibly worse, she was sort of going out with Frank Stenersen, or Frankenstein as he was known, since children—like a lot of adults—confuse Dr. Frankenstein with Frankenstein's monster. Frank was nicknamed Frankenstein because of his size and his somewhat formidable appearance, to which a barbwire-like dental brace added a particularly striking touch. In other words, Anne Beate preferred the tougher lads, the kind with Beatles boots and long hair, who smoked and swapped condoms in the bike shed.

Frank Stenersen fitted this profile perfectly, his meanness was the stuff of legend; he had a soul like a bloody beefsteak. Every other day he earned himself a visit to the headmaster, on one occasion because, in the dining room, he had gone so far as to deface the portrait of Trygve Lie, Grorud's famous son, with a stump of carrot. The most glaring example of his brutality was, however, the rumor that he had a fondness for hunting for songbirds' nests so that he could smash the eggs, those harmless little blue eggs. Who could do such a thing? To cap it all—although perhaps this really explained it all—his parents were communists. And everybody knows that to be a member of the NKP, the Norwegian Communist Party, in the sixties was truly to be an outsider; it was tantamount to hanging a sign on your door proclaiming utter godlessness.

How does one become a conqueror?

Jonas wanted to try to be one; he wanted to act like one of the tough guys, wanted to act big in front of Anne Beate Corneliussen, the ABC of Sex. He commenced his offensive during the autumn when they were in eighth grade, during a curious event known as "Get in on the Act." Jonas, who normally never performed in public, not even to play the piano, which he did rather well, had put his name down for this, and after having presented something quite different, something safe, at rehearsal, he made his move when they went live, so to speak, on the evening itself, in a stuffy gym hall so jam-packed that people were hanging from the wall-bars. Jonas did a kind of stand-up comedy act, with a routine that, in essence, involved reading out various fictitious letters to the headmaster from parents and fellow pupils. He put on a different voice for each letter, according to who had supposedly sent it, eliciting loud whoops and cheers from the audience—and from the other eighth graders in particular. The success of his turn may have been due not so much to the originality of his script, but to the lamentably low standard of the other acts. But if truth be told, Jonas had developed a certain talent for putting on different voices. This dated from the days when he had produced radio plays—a subject to which I shall return—and he won a well-merited round of applause for a lisping rendition of a letter complaining about how shocking it was, a proper disgrace to the school, that Miss Bergersen should have been seen coming out of Mr. Haugen's room with her hair all mussed up during last year's class trip. That this was not so far from the truth did not make the "letter" any the less piquant, nor did the fact that those lisping tones could so easily be traced to the staff room. The following lines were uttered through pinched nostrils, as Jonas mimicked one prim mamma: "Dear Headmaster: Please ask Miss Rauland to stop wearing blouses made from transparent fabric—my little Gunnar is forever locking himself in the bathroom these days." Stamping and clapping. Poor Guggen managed to slip out during the ensuing uproar. For a few seconds Jonas felt as if he had the hall, nay the whole world, in the palm of his hand.

And it worked. Jonas actually got to speak to Anne Beate. She sauntered up to him while he was at the drinking fountain during the lunch break the following day, bent her head down next to his and placed her fingers over the neighboring holes to make the jet of water leap higher. Out of the corner of his eye Jonas saw how her Setesdal sweater bulged under her open anorak. "Why are you so interested in your English teacher when you could be friends with me?" she said through moist lips. "Why don't we get together after school?" And when Jonas, after two seconds' thought, suggested that they meet in the basement of his block of flats, she agreed without hesitation, and Jonas knew what she was indirectly agreeing to: he would get to feel her tits.

During the last classes of the day he wasn't really there. He was an astronaut just before lift-off. He was going to see the far side of the moon. He was going to hold Venus and Jupiter in his hands. And Frankenstein didn't know a thing. That he might ever find out was not something Jonas wanted to think about. But he couldn't back out now; this was, as a Norwegian writer once put it, the whisper of the blood and the prayer of the bones, this was his chance, at long last, to discover for himself how "her ripe breasts shot out like lightning bolts from her body," as Daniel had read, whispered, from the top bunk, his nose buried in a book by Agnar Mykle. Jonas ran all the way home from school. Anne Beate had finished school an hour before him, he saw her bike parked outside the entry—balloon tires, everything about her was big; he opened the door and took a deep breath before descending into the underworld.

The basements. Many a tale could be told of the gloomy basements of Solhaug, the housing estate where Jonas grew up. They had served as the burial chambers inside pyramids where Jonas and Little Eagle had hunted for treasure, equipped with intricately drawn maps, scorched at the edges. They had been dripping caves inhabited by beasts and dragons, especially dragons. Those basements had formed the setting for the most wordless mystery plays, the venue for the meetings of secret clubs, where code words were whispered over flickering candle flames and rings set with glass diamonds changed fingers. They had been bunkers, especially after the weighty bombproof doors were installed—a delayed result of the Cold War. It is, by the way, quite amazing when one thinks, today, of all those bombproof doors and bomb shelters that suddenly became mandatory. The whole of Norway prepared for a life in the catacombs. Because it has already been forgotten that, although the fifties and sixties may in many ways have seemed a time of optimism, people—or at any rate all those who kept abreast of things—really did believe that an atom bomb could be dropped at any minute; it was an unpleasant fact of life, giving rise to a constant sense of insecurity which rendered the growing prosperity somehow even more intense.

So, behind those bombproof doors, Jonas and Little Eagle had also been the sole survivors, new versions of Robinson Crusoe and Friday, consigned to living in a dark, desolate basement. But now Jonas was willingly going to let himself be bombarded. He thought of the explosion that would occur as he laid his hands on Anne Beate. "Her breasts were like explosives under her jersey . . ."

He would not, of course, switch on the light, that went without saying. He closed the door, heard the hollow echo resound down the basement passage, the sort of sound used in films to create a sense of dread, of claustrophobia. It was cold. It was pitch-dark. The air was so fraught with tension that he could hardly breathe. He bit his lip, groped his way along the walls in which wooden doors, rough and flaking, punctuated the stippled surface at regular intervals.

They had arranged to meet in the center, on a landing that opened onto the next basement passage. His whole body was one great, pounding heart. Something was about to happen. He could hear a buzzing sound, like that from a transformer. Sensed danger. Lightning bolts shooting from breasts. High voltage. Something was about to happen. Two big tits, two hard nipples, switches that would turn his life around. He caught a whiff of something, the scent of an animal, a wild beast. Woman, he thought. A willing woman.

Something was wrong. But he could not turn round. He had to fight. He knew now what it was. He was ready to fight and not, in fact, afraid. He was all but expecting to be tackled from behind, for his legs to be knocked from under him. Nothing happened. He heard heavy breathing in the darkness. A fury. A fury that breathed. He was prepared to run into a body but was caught completely unawares by a fierce grip. A demonstration of raw power. A huge hand closes around his balls and pushes him up against the wall, a grip that holds him there, his limbs are paralyzed. He knows who has him pinned up against the wall. Frank Stenersen. A communist, a real, live communist, and inside the bomb shelter. What one fears most of all. An enemy within.

Frank Stenersen. Frankenstein. There was no doubt about it. A monster on some kind of high, induced by an adrenalin-coursing lust for revenge. The other's foul breath rammed Jonas's nostrils; he thought to himself that the stench must stem from bits of food stuck between the metal wires of his brace. Then he felt the grip on his balls tighten and a sickening pain spread throughout his body. Every boy knows what I'm talking about, every one who has been rammed in the groin by a football or a knee. "Please," Jonas gasped. "Try to talk your way out of this," Frankenstein hissed through the wiring on his teeth. "Stop messing about," Jonas groaned. "So you wanted to grope Anne Beate's tits, did you?" Frankenstein said, squeezing harder, a little bit harder all the time. Jonas thought of Frankenstein and the story about the birds' eggs. A soft squeal of pain escaped him. The pain was so bad that he saw stars in the darkness. Jonas felt that this entity that was him was merely a fragile illusion, that a firm grip on his balls was all it took to shatter it. "Write a letter to the Head about this, you lousy little prick!" snarled Frankenstein. He squeezed still tighter for a second, before letting go—tossed Jonas aside like a fish with a broken neck. Jonas heard footsteps, heard the heavy bombproof door open and bang shut again. He lay there in the darkness, weeping, consoling himself with the fact that there had been no one to see. I ought perhaps to add that, after this incident, Jonas would always feel a tightening of his testicles whenever he found himself in a tricky situation, not only that, but a contraction of his balls could actually warn him that trouble was brewing. Like a Geiger counter detecting uranium, his testicles signalled danger.

Jonas got up, tottered over to the door, afraid for a moment that he had been locked in; he screwed up his eyes against the light, dragged himself up the steps. It seemed to him that he climbed upwards and upwards, that he made the ascent of something more than just a flight of steps leading to an exit. He had been dead, and now he was alive again. Either that or he had undergone a transformation, emerged as another person. And already at this point, long before he would learn that Frankenstein was not the name of the monster but of its creator, Jonas divined that by shooting a bolt of lightning through his balls, as it were, Frank Stenersen had turned him into a monster, or more accurately: had made him see that he had always been a beast, that the drool-making thought of conquering two strutting breasts was, at heart, monstrous. And above all, in a flash, when the pain was its height, Jonas Wergeland had perceived how dangerous, how wonderfully fiendish and artfully treacherous and yet how indescribably delightful and desirable and, not least, mysterious, girls were.

As Jonas staggered like a cripple out into the light, he realized that Frankenstein's squeezing of his balls was not so much a punishment for chatting up Anne Beate as the penalty for having shown off on stage. For having made a boast that he could not live up to or for which he was not prepared to take the consequences. So even then, at the age of thirteen, Jonas Wergeland ought to have understood that performing in public, in the strangest, most roundabout ways, can get your balls in a squeeze.

Carl the Great

Is it possible to find a beginning, something that might have prepared us for the episode that shook, nay, stunned the whole of Norway? Might it lie in something as innocent as a journey abroad?

When, after four days surrounded by nothing but water, Jonas Wergeland stood on the deck and watched the green island slowly rise up out of the sea before him, truly rise up, as if it had been made for this moment, it occurred to him that this must have been how Columbus felt when he spied the first islands of the Caribbean—although he had been sailing for much longer and towards a quite different destination. Jonas had, nonetheless, the feeling that he was approaching an unknown continent. And as they slipped through the opening in the coral reef and found themselves, all at once, in Apia harbor, encircled by greenery, a green as bright as the slope running up to peaks he could not see—hidden as they were behind the first range of hills—the island on which he was about to set foot seemed to him like another Eden, a fresh start.

Why did Jonas Wergeland travel?

One day, Professor, someone will write a weighty treatise on the influence of Carl Barks on generations of Europeans. That's right: Carl Barks—not Karl Marx. No one should be surprised when, one day, some individual becomes, say, Secretary-General of the United Nations and, to the question as to what his or her greatest influences have been, does not, as expected, say *The Imitation of Christ* by Thomas à Kempis or the works of Leo Tolstoy but quite simply replies: some cartoon ducks. In other words: those incomparable stories from the pen of American chicken farmer Carl Barks.

Jonas read very, very little as a child and adolescent, but he did devour every single Donald Duck comic issued from the fifties until well into the sixties—for reasons to which I shall return—and although he knew nothing about the contributing writers and illustrators, it was Carl Barks's strips which made the biggest impact on him. So much so that certain stories were read as many as a hundred times, to the point where he knew them by heart; one might almost say they settled themselves as ballast inside him. Just as children of an earlier age had their hymns down pat, verse upon verse, Jonas knew the adventures of Donald Duck. Carl Barks opened wide the door not only onto the history of the world, including all its myths and legends, but also onto its geography. The countless expeditions Jonas undertook in the company of Barks's heroes represented a grand tour not unlike that made by Niels Holgersson and his geese. Barks's comic strips presented a first impression of regions and countries that never faded from Jonas's mind. Considered from a certain angle, it is no exaggeration to say that it was Carl Barks who gave Jonas the urge to travel and to travel far.

Of all Carl Barks's fantasies, there were few which Jonas liked better than those involving journeys to faraway places, to virtual Utopias no one knew existed: for example, that famed epic of the trip to Tralla La in the Himalayas, where money was unheard of, or the expedition into the forests of the pygmy Indians who talked in rhyme; or the trek into the mists of the Andes, where they stumbled upon the weird geometric universe of the square people. But Jonas also had a penchant for some of the shorter traveler's tales, especially those that took Carl Barks's trouser-less ducks to the isles of the South Seas, to islands where the people sang "Aloha oe!" and wealth was measured in coconuts. He particularly enjoyed the hair-raising trip to Tabu Yama, a volcanic island, where Uncle Scrooge had gone to search for black pearls in the lagoon.

I think, therefore, it is safe to say that Jonas Wergeland went—albeit unwittingly—to Polynesia to look for Carl Barks or to compare Carl Barks's creations with the real thing, although I'm sure this is not the reason he would have given. On this, one of his first long trips in the seventies, his prime aim was to visit a place that was as unspoiled as possible, relatively speaking at least. And when he stood by the rail of the boat, looking towards Apia and those green hillsides, the landscape really did seem to have a virginal air about it, the air of some last remaining paradise: Upolu, Apia, Utopia. But no sooner had that ostensible goal been achieved than he realized that he did not, in fact, have any idea why he had come here. In a way—and this is how Jonas Wergeland regarded most of his travels—he went there to discover why he had gone there.

Samoa may seem a long way away, Professor: very far, at any rate from everyday life in Norway. But we live in an age when all countries have become a part of all other countries. So I would just like to mention here that Samoa was, of course, not as unspoiled as Jonas Wergeland had thought or hoped: that Samoa has also had its part to play in the history of Norway. For it was here that a Norwegian by the name of Erik Dammann came to stay with his family for a while in the sixties, for much the same reason that Uncle Scrooge went to Tralla La, and to some extent it was here that he gained the insight which, not long afterwards, inspired him to write a book and, prompted by the overwhelming response to this book, to found a popular movement calling itself "The Future In Our Hands," one of the oddest phenomena in the history of post-war Norway, a movement which, at its height at any rate, seemed to suggest that a surprisingly large number of Norwegians were receptive to the idea of another way of life and a very different global distribution of commodities. So Samoa could, in fact, be seen as the starting point for this movement; it might not be going too far, either, to say that Erik Dammann was actually trying to turn the whole of Norway into another Samoa. Jonas's brother Daniel got particularly carried away—as was his wont—by such prospects for a couple of years, a phase which more or less overlapped with his involvement with the more extreme and far more puritanical and ascetic variant of these same ideals, namely, the Marxist-Leninist movement. Daniel subscribed to the more practical aspects of Dammann's credo with a fanatical fervour; he even gave up drinking Coca-Cola, something which, considering the amount of Coke he consumed at that time, must be regarded as the doughtiest of all his doughty feats in life and indeed one of the few times when, opportunistic bastard that he was, he actually made a sacrifice.

Jonas Wergeland was, however, blissfully ignorant of Erik Dammann's links with Samoa as he strolled along Beach Road, the main thoroughfare in Apia, looking for somewhere cheaper to stay than Aggie Grey's Hotel. It was hot and humid, and a sweet scent filled the air—not from spices, but from flowers. Apia itself was not much more than a large village: the church towers and spires rising above the white, two-story wooden houses with their corrugated iron roofs the only sign that this was, in fact, a town. Just five or ten minutes' walk from the town center the wooden houses gave way to *fale*, open-sided huts thatched with palm branches. The only familiar thing that Jonas could see was the bamboo, which called to mind his boyhood ski poles. He walked along Beach Road, clad in a neutral—one might almost say universal—tropical suit, glorying in the feeling of being a total stranger, a person whom none of the inhabitants of Upolu or Apia knew anything about. For all they know, I could be a young scientist, he thought, or the rebellious son of a billionaire, or—why not?—a writer looking for romantic inspiration, an excuse to get sand between his toes.

This sense of absolute anonymity was to some extent ruined the very next morning as he was eating breakfast at the guesthouse. When a young, hippie-looking man from New Zealand who, it transpired, had a neighbor of Norwegian descent, heard that Jonas was Norwegian, he immediately started blathering on about Ole Bull, wanting to know why in hell Ole Bull didn't establish Oleanna, his Utopian colony, on Samoa. It would have had a much better chance of success here than in America, of all the stupid, bloody places. "Can't you just hear it?" he said. "Ole Bull's violin interwoven with those lovely Samoan harmonies."

As a way of escaping from this conversation, later that day Jonas walked down to the market and took a bus out of town, a bus that looked more like a gaily decorated, open-sided shed on wheels. He got off at a random spot next to a banana grove, not far from a village, but these he skirted around and walked through breadfruit trees and bushes covered in exotic scarlet blooms, down to the sea, three to four hundred yards beyond the village. The beach was just as it ought to be, with palms bending over a crescent-shaped ribbon of golden sand. Jonas stopped to gaze in wonder at the lagoon, the seabirds sailing over the bands of foam where the Pacific broke against the reef. The sky was overcast. He discerned the top of a volcano beyond the hills, shrouded in mist, almost unreal.

Jonas feels a faint pinching of his testicles and turns around: a group of men are walking towards him. All are clad in *lava-lavas*, gaily-patterned sarongs, most are bare to the waist, a couple are wearing shirts. Some of them are carrying palm-leaf baskets on poles across their shoulders. Several are clutching *sapelu* knives, the kind used for splitting coconuts. Jonas's first thought is that his life is in danger, that he must have committed some dire offence against something or someone—thoughts of broken taboos flash through his mind—but he quickly realizes that the men seem happy to see him, that they aren't just happy, they look as if they can hardly believe their luck, they are all talking at once, pointing excitedly and yet respectfully, as if he were a stranded emperor. They keep up a constant stream of chatter, smiling broadly. He doesn't know what to make of it all. He says something. None of them speak English. They point to the sand, the palms, the reef offshore, nod their heads. They point to his tropical duds, laugh, point to his sunglasses, his hat.

"Matareva," they say again and again. And then, pointing to him: "Mr. Morgan."

Jonas introduced himself, pronouncing his name slowly, said that he was from Norway, repeated this in all the languages he knew, said that he studied the stars: this was at a little-known period in his life when Jonas Wergeland was attending classes at the Institute of Theoretical Astrophysics. He pointed to the sky, pronounced the words "Southern Cross," and wasn't it true, he said, or tried to say, that these islands were home to master navigators who sailed by the so-called "star paths," the *kaveinga*? They merely laughed, not understanding a word, smiled, bowed, went through the motions of embracing an imaginary woman, mimicking romantic scenes. "Mr. Morgan," they insisted. Jonas waved his hands in protest, but it made no difference; their expressions said he couldn't fool them, they knew who he was. So when Jonas heard the sound of a bus in the distance he jabbed at his watch and excused himself, then jogged off through the grove and up to the road. The men followed him, beckoning, as if inviting him to come with them to the village. He mimed a polite no, but this did not stop them from staying with him until the bus drew up, and when he waved goodbye, it was clear from their gestures that they were urging him to come back soon.

Jonas put the whole incident out of his mind until his penultimate day on the island. He had hitched a ride on a yacht bound for Fiji; he would have to leave earlier than planned. On impulse he grabbed something from his bag and caught the bus back to the village. He got there an hour before sundown. The littlest children spotted him straight away and led him around smoking cooking fires and through the aroma of baked taro to the headman's *fale*, to an elderly man lying on a mat with his head on a neck rest. When the formalities had been got out of the way Jonas was once more addressed by one of the young men from the beach—Jonas guessed that he must be the headman's son—and then invited to enter his *fale*. Before long more men appeared. Jonas was ushered to one of the mats inside the hut, an open construction sitting on a coral-stone platform, with a roof made from the leaves of the coconut palm. The others sat down, smiled at him as they had done before. One of them touched him, as if to check whether he was real. Beyond the uprights of the hut a bunch of kids followed the proceedings. A woman brought in a bowl of kava. As far as Jonas could make out this was not a traditional kava ceremony, they had some other reason for passing the half coconut shell to him, as if sealing a contract, or celebrating something that went beyond any stretch of his imagination, but he drank, he drank and nodded, felt it behove him to do so, drank the greyish-white liquid which tasted chalky and made his whole mouth numb. The men sat cross-legged, speaking sometimes to him, sometimes to one another, Jonas made out certain words: "Matareva" cropped up again and again, as did "Mr. Morgan." Jonas also thought he heard Gary Cooper's name mentioned more than once. He remembered that a number of films had been shot on the island and things began to fall into place.

As darkness fell some women came in carrying freshly cooked dishes wrapped in banana leaves and woven coconut-fiber baskets of fruit. The sky was the color of the hibiscus blossoms they wore in their hair. Soon the stars, too, appeared: unfamiliar constellations, seeming to offer endless possibilities for new ways of navigating. Jonas realized that he was a guest of honor. That this was no ordinary act of Samoan hospitality. No, it was more than that. They mistook him for someone else. He did not know who or what. Nor whether there was any risk attached to this case of mistaken identity. The men chattered incessantly, eyed him closely, nodded, smiled. He was an empty shell. They piled things into him. They turned him into someone else, a great man perhaps. All he did was to put up no resistance, make no protest.

Someone lit a paraffin lamp that hung from the ceiling. An array of dishes was set before him. He recognized fish in leaves, possibly octopus too, together with some indeterminate creamy paste. He spotted baked breadfruit, slices of taro in coconut milk, papaya and whole pineapples—he had no idea what the other things were. One person kept wafting the flies away from the food. Another brought him a dented cup containing some sort of cocoa.

The men cast curious glances at Jonas as he ate. On one of them he could see the edge of a big tattoo, the rest was concealed by his *lava-lava*. Maybe it was the glimpse of this strange design—either that or the night sky—that brought home to him something he had, without knowing it, learned from Carl Barks's traveler's tales: that we will always have the wrong idea about other cultures. We can never really understand them. We think we have understood something, but in fact we understand nothing.

The talk flew back and forth around him, the word "Hollywood" cropped up at regular intervals, and by putting two and two together Jonas suddenly grasped that, despite his youth, they thought he was a director, a film director searching for a location for a film. They thought he meant to choose their beach. He felt laughter well up inside him. Or was it fear? How amazing. They took him for a film director. Or so he thought. And in that instant Jonas Wergeland knew why he had come here: he had come here to be part of this very experience, to sit on a mat in a *fale* under a mind-reeling, star-studded sky and be treated like a great man, a film director. And suddenly all his embarrassment was gone and instead he found himself seeing this entire, grandiose misapprehension as an edifying experience, as something important, something from which he had to learn. This experience might prove to be every bit as valuable as a black pearl, he thought.

Jonas sat listening to a distant song, not knowing how to thank his hosts for their hospitality. But he did as he always did on such visits, a gesture which also accorded well with what was expected on Samoa. He gave them a present. The same present as always. When Jonas Wergeland went on his travels he invariably took with him a G-MAN saw, a frame and a blade, a product for which his family, or at any rate his mother, was, in a manner of speaking, responsible. So now he presented a G-MAN saw from the Grorud Ironmongers to these natives on an island in Samoa, in the South Pacific.

When Jonas stood at the rail of the yacht the next day, having spent the night in a palm-thatched hut before taking the bus back to town; when Jonas stood there and watched Apia and the rest of the island dwindling to nothing—tropical green sinking into blue—he felt relieved, happy. The previous evening he had lain awake, gazing out between the wooden uprights of the hut, and he carried away with him the memory of that vast, glittering night sky, which also represented an acknowledgment of the infinite potential for other names, other paths to take through the stars. And now, as Upolu vanished from view, he also found it possible to laugh at the whole crazy episode, although he could not rid himself of the thought that deep down there had been a danger there too, that one wrong word, one wrong move could have spelled disaster for him. He thanked God, in a way, that he had escaped before the misunderstanding had been discovered.

On the other hand his heart was heavy. He had a feeling that this confusion, being mistaken for someone else, was a formative experience, that in different guises this incident would keep on recurring throughout his life. His despondency was prompted by the thought that perhaps he should not bemoan this fact: that it was, on the contrary, his only hope.

Jonas Wergeland stood on the deck of a boat and watched a Polynesian island disappear. He had left Norway with hardware and was returning with software, to use terms that were not common parlance back then. You set out carrying goods and come back with ideas. And unlike Erik Dammann, Jonas Wergeland did not return home with a Utopian ideal of Norway, of a new way of life, but with a Utopian ideal of himself. This might be a side of himself—the great director, metaphorically speaking—of which he knew nothing. Maybe, he thought, I've been wrong about myself all this time.

And somehow Jonas sensed that this journey was not over, that no journey is ever over, that they go on, that, like Carl Barks's most thrilling adventures, they often end with a "to be contd."

The Pursuit of Immortality

The natural thing would, therefore, be to proceed to the trip to Jerevan, but if we're to follow the sequence I have in mind—that sequence that will, I hope, explain everything—then this is not the place for it. Nor for the story of the stamps, which another—dare I say?—less seasoned narrator might have presented at this point. Here, instead, we must turn to another island. This same thought had also occurred to Jonas Wergeland himself while he was in Samoa: that all the seashells around him reminded him of the large, burnished shells in the parlor of the house on Hvaler, souvenirs of his paternal grandfather's seafaring days, shells which, when Jonas held one to each ear, brought him the sound of the sea in stereo.

Jonas was not always alone with his grandfather on the island at the mouth of the fjord. His cousin, Veronika Røed, was often there too, especially in the last summers before they both started school, the house being just as much the childhood home of her father, known as Sir William because of his way of dressing and his aristocratic leanings. There were the two of them, Jonas and Veronika, and their grandfather. Just them and a storybook island abounding with treasure and dragons, with hedgehogs and kittens and bowls of milk, with baking hot rocks and jetties where you could spend half the day fishing for a troll crab only, when you finally caught it, to let it go again.

They often went out in the rowboat. Jonas loved to watch his grandfather rowing, loved to hear the rasp of skin on wood, the creak of the rowlocks; Jonas would sit on the thwart, admiring his grandfather's technique, noting how he flicked the blades of the oars and rested on each stroke, rowing with a rhythm that seemed to take no effort and made Jonas feel that they could go on rowing for ever. Actually, it was a funny thing about his grandfather's rowing: he didn't row forward, as was usual, he backed the oars, rowed backward so to speak, or rather, the reverse—he said it was easier that way.

Jonas's grandfather had once built a model of a Colin Archer lifeboat, an exact replica with the red Maltese Cross ringed in blue on the bow and all, and sometimes they would gently set this in the water. When the wind filled the tiny sails it would sail so well that, seen against the right bit of the background, it could have been taken for a real boat. They would row alongside it, and Jonas played that they were gods, watching over it, that his grandfather was Poseidon and he and Veronika his attendants. Which was not so far from the truth, because to Jonas his grandfather really was a god.

It was also while pottering about on the boats that their grandfather taught the children to tie knots: first a half-hitch and a bowline, then more complicated rope techniques such as splicing. He even showed them how to tie a double Turk's Head, the sort of boy-scout knot that Daniel tied in his Cubs neckerchief. Veronika slipped the knotted rope onto her finger and gave Jonas a funny look: "Now we're engaged," she said. Jonas had nothing against that. They were the same age, and Veronika was prettier than anybody else he knew, even darker and sultrier than Little Eagle's mother.

That summer Jonas was often to be found sitting against the sun-baked wall of the shed, looping bits of rope together. There was one particularly tricky knot which he never mastered: a clove hitch which, had he got it right, would have been almost as intricate in appearance as the drawings that Aunt Laura, the family's artistic alibi, had shown him, with Arabic characters intertwining in such a way that it looked like a labyrinth. Far easier, and really just as lovely was the square knot. Jonas could not understand how two simple loops could produce something so strong. He never forgot how to do a square knot, not after his grandfather taught him how to tie it by telling him a story about two wrestlers and how the one wrestler won both times.

But then Omar Hansen told stories almost non-stop, more often than not in the blue kitchen, in that room as full of gleaming copper as an Oriental bazaar. And sometimes when his grandfather was telling a story Jonas was allowed to pound cardamom pods in a brass mortar: spice to be added to the dough for buns. There was nothing quite like it, those thrilling tales combined with the knowledge that they would soon be having freshly baked buns. On his arm, his grandfather had a tattoo of a dragon, done in Shanghai, so he said, and before starting a story he always rolled up his shirtsleeves. "The dragon has to have air under its wings if the imagination is to soar freely," he said. And whether it was the dragon's flight that helped him or not, Omar Hansen never ran out of stories, he could go on telling them for as long as he could row; he seemed to have lived all his life for only this: to sit one day in a blue kitchen with saucer-eyed grandchildren sitting opposite him. And as he span his yarns, each one more amazing than the one before, he peered at a point that seemed somehow beyond time and space, in such a way that fine wrinkles fanned out from his eyes to his temples, as if he were also, actually, endeavoring to twine these tales into one enormous clove hitch, into the story, the crucial knot, that lay behind all the others and bound them together.

One day, when old Arnt had been left to keep an eye on Jonas and Veronika, Omar Hansen came back home from Strömstad—which is to say, all the way from Sweden—with a new treat, a wondrous thing: a peach. These days, when tropical fruit is taken for granted in Norway, when you can buy anything from mangoes to kiwis just about anywhere, no one would give it a second thought, but in those days peaches were a rarity—Jonas had certainly never seen one, nor had Veronika; they had eaten canned peaches with whipped cream on one occasion, but this was something quite different, this was the real thing. Their grandfather laid the peach on a silver platter. "This peach is from Italy," he said. "But originally the peach comes all the way from China."

It was one of the most beautiful things Jonas had ever seen: that groove in the flesh, the golden skin blushing pink on the one side. Their grandfather let them touch it, and Jonas held it tenderly, savoring the feel of the velvety surface; it reminded him of the fuzzy-felt pictures in Sunday School. From that day onwards he had no problem understanding how a complexion could be described as "peachy." Grandfather said it had to sit a while longer, it wasn't absolutely perfect yet. "We'll share it tomorrow," he said and solemnly placed the peach back on its silver platter.

They sat round the oilcloth-covered table, gazing at the fruit, which seemed almost to hover above the silver platter, while Omar Hansen outdid himself with a story featuring Marco Polo as its central character and Jonas and Veronika as his armor-bearers—or perhaps it was the other way round—and this peach as one of the props; it had something to do with a city in China called Changlu and a bit about the pursuit of immortality, a thrilling adventure, almost as thrilling as the peach itself.

Late that night—a warm, almost tropical night—after they had gone to bed, Veronika padded upstairs to where Jonas lay in the old bed in a small room in the attic. It's not easy to describe the relationship between two children, but there was something between Jonas and Veronika, something which caused their lips automatically to bump together when they played hide-and-seek in the dark in the barn, or when they came face to face in the tunnels formed by the dense tangle of juniper bushes on Tower Hill.

Outside of Jonas's room, the wide loft extended like a wilderness beyond the bounds of civilization. Here, old clothes hung over battered trunks plastered with labels from exotic cities, and weather-beaten chests from Zanzibar full of faded copies of *Allers Family Journal* and *The Illustrated Weekly*. And in one corner, under some nets, stood the most mysterious thing of all: an old safe, heavy and forbidding. An unopened treasure.

At the other end of the loft, deep in shadow, loomed a harmonium—what in Norway used to be called a "hymn-bike"—a memento of their grandmother who had, by all accounts, been a God-fearing woman whose heart had burned for the mission service. Actually it was on this instrument that Jonas's father had begun his musical career, one that had since led him to the organ in Grorud Church. When it was light, Jonas had been known to slip into the shadows and play triads, his feet pumping away at the pedals for dear life. It surprised him to find what a lot of noise it made; he pulled out some knobs and observed how more keys than he had fingers for were then pressed down, as if an invisible spirit were sitting playing alongside him. His grandmother, Jonas thought. The choral songbook, which for a long time he had believed to be full of songs about the sea and fish, was still there, shrouded—appropriately enough—in gloom and open at her favorite hymn "Lead, Kindly Light."

Jonas sits up in bed, can tell right away what Veronika has in mind. She cuddles up close to him, wearing a thin cotton nightdress with blue dolphins on it. "Why do we have to wait till tomorrow to eat the peach?" she says, smelling like no one else: sweet, confusing. Jonas isn't sure, he wavers: "But Granddad has to have a bit too, doesn't he?" he says. "He's going to let us have it all anyway," she says. "Couldn't you at least go and get it?"

Jonas tiptoes down to the kitchen, stands for a moment on the linoleum floor gazing in awe at the fruit on its silver platter, hovering in the bright summer night. A planet called China. He feels the pull it exerts on him. As if they belong together, he and the peach. He is Marco Polo. He picks it up and climbs back up to the loft, places it on the sheet in front of Veronika. They look at it. Jonas thinks it is divinely beautiful.

From an early age Jonas was always on the lookout for objects that were more than they seemed, things that in some way illustrated something he could not put into words. At home he had taken the works out of an old alarm clock. They sat on top of the chest of drawers. A tiny, transparent factory. He liked to look at the gears inside the metal frame, how the cogs turned, how they meshed with one another, not to mention the balance wheel, which pulsated like a little heart. Most mysterious of all was the spring, the spiral that powered all the cogs by slowly expanding. A coiled steel sling. "The only thing that spoils it a bit," Jonas told Little Eagle, "is that the works have to be wound up, that they don't run by themselves all the time."

Daniel had a similar set of clock workings, but he, of course, just had to try to unscrew the frame, with the result that bits went flying in all directions, a bit like splinters from an exploding shell. Jonas had gazed respectfully at the spring lying on the floor, ostensibly harmless and insignificant, almost a yard in length. He saw what force, what driving force it possessed. The secret lay simply in coiling it up.

The peach had some of this same quality about it. A tension. As of something compressed and capable of expansion.

"Take off your clothes," Veronika says. Jonas does as he is told, tells himself that the peach demands this, it is a crystal ball which will not reveal anything if he keeps on his pyjamas. Veronika promptly puts one warm hand around his balls. Jonas watches in amazement as his penis rises up, skinny and eager. She puts the other hand around the peach and shuts her eyes. Then she lifts the peach to his mouth. Jonas feels the soft, furred skin against his lips: down, velvet, silk, all at once. He is filled with a fierce hunger. He's got to have a bite of this fruit. The juice runs down his chin as he sinks his teeth into the skin. It's good, deliriously good. Veronika takes a bite before offering it to him again. They take bites turn and turn about, sharing it, with her hand cupped around his balls all the while.

Later in life, Jonas would say that nothing could hold a candle to those first bites of a peach. It was a delight, a treat, the like of which he would never experience again—not even when he dined at Bagatelle in Oslo, in those days the first and only restaurant in Norway to be awarded two stars in the Michelin guide. As the juice and the flesh glided over his tongue and down his throat Jonas felt a glow emanating from the very cortex of his brain, along with a taste in his mouth, which gave him an inkling of continents, spheres, of which he knew nothing.

Veronika looked adorable, sitting there in her flimsy nightie with its pattern of blue dolphins. Jonas beheld the soft lines of her body, her ankles, calves, the blonde hairs on her arms, brown summer skin covered in golden down. They snuggled up together, taking turns to eat, licking and sucking up every shred, every drop.

At last all that was left was the stone. It looked like a minuscule, worm-eaten brain. "Can I have it?" he asked, not knowing whether it was because the stone looked nice, or because he wanted to make sure that the evidence of the theft lay in his hands, even though he knew they could never wangle their way out of this particular jam.

Veronika let go of his balls, lifted up her nightie. She wasn't wearing any panties. She displayed her genitals. Jonas sat quite still and took in this sight, didn't touch her, just sat and looked, studying those lines, the gentle swelling, the fleshy softness, the dark slit. She spread those fleshy lips and showed him the inside. It occurred to him that the clitoris—not that he knew that word for it, of course—was a sort of fruit kernel. That this too lay at the heart of something juicy, a fruit, something that could cause the cortex of the brain to glow. At the same time, for some reason he thought of the Turk's Head knot, saw this thing before him as a knot, a circular knot. Veronika slid her finger a little way into her slit, or knot, then stuck it into Jonas's mouth. "Now we're spliced forever," she said. "Now nothing can part us."

Jonas slept soundly that night and wasn't really feeling at all guilty when he came down to breakfast. Veronika and their grandfather were already sitting in the blue kitchen, staring as if in mutual sorrow at the empty silver platter. Jonas knew right away that his cousin had told their grandfather a tale in which all the blame rested with him, Jonas, alone—all alone; no matter what he said, he would not be believed. So he said nothing. They ate in silence, bread with cold mackerel from dinner the day before, and he was on the verge of telling a story, but he couldn't bring himself to do it. He realized that the story was no good.

And afterwards? I don't know what to say about what happened afterwards, Professor. It would be far too easy to psychoanalyze it. His grandfather was calm, he was perfectly calm when he went out into the forest with a knife: "Only one thing'll do any good here—and that's a good old-fashioned taste of the birch," as he said; he was calm when he took Jonas up to the attic and demonstrated the use of the birch twigs on the boy's bare backside, rolled up his sleeves, giving Jonas the feeling that it was the tattooed dragon that was angry, that lashed and lashed at his behind; his grandfather brought down the birch again and again, beating steadily, with the same rhythm as when he rowed, as if he could keep it up for hours, but it was this very calmness that vouchsafed Jonas a glimpse of the towering rage, the almost berserker-like frenzy beneath the surface. There was something altogether a little too relentless, a little too self-righteous, a little too much solemn conviction in the blows his grandfather rained down on Jonas's behind. For, no matter how he looked at it, Jonas could not see how the eating of this peach, however cheated his grandfather might feel, could justify a grown man with a lifetime of experience behind him putting a terrified little boy over his knee and thrashing him—on his bare behind, at that, and for a long time, for far too long—with a bundle of birch twigs, ceasing only just before the skin broke and the blood ran. It was a brutal, nigh-on wicked act, thought Jonas, young though he was. And it was during those seconds that it dawned on him that there was something wrong, possibly even seriously wrong, with his grandfather. That behind all those stories and yarns, behind the patient backward rowing, there lurked some dark secret, a tricky, inextricable knot. And this suspicion grew no less when his grandfather stood up and gave a sort of a sigh before walking over to the harmonium in the shadows and, with his back to Jonas, proceeded to play "Lead, Kindly Light."

Don't put down your pen, Professor, I'm not finished. Because even when it hurt the most, Jonas knew that it was worth it. He would have done it again. For he had eaten the peach not just to find out how it tasted but also for another reason: to feed a craving that was more than physical hunger—just as the clock workings on the chest of drawers at home were more than just clock workings—and suddenly he knew that he was willing to endure a great deal in order to satisfy that craving. As he lay there, feeling the birch twigs strike his backside again and again, he sensed a mysterious power building up inside him, and when his grandfather allowed him to get up he felt a jolt run through his body, as if he had taken a huge leap forward, aged several years in one minute.

The next day, just for fun, he tried to tie that trickiest of knots, the labyrinthine clove hitch, and got it right the first time, as if he had been doing it all his life, as if he suddenly had those twists and turns of the rope at his fingertips.

Jonas kept the peach stone. He made believe that it was a dragon's brain. Dragons had tiny brains, he knew, but they could harbor a secret, like the safe in the corner of the loft. A pearl, maybe. One day, with

Veronika standing over him, he crushed it with a hammer and found another kernel inside the stone, something like an almond. "Would you like to have it?" he asked Veronika.

"If you plant it in the ground, it'll grow into a dragon," she said. "Come on, I know a place in the woods, just next to our rope ladder." And on the way there she stays him and, with what might almost have been tears in her eyes, says: "Did it hurt?"

The Vertebral Disc

Allow me, in this connection—and remember: the connections between the stories in a life are as important as the stories themselves—to tell you about a time when Jonas Wergeland felt real hurt or more correctly, about an incident which took place in the midst of that pain. It happened in the emotionally charged year of the EEC referendum, the year when Jonas Wergeland was due to sit his university Prelim—although the thought of sitting an exam seemed the farthest thing from his mind, not to say an absolute impossibility, at that time. He found himself at the northern end of Norway's largest lake, in the "dayroom" of a hospital, to be more exact, one of those rooms which, with their spartan, simulated cosiness seem more depressing and godforsaken than any other place on earth. As a small boy, whenever he saw a diagram of the human circulatory system Jonas would think to himself that the heart must be like a knot, and that was how it felt now. A knot tightening. Jonas Wergeland sat there, swollen-eyed, twisting a handkerchief round his fingers. Outside it was winter, and dark—as dark and impenetrable as life when it seems most pointless.

Jonas thought he was alone, but when he looked up, as if through water, there she was. She took him as much by surprise as a car you haven't seen in your side mirror, one that's been in the blind spot but which suddenly appears, seemingly materializing out of thin air, when you turn your head. He felt like asking her to go away, had a truculent "Piss off!" on the tip of his tongue, but bit it back. He shut his eyes. He sniffed. It sometimes occurred to Jonas that the reason he didn't take up smoking was because he was afraid he would lose the ability to inhale women: to let their scent flow into his bloodstream and excite visions. He had caught a whiff of this scent before, in Viktor's room.

She spoke to him: "Is there anything I can do for you?"

"No," Jonas said—curbing his irritation: "No, thanks." He kept his eyes shut, as if the world would grow even darker if he opened them.

But she didn't go away, she sat down on a chair next to him and placed her hand over his, thinking perhaps that he was a patient. She said nothing. Jonas inhaled her scent. Even with his eyes shut, even amid a maelstrom of black thoughts, he felt something seize hold of him, not of his hand but of his body, that something was drawing him to it, was intent on worming its way inside him: her, this unknown woman.

"What's the matter?" she asked.

He kept his eyes shut, his head bowed, thought first of leaving, but something made him stay, made him speak, say something, tearfully to begin with, but without it being embarrassing, about his best friend, about himself and Viktor, about the Three Wise Men, the bare bones only but enough for her—possibly—to grasp the magnitude of the disaster. She said not a word, simply sat with her hand on his. Jonas had the feeling that her hand led to light.

When she gets to her feet he looks up. The first thing he sees is a high forehead. Rationality, he thinks. Exactly what I need right now: rationality. A white coat hangs open over her indoor clothes. Her badge reveals that her name is Johanne A. She has just come off duty, is on her way out, home. She nods, gives him a searching look before walking off down the corridor. He follows her with his eyes, feels a faint pressure on his spine, a pressure that spreads throughout his body, like a tremor in the nervous system.

Jonas skipped school and stayed for some days in Lillehammer, in a town he would always hate. He met Johanne A. again. She was in her mid-twenties, a resident on the surgical ward—this was her first post. She told him what the neurologist had said about Viktor, about the depth of the coma and the swelling. Viktor was still on a respirator in intensive care. She explained the uncertainty of his condition, what treatment they were giving him, how things were likely to go from here. "I'm sorry," she said. "But there's nothing more we can do."

Shortly before he was due to return home to Oslo, Jonas was sitting on a bench in the Swan Chemist's Shop on Storgata, staring listlessly at a wall hung with portraits of generations of chemists. All chemists' shops reminded Jonas of his maternal grandmother, because always, on trips into town with her, they would purchase a mysterious ointment at the chemist's, the apothecary, on Stortorvet in Oslo—that one, too, with a swan on its façade: the symbol of immortality. And every time they stepped inside that shop his grandmother would throw up her hands in delight at the sight of the tiled floors, the pillars of creamy-colored marble and a ceiling decorated with symbolic paintings; and while they were waiting she would tell Jonas about the fine old fittings of mahogany and American maple, with drawers of solid oak. "Like a temple to medicine," she would whisper. For this reason, Jonas always felt there was something rather antiquated—something holy, almost—about chemist's shops, also now, here in Lillehammer. There was also something about the atmosphere of the place, the odor of creosote, of aniseed and essential oils, which reinforced this sense of a bygone, somehow alchemical, age. Even so, as he was washing down a headache tablet with a drink of water, he instantly recognized that other scent, it was as if he had been caught up in a whirlpool. He turned around. It was her. And there was something about Johanne A.'s figure, her dress and, above all, her high forehead that made her seem utterly anachronistic in those surroundings, like an astronaut in the middle ages. Nonetheless, he knew that there was a connection between her and the chemist's shop. Or to put it another way: all of Jonas Wergeland's women represented an encounter with the past.

Johanne A. invited him back to her place for coffee. She lived above the hospital, not far from the open-air museum at Maihaugen. They strolled up the hill. It was cold; it was growing dark. She was wearing a big hat, the sort of hat that made heads turn. In the hall Jonas noticed a shelf holding several other eye-catching pieces of headgear.

The flat was furnished in an unusual style: "avant-garde" was the word that sprang to Jonas's mind. The furniture in the sitting room looked more like works of art, architectonic concepts sculpted into chairs and storage units. The lighting too was highly original: little flying saucers hovering over glass-topped tables. Products from Bang & Olufsen—a television set and an expensive, metallic stereo system—seemed to belong to a universe unlike any Jonas had ever seen. Jars, vases, ashtrays—even the salt and pepper shakers on the shelf between the kitchen and the sitting room—appeared to have been designed for the atomic age. Jonas felt as if he had stepped into a laboratory, a room which proclaimed that here, within these walls, some sort of experiment was being carried out. "The world is progressing," was all she said when she noticed the way his eyes ran round the room in astonishment, occasionally glancing out of the window, at the old buildings on the hill, the vestiges of tarred-brown, medieval Norway only a stone's throw away.

She poured coffee for him from a transparent jug in which the grounds were pressed down to the bottom by a shining strainer. He pointed to an old microscope over by the window. "I've had that since I was a child," she said. "Pasteur was my great hero. These days, of course, viruses are the thing—electron microscopes." For a long time, while at university, she had considered a future as a research scientist but had abandoned this idea, was happy where she was now, expected to end up in general practice. As she was talking, Jonas studied the pictures hanging on the walls: reproductions of Rembrandt's *Dr. Tulp's Anatomy Lesson* and *The Raising of Lazarus* and a fine selection of Leonardo's studies of different parts of the body, all rendered strange and different by gleaming steel frames and by being interspersed with a number of stringently abstract pictures by Malevich. In one spot hung an artistic representation of the human head's development through various palaeontological stages, as if her pictures also aimed to underline her statement about the world progressing.

She broke off in the middle of a sentence: "I don't know what to make of you," she said. "You seem so ordinary and yet at the same time so different. There's a look in your eyes. Not at first, there wasn't, but now."

"It might have something to do with my back," he said. And because she was a doctor, he did not consider it unreasonable to tell her about an episode from his childhood, from the time when he would not eat. His parents had come up with all sorts of ploys to distract him during mealtimes, to get Jonas—inadvertently almost—to swallow a few morsels of food. On one occasion on Hvaler they had given him a box of buttons to play with while they shovelled food into him as best they could. Among all these different and interesting buttons one in particular caught Jonas's eye. His grandfather said that he had bought it in China and that it came from a dragon. "Imagine that, you little starveling: genuine dragon horn!" The Chinaman in the shop had told him that farmers sometimes came across dragon skeletons in desolate spots and sold the bones and horns. The apothecaries ground the bones into powder and craftsmen made things from the horns, including buttons. Jonas clearly enjoyed this story, because he promptly popped the button into his mouth—and swallowed it, to everyone's dismay. Jonas vaguely remembered his mother forcing him to sit on the potty, then examining his stools as keenly as a customs officer looking for bags of heroin, or as if he was the Emperor of China and his shit was sacred—but found no button. His parents were worried sick. They took him to the hospital and had him X-rayed. Nothing showed up on the X-ray plates either. No button had come out, and no button could be detected inside him, not by the X-rays at any rate. It wouldn't necessarily do any harm, the doctor reassured them, though secretly he guessed that the button had come out the other end long ago. "The body can cope with a lot more than we think," he said. "I'm sure you've heard stories of surgeons leaving this or that inside patients after an operation, folk have survived worse things than a button." Jonas, for one, felt reassured. As the years passed and he read about all the odd things that were inserted into people's bodies, from heart valves to silicone, he came to the conclusion that the body could accept one measly button, even a horn one. When he grew older, he would dream that it had slotted itself into his spine like a disc, that he was, in other words, equipped with an extra vertebra—had suffered more or less the opposite of a slipped disc. He recalled how proud he had been on attending one of his first school medicals: "You've got a remarkably straight back, boy!" the doctor had said. Several times, during bouts of depression, Jonas was to take comfort in this—in his belief that, in spite of everything, the button made him special. His grandfather had told him about a tribe in Brazil: when they reached a certain age the young boys of the tribe had wooden plugs put in their ears to enable them to pick up the dreams of the tribe. "Sometimes I think of the button as a pill," he told Johanne A. "A pill that didn't take effect for a long time." What he did not tell her, Professor, was that the effect of the pill was to exert a pressure on his spine, a pressure which sometimes altered his perception completely and gave him a glimpse of a world rich in possibilities.

"I knew there was something," she says, and without more ado she proceeds to switch off the lights, as if this anecdote has inspired her to undertake some unorthodox operation that needs to be conducted in the dark. She puts out all the lights, apart from one lamp in a corner, a sphere encircled by a metal ring, like another Saturn suspended over a table bearing little pyramids of colored glass. Normally, Jonas was frightened by dark rooms but not now, not with her beside him, not with that scent infiltrating his nostrils, filling him with a mounting sense of exhilaration. She sat on the white sofa, faint reflections from her eyes in the shadows. Two geometric earrings hung like satellites on either side of her face. She reached out her hands to him, he went to her, kissed her, felt a lock turn smoothly, as if they each possessed half of the key to something important which they could only open together, like you saw in films, where two keys were required in order to open a safety deposit box or fire a rocket.

She drew him into an adjoining bedroom, got undressed without a word, made him do the same. Her legs were smooth-shaven, she must have trimmed her pubic hair too, it looked a little too perfect in shape, or artificial, like something out of a retouched, chocolate-box picture. In the dim light the two halves of her buttocks looked to be made of crystal, twin globes that harbored secrets, future prospects, intimations that Jonas was about to make love to a being superior to himself, a visitor from a planet where evolution had reached a more advanced stage, where they did not play the old brutish game involving lots of primitive pawing and pumping in and out.

She did not invite any foreplay, pulled him down onto the bed, resolutely and yet controlled, almost cool, he thought to himself, and as he slipped inside her, he felt, as he always felt at those first, tentative thrusts, a friction that puts him in mind of a dynamo, a dynamo running against a bicycle wheel, activating a lamp, flooding everything with light; and he drifts around in this light, savoring not just the physical euphoria, but also the thoughts that promptly begin to come pouring into his head, thoughts of a most unusual nature, as if the extra disc in his spine—whether imaginary or real—also contains a secret program, impulses which only a woman can trigger.

Johanne A. was also in a state of extreme well-being, indeed she would later say that—although she had no idea why—this time with Jonas caused her to change her mind, revived her wish to become a research scientist after all, with the result that—as well as doing some remarkable work for Doctors for Peace and carrying out some pretty risky assignments for the Red Cross in war-torn regions—she wound up as an international expert on tropical diseases, a conqueror within medicine, within a field in which the study of microbes was central, the investigation of the influence of these minute organisms on people's lives, something which was about as hard to fathom as love, or the desire she was feeling now, a desire which, without any warning, almost made her take leave of her senses, to lie writhing under a man, hardly more than a boy, to whom she had only spoken for a few hours.

Jonas knew nothing of this, so preoccupied was he with the vigorous way in which she had gradually begun to move, with her vagina, which gripped him so tenderly, with the light, with the thoughts drifting into his mind, with words that passed into new words, images, a whole network of sudden similarities between widely differing entities. For if there was one thing Jonas had learned back in the days when Daniel used to lie in the top bunk and read aloud from Agnar Mykle's works, it was that sex is all to do with metaphors, with executing unexpected pirouettes in the imagination: to be able, one moment, to say that her small breasts "had a lovely shape, like the bowl of a champagne glass" and the next to gasp out the words: "her breasts were like explosives under her jersey." Jonas grasped very early on that sex had something to do with broadening the mind, of giving it span, that sex was not an end in itself, but a means by which to achieve something else, perhaps quite simply a means to creativity, a conviction which was now confirmed for him, here, as he lay on his back on the bed and she sank down onto him again and again, so warm and powerful that he could almost feel the springs in the mattress, even as something similar was happening to his thoughts, as she, or they together, transformed them into spirals, springs, with the ability to hop, free themselves from a chain that ran from A to B to C, and that was why he lay there, as she exerted a greater and greater pull on him, engulfing him even while seemingly trying to restrain herself, and felt how he built a bridge of metaphors, as from A to X to K, a bridge which suddenly led him to espy a similarity between his own erect penis and a lever, the sort of tool that enabled one to move objects heavier than oneself; and perhaps that was why, at that same moment, Jonas felt himself, or her, Johanne A., shrugging off something heavy, exposing some object that lay buried, braiding various fragments into larger chunks, and eventually a story, something about being in a forest, not in a modern flat, but in a primeval forest, much as this white apartment might conceal a mahogany chemist's shop, because lovemaking was alchemy, a commingling of irreconcilable elements, a fact which she proved by entwining herself around him with greater and greater ardor, surprising ardor, perhaps, uncontrolled even; by casting herself over him with an intensity that generated light and linked him to a story he both remembered and did not remember, thus he could recall that milk cartons had also been around ten years before, but not whether they had been printed with a red four-leaf clover design or not, and yet he knew, as he lay there savoring the light, drifting in it, that together they could set it rolling—the story that was hidden and yet right there: in the blind spot, you might say. And while Jonas was concentrating on remembering, or seeing; on letting his movements spark off associations, as they were weaving their limbs together into a writhing knot, he heard Johanne A., involuntarily, and possibly unwittingly, begin to snort, to utter sounds, hoarse grunts which, in a parenthesis in his train of thought, afforded room for surprise that a girl like her, the owner of this ultra-modern apartment, a woman who obviously believed wholeheartedly in man's potential for evolving into an even more intelligent being, that this woman could lie there like that, grunting wildly underneath him, as if her white coat came complete with a witch-doctor's mask. Howsoever that might be, this only made him even more aroused; he was conscious of how his thoughts struggled to get a grip on some sense of a whole, wove themselves together, how the friction slid over into a feeling of lightness, as if she were lifting him up and at the same time urging him to move with greater intensity, until she could hold back no longer, though she bit her lip until it bled—she came with a long drawn-out howl, a downright bestial scream which ended with her letting her arms flop to the floor, like someone fainting away, and whether this was what it took, or whether Jonas was just about there anyway, at that very second, thankfully and with his mind in giddy freefall, he discerned the thread connecting the whirl of thoughts which she, or the two of them together, had generated inside his head.

He was still inside her. "Didn't you come?" she asked on recovering consciousness, so to speak. Her voice was tinged with guilt. She was still out of breath, and one corner of her mouth was red with blood. "Did you get satisfaction?" she asked, as if it were important to her.

He lay there smiling: he too, out of breath, smiling for the first time in days. "Yes, I got satisfaction," he said at last. And it was true, although this word did not cover the phenomenon of orgasm in the normal sense. It's true that he was also interested in gaining satisfaction, but not the sort that could be measured in millilitres of semen produced. For Jonas Wergeland—and I hope to return to this—the act of love was not necessarily about ejaculation but about enlightenment, about being lit up, about seeing.

The Jewel

So what sort of stories were they that Jonas Wergeland recalled, or suddenly understood, while this woman was biting herself until the blood ran from sheer pleasure underneath him? Your wrist is aching, Professor, I can see that, but we cannot stop now. Remember, we've embarked on a serious undertaking here. It is quite simply a matter of life or death.

For years, Jonas dreamed the same dream. For a period during his childhood he would start out of sleep several times in a month with a particular picture in his head, an image he could not, however, make anything of, since it was somewhat abstract. It had no recognizable thread to it; it was more of an impression.

Jonas had this dream for the first time when he was sick with a fever—he must have been around four at the time—on a night when his temperature rose to almost 105 and the sheet was in a tangle from all his tossing and turning. In his head, and possibly also in his fingertips, he had a sense of forms, strands of wool or piano strings, which coiled themselves around one another, changing from a tight knot into looser, more amorphous formations, as from a ball of yarn to a tangle of string. The odd thing was that these shapes did not only represent something bad, a nightmare, but also something beautiful, like the reflections in a kaleidoscope: a mesmerizing pattern, ceaselessly shifting, though still within certain limits. Maybe I'm dreaming about God, Jonas thought.

Then, quite by chance, he stumbled upon a clue to the obscure signals from his nervous system. It happened on one of those Sunday outings that a number of the families in Solhaug used to go on together. And in the spring. For it wasn't just in the autumn that people went for walks in the woods—the autumn being the time when everyone seemed almost genetically programed to start gathering in stores like mad, by means of berry-picking and mushroom-gathering. In springtime too, on Sundays after church, Åse and Haakon Hansen, Jonas's parents, would don their well-worn walking clothes and rubber boots, not to mention rucksacks redolent of wartime and countless Easter skiing trips, gather the children together, meet up with the others and troop off to Lillomarka. Here, at different—but usually regular spots—practiced hands would light a campfire; then they would make coffee, cook food and sit around and talk—feeling, in short, that they were doing what was only right and proper: what was, so to speak, expected of them as good Norwegians. Picnicking in the woods was a part of their national heritage: you only had to look at Prime Minister Einar Gerhardsen and his love for the woods and the hills to see that. If you ask me, Professor, I think it would be just as fair to say that they were performing a ritual in memory of a not so distant past in which they had been hunters and gatherers, a theory which the stories they told round the campfire bore out, since these often had to do with hunting and fishing and the secret haunts of the chanterelle, interspersed with local legends about people who had lived here before and given the place its name. Be that as it may, Jonas loved being in the forest. He loved the smell of campfires and the unique flavour of grilled meat and roast potatoes served on scratched plastic plates along with slices of white bread covered in ash. He loved the way the adults were so keen to pass on the art of making pussy-willow flutes or bark boats. He loved sitting up in a tree and listening to the hum of the grownups' voices, mingled occasionally with the squawk of a portable radio as some major sporting event got under way. Even Five-Times Nilsen and Chairman Moen relaxed and forgot for a while the plans for communal garages when they sat on a log with their eyes resting on a black coffee pot set over a campfire.

Ørn—nicknamed Little Eagle—usually tagged along with Jonas's family. The forest was a fabulous place in which to play. Cowboys and Indians no taller than your finger looked perfectly lifelike if you just found the right slope, little ledges that played the part of cliff-top villages in Arizona or Utah. And if Little Eagle brought along his plastic animals, half the fauna of Africa, they could create a savannah among the tufts of grass. Just a box of used matches was enough. Tip the contents into a tiny stream and they had an arduous and perilous log-run that could keep them occupied for hours.

Ørn wasn't with them on this particular day. Little Eagle was sick. At least they said he was sick. The thought of Ørn bothered Jonas. The forest wasn't the same without Ørn.

What sort of sound does a dragon make?

It was a hot day, hotter than the day before, and while one of the fathers was telling off a couple of the bigger boys for setting light to a clump of heather—"Fire is dangerous, boys; remember what just happened at the Coliseum cinema!"—Jonas wandered about on his own, first playing at Robin Hood, with a long staff in his hands, then Tarzan: Tarzan heading deeper and deeper into the jungle. But he missed Little Eagle, and this niggled at him, turned him into a very destructive Tarzan, a king of the jungle who made ferocious swipes with his staff, knocking the top off bush after bush—gorillas, actually—while trying to find a suitable heroic deed to commit. And then there it was, his chance, dead ahead of him: a weeping woman in a ripped safari suit with her foot caught between the roots of a fir tree and a large rock. Jonas—or rather, Tarzan—had to roll the rock away, and there was no time to waste: for a lion, or better still, a fearsome dragon with slavering jaws was closing in on the woman. "Courage, noble maid," Jonas muttered and set his hip against the rock, it wobbled back and forth, but he still couldn't budge it, or only very little. He took his staff, stuck one end well under the stone and rested the other on a nearby hummock, to act as a lever, and when Jonas bore down on the other end he was quite surprised to find how easily the rock allowed itself to be dislodged, along with a fair amount of soil, a great clump, before rolling thunderously down the south-facing slope, leaving behind it a gaping hole.

Jonas knew right away: he had unearthed hidden treasure just as Oscar Wergeland, his maternal grandfather, had done in his youth. There was a smell of gunpowder, a smell of raw earth, a smell of gold.

He got down on his knees and peeked into the hole—possibly half-expecting to be disappointed—then he started back, just as he would do later in life when unexpectedly confronted with television footage of operations, shots of the brain or glistening intestines staring him in the face. A dragon's lair, that's what it must be: the thought flashed through his mind. There was an infernal roaring in his ears, but he wasn't sure that he had heard anything roar.

After the initial shock he simply kneeled there, staring. He could see deep into the heart of the tree root. Eventually, he realized what it reminded him of, this thing down in the depths: it reminded him of his mother's brooch. And I really ought to say a few words here about this jewel, since it played such an important part in Jonas Wergeland's life. Children have a unique capacity for being fascinated by things, for regarding—for inexplicable reasons—certain objects as magical. For an Albert Einstein, it was a compass, for others it might be a special stone. For Jonas Wergeland, it was a silver brooch.

There may well be a simple explanation for his fondness for this piece of jewelry: it was the first thing he remembered. His mother must have worn it a lot when he was little. She had been given the brooch, a so-called "round brooch," as a wedding present from Aunt Laura, the goldsmith. The surface was completely covered in an intricate tracery of ribbons that twined around one another, interlacing and seeming to form lots of "S"s or figure eights. "It looks like a gigantic knot that hasn't been tightened," Jonas would say, fingering it. This silver brooch was absolutely the most beautiful thing he'd ever seen—much more beautiful than the aforementioned clock workings on top of the chest of drawers. That little shield glowed, not outwardly, but inwardly, with a secret and powerful luster. In his imagination he thought of it as a weapon, a disc that, if one were to hurl it out into the cosmos, would set momentous processes in motion. For Jonas, in terms of latent power the brooch was a miniature atom bomb.

Jonas is on his hands and knees, gazing down into the hole laid bare by the dislodged rock. And what he sees there resembles the design on his mother's brooch: a coiling mass of ribbons. It's like looking down into the nerve center of the Earth, he thinks. Which is not so surprising, since Jonas is staring straight down onto a huge ball of snakes, nestling between the roots of the fir tree, possibly as much as five feet down. He can see it quite clearly, though, as if at the end of a narrow tunnel; an exceptionally large winter nest, containing at least fifty, maybe a hundred, adders—probably ring-snakes and slow-worms too, and even lizards and toads. All twined together in an enormous, tangled ball. Nature's very own clove hitch.

Jonas thought they were still deep in their winter sleep, but then he noticed that some of them were moving ever so slightly: this was obviously the day when they were going to wake up, now that the temperature had risen enough for the warmth to seep as far down as the snakes. Fascinated, Jonas knelt there, observing the ball of reptiles slowly coming to life. Just for a moment he considered running home to fetch the canister of petrol that was kept in the caretaker's shed, pour it over the nest and set light to it: create a living ball of fire. But why would he do that? These were timid creatures; they wouldn't do him any harm.

For ages Jonas sat there, seized by a sort of awe, watching this tangle of reptiles gradually stirring. He could make out the zigzag stripe along the backs of the adders, a pattern within a pattern. Some, presumably males, began to break away from the ball, wriggled sluggishly and silently up the tunnel, along passages that Jonas could not see. And at that same moment he realized that the ball of snakes reminded him of that recurring dream of his. He tried to pursue this thought but gave up. It fitted and yet did not. As a grown man Jonas Wergeland would be struck by the thought that on that spring day he had been confronted with an image of his own vast multitude of unrealized lives.

He didn't say a word about any of this when he returned to the campfire and his parents, with his trousers caked in muck. "Poor Jonas—looks like he's seen a wood nymph," said Chairman Moen, handing him a sausage wrapped in a slice of bread. Jonas sat down next to his mother, felt his hand trembling slightly as he took the cup of orange juice she poured for him.

It remained his secret, that spring day and that sight. Little did Jonas know what it would lead to. In any case, and thanks to the silver brooch, the ball of snakes seemed not so much frightening as precious. Jonas remembered it as a pattern, thought of it as a treasure. A jewel deep in the ground. A living jewel. Something swirling round and round, almost hypnotic.

Sonja and the Stars

It wasn't that Jonas Wergeland forgot that spring day in the forest, but it would be a long time before he could, so to speak, learn from it. To show you what I mean, allow me to remind you of the program on Sonja Henie, one of the twenty-odd chapters in that masterpiece, *Thinking Big*, Jonas Wergeland's epic television series on Norwegians who had won themselves a place in the world consciousness, whose names were bywords, rich in associations, in the international vocabulary.

Jonas Wergeland not only scored the highest viewer ratings ever recorded in Norway, he also, and much more importantly, achieved the highest viewer intensity. Expectations were always great, so to begin with—until they were won over, that is—people were a little disappointed with his portrait of Sonja Henie. The program contained no facile, sarcastic remarks about her father, the colorful and ambitious Wilhelm Henie, said nothing about those three incredible Olympic Golds, the ten world championships, the crowds at the Eastern Railway Station and the Royal Wharf when she came home to Oslo, nothing about her "Heil Hitler" salute to the Führer and her refusal to help Little Norway at the start of the war, nothing about Tyrone Power, nothing about the triumphant ice show at the Jordal Amfi Arena, nothing about two broken marriages, expensive mink coats, flamboyant jewelry, problems with alcohol, not so much as a word about the fashionable house on Hollywood's Delfern Drive and the parties held there, with swans carved out of blocks of ice in the swimming-pool and orchids flown in from Hawaii. Jonas Wergeland produced an all but silent program, a program that focused, basically, on just one thing: skating. With skating as dance, as acrobatics, as—yes, beauty. It was a scintillating ice-blue program. "It sent shivers down my spine like some eerie, yet beautiful, sight," as one reader's letter put it. And in case you have not guessed, Professor, this too has a bearing, of course, on the inconceivable factor round which we keep circling: a dead wife.

Originally, Jonas Wergeland had intended to build the key scene around a training session at Frogner Stadium, but instead he decided to set this scene—a fictitious one, naturally—on a tarn, a little lake in the forest, where the atmosphere was that much more magical. The camera captured an image of a clear winter's night with stars reflected on the glassy blue ice. Jonas commenced with a close-up of the skates, showing how forlorn they looked—a pair of battered skates, abandoned on the ice. Then he showed them being slipped onto two feet, the laces tied, and the transformation, as if they had been invested with spirit, before—steel blades flashing—they exploded into a series of turns, inscribing, as if by magic, an enormous "S" on the ice. The camera focused tightly on the legs the whole time, on the skates, on the blade slicing through the ice, etching out markings, figures, exercises from the world of the compulsory program: Mohawks, reverse Mohawks and double Mohawks, snaking curves and loops. The camera pulled up to reveal that the tarn was a circle upon which Sonja's dancing had etched flourishes and arabesques, an exquisite pattern; carved a gigantic, glittering brooch out of the very countryside of Norway.

This program had a strikingly erotic feel to it, distinctly at odds with the image of the girl with the baby-doll face. For the close-ups of the finer techniques of figure skating, they used the top female figure skater in Norway at that time. But the actress Ella Strand, who played all of the series' heroines, also did her bit, in a wig which bore a passing resemblance to Sonja's blonde curls, and with her own natural hint of a snub nose—as luck would have it she had figure skated herself as a girl, and still retained some of her old skill. Jonas had no scruples about making the most of her womanly silhouette, the line of her bust and her long legs, got her to wear a simple, tight-fitting dress with a short skirt—one of Sonja's many revolutionary innovations, as it happens. The camera dwelt on a woman spinning around, ardent and intent, dwelt on her thighs, almost caressing them, caught—with something close to awe—the suppleness that transmitted itself to the blade of the skate and made the ice fly up.

This was the program's key scene: Sonja on the little tarn, alone, in a wintry Norwegian forest, alone with her skates and the stars, executing a high-speed dance across a mirror-like expanse of ice. Jonas highlighted the physical nature of figure skating, the stamina it craved, by running the sequence without music, by amplifying the sound of the skates cutting through the ice, and that of Sonja's heavy breathing. With an adoring camera, Jonas Wergeland managed to convey the difficulty and beauty of, and the effort involved in, some of the figures from those days, for example the execution of three figure of eights in succession in such a way that it looked like just one. It was Sonja alone on the ice, encircled by snow-laden pine trees, skipping, gliding, swooping, in the midst of a strange display, like a rite, the blade of the skate etching figures in the ice, heavy breathing and the swish of swift swirling movement. "Talk about an undertow," was the cameraman's comment.

A lot has been said about Jonas Wergeland's intelligent filming—before that earth-shattering scandal, that is—about a producer who finally took people's intellect seriously. What rubbish! The truth is that Jonas Wergeland understood, better than anyone else, that television was first and foremost based on emotions, on the irrational. Jonas Wergeland knew that you conquered a nation not by appealing to its reason but by bombarding its senses. Which meant that you had to simplify. And the challenge, as he saw it, lay in coming up with the best, the most surprising form of simplification, the one which could, to greatest effect, reduce even a complex life to a few essential and comprehensible figures that could be etched out in a flurry of ice, like a figure of eight on a frozen lake: simple and yet infinitely fascinating.

For this reason Jonas Wergeland built his program on Sonja Henie primarily around the techniques of figure skating and, in the first sequence, on the jumps in particular: the axels, the lutzes, and the split jumps, soaring leaps rendered even more impressive by the lowering of the camera as Sonja took off. Over and over again. Almost dauntingly simple. And therefore so entrancing. Many viewers claimed to have experienced a feeling of weightlessness; and perhaps that, when you get right down to it, is what figure skating is all about: becoming weightless, suspending gravity, soaring up to the stars.

Jonas had Sonja conclude this part of the program with a move of her own invention, "the strip," in which she glided backwards, balancing on the toe of one skate and leaving a glorious groove in the ice, to simulate the way in which she had cut her way through the ice and the firmament, like a diamond through glass, to suddenly find herself in another world, the one place where she had always dreamed of being: Hollywood.

The Hollywood sequence concentrated on the first of the eleven films she had made in the USA, *One in a Million*. They reconstructed a number of meetings between Sonja and Darryl F. Zanuck, the redoubtable head of 20th Century Fox, and made much of the fact that she secured herself a sensational five-year contract and a stupendous amount of money for each film, even though she had no experience in front of the camera. They also showed a clip from *One in a Million*, the story of a country girl who becomes Olympic champion, then turns professional and scores an overwhelming success at Madison Square Gardens—in other words, pretty much identical to Sonja's own story. The film culminated in a lavish set piece, a forerunner to her ice shows, in which Sonja twirled and leaped in a skating ballet featuring hundreds of girls in extravagant costumes, as if in some glamorous opera on ice.

In also illustrating how this film was received, with an acclaim that fulfilled all expectations, Jonas aimed to make two points. Firstly, that Sonja Henie was the greatest Norwegian film-star of all time. In short, she conquered that most impregnable of all realms: Hollywood. And secondly—and it is surprising how often this is forgotten—Sonja Henie was a brilliant figure skater, a true virtuoso, three-time Olympic champion. And when she won such a victory—even in a silly film in which she spoke dreadful English and only had two facial expressions to choose from, with a script which was nothing but a mishmash of romantic drivel, sets composed of fake ice and artificial snow and the Swiss Alps as backdrop—it was thanks solely to her charm, her personality and her skating skills, the fact that she sparkled, did things on skates which the audience could not have imagined possible and which made them cheer in admiration. Even a few clips from this second-rate—and antiquated—film was enough to show viewers why Sonja Henie deserved to be called one of the western world's first superstars. There was no lack of response either—interestingly enough in a day and age when television channels strove so hard to encourage viewers to take an active part in programs: NRK, the Norwegian Broadcasting Corporation, was inundated with letters and faxes, the switchboard jammed by calls from people wanting to compliment Jonas Wergeland on how well he had comported himself on skates in his own regular slot and demanding that NRK show all of Sonja Henie's films immediately, which they duly did, to the great delight and satisfaction of the nation.

The transition from Hollywood to the program's closing sequence was a masterstroke: from thunderous applause straight into a soundless pirouette, a vertiginous whirl, and then, clearer and clearer, the solitary sound of the blade on the ice, Sonja alone again on the tarn on a winter's night in Norway, in a magical—some said, demonic—atmosphere. Jonas lingered particularly on the pirouettes now, the corkscrew turns, imparting a sense of how mind-reeling they were, ecstatic almost, as if executed by a seductive winter dryad or by a dervish attempting to throw himself into a trance. And for Sonja, figure skating had as much to do with mystery as it did with the dream of winning, of conquering the world. Jonas ran the turns in slow motion, very, very slowly, such that the shots of the solitary, pirouetting woman had as mesmerizing an effect as any big production number from Hollywood with its meticulously choreographed repetitions, duplications and symmetrical formations.

And then, again: Sonja Henie, zooming along, alone on the ice, alone with her skates and yet happy here, on the ice, with her dancing, her art. Jonas Wergeland took issue, indirectly, with the myth that said that all her life Sonja Henie was a lonely, unhappy child who never found real purpose. The way Jonas saw it, and presented it to the people of Norway, she did find happiness, here, in her pirouettes, in the total control, in the innate musicality of her movements, in the jumps, in speeding across the ice, when she tilted her body forwards or back—and anyone who has tried this, as in fact very many Norwegians have, has some idea of what an exhilarating experience this can be. During those seconds, Sonja became something that no one else was, or understood: when she used the toe picks to stop dead in the middle of a pirouette, then run forwards on her toes, throw herself into another jump, into flying spins and parallel spins, three corkscrew spins with an Arabian cartwheel. Again the camera captured the breathtaking speed, with close-ups of the skate blade, the tracks crisscrossing, steel suddenly scraping the ice and sending up a flurry of ice. A small camera had also been fixed to one of her skates, thus giving viewers something of the same thrill as that derived from watching a film shot from the front of a racing car, or a car on a roller-coaster. "My stomach lurched just watching her," people said.

Finally, Jonas got the camera to pull up slowly, pull high up to reveal that Sonja was dancing—almost sketching it out herself, the loops, the design, with her skating—on a huge painting by Joan Miró, projected onto the ice by means of trick photography. It was, aptly enough, a masterpiece by Miró entitled *Women in the Night*, one of the first paintings which Sonja bought for herself after meeting Niels Onstad—for this too was one of her gifts, a talent akin to the art of drawing lines on ice: she knew a good picture when she saw it.

What was Jonas Wergeland saying with this? He was saying that Sonja Henie's exercises on the ice, what she did, was just as childlike, just as lovely, just as mischievous and bold as Joan Miró's paintings. And I'm sure you have already observed, Professor, how this closing scene puts one in mind of Jonas Wergeland's experience in the forest as a little boy, the sight of a living brooch in the ground. It might not be going too far to regard the whole of the program on Sonja Henie as a silvery tracery of "S"s and figures of eight on an enormous brooch of ice—that, at any rate, is how one critic summed it up: "A real gem." And if you were to ask anyone what they remember from that program, this is the first thing they would mention, this shot of Sonja on the Miró painting; it has become a kind of national ornament, imprinted on the consciousness of the viewers.

Even those viewers—a fair number of older people—who had been negative to start with were delighted with Jonas Wergeland's slant on Sonja Henie's character. They realized what her unique talent had been when she was at her peak: to skate like no one else in the world. Sonja Henie elevated figure skating to an art form. She paired the essence of all things Norwegian, winter sport, with a global spirit. As a human being, and a Norwegian at that, Sonja Henie truly was one in a million.

Napoleon

Are you tired, Professor? Just one more story, then we'll call it a night.

At the end of the eighties, after the last program in the *Thinking Big* series had been screened, the plaudits rained down on Jonas Wergeland from all quarters. Advertisers felt that he had helped to color the nation's image of itself in that rare way in which only a troubadour can do with his simple yet unforgettable ballads. Teachers testified to the positive effect the series had had in terms of filling in the gaps in young people's knowledge of history. Another outcome, more interesting within our own context, was all the interviews which Jonas Wergeland gave at that time, and in which he repeatedly used the same expression in describing his first years in television: "A life of luxury." Time and again too, he compared the chance he was given to make his earliest programs with that of a trainee chef suddenly being given the run of a huge kitchen complete with every mod-con and all the world's freshest raw ingredients, where his imagination alone set the limits for what he could serve up. The descriptions of Jonas Wergeland's early days in television were positively aromatic, people said.

How does one become a conqueror?

The kitchen metaphor was not something Jonas had simply plucked out of thin air. The father of Jonas's best friend, Little Eagle, was in fact a chef. He didn't work just anywhere either, but at the imposing Grand Hotel in the very heart of Oslo. And not only that, but also at the very heart of the hotel, in a kitchen which, among other things, provided the sumptuous fare for one of the city's most distinguished restaurants, the Mirror Room. Everyone who was anyone at that time had, at least once, to have trod the red carpet under the crystal chandeliers of the "Mirror," as it was popularly called.

It was not uncommon for Little Eagle and Jonas to take the bus from Grorud to the city center along with Mrs. Larsen, and while Mrs. Larsen did her secret errands in the department stores or met a woman friend at Halvorsen's cake shop, she left the boys with her husband in the kitchen of the Grand Hotel, if he was on the early shift, that is—the Mirror opened at noon—and only with the blessing of the Italian chef de cuisine, naturally; he, like everyone else, had a bit of a soft spot for Mrs. Larsen. "Madam," he would say, kissing her hand gallantly. "Your name should not be Larsen, it should be Lollobrigida."

The kitchen was an enormous open space with white-tiled walls and two massive stoves, each standing under its own extractor hood. One stove was for the café and the Grand Basement, the other, at which Eagle's dad worked, was where the food for the Mirror and the function rooms was prepared. If there was one thing Jonas never tired of, it was this: to sit on a chair on the fringes of a bustling kitchen chock-full of pots, pans, ladles, sauce-boats and gleaming silver platters; to sit there and watch as many as forty chefs dashing back and forth between spotless shelves and cabinets, between all manner of raw ingredients and spices with names that were a fairytale in themselves; to watch and listen to how they chopped and sliced, whisked and stirred, how orders were called across the room, peppered with splendid French words, to result in mysterious dishes such as Fillet of Plaice Tout Paris, Tournedos Chasseur or Lobster Thermidore, usually after the work had been split into stages, with one chef doing the frying, one making the sauce and one arranging the garnish, while a fourth made a final, critical inspection of the plate before it was grabbed by one of the kitchen assistants and taken upstairs to the waiters. Almost like clockwork, Jonas thought.

Above this sizzling, seething world, with its odors to set the nostrils quivering and the stomach rumbling, in a glass-fronted booth, sat the chef de cuisine himself—first Hans Loose, and later the master chef Nicola Castracane—surveying the proceedings, as if from the bridge of a ship. Occasionally he might tap the glass with his pen and point to someone or other, for instance the trainee in charge of the sauce, whereupon the person concerned would immediately rush over with a bowl and hand this up to the booth so that the chef de cuisine could sample its contents and possibly issue an order in broken, but perfectly understandable, Norwegian: "You'll never learn, Syversen—a little more salt, I said!" It was like Father Christmas's workshop, Jonas would think as he sat there, engrossed in the hectic activity around hobs and ovens, the pounding and chopping, all the steam and the sputtering mingled with the shouts, not least from waiters fuming with impatience: "Get a bloomin' move on with that cod, will you, Anni!"

From where they sat, Little Eagle and Jonas could also keep an eye on the cold kitchen and pâtisserie section. Often they would sneak across to the counter in front of the latter—the main attraction here being the creation of the Grand's most celebrated cake. "Aha, a couple of spies," Mr. Metz, the pastry cook, would say. "Trying to steal the recipe for the best Napoleon cake in the world, eh? Well, well, then watch closely." Mr. Metz would give them a sly look and whisper in his Danish-accented Norwegian: "The secret is to make the cake on the spot." As if to demonstrate, he would then place a cake base on the worktop. "The bases must, of course, be baked that same morning, so that they have that very special crispness. And there has to be plenty of rum in the cream filling." Drooling at the mouth, Jonas and Little Eagle observed how elegantly Mr. Metz shaped the cream into a flat-topped cylinder in the center of the circular base almost like a bricklayer with his trowel. "And the icing should be added only just before it's served, so the base doesn't go all soggy. Like so. Here you are, boys, try one." Jonas stuck the fork with the first bite into his mouth, feeling like an invincible commander-in-chief—like Napoleon before the battle of Austerlitz.

What Jonas liked best of all was the feeling of having gone behind the scenes, as it were, to the place where the real action was. It was like being granted a peek into the innards of Norway. Or like visiting a factory: seeing where the values were formed. For this seething, reeking, hissing room here below, fraught with screaming and yelling, was just as much the reality as the mirror-clad restaurant and the smartly dressed diners upstairs. Jonas realized that, as with a coin, there were two sides to reality. And he didn't know which side he liked best. There was also something a bit scary about the kitchen, like the time when they were taken on a quick trip into the meat larder, where whole carcases hung in rows and people in heavy clothing were jointing the meat. This sight confirmed Jonas's impression of the kitchen as a kind of underworld, a hell as much as a paradise.

Ørn's dad was one of the kitchen's head chefs—"Three-Star Larsen" they called him—and Little Eagle was manifestly proud of his father, garbed in his chef's hat and jacket and, not least, his gingham-check trousers, bawling out orders to right and left: "For God's sake, don't scorch that sauce, Berg, it's for Mr. Mustad's fish." Or: "A Porterhouse steak for James Lorentzen the ship-owner. Remember, he wants it rare and with a good rim of fat." Sometimes he would come over to the boys, point to a mouth-watering plate: "That's for Wenche Foss, the famous actress," he would say with a wink.

On one occasion they were allowed to leaf through the menu. Jonas had no idea what all these things were: turtle soup Lady Curzon, Sole Colbert, Crêpes Suzette, Caviar Mallasol served on crushed ice. But what impressed him most were the prices. He had never thought about it before, how anyone could afford to eat here—that Norwegians like themselves actually entered these premises and sat down to eat under the crystal chandeliers. His parents had never been here, nor anyone else from the estate, as far as he knew. The Mirror, the Grand, was another world, like some dazzling Hollywood film set, a totally unimaginable realm—the exclusive province of the very rich or certainly the well-to-do.

And this, Professor, is one of the points of this story: how, when he grew up, Jonas Wergeland forgot this: how he thought nothing of frequenting the finest restaurants in Norway, in the world for that matter, and stuffing himself unconstrainedly with all manner of delights, without pausing for a moment to consider what a miracle it was, that he—only one generation removed from a breed of thrifty folk, scrimpers and savers—dined in restaurants as often as he ate at home; in the blink of an eye he had been transformed from a spectator, with his nose pressed against the restaurant's windowpane so to speak, to a gluttonous, gastronomic participant—now that is a story about Norway today, and it's something to think about.

Sometimes Jonas and Little Eagle went up to visit the waiters who held sway, in their dark-blue mess jackets, in the serving pantry. If there wasn't too much to do Mr. Gundersen would make the boys that exotic beverage, an iced tea, or he would explain how to use the mysterious cash register, when he wasn't over at the warming counter, teaching them a real fakir's trick: how to balance two scalding-hot plates on one hand.

What surprised Jonas most, on these visits, was all the fuss when somebody famous sat down at one of the tables. The shout would suddenly go up: "Sonja Henie's here," and everybody knew that a glass of champagne rosé would shortly be carried out to the lithe lady in the white fur, who sat with her gold champagne whisk at the ready. Occasionally, the waiters would also cluster behind the automatic swing doors into the restaurant, the opening mechanism of which could be overridden to allow them to peer discreetly at the diners through the two narrow panes of glass. Sometimes Mr. Gunderson would lift up Jonas and Little Eagle in turn and point out a particularly famous patron. "That rather starchy-looking gent over there is Francis Bull," he would say.

"And the handsome, curly-headed chap over by the dance floor is Toralv Maurstad." Another day a lanky-looking character caught Jonas's eye. "That's Leif Juster," Mr. Gundersen said. "He's got his dog underneath the table—don't tell anybody!"

One such moment was to have a certain bearing on Jonas Wergeland's life. More folk than usual had flocked excitedly around the door into the Mirror, including the ladies from the coffee kitchen half a flight down, and when the boys asked Mr. Gunderson what all the fuss was about—was it a government minister, a shipping magnate?—he told them, beaming with pride, that none other than so-and-so himself was sitting there in the restaurant, eating black grouse in a cream sauce. Neither Jonas nor Little Eagle recognized the name. Mr. Gundersen snorted. They must be joking! Did they really not know who that was? He was a presenter on the *Evening News*. "*He's on the TV*," Gundersen intoned respectfully, as if these words put paid to all questions, all doubt.

And eventually the boys were lifted up to the glass and Jonas saw this person, a newsreader whose name need not be cited here, since he has been completely forgotten, as a name that is, because he no longer appears on television, although he still works for NRK and now fulfils, it must be said, a far more important role. Let me remind you that this was in the infancy of television, when the *Evening News* wasn't even broadcast every evening. Some people may perhaps remember the opening credits: a globe with the program's title swirling around it in a streamer, accompanied by a fanfare of trumpets. This was a time when people regarded these NRK employees, these perfectly ordinary journalists, almost as being the voice of God Himself.

Jonas did not, however, react with the same awe as the waiters and the others. He did remark on the lovely light that fell on the newsreader, partly from the window and partly from the mirrors and the crystal, in such a way that a special aura seemed to hang about him; but what Jonas notices above all else is that in front of him, at this very moment, this personage has his dessert, has one of the Grand's celebrated Napoleon cakes, as if—through his choice of dessert—wishing to underline his status as a modern-day conqueror.

Only later was the significance of this episode brought home to Jonas. He realized that television did something to people. Or, more importantly: it had never occurred to Jonas that a person could sit quite still in a chair, yet still be out there conquering. You hardly had to do a thing. All you had to do was to read from a sheet of paper, all you had to do was show your face. Your power stemmed not from wealth or knowledge but from being seen. Could there be any cheaper form of fame? Unbeknown to himself, once he had comprehended this Jonas felt an unutterable sense of relief.

This lesson did not sink in, however, until much later. In the first instance, it was remarkable that Jonas, despite having seen the restaurant and these famous people, did not for a moment cherish a dream of one day sitting there himself, or think that some day there might even be a couple of lads sitting in that kitchen who, when someone said: "This chateaubriand is for Jonas Hansen," would cry out: "Wow! Jonas Hansen!" No, after these visits, Jonas had only one thought: he wanted to be a chef.

After Jonas, his surname long since changed to Wergeland, had made his first appearance on television, as an announcer, when he had in other words taken the first step towards a degree of celebrity the like of which has rarely been seen in Norway, one of the first things he treated himself to was, however, a meal at one of the capital's finest restaurants. One could, therefore, ask oneself whether Jonas Wergeland perhaps denied his own boyish instinct, which said that a skilled chef was much more to be admired than a face that simply read from a sheet of paper. It might look as though his aim was not to serve but to be served. Or, to put it another way: as though he chose the side of reality's coin which showed the golden surface, rather than the clamorous, steaming, value-forming chaos on the reverse.

Maybe I'm being unfair. Because, in the studio, Jonas Wergeland never quite rid himself of the feeling that he actually found himself in a vast kitchen, that in making programs, his ideal was to dish up tasty, aromatic food for the people of Norway—they were, so to speak, patrons in his restaurant, a chamber full of light and magic mirrors.

I—yes I, the professor—feel compelled to interrupt here. I feel a powerful need to apologize for what I would call the form of the preceding pages, which is not at all like anything else I've ever written. I have weighed up the pros and cons, I have tried every alternative and still, believe me when I say: this is the best solution. For all concerned.

In other words, it was not me personally who took the initiative for this project. I was contacted, not to say headhunted, by the publishers, to write as they put it, "the definitive Wergeland biography." They assured me, in the most fulsome terms, that I was the "perfect" man for such an assignment, and since the prospects of commercial gain seemed more than fair, they made me an offer I couldn't refuse—to coin a phrase from less law-abiding circles.

That said, I cannot deny that I was tempted, that the thought had already crossed my mind. For a long time, even after everything came to light, I had felt a certain sympathy for, and possibly a distant affinity with, Jonas Wergeland. Besides which, it really got my back up to see how he was treated. Thanks to a combination of a major success and a painful divorce, I know how it feels to be hounded by sensation-hungry reporters.

I think we can safely say that the year 1992 was an *annus horribilis* not just for the British queen but also for Jonas Wergeland. Who does not remember the shock, the disbelief, on that spring evening when the killing of Wergeland's wife, Magrete Boeck, was the lead item on the *Evening News*? Even the newsreader looked profoundly affected, stunned almost. Like most people, I followed every news broadcast during the days that followed, feeling both fascinated and appalled. And there was plenty to hold our interest. I cannot recall ever having seen such an explosion in the media before, with extended television broadcasts and extra editions of the tabloid papers; anyone would have thought, from the headlines, that the royal palace had been blow sky-high—yes, that's it: you'd have thought some accident had befallen the Norwegian monarchy.

Shocking news stories come and go, and some people may already have forgotten the whole thing. Allow me, very briefly, to remind you of the intriguing spreads in the newspapers, featuring faithfully rendered sketches of the crime scene, Villa Wergeland, with arrowed boxes containing descriptions of each room, not least the living room, where even the outlines of a polar-bear skin and the body of Margrete Boeck were depicted with an astonishing wealth of detail and graphic bravura. There was a welter of theories, a welter of voices all striving to understand, explain, comfort. Both friends and opponents of Jonas Wergeland, even the odd relative, made effusive statements. What everyone longed for, was positively screaming out for—not surprisingly—was some comment from Jonas Wergeland himself, seeing that it was he who had found her, he who had reported her death. It was as if they expected, more or less demanded, that he answer questions along the lines of: "What did you feel when you arrived home from the World's Fair in Seville and found your wife murdered?" Only after some days did word get out as to what had happened when the police arrived at the villa on the evening of the murder: Jonas Wergeland had broken down completely and had had to be admitted to hospital. When it became known that Norway's top television celebrity was lying in Ullevål Hospital, practically in a state of shock, it is no empty platitude to say that an entire nation felt for him.

The police were not giving away much. They had a few vague eyewitness accounts from neighbors and some other tips, but all of it conflicting. They issued no descriptions of people whom they wished to question in connection with their enquiries, no Identikit pictures. The police were, however, operating on the theory that Jonas Wergeland's wife had probably been taken by surprise—word leaked out that the killer or killers had battered her head against the wall before shooting her. It was rumored that the police were pursuing a line of enquiry that led back to Margrete Boeck's past, in another country no less. They concentrated on the murder weapon, issued pictures and descriptions of it. Then things died down. Jonas Wergeland was discharged from hospital but refused to speak to anyone. Weeks went by without any sensational developments in the case, and when there's nothing new to report, interest tends to wane—such is the implacable law of the media.

So much for the event itself. Jonas Wergeland's tragedy, his destiny, one might say. Because the whole sequence was not altogether unlike a Greek drama. I suppose even back then I had in mind a story in which hubris played a large part, in which dark powers were underestimated.

So when the publishers approached me I jumped at the chance. I did not have to think too long before signing on the dotted line.

I decided to follow my usual procedure: one year for the groundwork, followed by another year for the actual writing. That ought to be enough, I felt, it certainly had been in the past, to produce studies of lives which, in the grand scheme of things, will surely prove to be of more consequence than Jonas Wergeland's. I started gathering material, conducted interviews, traveled, read, sorted and sifted and wrote notes. In any case, I knew right from the start what my aim ought to be: to shed light on the mysterious creative process behind Jonas Wergeland's television programs. If I could understand that, I might also be able to understand this other thing. I sketched out a framework, came up with a couple of intuitive hypotheses—things seemed to be shaping up nicely.

I live, as I suppose most people know from various newspaper and magazine articles, in the Oslo suburb of Snarøya, on one of the highest points in the area. My study is in a sort of turret at the top of the house. The house itself was modelled on Fridtjof Nansen's mansion at Polhøgda, not that far away. From my desk I can watch the planes landing and taking off at Fornebu Airport, on the south-western section of the runway, as well as the boats sailing up and down the coastline of the Nesodden peninsula. It's an inspiring vista: it makes me feel as though I am at a junction, that I am sitting in a control tower from which I have a complete overview. At times I can almost believe that all this activity around me is generated by my writing.

This illusion was soon shattered. The first sign that the biography of Jonas Wergeland was going to be different manifested itself in a pressing need to devote an extra year to the collection of material. And when I did finally set to work up here—after, that is, having gone through the phase in which I commit key points from my notes to memory, almost letting my brain soak up all my lines of argument—I saw that none of my hypotheses held water. And what was worse: that I could not come up with any new ones.

I sat in my turret, feeling hamstrung, or rather, that I had bitten off more than I could chew, staring at the stacks of papers and books round about me, the notice boards covered in cryptic notes and maps of Cape Town and Jaipur; the best encyclopaedia on the market lay next to a commemorative history of the Grorud Ironmongers, works on everything from woodcarving and organ music to Duke Ellington and the moons of Pluto. Chapters had been studiously plotted out on index cards that were then neatly filed in boxes and ring binders in a particular order, all of it adhering to a detailed chronological framework. Drawers and filing cabinets were brimming over with cuttings, copies of articles, transcripts, photographs, letters. The place was littered with audiocassettes and videotapes containing recordings of interviews and film footage. I sat in the turret and tried to take in all of this contradictory, unrelated, bewildering data. I soon realized that it would take me years merely to read such a volume of material. How to select those details that were significant? How to build a life out of all those boxes and binders bulging with television reviews, items on local history, snippets about women friends and the unreliable recollections of old friends? And above all: how was I to link together this mass of bits and pieces? When I eventually sat down to write, determined to make a start somewhere at least, I found myself absolutely and utterly stuck, my fingers refused, quite literally, to strike the keys.

I was at my wit's end. I sat in a room packed with information. Around me loomed all sorts of fancy equipment: fax machines, photocopiers, video players, printers and, not least, computers, providing access to diverse networks—what I lacked, though, was the mental software necessary in order for the combination of data and hardware to produce some result. What should I include and what should I leave out? I could write a score of pages simply on Jonas Wergeland's penchant for tweed jackets. At one point I felt tempted to do more research, take a trip to Tokyo, for example, see whether I could discover any clues to what had actually happened there—maybe that would break the block, endow me with a flash of crystal-clear insight—but I knew I would only be running away, putting things off. I could not afford to dilly-dally like this. The publishers were on my back. The press had got wind of the project, and the biography was already being described as a really juicy exposé. Everyone was waiting.

I had been suffering for some weeks from this attack of writer's block when help arrived. It was a Sunday evening, with a thick fog outside. I had just lit a fire, wondering, as I did so, at an unusual and fierce burst of dog barking, when the doorbell rang. This marked the start of the strangest week of my life. On the doorstep, seeming almost to have materialized out of the fog, stood an enigmatic individual swathed in a black cloak, a figure that conveyed an instant sense of authority and dignity. "I have come to your rescue, Professor," this person announced bluntly and walked straight in before I could say a word. "I assume your study is up in the turret." The figure proceeded resolutely up the spiral staircase. I had no choice but to follow.

After removing the cloak with a flourish that put me in mind of a bullfighter, the stranger promptly sat down in the best chair in the study and ran an eye over all the clutter, all of that ridiculous, and so far useless, equipment. "Could I ask you, please, to dim the lights?" this person said, almost as if disgusted by the shambolic scene, by the desk buried under papers and books—this sea of details, so impenetrable that I referred to it as "my dark sources." I could see that the stranger was impatient, that this person, no matter how odd it may sound, gave the impression of having eaten too much, of being full to bursting. "I know you are working on a biography of Jonas Wergeland," the stranger said. "I also know that you have got bogged down. So I am going to help you. I am used to chaos." This person pulled the chair closer to the fire. "I am not blessed with omniscience—but I know a great deal. I hold, among other things, the key to the riddle of Jonas Wergeland. Or, not to beat about the bush, I carry, if I may make so bold as to say, the whole of his story in my head." It may have been because I was confused, but I thought I detected a slight accent, as if Norwegian was not my visitor's mother tongue.

"That is why I have come to you, Professor. You see, I cannot write, only recount."

"Why are you doing this?" was the first thing I managed to say.

"Out of pity," my visitor said. "Sheer pity."

I was not sure whether the stranger was thinking of me or of Jonas Wergeland. "And your purpose?" I asked, putting the same question in another way.

"To save a life. Otherwise there would be no point."

I still couldn't tell whether the stranger was referring to Jonas Wergeland or myself. And it took some time for it to dawn on me that this person was actually offering me a job as chronicler of Jonas Wergeland's story—on two conditions: that I undertook not to deviate from the order in which the story was recounted and that I wrote it by hand.

"Can't I use a tape recorder?" I said.

"No," the visitor replied. "I'm old-fashioned. I belong, so to speak, to another age. I do not wish to talk into a machine. I wish to talk to a face, I must have a person—call it a scribe if you like—to whom I can tell the story. I don't trust machines."

"I just thought it might be handy to have the tape as backup," I said. "In case I missed anything."

"You don't understand," the stranger said. "That's the very possibility I mean to deny you. I said I would help you, not write the book for you. I don't expect you to quote me word for word. I'm not looking for a copy. I want you to interpret what I say as you write. The stories will not be as I tell them but as you perceive them. If you do not get it exactly right, if you have to rely on your memory, then all to the good. And you are, of course, free to add things gleaned from your own material to improve upon it."

I accepted. I had to accept if the publishers were ever to get their biography. At the back of my mind I thanked my stars for the fact that I had once, in a previous career, been ambitious enough to learn shorthand, had attended a course run by the Norwegian parliament, no less. Although for a long time I could not be sure, I have come to the conclusion that my visitor must have been aware that I was proficient—or at any rate moderately proficient—in this rare skill.

"Well, we might as well get started right away," the stranger said, as if in the habit of giving orders. "Hurry up, I have the entire sequence worked out in my head, and mark my words, Professor, in this case the sequence is crucial; only by following it can you hope to understand anything at all. So please do not distract me; just one story out of place and it all falls apart."

These words, the way they were uttered—with a kind of, how shall I put it, pent-up aggression—gave me the feeling that the stranger had something against Jonas Wergeland, almost hated him, in fact. The figure kept a close eye on me from the chair by the fire as I fetched my spiral-bound notebook and a pen, staring at me as intently as a juggler with twenty balls in the air. Then the stream of stories began, and though during the course of their telling I still felt an urge to cry out, to protest, to pose questions, to ask their narrator to stop, I managed to refrain, to confine myself to taking notes, tried to get down as much as possible. I'm sure I hardly need add that this was the longest and most arduous single bout of writing I had ever undertaken.

Nonetheless, it was a relief to sit there with a blank sheet of paper in front of me, to have the chance, in a way, to start from scratch again. The results of that first evening, of our joint efforts, can be read on the preceding pages. And I believe the stranger was right: there was something about being forced to write, almost without thinking, as my visitor talked, that had a fruitful effect, so much so that I even managed, during short pauses, to jot down brief notes that I could enlarge upon later, points I suddenly recalled from my own research. The stranger created the necessary distance, enabling me to discern things from fresh angles, in a new light. Besides which, I liked the constant use of my title: "Professor"—no one has called me that in fifteen years—as if my unknown visitor was, above all, well aware of my past. This gave me the confidence, at a later stage when I was transcribing my notes, to rework the text, sometimes quite drastically, on the basis of data from my own sources. Sometimes, when I read through the stories I found myself wondering whether this was what my visitor had said. Or whether, in the writing, even in those passages where I believe I have copied down the stranger's exact words, somehow or other the story has gone from being half-true to being half-false.

The second evening on which the stranger sat down in the chair by the fireplace, rather like a general commandeering my house, this enigmatic character started without any preamble—and with eyes riveted, so it seemed, on the darkness, if not, that is, on the tall pine tree outside the window overlooking the fjord—on a story that was totally new to me.

Outer Land

One day Jonas Wergeland was quite suddenly sent reeling. He knew he was seriously ill but was incapable of doing anything, nor did he feel like doing anything, he hardly seemed to care. He lay on his back, staring up at the sky, up at the clouds, up at woolly floes that were forever changing, moving too fast, careening towards him. He was far from all help, far out on the Mongolian steppes, surrounded by nothing but a rippling sea of grass and a sky fraught with wind.

An odd-looking face leaned into his field of vision, a Mongol, but he had something on his head, antlers; he looked like some sort of weird hybrid, a dragon, was Jonas's first thought, no, a spirit creature, half-elk, half-man, a figure which began to move, dance in a circle around Jonas.

He was ill, dangerously ill, had been suddenly stricken, something to do with his head, his brain maybe, an inflammation of his most vital organ, deep in a foreign country. He was afraid, and yet not. His body had been invaded by worms, ribbons that slithered around, wove in and out of one another, ribbons that slowly tipped him over into an abstract state, a reality in which undulating patterns took over from the known world. "Help," he cried, or whispered, or thought.

He tried to pull himself together. He recognized the dancer. It was Buddha. He had to hold on to that thought. Buddha. And Mongolia.

Only the day before, everything had been fine. Not just fine. Wonderful. Jonas and Buddha had been stretched out on the heights of Karakorum, as was their wont, peering down into the valley below. "Isn't that a caravan we can see down there?" Jonas might say. Buddha would gaze long and hard, as if listening for something on the wind, might pluck a blade of grass and proceed to chew on it: "No, I think it's a procession of monks on their way to the temple," he would say at last. When Jonas strained his eyes he could catch a glint of gold from the roof of a temple in the distance.

They lay back on the grass and gazed up at the clouds, at the birds in flight, and listened to the sounds of the wind. They had all the time in the world and no particular plans. "There's a good dragon flying over us today," said Buddha, meaning simply that the weather was nice, with clouds drifting by overhead. They were in the midst of a boundless space, with wide plains stretching out on all sides. From their *ger* fluttered a long, fringed pennant. Buddha lay there purring like a cat. Or a prayer wheel. Buddha was the only person Jonas knew who had this ability. He could curl up in a ball and be so content that he positively thrummed inside. And nowhere did Buddha feel happier than up here on the heights, on the steppes, in a landscape where the sky dominated one's field of vision—if they were lucky it was breezy too; and the wind seemed to enhance Buddha's sense of freedom and well-being. "Know what I like best about Mongolia?" Jonas said. "You'd have to walk a hundred miles if you wanted to hang yourself."

The day before, Jonas had dozed off for a while when they were lying like this, had not woken until Buddha was standing over him yelling, "Get up, lazybones, time to wrestle." Buddha was ten years old but already strong. They wrestled Mongolian-style. The first one whose knee or elbow, back or shoulder touched the ground had lost. Jonas allowed a puffing, panting Buddha to bring him down, whereupon Buddha proceeded to run around, whooping triumphantly. "Hey, stop all that jumping about and come and help me get things ready for the night," Jonas said, wanting to calm him down.

They crawled into the *ger*, through a door facing due south. They always carried a compass. A *ger* was supposed to be an image of the universe—the ancient universe, that is—with the stove, like the sun, at its center. There was a place for everything; Jonas and Buddha slept in the area that faced west. To the north lay the sacred objects; Buddha usually brought a box full of different bits and pieces or maybe a picture. On this occasion it was a portrait of Agnetha Fältskog from the pop group ABBA.

All of this had originally been Jonas's idea. Or so he thought. Ever since Buddha was a baby, whenever his brother had been taken along to social gatherings, it had vexed Jonas to see how people automatically looked down on him. As Buddha grew older and began to display what were, by his own standards, rare gifts, they had hatched a plan. In any given situation Jonas might ask the others present if they knew what a *dell* was, or a *gurtum*—and *naadam*, ladies and gentlemen, what might that be? The others could not, of course, answer. But Buddha, aged seven or eight, could hold forth for minutes on end, describing a *dell*, a national costume in a variety of different styles, the trimmings, the nine buttons, the bright blue, red, yellow and green hues; or explain in detail what took place during the *naadam* festival, not least the horse-riding competition. This soon put paid to that slightly indulgent, benign attitude; and Buddha was treated, if not exactly the same as everyone else, then certainly with a new respect, not to say awe. And awe was, after all, better than condescension or that unappetizing blend of pity and curiosity which reduced Buddha to a cute, innocent mascot.

As time went on, Jonas and Buddha created a common domain that was theirs alone; they were both citizens of an imaginary Mongolia, "land of the brave, proud men." As often as possible they would take themselves off to Lillomarka to indulge their Mongolian inclinations: to be nomads on a boundless plain, nomads who loved the wind and the freedom found under those clear skies, who would quite spontaneously compare sheep viewed against a lush pasture with pearls on green velvet. Over his bed in the new villa, just a stone's throw from Solhaug and their old flat, Buddha had a large-scale map of Mongolia and across this they made many an arduous trek before he went to sleep. In due course, Buddha memorized the names of most of the country's towns and provinces, mountains and rivers. He was also one of the very few people in Norway who knew the meaning of such utterly elementary words as "*khalka*," "*tugrik*," and "*urga*." Jonas never could tell how much of all this his brother understood, but he certainly remembered it, used the words properly—it could of course have been put down to his marvellous gift for mimicry, which also made him an uncommonly good ABBA imitator—his renderings of numbers such as "I Do, I Do, I Do, I Do, I Do" were quite priceless. Buddha could well be called an expert in his field. Jonas took a certain pleasure in this: that, in one area at least, his brother knew more than most people. The strange thing was that Jonas, too, became captivated by this universe, as if it were an outer land, an Outer Norway, just beyond the boundaries of the realm in the same way as there was an Outer Mongolia. Jonas had, in fact, known it from the start: his brother possessed valuable gifts into which it would be difficult for him, Jonas, to gain any insight.

Jonas lies in his sleeping bag, bathed in sweat, understanding everything and understanding nothing, both remembering and not remembering where he is. He is burning up inside his skull. His heart is beating irregularly. His thoughts are in a whirl, drifting with the clouds, causing him to forget that he may be mortally ill, that this could be the end—if, that is, the figure dancing round him, the figure with the antlers on its head, cannot save him. "Help," he cries, whispers, thinks.

Who was the most important person in Jonas Wergeland's life? It was Buddha. Of this I am in no doubt, Professor: it was Buddha.

Over a number of years in the mid-seventies, Jonas and Buddha created a little slice of Mongolia for themselves in the heart of Lillomarka. They would strike off from the forest track down at Breisjø Lake, cut through the ruins of the monastery in Bispedalen—which turned, as if by magic, into a lamasery filled with the sounds of murmured prayers and resounding gongs—and continued up the slope until they reached the top of Revlikollen. Being so high up, on what was, in those days, a bare hilltop, gave them a pretty good illusion of standing on a mountain plateau, and it was easy to make believe that they were not far from Karakorum, site of Genghis Khan's old camp, the very heart of the world. Here they pitched their tent—not a felt *ger*, unfortunately, but a tent all the same. It was no coincidence that Jonas should have written, around this time, a singular and controversial study paper on the architecture of tents. "I do believe you could have stirred up a minor revolt among the Bedouins with that," commented one of his tutors at the School of Architecture.

I really ought to make it quite clear, here, since it could be misinterpreted, that it was not escapism, all this, but a form of communication. Or an advanced sort of game. Not only that, but it was something these two had conceived of together. Which is to say: to begin with Jonas thought that Buddha had picked it up from him, from all the stories he had told his brother over the years, about the uses of such curious inventions as the pole lasso or the sweat scraper, or about camel nose pegs and the laborious process of felt-making. But as time went on Jonas began to wonder. Because Buddha reacted in an unaccountable manner to some things. When just a little boy he had evinced an unusual fondness, not to say passion, for some coral and turquoise stones at Aunt Laura's flat. It was all they could do to get them away from him. Only later did Jonas discover that stones like these were used in Mongolian jewelry. Another time, or rather lots of times, Buddha was to be found sitting in some green spot, arranging a circle of stones around himself. Every now and again Jonas would count the stones: there were always 108, neither more nor less. And the first time Buddha used chopsticks in a Chinese restaurant, he—this boy who had fumbled for so long with knives and forks—ate perfectly with them, as if he had never done anything else.

And who could explain his astonishing way with horses? Not to mention his talent for archery?

In the evenings, after long, hard days spent milking, branding cattle, breaking in horses, whittling pieces of wood into horse-head violins and so on, they would lie in the tent and eat juicy lamb chops—it had to be sheep meat—cooked in a frying pan over the primus stove in the center and drink *kefir* from a thermos—*kefir* was the closest they could get to the Mongolians' fermented mare's milk. "Have some more *arkhi*," Jonas might say before pouring *kefir* into Buddha's little wooden bowl. Other meals consisted mainly of yellow cheeses: Gouda, Cheddar, Emmenthal, although they weren't dried like the Mongolian cheeses. They also drank tea, tea mixed with a little butter and salt and new milk.

"Tell me the story about Basaman," Buddha would say, as they lay like this in the tent, regaling themselves. And for the hundredth time Jonas told him the tale of how, in 1936, Basaman the shaman from Solon was killed by a Japanese locomotive when he attempted, a mite optimistically, to stop it. Alternatively, Jonas might tell of the time when Dölgöre the shaman magicked all of the spirits over which he had control into two Russian padlocks. At such moments Buddha would lie fingering the animal bones he had found, raising them to his lips as if they were flutes, or contemplating the elk's antlers that he had been hanging on to for so long.

They had made many such treks across the Mongolian steppes. The previous day had been no different in that respect. But this morning Jonas had woken with a fever, and it was getting worse and worse; he didn't know what was wrong, only that it was something to do with his head, at the very worst meningitis, something serious, something that progressed fast and could be fatal. "Help," he managed to say to Buddha, or whisper, or think.

He had slipped into a delirium, slipped down among sinuous shapes, lay reeling in his sleeping bag with his head sticking out of the tent opening, above and below the clouds at one and the same time. Buddha kept his head; first he sat for a while drumming with a stick on a saucepan. From when Buddha was very small, Jonas had remarked on his brother's way of playing his toy drums: monotonously, mysteriously, as if he struck them not to make a noise like other children but to generate silence. And now, as he drummed on the saucepan, Buddha had gone into a sort of trance, had been transformed, this much Jonas grasped. Buddha fixes the elk antlers on his head, gets to his feet and starts to dance, even puts a stick between his legs so it looks as if he is riding a horse, dances, or rides around Jonas, not Buddha himself that is, but this thing inside Buddha, this thing of which Jonas knows nothing, this thing that hails from other, outer, spheres; and Jonas becomes aware, after an hour, possibly two, when Buddha is once more sitting quietly by his side, holding his hand, of how the fever slowly loosens its grip, of how his thoughts begin to run along their normal lines, of how the breeze suddenly feels cool and refreshing on his brow. “Thanks,” he says, or whispers, or thinks.

Jonas never found out whether this nasty turn in the woods—or up on the Mongolian steppes, depending on your point of view—could have proved fatal. And it was never mentioned between the two boys. Jonas suspected that Buddha had saved his life that day. Not that it made much difference, really. Buddha had saved his life anyway. When you get right down to it, there was only one true hero in Jonas Wergeland’s life, and that hero’s name was Buddha.

Made in Norway

Which reminds me: I must tell you about the attack in Istanbul, but first I need to recount the tale of the Three Wise Men. You see, Jonas himself once had a go at being a shaman. Not by dancing but by reading. For even though Jonas Wergeland only rarely opened a book, there was a period—a long period—when he used to sit with the same thick book in his hands. And he wasn't reading to himself, either; he was reading aloud, to another person, for the ears of that person who sat, or as good as lay, in a chair. And despite the fact that his companion's eyes were fixed on a blank television screen, Jonas read: "For the seven lakes, and by no man these verses: / Rain; empty river; a voyage, / Fire from frozen cloud, heavy rain in the twilight," he read and scanned the face opposite him, a face that remained as immobile as ever, eyes that never blinked.

Jonas Wergeland was sitting in an institution in Oslo, reading to one of his best friends. He read aloud and at length. Jonas Wergeland was not a good reader, he recited in a flat monotone, softly, nonetheless he read, read with a dogged determination, from an endless poem, laying stress on, nay, instilling hope into, every word. As far as I know, this was the only time when Jonas Wergeland read because he felt that it really mattered, although he did not understand one word of what he was reading. He would read from this weighty tome, read these, to him, incomprehensible stanzas, for decades, at least once a month. Words such as: "Under the cabin roof was one lantern. / The reeds are heavy; bent / and the bamboos speak as if weeping."

Jonas put down the book and stared deep into Viktor's pupils, as if hoping for some sign of life, much as coals can sometimes give off a faint glow just when you think the fire has gone out. "I wish I could have brought you a bottle of aquavit—a bottle of Gilde's Non Plus Ultra," he says. "But it's not allowed, you see." No answer. Never any answer. Black coals.

"I'm married now," Jonas said. "D'you remember I told you about Margrete, the one who dumped me in seventh grade?" he said. "We have a baby," he said. "Oh, by the way, I'm going to be doing a program for television soon—got any good ideas?" Jonas refused to give up, always spent a long time talking to Viktor, pausing briefly every now and again, as if listening to his friend's replies: "You were right," he might say. "*Pet Sounds* is a more important album than *Sergeant Pepper*." Short pause. "And I've been thinking about it: as an ideology, Merckxism could definitely take over from Marxism." He may also have endeavored to develop his argument, although not, of course, the way Viktor Harlem himself would have done it—if those coals had not been extinguished.

They were sitting in a nursing home in Oslo, a totally characterless room that fitted well with Viktor's own characterlessness, the eyes fixed on the blank television screen in the corner. For Viktor Harlem, time had stopped. He still looked as he had done at the age of nineteen, when in his final year at Oslo Cathedral School. He—Viktor the Taoist—had attained his goal: he had become immortal. Jonas had the idea that, in spirit, his friend was actually somewhere else, that this was why his body remained the same—because there was nobody there, inside it. Viktor sat absolutely still, staring into space. There didn't seem to be any point, but Jonas knew, hoped, that something was going on behind those black pupils. Something must register, surely, and this "something" might, in the long run, generate a glow. "Remember what I said about the Middle Ages being a golden age in the history of the West?" Jonas said. "It was a bluff. One of many. It was something I lifted, just a quote from a book of lectures by Friedrich von Schlegel."

No reaction. No glow in Viktor's pupils. His face as blank as the television screen in the corner.

Occasionally, when they were in the lounge, Jonas would sit down at the piano and play one of the standards, "Someone To Watch Over Me" maybe, striking chords that would have made anyone else raise an eyebrow.

No response. An outsider would never have guessed that this human vegetable in the armchair had once, ten years earlier, been a regular firecracker, fizzing with ideas and flashes of inspiration, one great scintillating ball of energy; that this figure had been the natural leader and spokesman for a remarkable group known as the Three Wise Men: the sort of baffling individual, one in a hundred thousand, who in third year at high school, at the drop of a hat and without turning a hair, would proceed to sum up—to pick a subject at random—the ins and outs of analytical, phenomenological and hermeneutic philosophy.

How does one become a conqueror?

Jonas often thought about Lillehammer. He hated that town. As far as he was concerned, it was no surprise that Lillehammer should have been the scene of the first terrorist attack on Norwegian soil—the assassination of an innocent man, carried out by the Israeli intelligence service, Mossad. Ten years earlier they had walked there arm in arm, Jonas, Axel, and Viktor, the Three Wise Men, on their way home from an eventful skiing holiday farther up Gudbrandsdalen, on their way home to the wilderness of the Cathedral School and the ominous advent of the university Prelim. Unlike Axel and Jonas, Viktor was very fair and had already begun to lose his hair. Caricatures in the school newspaper invariably depicted him as a light bulb screwed into a black polo neck sweater. And it was true, he always seemed lit up, incessantly sparkling with theories, exuberant notions—on that day too, just before it happened, as they, but mostly Viktor, were walking along, debating possible future demonstrations, the stream of talk punctuated by hoots of laughter as he reminded Jonas and Axel of some of their previous, highly original raids: because, despite what many might say, and despite a rather reckless approach to life, the Three Wise Men were warriors at heart, young men who were ready to revolt at the first sign of injustice and social folly and who devoted almost as much time to making sense of the world as they did to changing it.

One of these latterly so legendary demonstrations was staged in Oslo on an autumn evening in 1969, as a protest against the situation in Biafra. I ought perhaps to say something here about Biafra, Professor, since disasters of this nature have a way of elbowing one another out of the collective memory. But Biafra constituted the real watershed. Biafra was nothing less than the first unthinkable famine to come sweeping into the living rooms of Norway by way of the television screen with the result that for years Biafra was to represent the epitome of world want. And remember: this was before such disasters were turned into light family entertainment, into Live Aid concerts and the like. Being confronted with the Biafran tragedy was like seeing one's first horror movie, that sense of actually feeling one's nerves fraying at the edges.

The Biafran war held special meaning for Jonas, since it was this event that opened his eyes to the change that had occurred in his own home. Ever since his father, lured by the advertisements, had bought their first television set in order to watch the speed skating in the winter Olympics of 1964, Jonas's parents had spoken less and less to one another.

The hum of a perpetual conversation, a sound like the low thrum of a power station, so much a part of his childhood, was now replaced by the hum of the television set. And the chairs which had once sat facing one another were now ranged side by side—not only that, they had bought new chairs, of a type specially designed for television viewing.

One evening in particular was to be of crucial significance. Jonas had been doing his homework and was on his way to the toilet when the usual metallic murmur prompted him to peek into the living room and thus he found himself confronted with a scene which he would never forget, one which stuck to his cerebral cortex like an icon: for there in the living room sat his parents, each in their chair, their eyes fixed on a screen filled with ghastly, heartbreaking reality, and yet they were so silent, so apathetic almost, that they might have been watching the Interlude fish in their aquarium. Although it's only fair to say that when the first reports from Biafra were screened, Jonas's parents too were, of course, appalled, they may even have wept, but by this time, six months later, their senses had become strangely blunted, they sat back in their chairs, staring listlessly at the television as if they were actually waiting for something else to come on, and this despite the fact that their eyes rested on one of those images which would be replayed again and again, with only minor variations, in the course of every famine disaster: a little girl with flies crawling over her eyes, weak from hunger, and on the ground right next to her: a vulture. Here, Jonas received an epiphanic vision of the true nature of Norway: this sight multiplied thousands upon thousands of times—people sitting in armchairs in front of televisions showing pictures of starving children far away.

It seems likely—and this is just a theory—that this was the evening on which Jonas Wergeland formed his overriding perception of Norway: of Norway as a nation of spectators. Finally, Jonas understood what his parents' generation had been building on those community workdays in the 1950s: a grandstand in which they had now taken their seats. All of Norway had become what it could indeed appear to be when seen from space—a 1200-mile long granite grandstand packed with armchairs. *Window On Our Times* was the name of the program, and people truly did sit there in their chairs as if staring through a window in the wall at the world outside, following all the suffering in the world from the sidelines as it were. Television was, quite simply, an invention eminently suited to a country which lay thus on the periphery, which was used to witnessing events from a safe distance.

"The screen tricks us into believing that we don't live a sheltered life," as Jonas Wergeland once remarked in a debate. The Norwegian word for television is "*fjernsyn*"—meaning "distant vision." And because the *fjernsyn* gave such a blessed illusion of beholding some distant vision, one could hold onto the blissful sense that one was merely a spectator and never an active participant.

This experience—I am in a position to reveal here—also lay behind one of Jonas Wergeland's earliest programs for television: one in which, so the advance publicity promised, he would take a look at the most quintessentially Norwegian product ever. Everyone was sure this would be something like Bjelland's fish balls or possibly one of Frionor's frozen seafood dishes, but in fact it turned out to be a product made by Ekornes, the successful furniture manufacturers from Sunnmøre on the west coast. In this program Jonas Wergeland stated, not without a trace of irony, that Norway's greatest contribution to the world in recent times was not the cheese-slicer, nor the plastic keycard, but the Stressless chair, first launched onto the market in 1971—an invention worthy of a land of spectators and indeed one for which the national spectator mentality was an absolute prerequisite. Because the Stressless patent was—and still is, I might say—brilliant in all its simplicity. The innovative feature, no less than a revolution in the relaxation industry, was that you could assume different sitting positions merely by shifting your body. A lazy nudge of the hip was enough, a little wriggle. You no longer needed to stretch your hand down to a lever. The position was adjusted by the weight of the body itself. Jonas filmed a lingering sequence demonstrating the merits of the chair—which was set in front of a television: a comical scene that did not fail to provoke a lot of bitter complaints to the NRK management from the furniture industry. But Jonas was perfectly serious. "We ought to design a new Norwegian flag," he said. "White as innocence and with a stylized Stressless chair in the center, just as India has the Emperor Ashoka's wheel on its flag." Jonas had no doubt: in a hundred years the Stressless would be on display in museums, hailed as a national symbol on a par with the painting of "Bridal Procession in Hardanger."

What I am trying to say is that the Biafra disaster occupied a nigh-on traumatic place in Jonas's consciousness, which is why he reacted so strongly when Viktor announced that autumn, that Norwegian missiles were being used in the war down there in tropical Africa. And do please pay attention here, Professor, because if there is one thing I know a little bit about it is the evil acts of which mankind is capable. Viktor read everything and anything and had contacts everywhere. Viktor was the sort of character who walked around with *Le Monde*'s weekly digest sticking out of his jacket pocket. He had an acquaintance in England who worked for a publication entitled *Peace News*, and in this paper, in the forthcoming November issue, it was reported that arms manufactured in Norway were being used in Biafra. Viktor had a copy of the article. He was outraged. It had, of course, been rumored that NATO ammunition was being employed down there, but this had elicited no great outcry. Any suggestion that these weapons might in some way be connected to Norway had nonetheless been denied. But now. In England they had a photograph, proof that the name of Norway was branded on the Biafra conflict for all time. In other words, that for once Norway was not a mere spectator but also, in fact, a participant of sorts. The picture showed the casing of a 40mm shell, stamped with the legend USN (NORWAY)—Norway, typically, only as a parenthesis but there all the same. "They ought to make miniature copies of this shell-casing," Viktor felt, "for Norwegians to sit on top of their television sets."

The Three Wise Men were never in any doubt: this news had to be made public. But how? Not surprisingly it was Viktor himself, with his mysterious network of contacts, who came up with the solution and set the stage for the triumphant evening when the three friends came walking—arm in arm then too—along Karl Johans gate, like three gunslingers in a western striding down the main street of some lawless town. They had come across Egertorget, passing underneath the splendid neon sign for Freia Chocolate, at which Jonas had so often gazed in wonder as a child, and were making their way over to the Eastern Station. And there—dead ahead of them—as if inscribed across the dark evening sky—was the message, sweeping past the eyes of everyone who was watching, like the Northern Lights: NORWEGIAN SHELLS USED IN BIAFRA. How Viktor, undoubtedly with the help of some reporter, had succeeded in keying the headline into the telex machine at the *Aftenposten* offices on Akersgata, onto the tape which, by transmitting the data down a telephone wire, converted it into glowing letters running round the top of the Eastern Railway Station façade, remained a mystery—not least to the owners of the newspaper. There it was, however, the writing on the wall, as clear as it was inexplicable, presented as it was on the largest electric headlines sign in Norway. Every bit as impressive as the Freia Chocolate sign. A whole twenty-six yards of panels, nine thousand light bulbs, revolving round and round. The Three Wise Men stood at the bottom of Karl Johans gate along with a good many other people, gazing up at the building across from them, as if mesmerized by the incomprehensible, impossible, outrageous, insolent legend that swept past their eyes at regular intervals, picked out in blazing light bulbs: NORWEGIAN SHELLS USED IN BIAFRA, again and again, between an advert for Adelsten Ladies and Menswear and a subscription special offer.

Several members of the press had also seen it. To be on the safe side, Viktor had tipped off one of the city papers and sent them a copy of the article in *Peace News*. A few days later it made front-page headlines. People refused to believe it, of course. They simply could not credit it. To begin with, the Ministry of Defense also denied the assertions but later issued a statement confirming them: the arms had been produced by the Norwegian company Raufoss for an American client. A long and involved explanation was given for how this could have happened, together with an assurance that Norway had not, of course, sold these shells to Nigeria.

Not that anyone believed that either. The Three Wise Men did not mean to moralize; they simply wanted to show that Norway was involved with the outside world. As long as the wealth was filtering into the country—not to say pouring in, or rather, being sucked into Norway—you could be sure that, in global terms, we were on the side of the lawbreakers, not to say the vultures. It was this fact which, incredible though it may seem, the people of Norway succeeded in suppressing and go on suppressing, as they sit there deeply ensconced in their comfy Stressless armchairs. Hence the reason that they are regularly taken so completely by surprise when arms fabricated in Norway, some small component, shows up where it shouldn't—be it, as past history has shown, in Cuba, in Israel, in the Soviet Union or Turkey. Or when it is discovered that some nice, respectable Norwegian concern has set up shop in a bloody dictatorship. Norway cannot stay an innocent bystander, sheltered from events forever. One of the things that was shot to pieces in Biafra, in that blessedly far-off conflict, was Norway's innocence. Thanks to Viktor Harlem, this blot on the virtuous face of Norway was placed, as it were, on record, to endure for all time.

And now, nearly three years after this exploit, the Three Wise Men are walking the streets of Lillehammer after a glorious skiing expedition in Gudbrandsdalen, another exploit which I should like, if I may, to describe in detail later. Now though, as I say, they are walking side-by-side, arm in arm, gleefully firing off suggestions—each one crazier than the one before—for new and momentous demonstrations, fresh disclosures concerning woeful situations in what they call the Potato Monarchy. In later years, both Axel and Jonas would recall that Viktor—it may have been the Taoist in him—had had his misgivings about that day, that he had anxiously consulted his diary—otherwise known as his seventh sense—wherein the date was circled in bright red, and shaken his head. So now he was treading rather warily, as a superstitious person will avoid stepping on the cracks in the pavement, and all of a sudden, on a side street, he swaps places with Jonas, takes Jonas's place in the middle, playing "all change," like when they were boys, and then it happens, what so seldom happens, and yet now and again does: a chunk of ice slides off one of the roofs, a large, hard chunk of ice comes hurtling through the air, inexorably, and hits Viktor—of all people Viktor, who is walking in the middle—on the head.

Viktor instantly fell to the ground, unconscious, and lay still. Axel, quick-witted as always, sprinted into a shop and called an ambulance. When it arrived he got in along with Viktor.

Jonas stayed behind. Picked up, of all things, the block of ice. Thought for a second, perhaps, of the old party game, Spin the Bottle. The whim of chance. Thought, perhaps, incensed by his own impotence, of smashing a window, all the windows in the street. He felt a burning urge to climb up onto the roof, to see that spot where the chunk of ice had broken off, from which it had fallen, the cause of the accident. Instead he stood where he was, regarding it as if it were a crystal ball, offering the prospect of an answer, and he did, in fact, glimpse something inside the ice. He took it back to the guesthouse in which they were staying and put it in the washbasin. Only then, with the bathroom light shining on it, did he spy the earring inside, one of those big pearl earrings, fake, cheap. Or maybe it was genuine, he thought. Jonas had no idea how it could have got there. How do things ever find their place? By a process that was possibly just as inexplicable or as logical as Norwegian shells winding up in Biafra.

Axel was sitting in the corridor when Jonas arrived at the hospital; distractedly running his fingers through his hair, as if trying to straighten out his black curls. Viktor was still unconscious, undergoing clinical tests in Admissions. The X-rays of his head had revealed nothing. They could hope. But both Axel and Jonas knew that a head was every bit as fragile as an electric bulb. They sat wordlessly side by side. Jonas rubbed his forehead; Axel fiddled with his hair. A kindly doctor asked them to come back the next day. Axel had called Viktor's mother. She was on her way to Lillehammer.

At the guesthouse the chunk of ice had almost melted away. Jonas told Axel about the earring, but when he looked for it, it was gone. "Don't kid around with me now," Axel said.

After a week Viktor regained consciousness, but that was all. He said nothing. He was somewhere else. Even though he could dress himself, could walk, could eat, he still needed help. He was there, and yet not. There was no reason why it should have been so, but so it was. He was a mystery to medical science, as they said. Jonas took it hard, even harder than Axel. Six months later, when he went to Timbuktu, there were those who said it was because he felt so bad about Viktor.

Viktor eventually wound up in an institution in Oslo, and it was here that Jonas visited him regularly, year after year. "Behind hill the monk's bell / borne on the wind. / Sail passed here in April; / may return in October / Boat fades in silver; slowly." No response. Viktor sat utterly motionless, staring into space. An extinguished light bulb.

Ironically enough, Viktor's mother had bought him a Stressless Royal. Here, in this chair, Viktor spent the greater part of his life from then on. All he did was eat and watch TV, nothing else. He, who had never looked at a television before, who was never still, sat there like an inert king. One might almost say he had become the perfect Norwegian, Jonas thought. The quintessential spectator. Who saw and yet did not see. Who could watch anything at all without it making any impression. An exponent of *wu-wei*, non-action. And even now, ten years after the accident, Viktor looked as young as ever; he might still have been in his third year at high school, about to sit his university Prelim. It was true: Viktor had gained eternal life but at what a price.

"Do you remember Master Tung-hsüan-tzû and the art of love?" Jonas said.

No glow in the eyes before him, eyes which had sparkled when Viktor had told Jonas about the Taoist metaphors for the different ways of thrusting into a vagina—like a wild horse leaping into a river, like a sparrow pecking up rice in a field, like large rocks sinking into the sea, or like the wind filling a sail—images which showed Jonas, as Daniel's examples had done, that the act of love posed the greatest challenge to the imagination, or was it the other way round?

"You know Svein Rossland, my old teacher, knew Niels Bohr?" Jonas said. "They worked together in Copenhagen."

No response. For the first few years, Jonas had talked a lot about this, hoping that it would ring a bell somewhere inside Viktor's head, hoping to find a switch that might turn him on.

"I often said that Pluto had to have a moon, but everybody laughed at me," Jonas said. "Now they've discovered it, the Americans."

No response.

In a final attempt to rouse his friend, and one that was about as dangerous as tampering with an unexploded bomb, Jonas asked, "What was the name of the marshal in command of Napoleon's I Corps at the battle of Austerlitz?"

No response.

After the accident, after the Prelim, after Timbuktu and after national service, Jonas started at Oslo University. Jonas suspected that he might have chosen to study astrophysics because he wanted to learn more about the universe, that universe which causes two people to swap places, then makes a chunk of ice drop out of the sky. He wanted to learn the ways of the universe—or its Tao, as Viktor would have put it—and mankind's place in this design.

"Comes then snow scur on the river / And a world is covered with jade."

Criminal Past

Why wrestle with mystifying chains of cause and effect? There were times in his life when Jonas Wergeland was less concerned with questioning how the universe came into existence than with charting his own existence. As, for example, on one of the few trips he made together with his wife, when they managed no more on their first evening than to take a taxi across the bridge and ride up to the restaurant at the top of the Galata Tower where, thanks to Margrete's whispered conversation with the maître d', they were given a table by one of the windows overlooking the old town. And as Jonas was sitting there with his glass of raki and the taste of fried clams in his mouth, waiting for a helping of osmanli köftesi—recommended by Margrete—it struck him that he could have left for home the next morning, had he been an ordinary tourist, that is, because this, the sight before him, had to be the paramount and most enduring image of Istanbul: the silhouettes, the Oriental skyline—an almost stupefyingly beautiful prospect, triggering a myriad of associations. He ran his gaze over the array of domes and minarets and thought of Aunt Laura; thought how he was sitting in a city where Europe and Asia, and possibly also the medieval and the modern world, intertwined. And, in the midst of all this, as his eye fell on master architect Sinan's massive, nigh-on tumescent, Süleymaniye Mosque, he felt a twinge of guilt because it reminded him of a dream, a calling which he had forsaken.

"I think I like the Blue Mosque best," he said, his eyes flitting over the floodlit buildings on the other side of the water.

"Just because it has six minarets?" said Margrete. "You're like a little boy. Going for the battleship with the most guns."

Why did Jonas Wergeland travel? His travels had something to do with memory, with visiting places that were a part of him but which he could not recall. Jonas Wergeland always set off on a journey with a suspicion that he was, in fact, going home. And when they were making love in the hotel room in the old town, not very far from the large, covered bazaar, it seemed to him that Margrete was making love to him in a different way, as if she were bent on urging his imagination to follow new and eccentric paths, with the result that, afterwards, when he thought of the mosques, it suddenly struck him that they looked rather like giant crabs, either that or Samurai helmets flanked by the tips of lances. And this stroke of invention could not simply be ascribed to the shabby, though elegant and exotic interior—the ceramic tiles in the bathroom with their reproduction of a famed Iznik design, the bunch of tulips on the marble bedside table—which could have made him feel that one of the recurring dreams of his youth had come true and he was actually spending a night in the harem with one of the sultan's slaves. There was something about this city itself, about making love here, which filled him with a rare and weighty awareness of being "in place," as if he had completed an invisible circle. And as they lay there listening to the muezzins proclaiming the hour of late evening prayers Margrete asked him why he was so pensive, why he lay there smiling in the darkness, and he said, "Because I have roots here." For so it is: not only the sins of the fathers but also the blissful experiences of the parents are visited on the sons.

Neither the Blue Mosque nor the Topkapi was at the top of Jonas's list of sights to see, however. The following day he took Margrete to a hotel on the other side of the Golden Horn, the narrow inlet separating the old part of the city from the new; to the Pera Palas, a hotel built to accommodate passengers off the Orient Express in the days when Istanbul was the most cosmopolitan of all cities. Margrete laughed at his eagerness, thought he meant to show her the suite in which Kemal Atatürk or Mata Hari had stayed. "Why did we come here?" she asked out of politeness. "Because . . ." Jonas said and left a lengthy pause for dramatic effect, as they stood there, directly across from the pale-green, cubic building. "Because my parents once stayed here."

Not many couples from Grorud visited Istanbul in the early fifties, but Åse and Haakon Hansen did. And it was mainly Jonas's mother's doing. Åse was an avid reader of detective novels, and there was one very good reason why Istanbul held such a particular appeal for her. It is true that Jonas came from a more or less bookless home, but that was only because these paperbacks, most of them in English, never made it onto any bookshelf; they came and they went, leaving no trace—the majority of them were of course borrowed. Most notably during the run-up to the Easter break, true to a singular Norwegian tradition for reading crime novels over this particular holiday, his mother would gather together a pile of dog-eared English books with garish covers—as if inspired by the Church's gory Easter story; as if in need of a secular counterweight, so to speak. For a long time as a small boy Jonas felt that the Crimea would have to be the perfect spot for Norwegians to spend the Easter holidays.

One of his mother's favorite writers was Agatha Christie, and of all her books she liked *Murder on the Orient Express* the best. So when—thanks to Uncle Lauritz the pilot and his connections with the newly formed SAS airline—she was offered the chance for her and Haakon to fly to Istanbul, she jumped at it. To cap it all they were to be put up at the Pera Palas hotel, where Agatha Christie had written the aforementioned book. Although the timing was not of the best, his mother insisted on making the trip—heartily supported by Aunt Laura, who offered to look after Rakel and Daniel, the latter of whom was still being bottle-fed. And I'm sure you can tell where this is leading, Professor.

His parents had been given a room on the fourth floor with a view of the Golden Horn above the Atatürk Bridge and the Fatih Mehmet mosque, the mosque of the Conqueror himself, sitting dead center on the hill on the other side. They had never said anything, but Jonas had worked it out for himself: "I must have been conceived in the Pera Palas Hotel," he told Margrete exultantly and drew her through the dark wooden doors into a hotel where, though it had lost something of its luster, one could still catch a whiff of bygone grandeur, not least if one peeked into the banqueting hall just off the lobby: like something out a dream with its pillars in two sorts of pale-brown marble and a cupola clad with wood panelling inset with latticed windows. "Imagine being granted the gift of life right here," he said. But when Margrete tried to lead him round the side of the reception desk and over to the ancient, openwork wooden lift to see Agatha Christie's room on the fourth floor, he would not go; instead he dragged her into the Orient Express Bar where they found a table next to the octagonal aquarium in the center. To see the fourth floor, where his parents had also stayed, the prospect of the Conqueror's mosque, would be going too far, it would be a form of sacrilege, like poking one's nose into the mystery of life itself, much as today's genetic scientists are doing. And besides, Jonas's own feelings on the matter were a mite ambivalent. Both because a book, even a bad book, could prompt a person to travel to a distant country—hence the reason, perhaps, that Jonas, throughout his life mistrusted books so—

and because he disliked the thought of being conceived, to all intents and purposes, out of the heady thrill induced by pulp fiction; of being not highborn, but lowborn.

As they sat in their armchairs in the Orient Express Bar, surrounded by terracotta walls covered in Islamic ceramics, each with a cup of Turkish coffee in front of them, he toyed with the idea of staying here, on this spot where Europe and Asia seemed to lie fondling one another. He had a vision of the exquisite drama which must have been enacted in the brass bed in his parents' room, possibly even on the oriental rug with which he knew every room to be furnished, this act of love that had produced him, Jonas Wergeland. And in a way it fitted: there was something of the European about his mother and something of the Asian about his father, such an intertwining had to—was bound to—give rise to something extraordinary. This he liked, could not hear the name of the Golden Horn without feeling that it was in some way connected with his father, that his father must have had "a golden horn" on that very night, since it had expelled the spermatozoa which fertilized his mother's egg, thus tying the first knot on the carpet that would be his life. In olden days the area on this side of the Golden Horn was known as Pera—which means "the other side." He, Jonas, had therefore come into being "on the other side." He sat in a bar in Istanbul, in the hotel of his conception, and hugged the notion of being an outsider. Because, in case you haven't yet realized it, Professor, Jonas Wergeland had an almost pathological need to feel different.

Is this, then, where the story of his jealousy begins?

Immediately afterwards, as they were strolling down to the harbor on the Bosphorus to watch the people fishing and the ferries coming and going, with the mosques straight ahead of them again, Jonas was seized by a sudden euphoria. He had come into existence between two continents. Suddenly it came to him: that was why he had been so drawn to that peach as a boy—because it belonged to him, a child of the Orient. It was as if Jonas had suddenly been presented with the explanation for his feel for mosaics, for ornamentation. From then on he would never have any trouble understanding the criticism of his television series *Thinking Big*: that the individual programs were not all that special in themselves, that the impact derived from the element of repetition, which caused these twenty-odd programs to form such an intriguing pattern. And wasn't the television picture, if magnified, a mosaic of colored dots? "*Ich bin ein Byzantiner,*" Jonas cried, his words directed at the panorama before him, with something of the rhetorical fervour once evinced by the blessed John F. Kennedy in another city.

A couple of days later, still filled with this euphoria, this heaven-sent euphoria, he was strolling with Margrete along the main street, Istiklal Caddesi. On impulse, just beyond Galatsaray Square, he turned down a side street and found himself in a stinking, pulsating fish market that ran out into a maze of narrow lanes and alleyways; at this time, early in the day, it was surprisingly quiet. Margrete had stayed behind in a shop to look for a present for Kristin. Jonas sauntered on, marvelling again, for the umpteenth time, at Margrete, this person whom he loved with an almost blasphemous passion, with all his heart and all his soul and all his mind. The previous day they had been standing inside the Great Church of Hagia Sofia, contemplating the light that appeared to come more from within than without, looking up at the dome which everyone said appeared to hang down from heaven, to float in midair. Jonas was gazing open-mouthed at this sight, utterly enraptured—for one thing because the dome seemed to be wheeling round, spun by the light—when Margrete nudged him in the side and said: "Let's get out of this geometric bunker, I feel like I'm inside the stomach of a giant beetle." He could not make her out. À propos Kristin—à propos conception, come to that—he remembered the day when Margrete had stood before him and announced: "I am with child." What an anachronistic way to put it. With child! And yet so like Margrete. As if she quite naturally wished to elevate these tidings into something wonderfully solemn and Biblical.

Jonas was halfway down the narrow back street, a curving downhill slope, an alley where washing was hung to dry on lines stretched out high above, beneath cockeyed television aerials, and the air reeked of cooking oil and rotten melons. His interest had been caught by some dilapidated oriel windows jutting out from the house walls. Suddenly there's a man standing right in front of him, asking Jonas, quite politely really, to hand over his cash. A knife hovering dangerously close to Jonas's stomach makes it clear that he is not fooling around. Jonas remains surprisingly calm, despite a horrid contraction of his testicles. In a way, it seems only right and proper that he should be confronted with crime in some shape or form in this city, bearing in mind his mother's motives in visiting it. In any case, something about this man tells Jonas he'd better not try anything, that this is one of the Beyoglu quarter's shadier sons. He takes out his wallet and promptly hands the man all his paper money. The man glances at it, seems satisfied, is about to stick it in his pocket when he notices one banknote that is not Turkish—a Norwegian thousand-kroner note. He studies it, the reproduction of Peder Balke's dramatic painting of Vardø lighthouse, turns it over, lowers the hand clutching the knife. "Where are you from?" he asks in excellent English. "Norway," says Jonas. "Who is this?" he says. "Henrik Ibsen," Jonas says. "What about Knut Hamsun—is he on a banknote too?" the man says. Jonas shakes his head. The man's face suddenly darkens, he points the knife at Jonas. "Are you telling me that Hamsun, one of the greatest writers in the world, doesn't appear on your banknotes? What sort of a country do you call that?" he says, then launches into what sounds like a virulent lecture, or indictment, delivered at such a speed that Jonas doesn't manage to catch it all—partly, of course, because he is so terrified, because of the knife and because of a thief who, instead of hightailing it out of there, proceeds to discuss which writers deserve to appear on Norwegian banknotes. This latter aspect actually scares him most of all, since he takes it as a sign that the guy must be stark raving mad and capable of absolutely anything.

As the man was finishing a harangue on what an indelible impression Hamsun's novel *Hunger* had made on him, a poor man from the slums of Istanbul—Jonas thought he could almost see tears in the mugger's eyes—Margrete came walking down the alley. Jonas turned his head: "Get out of here," he hissed as loudly as he could. "He's got a knife." Margrete did not react, calmly strolled straight up to them. This seemed to throw the man too. He crammed the money into his pocket, shifted his focus from Jonas to Margrete, even lunged at her with the knife. It all happened very fast, but later Jonas tried to recall those seconds, which gave him yet another reason to marvel at his wife. For as the man darted towards her, jabbing with his hand, she sidestepped, and Jonas seemed to recall that it had been a graceful movement, more like a dance step, backwards; a little jink which stood, in his memory, as a greater feat than the hold that she suddenly took on the man's arm and the way she positioned her body in relation to his, in order, the next instant, lightly, as if it cost her no effort, to hurl him through the air, positively send him flying—as Jonas saw it—while still keeping a firm grip on his arm, thus forcing him to let go of the knife, with a hideous shriek of pain betraying that she had in fact hurt him in the process, and all of this before he hit the ground with a thud and, hurt or no hurt, promptly scrambled to his feet and vanished with the same baffling suddenness as he had appeared.

Margrete took Jonas's hand and, with a faint air of impatience, strode out of the alley, leaving the knife where it lay. "He took my money," Jonas said when they had turned the corner. "Who cares, it wasn't that much, was it?" she said. "Come on in here, I think I've found something for Kristin—look at this lovely brass dolls' tea-set!"

For the rest of the day, while walking round sunken palaces and subterranean mosques, the ruins of the city walls and aqueducts, in the spice bazaars and the mosaic museums, Jonas thought about Margrete, about how little he knew of her. Against his will, he recalled some of the rumors he had heard about the years when she was living abroad, as the daughter of a diplomat and later as a student: rumors he had tried to ignore, to suppress, but which had stuck to his subconscious nonetheless. What he had seen back there in the alley accorded with the story that, as a teenager, somewhere in the Far East, she had studied the martial arts. Occasionally in the summer he had noticed how, when she thought no one was looking, she would do what looked like callisthenics on the lawn, smooth, controlled movements, like a balancing act in slow motion. He had heard so many things, didn't know what to believe. Not even of what she told him herself. Jonas walked around Istanbul with his mind in turmoil, a state which possibly mirrored the confusion of smells in the city streets: everything from mimosa, exhaust fumes and roasted nuts to the eternally rotating kebabs on the roadside stalls and every kind of fried fish. It was said that she had once written a wonderful book—someone had heard her read bits of it—the manuscript of which she had thrown away or lost, or burned and then scattered the ashes on the Ganges—accounts varied. Was it true that at one point she had had a pet snake? And had she really danced with a famous rock star, on the stage, during a concert? When he asked her about such things, she would laugh. "You're just jealous," she would say. And she was right, that is exactly what he was. Because she was the sort of woman you saw, even in the heaving mass of bodies in front of a stage.

With Margrete you never knew what to expect. While Jonas wandered reverently around the Topkapi Palace, feasting his eyes on everything from Mohammed's footprints in a stone to the beautiful doors of the harem, patterned with tortoiseshell and mother of pearl, Margrete was more interested in the guards and their tiny, crackling walkie-talkies and all the Turkish women with their covered heads: "Do you remember what sort of headscarf your mother used to wear?" she would whisper to Jonas, as if all of this only served to remind her of Norway's recent past.

It may have been in the harem itself that a troubling thought entered his head: all that talk about how sexually liberal she had been. "She just can't get enough of it," someone had once said, a man whose teeth Jonas had only just managed to stop himself from knocking out. He had tried to close his ears to the snippets of information he had picked up, of other boyfriends she had had; talk of men who, literally or figuratively, would have cut off their ear lobes for her. Fragments which, when he put them together, formed a picture of a monster. He had been more alarmed than impressed by the little display she had given in the alley, feared that she might one day do to him what she had done to that thief. She's downright dangerous, he told himself.

Jonas walked through a city on the border between two continents, teetering between doting admiration and a niggling sense of uncertainty. He couldn't make her out. He found this blend of naïvety and sophistication particularly confusing. She was an ingenuous reader, a bit like Axel; prepared to believe anything—this woman, a rational doctor who wrote articles for medical journals, could lie stretched out on the sofa, so absorbed in the plot of even the worst book that she would utter screams, cries of protest, cheers. Jonas hardly dared to go to the theater with her; she always seemed on the verge of shouting at the actors, like a child almost falling of its seat in its excitement: "Watch out, the fox is right behind you!" And yet she was such a woman of the world. Jonas had noticed with what aplomb and savoir-faire she had eaten all of the exotic dishes set before them in Istanbul—whether it was sucuk: fried garlic sausages, or a pilaf of lamb and almonds, or aubergines done in every conceivable way. Margrete's nostrils quivered with delight when she cut into a börek, as if it were a lucky bag of aromas, and she could judge a square of freshly-baked baklava purely on its appearance: knew whether the syrup would ooze out if she pressed the paper-thin layers gently. Jonas could only shake his head at the ease, the poise, with which she made her way through the Kapali Carsi, the huge bazaar right next to the hotel, where the little domed roofs gave one the feeling of being inside a gigantic beehive. He followed her with his eyes as she stood amid glittering gold or soft falls of carpet, fragile alabaster or warlike swords, depending on which passage she happened to find herself in; he watched as she demonstrated the use of an astrolabe to the owner of an antique shop, taking it apart, disc by disc—an astrolabe! Jonas beheld her as though he were watching a film about a stranger: how, in another shop, she began to haggle lightly and laughingly over the price of a chessboard with Ottoman pieces of brass and copper, while the stallholder plied her with apple tea. To Jonas the place was a maze and a daunting one at that. To her, it was obviously a familiar world, one that she could read like the back of her hand; she seemed, in fact, to come to life, like a creature suddenly rediscovering its proper and much longed-for element. Something she could not find in Oslo, not in Norway. And what Jonas feared most of all: not with him.

On the plane home, with Margrete asleep in the seat next to him, a book lying open in her lap—a second-rate detective novel, Jonas guessed—he sat gazing out at the layer of cloud and thinking: I can never be good enough for her. I'm going to lose her. The optimism he had felt in the Pera Palas seemed to have deserted him. Just before they landed in Copenhagen he stole a glance at her again, with a love so desperately deep that it was almost like torture to him: If you leave me, I'll kill you, he thought.

Little Eagle

Jonas Wergeland did have his disturbing sides, no two ways about it. We have now worked our way forward—please note: not back, but forward—to his tenth year, so I could, in other words, tell the story of the accident on the ski-jump slope or the trip in the rowing boat with Veronika or the illicit climb up the tower on Robber Hill—many people would find this last one particularly appealing. There is, however, no doubt in my mind that I must opt for Jonas's friendship with Ørn and in that connection not, as you might expect, the breathtaking dive in Grorud Pond or their fateful spying on Ørn's mother—not even the terrible forest fire. The right approach, and not just because of the link with the banknote bearing Ibsen's portrait, is to focus on Ørn's interest in the javelin thrower Egil Danielsen.

In Norwegian the word "*ørn*" means "eagle," so Jonas Wergeland's best friend when he was a boy was, in fact, called Eagle, though he was no Red Indian. His full name was Ørn-Henrik, but he was known simply as Ørn—which is to say, Eagle—and hence, Little Eagle. And let it be said at the outset: no one could have been less suited to bear that imposing name, so redolent of history and Viking times. In Norway, you can get away with being called a bear—Bjørn—or even an elk—Elg. But an eagle—that's a tough one. Sparrow would have been a better name for him. Not only was Ørn small and scrawny for his age—he was also what can only be described as scruffy. And yet in certain situations, not unlike a lemming, he had an incongruously belligerent air about him that tended to have a provocative effect, especially on the bigger boys. To be called Eagle—and look the way Ørn did—was an insult, it was like asking to get beaten up. And beaten up he was.

As his nickname suggests, Ørn was doomed to play the Red Indian in all of the fierce battles fought by the children of Solhaug. Times without number he had hidden himself in some hopelessly obvious spot, with two crow feathers in his hair, only to receive a hard and ruthless knock on the back of the head with the butt of a revolver—absolute realism was the order of the day. For Little Eagle, it was an everyday occurrence to be thrown into patches of nettles or enormous anthills, or to be tied to trees and subjected to the cruellest torture, not least by Petter—later Sgt. Petter—and his gang. On one occasion they even lit a fire at his feet—only the keen noses of a couple of vigilant parents averted a tragedy. Little Eagle didn't do the scalping; he got scalped. Never did an eagle have its wings so well and truly clipped.

In the playground, too, Ørn was the communal punch-ball. At least once a week he would get into a fight, find himself—always undermost—in the middle of a ring of boys which rapidly degenerated into a cheering, chanting mob until the teacher on playground duty finally broke the enchanted circle, and the two boys in the middle were grabbed by the scruff of the neck and marched off to the headmaster's office, as if Little Eagle, he, the sparrow was as much to blame as the firebrand by his side. There would be a little smile on Ørn's face, of defiance or possibly satisfaction. Such a character was hard to fathom because, despite that maddening aggressive streak, he had a fawning, almost servile, air about him. This may have been why he liked being with Jonas; they spent every day together—until the accident, the major collision, occurred.

Why on earth did Jonas choose Ørn as his best friend? To say that Jonas wanted someone he could boss about, someone he could tell what to do, would surely be an oversimplification. Nor could it be compared to the phenomenon sometimes found among young girls, where a pretty girl will choose a plain friend, thus making her own good looks that much more apparent. Maybe—it's a point worth considering—it all had to do with the chance of getting his hands on the treasures to be found in Eagle's living room.

Thanks to a well-placed relative, Eagle owned every Donald Duck comic issued from 1948 onwards, in bound volumes at that. These magnificent albums were ranged on the bookcase in the living room alongside Aschehoug's splendid encyclopaedia and took up nearly as much space. Later in life, Jonas would regard this arrangement as a natural upgrading of the worth of these comics. One which was well-deserved, since they were in many ways Jonas's main work of reference, a source of information which came in handy in all sorts of situations, not least as an aid to the art of conversation. At the same time it gave Jonas an inkling that even an encyclopaedia is nothing but a pure fabrication. Not only that—if, for example, he looked up "The Flying Dutchman" or "The Incan Empire," he found the relevant entries dull and heavy-handed compared to the Uncle Scrooge stories concerning these same subjects.

Jonas would always remember those hours spent lying on the carpet of the Larsen family living room as special moments, hours when his eyes were drawn unresistingly from picture to picture through the wondrous world of the cartoon strips, most of all in the fantastic stories by the aforementioned Carl Barks. This heady pleasure was, moreover, often accompanied by a sound that enhanced the sense of having embarked on a fabulous journey into the realms of fantasy. Because it so happened that Ørn's dad, when he had time off from his pots and pans at the Grand Hotel, would often sit in the living room, listening to one of his numerous Linguaphone records. Every winter Ørn's dad—Three-Star Larsen—dreamed of setting out an extended tour of Europe in the summer holidays, though he never went any further than the southern tip of the Royal Wharf, never got beyond these courses, the patient repetition of crackling recorded phrases in Italian, Spanish, or Greek. Mr. Larsen could say "What time is it?" and "Can you recommend a restaurant?" in eight languages, though he never got the chance to put his skills into practice. Nonetheless, like the sound effects in a radio play, he helped to expand the space around the reading boys.

One day when they were ten years old, a spring day with a gentle rain washing away the last patches of snow outside, Ørn had done something unexpected. Or perhaps it wasn't. Looking back on it, it occurred to Jonas that he had known it all along. That this was why he was friends with Eagle: that this was his reward, so to speak, for long and faithful service. Eagle had pulled a heavy book from the shelf, a volume that proved to be a fine, tooled leather album with gilded pages. A Bible, thought Jonas, a holy scripture. For is it not the case, Professor, that every person has a story, does something which shows that he is an Ankenaton, a unique human being; the sudden revelation, coming as a shock to everyone around them, that a person worships the sun, is a monotheist, when everyone else is praying to a whole host of gods—that he holds one idea above all others, one which he pursues faithfully and single-mindedly and for which he would willingly wipe out everything else?

Eagle opened the book, or album. It was not filled with photographs or scraps, football or automobile cards, as Jonas had expected, but with stamps: with transparent sheets of paper overlaying tiny, bright-hued miniatures. Jonas looked at Eagle, saw how all at once his face was glowing, as if illumined by a light—not to say a sun—shining out of the album itself, from beneath, like something out of a painting by Rembrandt. Jonas suddenly felt that he was being granted a glimpse of Eagle's inner being, of a hidden majesty, a unifying vision.

Stamps. The English word is so flat and square, smacking of repression. Not so the Norwegian word: "*frimærke*"—"free marks," marks that make one free. This must be why nothing could daunt Ørn, even when nothing else was going right for him: when he got inkblots all over his handwriting primer or scored an own goal at football. Jonas looked more closely at the stamps, understanding and yet not. Because the surprising thing was not that Eagle collected stamps, pored over them with tweezers and magnifying glass. Most boys have collected stamps at some time in their lives, for a week or so, or a couple of years. But Jonas realized that Eagle was the type who would go on collecting stamps all his life, and what was more: that there was a system, a concept of some sort, behind what he was seeing.

Jonas had himself taken a couple of tentative steps into the labyrinth of philately. For a while he had zealously cut up envelopes, filled the bath with water and scattered the corners with the stamps into it, so that the bath looked like a huge pot full of steeped slivers of flat bread, like the dish they ate on Christmas Eve before going to church, "mush" they called it—and that was what this was, a mush. Jonas soon came to the conclusion that such a muddle was more trouble than it was worth: an ocean of stamps and only a bath to put them in. Besides which, there seemed to be no way of getting to grips with such a multiplicity of stamps, not to mention all the duplication: what does one do with two hundred stamps bearing the king's head; or shoeboxes full of 35-øre stamps depicting whooper swans, all commemorating Nordic Day?

Eagle had understood something that Jonas had not: you had to set limits for yourself. As he leafed through the album Jonas realized that Eagle had discerned a pattern in the chaos, for here the first sheets were covered with stamps depicting the Norwegian landscape, then came stamps featuring flowers, birds and animals, after which Jonas could run his eye over the history of Norway: from miniature images of rock carvings and ancient gods to tiny illustrations of Viking ships and stave churches which, in turn, were followed by stamps dedicated to kings, celebrities, buildings, all meticulously arranged in chronological order right up to the Second World War—a splendid geography-cum-history book, an alternative social history told through stamps. A bit like a comic strip, Jonas thought.

But it was a separate collection at the back of the album that came as the greatest surprise. Jonas stared and stared, but he couldn't figure it out. "A collection of Norvegiana," Ørn said. It sounded alien and mysterious, as if he were talking about a dreamland.

"What's that?"

"Stamps from other countries featuring images with some sort of Norwegian connection."

It had never occurred to Jonas that people in foreign countries might have any interest in Norway. He examined the stamps more closely and found Sigrid Undset on a Turkish stamp issued in 1935. On another page he spied Roald Amundsen's profile on a stamp from Hungary issued in 1948. And there, on a Cuban stamp, a picture of Armauer Hansen. Henrik Ibsen graced stamps from Bulgaria and Rumania, and Grieg was portrayed on one from the Soviet Union. The most baffling subject of all, though, was Egil Danielsen, honored for his gold-medal win in the javelin event at the Melbourne Olympics— on a stamp from the Dominican Republic! Who would believe it! What did the peasants in the Dominican Republic think when they stuck this on their letters: Egil Danielsen captured at the very moment that the javelin left his hand? Jonas was dumbstruck. These stamps, all this foreign interest, left him quite bemused; trains of thought wove in and out of one another inside his head. I need hardly stress, Professor, that this was a decisive moment in Jonas Wergeland's life.

Ørn began to tell him about the postal system and the stamps, about how amazing it all was. This worldwide network. Proof of the possibility of peaceful coexistence. Ørn was all lit up, Jonas hardly recognized his friend. Ørn stumbled over his words, sounding old beyond his years as he breathlessly explained: "You see, stamps reflect the soul of a country."

"Great," Jonas said, slamming the album shut. "That's great, Eagle, but can't we do something else now? What about going down to the corner shop? I've got a couple of empty bottles."

He could tell that Eagle was disappointed, saw the light in his friend's face fade. "Okay, we could pop down and get some chewing-gum," Eagle said, putting the album back on the shelf. Jonas noted its position, between *The World of Music* and *Gone with the Wind*.

Although they had many another reading session on Ørn's living-room floor that spring, Ørn never showed him his stamps again. And Jonas never mentioned them.

Where are the dark holes in Jonas Wergeland's life?

One day Little Eagle didn't come to school. He wasn't there the next day either. Jonas called at the house to ask after him. Ørn-Henrik was ill, his mother said. He was off school for a whole week. When at last he returned everyone could see that he must have been really sick: his eyes were a nasty red color, as if he had spent a long day in the chlorinated water of the Frogner Baths. And he had changed. Not that he was any less scrawny, but there was something else there too now.

Jonas noticed it too. Ørn was moody, withdrawn, he seemed both utterly crushed and mad as hell, turned away huffily when Jonas spoke to him.

One afternoon on the way home from school Eagle finally opened his mouth: "My stamp album's gone," he said. "Completely disappeared."

It was springtime, he kicked some sand, stopped, spun round to face Jonas: "I can't understand it. I can't find it."

"Burglars?" Jonas said.

"No, that can't be it," Eagle said. "I just don't get it."

They walked on, said no more about it. Some girls were skipping, smack, smack, a heavy rope, a line lashing the ground.

Over the days that followed, Eagle grew more and more antagonistic, even towards Jonas. Any approach met with a surly, almost abusive, response, as if he wanted to pick a fight.

Then something even more mystifying happened. Just before May 17, that combination of spring rite and gala day, Little Eagle turned up at school with his head shaved, which is to say: with a strip of hair running from the middle of his forehead to the nape of his neck. Like a real Red Indian, a Mohawk or whatever tribe it was that wore their hair like that—a hairstyle which the punks of a later generation would copy and dye orange or bright green. It is no exaggeration to say that this hairstyle, Little Eagle's hairstyle that is, seemed even more provocative—shocking, in fact—back then. You have to remember that this was before the Beatles grew their hair long. You could say that Little Eagle was one of the first punk rockers in Oslo.

Nobody knew what to make of it. Little Eagle's act of rebellion was so awesome, not to say so totally loony, that even the older boys left him alone, as if they understood that this was not the old sparrow, the punchball, but a walking hand grenade with a dangerously loose pin. Little Eagle paraded through the streets of Grorud in May with his head held high, wearing his blazer and his Mohican hairdo, to the consternation of all and sundry, leaving people whispering in horror on the pavement. He had stopped talking, wouldn't even speak to Jonas. So Jonas was surprised when, some weeks later, Ørn asked him to come with him up to the woods—Ørn had something he wanted to show him. It was Midsummer's Eve, no less, in the morning; and Jonas was nervous because he was performing in a skit later that day.

They had struck off into the woods at Hukenveien, at the spot where Little Eagle had once been tied to a tree and Petter had shot at him with a bow and arrow. It was only by luck that Eagle wasn't blinded. They stand there on the grassy slope beside the stream that flows down from the swimming hole. Jonas waits, hasn't the foggiest notion of what's going on, what Eagle wants to show him. Then, out of the blue, Eagle starts laying into Jonas. Goes totally berserk. Punches and punches him, even though it's no use, Jonas is bigger than him, brings him down without any trouble. But Eagle will not give in, wriggles like a worm on a hook. Jonas can see that he is mad, blazing mad, so mad that he's in tears, although Jonas knows he's not hurting him, he's just holding him down, and maybe that is why he's in tears, because Jonas is just holding him down, doesn't punch him in the face like the others would, just keeps a firm grip on him, a vice-like grip, with his knees and hands. Eagle writhes about for some time, struggling and struggling, while the tears rain down. Jonas thinks Eagle looks ridiculous, mainly because of the Mohawk, which gives him the illusion of fighting with a real Red Indian, or a being not of this world. Jonas feels his contempt subsiding and in the midst of all this he suddenly has the idea of altering a couple of lines in the sketch he's going to do, a little twist that will turn a rotten skit into a pretty good one.

At long last Ørn lies still. His eyes are closed. There's snot on his upper lip. He's a sorry sight. They lie quietly for a long while, Jonas on top of Ørn.

Little Eagle opens his eyes, looks straight up into Jonas's eyes. His gaze does not waver. He never used to do that. He stares long and hard at Jonas. Jonas looks down at Ørn. He knows what he is seeing. Never in his life has he seen it before, but he knows what it is: hate.

"You bastard," Ørn says.

Just the once. And not all that loudly.

They go on lying there. Ørn gazes into Jonas's eyes. For ages they lie there. Jonas thinks it's funny, but he doesn't laugh. Something about the situation stops him from laughing.

Then he gets up. Little Eagle clambers to his feet, turns and walks off. Jonas waits for a few minutes before following him down the road towards Solhaug, catches a glimpse of Ørn's back as he turns in between the blocks of flats. Jonas went home to change his clothes, shut his eyes to go over the new lines for the sketch that he was going to be presenting outside of Number One, in front of all the grownups.

Ørn didn't come to see it. Jonas did not see Ørn that evening—not even then, on Midsummer's Eve, the longest, lightest day of the year.

Soon afterwards Ørn moved away. Little Eagle, it transpired, was gone forever.

Cain and Abel

Stamps illustrate the uniformity of an era. For months, years maybe, everyone, millions of letter-writers, stick identical images on their envelopes. Stamps were the forerunners of the mass media: there too, for weeks on end, one sees the same face, the same picture, everywhere. It was against just such a background that Jonas Wergeland's programs stood out; he produced a stream of images unlike anything ever seen before, on NRK or any other channel.

After the scandal broke, Jonas Wergeland's television programs were pretty much put under the microscope, as if people were searching for clues, some warning of what was to come. The program on Niels Henrik Abel, in particular, with its unforgettable opening shot of the Pont Arts in a grey, December-chill Paris—the eyes fixed longingly, almost pleadingly on the façade of the Institut de France—was subjected to a lot of scrutiny. Initially, its pointed visual statements were construed as a sign of admirable commitment—something singularly lacking in most TV programs—but the prevailing, hypocritical consensus later was that here Jonas Wergeland had gone over the score, that this out-and-out caricature of Frenchmen and all things French was far too spiteful by half. "Behind the virtuosity of this program one discerns something dark, hateful even," one famous opportunist would later write. However that may be, the story of Niels Henrik Abel formed the basis for the most subjective and aggressive of Jonas Wergeland's programs.

I can now reveal, Professor, that there were personal reasons for this. And here I am thinking not of stamps, although I'm sure you have already spotted the connection, you may even own one of the stamps issued on April 6, 1929, to mark the centenary of Niels Henrik Abel's death. No, I am referring to one of Jonas Wergeland's first and little-known trips abroad, to that same city of Paris. He was feeling nervous even before he had gotten through passport control, as if he was prepared for anything to happen at an airport named after Charles de Gaulle. This insecurity, which he thought must spring from some sort of national inferiority complex, grew even more palpable as he was passing through Customs, where a man in uniform eyed him sternly. And it was at this point that Jonas, as he saw it, made his big mistake: he smiled. The customs officer promptly called him over and asked to see his luggage. Jonas had the feeling that the man was doing this purely out of resentment—he wasn't going to have any stupid Norwegian smiling at him. He didn't conduct a neat search of Jonas's suitcase either but rummaged around in it as if sure of turning up something, and when he found nothing, Jonas was led into another room where the first man and another officer proceeded to interview, or virtually cross-examine him—that, at least, is how it seemed to Jonas. "Here in Paris I'm not a Norwegian, I'm a nigger," Jonas said to himself. I would like to emphasize that I'm sure such things did not happen very often, that this was in all likelihood a cosmic exception to the usual hospitality of the French passport and customs authorities. Nonetheless, it did happen. Jonas spoke to the two officers in his best French, but they acted as if they did not understand, interrupted him with curt, antagonistic orders, out of sheer bloody-mindedness, Jonas kept thinking; and this they did even though they knew he hadn't done anything, this they did because they had every right to do so, Jonas could be a dangerous character, a big-time smuggler. Jonas had smiled: now who would smile at a strange Frenchman if they had nothing to hide? They asked to see his tickets, inquired as to where he would be staying, how much money he had with him, he understood what they said, they did not understand what he said, although they should have been able to; several times Jonas heard the word "*zéro*"—not "*rien*," but "*zéro*"—and automatically assumed that this referred to him; I'm not sure, Professor, but it isn't altogether inconceivable that they also asked him to undress, that they also searched his person in the most thorough and humiliating way and still with every right to do so, I say again, even though he had done nothing wrong, "*il est nul*," but he had smiled, he was suspicious, a pathetic Norwegian, a nigger in Paris, they had sussed out that he was a nothing trying to make out that he wasn't just a nothing, they simply would not have a nothing in their country, in France, a land of ones, the cradle of European civilization; Jonas felt that they were laughing at him the whole time: at his clothes, his sad excuse for a suitcase and not least his halting French, which had been good enough at school but a joke here. "*C'est un zéro en chiffre.*" They let him out of the room with a little laugh, and even though they did not find anything,

Jonas felt that they had exposed him, that they had stripped him bare, in more than one sense. "They raped me mentally," he said later. Even if he was not a nothing, they made him feel like a nothing.

Am I on the right track? Why else would Niels Henrik Abel, as played by Normann Vaage, walk around Paris made up to look like a Negro? Jonas Wergeland's story about Abel was a tale of intellectual racism, of the degradation of a small nation, of the world's doubts that anything good could really come out of Norway. There was a personal reason for the underlying rage in the program, but that is not the whole explanation. Jonas Wergeland was on safe ground here—for who could help but feel outraged at the thought of how Abel was treated in Paris?

Jonas Wergeland could, of course, have centered his program on Abel around the discovery of elliptical functions and the heart-stopping race to beat Gustav Jacobi to the post, but from the very start he knew how to angle this program in his series on heroic Norwegians, *Thinking Big*: he would focus on Abel's waiting. Niels Henrik Abel was, in short, a brilliant scholar, a man who, in the words of one mathematician, was in the process of "discovering Magellian passages to huge areas of that same, vast analytical ocean." An individual who, in his short life, would establish a legacy "which will keep mathematicians occupied for five hundred years," as another put it. The program captured this unique person at the point on his grand tour when he arrived in Paris, the mathematical capital of the day, to present what has since become known as the great Abelian theorem, his masterpiece, to the French Scientific Society, in hopes of seeing it published in their *Mémoires des savants étrangers* and thereby winning international recognition and a university lectureship, as well as the chance to develop all of the other ideas proliferating inside his head to an extent unseen in any other mathematician at that time. Abel is in Paris. This is his moment of truth. The only problem is that he comes from Norway.

Jonas had focused particularly on the moment when a bowing Abel hands over his paper on algebraic functions and their integrals—a theorem of such enormously far-reaching importance, regarded by some as the most significant mathematical work of the nineteenth century—at a meeting of the French Scientific Society at the Institut de France, in October 1826, where Augustin Louis Cauchy and Adrien Marie Legendre, the two men who would decide his fate—all shame on their names—were appointed to assess his paper: a scene in which Jonas made much of the Institut building, the solemn atmosphere of that room steeped in centuries of scholarship and the blasé faces of the assembled company, their skeptical glances at Abel, as he stood there, made up like a Negro. From this Jonas cut to a close-up of the front page of his manuscript, showing what was for him, Jonas, the obvious key to Abel's failure. After his name Abel had added: *Norvégien*. From Norway. Norwegian. Could those grand gentlemen have been in any doubt? This addition was their guarantee that they were looking at a manuscript they did not have to take seriously, which they could, therefore, treat with the greatest indifference.

Abel's hopes, on the other hand, were high; he expected to receive an answer within two weeks. The program dwelt on Abel during this period of waiting as it dragged out, stretched to three weeks, then to four weeks; the camera followed Abel as he roamed the streets of Paris, waiting, lonely, hungry, waiting desperately, on tenterhooks, for the judges' verdict. From time to time one was given a peek into Cauchy's study and saw how Abel's brilliant work on transcendental functions sank further and further down into a heap of papers, a situation almost as reprehensible, not to say stupid, as an Egyptologist having the Rosetta Stone fall into his hands right at the start, then forgetting where he's put it. Cauchy—all shame on his name—was too taken up with his own works to look at the jottings of a young mathematician from Norway, a country where, by definition, scholarship was still languishing in the Stone Age.

In the meantime Abel, this Norwegian, was seen sitting in the cafés around St. Germain des Prés, lodging as he did with a poor family who lived not far from there, in a street which no longer exists, as if the French, consumed by guilt, wished to erase all memory of Abel. He sits in cafés, writes letters that, typically, he dates with a mathematical problem. We see Abel, a Norwegian, walking the streets of a Paris that grows colder and colder; in the background we hear the sound of bells—a sound that dominates the whole program—church bells ringing; we see how cold Abel is, shivering with cold, we hear him coughing, a cough that gets worse and worse; we see him circling, trembling with cold, around the Institut de France, stronghold of arrogance, where Jonas showed men walking out of the main door and shaking their heads dismissively, Cauchy among them—all shame on his name—at Abel who stands there waiting, humble, head bowed, made up like a Negro. The camera stuck with Abel, following him on his walks through the Jardin du Luxembourg amid the chiming of church bells, and from there back to the Institut de France, always back to that spot, around that building, coughing and coughing, then into the Café Procope, just round the back in the rue Mazarine, the haunt of all manner of individuals: Diderot and Rousseau to name but two; and here Abel, their equal, algebra's answer to Rimbaud, scribbles on a sheet of paper, mulling over difficult mathematical questions. So here walked, here sat, a genius, an unacknowledged genius, a supposed nothing who was, in fact, a number one. And what was it they overlooked, these pompous Frenchmen, these budding Napoleons blinded by their own excellence? They overlooked a man with a unique gift for spotting profound connections between mathematical groups, how they affected one another; for turning tricky questions on their heads, seeing things from new angles, as when—instead of solving the problem of fifth-degree equations, he showed that generally these could not be expressed in terms of radicals. Similarly, with elliptic integrals: instead of studying the integrals themselves, he looked at the opposite, or inverse, functions, the elliptical functions. Suddenly, thanks to this magnificent device, everything looked different. Abel is brooding on a whole host of projects. There is just one catch: he has the misfortune to have been born on the periphery. Abel, a Norwegian, wanders around Paris, waiting and coughing, he waits one month, he waits two months, on a visit to a doctor he is found to be suffering from tuberculosis, but still Abel hangs on patiently in Paris for as long as his money lasts. Then he has to leave, traveling home by way of Berlin.

Not until word of Abel's death reached Paris, a good two years later, was his paper unearthed by Cauchy—all shame on his memory—and dealt with post-haste, although it was not published until 1841, fifteen years after its submission. To crown it all, the publishers then added to the catalogue of crimes by losing the manuscript immediately thereafter.

Perhaps it's not so strange that Jonas Wergeland, after working on Abel, had an even greater hatred of all things French, from the guillotine to their pompous, incomprehensible post-structuralism with its obscure terminology, all those arrogant Frenchmen, in fact, who, God help us, couldn't even see that their own composer, Berlioz, was a genius; although Jonas Wergeland did possibly go too far in declaring in a promotional interview that the French were the most cynical and arrogant of races, that it was hardly any wonder they were the most detested and corrupt of all colonialists, or that they had no qualms about carrying out nuclear tests anywhere, as long as it wasn't their own country. "And if you're a corrupt dictator in the market for arms," he was reported as saying, "you can be sure that France will be happy to oblige, in their eyes no tyrant is too rotten." One of the film crew later maintained that, during the regular spot in which Wergeland himself entered the scene, he had spat on the Institut building—a shot which was edited out of the final version. Jonas Wergeland was sure he was right: France had killed a Norwegian, one of the greatest Norwegians of all time.

In the program's closing scene, Jonas Wergeland showed his hero standing just beyond the Pont Neuf, at that triangle where the two channels of the Seine run into one, gazing at the Institut de France. As a viewer, one senses Abel's feeling that he is faced here with two choices in life, that he stands at a crucial parting of the ways. And yet one also sees what an ocean separates this coughing, shivering, starving figure by the bridge from those blind, self-righteous, shameless men shaking their heads outside the Institut de France. For the whole of the final minute Jonas showed fragments of Abel's calculations projected onto various shots of Paris, not least of the Scientific Society building, televised images which made it look as though the buildings of Paris, the entire city, were covered in mathematical formulae, in Abel's equations and elliptical functions, almost like graffiti, a rebellion, vandalism. An algebraic conquest.

Disoriented

One thing that comes to no one as a matter of course is love, far less that hormonal jitterbug inside us so feebly termed "being in love." After Jonas's dream, that somewhat morbid dream of getting his hands under Anne Beate Corneliussen's bulging Setesdal sweater was, as it were, squeezed to bits, he suffered for some time from feelings of unfulfilled desire, and certain girls in the parallel class—this was before mixed classes became the norm—were the object of many a long look. Not unnaturally, it was one of these girls who eventually caught his attention or, more accurately, grabbed Jonas's attention. Henny F. was a pretty ordinary girl, and Jonas did not take any real notice of her until the class trip in eighth grade, in March of that year—and, I should add, with the entire class in the throes of puberty—when they spent a whole tremulous week up in the hills near Vinstra, where the attraction between the sexes was strong enough to start an avalanche and a number of new pairings saw the light of day or rather, the dark of night. There was one dinner in particular at which Henny F. made a big impression by displaying her talent for tying knots of spaghetti in her mouth with her tongue. What would it be like to kiss such a girl, Jonas mused.

The big breakthrough came on May 17, on the morning of Constitution Day itself, after they had been running amok with firecrackers for hours, destroying diverse bike handlebars and postboxes, as well as scorching the stockings of some of the mothers quite badly with the more capricious "jumping-jacks," which shot dangerously this way and that—exploding, as they did, several times. Jonas attended the traditional ceremony in the Memorial Grove, where the Grorud School girls' choir arranged themselves on the steps of the church and sang—at the top of their voices, as they say—"Now See the Groves Awaken," no more, no less, and there stood Henny F., wreathed by green birch leaves, along with the other girls in their thin white sweaters and red skirts and, not least, red bonnets which looked so totally out of place and yet utterly irresistible, especially on Henny F., and they sang, they sang so beautifully that Jonas felt his body go numb with delight. For there was something mystical about songs sung in harmony, he had discovered this for himself in first grade, when their teacher had taught them to sing "All the Birds" in two-part harmony. With tireless patience she had taken half of the class out into the corridor and rehearsed the second part with them one by one. And when they sang this song that they had been practicing and practicing, "All the Birds," for the first time altogether, it went surprisingly well, it didn't merely sound twice as beautiful, it sounded ten times as beautiful, so beautiful that it made Jonas's scalp tingle. This was an aesthetic milestone and a preparation for the day when Jonas would discover how much finer things became when you simply wove two of them together. But here was the girls' choir, not the world's best girls' choir perhaps, but they were singing in harmony, singing "Now See the Groves Awaken," a song Jonas had heard many times but which now, because of Henny F., standing there with a look of such fervour on her face, all-aglow in the midst of the group of girls, Henny F. with her throat straining eagerly and Jonas's eyes fixed on her larynx, sensing as he did that this was the seat of her magic, acquired the semblance of pure beauty and gave Jonas a musical experience that not even Wagner at his most grandiose and extravagant could top. Standing there in the Memorial Grove, Jonas felt a pressure on his spine, felt something seizing hold of him body and soul, even though he had not yet deciphered the signals from the dragon-horn button he had swallowed as a little boy; and for the first time—or the second if one counts Margrete, a relationship which Jonas himself had pushed to the back of his mind—he understood that girls were different, that what he was now feeling, this longing, this throbbing, all-consuming desire, was something other than the more limited randiness triggered by Anne Beate Corneliussen's pneumatic allurements. This was not the ABC of Sex; this was the Alpha and Omega of love.

He started walking home from school with Henny F., liked to hear her talk, this in itself enough: her voice caressing his ears, making him go all funny inside. Although these were the days of colorful, almost psychedelic, Flower-Power garb, she often wore more theatrical clothes than other girls, as if for her the world was a stage. On one occasion she invited him to her house, and he was introduced to her father, a violinist who, as one might expect, looked kindly on a son of the organist from Grorud Church. Jonas also got to see her room where, apart from a couple of diplomas for ski jumping, the walls were completely covered in pictures of pop groups cut from the countless music magazines that flourished during these years: groups Jonas knew next to nothing about, even though many of the same pictures were also stuck up on Daniel's wall—and on the ceiling—at home. He noticed that the Hollies were much in evidence, a group which—as I'm sure even you are aware, Professor—was, not surprisingly, particularly strong on the vocals. She played him some singles: "Look Through Any Window," "I Can't Let Go," "Bus Stop," songs in which Allan Clark, Tony Hicks, and Graham Nash created their distinctive harmonies, and to which Henny F. added an upper part, even higher than Graham Nash's—no small achievement, had Jonas but known it. "Maybe you'll be a star too one day," he said and pointed to a picture of Cilla Black sporting long, false eyelashes, "I mean, you're so musical." She shook her head shyly: "Who me? No!"

Nevertheless she blossomed under his importunate attentions. To the surprise of her friends, at the eighth grade end-of-term party, to which their parents were also invited, she did a turn with another girl; they played nylon-stringed guitars and sung one of the year's big hits, "Somethin' Stupid," in two-part harmony. For this they reaped, not surprisingly, a spontaneous burst of applause with lots of cheering, whistling and stamping of feet. Very few could have suspected, however, that at a later date this same girl—and this may not be entirely unconnected with her having known Jonas—would become one of Norway's greatest singers—a lyric soprano, a diva, so they said—who spent part of each year abroad and had engagements on all the world's most famous stages. Jonas stayed close to her throughout the evening. She was wearing an eye-catching and rather unusual mini-dress of deep-red velvet. In the crush he ran a stealthy finger over her shoulder, saw how it left a trail, like a signature.

On one of the first days of the summer holidays Jonas invited Henny F. to go orienteering with him. In a move to encourage people to try a different form of exercise, the Grorud Athletics Society orienteering club had set up a series of control points in Lillomarka. If you visited a certain number of control points in the course of the season, you won a badge. For Jonas this was, however, only an excuse; he borrowed Daniel's map and compass and there they were, Jonas and Henny F., on a hot summer's day in the woods, both tense with an expectancy that had nothing to do with orienteering.

Jonas wasn't particularly handy with a map and compass and at one point, after finding five control points and punching their card amid rather exaggerated whoops of glee, they lost their way somewhere in the hilly terrain between Breisjøen and Alunsjøen Lakes: or rather, they had wandered on to the top of an out-of-the-way hill, a small mountain almost, where there should have been a control point, but where there was no control point, whereupon Jonas bombastically declared that this hill was not on the map, that they found themselves, in other words, in an uncharted region of Norway.

Henny F. has nothing against this. She removes her rucksack, pulls out a large chequered traveling rug and unfurls it, as one might cast a net, onto the grass. "Come on," she says, "let's soak up the sun for a while." They are in a totally secluded spot and she promptly proceeds to take off her clothes, lies down in just her bra and panties, cotton garments with a pattern that gives them the look of a bikini. Jonas strips off too, sits down beside her in his underpants, which all of a sudden seem far too small. Both are pale-skinned.

"What sort of sound does a dragon make?" Jonas finds himself asking.

She turns and looks at him. Says not a word. Just looks.

"That's right," Jonas says. "No sound."

He fell to studying the terrain, appearing terribly interested in something, placed the compass on the map and took his bearings, sat like this until Henny F. swept them off his lap with a resoluteness, bordering on resentfulness, that surprised him. "Forget that," she said, as if making a protest against all attempts to put the world in order at this moment. Jonas stayed perfectly still, forced himself not to glance down at Henny F., lying there next to him with her eyes closed, an outstretched girl's body clad only in a few square inches of cotton. Jonas sat in a piece of uncharted Norway, feeling something he had not felt since Margrete: that he was positively shuddering with desire. Or confusion. Or bewilderment. If he had not realized it before, he saw now that behind all the fine theories about reason and intellect, human beings consisted to just as great an extent of chemicals and electricity, that people could at times be turned, at the push of a button, into a factory buzzing with hormones, all wilfully going their own way.

He slid down onto the traveling rug, on his back. A moment later he felt her finger brush his hand, her fingertips, and it is not much of an exaggeration when I say that this situation, from a subjective point of view at least, is reminiscent of Michelangelo's fresco of the Creation, fingers touching, life coming into being. Because that is what it was like and that is how it would be every time a girl touched Jonas: as if he suddenly awoke, became someone else; he was no longer an ordinary boy, he was something very special.

He had to turn over onto his stomach, for several reasons. She began to stroke the back of his neck, his shoulders. Touching him ever so lightly, allowing her fingertips to no more than graze the hairs on his body. He had the idea that his skin had turned to velvet, that the pressure of her fingers had left a trail. She kept this up for some time, before lying back and starting to hum, possibly a Hollies song, "I'm Alive," Jonas couldn't have said.

He propped himself up on his elbows, leaned over her and, at long last, he did it, he kissed her, experienced a parallel to the phenomenon of two-part harmony: how, when they meet, two ordinary pairs of lips become more than the sum of their parts, so much so that suddenly he was drifting in all directions, he was both lying there and yet not lying there, because her tongue could not only tie knots in spaghetti, it could also suspend gravity and all the laws of cause and effect, besides showing him that the mouth was linked to every other part of the body, that there had to be cross-connections from the groove between his upper lip and his nose to the line bisecting his scrotum, as if they were, so to speak, on the same meridian. To Jonas's mind the whole of his explosively randy body, every molecule, was invested in that kiss. And as if to reciprocate he worked his way down to her neck, her throat; was so worked up that, without meaning to, he gave her a huge love bite. He hoped, however, that she would interpret this as a stamp, a watermark, a sign of true love—something which need not be hidden underneath a polo-neck sweater but should be paraded like a medal: "Look, I've been kissed; I've been kissed by a randy, besotted boy!"

He slid into a rapturous haze, he was someone else, experienced for the first time the thrill of flipping up the cup of a brassiere, so surprisingly easy, as if the impulse were stored in the genetic makeup of his fingers, in the same way as a newborn baby instinctively knows how to suck. And Jonas Wergeland was finally treated to the delicious tactile sensation of a soft girlish breast filling the palm of his hand, and he didn't even try, he knew he could never describe the feeling of that little nipple against the spot where the heart-line almost meets the lifeline. Nonetheless, he understood—even in the somewhat cooler light of hindsight—that he was experiencing one of life's high points, that that invisible cup-shaped imprint, every bit as unique as a fingerprint, had been branded upon the palm of his hand: that the spot which the nipple had touched, between his heart line and his indistinct life line would bear the mark like a tattoo forever.

And now, still with his hand inside the cup surrounding the soft stupa of her breast, as if conducting a religious act, receiving something, a gift, he let his eye flicker down over her crotch to the enticing mound beneath the cotton, where he could even make out the frizz of hair, a sight which left him breathless, although he knew more about Olympus Mons on Mars than about this bulge and could have told you more about the Marianas Trench in the Pacific Ocean than about the cleft that opened up underneath it. And as he tentatively slipped his hand inside her panties and she did not protest, and as he then slid it further down through the rather sparse bush of hair towards that dome, he could not help thinking of Daniel reading aloud, thought to himself that now he was fondling "her secret recesses"—an expression which, in fact, perfectly suited this intimate moment's blend of solemnity and modesty, the very fine line between crippling shyness and wild hysteria. In any case, when at long last, after years of speculation, his finger closed in on that mysterious little organ, equivalent to the point at the very top of a Gothic arch, the "clitoris," a word he had never dared to utter out loud, he had the feeling that he had merely grazed the surface of something greater, something mighty, which lay hidden inside her body, as if it were the top of a pyramid buried in sand, and this was, for Jonas, confirmed by the sounds she made, issuing from her larynx, as if from an incredibly complex instrument: noises which, as far as Jonas could tell, sounded like songs coming from deep down in the secret vaults of the body or, indeed, from the depths of the soul.

The sun went behind a cloud. Henny F. wrapped the ends of the plaid around them and snuggled up close to him. Two ordinary people, Jonas thought, two nothings who, when curled up against one another, formed a recumbent figure eight, symbol of infinity: who, together, became something else, a bigger figure. He liked that. He felt a rush of tenderness towards her, could not imagine how upset she would be when he "broke it off" some months later, rather brutally perhaps and for no real reason, that she would be completely beside herself with grief, that there would be rumors that she had tried to kill herself, some mention of her mother's sleeping pills; Jonas could not foresee all that now, was far too preoccupied with what she was doing to his ear, because she was kissing it, but at the same time seeming to sing into it, knocking him right off-center and into a mind-reeling, almost vibrant state, despite the fact that he was lying safe and sound on the ground, so much so that when he tried to say something, it came out in a husky, unfamiliar voice, as if even his vocal chords were involved in this process. Jonas could not help thinking of the Japanese prints which Aunt Laura had shown him, of men with penises as big as gnarled tree-trunks; that was how he felt: pumped up, blown out of proportion, ridden by a lust that left him gasping for breath. All in all, this overpowering passion, exaggerated and yet undeniably genuine, was not unlike what he would later discover in opera.

Heart pounding, he rolled over onto his back and felt, with alarm almost—the alarm of anticipation, alarm at his own arousal—how her hand groped its way into his pants: how, with her eyes averted, she wrapped her fingers around his straining member and held it, gently, as if she didn't know what to do with it, she just held it, softly but firmly, that was all, just held it, felt it. Jonas lifted his eyes to the treetops, the network of branches, felt his thoughts running along similar lines, spreading out and criss-crossing. For the first time he was conscious of his mental processes taking a particular turn when a woman touched him, as if his penis were a lever, flipping his whole intellect over into another dimension, one full of unsuspected connections. They, the women, moved him to fantasize in a different way by opening, with their touch, hidden doors in his memory, by quite simply setting in train the strangest stories. Suddenly he spied links between things that were far removed from one another, or the distance between things that lay close together; his thoughts darted here and there in explosive leaps—like those jumping-jacks—up and down between different levels of the brain, thus forming chains, ever longer chains of thought, forged by recollections, half clear, half blurred, which were tucked away in his memory and whose compass he did not comprehend until such moments; and that must have been why, perhaps because of the rug wrapped around them, he recalled the tent, while the sounds from her larynx made him think of songs, joyous songs, and the quaking inside him put him in mind of madness, or no, not madness, but the sense of being on the brink of something incomprehensible and yet so important that one burst into a language beyond all languages, trying if possible to fathom it, become another, others, someone. All these things that were racing around in his head were a result of the heady thrill she induced in him simply by clasping her fingers around his penis. Thanks to Henny

F., he was not just lying there on some unknown hill in Lillomarka, he was also on the verge of transcending a crucial new barrier; he was, in short, on the trail of a story, pursuing the certainty that there was more to him, potential he had yet to realize.

Possessed

For a child, there was any amount of things to do at Hvaler in the summer, from teasing the terns—those little dive-bombers—to going out in the pilot-boat in a stiff breeze. But if Jonas had to pick a favorite, it would either have to be Strömstad or the attic. At least once during the summer they would sail over to Strömstad in Sweden, the main attraction being the market in the town square: a kind of Scandinavian Marrakech with seedy stalls selling all sorts of cheap rubbish from packs of magic playing cards comprised of nothing but Jacks of Diamonds and Phantom rings with red glass eyes to disgusting stink bombs and the very latest in toy cars with flashing lights, and speedboats with real, battery-driven outboard motors, treasures beyond compare, even though most of them fell apart in the boat on the way home.

The attic, mysterious and fascinating as the props cupboard of a theater, was a place where Daniel and Jonas were only allowed to play when it rained. They were forever finding different stuff up there, boxes within boxes, old sea charts, photograph albums, a broken accordion, bottles of medicine with illegible labels and stupefying smells. One summer Daniel stumbled upon the little safe deep in a corner, like an overgrown temple amid the attic's jungle of nets and mildewed old clothes; they immediately fell to wondering what fabulous treasures it might contain. Their grandfather merely laughed when they told him of their find and got them even more steamed up by telling them one of his tallest tales: "In that safe, lads, I put a diamond given to me by the German Kaiser. Bigger than the Cullinan diamond it is! As big as a seagull's egg!"

One day, when the rain was coming down in buckets outside, something unexpected happened: Daniel managed to open the safe. Although he had been lying with his ear right up against it, listening intently, the way he had seen in films, it was only by pure luck that he happened to turn the dial to the correct three numbers—much in the same way, perhaps, as one could sometimes be jammy enough to crack the combination lock on a friend's bike just by turning the discs this way and that, without really thinking about it. Inside the safe they found a pretty, black lacquer casket inlaid with mother-of-pearl. But just as they lift the lid of the casket to reveal a grubby canvas bag, which prompts Daniel to form the word "pearls!" with his lips, their grandfather, prompted by sheer intuition so it seems, comes bounding into the attic, and before they can draw breath he has snatched the bag out of the casket. "I'll take that," is all he says, oddly agitated, panic-stricken even, then disappears again.

Daniel was seriously put out by this, which is probably why he did not object to Jonas taking the casket. Their grandfather, too, said that Jonas could keep it. "I bought that in Japan," he said. "See this glossy surface? It was once the sap inside a Japanese lacquer tree." For Jonas, the casket was, in itself, a treasure and not just because of the mother-of-pearl dragon on the lid; if there was one thing he never tired of, it was gazing at the layer upon layer of black lacquer, as if peering into a deep gloom: transparent, endless, an opening onto an unknown universe. When Jonas returned home at the end of this summer holiday he knew straightaway that he had to find something of value to put in the casket. He considered the clock workings, that enigmatic skeleton of cogs that sat ticking away on top of the chest of drawers, but dismissed that idea. What he really wanted was a pearl. After lengthy deliberation he came to the conclusion that only one object was worthy of this place of honor: his mother's silver brooch. With her blessing, he placed the round brooch with its intriguing tracery of ribbons in the casket, as if consigning it to a black, bottomless pit.

How does one become a conqueror?

There was no doubt as to the Brothers Grimm's favorite form of relaxation during the holidays. To Jonas's cousins—as ugly as their younger sister was pretty, hence the name—no stay on Hvaler was complete without a visit to one of the clamorous tent meetings on the neighboring island of Nedgården. One of the first things they did when they came to stay just after the incident with the safe was, therefore, to fill the rowboat with friends and set off across the sound. Jonas, too, was among the party when it reached its objective, after a walk though the pine forest. For here, on a flat stretch of ground not far from the steamship wharf on Nedgården, stood the big tent. "We're off to the circus," the Brothers Grimm said. And what a circus it was.

Jonas never did discover what manner of people they were, the spiritual nomads—I almost said Mongols—who arranged these meetings:

whether they were Pentecostalists or what. They certainly didn't look much like the dry and dusty congregation in Grorud Church on a Sunday morning. These people really swung, Jonas could not think of a better word; the atmosphere was electric, the noise level high as they slipped through the tent opening to find themselves standing under the dome of white fabric, the air heavy with the odors of damp grass, earth and sweat—the sweat of ecstasy, that is. For there before them, in the ring or whatever you want to call it, were both musicians and people who were in some way performing, and it was this "entertainment" that the Brothers Grimm had come to see. Because the faithful did not sit mouthing hymns the way they did in church: they sang, or no—they didn't sing, they exulted. You got the feeling that the canvas of the tent was all puffed up by the pressure of their voices and the rhythmical guitar accompaniment. And in the front rows you could see girls of whom it was said that they were so freshly redeemed, so flushed with redemption, that when asked at school to name the capital of Hawaii, they were quite liable to cry out "Hallelujah" instead of "Honolulu."

As usual the Brothers Grimm slid down onto the bench at the very back, where they could hunch down out of sight. To tell the truth, they didn't just hunch down, sometimes they had to lie flat-out on the grass; they lay there on the ground, bent double and racked by laughter at what they saw and heard. For this was the best kind of fun, it beat any television program or any other show for that matter, even the films of Old Rubber-Face himself, Jerry Lewis.

I may not be the right person to recount stories from this side of life, Professor, nonetheless I must make an attempt, if the pieces of Jonas Wergeland's life are to fall into place: because you see, on this bright evening, with the sun still hovering on the horizon and the sea perfectly calm outside, but with a spiritual storm raging inside the tent, a missionary was making a guest appearance. This was probably not such a common occurrence at the summer revival meetings, where the proceedings generally tended to follow a very simple, tried and tested format, with the clear aim of getting as many people as possible to "cast themselves into the Savior's arms." but this must be how it happened: it may be that the missionary just happened to be home on leave and was asked to speak at the meeting that evening. And the missionary, who might even have been sponsored by the brethren on the island, probably thought it only natural to weave stories of his experiences in the missionary field into his speech, because when Jonas and the Brothers Grimm sidled into the tent, he was in the midst of describing an exorcism which he had attended down there, in a country full of heathens: a pretty colorful story, a glowing and, in parts, extremely vociferous testimony to the inimitable power of the Lord.

Within seconds, on principle almost, the Brothers Grimm were fighting to control their laughter, as if they thought the tent was full of laughing gas—possibly because of all the "Praise the Lords!" being breathed round about them. Jonas, for his part, had been just as swiftly filled with curiosity. He had been interested in demons for a long time, ever since the first time when, half-asleep, he had heard them spoken of from the pulpit in Grorud Church, one second Sunday after Lent as it was called. He had been sitting upstairs in the balcony as usual, with a view of his father's organ playing and the pulpit, when the vicar began to talk about a boy who was possessed by an unclean spirit. Jonas had pricked up his ears. Till then he had associated the word "spirits" with the stuff grownups drank at parties, although his sister's obsession with the spirits in *The Arabian Nights* had led him to suspect that "spirit" might also mean something else, something dreadful. And right enough, here was the vicar describing how the unclean spirit caused this poor child to roll around on the ground, foaming at the mouth, and it was on this occasion too, or was it in RI class, that Jonas heard about Mary Magdalene, who was possessed by seven evil spirits, and, even more thrilling, the deadly spirit whose name was Legion, because he—the spirit, that is—was, in fact, many. Jonas had puzzled over this for ages, he even gave up playing with Legos, thinking as he did that Legos must have something to do with demons—and he may actually have been onto something there, since Jonas had a habit of building tall, reckless constructions with his bricks, models that could easily conjure up thoughts of a presumptuous and sinful Tower of Babel.

The Brothers Grimm are not listening to any of what's being said. They are already almost flat out on the grass, red in the face from stifled—I almost said demonic—laughter. They are having a whale of a time. And although this is, as I say, a revival meeting, something extraordinary is in the offing on this summer evening on the island at the mouth of the fjord—the congregation, the faithful, sense it too; several of them spontaneously begin to speak in tongues as the preacher, which is to say the homecoming missionary, builds up his speech, by way of a succession of Biblical quotations, to a dramatic climax; they burst into long strings of incomprehensible words which send the Brothers Grimm into paroxysms of giggling—Preben confessed later that he had actually dribbled into his pants. For the cousins, this was one of the summer's absolute high points when it came to entertainment. "Oh, gawd! This is funnier than all of Einar Rose's and Arve Opsahl's jokes rolled into one!" Stephan exclaimed. Jonas was equally enchanted but not for the same reasons as the Brothers Grimm. He realized that this language, this glossolalia, was not the senseless gibberish his cousins took it to be, but an attempt to stretch language as far as it would go, into a vacuum where rules and reason had to admit defeat. He also had the feeling that something big was about to happen. That something was going to lay itself open for him, just like the safe in the loft; that he would be presented with a dark casket which—who knew—might contain a precious pearl.

So he did not drift out of the tent-opening along with the Brothers Grimm and the others as the singing, a Norwegian version of gospel, and the guitars took over again, and the meeting moved towards its conclusion—after, that is, urgent appeals for people to come forward and bend the knee to the Lord or, in plain words, be saved. Jonas remained standing next to one of the rearmost benches, watching the people, quite a lot of them, who made their way towards the middle of the tent and kneeled down, a good few young people among them as it happens, and it was then, at this post-meeting as it was called, at this relatively chaotic stage of the proceedings, that something occurred which does not normally occur at these summertime tent meetings: all at once a young man cries out that he is tormented by evil spirits. Now a normal Pentecostalist, or whatever they were, might not have made any attempt to deal with this situation or only dealt with it in the most superficial manner, but here was this missionary, with his truly hair-raising experiences from the mission service and his work among "the savages," far more dramatic than this, and—somewhat taken aback though he might have been—he walked purposefully up to the young man, placed his hands on his head and began to shout things, or rather, to issue orders which Jonas did not understand: "In the name of Jesus Christ, I command you!" and the like, so write, Professor, write as if your life depended upon it, because it was awesome; Jonas would never forget it. The young man's knees gave way, he keeled over and as he did so the missionary was thrown backwards as if he had received an electric shock. Jonas truly felt that powerful forces were present in the tent; there was a pressure, the sort of atmosphere that prevails immediately before a Biblical thunderstorm.

The man on the ground is grunting and writhing about, shaking. Jonas believes he sees his face change, at least seven times, as if it belongs to different people and not only people but animals too, wild beasts. The missionary bends over him and grips his head tightly, almost tearing at him. To Jonas, it looks like a battle in which one of the combatants is invisible. That said, though, it was a nice, clean fight, and for the record let me just say that it bore little similarity to the commercialised versions one is presented with in films, in which little girls speak with harsh male voices and heads spin round and round. In short, Jonas was observing an individual in obvious torment and a man who was endeavoring to do something about this torment. And did so. All at once, after a violent shudder, the young man relaxes, and a smile spreads across his lips. He stands up, raises his arms as if in thanks to heaven, before dropping onto his knees in the grass, with his elbows on a bench and his eyes shut, while the elders stand around him praising the Lord.

Jonas left the tent, filled with the same blend of exultation and sadness as when he had to leave the copious market in Strömstad. He caught up with the others among the pine trees on their way to the boat. They were still laughing, slapping their thighs, roaring their heads off, had to keep stopping to stand doubled up with laughter. Jonas walked along quietly at the tail end. He was thinking, no, not just thinking: pondering. And what he was pondering upon, more than anything else, was whether such spirits always had to be evil. To tell the truth, this evening marked a turning point for Jonas's notion of what it means to be a human being, although this perception still lay far out on the fringes of, or possibly beyond, language, rather like speaking in tongues. Looked at in this light, Jonas Wergeland was also saved at that meeting. He sauntered down to the rowboat, feeling strangely relieved. Who's to say there's only one of me, he thought, knowing what this meant: that other avenues were open to him, possibly even other lives.

So Jonas did not wish, like the young man in the tent on Nedgården, to rid himself of these possible spirits; he wanted to cherish them, get to know them. He hoped he had at least seven spirits within him, like Mary Magdalene. Maybe even a wild beast. He could do with it: he whom everybody said was such a good boy. Several times that summer his mother would surprise Jonas when he was sitting talking to himself, using different voices. And this boy who, for years, had been such a fussy eater, suddenly started tucking in at mealtimes. Not only that, but he varied his diet, helped himself for the first time—oh, wonder of wonders—to boiled vegetables and didn't even gag. So, whichever way you look at it, this was the summer when Jonas turned from a fairly puny little kid into a lad who rapidly shot up, bursting with health. And not only that: from that summer onwards Jonas Wergeland was possessed. He was on the trail of his true self. Or rather: his true selves.

I—the Professor—remarked on one word that cropped up in every newspaper article on Jonas Wergeland: demonic. This was after the whole thing blew up anew, again when no one was prepared for it, as if it were all part of a carefully planned two-stage rocket launch. It would be wrong to call it a bombshell. To the general public, despite a certain shock factor, it was more in the nature of a spectacular fireworks display.

I'm sure I wasn't the only one, during the first phase of the case, to be titillated by a couple of unexplained details. Why had Margrete Boeck not put up any resistance—especially when one considers her, albeit latent, self-defense skills? It could of course be, as one theory had it, that she had been taken totally by surprise. But couldn't the caller be someone she knew, who banged her head against the wall, knocking her senseless before she realized what said caller was up to?

Then there was the information the police eventually released regarding the murder weapon, the mysterious Luger. There were no fingerprints on the pistol, but the newspapers cited a number of theories as to its origins and ownership. This aspect gave rise to numerous in-depth reports on neo-Nazi organizations, including interviews with militant leaders and revelations concerning arms training and mail order companies. It became disturbingly apparent that even in Norway there were people who held secret meetings at which they reverently watched old documentaries about the Führer and gave the "Heil Hitler" salute, while at the same time guarding items of Nazi memorabilia from the war as if they were holy relics. But everyone, even the right-wing extremists who had launched a menacingly worded attack on Jonas Wergeland's final program—the one on immigrants, a program which, not surprisingly, was shown again immediately after the killing—denied having anything to do with this brutal crime.

Then came the silence, or lassitude: a kind of collective mental state like the way you feel on getting up, stiff and slightly dazed, to switch off the television late on a Saturday evening. The public could not know it, but it was at this point that Jonas Wergeland's brother, Reverend Daniel W. Hansen, contacted the police—"after lengthy and painful consideration"—having also seen the picture of the Luger in the paper. At police headquarters he had no difficulty in picking out the murder weapon from a selection of pistols and thereafter gave the name of the Luger's probable owner. Reverend Hansen was, by all accounts devastated. But as he had said on arriving at the police station: "Here I stand, I can do no other."

From that moment on the entire media picture—a picture which can safely be filed under the heading of New Expressionism—was dominated by one news story: Jonas Wergeland had been arrested, charged with the murder of his wife. The press promptly resorted to such phrases as "Norway's crime of the century." At any rate it was the perfect event for a well-developed information society. For a couple of days the country was in the grip of something approaching mass hysteria. The reaction to Wergeland's arrest even exceeded all the commotion surrounding the death of the old king the year before, certainly in terms of column inches and television coverage. Reports on the *Evening News* showed people weeping openly in the street and taking photographs or shooting video film outside Villa Wergeland in Grorud, as if this were Hollywood. Some fans even went so far as to light candles outside the fence. A number of newspapers gave readers their own page in which to express their thoughts and feelings. An entire nation appeared to be ripe for counselling.

Everyone attempted yet again to get in touch with the person at the center of it all. An interview, just a couple of quotes even, would have been the scoop of the year. But Jonas Wergeland had been remanded in custody, barred from receiving mail or visitors; and when this ban was lifted he would not speak to anyone apart from close family. His mother came to see him, and his little brother, known as Buddha. Indeed Buddha visited Oslo District Prison as often as was practically possible and was soon well acquainted with everyone there. Nonetheless, and even though the prison staff felt bad about it, they had to confiscate several of the odd presents he wanted to give Jonas. On one occasion he brought a kite. "What's your big brother going to do with that?" they asked. "I thought he could fly it from his cell window to drive out evil spirits," said Buddha.

The first person who was allowed to visit Jonas Wergeland, however, was Kristin, his daughter—a fact that did not go unnoticed in certain of the tabloids. Jonas Wergeland's mother had shielded her from the worst instances of invasive reporting by taking refuge on Hvaler. But it was the girl herself who had asked to see her father, not only asked, in fact, but insisted. And what did they talk about? They talked about trees. Yes, trees. According to my source, they spent a whole hour chatting about trees. When her time was up, Kristin left with her father a drawing in which the tree underneath the ground, the root system, was as big as the tree itself.

But to return to my starting point, to the way in which the media gloated over the fact that the heroic image of Jonas Wergeland was crumbling like an icon riddled with rot, and how the lowest common denominator in every article was the word "demonic." It was this particular expression that had—I can find no better word—arrested my attention and to some extent influenced my decision to accept the publisher's almost unnecessarily lucrative offer. That had to be the deepest aim of the biography, the litmus test of its originality: to explain the nature of Jonas Wergeland's demoniacal side. And that may have been why I got so bogged down, if you like, in all the material I had assembled since it did not offer the faintest glimmer of an answer to questions of this type. Until my rescuer showed up, what I had lacked, above all else—strangely enough, considering the panoramic view from my study window—was the perspective which would bring the lines of Jonas Wergeland's life into relief, show me a theme and hidden passages instead of screeds of place names and dates. Due to these unexpected problems I had also begun to worry about another eventuality—something which my visitor, not without a touch of sarcasm, had hinted at on our very first meeting: that this assignment might be on the difficult side for someone who had hitherto wrestled solely with the past. Was it possible for me, with my background and experience, to disclose the essence of modern life?

Or, as my unknown helper—I almost used the word employer—said at the beginning of the third evening we spent together in the turret at Snarøya: "Every life seems banal the minute one tries to sum it up." Despite repeated offers of some refreshment—I humbly suggested a little Stilton and a glass of port—all the stranger asked for was a jug of water. "My only trouble is that I suffer from an abiding thirst," my visitor said with that barely discernible accent. "By the way—I would appreciate it if you would light the fire as you usually do; it's so damned cold in this country."

As soon as the logs caught light my visitor stretched hungry hands out to the flames, at the same time eyeing a caricature of myself that hung on the wall. Like President de Gaulle, I am always drawn with the face of an elephant, because of my prominent nose and big ears. I prefer to think, though, that it's because I have an excellent memory—something I most certainly had need of at this time.

As usual the stranger was dressed in black, a color that accentuated an almost startling pallor; and, although that face had the aspect of a scholar, I cannot say that I liked the person sitting across from me. I noted that the hands were covered in little scars, and the clothes emitted an indefinable odor reminiscent of burnt horn, or possibly it was the reek of a chemistry lab. This person told me nothing about who they were; merely stared at me, eagerly, expectantly almost, again apparently so brimful of stories that those lips could barely contain them.

"This matter . . . engages me, Professor. Greatly. Personally." There were times, especially on those first evenings, when the stranger faltered or groped around, as if unable to remember or not knowing the right Norwegian word.

"Would it be impolite of me to ask why?"

"What if I were to tell you that I am involved in it, that I may unfortunately be partly to blame for Jonas Wergeland's actions," the visitor said, sending me a glance that frightened me. "Would you believe me if I said that it was all the result of a wager? How could we know that it would have such—how shall I put it—unfortunate consequences?"

"And what was this wager about?" I ventured to ask.

"It might be a bit difficult to explain on what plane it lay—I mean, to explain it to you. I could say that I, moving as I did in an entirely different sphere, as it were, quite simply bet that Jonas Wergeland would become a great man, "make a name for himself" as they say. My opposite number, if that is the correct term, bet that, with what talents he had, Jonas Wergeland would never amount to anything. You could say that we were betting on whether he would become a dragon or a sparrow."

I was on the point of asking what the stakes in this wager had been, but my visitor had already embarked upon a preamble which was clearly meant to lead into that evening's stories: "You might not think it of me, Professor, but I actually regard it as my duty to help you. Just because the image of a hero has been shattered doesn't mean that it cannot be put together again, albeit as another image."

From the turret we could see the planes gliding in or taking off, so close that until darkness fell the logos of the different airlines were clearly visible; and if we turned round we could see the fjord, the boats slipping past, with an occasional, brilliantly illuminated colossus looking too big for the narrow channel.

"Somewhere in Jonas Wergeland's life there is a pattern," the stranger continued. "A pattern that generated the energy which, in turn, gave him the power to do what he did. What stories then, what series of events was it, that made Jonas Wergeland, a perfectly ordinary human being, capable both of creating that magnificent and inspiring television series and of being arrested and charged with murder? Because whichever way you look at it, no one can say that they did not appreciate the high standard of these programs when they were broadcast, that they were not uplifting. And no matter what people may claim, no one, not even the most zealous inquisitor, knows anything about Jonas Wergeland's motives—I'm talking here about his innermost motives—on that evening when he returned home from the World's Fair in Seville."

I could tell that I was tense, almost involuntarily tense. And at the same time grateful to be experiencing something I believe many people spend all their lives longing for: to meet a stranger who asks you to take a seat by the fire so that he or she can tell you what it's all about.

"This first story shows that to call Jonas Wergeland demonic is an oversimplification as outrageous as that of calling a dragon a monster," the stranger declared with fire reflected in those pupils and a concentration which made me feel the story was at that very moment being pulled out of its waiting room in the storyteller's memory.

Radio Theater Presents

On one of the threads that forms a spiral in Jonas Wergeland's life he killed a dragon. And if we enter one of the coils in this spiral we find the following story:

They were going to put on a radio play. Not the way they had done as little boys, when they caught bumblebees and held them, buzzing and buzzing, inside shoeboxes. No, proper radio theater. Jonas and Little Eagle were about to undertake a project that would represent the culmination of their career; they were going to record a play of their own writing, based on the story of St. George and the Dragon. This undertaking did, however, present lots of challenges, and the greatest of these, aside from the different voices, was of course posed by the background noises, referred to in the trade simply as "background": the sound effects which enable listeners to picture rafts heading towards dangerous rapids, or skiers in a snowstorm, if that is what is required. That was Ørn's job, the sound effects; he was what you might call the floor manager. "There's no sound I can't make," was Ørn's motto. I don't know whether I have to spell it out for you, Professor, but when it comes to the question of which person has exerted the greatest influence on Jonas Wergeland's life, the answer has to be Little Eagle—alias Ørn-Henrik Larsen.

It was actually Daniel who had told them about St. George, because Daniel was in the Cubs and they had recently celebrated St. George's Day with much pomp and ceremony. Jonas and Ørn instantly fell for the story of the knight who sets out to rescue the princess from the dragon. They had originally been thinking of recording a simplified version of Jack London's *Call of the Wild*—with Colonel Eriksen the elkhound playing the lead—but soon found that this presented certain insurmountable problems as far as the sounds were concerned. It was one thing to get an extremely placid Colonel Eriksen to bark in the right places, or even howl; manufacturing a whole pack of wolves was something else again.

But what sort of sound does a dragon make? Or to put it another way: what is the creepiest sound you can think of?

The tape recorder they were using, or "*magnetophone*" as Mr. Larsen grandly referred to it, had only one track, which meant they had to record the voices and the background noises at the same time. Incidentally, this machine, acquired for Mr. Larsen to brush up his "Can you tell me the way to the nearest restaurant?" in eight languages, was itself a little marvel. I take it, Professor, that you recall the Tandberg tape recorders of the mid-fifties? TB2s they were called: like little temples to sound with their mahogany casings and loudspeakers installed behind latticed glass panels.

Actually it would not be entirely out of place to dwell for a moment, here, on the name Tandberg: on the company's founder, Vebjørn Tandberg, a prime Norwegian example of the pioneer spirit and industrial farsightedness, and perhaps even more on the blissful feelings of nostalgia which Tandberg's products arouse within a large proportion of the Norwegian population. Say "Silver Super" and you trigger a collective landslide of memories, mental pictures of casings in highly polished, lacquered wood, possibly shot with the memory of the feel of a fingertip turning a tuning dial or even the give of the buttons when pressed. Newer models produced around this time were a delight to the eye as well as the ear, not least the real battleship of the Tandberg fleet, the "Huldra," the ultimate expression of tasteful design, a Norwegian equivalent of Denmark's Lego, an object which, when set in its place in the living room, raised the whole house several rungs up the ladder of modernity and sophisticated elegance. With its knobs and lights, its teak casing and its wood-nymph name, it imbued an apartment with an air of space age, tropical island and mysterious forest combined.

We find ourselves, therefore, in an era which already seems remote, a time when the living room was still arranged around the radiogram, the wireless being the household altar, occupying the place soon to be accorded to the television set, when people switched religions as you might say, swapped old gods for new. And when Jonas Wergeland was a boy, the most eagerly awaited radio program was the *Saturday Children's Hour*, and best of all, like the trinket in the center of a lucky potato: the weekly serial. Jonas could never get enough of these, especially the noises in the background which one could barely hear but which acted like drum rolls on his nerves, made him bite his knuckles—creaking doors, footsteps on stairs, matches being struck inside dark caves—his brain fairly seethed, he saw those scenes, clearer than he ever would later when he saw, with his own eyes I mean, those notorious pieces on television's *Armchair Theater*: the Finnish plays, for example, with their hilariously exaggerated sounds of feet scrunching through cold snow. All those afternoons spent in a chair pulled up close to the radio—breathtaking hours of listening to *The Road to Agra, The Jungle Book, Around the World in Eighty Days*—taught Jonas that sounds have an unconscious effect on us, just as a song can tip an incident over into a whole other dimension—like the time, one May 17, when Wolfgang Michaelsen, under duress, of course, and blushing furiously, played an infernally strident clarinet during the singing of the national anthem on the flag green in the morning, thus inserting an ironic, not to say anarchic, element into the pompously patriotic tenor of the day: the chairman of the residents' association, standing there in his new suit, May 17 ribbons fluttering, all the children in their Sunday best with money burning a hole in their pockets. All things considered, it was the radio, and more specifically the radio plays, which truly taught Jonas Wergeland about the power of illusion, how little it took to fire people's imaginations. "It's really quite amazing," he said to Ørn, "how the mere sound of somebody crumpling a bit of paper can make you so scared you pee your pants."

So what sort of sound does a dragon make? Like a hundred lions? Or like a peach stone scraped across a blackboard?

The voices for the play about St. George presented no problems, because Jonas did them all. Jonas was a master when it came to mimicry, to putting on different voices. And after the visit to the Pentecostalists' tent he was even more conscious of containing a whole gallery of role models within himself; it was almost as if he had been "possessed" by the spirit to perform radio plays involving a host of voices.

The challenge therefore lay in the sound effects. And Jonas and Little Eagle were perfectionists. For months they had been completely taken up with this new hobby, every day after school. They could spend a week finding the right sound for their own dramatization of the ascent of Tirich Mir, based on the book by Arne Næss. At last they hit upon it: to give the listener the picture of a mountaineer digging his crampon into ice, they stuck the tip of a pocket-knife into a lump of resin. In their eyes this was an achievement on a par with the ascent itself, and they were quite sure that philosopher Arne Næss would also have applauded it, perhaps even embarked on fruitful speculations as to the link between resin and Tirich Mir—looked upon it as an incitement to climb still further in his thoughts. "I probably get as much pleasure from a good sound effect," Ørn once said, "as a counterfeiter gets from looking at a perfect forgery of a hundred-kroner note."

So far nothing had had them stumped, not thunder, not lightning, not fire—they used rustling cellophane for that—not even steamy love scenes: Ørn's simulated kiss was in the Casanova class. Ørn was also a wizard at imitating cars—right down to the different marques. They walked about with their ears on stalks; every noise was a potential sound effect for a radio play. It reached the point where they begged Ørn's mother to let them cover the living-room walls in egg boxes to get rid of an annoying echo. And although she refused, she had to turn a blind eye to the mysterious disappearance of a whole host of things from the kitchen: a hand whisk, grease-proof paper, brushes and pans—even the vacuum cleaner. You needed more than a few measly props for a masterpiece such as *In the Sultan's Harem* or *Napoleon and the Battle of Austerlitz*.

In the play about St. George, they endeavored to get to the forest scene as quickly as possible. This was the part where they could give their imaginations free rein. They pretended that they were inventors, freely experimenting with every conceivable, and inconceivable, device from bicycle pumps to balloons. They did not, however, use coconut shells to emulate the sound of a horse walking or galloping, Ørn reproduced this perfectly by drumming his fingertips on the coffee table. One small stroke of genius, though, was the chirping of the birds at the beginning, before things began to get creepy, which Ørn produced by rubbing a damp cork against a bottle—for a whole afternoon they amused themselves with producing the distinctive calls of various different birds, taping them and chortling delightedly at all the lifelike results. As the drama grew darker they added more wind—the radio tuned to a station that was off the air—and the rustling of leaves on swaying branches. Peas in a cardboard box sounded like a shower of rain, a couple of tin cans gave the chink of armor. Ørn was a sight to be seen, bouncing back and forth like a yoyo between his various "instruments." "When you're finished with this you'll be able to get a job as the ball in a pinball machine," Jonas said.

The real—the nigh-on insoluble problem—was still the dragon itself. For what does a dragon say? They both tried roaring in different ways, but it sounded as silly as having a lion bark like a poodle. They tried using Ørn's mother's Mixmaster, they tried spray cans, they considered—talking of hissing sounds—dripping water onto the cooker hotplate, but were not allowed into the kitchen. Their best solution involved Ørn sitting with his head inside a tin pail, it sounded bloodcurdling enough and would do at a push. By shaking Ørn's dad's leather jacket in the air—didn't it even reek a little of dragon?—they managed to replicate the sound of leathery wing-beats. Finally, Jonas added the crowning touch to their inventiveness by bringing along Daniel's kerosene lamp which, when they lit it, gave the most glorious sense of fire being breathed.

After numerous dry runs, mainly to get the coordination right, they were ready for the final take. If it turned out well, they were to let the little kids hear it; with any luck they'd scare the socks off them. The introduction went like clockwork, Ørn struck the largest pot lid with a ladle, and Jonas announced in a deep, dramatic voice: "Grorud Radio Theater presents"—then left a nice pause for effect before intoning in an, if possible, even deeper voice: "*St. George and the Fearful Dragon.*" Another clang of the pot lid. The first part also passed without a hitch, went better than ever before; Little Eagle flew back and forth between the various articles scattered around the room and on the table, screwed and scraped, wafted and rattled, he was the soul of confidence, drumming with his fingers on the tabletop and shaking boxes, ripping clothes—it all sounded quite professional.

St. George draws near to the dragon's lair, in the middle of a dark and forbidding forest; the wind howls, the leaves tremble, the air is rent by a scream: Jonas makes his voice as high-pitched as possible, a princess's cry for help, a maiden in distress, Jonas switches to the narrator's neutral, but no less compelling tone, tells how St. George leaps off his horse, walks through dry leaves—Little Eagle rakes through strips of paper—sees the dragon come flying towards him—Ørn waves the leather jacket frantically in the air, it sounds good, it sounds really great, this is going to be such a success—the dragon lands with a thud—Ørn jumps off the sofa onto the floor, the dragon comes charging through the undergrowth—Ørn stamps orange boxes to smithereens—they had practically had to go down on their bended knees to get these particular, orange boxes, with slats of just the right thinness, from the grocer—it sounded diabolical, like an elephant, a dinosaur, or yes, a dragon approaching. "Now you shall die!" Jonas cries in St. George's heroic, fearless voice, a challenge which is supposed to be followed by the dragon's spine-chilling, stupefying fiery breath; Ørn is right on schedule with a lighter held in front of a blowlamp which has so far been used for nothing more exciting than melting Swix ski-wax, but which will now make small children turn weak at the knees; in his mind Ørn is already over by the pail that will lend resonance to the dragon's hideous roar, but first a terrible blast of flame, the only problem is that suddenly the lighter won't work, it only goes click, click, Ørn tries frantically, but it's no good, click click it says, Jonas gazes at him in desperation, it had all been going so beautifully up until now, and there is something about this situation which makes Ørn laugh, to roar with laughter, to laugh in a most particular way, almost gloatingly, spitefully is perhaps the word or carelessly, because he doesn't take this quite so seriously as Jonas; Little Eagle laughs and laughs, as if he can't believe this is happening, laughs resignedly, in disbelief, howls with laughter, pops the tin pail over his head in an attempt to smother his mirth, but carries on laughing inside it. "You don't scare me, vile dragon, foul abductor of innocent women," Jonas continues in St. George's voice, doing the sword-out-of-scabbard sound, wanting to see the play through to the end for the practice, if nothing else, runs a bread knife over the vacuum's metal tube, while Little Eagle just laughs and laughs, so hard that he topples off the sofa and knocks over the table, and all his props, including the microphone, making a deafening racket, and they have to stop, switch off the tape recorder. "Damn, that's just like you, Ørn," Jonas fumed, "ruining the very end."

Jonas runs the tape back, though, wanting to hear the recording anyway, to be on the safe side. And it is then, when they come to the fatal point, that it dawns on him: It's perfect! The clicks sound sinister, you would never guess it was a lighter, it sounds as if the dragon is doing something venomous, working up to something, with its forked tongue. And Ørn's laughter heightens the tension, not least because it is unintentional, and preceded by a hair-raising pffffft—Ørn's involuntary reaction actually gave the impression of an honest-to-goodness dragon, a rather menacing, utterly surprising sound, from inside the pail in particular it bordered on something beyond their understanding, a kind of smiling malice, something even more dangerous than a roaring, fire-breathing dragon. Brilliant. And the din produced when Little Eagle knocked everything over provided the cataclysmic soundtrack to a swift but fierce battle in which—no one could be in any doubt—the dragon was killed.

What sort of sound does a dragon make?

An apologetic little laugh?

This was the day on which Jonas learned that creativity can lie in the unexpected, in things one hadn't thought of, and above all else: in simplicity. Not only that but it might even be that a dragon was killed—for real. He felt proud when he stood with that tape in his hands. To some extent he understood that this spool of tape, this discus of invisible tracks, was more important, that in the long run it also stood for something more valuable than the actual machinery, the tape recorder. At the back of his mind he was also haunted by the thought that these background noises, when isolated, would form the basis for a very different story.

They ran the play for some of the little kids as planned—against their mothers' will, no doubt—and scared the living daylights out of them. No one could understand why a number of younger children at Solhaug suddenly started waking up in the night, crying and muttering about dragons and not letting them get them. "There, there," their mothers said. "There's no such thing as dragons." And having thought about it for a moment they might have added: "Not in Norway anyway."

Mysteries of the Milky Way

Jonas, too, once had a nightmare. But he was not dreaming. Someone presented him with a dragon, an unnatural creature, and said it was his brother. No talk here of the wrong sound, though, this was a total misconception, a minor addition at the most elementary level of life: one "x" too many so to speak.

Where are the dark holes in Jonas Wergeland's life?

More than one person has been prepared to state that Jonas Wergeland was incapable of loving anyone. I don't know what to say to that, Professor—there were undoubtedly a lot of people whom he truly, deeply loathed. But there was no one whom he hated more bitterly than Buddha.

When Buddha was born Jonas was devastated. Buddha might have been a meteorite from above which, small though it is, can inflict mysteriously large wounds on a landscape. Usually it is the parents who suffer from shock in the wake of such a birth, who are left stunned by the doctor's announcement that their new baby is not like other babies, but in the Hansen family no one was harder hit by this news than Jonas. He was so stricken that he took to his bed. It was he, not his mother, who had trouble with the "afterbirth."

For weeks Jonas lay in bed, tossing and turning in anguish. Why? Because he felt responsible for this child. In his own eyes, Jonas was the boy's father.

And yet—this sense of responsibility was soon overshadowed by hate. Pure, unadulterated hate. The kind of hate he had once seen in Little Eagle's eyes. For days and days Jonas sat on his own, wondering, quite seriously, how he could do away with his brother. You often hear about the jealousy felt by the older children in a family when a new baby arrives and steals all the attention. But this was different: Jonas was fourteen years old.

Time and again he stood over Buddha's crib, looking down on that unsuspecting face and despising himself because he could not bring himself to put his hands around the infant's throat and squeeze or place a pillow over that awful visage, hideous in its innocence. Alternatively, he considered taking his mother's brooch from the black lacquer casket and poking out his own eyes with the pin: that way he would at least be spared having to see that apparition, the head whose tiny ears were already starting to take on the protuberant form that prompted thoughts of other planets, but he couldn't do that either. The only thing he was capable of was hating, subjecting this little toad to black, bottomless hate.

Over the years that followed, Jonas noticed how his whole body would contract at the slightest glimpse of his brother—that moon face, those ghastly ears, the slanted, slightly skelly eyes, the tongue that flicked in and out like that of some long extinct lizard. The others accepted the drooling creature right from the word go, they were perfectly happy with Buddha. "A baroque gem," Rakel said. The new member of the family had even winkled his parents out of their TV chairs. "He's saved us from the magic mountain," his mother said one evening when she and his father were sitting chatting the way they used to do, with their armchairs facing one another. It was actually Daniel who started calling their little brother Buddha, because of the brat's fondness for rice. And even though there were times when Daniel might be embarrassed by Buddha, Jonas was alone in his murderous antipathy.

In terms of natural gifts, Buddha was very well endowed, but as one might expect he did develop more slowly than other children. At the age of three he was only just starting to toddle about on little bandy legs, and he said nothing, apart from some sounds or cryptic onomatopoeics that could have been interpreted as "Mamma." Something did, however, happen to his concentration when he played with the sugar tongs or chess pieces, particularly the knights. Little mirrors and bells also elicited an animation, accompanied by loud crows of delight.

Mainly as a means of humiliating his brother, Jonas decided to try to teach Buddha to say just one word. In order to prove that it could not be done, that—as an act of pure compassion—the poor soul ought to be done away with as soon as possible, either that or be consigned to some distant solitary cell. In a flash of spite Jonas decided that he would get the boy to say "milk," the most basic element in any child's life. "Milk," said Jonas each time he handed Buddha his feeder cup. "Milk, milk, milk, milk. Can you say it? Milk. M-i-l-k."

Buddha merely broke into his usual happy grin. Like a dog about to be fed. This was something else Jonas hated: that Buddha could not sense his hate.

"Milk. It's milk. Say it, stupid."

Buddha just smiled.

For six months they went on like this. Jonas must have said that word to Buddha a thousand times, and each time Buddha responded by smiling blankly, when even a dog, out of sheer exhaustion almost, would have been moved to utter the word "milk." Jonas should have been satisfied—he had proved beyond a doubt that his brother could not be taught—and yet Jonas was not happy. It became an obsession with him, to get his brother to say at least one word. Then they could get rid of him.

One Saturday morning Jonas was at home alone with Buddha. It was raining outside, rain bucketing down, the windows seemed to be covered in transparent, wet plastic. As usual when they were eating, Jonas placed the cup next to Buddha's stubby fingers and said, almost without thinking—as if he had long since given up: "Milk. Look. Milk. This is milk. Say milk, blast you. Milk, milk, milk. It's not that hard. Look at my lips. Milk. Mmmm-iiii-lk. MILK. Milk, you rotten little sod, you moon-faced little git!" He felt like smashing the cup into the face of the creature sitting across from him.

Rain streamed down the windowpanes, soundlessly. Buddha looked at him. He looked at Jonas in a new way. For a long time Buddha looked at his brother, deep into his face, right through his face.

Then he said it. So banal and yet so obvious: "Jonas," he said. Not all that clearly. His tongue rather in the way but clear enough all the same: "Jonas."

Jonas tried later to describe what happened next. It was as if a landslide swept through him, he said, backwards, upwards, slowly. It was as if a dozen different emotions flowed through him, all shooting off in different directions, or were dispersed, leaving a huge hollow space in the center, and then it all flowed back again, only this time as one feeling: warmth. An abundance of warmth.

All that hate, all that cursing, and Buddha's first word was a name. A declaration of love.

Buddha was on his feet, stood with his arms wrapped around his big brother. Said it again, his name. The rain streamed down the windowpanes. The landscape outside was little more than a blur, glimpsed as if through a plastic bag full of water. Jonas cupped his hands around Buddha's face. Had the whole world in his hands. He realized that he was crying. He could have been crying for some time, he didn't know, he cried his eyes out, soundlessly. Filled with a sudden, all-pervading emotion he had not known that he owned, a quite inconceivable love that would surely endure everything, hope everything, move mountains and things still bigger. And the object of this incomprehensible love was the figure before him. The defenseless bundle that he hated so much.

Buddha stroked Jonas's damp cheek with his finger. "Milk," he said. "Milk."

It is no exaggeration to say that, not counting his parents and Kristin, in all his life Jonas Wergeland loved only one person, and by that I mean with all his heart and without any ulterior motive: Buddha. Possibly because he had never hated anyone as fiercely either.

Buddha was a genius. A genius at love.

And I think I know why: Buddha was the product of a broken heart.

The Erogenous Battle Zone

Now we have to tread warily, Professor, because this—the fateful consequences of that broken heart, I mean—constitutes a story that belongs elsewhere, though an imprudent narrator might have told it here, not realizing that such an artificial splicing would put the whole account of Jonas Wergeland's life at risk. One tiny alteration can make all the difference; Buddha is living proof of this.

At this juncture, however, another tale impinges, so strongly that I can positively feel how it—physically—grabs hold of the last sentences above. Ergo, the following story is also about love, or about what, for a long time, Jonas mistook for love.

In the latter half of the seventies, during the years when he was studying architecture, Jonas often visited the Museum of Cultural History on the island of Bygdøy, to sketch the historic buildings on exhibit there. He had a peculiar weakness for this place, always felt, as he passed through the tunnel-like entranceway with its ticket windows, that he was entering another zone, a zone in which several ages existed simultaneously—rather like the three levels of the human brain. And what he felt most in touch with, as he strolled among old buildings reeking of creosote, sketching a cog joint from Numedal here, a corner post from Hallingdal there, was his reptile self, the oldest level of his consciousness. Given the choice he would have said he liked the Setesdal farmstead best, possibly because it was situated close to the entrance, or because it had the look of a street, with a row of buildings on either side of the path—either that or it could have had something to do with the notion of Setesdal as somewhere so totally cut off, the thought that here he had found the perfect picture of Norway and the nation's history.

That afternoon, a weekday in early summer with sunshine and scudding clouds, he happened to wander into the Åmlid farmhouse, into a room that was surprisingly cool. There were no windows in the house; the only light fell through the smoke hole in the ceiling. He stood with his feet on hard-packed earth, studying the open hearth in the center of the room, trying to imagine all the smoke that must collect in the room when a fire was burning. The ceiling beams were completely blackened. This was how people had lived in the Middle Ages—although in Setesdal, because it was such an out-of-the way spot, people had lived liked this until well into the nineteenth century. Jonas could not rid himself of the thought that, in their minds, many Norwegians were still as cut off from the rest of the world.

An elderly couple, Danish pensioners, climbed over the high threshold and a guide, a girl whom Jonas had not noticed, stepped out of the shadows clad in folk costume. Jonas stayed where he was and listened to the way in which she explained to the Danes about the *gjøya*, a thick pole suspended over the hearth on which to hang pots. "As you can see," she said, pointing, "the pole is shaped like a horse, because on the farm the horse was regarded as a fertility symbol." Jonas saw how she glanced in his direction, giving him the once-over even as she went on talking, showing the Danish tourists how the pole pivoted on a huge wooden hinge. One of her eyebrows sat higher than the other, as if in constant surprise.

Once they were alone she walked over to him: "I know you," she said. To begin with, due to the respectful look in her eye, he thought she had mistaken him for someone else, that this was a variant on the Samoan incident. "We went to the same school," she said. Her voice was commanding but pleasant. Jonas fixed his eyes on a corner, thought of cog joints, thought of the perfect way of fitting wooden logs together. As if she felt it was time to switch from defense to attack, she reminded him of something he had apparently said once, during a discussion with the Young Socialists in the schoolyard, something to the effect that war could be limited because it was merely the continuation of politics, albeit by other means. She was not to know that this was based on a quotation, the only brief passage from Carl von Clausewitz's *On War* that he had read and memorized. "I've thought a lot about that and decided that I don't agree," she said.

Recognition was slowly dawning on Jonas; he remembered that her father was in some top post in the government. He also recalled something about a conspicuous scar on her neck, looked for and found it even in the gloom. She had been in a parallel class to his; they had met at a few parties—he even remembered seeing her in folk costume at a May 17 breakfast.

He had wondered at this, a city girl with a fondness for wearing the traditional bunad. And here, in the gloomy Åmlid farmhouse he noticed what a difference the folk costume made to her, all at once she was a girl from old Setesdal. She told him that she was at university, writing a dissertation on the Soviet Union. He never took his eyes off her. Although he had seen her before he had never really taken any notice of her. But now—the folk costume, this room seemed to present her in a strange new light or endowed her with a shadowiness she had not previously possessed.

He went outside, had to duck his head to get through the low doorways. He strolled on, looked into rooms on other farmsteads, peered through ancient leaded windowpanes, buckled glass that made the world look different, distorted it, turned it into the setting for a drama about buried instincts. He sauntered about, made a few sketches in his book, of details, the design on the door of a storehouse, the lines of a bowl, the rose painting on a cabinet, but found it impossible to concentrate; snakes writhed in his stomach, he could think of only one thing, contemplated the planks, the boards, staves and logs, the traditional Norwegian building style; wherever he turned, staves and logs and the landscape outside the ridged windowpanes taking little leaps when he moved his head, just for the fun of it, he thought, out of sheer, giddy wantonness.

Late in the afternoon he found himself back at the Setesdal farmstead. He could not help himself, stepped inside the Åmlid farmhouse, thought at first that it was empty, then realized that she was sitting on a bench between the bed and the cabinet. Light filtered down through the opening in the roof and spread around the room that remained, however, shadowy. There was no doubt: he felt that pressure on his spine, as if a switch had been turned on, his whole body put into a state of receptivity. He said nothing, his thoughts went to Louis Kahn, darkness and light; he took out his sketchbook and proceeded to sketch a simple shelf holding some wooden vessels. He could not see well in the semi-darkness, gave up, turned his eye to the *gjøya*, shaped like a horse, the fertility symbol. The place smelled of ancient wood. The logs were enormous. Everything in here was thick, even his fingers felt thick.

She spoke, he answered, had no idea what he answered, felt thick all over, thought only that she was a perfect guide: her figure, the costume, her eyebrows, her voice, a perfect guide to Norway, everything Norwegian, these thick logs, massive corners, the cogging, the idea of raping her occurred to him, yes, rape, an uncontrollable sense of having no choice, of not being in control, this dim room, too dim, almost dark, especially now, with the sun disappearing behind a cloud, as if someone had turned off the light; he felt afraid, for a second, afraid of he knew not what, turned around and saw that she was glowing, she stood in the shadows radiating light, then she walked towards him with the same resolve that she would later display in her chosen career, although it could be that she became possessed of it at that very moment, because Ellisiv H. surprised everyone at university, including herself perhaps, by making an abrupt about-turn and entering the Officers Training School, which had only just opened its doors to women; and she would raise even more eyebrows when, after her obligatory year as a sergeant in the Signal Corps of N Brigade, she went on to Military Academy, thus laying the foundations for a notable military career which not only made her a trailblazer for other women in the Norwegian armed forces—it was thanks to her, for example, that girls were finally allowed to join the Royal Lifeguards—but eventually also led her to an unprecedented high rank in the army and a top post with NATO in Brussels, so in a way you could say that she conquered Europe; but first there was Jonas Wergeland, whom she quite simply overcame by putting her arms around him and squeezing him, with a physical strength that would also surprise her future fellow officers when she beat them in competitions and exercises; Jonas just let his sketchbook fall to the earth floor, overwhelmed by a pounding at his temples that made everything go black while at the same time turning his member into a log, shaped like a horse; she locked both doors, it was closing time anyway, they were alone, them and the gloom, which sparked with tension; she kissed him, tugging at his clothing as she did so, tore them off, tore off her apron, and everything she was wearing underneath, including the thick stockings, kept on the black headscarf, rolled him around the floor of the cool room, as if it were a wrestling match, she was raging with desire, her eyes clouded, she said something in a husky voice, was trying to climb on top of him, coiled herself around him, knocked over an ancient log chair, clambered up, dragged him up onto the solitary bed in the corner, hauled off the coverlet and lay back on a fur pelt, a sheepskin which was spread across the straw mattress; Jonas felt raw, raw and primitive, and he loved it, loved every bit of it, was almost aching with throbbing desire when he saw how the light fell down from the roof and glinted off a thick gold chain around her neck and, further down, off her fair pubic hair, a rich, luxuriant tuft; a sight which drove him wild, drove him to grope around in that triangle with his hand, poke a finger through the ring of damp fur, let it sink in until it began to drip with gold, as from Odin's own ring, Draupner, itself.

He could feel that she wanted him, that her whole body wanted him. When he hesitated she muttered something about a coil, that she wore a coil, and that was how it seemed to him too, as she dug her fingers into his shoulders and dragged him down on top of her, that it was not a case of moving in and out but of being led round the round the turns of a coil, upwards or downwards, outwards or inwards. And again he had the impression of a light, as if in touching her clitoris he had flicked a switch. This was not lovemaking, this was illumination; she twined herself around him, made love to him passionately, as if grateful for the pleasure welling up inside her, accentuated perhaps by the unusual way in which Jonas Wergeland penetrated her, from another angle so it seemed, something which Jonas, when asked once, ascribed to the dragon-horn button which he had swallowed as a little boy and which he thought might have wedged itself in his spine, as an extra vertebra: a phenomenon which not only enabled him to pick up signals from certain women but also forced him to hold himself at a slightly different angle during sex; however that may be, he made love to her in such a unique way that she endeavored to do likewise to him, pressed him so tightly to her that Jonas felt as though he was being transformed, acquiring a different, finer caliber, that something was happening to him, to his way of thinking, that the spittle in her kisses was an elixir which affected his memory more than his body, causing him to recall something, something very special, in a new way.

She grew wilder and wilder, clawed at him, leaving bloody welts down his back; this in turn drove him, unwittingly, to pull her hair as he rode her, pitching in to her, seized with an urge to be violent, in the grip of unbridled forces which simply surged up out of nowhere. "You're killing me," she moaned, licking his throat compliantly and holding him in a muscular, vice-like grip; he plunged in, far in, again and again, not knowing whether they were fighting or making love, ramming into her so hard that the room rang with what sounded like the slapping of a wet floor mop. Suddenly she began to pull back every time he drove into her, as if taking evasive action, a strategy which goaded him into making a massive attempt to outwit her, to pursue her, hard, at different tempos, but to no avail, not until she did another about-turn, as it were, and went into the attack, threw herself at him with such ferocity that she screamed out loud. He made to respond, but all that came out was a snarl. He was incensed, or no, not incensed, he was aflame: filled with a frantic ardor, he was on the track of a cause, or in the act of inventing a cause, actually creating himself, re-creating himself, becoming someone different from the person he had been at the start of their lovemaking.

She was working in a daze, making love to him as if intent on sucking him up, laid bare her throat in such a way that he caught the gleam of her scar, a long gash running crosswise to the gold chain; she dug her nails into his shoulders. "I think I'm going to die," she whispered just before her body went taut, as if with a pleasure bordering on the unbearable, then caught her breath as her back arched and stiffened convulsively into a bridge which conducted him across to another world, far beyond that dark room, and yet composed of inexplicably similar elements. For, just as the sound of a cork rubbed against a bottle could, thanks to the imagination's ability to make leaps, become the chirping of birds in a radio play, the friction caused by his penis moving inside her vagina made him think of a clearing in the forest; there was something about the smell of earth, the hearth, the charcoal, not least the way she coiled herself around him, which had long since conjured up the threads of a memory, a significant story, a narrative he might almost have been said to weave into being, using his member as the shuttle. Jonas Wergeland was not quite like other men. Ejaculation never came to him as a release, a feeling of something being loosed. To him it was more like a knot—a knot in which lots of threads were gathered together—drawn tight.

They lay quietly, still intertwined. Jonas strove to memorize this moment, to fix these images in his mind. He became aware that she was crying softly. He took this to be a sign of happiness, a reaction to overwhelming contentment. Like something bursting, but in a good way. Looking back on it, though, he was not so sure. He was never quite certain that he construed such situations correctly.

My Dear Fellow Countrymen

The threads he was tying together had to do with having ambition, with the mystery inherent in that a person can be moseying along one day, perfectly content with life, only the next to be seized by an unquenchable urge to do something, be someone, make a name for himself. Where does this impulse come from? Could there be a little steel coil inside the body that can suddenly be wound up like the spring inside the workings of a clock? And furthermore: is it possible to determine the precise moment when a person chooses his main path in life? In Jonas Wergeland's case, it is. And, I hasten to add, to avoid any misunderstandings: it was not me who talked him into it.

To questions from well-meaning relatives as to what he wanted to be when he grew up, throughout his childhood Jonas always answered without hesitation: "A pilot!" or "A chef!"—thanks to Uncle Lauritz and Three Star Larsen, Ørn's father, respectively. In time, however, he came up with a more original occupation, one that invariably made those selfsame relatives smile: "I'm going to be the Father of my Country," he would say. Now this idea had not been plucked completely out of thin air: Prime Minister Einar Gerhardsen lived in the same building as Aunt Laura on Sofienberggata in the Tøyen district of Oslo. To be the Father of one's Country, to lead the people, seemed to Jonas a promising—and by no means unattainable—future calling, to stand before a sea of people and say, as Gerhardsen had done, with a slight catch in his voice: "My dear fellow countrymen." And though this may have been a childish notion, yet it speaks of an exceptionally high level of ambition, a dream of achieving something great, which cannot be put down to his aunt's Tøyen address. The explanation must have lain to as great an extent in his mother's stirring stories—have patience, Professor, I'm getting there—not to mention his grandfather's incessant stream of yarns, in which Jonas was always the hero, a fabulously well-equipped dragon slayer.

Jonas was sitting on his own, up in the little quarry in the forest hard by the People's Palace, which doubled as the local cinema. According to the calendar, it was the end of April; the snow had melted, and the sun was getting stronger. All around him buds were bursting open; he almost thought he could hear the sound of popcorn hissing in oil just before the popping starts. He pulled off his jersey, sat there in just his shirt, a Davy Crockett T-shirt that would soon be too small for him. Jonas had spent most of his time alone since Little Eagle went away. He was considered to be a bit of a lone wolf, and the sort of unpredictable, aggressive wolf you didn't dare tease. Jonas sat on a ledge in the middle of the quarry, sat there drowsing in the hot sun with granite crystals glittering all around him. The slope of the mountain formed a natural amphitheater; Jonas sat there, peering down at an empty stage. In fact, had he been in the mood for it, he could well have pretended that he was standing among the market stalls on Youngstorget in Oslo, about to make a speech, as practiced as another Demosthenes with pebbles in his mouth: "My dear fellow countrymen."

The particular attributes of this spot made it something of a holy place for the local community. The stone for Grorud Church had come from quarries in this area. Jonas might well have been sitting in a matrix for the church where he had been christened, the spire of which he could just make out above the treetops. The scouts often used the granite amphitheater on ceremonial occasions, for rites that could bring a lump to many a young lad's throat, on St. George's day for instance, or for the swearing-in of new scouts, when the place was decorated with flags and banners and candles, and the stone sides resounded with the murmurings of "Isolemnlysweartodomybest . . ."

Jonas was feeling down in the dumps. For the first time in his life he was truly depressed. The previous weekend they had had a visit from Sir William and family, who would shortly be leaving for Africa. And during Sunday dinner, the usual cold roast with brown sauce, his uncle had turned to the subject of Veronika and her rare gifts. "Mark my words, one day that girl is going to make it big," he intoned, while Jonas's cousin kept her eyes fixed coyly on the tablecloth. "What about me?" Jonas was foolish enough to ask to the obvious, malicious glee of the Brothers Grimm. "You, Jonas," Sir William had replied at length, after adjusting his silk cravat—as if he, this heartless individual, was for once considering biting back a spiteful remark—"you'll never amount to anything. You're the commonest little mongrel I've ever met, you're a perfectly ordinary little boy and you should be content with that." Although none of the others took this as anything more than a jovial quip, or at least: no more than just another of his uncle's almost pathologically crass remarks, his words had echoed in Jonas's head for the rest of the meal: "Perfectly ordinary." The words ran round and round his head in a never-ending loop, like an electric headlines sign. "Perfectly ordinary . . . common . . ."

Jonas knew why Sir William's summation of his character had affected him as it had. It was because he had realized—only at that moment, in fact—that for him, Jonas Wergeland, to be ordinary was the worst of all possible fates. At the same time it had dawned on him that his uncle was right. He was ordinary, he was common. And not only that: he was as common as common could be. He had known it for some time, although he couldn't have put it into words. His only talent lay in his voice. And maybe an extra vertebra in his spine. Hardly the makings of a Father of the People. The best he could hope for was to be an announcer at the Eastern Station. Better, then, to be like Ørn, he thought hopelessly. Better to be a loser. Sooner a "Fail" than a "Fair to Middling."

So here he was, sitting in the amphitheater, in a granite grandstand, as if in illustration of his fate: he was to be a spectator, he was doomed to be a spectator for the rest of his life. He slumped back, feeling flat, felt himself becoming one with the bedrock, grey on grey. The sun was so hot that the air actually smelled of sun, of spring, of stone. The living world seethed round about him, like in a laboratory, giving him a sense of tremendous pressure, a feeling that something stupendous was about to take place. He sat, or sprawled, there, filled with a burning desire to be transformed.

This yearning, or rather, this heartfelt prayer, could be traced back to a crucial flash of insight which he had been granted not long before—he must have been in a particularly receptive state, antennae working frantically, after his uncle's prophecy. In biology class their teacher had been talking about diamonds, told them that diamond, the hardest of all substances, was a mineral consisting of pure carbon, as was graphite—except that graphite was very soft. "Carbon is, therefore, polymorphous," the teacher said. Although Jonas did not know the meaning of this expression: that carbon could crystallize in different ways—in other words, that diamond could be formed only under great pressure, while graphite was a low-pressure variant of the same substance—he got the main point: that carbon could assume a number of forms. This had brought him much-needed comfort—to know that plain, ordinary graphite, as he knew it, for example, in his own pencil, when subjected to a different level of pressure could become a diamond—become what the Greeks called "*adamas*," meaning invincible. Was there any reason why he might not contain similar potential?

How does one become a conqueror?

Jonas is lying there in a drowse when he becomes aware of a movement on the edge of the clearing below him. He opens his eyes wide and sees two adders slithering towards a flat rock dead ahead of him, only ten yards away. He sits stock-still, feels how his heart pounds at the sight of the snakes—not because they are dangerous, but because he knows that a drama of the utmost significance is about to be played out on the stage before him.

Suddenly the two snakes raise the front parts of their bodies into the air and begin to sway towards one another, for some time they do this, as in some strange dance, before they almost—so it seems to Jonas—twine themselves around one another, though without touching, and still with their bodies lifted off the ground. Jonas was thrilled. He had heard of snakes "wrestling": rival males wrapping themselves round one another. But as far as he knew this usually happened in the grass, horizontally. The confrontation he was witnessing here was being conducted in a semi-vertical position, this surely had to be something of a miracle; adders were not actually all that flexible, they didn't have the cobra's ability to raise its body high into the air. The snakes seemed to Jonas to be bathed in light, a golden glow. A promise, he thought to himself, it's a promise.

Jonas knew right away that this sight, this upward-straining intertwinement was vitally important, that it had the power to heal him, in the same way as the serpent of brass Moses set on a pole in the desert. The way he saw it, this moment, those seconds when they raised themselves into the air and formed a double spiral, had been created for him—and him alone. These creatures were doomed to crawl on their bellies, but they had risen up, right in front of him, held up their heads as it were, defied the biblical curse, did the impossible—yes, that was it: the impossible—defied their biological limitations and lifted themselves up, a zoological miracle on a stage of granite. Later it would occur to Jonas that they had formed what looked like a section mark, that he had caught a glimpse of the essence of life, of the first clause in the law of life.

But what cheered him most of all was that this spectacle corresponded with—you might almost say, consolidated—an image he had had in his head for a long time, an image or a tactile sensation which stemmed from a feverish dream and which could be compared only to the feeling of running a finger along a corkscrew. Also, he had immediately made the connection between the two snakes in the clearing and the ball of snakes he had stumbled upon the year before. This dance was a continuation of that incident, a clarification of something of which the ball had allowed him a mere glimpse: two spirals intertwined. The principle of leverage, of something that could set mighty things in motion, raise him to undreamed-of heights. He stared at the snakes for so long that they slithered through his eyes and into his head. At any rate, suddenly they were gone, dissolved into thin air so it seemed. The snakes, or a double helix, had taken up residence in his brain. "Inside me I carry a new way of thinking," his heart sang. "I am different."

At that very moment—believe me, it's true—Jonas heard a voice, or perhaps something more akin to the deep scale of notes from an organ, which said, or told him, in no uncertain terms that he would be a conqueror. He always maintained that that voice or sonorous peal came from the very granite on which he was sitting, almost oozed from the crystals—so clearly that he could positively feel the vibrations, as from the membrane of a loudspeaker. And at that instant he knew, as if it were an integral part of the experience, what his weapon in this conquest would be: that intertwining form.

I know this sounds a bit high-flown. But everyone experiences—to a greater or lesser degree—mystical moments, when they receive a clear and inescapable message—or whatever you want to call it—and for Jonas Wergeland this was how it happened. From that day onwards he knew for sure. He was not going to be a chef or a pilot, nor even the Father of his Country; he was going to be a conqueror. By the time he stood up and set off for home he had carved out a calling for himself, as solid as a granite church.

You look surprised, Professor, because you have never heard of this, such a pivotal episode. Perhaps I did not express myself as well as I might have done on an earlier occasion, when I said that Jonas Wergeland did not recognize the significance of these events until they cropped up again, thanks to some woman. What if he had not experienced these things at all? What if he had merely imagined them, dreamed them up, during those acts of love, but so vividly and with such powerful conviction that he seemed to have experienced them. Whatever the case, Jonas Wergeland felt that these women somehow enabled him to relive many fundamental stories upon which he was able to draw later, use as springboards to a changed life. It was as if he had been given the chance to travel back in a train and get off at stations he had run past first time round. So you see it could well be that Jonas Wergeland's later success, his inimitable chain of television programs was forged from causes—stories—which never were but which could be reconstructed, like Gleipne, the chain in Nordic mythology: it too was made from things that did not exist.

It might be more correct to say that at a certain point—possibly not until that coupling in a dim room in the Museum of Cultural History—it was brought home to Jonas Wergeland that one was not doomed to be the person one was, or at least not only that person. One could become more. We are not, he thought, we form ourselves.

One thing that is certainly true is that when he got home from the quarry he wrote his name on a sheet of paper, and to his amazement he found that his handwriting had changed. On impulse he had also put a "W" between his first and last names, "Jonas W. Hansen" he wrote and discovered that he had made a new name for himself: that one letter could be all it took to change everything, just as the little prefix "un" before the word "common" produces something uncommon. As he contemplated the "W" Jonas could not help thinking of a machine of some kind which could cause him too to stretch himself, much as a leg that is too short can sometimes be made longer. The "W" had the appearance of a coat of arms or a royal emblem—Jonas VI or something of the sort. His initials, too, looked exceptionally powerful, nigh-on divine. There was something about the sight of these three characters which instinctively prompted him to clear his throat and say, in all seriousness, as if carrying out a voice test: "My dear fellow countrymen."

The next day he cycled to school, even though he hadn't passed the proficiency test. He was bursting with newfound self-confidence. At the school gate he collided with Margrete Boeck, the new girl in the parallel class to his own. Turn a "W" on its head and you get an "M." He didn't know it then, but his life had already changed.

From the Caucasus?
Beams My Soul from the Caucasus?

(Henrik Wergeland: *Det Befriede Europa*)

Why did Jonas Wergeland travel? It cannot simply be because he wished to conquer new lands? Or change his life, come to that. Jonas himself believed that he made each journey merely so that he could tuck it away in his memory and bring it out again later, always as a different journey, because it altered character from one time to the next. Viewed at a distance, a journey became something different, often something vague and, above all, pungent, like the aftertaste of a fine cognac.

Jonas sometimes wondered whether he had been to Yerevan three times or just the once. He remembered standing on the hillside outside a remarkable-looking building known as the Matenadaran, looking out across the city. The Armenian Soviet Republic had come as a pleasant surprise, despite the time of year and its strained relations with its neighbor state, the Muslims to the East. Yerevan had proved to be an astonishing oasis after the barren desert of Moscow, with a completely different atmosphere and mentality—and the shops here were full of merchandise. Jonas had walked to the Matenadaran from the Hotel Armenia and the impressive circular Lenin Square in the city center, so that he—the architect in him, that is—could take in the exceptionally well thought-out and well-executed layout of the city along the way. He nibbled on dried apricots sprinkled with honey and almonds as he strolled along admiring the buildings, many of them—like the hotel—built from the local tufa stone in varying tones of red and pink and decorated with fine carvings: interwoven branches laden with fruit. This, like Grorud, was stonemason country. Jonas felt very much at home here, from the very start he had felt a powerful sense of belonging: here, he thought, here I could actually settle down for good.

He stood on a terrace at the top of a long run of steps leading down to the road. He shut his eyes and listened. Possibly because of his early interest in sounds, listening was one of the first things he did in a new place—as if endeavoring to wring from the background noise some secret about the landscape, some knowledge hidden from the eyes; or he may have thought that, just as the same sound effects can be used in different plays, these sounds could form the background to more memories of the place.

As he was standing there, ears pricked up, just as he was actually thinking that he had heard a sigh, somewhere under or over the ground—a sigh reminiscent of the sound created when his father switched on the organ, which is to say, started up the fan, allowing the air to flow into the pipes—a figure approached him, slowly and with an inquiring look on his face. A man in a heavy, military-style overcoat with a sort of beret on his head. "You are a tourist, perhaps?" he asked hesitantly in French good enough for Jonas to understand him. Jonas was doing a tour of those parts of the Soviet Union that lay close to the Black Sea, under the reassuring auspices of Intourist. The trip was intended as a relaxing break, not to say a reward, after years of working himself half to death on NRK's prestige project, *Thinking Big*, which was to be broadcast in the New Year—a television series which may have had its beginnings in a stone quarry, an amphitheater of reddish granite.

Jonas told the man where he came from. The man nodded, had managed to light his pipe, stood looking out across the city in the same direction as Jonas, his rich enjoyment of the tobacco written large on his features. "Do you know what my name is?" he said at last. Jonas shrugged, how could he possibly know? The only Armenian name he knew was Khachaturian, because as a boy he had played some unusual pieces for the piano by this composer.

"My name is Nansen Sarjan," the man said and eyed Jonas expectantly, as if awaiting a reaction from Jonas, although he could not have known that it was precisely because of Fridtjof Nansen that Jonas had wanted to come here; it was because of him that Armenia, or rather the Armenian people, were so much on his mind.

"Your first name is Nansen?" Jonas said.

"My father was so grateful for what Nansen did for our people that he named me after him," the man said. "There are quite a number of people in Armenia whose first name is Nansen."

Jonas was touched; he found this very moving. He had heard of people in Brazil calling their children after national football players, no matter how farfetched their professional names might be. If one admires a person, no name is too improbable. An Armenian boy could well be christened Nansen.

The man seemed gratified by Jonas's interest and proceeded to tell him about his father, the hardships his father had suffered in the years after the First World War, and about himself. He pointed to the other side of the city. "I work in the distillery you can see over there. Have you tried our famous brandy? The very finest quality."

Jonas was feeling a little chilly; he wouldn't have minded a small glass of cognac.

"Troubles or no troubles, you have to learn to enjoy life," the Armenian said, pointing to his pipe. "Have you read Nansen's book, *First Crossing of Greenland*?" Jonas shook his head, did not dare to mention that in his program on Nansen he had focused on things that had absolutely nothing to do with skiing.

"You know," Nansen Sarjan said, "the truly great achievement, where the Greenland expedition is concerned, is not the actual ski crossing. The real work of art is the book, especially the passages in which Nansen describes the team's pipe-smoking: how they spun out their Sunday ration of tobacco. Do you remember? First they smoked the tobacco, then they smoked the ash and wood in the bowl of the pipe, and after that they stuffed in tarred rope and smoked that." The man laughed. "And when they finally reached the west coast and the icecap was behind them . . . I'll never forget how Nansen describes the pleasure of feeling earth and rock under his feet again, the glorious smell of grass. And then, to crown it all, how they stretched out in the soft heather and, with the greatest relish, puffed on pipes filled with moss. You have to read it; it's quite amazing. It must have something to do with the joy of being alive. It was after reading that book that I took up the pipe."

Jonas smiled. For some reason he found this quite splendid. Standing here. Him and this man. Why had he come to Yerevan? Perhaps to hear a total stranger wax eloquent about a passage from a book that extolled the joys of pipe-smoking or to hear that name, Nansen, to hear that it lived on here, had survived here, hundreds of miles from Norway. Was a part of the language. Flesh and blood. For some unknown reason, Jonas felt a rapport with the man standing next to him, as if, although he didn't know it, he owed his life to Nansen Sarjan; he stands there surveying the lovely city of red stone, still listening to the sighing all around him: it sounds like the hum of a huge fan, a hum that carried within it a sense of anticipation, of preparing for something big, in exactly the same way as when his father pulled out the stops on the organ before, like a delicious shock, he broke into the prelude. Jonas remembered that there had been a little organ on board Nansen's ship, the *Fram*, on the first polar expedition. Was it Nansen himself who had played it? Jonas peered down at the city. It was winter, but there was hardly any snow. He took a deep breath, felt powerful, confident, as if he were at a point in his life when anything, absolutely anything, could happen.

A journey need not be long, in terms of time, to turn everything upside down. A day or two in a strange place can change your life.

A National Monument

It takes no great stretch of the imagination to spot the connection between this point, a conversation in the Caucasus, and a winter's tale from long before, in Norway—between two episodes so well-suited to demonstrating that each new moment is only one of many possibilities.

Jonas liked ice, especially the ice in late autumn. After the first few days of hard frost he and Little Eagle always ran up to Steinbruvannet to see how the water had somehow stiffened, acquired a film of gleaming crystal. His limbs trembled with suspense as they slid warily out onto the ice, listening all the time, like animals, for a warning snap. Jonas never could understand how ice this thin did not break, not even when it gave underfoot: that this fraction of an inch was enough to bear his weight. Ice always gave him an uneasy sense of being part of the lightness of being.

They tended to stay close to the shore, where the water was shallow, crouched or lay down to scan the pond bottom and the fish beneath them. Jonas and Ørn played that they were lying on top of a gigantic television screen, immersing themselves in it from top to toe. Either that or they felt like Captain Nemo drawing back the curtains on his submarine, the *Nautilus*, to suddenly be brought face to face with the drama of the deep.

Once the ice was safe and before the first snow had fallen, the lakes in the surrounding countryside became a Mecca for skaters; it was on Steinbruvannet, with the aroma of his parents' beef tea in his nostrils, that Jonas learned to master the Norwegian national sport, stage by stage, so to speak, working his way from triple-bladed trainer skates to speed-skates. From the very first he loved it, adored the zing of the fresh, clean ice, the vibrant chime each time the blades sliced through. Most of all he loved to spin—not least when he was skating across ice-bound water where no one had been before him—and examine the patterns left by his skates. "It's a sort of secret writing," he said to himself. "Symbols that have to do with conquest."

It was on such a day, late in the autumn of the year when he was going with Margrete, that Jonas made his first tentative attempt to build a monument, a monument of glittering ice—an impulse which ought probably to be viewed in the light of the new-won self-confidence with which he had been filled after the incident in the quarry eighteen months earlier. And I really do not think, Professor, that we should attach too much importance to the fact that this monument was founded on frost, on cold.

The way had been paved for this sudden entrepreneurial urge by a bet made by the grownups at Solhaug. Late one night during a gents-only get-together in Five-Times Nilsen's cosy living room to christen the normally so diffident salesman's latest acquisition—a magnificent bookcase complete with that last word in luxury: an integral drinks cabinet—Five-Times Nilsen had got a little above himself and announced that he was going ice bathing, so help him he was. And since the others didn't believe he would do it, they ended up making a bet—with a fair bit of money in the pot, I can tell you, a sum that confirmed the Norwegian people's strange mania for gambling and penchant for lotteries of any description. Jonas had, in fact, seen the drinks cabinet on one occasion, one time when he was selling flags, which is to say: suffering the torture to which all children are subjected, of having a tray full of flags hung on a cord around his neck and being shooed off to sell or, no, not sell: beg. Jonas hated this, hated standing on people's doorsteps with his head bowed, this yoke around his neck, and a "Pleasewillyoubuy" on his lips. It ought to be said, though, that Mrs. Nilsen was the saving of every desperate flag-seller, or their victim rather; the textured wallpaper in the Nilsen's hall was like a pincushion, studded with flowers from the TB Association, Lifeboat flags, pins for Cancer Research and the Children's Ski Foundation. And it was on one such call, while Mrs. Nilsen was fumbling with her small change, that Jonas caught a glimpse of the new marvel in the living room, a proper little Soria Moria Castle, with a lid that folded down, built-in lighting and a mirror at the back, giving the impression of double—nay—infinite enjoyment, not least due to the brightly colored contents of the various bottles, which reminded Jonas of his father's extraordinary collection of aftershave lotions, since this too was connected with scents, with men in white shirts and braces getting all het up; and on a shelf at the very top, if it was not a mirage, Jonas discerned the most renowned items of all: the highball glasses with the scantily clad ladies on the outside who, when viewed from the inside, were stark naked. So Jonas had no problem, later, in understanding how Five-Times Nilsen could have become a mite loose-tongued after a few highballs—and this was in the days when a highball really was a highball, served in a raffia sleeve which conjured up thoughts of grass skirts, lagoons and warm water—that Five-Times Nilsen should declare, possibly while peering through his whisky at the naked lady on the inside of the glass, like an enticing reward in the distance, that he was going ice bathing, so help me, anyone wanna bet that I won't!

And go ice bathing he did. One Sunday morning, at a relatively early hour to save attracting an embarrassing crowd, a few of the fathers made their way up to Steinbruvannet. Chairman Moen had even got hold of an ice bore and a good old-fashioned ice saw, so it didn't take long to cut out a fairly large, square hole—the ice wasn't all that thick at that time anyway. And let it be said right at the outset, since this is only a side-story, that Five-Times Nilsen actually did take a dip in the icy water—carried it off with considerable panache, in fact, and to the great glee of his neighbors. Not only that, but his wife, the rather pettish, but kind-hearted Mrs. Nilsen, insisted on him staying home from the shop for a week, quarantined him, would not open the door to anyone, not even a poor flag-seller with his yoke around his neck; she was too busy squeezing oranges to save her husband from catching a cold or perhaps to give him the illusion of more tropical climes as he lay on the sofa with his face turned to the drinks cabinet's scintillating solar system. There were those who were sure that he too was well and truly squeezed that week; word was that Mrs. Nilsen would stop at nothing to warm him up again—there were even a few on the estate who wondered whether they ought not to rename him Ten-Times Nilsen.

In any case, the upshot of it all was that lots of blocks of ice—fragments of ice is possibly a better description—of all sizes lay strewn around the hole where the ice bathing had taken place, when Jonas and Margrete went up to Steinbruvannet to skate, on the afternoon of that same Sunday.

With Legos, Jonas had always found the transparent bricks the most fascinating—as a small boy he constantly dreamed of being able to build a whole house solely out of them—so the minute he saw those beautiful, gleaming blocks lying there all ready and waiting he knew he had to build something out of them. If he were honest with himself, he had been rambling on about doing something of the sort as they were walking up to the lake; after Margrete had turned those black and faintly Oriental eyes of hers on him and told him that when she was nine—before the family moved back to Norway, that is—she had visited Harbin in China with her father the diplomat and seen the fabulous ice sculptures and ice lanterns created for the New Moon Festival held there: thirty degrees below and a whole park full of shimmering ice structures. "It was like being on another planet. Triton, or somewhere like that," she said.

Only a girl like Margrete could think of mentioning one of the moons of Neptune in a sentence. She was wearing earmuffs over hair so black that it had a bluish sheen to it, like Cleopatra's in the strip cartoons. Jonas stole a glance at her, so in love that it hurt.

What makes a murderer?

He forgot all about his skates. There weren't many people on the ice apart from them anyway, only a couple of guys playing ice hockey way down by the dam. Jonas carried the blocks away from the hole, further out onto the ice, seeing in his mind's eye a palace the like of which had never been seen before. On this particular Sunday the temperature was hovering just above—rather than below—zero, so the pieces of ice had not had a chance to freeze solid, instead they were slippery and slightly wet on the surface. Jonas started to build something, took a sheath knife from his rucksack, cut and pared the ice as he saw fit. Although for the most part he could use the pieces as they were, since they were all different shapes to start with. The hardest part was to stop the blocks from sliding off one another. "What do you think I should make?" he called to Margrete. "Oslo Town Hall?"

"The Crystal Palace," she laughed.

While Jonas was building, with no particular plan to begin with, Margrete danced around him on her figure skates, like a good fairy giving the work her blessing. She could do some simple figure skating, and she was a lovely, and really quite sexy sight in her stretchy ski pants and tight woollen sweater. But Jonas had no eyes for her, or rather: he was more keen on showing her that he was a conqueror, that he could create something magnificent, something of which she would never have dreamed him capable; he was totally engrossed, worked like a soul possessed, saw that the structure was starting to resemble a stave church, or maybe it was more like a slender ziggurat, a sacred building; he employed his knife like a woodcarver's gouge on the hard ice, endowing those pieces which were to sit on the top with a more distinctive form, like little spires. On the very pinnacle he placed one chunk, totally transparent, and as he lifted it into place he noticed that there was a pearl embedded in it. Or not a pearl, but one of those little pearl ear-studs. He couldn't imagine how it came to be there: trapped, as it were, inside an ice-cold giant clam. Maybe someone had dropped it; there was no way of telling. Most likely it wasn't a real pearl either, he thought. Probably just some cheap junk. He wasn't going to check right now, anyway, because he was finished, just as the last rays of the sun made the ice palace almost luminous; its walls and towers glittered and gleamed as if they were made from precious gems, or prisms. It was the sort of structure in front of which, at a later date, someone would place a vodka bottle, to produce a fabulous advertising shot. Jonas, for his part, thought fleetingly of a mirrored drinks cabinet.

Jonas calls out happily to Margrete, who is circling around further out on the ice. She does not hear him, is practicing a jump. They are alone now; Jonas cannot see anyone down by the dam. It's getting colder. He is glad of that, knows that this will cement his rather frail, unsteady construction. He calls out again, feeling proud, wanting to show off his masterpiece, a marvel of consummate symmetry. The sun is sinking lower and lower, soon only the tops of the spires will flash in the light of the last rays piercing the tops of the fir trees in the west. But it looks fantastic, a combination of stave church and a sort of ziggurat—truly a national monument—that might have been built out of transparent white marble, or air. A building from the land of fable. Jonas beholds it in the light, totally transparent, almost floating above the ice.

He heard the sound of skates, turned round, and at that very moment, as Margrete was making her way towards him, arms outstretched, smiling, black hair shot with blue—in his moment of triumph—disaster struck. Jonas would never understand how it could have happened, where it came from, who had sent it—although hadn't he perhaps seen a shadow after all, someone who hadn't gone home, down by the dam? For just then a puck came gliding towards him; Jonas spied it while it was quite a long way off, a dot, a tadpole, it should have ground to a halt long ago, but it glided on and on, not moving all that fast, but not slow enough for Jonas to get to it and stop it, he was too far away from the ice structure, he tried, but his legs kept giving way on the ice, it looked hilarious, and meanwhile the puck, "out of nowhere" he thought, glided relentlessly towards the ice palace—which at that moment was shimmering with an almost unearthly luster, as if it were made from frozen air—and rammed one of the nethermost blocks sideways on, knocking it just enough out of place to bring Jonas's work of art tumbling down, with infinite slowness so it seemed to him, and with a lovely tinkling sound, like sleigh bells, he thought later, sending all the little pieces slithering in every direction, a long, long way in every direction; and in some measure—Jonas had to admit it, even though he was half in shock—the actual destruction was as fascinating an experience as the building of it, that glorious instant of utter collapse, a shower of bright sparks and the music created by the sound of tinkling ice.

And Margrete, what did she do? Margrete had almost reached him when the structure collapsed, she stopped and stared at Jonas, but while he was still standing there, stunned, long after the shards of ice had ceased to jangle and halted in their star-shaped flight, she did a few neat steps on her figure skates, began, in fact, to dance around him, as if through this, her dancing, she was trying to tell him something, forcing him to view this fiasco from another angle. Not only did she dance, she smiled, smiled in a way that, for the first time, led Jonas to suspect that there was a complex, possibly even dangerous, side to her: something he would never understand no matter how hard he tried. She started laughing, could see Jonas was hurt by this but could not stop herself, laughed at him, danced round and round him, laughing out loud, a laughter he would never forget.

So I ask you, Professor: is it possible, if one considers it from a great enough distance—I was on the point of saying from the ice planet Triton—that Jonas Wergeland killed her way back here?

Right then, Jonas—as he saw it, at least—was less concerned with Margrete's odd behaviour than with finding the piece of ice containing the pearl stud. He hunted frantically, he ran hither and yon, combing a wide radius, lifting blocks of ice up to the fading light, but no matter how hard he looked he did not find that one piece. He was desperate, it was as if he knew that he had to find this fragment of ice again, that for some reason it was absolutely vital, that if he could lay hands on it he would be able to avert a catastrophe, that no matter how fake and cheap the pearl was, something of tremendous value would be lost if he did not find it.

It was a very crestfallen Jonas who slid back to the center, to the point where the ice monument had stood and where the puck now lay, like a full stop on a huge sheet of paper, putting an end to his endeavor to make an impression. He picked it up, hefted it in his hand, studied it. And I don't think I'm giving too much away if I say that this black disc was to become a talisman for Jonas Wergeland. Indeed, he was instantly intrigued by all the scratches, the patterns on its surface. "It looks like a scarab," Margrete said, looking over his shoulder. "The sort of beetle they used to place over the hearts of the dead in Ancient Egypt."

After saying a bewildered goodbye to Margrete at the junction with Bergensveien, with the dreadful feeling that their relationship was unlikely to survive the skating season, Jonas went home and took out his own personal Kaba, the black lacquer casket with the mother-of-pearl dragon on its lid. Acting on instinct he lifted out his mother's round brooch and set it on top of the puck. It was almost the same size in diameter; it fitted astonishingly well. A silvery disc and a black disc. Jonas looked. And what he was looking at was bafflingly beautiful. A brooch, with all of its associations, atop a puck with all of its possibilities, not to say stories. He immediately perceived that, like alchemy, when put together these two became something more than a gem and a puck. A spark had been ignited inside him as he placed the silver brooch on top of the black surface; ideas had taken shape, so disjointed and inexplicable that it made him jump. Maybe that was why the next second he picked up the clock workings from their place next to the box on top of the chest of drawers and threw them into the wastepaper bin. All of a sudden the frame and all those cogs seemed somehow hopelessly old-fashioned and mechanical. Like a psychological steam engine, he thought, something that is no longer of any use to me.

He eyed this new object, a tracery of silver on a black circle. He stared at it for a long time, so long that he began to discern the corner of something unforeseeable. He felt almost afraid, as if he had discovered something dangerous, an unknown weapon with enormous potential.

Jonas Wergeland had produced his first program.

Venus and Mars

It would not be totally amiss to look upon Jonas Wergeland's magnificent television series as an extension of sorts of the project at Steinbruvannet, slivers of ice set at different angles to one another to create a three-dimensional space. Or, if you will: a national monument constructed out of crystalline fragments.

Jonas Wergeland's programs were, as I say, subjected to vigorous reassessment after his arrest. Suddenly it seemed that everybody and their uncle could see that *Thinking Big* was a mass of transparent segments and felt, therefore, duty-bound to sing out like the little boy in "The Emperor's New Clothes." One after another they came forward to prove that this "monumental work," as it had been called, was both cold and cynical and fell into a million pieces at the slightest, critical touch.

One of the few things which might merit our attention is an interview with one of Jonas Wergeland's closest colleagues—an exception, this article, in that the emphasis was placed not on Wergeland's arrogance and effrontery, or his brutality: the fact that he would trample over anyone who got in his way, not unlike the case of the Emperor Qin Shihuang and the Great Wall of China. Instead what was communicated here was an ill-concealed bitterness over the fact that Jonas Wergeland had taken all the credit. This colleague claimed that Wergeland never knew where to draw the line; while he might well have been a wizard once everything was in the can and the post-production work begun, he needed the assistance of a critical eye at the actual planning stage. Jonas Wergeland's great failing was his tendency to want to include too much, to bite off more than he could chew. His colleague used the program on Sigrid Undset as an example, and I think it is worth our while to dwell for a moment on this program, seeing that it turned out to be one of the series' real tours de force, the one which was bought by the greatest number of television channels worldwide.

Originally, if this source is to be believed, Jonas wanted to include scenes from Sigrid Undset's sojourn on the Swedish island of Gotland

and her later visit to Carl Linnaeus's home, Hammerby Manor near Uppsala, its rooms papered with drawings of flowers; Jonas was particularly keen to highlight the legendary moment when she leans down in this chapel to nature and kisses von Linnaeus's desk, just as pilgrims kiss the statues of saints. In his head Jonas had a clear idea of how telling this scene would be: Undset virtually kissing the ideal of the Grand Scheme of Things, the Great Classification, in which everything falls neatly into a certain order—a parallel to Catholicism; but his colleague had managed to foil this suggestion, thereby, as he saw it, not only saving NRK the considerable cost of a trip to Sweden, which was now cancelled, but also laying the foundations of a better program—and receiving no credit for it. To his mind, he was the Ezra Pound to T. S. Eliot's *The Waste Land*.

I am not sure that he is right, Professor. If you examine the key scene in the Undset program, the walk through an English forest, you will notice how it seethes with botanical life; one could quite safely say that this scene was a visual kiss from Linnaeus. I think his colleague underestimated, and misunderstood, Jonas Wergeland's creative genius: was blind to the way in which he was forever reworking his original ideas to produce simpler and simpler solutions, moved by a desire—ideally, at any rate—to reduce the chaotic raw material of each life to a few surprising strands, preferably no more than two, which he could twine together, like a double helix, in such a way that they nevertheless provided a picture of a complex, organic life.

You could say that with their "unveilings" the newspapers were only giving Jonas Wergeland a taste of his own medicine, since that's exactly what he set out to do to his heroes, to unveil them, as in removing the veil from them. This is demonstrated in exemplary fashion in the opening scene of the Undset program in which the central character slowly, lingeringly, looking straight at the camera, unbinds her coil of hair, that characteristic braid so often seen in pictures of her, and lets her long locks tumble down over her shoulders—this in itself coming as a shock of relief to many viewers, especially faithful women readers of Sigrid Undset's books who were used to the standard book-jacket portraits: the chaste features and the hair pinned up tightly on the top of her head, like a crown of thorns, an image which, even before one opened the book, spoke of a content suffused with momentous gravity, with the weight of the dark weft of human lives. Right at the very start Jonas Wergeland shattered this main cliché about Undset and showed her to be—apparently, at least, and thanks largely to Ella Strand's magnetic presence—a lusty woman, a woman capable of torrid embraces and passionate kisses, of enjoying a drop or two, of laughing even.

A nigh-on impossible thought: Sigrid Undset laughing. It was almost indecent, like being offered a peek inside the legendary Undset shell. But this was the very aspect which Jonas Wergeland highlighted, because in his eyes—and setting aside her undeniable gifts as a storyteller—the key to Undset's artistic success lay in her sensuality, her recognition of the power of the senses, of love as an unstoppable primal force, reminding one not so much of historical novels as of the books of an author she herself greatly admired: D. H. Lawrence. In a way—and this is something which many people considered paradoxical—the program on Sigrid Undset was the most erotic in the whole of Jonas Wergeland's television series with its undercurrent of almost startling lust, a covert voluptuousness which was perceived more by the intuition than by the eye.

Personally—if I may say so—I consider the Undset program as a prime example of how well Jonas Wergeland succeeded in conveying the essence of a life simply by twining two aspects together to good effect. One of the program's two main elements was a walk around the National Gallery in London, the other a stroll through the vestiges of an ancient oak forest outside the city in Middlesex—in Sigrid Undset's life both of these events took place on her honeymoon in 1912, during the six months spent by the newlyweds in England, possibly the happiest half-year of her life, a time when she herself was in love, when she made mad, passionate love—a thought almost as alien to her readers as the idea that their own parents must once have had sex.

Sigrid Undset strolls among the huge, old oak trees, through the countryside in which she felt most at home, just as Shakespeare and Chaucer were possibly her greatest sources of inspiration. She is walking with her husband, the painter Anders Castus Svarstad; it is late summer, she is pregnant, although it doesn't yet show. The scene is vibrant with light and color; the camera cuts occasionally to shots of wild flowers and small birds, all the things in which Undset took an interest. Jonas spent a lot of time working on the mood of this scene, to give the viewers an impression of how the forest embodied both light and dark, how it was positively vibrant with mythology and history—and, not least, with the spirit of the age of chivalry. It was during this stay that Sigrid Undset started making notes for a book on King Arthur and the Knights of the Round Table. At one point the couple stop in their tracks, and one hears the distant sound of battle, sword on sword. Through the use of trick photography Jonas suddenly showed them walking along clad in medieval dress, Sigrid Undset wearing a striking brooch pinned to her dress, on loan from the University Museum of Antiquities: a round, silver brooch ornamented with an exquisite tracery.

In the second sequence, a parallel walk which was woven, or cross-cut, into the first, one saw Sigrid Undset strolling through London, an industrial city full of the clamor of machinery, with a book in her hand, smoking a cigarette; Sigrid Undset, a modern woman, walking through the doors of the National Gallery—she had originally wanted to be a painter—where the camera followed her through rooms filled with pictures, this too a mythological forest of sorts, until she stopped in front of Botticelli, one of her favorite painters, in front of his "Venus and Mars," a painting which depicts the almost transcendental character of Nature and of the two figures resting in the forest.

These two elements merged together, therefore, when the newly-weds—back in the strand formed by the first sequence, came to a clearing in the forest where they sat down on the grass, Svarstad leaning back with his eyes shut, she looking pensive, such that they assumed exactly the same positions as Venus and Mars in the Botticelli painting in the gallery. Jonas had Undset glance fleetingly at the sky, as if she really were looking in the direction of Venus—not knowing, of course, that a crater on that planet would one day be named after her—before letting the couple drift into a passionate embrace. This scene encapsulated two key ingredients in Undset's universe: a couple succumbing to carnal desire, in rapturous performance of the sexual act, and the dense forest in the background, a symbol of the inescapable dark side of life. The program closed with a blatant sex scene, lingering kisses and ecstatic embraces in the grass, on the bounds of the permissible, and yet with a touch of the religious about it, as if there were a connection between physical love and religion. Not unexpectedly the NRK management had to put up with complaints from the Christian Broadcasting Circle.

Towards the end of the scene Jonas had the camera pull up to reveal that the couple had now moved—if, that is, they had not been there all the time—to the Palace Gardens in modern-day Oslo; the camera panned across the city, down towards Karl Johans gate and the Parliament building. It is not unreasonable to imagine that, with this surprising device, Jonas Wergeland wished to make a point about Norway being stuck in a permanent Middle Age.

Because that is what Undset had taught him: that Norwegians, even those people walking down Karl Johan with their mobile phones and their laptop computers, were living in the Middle Ages, mentally at least and to a greater extent than other nations in Europe; that they were barely done with the sagas, that deep down they were at odds with their own time. Norway had gone from the Middle Ages to a welfare state in the atomic age in just one century—in other words, so quickly that they were still stuck, psychologically speaking, in the medieval peasant society, still had their roots in the earth. Like Undset, most Norwegians cherish an ineradicable mistrust of everything that smacks of a belief in progress and hope for the future. Like Undset, deep in their souls they believe in a static human nature, a heart that never changes. Undset had, in fact, made an invaluable contribution to the understanding of the Norwegian identity: the citizens of Norway—even those sitting back in their comfy new Stressless chairs—are medieval people. There is a very simple reason why Norwegians perceive Sigrid Undset's historical novels as contemporary fiction: the people of Norway are still living in the past.

To be fair, though: viewed from another—one might almost say, opposite—angle, it could just as well be that, by dint of that same device, Jonas Wergeland wished to say something about what was possibly Sigrid Undset's greatest achievement: she dragged the Middle Ages out of the darkness so to speak, out of oblivion. She believed that the Middle Ages should be able to shed light on modern-day problems—individualism, materialism, the idea that mankind could be used as a yardstick for the universe—since many of the things lacking in modern society could still be found in medieval beliefs and culture. Sigrid Undset's positive view of this era anticipated the general reassessment of the Middle Ages made by researchers many years later.

In any case, Jonas Wergeland also realized something else: that there could be no better reason for working with television than this, since television was the perfect medium for "medieval people," folk who lost themselves in fictions, who yearned for simplicity and coherence. Now and again he had the feeling that Norwegians did not regard the unique individuals around whom he built a television series as heroes, but as saints: that in all secrecy, when no one was watching, they kneeled down in front of the TV screen and kissed those images.

Cold, Calm, Clittering As Ararat's Topmost Chunk of Ice

(Henrik Wergeland: *Det Befriede Europa*)

Jonas sometimes wondered whether he had been to Yerevan three times or just the once. He remembered standing outside the Matenadaran, a building not unlike a temple, situated a little way up a hillside in the north of the city, surveying the scene below and feeling a kind of light washing over him, something which, for want of a better word, we will have to call a religious experience. It was December, but not uncomfortably cold. Beneath the landscape there sounded a low, barely audible note, or a hum, as if from a colossal dynamo lying somewhere deep under his feet.

In his memory he could see a person, a man smoking a pipe, but occasionally all he recalled was the sight of the mountain before him. Because there, just across the border from Turkey, lay Ararat's vast massif—Little Ararat to the left, Great Ararat to the right, the latter almost 17,000 feet high, Little Ararat roughly 4,000 feet lower and more conical in shape, not unlike Mount Fujiyama in Japan. It was not hard to guess that this had in the past been a volcanic region. From where Jonas was standing, right below the Matenadaran, the two peaks seemed almost transparent, like a mirage, and the way the sunlight glittered on the glacier at the very top of Great Ararat made Jonas think of Theodor Kittelsen's painting of the boy standing gazing at Soria Moria Castle, the golden glow on the ridge facing him: "A long, long way off he saw something glittering and gleaming." Jonas stood there, quite certain of what he would find in the sparkling chunk of ice at the very top—were he suddenly, magically, to find himself up there: a pearl, a pearl ear-stud encased inside the ice.

But there was something else too: something special about that mountain. Tradition had it that Noah's ark had been left high and dry on the top of Mount Ararat when the floodwaters subsided. A number of expeditions had set out to search for remains of the ark in the glacier at which Jonas was gazing. He had always been fascinated by the story of Noah. It was a tale of survival. About being many and then all at once so few. Being chosen. Like being born again, being given a second chance. Jonas gazed at Mount Ararat, was put in mind of a slumbering dragon, could not take his eyes off that mighty silhouette. He had planned to spend a couple of days in Armenia, but suddenly he felt like staying longer, in some way that he could not explain he felt at home here. If one believed in the legend of Noah, this place was also the cradle of mankind. And there were plenty of down-to-earth historians who maintained that the Indo-European race had its origins in this part of the world. If they were right, and if he were to go far enough back in time, Jonas actually had a distant link with this place.

He stands there gazing out across the town, listening spellbound to the deep thrum beneath or above the landscape, like the note produced by the pedals of an organ: a dark note, or voice, emanating from the very bedrock. The confirmation of a calling. Anything, absolutely anything can happen, thinks Jonas. Anything is possible. At any moment.

Why had he gone to Yerevan? He went there to see this almost transparent mountain on the horizon, an unbelievably wondrous sight. Jonas stood under a distant sky and looked at a mountain, let it take up residence inside him, seep into his body. Jonas Wergeland was struck by the pure sense of being alive and the knowledge that the meaning of life could be something as simple as four minutes one morning in December when one is thirty-five years of age, at the zenith of one's life—that the intensity and beauty of those four minutes could define an entire life, in the same way that a pretty unexceptional book of seven hundred pages might have four lines on page 351 which lift the whole thing up onto another plane, which have the power to transform both past and future.

A journey need not be long, in terms of time, for it to turn everything upside down. A day or two in a strange place can change your life.

Blowin' in the Wind

What a wealth of cross-connections! I can see a hundred paths we could take from here, but for the moment we must stay with matters Biblical, albeit with a Bible of a different sort. No one was surprised when Jonas's brother, Red Daniel, that uncompromising Marxist-Leninist, virtually took refuge aboard a Noah's Ark of sorts by finally completing the university course he had dropped out of in the seventies—in theology. The leap from theology to the Marxist-Leninist movement had been as painless as the somersault back again—in both cases because of an unshakeable faith, also known as fundamentalism: *Das Kapital* by Marx, volume I, page 49, the Gospel according to Mark, chapter four, verse nine.

I think I ought to say something about why Daniel forsook the Norwegian Marxist-Leninist Party, since this did not, as some have maintained, have anything to do with him falling out with those cadres who defended the support given to strikes staged by well-paid workers—people earning two or three times as much as Daniel knew he could ever hope to make. And even though this ought to have been reason enough—since only a fool could claim that the aim of socialism is to line the pockets of prosperous high-achievers—it was a lesser, but equally shocking matter which finally made Daniel see the Marxist-Leninist movement for what it was: sheer cretinization masquerading as ideology.

One day Daniel heard something which he could not believe to be true but which did in fact prove to be so: that Dag Østerberg—whom Daniel, even in his most one-dimensional Marxist-Leninist phase, could not have brought himself to imagine was anything other than a brilliant sociologist, best known as the translator into Norwegian of Thomas Mann's *Doctor Faustus*, one of the books which had inspired Daniel to study theology—that this man did not get the post at the Architectural College in Oslo for which he had applied, a lectureship in architecture and sociology, tailor-made for a man of Østerberg's caliber. The teachers had, of course, been all for Østerberg, but the members of the Students

Council—which is to say, the people who would have derived the greatest benefit from being able to consult such a mine of information—were unanimous in rejecting him and instead ensured that the post was filled by an applicant with the right Marxist-Leninist credentials: a perfect example of *Berufsverbot* in reverse, one of the most shameful blunders in the history of Norwegian further education. It was too much, even for Red Daniel—after this demonstration of Maoism in practice he basically stopped taking any active part in things, although it was a while before he actually left the party.

What sort of person was Daniel? I admit that even I, of all people, find it hard to curb my curiosity when it comes to Daniel W. Hansen, the man who actually informed—if that is the right word—on Jonas, saying that it was for his conscience's sake. Personally, I think Daniel must have felt very relieved to find himself back in the theology faculty reading room, cut off from the world by a wall of concordances and synopses, dogmatic outlines and summaries of ecclesiastical history, making great forays into the frontiers of language, or logic rather, where one had to walk the fine line between the concepts of Christ as being "uncreated" and yet "born" and be able, at the drop of a hat, to explain the impossible parity between *tres personae* and *una substantia*. Having first sought in vain for the truth somewhere in the gap between the historical figure of Jesus and the fantasy fostered by the early Christians, he began increasingly to home in on, or back towards, the study of the Old Testament because, as with the abbreviation for a certain type of car, the initials GT—standing in Norwegian for the *Gamle Testamente*—tell you that here you can step on the gas, here you can really have some fun.

After taking a first-class degree Daniel got a job as a research assistant, commonly known as an RA, and began to concentrate in earnest on the Pentateuch, which was neither an engine nor a camera, but the Greek name for the first five books of the Old Testament, traditionally ascribed to Moses: a fretwork of accounts by different authors and a real treat, not to say a genuine playground, for any ambitious researcher. One soon realized that Moses could not possibly be the source of all these texts: very few writers actually describe their own deaths, after all, and it had gradually become customary to operate with at least four different levels of text—the Four-Source Hypothesis—denoted by the abbreviations J, E, P and D. With childlike enthusiasm, the student Daniel had made different colored marks in the margins of his Bible Hebraica to indicate the different layers, interlocking like some intricately designed zip-fastener—there were places where the chapters looked exactly like rainbows. Anyway—to cut a long, a very long, story short, Daniel was most interested in J, which is to say the Jahwist strand, which probably also represents the oldest source. That a later theory also suggested that J was a woman only goes to show that Daniel had not lost his touch.

Daniel had had an idea: one of nigh-on Faustian proportions. He would pick out all the Jahwist passages, like threads out of a weaving, and splice them together to form one unbroken account. And not only that: he would uncover a new and more primordial narrative in this story, especially concerning the wandering in the desert, from Exodus onward, believing as he did that the current version was illogical. Daniel, who only a few years earlier had cherished dreams of the proletariat's armed revolution, now sat in his office contemplating a work that would revolutionize Old Testament research, all but disarm white-haired professors, including the ghosts of such great authorities as Wellhausen and Gunkel. Thus he set about the hard, painstaking slog—not altogether unlike a tramp through the desert—of cutting up copies of the Hebraic text and laying what he believed to be the Jahwist passages round about him in various, tentative sequences. But before he could glue them together again—in their new order, I mean—he had to work out the correct sequence.

Excuse me for laughing, Professor, but this reminds me that Daniel's interest in cutting things out had started long before this and continued for a good while after—and we're not talking Biblical texts here. Daniel was what one would have to call over-sexed; it was as if listening to the chapel hymn with the refrain "Dare to stand like Daniel" had left him with a permanent erection.

While his father was an organist, Daniel was an onanist on the grand scale, obsessed throughout his adolescence with whatever could get him worked up, inwardly and outwardly. The one thing he had in common with his father was an interest in fingering: which fingers to place where on the instrument—in his case what the Chinese referred to as the "jade flute"—and the tempo, which Daniel also defined in musical terms, from the lingering andante of the overture to the allegro furioso of the last movement. As a teenager, lying in the bunk bed above Jonas, Daniel would launch into half-whispered discussions, or monologues, on what would be the optimum substitute for a vagina. A padded mitten? A roll of elastic bandage? "Boy, do I envy Guggen," he said one night. "Finding Anne Beate Corneliussen's scarf, carrying it about in a daze, pressing it to his nose like a glue-sniffer, then coming up with the idea of tying it round his dick—can you imagine it, the softness and the scent of it!" What Daniel did not know was that this experiment had left Guggen with a member so swollen and covered in friction burns that his anxious parents had had to take him to the doctor. According to Daniel, Guggen had also experimented with minced meat in a plastic bag which had first been submerged in warm water—a forerunner to such phenomena as the "Throbber battery-operated, travel-size vagina" which appeared on the Norwegian market ten years later.

And yet nothing got Daniel more worked up than pictures. He began collecting them at an early age—starting with innocent lingerie ads, then progressing to various rather more daring publications, acquired partly on secret summer expeditions to Strömstad and partly through chums who stole them from suspect stepfathers: pornography of a raunchier flavour, in keeping with the names of the magazines for which Daniel swapped it: *Texas* and *Wild West*. From these magazines he cut his favorite pictures, which is to say the ones that stood the test of turning him on time after time, inducing that hot itch in his groin. Because that was the whole point; to get a big hard-on, to stock up on pictures which could act as an aid to masturbation, photos which—when laid out in the right order, that is—contributed to an accumulated randiness which in turn, as he ran his eye down the line, prompted a more vigorous working of the hand: a pictorial plot which culminated in the perfect orgasm, setting a full stop in the form of a warm discharge fired at the cleavage of the dream woman who was the sum of all the pictures in front of him.

For Daniel, masturbation was not—as it was for other boys—a pursuit conducted in the manner of the baboons in the zoo. No, for him it was a science—not least when it came to the selection of pictures. He had a particular preference for breasts, and these were evaluated according to the most stringent criteria. Breasts constituted the leitmotif in Daniel's otherwise so inconstant life, from suckling onwards. Besides having a preference for a very specific and totally irrational shape and size, he had a breathless fascination for the nipples and the area round about them, and for their color, as if there was talk here of a target, or—with a bit of good will—a kind of mandala on which to meditate.

But where to hide the porn? This brings us to one of the many singular challenges posed to the boyish imagination, and there were endless strategies: one could, for example, cover the magazines, camouflaging them as jotters in one's schoolbag; or one could conceal the judicious selection of pictures in a hollow tube, in itself an erotic act, or simply slip one's issue of *Cocktail*, most symbolically, inside the sixth volume of *My Treasury of Tales*. For months Daniel's collection reposed safely in Paradise.

In the days when Daniel's radicalism extended only to his learning the songs of Bob Dylan, he used to practice playing the guitar in the loft at Solhaug—an arrangement which suited him perfectly, since this was also where he kept the cut-outs of his favorite women, tucked inside a dilapidated old mattress, a real lulu, which some smart advertising people had dubbed the Paradise Mattress. Daniel was a terrible singer, even if his nasal drone did sound a bit like Dylan's, and could produce from his harmonica no greater range of notes than a little kid pretending to be a fire engine. So he often ended up sinking down onto the mattress's battered springs to console himself with his imaginary hordes of female fans, allowing them to pass before his eyes in the preferred, well-tried order, warbling at him à la Roy Orbison and thereby inciting his hand to move faster and faster until the picture of the last girl, with her—according to Daniel's subjective yardstick—divine tits caused his balls to contract in a blissful blow-out. Poets have written of that stuff of which dreams are made. For Daniel they were made of paper.

Then, one Midsummer's Eve—ironically enough just after Daniel had more or less mastered Dylan's "Blowin" in the Wind"—something terrible happened. Moments before the bonfire was to be lit, Daniel was standing on the green, waiting expectantly with everyone else from the estate when, to his horror, he saw his father running out with the old mattress, to throw it on the pyre, knowing nothing, of course, about its precious stuffing. Acting almost on instinct, or maybe more like a sultan attempting to save his harem, Daniel leaped forward and gave the mattress a hefty tug, trying to wrest it out of his father's hands, with the result that the ticking ripped even more and out fluttered all of Daniel's treasured pictures, to be caught by the breeze and sent flying into the air, and for a moment the heavens seemed, from Daniel's point of view at any rate, to be filled with a host of angels, before they were hastily collected by the estate's more morally upright residents, not least the mothers, and thrown onto the fire, where they were, so to speak, burned as witches.

I have, as it happens, an alternative explanation for why Red Daniel returned, like the prodigal son, to the study of theology. The fact is that he experienced a belated high point in his cut out career as late as 1975, which is to say long after he had given up collecting pictures. Some will remember 1975 as the year when the Suez Canal was reopened; Daniel remembered it for Ingeborg Sørensen. There are times when I think that there was only one point in his life when Daniel was proud of being Norwegian: when Ingeborg Sørensen graced the centerfold of America's *Playboy* magazine and, in a sense, conquered the United States. Several Norwegian women have in fact been Playmate of the Month, but Ingeborg Sørensen was the only one to come to Daniel's attention. He sneaked into a newsagent's, despite nightmares of being spotted by one of the Women's Libbers, and bought the March issue, to bring him comfort in his bleak, self-proletarianized existence; secure in the knowledge that Ingeborg Sørensen had not prostituted herself to a worse degree than he himself had been doing for some years—in one shot she was even pictured wearing a hard hat and boiler suit, like a worker. Daniel was so bowled over by her beauty that he actually cut out the picture of her in the bath with her breasts sticking out of the water like two island paradises in a sea of foam. So perhaps it was really Ingeborg Sørensen, and the lines of what, for Daniel, represented the embodiment of the perfect breasts which—that same year—showed him the way home; persuaded him to drop the Marxist-Leninist Party and resume his theological studies, as if she represented the naked truth, drove him back to the genesis of Paradise, to the GT and the Jahwist source.

It is not, therefore, beyond the bounds of possibility that—by demonstrating the heights a Norwegian could attain—she also fired Daniel's scholarly ambitions; that the thought of Ingeborg Sørensen and his youthful hobby also lay at the back of his mind when he was cutting passages out of the Old Testament in his efforts to discover a new, an utterly brilliant sequence which would overturn everything hitherto postulated by researchers on the subject of the Jahwist source. For months Daniel pored over scraps of Hebraic scripture spread out on the large table he had set up in his office, switching the slips of paper about again and again, continually altering the pattern—until one day, almost by accident and so abruptly that it came as a shock, it all fell into place, or nearly into place. The obvious sequence, just around the corner. For a few seconds he felt as light-headed as Crick and Watson must have felt the moment before they stood back and surveyed their completed model of the DNA structure. He could hardly believe it; had a vision of what this would mean. "I'm famous," he thought to himself. "My God, I'm about to become famous."

But as the saying goes: "how long was Adam in Paradise?" It is a warm spring day, just after Easter, the world is full of hope, and Daniel is sitting by an open window. And of course a girl comes in—a lot of female students tended to pop into his office—and in her eagerness to ask some burning question she knocks on the door then walks straight in, causing all of the scraps of paper spread out on the table to fly up, positively whirl into the air, some of them even vanishing out of the window, before coming to rest again in the most woeful disarray; he finds the whole thing suspiciously reminiscent of that time, as a boy, when he was stupid enough to unscrew the workings of a clock and all the parts were sent flying around the room. Daniel knew he was beaten. He would never get so close to the right sequence again. He eyed the jumble of paper around him—suddenly, with merciless clarity, it seemed to illustrate the futility of the entire undertaking and in many ways also anticipated developments in Pentateuchal research, which came more and more to assert the impossibility of "going from the omelette back to the eggs." In other words: he gave up. There was more to life than bits of paper. A new challenge, not to say two new challenges, stood before him, in the flesh.

I should perhaps remind you here of Daniel's idiosyncrasies, again where breasts were concerned: remind you of the time when, as a boy, he used to lie in bed briefing Jonas on which fabric provided the most provocative covering for the female breast. Daniel, as we have seen, favored wool and it's an ill wind that blows nobody any good, as they say—because the woman who had opened the door and caused the draught was wearing nothing but a fine wool sweater over her breasts: two gambolling lambs, Daniel thought, putting a little twist on *The Song of Solomon*'s paean to the same phenomenon. Daniel never did anything by halves, and this whole story eventually culminated in a happy Exodus: he married the agent of his downfall, this girl who even as a small child had been described as "a whirlwind"—and, I might add, they had four sons in rapid succession, whom Daniel with a certain self-irony, called the Four-Source Hypothesis.

Daniel left research and entered the church. And even though he was tone deaf he insisted on singing the Litany during services. When Daniel was droning on in that hoarse, nasal voice of his, it always sounded to Jonas as if, standing there behind the Communion-rail, leading the congregation, his brother was singing: "The answer, my friend, is blowin' in the wind."

The Tail and the Sheath

Supposing one were a conqueror—what would one win? The world? A little peace of mind? A name? Immortality? Oneself? Power? Women? There were times in Jonas Wergeland's life when he felt there was only one thing worth striving for: Health. To be fit and well.

Despite all of Daniel's sexual excesses—and as an adult he committed many sins far worse than fornicating with paper images—he never made, I almost said, a complete mess of things. Jonas, on the other hand, did.

Some stories have to be told more than once. You think you are finished with them, but then they pop up again like twists and turns that have lain low all the way along, only suddenly to wriggle up to the surface again. So this, Professor, is of course a continuation of the Istanbul story—and do not be misled into thinking that it deals with an earlier experience.

The more Jonas learned about his wife, the more he knew how much he didn't know. There are two types of people: those who know how to mix a dry Martini and those—by far the biggest group—who do not. Margrete knew how to make a proper dry Martini, and this troubled Jonas; it gave rise to all sorts of misgivings as to what else she was capable of but kept secret from him. And yet Margrete was the last person Jonas would have suspected of infidelity, and while you may laugh at such naïvety, Professor, do not forget what she worked with day in, day out. She was a dermatologist, or to put it another way: she worked with sexually transmitted diseases.

Does the story of the jealousy start here? Deep down?

Jonas himself had only visited the Oslo Health Center once. True, he had walked past the striking new building on St. Olavs plass every day on his way to and from the Cathedral School, but he had never given any thought to what delicate matters and contrite souls lay hidden behind the natural concrete of its facade.

Five years later, however, he had no choice but to take the Canossa way or, as some would have it, the Casanova way to the inner chambers of the aforementioned Health Center: which is to say he was saved from having to crawl, and instead took the lift to the fifth floor and pushed open the door bearing the daunting sign "Department of Dermatology and Venereal Diseases." The reason for this ignominious visit was, as far as Jonas himself could tell, a good old-fashioned dose of the clap. Well, not good—of the worst possible kind.

Tempting though it is, I do not propose to dwell at any length on the psychological gauntlet many people feel they are running when they enter the waiting room of such a department, with pus seeping into their underwear. Nor am I going to make fun of the sudden reluctance to give one's name to the nurse filling out the card, as if one is half expecting to be charged with some dreadful penance or imagines that one's name is being entered in some sort of Sinners' Register.

What Jonas remembered most clearly was the moment when he walked into the doctor's surgery, a rather poky, nondescript office, to find himself looking at a woman—and not only that, but looking at what he would later describe as a fine figure of a woman, who—on the basis of a postcard tacked to the wall, of Van Gogh's *Starry Night*—he immediately assumed to be a connoisseur of art. He had automatically envisaged a male doctor but promptly thought to himself: why not? Why shouldn't a female doctor treat male patients too?

She—Dr. Kleveland, according to the badge on her white coat—greeted him politely before inquiring what the trouble was, asking a few professional and yet personal questions which instantly gave him full confidence in her: nay, filled him with gratitude almost for being allowed to get things off his chest, somehow confess, as if he were a Catholic and she was the priest behind the screen in the confessional. He explained, a little longwindedly perhaps, while she nodded and told him to take down his trousers and lie down on the couch over against the wall. And I'm sure quite a few people in Norway would have liked to witness this sight—Jonas Wergeland lying there with his pants down, presenting his afflicted member, humbly and possibly a little shamefully. "I'd never have thought it of her," he said.

Dr. Kleveland put on a pair of latex gloves with a snap that made Jonas think of washing-up, or feel that at any minute she was going to pick up a scalpel and remove the whole lot, cut the evil off at the root, as it were. For a fleeting moment it seemed to him that she weighed his penis in her hand, as if comparing it to others she had seen, or as if it was a fine work of art and the whole point of the gloves was to prevent it from being sullied by sweaty or greasy fingers, just as curators wore gloves when restoring valuable old masters. It would probably be truer to say that Dr. Kleveland was much more interested in the inner state of Jonas Wergeland's penis than in its outward appearance. "Could you pull back the foreskin?" she said. This he did, feeling as though he were raising the curtain on a tragic drama.

I will not go into the details of Dr. Kleveland's skilful handling of the urethral spatula, or attempt to describe the tiny stab of pain or the thoughts that go through one's head when a charcoal brush is pushed almost an inch into the urethra, merely say that Dr. Kleveland—making no comment and closely observed by a rather worried Jonas, brushed the pus onto a cover slip which she then dried before coating it with a so-called Löffler dye and put her eye down to the microscope—it was all over in a couple of minutes.

"Ah, yes, gonorrhoea," said Dr. Kleveland.

After Jonas had swallowed half a dozen tablets and given the name of the infection source—something about which he had no qualms—and been told to contact the person concerned himself and ask her to call at the Health Center, he made a remark, out of relief really, which clearly annoyed Dr. Kleveland and caused her, for once, to lose a little of her professional demeanor: "Oh well, that's not so bad really," he said.

Like other doctors, Dr. Kleveland was adept at differentiating between the performance of her duties and the temptation to lecture her patients. But on this particular day, prompted perhaps by sheer wisdom or what is known as feminine intuition, Dr. Kleveland simply saw red and did something she had never done before and would never do again—she took down a book from the office bookcase: it immediately put Jonas in mind of Ørn's stamp album or the family Bible at home, but he could not have been further off the mark, because it proved to be a textbook on venereal diseases, a classic work in fact, as Jonas would later discover, and this she dropped with a demonstrative thud onto the desk in front of him: "Have a look in here," she said, "and then we'll see if you're still saying 'Oh well.'"

Jonas leafed through the book while Dr. Kleveland prepared the sample which, to be on the safe side, was to be sent somewhere else for testing. The sight that met Jonas's eyes was not a pretty one, but the pictures were mesmerizing, every bit as mesmerizing as Gustav Doré's illustrations in the family Bible, in fact they could have been used as an addendum to the chapter on Sodom and Gomorrah: black, avenging angels, photographs illustrating the different venereal diseases, including those cases which had gone too long without treatment. In full color. More than anything else they made him think of leprosy, especially the male organs, which looked as if they were about to drop off, like half sawn-off branches. These images were in fact so hideously grotesque and spoke of such pain that Jonas could not bear to look at them—possibly also because it was the most sensitive area of the body that was affected and because, paradoxically, what he was seeing here was, in many cases, the fruits of pleasure. He had been given a glimpse into a gruesome world that was the exact opposite of Daniel's Mykle universe, the whispered recitals of his youth, lines such as "with deeply tremulous reverence to fondle her secret recesses."

Jonas closes the book, or rather: his body closes the book, refuses to see any more. Dr. Kleveland is also finished with what she was doing, says nothing, can tell from Jonas's face that she doesn't need to, she simply gives him a couple of practical instructions before he bows out backwards.

It was, therefore, this not exactly pleasant story that lay behind Jonas's nigh-on blind trust in Margrete, his firm belief that she would never be unfaithful. The way he saw it, she simply had to be immune to adultery. She worked at the Health Center, after all, he reasoned, in the same department, Dermatology and Venereal Diseases, which he himself had once attended, shaking in his shoes. And how, he asked himself, could a woman who saw that sort of thing every day, those rot-infested, throbbing, suppurating, fungus-ridden genitals—a great many of them the result of infidelity—how could she ever contemplate exposing herself to or even get anywhere close, to such an eventuality?

Margrete seldom talked about her work at home. Jonas all but forgot that she was even a doctor, never mind a derma-venereologist. Or maybe he simply blocked it out, had no wish to think about what went through the heads of the men who had the honor of resting their penises, occasionally healthy penises at that, in Dr. Boeck's lovely hand, as if on scales of purest gold. If she did mention her job, it was usually to tell some anecdote about skin, or skin disorders—a safer topic. Because she did work with these too, for half of each day to be exact, dealing with everything from acne to all manner of rashes and eczemas, carrying out prosaic little operations camouflaged by such obscure terms as "biopsy" and "cryotherapy." Jonas always felt that this must be why she attached such great erotic importance to skin, she would spend whole evenings just stroking him with her fingers, enabling him to experience a closeness he had never known before. "No sexual organ can hold a candle to the skin," she said. At such moments he thanked his lucky stars, to be so privileged: to be married to a woman unlike any other in the world.

Jonas didn't ask much about Margrete's work either—his experience at the Health Center, the knowledge of what hurts that elegant façade could conceal seeming to have scared him off such topics for good and all. He followed her career more or less on the sly, knew for example how interested she had been, when he met her—at the time when she was doing a supplementary course at the University Hospital—in a "new" disease called chlamydia. He could not rid himself of the suspicion that her pleasure lay, as it were, in the venereal. How else to explain why she sometimes came home all-aglow to tell him that they had had a case of syphilis that day—a rare occurrence now—and then launched into a gripping and very detailed description of the image in the microscope, in which the corkscrew forms of the spirochaete stood out clearly against the dark background: an image which, by the way, she compared to a starry sky, delighting in the discovery in a way that reminded Jonas of his own days as an enthusiastic student of astronomy. But normally she said very little. Understandably. "Well, it's hardly the most scintillating dinner-party conversation is it—entertaining everyone with the latest news on the condylomata or herpes fronts," was the excuse she gave on one occasion.

If she said anything about the everyday goings-on at the Health Center, it usually had to do with what she saw or heard, rather than with the diseases as such. She might, in strictest confidence, tell him about the medical students who came by the center, the questions they were liable to blurt out in the heat of their enthusiasm, not to mention the embarrassing, often astonishing, networks disclosed by particularly active infection sources. "It's at times like those that you realize how much mischief one person can do, how quickly things spread," she said. "Or see that, at the genetic level, we are still ninety per cent animal." But more often than not, when Margrete gave in to temptation, it was to tell the stories that men in particular, patients that is, could come out with when they stood there with their trousers round their ankles, unwinding the bandages from their cocks, as if they felt that only the most fantastic tale could explain how on earth their bowsprit could have sustained such damage. Jonas knew that Margrete was in a class by herself when it came to the greatest challenge in her profession: establishing a rapport with a patient. She could make a shamefaced boy relax, an unscrupulous, cynical man open up and give her his confidence. And there were times when Jonas suspected that this was the underlying reason, maybe even the real reason, why she enjoyed her work so much: the fact that she got to hear all those amazing tales, as if she were working not at the Health Center but in a bazaar. "Do you know anything about taking precautions?" Margrete had asked one man with a severely wounded penis. "Oh, yes," he said. "After I've been with a woman I always wash my dick with cognac." Margrete had eyed the man up and down: "And do you think that's good enough?" she said. "Well, it should be," the man replied indignantly, "it's three-star!"

But to get back to where we came in: Jonas Wergeland had got it into his head that, with her day-to-day insight into the grislier aspects of sex, Margrete would never allow another man to stick his penis inside her. He had, in other words, forgotten with what warmth and devotion she had welcomed his rigid manhood—that same organ which had once run with pus. It never occurred to Jonas that in the very course of her work Margrete would have learned some simple way of protecting herself. Or that this was exactly why she appreciated having a nice, clean man with a healthy, pulsating member between his legs.

It Looks down on Earth While My Heart Stands Still

(Henrik Wergeland: *Det Befriede Europa*)

Sometimes Jonas wondered whether he had been to Yerevan three times or just the once. He remembered standing outside a distinctive building called the Matenadaran, an institute for the preservation of ancient documents. And although he vaguely recalled something about a conversation, and possibly something about a mountain—like a white arc in the blue—if he thought hard enough about it, all he remembered was the script.

He had stopped without thinking next to a statue on the terrace just below the entrance, struck by a feeling that his body was full of letters. The statue showed a pupil kneeling before Mesrop Mashotots, the man who was reputed to have created the Armenian alphabet, the characters that were carved into the wall behind him: an alphabet that had never been used by any other people. It was a script that appealed to Jonas; the capitals in particular had an unusually regular and stylized form that at the same time made the characters seem somehow to have been reversed. A script for outsiders, thought Jonas, befitting a proud and hard-pressed people.

Inside the copper doors of the Matenadaran he and the guide had wandered through its rooms, looking at ancient manuscripts from monasteries, handwritten copies of the works of Armenian scholars and of foreign books. Some texts from antiquity had only survived in their Armenian translations—a chronicle by Eusebios of Caesarea, a treatise on nature by Zeno. As if the script itself were a sort of Noah's ark, thought Jonas, examining one fragile parchment volume: the Gospel of Lazarus. He felt as though the lovely letters were exerting an influence on him, trying to tell him something, although he did not know what.

Why had he gone to Yerevan? Perhaps simply to see this wilful alphabet. For the first time since elementary school he felt something for letters, had the urge to write, abandon television, even. It may be that this was precisely what this almost otherworldly script was telling him: that nothing was fixed. That anything was possible. What if I were to settle down here, he thought, break all ties and do something completely different?

Jonas had remained standing outside the institute, gazing down on the city and listening to a deep murmur emanating from beneath or above the landscape, as if some massive plates he could not see were turning or grinding against one another. He thought of Fridtjof Nansen, pack ice, he thought of Ararat, the glacier, he thought of the year ahead of him, he thought of the television series which was shortly to be broadcast, he thought of Margrete—he thought of Margrete, not knowing that, because of her, he would find himself at the center of a sensational scandal, that he would discover how it felt when something he believed to be solid and permanent suddenly shifted under his feet. He could not know, was too busy savoring this slow moment of revelation, the sensation of being at a point where everything trickles down and converges, like sand in the narrow neck of an hourglass.

His reverie was interrupted by a man—because there was something else, not only a script, not only a mountain, but a person. Nansen Sarjan—almost having to shake Jonas awake and telling him that he had to leave, now, this very instant. "But why?" Jonas asks lightly, despite a faint contraction of his testicles, "I'm leaving for Leninakan this evening." Leninakan was the largest city in Armenia after Yerevan, and Jonas meant to visit the university there the next morning. "Because you must," the man says adamantly and knocks out his pipe against his heel. "I just know, that's all. You must not stay here one second longer."

Jonas did not know why he allowed himself to be persuaded, why he permitted himself to be escorted, led by the hand almost, back to his hotel, where an impatient Nansen Sarjan had an earnest conversation with the Intourist representative, whereupon Jonas's ticket was changed and he was driven straight off to the airport, without even stopping for a bite of lunch—maybe it was the thought of Nansen, Fridtjof that is, or of Noah, or of that enigmatic script which stopped him from protesting. Whatever it was, a sudden shunt, he arrived in Moscow that same afternoon. As the plane bumped down onto the runway he seemed to wake from a hypnotic trance.

Sometimes Jonas Wergeland doubted whether he had been to Yerevan at all.

The following day he heard rumors, but it wasn't until he returned to Norway that he heard the full story: news of the disaster was all over the papers and on television. The morning after he left, Armenia had been hit by a severe earthquake, the worst experienced in the Caucasus in eighty years; 25,000 people had been killed, 12,000 were hospitalized, half a million people had been left homeless. The quake had wreaked particular havoc in Leninakan; large parts of the city, including the university, had been completely flattened.

Jonas Wergeland knew it: we owe our lives to other people.

A journey need not be long, in terms of time, for it to turn everything upside down. A day or two in a strange place can change your life.

I—the Professor—do not know whether or not to call this the irony of fate. Jonas Wergeland escaped disaster that time, but nothing could save him from the media earthquake triggered by his arrest and later trial—not surprisingly perhaps, seeing that Wergeland himself was the instigating factor. The public hoped, of course, for as long as they could, hoped that something was wrong, that someone, somewhere had made a terrible and most unfortunate mistake. Rumor had it that Jonas Wergeland remained silent—and, others added, unmoved—and he refused to make any sort of statement to the police. He had accepted the lawyer appointed to defend him without demur and would not hear of engaging one of the big-time lawyers whom Daniel was sure would be able to help him.

I think everyone, including myself, awaited the trial in such a state of suspense that you would have thought the honor of Norway was at stake. At times, the interest in the case could almost be compared to the hullabaloo surrounding the winter Olympics at Lillehammer that would shortly be coming to a close. It seemed as though higher powers wished to reward the Norwegian people by treating them, for a short time—en masse, as it were—to not one mammoth spectacle but two: a thought-provoking reflection of Jonas Wergeland's theory that Norway was "a nation of spectators."

I do not know whether it is possible to say anything about the proceedings in the High Court beyond all that has already been reported, all that has been written, all the pictures that have been published—not least those risible sketches from the courtroom, like illustrations from cheap crime magazines. One can ask oneself whether there was anything about Jonas Wergeland that did not come out during the trial—a kind of inverted version of *This Is Your Life*—thanks to the prosecution's dogged efforts to prove his guilt. The most surprising part was probably the fact that Jonas Wergeland also chose to remain silent, as if he considered this his best mode of defense, or his only mode of defense: something which lots of people naturally interpreted as a black mark against him. Nonetheless, there was no doubt: through everything that came to light, everything that was relayed by the media and greedily watched, read, listened to and, not least, discussed everywhere, Jonas Wergeland seduced the Norwegian people anew.

By the time the case came to court a number of books about him had already been published, with titles such as *The TV Demon* and *All That Glisterns*: superficial, hastily penned "biographies" produced with only one aim in mind: to make money. Well, it was a very tasty story, almost worthy of Shakespeare himself: the vertiginous plunge from the peaks of distinction to the pit of hell. And yet the trial managed, indirectly mind you, to produce fresh details, whole stories in fact, primarily of the murkier sort, the relevance of which was skilfully argued by the prosecution—everything from a boyhood story about the theft of a stamp album to that of an embarrassingly degrading taxi ride about a year before the killing. The prosecutors also received plenty of help from Gjermund Boeck, Margrete's father, and William Røed, Jonas's uncle who, in their respective capacities as the Norwegian king's ambassador and a director of Statoil presented their testimonies with great authority: his uncle, known within the family as Sir William, impeccably attired in a blazer with a gold silk cravat at his throat, painted a particularly lethal picture of what he called "Jonas Wergeland's complete lack of character." Few would disagree with the newspapermen's refrain: "If anyone in modern times has been put in the stocks, then it's Jonas Wergeland."

In all fairness it has to be said that a few critical voices did say that it all went too far, as when an ex-girlfriend appeared in court and told—she, with her natural bloom and expressive features—of their six-month affair, a testimony in which their sexual escapades were more than hinted at. She had been called as a witness—this was a point which a tireless prosecutor emphasized at great length—because of a brutal tale, a quite shocking business, if it were true, which would possibly provide absolute proof of Jonas Wergeland's terrible temper and violent tendencies. These revelations were all the more sensational since the woman concerned was now one of Norway's best known film actresses, one of the very few to achieve international stardom—and as if that weren't enough she had recently married and had a child by an Oscar-winning American director.

I would like, if I may, to slip in here a little information about this person drawn from my own material: Jonas Wergeland met Ingunn U.

while she was at drama school, when her temperament was at its most volatile—if that is any excuse. She was the type who was liable to bathe in fountains and simulate scenes on the tram. If my source is correct, she went so far on several occasions as to have sex with Jonas with her face heavily made-up, wearing theatrical masks from a variety of roles; according to Jonas himself, the first time he was about to enter her she apparently murmured one of Juliet's final lines: "O happy dagger—this is thy sheath!" As far as I can judge Ingunn U. was a person who was more or less continually out of context. When Jonas broke up with her, she would stand all night outside his window in Hegdehaugsveien, bawling and shouting and waking up half of Homansbyen until the police finally took her in hand. Whether it was acting or genuine hysteria no one ever knew; that was her secret, as it was on the stage or on film sets later in her career.

All in all, a lot of things seemed to be taken to the extreme, blown totally out of all proportion. The whole sensation industry that fed on this case lent it the character of a farce, of something unreal. More and more people had the feeling that something was fundamentally wrong. For a start, the motive seemed unclear. Why would Jonas Wergeland kill his wife? This seemed even more inconceivable to all those Norwegians for whom the thought of Jonas Wergeland and Margrete Boeck conjured up a picture of the ideal couple, snapped at premieres and parties, a regular feature in weekly mags and newspapers year after year; the television personality and his wife, a dark beauty who also happened to occupy the highly respected post of consultant physician.

"Do you know what the most surprising thing of all is?" my guest asked on the fourth evening on which she visited me, clad in her usual elegant black and as earnest as always. "The most surprising part of all this washing of dirty laundry in public was one question that was never asked. Obviously because it had nothing to do with the case. And yet it gets to the very nub of the matter. Because, if it were true that Jonas Wergeland possessed all those failings and evil inclinations, how could a whole nation fall under his spell? And that being the case, does this not say everything about Norway, the cultural level of this country in the last decade before the millennium? That such an individual could wangle his way to such enormous power and popularity, I mean?"

This evening she was in less of a hurry to launch into her unstoppable monologue; for the first time she wandered round the turret room, taking everything in. I have to be honest and admit that I was warming to her, that she was actually starting to intrigue me, those bright red lips in the pale face and the blazing eyes framed by such a remarkable mass of black; the way she moved, with the dignity of one of royal birth. As she passed me I tried again to place the indefinable odor that hung around her—it seemed to hail from some other land—but with no success. She stopped in front of one of the bookcases, pulled out a couple of the biographies I have written, leafed through them, smiled. "Well, you've certainly not been idle, Professor."

No I haven't. I have always worked hard. I do not know whether it is necessary to mention this, but I am regarded as a pioneer within my field, my original field that is: historical research. I think I can safely say that I was the first, or certainly the first clear representative in Norway of what is now referred to as the Annales school: a form of historical research with the emphasis on research which, simply put, concentrates more on the long lines of history, the currents below the surface, than on individual lives, and endeavors, above all else, to eschew any kind of storytelling, especially of stories depicting political or military events as the illustrious deeds of great men. "Structures rather than events" was my motto. Where the nineteenth century, my own specific field of study, was concerned, I took up the fight to tone down the focus on nation-builders and looked instead at the more economic and social aspects. My best known work, which is still cited in international history circles, is the treatise *Broad Sail*—the title meant to give an idea of the book's subject matter and its scope—in which I shed light on the Norway of the nineteenth century by writing about the shipping trade and the south coast of Norway, though with wider reference to the whole period from 1536 to 1870. It is as much a study of the region as it is a work of history, an investigation of the relationship between the people and the country along the south coast. The first—and most highly praised—third of the book deals with the district solely from a geographic point of view: the climate, the coastline and the interior, islands, harbors and towns, land, and seaways. The aim was to view the whole of the North Sea as one vast region in such a way that the relevance of Britain to what happened in Norway became apparent. By dint of interdisciplinary methods I describe everything from food, clothing, housing, tools, wages, and prices, to the family circle, customs, religion and superstition—and even idioms peculiar to the south coast, not least seamen's expressions. Some said that the treatise's central character was not man, but the ship, or the sea.

My apologies for this brief discourse, but I feel a need to underline that it was not a betrayal of, but doubts about, this method which led me to make a fresh start, whereby I would once more attempt to center my account around people, those people whom I had, until now, working from my Olympian perspective, treated almost like insects, or as a "sum." Perhaps—I say perhaps—this could be attributed to a new realization that you cannot discount the story from a description of historical events. In any case, this resulted in a string of books that could be said to be well known and that I suppose could be called biographies since they deal with figures of consequence in the history of nineteenth-century Norway. And while the general public had never heard of my four major scholarly works, not even *The Structure of the Bureaucrat State*, sales of the first biography, of P. A. Munch, simply skyrocketed. Two years later *The Norwegian No*, a book about Søren Jaabæk, appeared and repeated the success.

Although I did try later to explain the success of these books by saying that I just happened to hit the biography boom which began around this time, satisfying the public's apparently insatiable need for coherence, for a mirror they could hold up to their own lives, the real reason was obvious: the Norwegian people, the Norwegian general public at least, wanted histories not History. And maybe they are right: maybe our existence is best understood as a story. To some extent this depressed me, to some extent it heartened me. I confess, however, that this voracious interest took me by surprise, and what is more: it was this longed-for wider recognition that tempted me to resign my professorship in order to devote myself to writing biographies fulltime. And if I were a Judas, selling out my beliefs, then I didn't sell them cheap; I made a fortune out of it. Forgive me, I'm only human—vain too: I willingly let myself be flattered by people who praised my gift for popularization, for taking a fresh slant on things, by reviewers who maintained that I had done for a number of prominent Norwegians what Lytton Strachey did for a bunch of his countrymen.

So I was wary of any tinge of irony in her voice when she addressed me as "Professor," as if I were continually hearing myself being accused of having abandoned my true calling. Eventually, though, I began to interpret it more as her way of invoking, not to say appealing to, my academic abilities. I regarded her with bated breath as she flicked desultorily through my biography—the one I am most pleased with—of historian Ernst Sars: *Prospect of a Life*. "Do you think that so-called great people have to be out-of-the-ordinary?" she asked, and then, as if not expecting a reply: "What if they were perfectly ordinary. Or downright weak." She put the book back. "Could one, for example, admire a man who might be a murderer?"

The ferry to Denmark slipped past, out on the fjord. It may have been its glowing lights that prompted her to move over to the fireplace where a fire was burning. "I hate this cold," she said again, although the temperature outside was only around zero, and then, seeing my look of surprise: "I'm used to much warmer conditions."

As I was putting more wood on the fire she bent an openly appreciative eye on the mounds of papers on my desk, piled up so high that I could barely see out of the window when I sat down. There too lay all sorts of statistical surveys, official documents, fat works of reference, economic reports, a history of television, the yearbooks of various professional bodies—as if the room belonged to a social scientist or social anthropologist rather than a historian. I realized that, in my uncertainty regarding my project, I had fallen back on my old methods—I almost said: my old sins. Could it be that all along, without knowing it, I had been afraid that I would not be able to discern a clear storyline in the life of someone from our own century and had, therefore, accumulated all this material, just as I had done for my earliest works—on an epoch, on a country—as if hoping that somewhere in there I would spot one long thread winding its way through the mass of information. Or maybe I suspected that Jonas Wergeland was just another name for a—what shall I call it?—a way of thinking, that he was the symbol of a national trend: that, like Abraham in the Bible, he personified the whole history of his tribe, that he represented something more, except that I could not see what it was. And yet, surprisingly enough, she seemed to approve of my method. "I need someone who takes a man seriously," she said, "who understands that a man amounts to more than his own life."

Before she came on the scene, I had had the feeling that I had in my possession the annals of Jonas Wergeland, but that I wasn't getting anywhere. I lacked the structure: which is to say, the secret thread of life on which the stories of his life could be assembled like pearls on a string. Inevitably I had begun to wonder whether there could be a crucial difference between a life of today and a life from the previous century. It might be that one could now amass so much material on a life that it was no longer possible to recount it. Or was there a simpler explanation: that I was clinging to the past, to old-fashioned expository models, outdated theories on just about everything. The perpetual rumble from the airport occasionally made me feel as if I was sitting next door to a prehistoric zoo, full of dinosaurs.

Whether my fears were justified or not, my visitor's stories forced me to see that I might have been on the trail of a story that was too big. She showed me that it was also possible to arrive at insight into a life through something seemingly fragmentary, strings of stories which at first sight are totally unconnected but which, when you get right down to it, constitute a new form of coherence and unity. Something seemed to dawn on me, especially when I was writing for all I was worth, trying to follow her disjointed narrative, and I was unwilling, off-hand, to call it an acknowledgement of inferiority. Maybe that's just how life is, how it must be.

When I mentioned the trial to her, she sat down in the chair by the fire and laughed: "There was at least one story that did not come out there, Professor."

I dimmed all the lights, apart from the lamp next to my own chair. She shifted closer to the fire and fixed her eyes on a spot outside the windows, as if fire and darkness were the very prerequisites of the storytelling. I put pen to paper just as a plane was taking off from Fornebu. I knew as little about where it would land as I did about the tales she proceeded to tell.

Because It Was There

Jonas's family often went on holiday jaunts around Norway. Because, you see, they had a car. Children today would hardly consider the fact of having a car anything to shout about, but back then it was a real event when Dad came home, proud as a stag in rut, with a new automobile, usually the first ever; people hung out of their windows and everybody, or all of the male residents of the estate at any rate, had to troop out to view this object of wonder and stand with their hands in their pockets asking questions about the technical details before the family went off for the ritual trial run, cheered on their way like a ship on its maiden voyage. Rakel liked the old Opel Caravan best, because of the name's associations with the Arabian Nights world in which she lived, while Jonas was for a long time a fan of the Opel Rekord, mainly because it had a speedometer on which the indicator, a horizontal line, started out green, then magically turned yellow and eventually red, depending on how fast you drove. The future Red Daniel, true to form, was forever yelling: "Into the red, Dad, drive it into the red!"

How does one become a conqueror?

More often than not the destination on the weekend jaunts the family took when Jonas was a boy was determined by his mother or rather, his mother's stories. Åse Wergeland was not one for lulling children to sleep with nice, wholesome bedtime stories. In the evening, when their sister was tucked up with her *Romance* magazine or the *One Thousand and One Nights*, Åse was in Daniel's and Jonas's room, telling them tales of the Vikings' bloodthirsty world, stories which she claimed were taken from the Norse sagas. As a little boy, Jonas used to connect the word "saga" with the Norwegian word for a saw: "*sag*." Thus he thought that his mother's liking for the old legends must have something to do with her interest in saws and her work at the Grorud Ironmongers. Not an unreasonable conclusion, since his mother fought hard, with sword in hand you might say, to ensure that a product such as the G-MAN saw would conquer the market.

Jonas had always been particularly fond of the line in the Norwegian national anthem where it says: "and with that saga night that falls, fall dreams upon our earth." Almost every evening for years during his childhood his mother told the boys stories from Norway's glorious Viking age before they went to sleep with—at Jonas's behest—her round silver brooch pinned to her chest, as a kind of prop. What the boys did not know was that their mother's stories were recounted freely from memory, she mixed up people and events and also had a tendency to render the tales even more exciting and dramatic if that were possible—and more brutal—by drawing on the arsenal of intrigue and misdeed she had built up thanks to years as an avid reader of detective stories. Nonetheless, they were fed, albeit in the wrong contexts, most of the most famous lines from the sagas: all Jomsborg's Vikings are not yet dead, a fall means good luck, you have struck Norway from my hands, the King has fed us well, the roots of my heart are still fat—all of those matchless old saws. They were also wont to quote them at appropriate moments, as when Daniel farted and inquired: "What cracked so loud?"

The question is, therefore, particularly when one bears in mind the formidable capacity which stories have for forming an individual, whether the most important person in Jonas Wergeland's life was not, in fact, his mother and whether, by admitting this, I am also shifting the focus of my account. Because most heroic tales can awaken forces which until then have lain fettered inside a person; they can unleash a spontaneous urge to emulate the hero's deeds—as, for example, when Daniel, tried to imitate the Viking king Olav Tryggvason by walking along the oars while Jonas was rowing, and very near drowned. The great ideal, though, was Einar Tambarskjelve, at least for Jonas who liked archery and who, even that early on, may have been aiming too high. For once, his mother had actually matched the right words with the right person, all the way from Einar's answer to King Olaf Tryggvason's question as to what had cracked so loud: "Norway, from your hand, lord king," and the part immediately after this, when he is handed the king's weapon: "Too weak, too weak the king's sword is," to the words he speaks just before he dies: "Dark it is in the king's moot hall." The boys' blood used to run cold at the savagery of their mother's stories; folk swearing that they would heap body on body before they would surrender, teeth jangling on ice as men clove open one another's skulls, foreign weaklings praying to God to be spared from the wrath of the Norsemen. So it was thanks to many years spent in the company of the figures in his mother's more or less unlikely stories that Jonas Wergeland not only vowed to go to Miklagard, otherwise known as Istanbul, but was also imbued with a latent impulse to become a conqueror, expand boundaries and possibly also a taste for a certain belligerent lack of restraint, like the character in the Icelandic saga who kills a thrall simply "because he was there." When you get right down to it, it would not be altogether wrong to say that it was Jonas Wergeland's mother who turned him into a potential murderer.

The stories which their mother embroidered upon for the boys had been told to her by her father, the only difference being that Oscar Wergeland had read from the sagas, both from Snorre Sturlason's tales and from the Icelandic family sagas, so he had passed far more accurate versions of the tales to little Åse and Lauritz—the latter conscientiously followed up this upbringing, of course, by becoming the captain on a succession of DC planes in the SAS fleet, all named after Viking heroes. And Oscar did not just read them stories, he also told them stories from his own life that, in their turn, had given him his insatiable interest in the sagas and the Viking age in general.

In his youth, Jonas's maternal grandfather had from time to time visited an uncle who had a farm down near Onsøy. On one such occasion, when he was helping prepare the ground for the building of a new house, they came upon the remains of a ship, along with various artefacts. While it could not match the greatest treasure trove found in Norway: gold weighing a total of five and a half pounds, it still fired the imagination; there had been one sword hilt in particular which his grandfather had been much taken with—years later he was still able to sketch it on a piece of paper for his children.

Their mother had to tell this story for Daniel and Jonas time and time again; for all I know she may well have thrown in a couple of elements from Oehlenschläger's poem about the Golden Horns found in Denmark. Jonas could just picture it: you go out to the field one day to plough or lift potatoes and suddenly you're unearthing the history of Norway. Jonas never really got that out of his head: it could even be that he also applied it to other areas of his life. After all, since large amounts of gold had been buried during periods of unrest in Viking times, and since most of it still lay hidden in the ground, with a little luck at any time you might stumble on something valuable. Jonas had fantasies of finding treasures of undreamed-of worth if he so much as rolled away a stone in the forest. He also knew how these things would look: exactly like the bowl-shaped dragon brooch Aunt Laura had given his mother, with its pattern of intertwining lines.

As I say, it was his mother, or his mother's stories that determined where many of the family's trips took them—even his father and Rakel, who were really both living in worlds of their own, meekly went along with her choices. Daniel and Jonas called these jaunts Viking raids, and that's possibly quite true: these trips were a combination of holiday and business, colonization and fierce combat—the boys taking care of the latter. In this way the family had covered the length and breadth of southern Norway, seen everything from rock engravings and cairns to ancient roadways and battlefields, from the tumulus at Haug by the shores of Karmsundet just north of Hafrsfjord, to Kaupang in Vestfold, from Raknehaugen Barrow in Ullensaker to the rune stones at Vang Church in Valdres. On these trips they immersed themselves so deeply in the world of the sagas that on one occasion, after they had pretty much cleaned out a roadside hotdog stall, Daniel had burped contentedly and said, "The King has fed us well."

This interest in the Vikings went so far that their mother even took the boys down to the Akers Mek shipyard at Pipervika one day late in the autumn of 1966 to see the oil rig *Ocean Viking*, which was nearing completion. "These will be the new Viking ships," she said reverently, having gazed long in wonder at this giant.

And now, on a day in May of that same year—a month full of long holiday weekends—they were on the way to Stiklestad, scene of the famed battle in which King Olaf II was slain. Jonas was in a bad mood. He had been a bit tetchy—spoiling for a fight, you might say—for some time, mourning as he was for his lost love, for Margrete's treacherous rejection of him and ditto departure from the country. They stopped for the night at Røros, also in its way a historic monument, albeit of more recent date than the Viking remains. The old mining town had an unreal beauty about it, as it lay there bathed in the copper light on the plateau, so unique that it would come as no surprise to anyone that it would soon be added to UNESCO's World Heritage List, right up there alongside the Great Pyramid of Cheops and the Great Wall of China.

Each time the family arrived at a new place they followed the same two-fold ritual. The first thing they did, therefore, was not to visit the slagheaps or the old mines at Bergstaden but to march straight to the town ironmonger in a body, to check that they stocked G-MAN saws and possibly ask whether they had remembered to place a new order with the wholesaler if they had run out. In other words, half an hour after their bags had been lugged into the guest house, the Hansen family were to be found in the Bergmannsgata premises of M. Engzelius and Son, one of Røros's time-honored establishments, asking stern-faced and as with one voice almost, to see their selection of saws, and at least four members of the family breathed a sigh of relief when a baffled sales assistant showed them the wall on which the G-MAN saws were displayed exactly as they should be, because they knew that their mother showed no mercy if anything was missing—particularly if it was the new G-Mini saw, the very flagship of the Grorud Ironmonger's range, called after the Gemini space rocket and equipped most ingeniously with two different blades, so that it could be used either for meat or logs, an innovation which was nothing short of world-shattering. Entire holidays could be ruined by ironmongers with negligent buyers, or shopkeepers who simply did not stock "the world's best saw." Sometimes their mother would go quite berserk: "Haven't you heard about the drive to sell Norwegian-made products!" she would shout, shaking her fists at a terrified shop assistant.

In the second part of this ritual, which was almost a way of conquering the town, they trooped after their father up to Bergstaden's mighty white Ziir, which is to say the octagonal stone church. Their father had called from the guest house and made an appointment with the organist, so that he could at least see the famous old baroque organ that, sadly, had just broken down and would have to be repaired. Instead he was allowed to try out the brand-new, Czechoslovakian main organ. "Play some Bach, Dad!" Daniel yelled up at the little door in the side, behind which his father was taking his seat, as if here too the whole point was to put the speedometer into the red. And their father played Bach while the rest of the family sat proudly in a pew in the center of the lovely, light church, listening. Thinking back on it as an adult, it seemed to Jonas that his father made love to churches when he played. That his father made conquests of churches rather than women. That his aim in life was to play in as many churches as possible. Haakon Hansen may have been a sober-minded character, but when it came to organs he was a real Don Juan.

So, for Jonas, Norway was a network of organs and ironmongers, music and steel—he had a feeling that life itself must consist of just such a combination, of something soft and something hard. And no weekend jaunt was more perfect than on those occasions when his mother's and his father's interests conjoined, in places that had both a fine organ and an ironmonger stocking a wide range of G-MAN saws—plus, since this was of course their excuse for being there, an interesting rune stone.

Although Jonas liked Røros—the buildings and the landscape appeared so alien and intriguing that he pretended he was in Ulan Bator in Mongolia—he was feeling a bit despondent that night as he stood alone in front of the mirror in the bathroom. They had booked in to one of those atmospheric inns in the museum-piece street that ran down to the church, a place that had retained some breath of history from the days when Røros had been a pulsating mining community. His parents were sleeping in one room, the three children in another, with a shared bathroom.

As Jonas stood there in his pyjamas, brushing his teeth, his thoughts turned to Margrete, back to Margrete, who had chucked him; and it was then, as he was standing there, cosseting his broken heart, that he noticed the strange box on the shelf below the mirror, and it couldn't possibly be a powder compact, so he had to open it. He was not so stupid that he didn't recognize it for what it was. His mother's diaphragm. He gazed at the rubber ring, at first panic-stricken because for a second or so he thought that it was the same size in diameter as the vagina and could not imagine how his little penis could ever fill such a huge space. On reflection, though, he realized that that could hardly be the case. A sudden surge of excitement hit him, a sense of expectation not unlike the thrill he had felt the first time he found his mother's pack of sanitary towels on top of the geyser in the bathroom at home: Sheba, the name alone had set his spine jangling, set him thinking about realms which seemed as exotic and remote as the queen's little blue face, Egyptian-like on the pack.

Jonas stands in that bathroom in Røros, staring at himself in the mirror, then drops his gaze and spies something else lying next to the diaphragm. His father's razor. These two objects represented a mysterious beauty, like a dome and a minaret. Or something soft and something hard. Jonas felt that this situation called for a creative act, a combining of these two objects. The sight he beheld here cried out for a make-believe fight, with the razor as a sword and the diaphragm a shield clashing together in a great battle—on the field at Stiklestad for example. Alongside the razor lay a razorblade. With his fingertips Jonas lifted it, made a cut in the thin rubber membrane of the diaphragm, not very long and close up against the elastic ring, where it was all but invisible; he put the diaphragm back in its box, closed the lid. The way he saw it he had pressed a button. Now what would happen?

He lay in bed—Rakel and Daniel were already fast asleep—listening to his mother and father in the bathroom, could hear that they were in high good humour, laughing softly, that it was one of those nights. Jonas lay on his back, looking up at some knotholes in the boards of the ceiling and smiling to himself in the grey half-light. It was as if only now did he understand the wisdom of the sagas, those pithy sayings. Because if he had ever been asked why he had done what he did, he wouldn't have been able to come up with any other explanation either, except: "Because it was there."

At breakfast, while Rakel was studying the map and his father was wondering whether he would be allowed to play the organ in Nidaros Cathedral, their mother told them about a dream she had had. "I met a white elephant," she said. "And would you believe, I dreamed that it wrapped its trunk around me and lifted me high into the air." She laughed, nudged their father in the arm. "Pass me the jam, Daniel, and stop playing the Battle of Stiklestad here at the table at least."

Only Jonas suspected that she might have been impregnated by that white elephant, that for several hours now a Buddha had been in the making.

Cape

Whence come our dreams? The past or the future?

It is a bright, clear morning, already warm, and he is making his way into the center with all his senses in top gear. He strolls through the vestiges of the Company's Gardens and on down Adderley Street, then turns right into Golden Acre, the new, ultra-modern shopping center and there, ahead of him, is the Grand Parade, an open square with a low and not particularly impressive fortress in the background. The air is heavy with unfamiliar smells. He is tense, tries to shake the feeling off, but he is tense. He sees stalls selling fruit and vegetables and, on closer inspection—yes, sure enough—next to them a flea market. It all fits, he thinks. So far.

It was the first morning in a new city, and the dream had been fresh in his mind when he woke up. He had dreamed that he met a woman dressed in white at a flea market and that she had asked him the way to Greenmarket Square—he remembered this with strange clarity: Greenmarket Square. And that she was wearing a labyrinthine brooch. Jonas did not set any great store by his dreams, unless it was for their entertainment value, but suddenly it occurred to him that this could be important, not to say crucial, as far as his life was concerned. After breakfast, just to be on the safe side, he enquired at reception as to whether there was a flea market in the city. He was in luck, they said, it was Wednesday, so there was a market on the Parade. "Do you have a map?" Jonas asked, not so much intrigued as perturbed.

So there he was, threading his way between tables that were, for the most part, covered in junk, when a young woman—obviously a tourist like himself and dressed in clothes that seemed far too white, giving her the appearance of an angel paying a visit to a trouble-torn world—approached him and asked him the way to Greenmarket Square. Jonas had studied the map and gave her exact directions, possibly too long and involved—partly to mask his own inner turmoil—on how to get there, all the while with his eyes riveted on her brooch, as if a much more interesting map lay hidden there, in its pattern. She thanked him with a laugh, she too a little confused. For the rest of the day he walked around in a daze, with no idea of where he was; he was simply waiting for the night, for new dreams.

No one can say that Jonas Wergeland rested on his laurels. In the midst of his triumph, in the year when the television series *Thinking Big* was broadcast to great general jubilation, he was to be found in South Africa, armed with a visa and the blessing of the Norwegian Foreign Office. He was on his way home from South Georgia where they had just finished shooting a program on the old Norwegian whaling stations and had made a brief stopover on the Cape. To celebrate the success of the shoot he checked into the hotel in Cape Town, the Mount Nelson, which, with its stately atmosphere and its situation on the hillside above the city center truly was a place fit for a lord.

The following morning he sat at the breakfast table deep in thought, reviewing his night. He had dreamed that he was a hairsbreadth from being run down by a white Ford. The grapefruit he was eating reinforced a sour-sweet sensation inside him; he also noted how the halved fruit resembled a wheel. He was possibly overreacting, but he decided to tread warily, took care when crossing the road that same morning when looking around the Bokaap district of the city, the old Malay quarter where the city's Muslims had made their homes. Having first visited the Auwal Mosque on Dorp Street he then attacked the steep, narrow streets climbing up the slope to Signal Hill.

He was about to cross the street just next to one of the little mosques in Chiappini Street when his attention was caught by a spicy aroma. This moment's distraction was all it took for him almost to be hit by a white Ford that came racing down the hill. The driver banged on his horn, and Jonas jumped back onto the pavement. And as he was standing there gasping for breath, with people staring at him and his heart pounding, he realized that he liked this, these sudden tie-ups between dreams and reality. He was actually more exhilarated than shaken, as if he had just come alarmingly close to an irascible rhino on a safari where everything, even those things which seemed dangerous, was safe and stage-managed.

But he did not know what to think when he was jolted out of sleep at dawn the next morning in his bed at the Mount Nelson; his testicles felt has if they had been caught in a nutcracker. He had dreamed of falling, of riding on a cable railway, dreamed that the car he was in fell down, fell and fell until it smashed to pieces on the ground.

Jonas had not been planning to do it, to take the trip up Table Mountain, he was afraid of heights. Now he had to. His whole body craved it, his throat constricted with excitement. Why did Jonas Wergeland travel? To say that he wanted to expose himself to risk, to rebel against his innate penchant—not least as a Norwegian—for security, is only half the truth. There were some moments when Jonas Wergeland actually believed that travel was training for death. Training in cutting all ties. As a boy, when they played "knifey" he was never as interested in winning a bigger slice of territory as he was in the knife itself, everything which the knife, the sharp steel, represented in terms of danger and fateful possibilities; one quick slash through normality and all at once you found yourself in the complete unknown.

While still in the taxi on the way up to the lower cableway station on Taffelberg Road he noticed how his senses were stimulated by the forthcoming feat of daring, how he was seeing in a new way, spotting the oddest details in his surroundings. He also registered a flutter of impatience, as if he were keen to get this over as quickly as possible, as if he were longing to die. Once he was actually inside the gondola he forced himself to look down into the void while he thought about his dream, all the way up, for six or seven minutes, even thought he hated it, felt sick with fear. Or no, not fear. The whole experience was more like being on a high: being hauled through the air by a cable while the seconds tick away, a question of will it, won't it, will it, won't it; but nothing happened. Naturally nothing happened. And yet: it could have happened.

He alighted at the upper station, wandered around for half an hour on the top of the vast landmark, over three and a half thousand feet above sea level, a mountain so flat that from the sea it looked like a table covered with a tablecloth. His grandfather had raved about it. Jonas walked about, reading posters but not taking in anything of what he was reading, surveyed the view without seeing what he was surveying, looked into the restaurant and the souvenir shop without really being there, without buying anything. His feet were on solid ground, but he felt as if he were balancing on a knife's edge. A narrow promontory that could split his life in two.

It happened on the way down. He was alone in the gondola with an elderly man who stood with one hand tucked inside his jacket, like another Napoleon. Few tourists visited the country in those days, even fewer at that time of year. The wind had risen a little, but the weather was fine; the sea sparkled brilliantly in the south, as a reminder, almost, of how rich in diamonds the country was. The man immediately struck up a conversation, he was from Cape Town himself, brightened up when Jonas mentioned Norway, showed him his stick: "See what that is?" he said eagerly, nodding at the handle. And then, triumphantly: "Whalebone."

It might have been because of his grandfather, but Jonas could almost foresee what happened next. The man pointed down at Table Bay and the harbor and began to tell him about all the Norwegian whale fishermen who had passed through the city. "Some of the harpooners lived here all year round, you know." The man knew something of the whaler's life, he had delivered food to the ships when they were bunkering. "Canned fruit was popular," he said. "Peaches especially." Within a couple of minutes he had told a great deal about Norwegians and Cape Town. "And it's no secret," he chuckled, "that a fair number of babies with Norwegian blood in their veins have been born here."

They were a third of the way down. Jonas observed that the wind had freshened; the gondola was rocking noticeably. He felt afraid, and yet was conscious of how concentrated everything was, even what the man was saying. A life crumpled up into a few seconds. Usually Jonas preferred to maintain a discreet silence on the subject of Norway and whales. The images from South Georgia were still fresh in his mind: the ghost towns at Husvik and Grytviken, the rusty storage tanks, half-sunken whaling ships, a deserted flensing plan forming a slanting dance floor for the penguins. The whale population around South Georgia is still as little as ten per cent of what it once was. In some seasons nigh-on 8,000 whales could be caught in those waters. A total massacre.

"Great city," the man said, peering out. "Shame about all the blacks, ruin everything so they do. Fucking and fighting's all they know. Animals. Bloody animals." The man's knuckles whitened around the handle of his stick.

Jonas did not feel like getting into a discussion with this character, he merely shook his head, unconsciously almost, and went on gazing at the view.

This only goaded the other man: "And please don't talk to me about racism. I happen to be one of those people who rate the whale very highly among God's creatures. I think it really is as intelligent as we are. But I'd never dream of criticizing you lot for hunting it. So you can't bloody well blame us for doing to the kaffirs—inferior beings that they are—what you've done to the whale. In fact, we ought to take a leaf out of you Norwegians' book. Do a really radical cull."

Just as Jonas was about to protest at this comparison, out of common decency, if nothing else, the gondola stopped. A twang. Like a pizzicato note from a violin string. Something was wrong.

He tried not to look down and instead gazed out at the water, a carpet of diamonds; he had never seen an ocean sparkle like that, so bright, so dazzling. But the man was not to be sidetracked; he was visibly incensed. "Don't you come here acting all holier-than-thou," he said. "We're the same, you and I. Your lot got rich on whaling. We got rich through the blacks. You should be downright proud of Svend Foyn. Inventing the grenade harpoon puts him in the same league as Hiram Stevens Maxim, the man behind the machine-gun."

They hung quietly between heaven and earth. Jonas was waiting for the jerk, a twang, as from Einar Tambarskjelve's bowstring, and then the fall, one fleeting second and it would all be over. To win a new land: death. "But you're forgetting one thing," he said stubbornly, or as a way of escaping his fear. "We don't really hunt whales any more."

"Well, there'll never be an end to apartheid, that's for sure," came the other man's curt, bitter reply. "Never. We're going to keep the blacks down for ever."

At best, if this was a valid comparison, then perhaps one day the prosperous white areas around Sea Point would lie as deserted as the rusty ruins in South Georgia, Jonas thought. He could not know that things were happening behind the scenes in South Africa, that great changes were afoot, that just after New Year speeches would be made in the South African parliament, in this same city below him, which no one could have predicted and which would make a whole world believe that one truly could round a cape by the name of Good Hope.

Jonas could not resist it; he had to look out, down at the steep scree beneath them. His life hung, quite literally, by a thread, a cable.

His whole life depended on cables. He had known it for a long time.

There came a jolt. In his heart too. An echo inside him. The gondola started to move. Minutes later they were down. He stepped out, but his legs would not carry him; he dropped down onto a bench. The elderly man got into a waiting car, raised his stick to him before he drove off. Jonas couldn't have said whether this was meant as a threat or a salute. But one thing he understood: we know nothing about what our dreams mean. And we know nothing, thank heavens, about what the future holds. We can never know what will happen the next second, the next day, the next year.

On the way to Greenmarket Square, moments after they had barely missed running into a man who dashed across the road, the taxi driver told Jonas that he had had the same dream three nights running: a whale swam in from Robben Island—the driver pointed across the glittering waters to the north-west—and coughed up a man on the beach at Sea Point, a black man wearing a royal crown. Now what did Jonas make of that?

You Should Have Heard That Chord

It was not until the end of the sixties that Jonas Wergeland's decision finally ripened, the one for which he had been searching for, dreaming of, impatiently and more or less constantly, ever since that day in the quarry years before: it was within the realms of music that he would become a king, conquer new territory.

Jonas had been playing the piano since the start of second grade and unlike a lot of children he actually enjoyed it. He did not think this had anything to do with his father, with having watched his father's blissful face bent over the keys for as long as he could remember. It had to be due to a talent, to skills that had been slumbering inside him and which were now, at long last, being awakened. He had also been taking lessons, though with a different teacher from Daniel—both out of an inveterate need to do the very opposite of his brother and out of a sense of premonition. Daniel went to a lady who lived at the top of Bergensveien, while Jonas went in quite the opposite direction, to a teacher who lived on the other side of Trondheimsveien. As their names suggest, these were two widely diverse addresses: almost, so it would prove, like two different continents. Not surprisingly, Daniel chose his piano teacher according to his own, monomaniacal criteria, which were based more on an assessment of her physical attributes than her gifts as a teacher. So while Daniel had a teacher who tickled the hairs on the back of his neck with jutting breasts every time she leaned over him from behind to show him how to play the part over which he had just stumbled—more often than not on purpose—Jonas had a musical cicerone who galvanized his ears with lilting notes. And while for Daniel, right from the start, practice was a chore—his "I" pitted against the piano—exercises were sheer hell, and the pieces themselves pearls cast before swine, Jonas experienced some of the pleasure promised by music books with titles such as *The Piano and Me*, *Exercises are Fun*, and *Pearls from the Baroque*.

What sort of sound does a dragon make?

Jonas's teacher lived in a spacious villa next door to the vicarage, on holy ground you might say, where lessons were overseen, not to say inspired, by "the four greats": Bach, Haydn, Mozart, and Beethoven, whose semi-divine visages looked down from their frames on the living-room wall. If Jonas turned his head he could see the whole of the Grorud Valley spread out before him outside the window, as if the music lifted him up to the heavens, an impression which was reinforced by the smell of the place, since the kitchen always contained some freshly-baked wonder, plump Christmas cakes or plaited loaves, and thus the dances and ballads, marches and rhapsodies gave the illusion of making his mouth water. As a way of rounding off the lesson he would often sit with a fresh slice of coffee ring in his hand, listening while Fru Brøgger, who had the longest, slenderest fingers he had ever seen, demonstrated how Chopin's "Minute Waltz" really could be played in a minute—a feat so incredible that his ears just about fell off.

Fru Brøgger and her sensitive fingers may have been something of a rarity, who am I to say; at any rate, she was quite liable to interrupt a lesson so that they could watch the birds on the bird table in the garden instead; sometimes they even went out onto the steps to hear them singing, especially in the spring. Her real stroke of genius, however, was that as well as teaching him the obligatory short pieces, she also allowed Jonas to feel his own way into the world of music, making it a kind of game in which he could discover all its different elements: triads, tempo, dynamics or the mystery of major and minor. She allowed him, to use a high-flown word, to improvise. So—my apologies for getting carried away here—God bless the exceptions like Fru Brøgger, and the Devil take all those who kill an inquisitive child's pleasure in playing the piano by making them slog away at exercises in fingering and legato playing—not that these aren't necessary at a certain stage, but at other times they act as a total barrier to the art itself, to what music is: timbre, rhythm, melody.

With Fru Brøgger this was how it worked: instead of having to struggle through a saraband by Bach come hell or high water, particularly if she could hear that Jonas had not practiced enough, they might play with the cycle of fifths—if, that is, she wasn't telling him something about harmonics or the demanding nature of the contrapuntal technique. And in due course she introduced Jonas to the liberating world of jazz, with the aid of composer Maj Sønstevold's little, but extremely stimulating, *Jazz ABC*. Nor did Fru Brøgger neglect to tell Jonas an anecdote that taught him something important about the love of music and a certain way of looking at life. Briefly told, it was a story about Maj's husband, Gunnar Sønstevold, also a composer, who had come home one day and told his wife that he had been helping to move a big piano, only it had slipped out of their hands on the bend in the stairs and flown out of the window on the fifth floor. And in describing this incredible incident to Maj: how the piano had hit the ground with a crash, all he said was: "You should have heard that chord!"

After all these years with Fru Brøgger, with birds and minute waltzes and fresh-baked coffee ring, it was not surprising that it should be within the field of music that Jonas would spy a potential for conquest, or that he should first consider chords as posing the greatest challenge. It came to a point where he was practicing for as much as two hours every day, to the great annoyance of the rest of the family. Buddha, when he appeared on the scene, was the only one who could not get enough of it, especially when it came to chordal improvisations, always crawled over and sat close to the piano when Jonas was playing.

And so it was in that legendary year of revolution, with students all over the Western world seething with unrest, Jonas Wergeland had his—oh, why not: revolutionary—musical vision, and it struck him with such force that he almost fell of his stool. For once he was alone at home, sitting at the piano, running his fingers over the keys when he—or rather: his fingers, his body—suddenly began to produce rhythmic patterns, he tried alternating between the white keys and all the black ones; the resultant effect went straight to his head, he produced increasingly electrifying tones, kept repeating the chords, building them up into a crescendo while continually altering the rhythm; it was amazing, he got more and more carried away, discovered new harmonies, new rhythms, felt his body all but lifting off the piano stool, felt himself becoming hypnotized by what he had created, rhythms that grew more and more frenetic, according with everything going on inside him, the turbulent events of the last few years, not least an upsetting incident that had occurred only a few weeks earlier—we're getting there, Professor, we're getting there—one which was in no way eclipsed by the sight of a piano crashing to the ground from a fifth-floor window. He also understood, for the first time, the extract he had copied down earlier from one of the books sitting disregarded in the bookcase—a legacy, a score of old volumes—from the postscript to Hector Berlioz's memoirs, to be precise, which said that, as Berlioz saw it, music comes down to passionate expression, inner intensity, rhythmical drive, and a quality of unexpectedness. All at once Jonas felt strong, full of self-confidence, like a Hector, a hero, a giant.

From then on he gave himself up to composing. He was only fifteen, but pretty well schooled in musical notation. He learned the most complicated passages by heart anyway, if they did not simply stick in his memory after a few playings. That whole year, spring, summer, autumn, he was obsessed with this, he was convinced, in the mind-reeling way one can only be at the age of fifteen, that he was in possession of an explosive idea, something that had never been heard before, nothing less than a brand-new path for music to take, an incredibly bold concept, and one which called, above all, for courage. By God, it would have consequences for the whole concept of what music is, Jonas thought.

He knew it would take time, that it would take him years, but he wanted to proclaim his discovery now, as if he were anxious to take out a patent for this sensational invention as quickly as possible. And so he devised a way of trying out his magnificent vision in a simplified form: a piece for the piano he called "Dragon Sacrifice," to be played on Pupils' Night, the concert that rounded off the autumn term.

I do not know if the words "Pupils' Night" make you shudder, Professor, but you can take it from me that such evenings were pure torture, even at Fru Brøgger's, a kind of purgatory that had to be undergone before one attained the paradisiacal state of the holidays. On such evenings the mums and dads made up the audience, and the bunch of spruced-up children had, as it were, to show their parents that their money had been well spent or, what was far more difficult, that all that fractured pounding on the keys which had disturbed their newspaper reading had actually borne fruit. As I say, most people's idea of a nightmare.

But not for Jonas Wergeland, or at least not on this December evening, because he was about to give the assembled company a foretaste of his triumph, something which they would recall as a milestone, a work which maybe—he thought, he dreamed—even at this stage would be seen for what it was: a change of course, the cutting of the first sod for a totally new road.

Pupils' Night arrived. In the one half of Fru Brøgger's L-shaped living room sat the expectant parents—from Jonas's family his father, Haakon Hansen—and at the other end, out of sight, the nervous pupils huddled together in panic-stricken solidarity. In the middle, for all to see, stood the grand piano, which was only used on such grand occasions, that in itself a responsibility—one which was further underlined by the fact that the lid was raised, like the sail of a majestic black ship. Fru Brøgger, almost unrecognizable in evening dress, introduced her pupils with a few kind words meant to lighten the mood—to no avail, of course.

The youngest children played first, little more than scales really, to loud applause no matter how often they stumbled. And so it progressed, in ascending order of difficulty rather than age, perhaps. Fru Brøgger was saving Jonas for last, even though she had not heard his piece, he had simply asked if he could play one of his own compositions. "It's better than that blasted Rachmaninoff prelude," he declared. A tolerant and in truth rather curious Fru Brøgger yielded to this shameless show of bravado.

It went well; children played études and minuets, some very well, others making ghastly mistakes, one of them even had a total mental block—the one thing everybody dreaded. And then it is Jonas's turn, the audience know he is good, son of the organist, they have heard him play before, remember the time he played the second movement of the "Pathétique" sonata so beautifully that it brought a lump to the throat, they nod and whisper to one another; Jonas steps out, catches a glimpse of the whole Grorud Valley spread at his feet and glittering like the promise of a reward outside the window, before he bows and people clap; he is a conqueror, he is about to present his new kingdom, he sits down at the grand piano, as if at a gigantic lacquered casket, from whose lid he will call up a dragon. Or—the thought suddenly strikes him—a radio play.

He is trembling with excitement. But also with self-confidence. He feels the approving eyes of "the four greats" on his back.

He strikes the keys. A shock attack. An explosive clang, varied and repeated in unconventional rhythms. He is aware, even though he is concentrating on his playing, of the jolt of surprise that runs through the audience—many of whom he knows. For this is no safe invention by Bach or a nice little sonata by Mozart and most definitely not an old chestnut like the second movement of the "Pathétique" sonata, but Jonas Wergeland's own bold composition; it is Pupils' Night and one of the darkest days of the year, aptly enough, since Jonas Wergeland is playing "Dragon Sacrifice" on a black grand piano: an evocation of the battle between weak, waning light and vast darkness. The music has to do with harvest, with people holding a sense-inflaming sacrificial ceremony: Vikings perhaps, pagans who worship the forces of nature; a savage ritual designed to compel the light to return, or to achieve complete and utter darkness, who knows; a ceremony which will grow wilder and wilder.

Rhythm is the cornerstone: rhythm and not much else. It is music for a new age. Jonas has created startling, jangling chords that he builds into a variety of rhythmic progressions, at the same time alternating between different tempos. Now and again, particularly towards the end, he plays the same discordant—to the listeners' ears, that is—tone again and again, at a furious tempo for over a minute, he feels people starting to squirm in their seats, clearly ruffled, or riled, as if this is like torture to them, or a kind of rape. He has also discovered something he calls "laughter harmony," a combination of two different, conflicting chords played high up on the descant, a glorious, devilish dissonance which he slams out at regular intervals, like a spark in the darkness, wanting to give the audience a sensation, through their hearing, of something very, very primitive, something revoltingly immoral, something which is going totally berserk. And yet, as he sits there, conscious with one part of his mind of the gleaming, black surface of the piano, so like the lacquer on his grandfather's old casket, he is suddenly overwhelmed by the beauty of this barbaric piece of music. With something close to alarm he notices how it becomes more and more beautiful—to his ears, that is—how an inexplicable, ecstatic sense of well-being spreads throughout his body as he hammers out these dissonant chords, producing a sound which borders on the threshold of pain, the whole thing culminating in a crescendo that goes on and on, one which, in his own mental picture of the music, does not stop at one lousy *fortissimo* but has an *ffff* written into it; and finally, with both forearms and the pedal, he bangs out a chord that sounds like something huge and heavy, enormous black wings, crashing to the ground—a dragon. It's marvellous, it's crazy. It's brilliant, he thinks to himself. He stands up, bows. He knows what they will say when they get home, or when they tell their friends about it: "You should have heard that chord!"

No applause. Utter silence.

Haakon Hansen clears his throat. Claps.

God bless fathers like Haakon Hansen.

Fru Brøgger begins to clap too. Everyone else claps, hesitantly and not for long. Fru Brøgger smiles. A genuine smile. "Well, I must say . . ." she begins, "that really was . . ." She has to let her long, slender fingers form the words she cannot find. "But now it's time for a bite to eat," she says, because refreshments were always served after the actual concert: smørbrød, incomparable freshly-baked coffee ring, of course, lemonade and coffee, before the evening continued with some informal games, usually including one in which you had to run around finding little pictures of birds and putting names to them.

Jonas walked home with his father, the latter with his arm round his son's shoulder. Haakon started to say something then stopped and instead gripped Jonas's shoulder even tighter, gave him a little shake.

God bless fathers like Haakon Hansen. Fathers who could say something, and would be quite right, but do not say anything.

So it was left to Fru Brøgger to bring Jonas back down to earth, or whatever you want to call it. He had one lesson left before Christmas and was looking forward to discussing his composition. When he entered the living room Fru Brøgger was standing with her back to him, watching some great tits hopping about among the bushes in the snow-covered garden—an idyllic Christmas-card scene. "Come here," she said. "Look." Jonas positioned himself next to her. Without turning she stroked his back once.

"I'm not sure I ought to be doing this," she said, walking over to a cupboard and taking out a record. "But I think it's for the best. In the long run." Jonas watched as those long, slender fingers removed the black record from its sleeve and right away he knew that this was another puck, a black disc that would shatter a dream. She put on the record, turned up the sound. Loud. Jonas listened with pounding heart to the music that poured out of the two loudspeakers at the other end of the room.

He gave a start. He could not believe it. He started because he was hearing his own piece. Not exactly the same, obviously. And the parts that were similar were, of course, a lot better. An awful lot better. But still. His own piece. The concept. They stood and heard it to the end. A torment and a shock. He thought of a puck skimming silently across the ice, appearing out of nowhere, and an exquisite monument crashing down in a cascade of light, shards flying in all directions, a pearl he would never find again.

"Igor Stravinsky," Fru Brøgger said. "We haven't played anything by him yet."

"When?" was all he said, his last hope—a straw—that the answer would be last year, yesterday.

"Before the First World War," she said. "Fifty-five years ago." She didn't need to add this last, but she said it, knew she had to say it.

Jonas stood there in the center of the room with "the four greats" in their frames behind him. He heard a quick laugh. A devilish harmony played high up on the descant. A dragon. Or a chord from a piano crashing to the ground from the fifth floor—he could not say. Someone had had his groundbreaking idea about music half a century ago. For years, someone, a whole world had inhabited that landscape which he had imagined to be deserted. The concept had been perfected, used up, milked of all potential.

He was devastated. He felt—and only a poet's analogy can capture his state of mind—like a Napoleon crippled in his first battle. In his mind, his whole future had been based on this: that he had the power to create something new. He could always improve upon his technique, but he now knew that he did not possess the one thing that really counted: a capacity for original thought. One could of course say that Jonas Wergeland was not being fair to himself, that one cannot judge one's life at the age of fifteen, that it is perfectly possible to think along new lines even when one has never done so before—the early works of many great composers weren't all that impressive either—but for Jonas the impatient, for Jonas Wergeland the perfectionist, this, this composition was his to be or not to be. Fru Brøgger's revelation confirmed what he had, deep down, feared most of all: he was a mediocrity. The commonest little mongrel, as his uncle had once said. That was his fate. He just knew it. He could postpone it, fight for ten years at least against this knowledge, but the verdict would still be the same: he would always be a charlatan. One who, although he managed to hide it from an audience—other mediocrities—merely imitated the creations of true conquerors. He would have to wrestle with the worst of all fates: to have planted within him a lofty goal, a goal so manifestly right, so enticing that he could never forsake it, but at the same time lack the aptitude to achieve it.

He could not bear to stay there, Fru Brøgger walked him to the door, stroked his back again. Wordlessly she handed him a slice of coffee ring, as if he were a little kid, he thought, a little kid in need of comforting. "Give it to the birds," he said and was gone.

He had never seen as many great tits as he did on the way home. The males were strung out like infuriating yellow notes along the black lines of the tree branches. The words rang in his head: Great tit! You great tit! He swore that he would never touch a piano again.

It was snowing. On impulse he made for the church, thinking of suicide, thinking that he was on his way to his own funeral.

What cracked so loud? He heard the question sung out all around him? Norway from my hand, he thought.

Bronze Age

But then there came those unexpected ups, signs that there was more to him. Could be more. He might be standing, let's say, in the middle of a heap of stones and suddenly feel a pressure building up, feel all of his ordinariness, the various bits that went to make up his self shuffle themselves around and fall into a new pattern—or, why not: crystallized in a different way—so that he positively sensed, in every bit of himself, the possibility of assuming a different carat. Or, to be more specific: I'm talking about the summer out on Hvaler when he met Liv H. up at Røsset, a girl with a peeling nose and hair pulled into a thick plait that hung down her back, as bright as burnished copper. She was in high school like him, came from Larvik and was holidaying on a neighboring island. Jonas felt a button being pushed. Her I've got to have, he thought. No matter what.

"Røsset"—the reason why Liv H. had made the trip across the sound—was a Bronze Age barrow, one of those man-made mounds of stones that can be found up and down the Norwegian coast. "Wouldn't that be wonderful," she said, sitting down on the top of the landmark and looking out across the fjord towards Færder lighthouse. "To be buried under thousands of round stones shaped by the sea. And in such a fabulous spot." Jonas eyed her curiously. It turned out—he could almost have guessed it—that she wanted to study archaeology after she finished high school; nothing could be more exciting than digging into the past, she declared. And Liv H. would stay true to her dream, would in fact end up as an archaeologist of wide renown, an authority on ancient Norwegian settlements abroad, in England, Normandy, America, dating from the time when the Norsemen were usurpers, when they were conquerors. She would become famous for taking direct issue with the established research community, and for the unorthodox methods she employed in order to prove her theories: adventures that eventually also secured her membership of the celebrated Explorers Club. "It must have been some job," she said—now, I mean, talking to Jonas. "Lugging all those stones up here. I bet there's a great story hidden in this mound."

It had never occurred to him that these stones could be more than stones. It was a weird phenomenon, certainly, but the main thing was that it offered a great view of the island and the sea beyond. "Ships could probably sail in through there in the old days," she said, pointing out to the channel where the sun turned the water into silver paper. "Strange-looking vessels once dropped anchor down there and Bronze Age people came ashore to bury a great man, a chief maybe." Jonas tried to picture it, boats like the ones you saw on rock engravings, maybe with prows shaped like dragons heads. "Do you think we would find anything valuable if we managed to move away all these stones?" she asked brightly, as if she really wouldn't mind having a go, would start right away, in fact.

Although she did not know it she had made Jonas feel better. His grandfather was dead, and Jonas felt heartsick at being here now, and a bit disappointed too perhaps, since now he would never learn Omar Hansen's secret: what had been concealed in the canvas bag they found in the safe. Not only that, but he missed all the stories, the yarns from his grandfather's days with the Wilhelm Wilhelmsen shipping line. Jonas took a long look at his companion. Her skin was like bronze, her hair thick with salt, with wind and weather. Although a fresh sou'wester was blowing, she was wearing shorts and a thin, old anorak. He could clearly see that there was nothing under the anorak but her own soft curves. "Where do you think these stones come from?" she asked. "And how many years did it take the waves to grind them so smooth?" She clasped a stone in each hand, as if they were large eggs which she intended to hatch, reveal their secret. There was something in her eyes, a curiosity, an eagerness to learn which he found immensely attractive. "Archaeologists dig and dig, brush the dirt off thousands of fragments in different places," she said. "But somebody has to put all of the pieces together." He knew who she was talking about.

Liv H. had a small and rather rickety sailboat of indeterminate make, and Jonas accompanied her on several expeditions around the skerries in the weeks that followed. He soon found out that there could hardly be anything lovelier—for a teenage boy, at any rate—than a sun-bronzed girl with a peeling nose, her hand on the tiller and her eyes screwed up against the sun. One day when they had pretty much left the boat to make its own way around the marker buoys, steered by the wind and the current, they ended up off Akerøy, further north in the archipelago, with Akerøy Fort lying on an islet next to it, a building which had lain in ruins for years but was now to be restored. Liv H. scanned the fort closely and made some observations about ancient fortress styles that made Jonas's mind boggle, before they went ashore on Akerøy itself, a nature reserve with only one white house nestling among rocky knolls and soft grassy hills, a cottage used in the spring and autumn by ornithologists because the island was a vital resting place for migrant birds.

They were alone, apart from a figure walking to and fro among the heather and juniper some way off. "A thinker," Liv H. asserted after watching him for a while.

At one point they crossed paths with this other person, who proved to be an elderly man in an old-fashioned windcheater: tall and thin, wearing horn-rimmed glasses under a deeply furrowed brow. They fell into conversation with him, and he told them that he had recently bought a place down by the sound that ran between the two large islands just to the east, but that he had spent many a summer in the house they saw here on Akerøy. The man looked a bit like a bird himself, he had a lean head that was never at rest but kept dipping this way and that—as if he couldn't help it, Jonas thought, maybe he had some disease.

"What do you do?" asked Liv H., direct as always.

"I'm writing a book," the man said.

"A book about birds?"

"A novel."

"But why all this roaming round and round?"

"Because I think best when I'm walking, it has something to do with the rhythm."

"So in a way your walks generate stories," she said, the idea seeming to excite her.

"Well, I don't think I'd put it quite as strongly," he said. "But sentences, yes."

He had obviously taken a liking to Liv H., smiled when she told him she meant to study archaeology and especially the links between ancient cultures. "Impressive. The whole world as your field," he said. "Personally I find the question "Who am I?" is more than enough for me. You might say I'm an archaeologist who investigates the complexities of the mind. That I search for connections there."

"Such as what?" Jonas ventured to ask.

"Such as the inexplicable leaps, the hidden link, between childhood and adulthood. The bridges between the continents of the psyche are challenge enough for me." He regarded Jonas, appeared to be enjoying himself. "What if one were two? Had two identities? What would be the link, then, between 'self' and 'self'? Would it be possible to sail a conciliatory raft between the two? Show that they did still belong together, were part of the same civilization, so to speak?"

The man gazes at them intently, as if he envies them—a boy and a girl on an islet at the mouth of the fjord. "I'm thinking of bequeathing my body to the archaeologists of medicine," he says, "let them dig around a bit in there. I'd like to know what they would find. Maybe that I have a Chinese heart. That I have the large intestine of a Negro."

Although they did not know it, Jonas and his new girlfriend were standing on one of the most important islands in the history of Norwegian literature—on that island, I think it is safe to say, where most of the loveliest short stories about love have been conceived. And this man was of course Johan Borgen, who had just purchased Knatten House on Asmaløy and who, this summer, was working on a new novel.

Maybe it was Johan Borgen who really brought these two young people together, who can say? At any rate they began going for evening strolls with other teenagers, a number of them equipped with transistor radios that, because of their aerials, reminded Jonas of creatures with feelers, alternative modes of communication. They sauntered along a cart-track, buoyed up by the strains of that summer's hits, only one of which Jonas would be able later to recall: "The Long and Winding Road." Because he was becoming more and more besotted with Liv H., yearned for her body, although he didn't let it show, walked beside her among fir trees and wild flowers, laughing and joking and wondering how on earth he was going to conquer her.

One bright summer evening when they are standing on the jetty waiting for the last ferry, surrounded by seagull cries and the pungent smells of a beach at low tide, the talk comes around to school and this brings her back to her archaeology plans. "I've always wanted to seek out similarities," she says. "Some sort of correspondence, even across great distances."

"The way it is with boys and girls," he says, inspired by Johan Borgen. On his spine: that pressure, a crystal-clear sign.

She looks at him. "I hadn't thought of that." And then: "But now you mention it."

Why did these girls fall for Jonas Wergeland? I think it must have had something to do with that pressure inside him; it made an almost chemical impact on them which was as unmistakeable and effective as the visual signals of the animal kingdom, like the elephant seal's inflated nose or the peacock's tail.

One evening they wound up on Svanetangen, right on the tip, looking out to the open sea, just the two of them. Far out on the water an old fishing smack chugged past, thud, thud, thud, like a sea-borne heart. They sat down on a pebble beach, a sudden break in the rocks on which Jonas had spent many a day with his grandfather, and with Daniel who liked to build huge bonfires out of all the driftwood, onto which he could throw any tin cans that had been washed up and see the flames send them shooting gloriously skywards. To Jonas this was a beach rich in adventure and explosions, a view that evening would do nothing to diminish.

A fresh breeze was blowing, but it was not cold. She settled herself with her back against his legs, sat quietly for a long time, just watching the waves that came rolling in to break on the shingle at the water's edge, seemed mesmerized by this, the sea spray falling just short of them. All at once she began to tell him about the Gulf Stream, about a theory she had come up with, a crazy notion as to how Norway had been populated. What if people had drifted here with the Gulf Stream? From England, Scotland, Ireland. They might have done, if they had had sea-going vessels earlier than we thought. She launched into a long discourse on the possible Celtic influence on Norwegian culture, but Jonas lost the thread of it, was too preoccupied with other forces, stronger than any ocean drift: the current that flows from a boy to a girl.

She found a hollow among the pebbles, like a sort of large deck chair still warm from the sun: smooth globes patterned with lichen, like maps of unknown worlds. He lay down, she remained sitting: or rather, she put a finger to her lips, silently shushing him, before unbuttoning his trousers and pulling them down to his knees. She stroked him tentatively with her fingers, making his penis rise up, studied it for a long time, as if she were surprised, as if his member was an obelisk covered in hieroglyphics, a unique archaeological discovery. And as if intent on examining it more closely she proceeded to lick him, all over, lingeringly, paying particular attention to his testicles, sucking his stones into her mouth one after the other, as if to shift them, to uncover a treasure.

He lay back in the hollow, lapping it up: the tang of seaweed and salt, the warm fingers on the thin skin of his penis, her lips, the tip of her tongue endeavoring to trace figures on his genitals, the wind brushing over the damp patches, all while he listened to the waves breaking on the shore, a slow, steady rhythm which matched the way she was kissing him, long kisses, until—as if wishing to assure herself of a share in that organ's potency—she whipped off her shorts and climbed on top of him with her back to him, and guided his penis inside her, beginning, as she did so to roll away from him, then back towards him, heaving up and down until he began to hear gurgling sounds, or the waves made him think he heard gurgling sounds.

He looked at her naked bottom below the hem of her anorak, eyed the back of her neck, the thick plait swinging back and forth on her back. His senses were so alive, so receptive, that he was sure he could feel her clitoris rubbing against his glans as she all but rolled away from him, he remembered that the Romans had had another name for the clitoris—*naviculus*, little boat, which seemed most apt, since he had the feeling that she was taking him on a voyage, across a great ocean.

Jonas experienced an indescribable pleasure from being made love to like this, amid sea pinks and driftwood, sea spray and round, warm stones which by now seemed quite soft. She rocked and heaved before his eyes, and each time she sank down he felt as though warm water were washing over him. Jonas had never made love to anyone who moved like this, sailing off with him, you might say, riding him over the rolling waves, an image which was enhanced by the fact that the wind buffeted her anorak, so that she appeared to be sitting on a little raft, using her own body as the sail. And then it came, as it always did; she must have activated him, he thought, just as the puck was activated when he laid the brooch on top of it; something rose to the surface, suddenly, and with utter clarity. It may have been the sight of his penis that made him think of a post he had once seen. And something about a ship. Because when he made love like this he truly did feel that he was drifting along, traveling, going beyond himself. Or shortened the distance between what he was and what he could become. He sailed on until he felt that he was floating, that with her body she had lifted him into the air, that they were flying, like swans, yes, that was it, swans, into the realms of the imagination, to find a connection, the actual story, between his self and his self. For within his own stones too a tale lay buried.

In a flicker of delight he saw how she raised her hands, as if she too wanted to rise upwards; she was a boat, half-flying, half-drifting along, in a way that might have prompted her to say, as another girl did say in a similar situation: "It's like your cock has wings." Because not even in the midst of the most passionate lovemaking did any woman see Jonas Wergeland's penis as an organ built for striking or stabbing. None of his women would ever have thought of crying, as they do in the fantasy world of porno movies: "Fuck me harder!" They were more likely to say: "Love me lighter, softer." Or, as they frequently said: "Lift me higher!"

The way she sat, with her back to him, made Jonas think that he was being made love to backwards, and as the semen left his body, he did not feel as though he were spurting something out uncontrollably, but rather as if he were brushing something onto a background, that this was a process akin to tracing, summoning up, something: figures, patterns that lay hidden inside him.

The Academic

For so it is: even though life is lived forward, it is always understood backward. You turn around and behold—in awe or fear—a pattern that you are not aware of having made. Not until Jonas Wergeland killed a dragon did he understand that the following chapter was part of that story.

Jonas developed an interest in design and ornamentation at an early age, thanks to an aunt who was a goldsmith. There were periods when he spent more time in her flat in Tøyen than he did at home. And when Aunt Laura was sitting in the workshop corner of her living room, wearing her elk-skin apron and hammering silver or gold into original and much sought-after pieces of jewelry, in a light so mystical that it made Jonas think of the smiths in Norse mythology, he sat at the big table, working with charcoal—until his patience ran out, and for the hundredth time he asked her if she wouldn't tell him a tale of Samarkand. His aunt was always happy to tell him stories of her travels in the Middle East and Central Asia but never about Samarkand. She steadfastly refused. "You'll have to go there yourself," was all she said. "The day you reach Samarkand, your life will be turned upside down."

In this, arguably the most important of all the rooms of his childhood, with walls covered in copper and brass and Oriental rugs, and with a scent found nowhere else in the whole of Norway but here, since his aunt prided herself on never owning a perfume that any other Norwegian woman might own, Jonas would often sit covering large, white sheets of paper with charcoal drawings or sketches for which he used soft pencils—always with the certainty at the back of his mind that it was but a short step from graphite to diamond, since both were forms of carbon, consisting of different crystalline patterns. Aunt Laura kept pulling out more books containing reproductions of works by famous artists and laying them in front of him: "Try copying these, Jonas, now there's something to strive for." Jonas liked the feeling of the stick of charcoal on the slightly rough paper, the sight of the black particles spreading finely over the fibers of the paper—strokes which, when magnified, were revealed to be tiny, unexpected works of art in themselves; and he always felt proud if his aunt was pleased with his drawings, which is to say: if she took them into another room and fixed them. He was good at copying, much better at that than at drawing free-hand, and—apropos a certain debate in Norwegian art circles—I can tell you that Jonas Wergeland actually could draw a hand—thanks to the many attempts he had made to copy Dürer's hands. Because when it came to drawing, Dürer was his favorite—along with Rembrandt and Ruskin. Nonetheless, and however unlikely it may sound, Jonas was soon to discover lines which he found even more entrancing, and in Norway at that.

This tale began in the summer between fifth and sixth grades, on a day when he played the tourist in his own country, a day when Aunt Laura, in broad-brimmed hat and flowing garments—and made up like the Queen of Sheba—took him to the Viking Ship Museum on the island of Bygdøy, a visit which he had been looking forward to, since all of the museums he had seen up to this point had, generally speaking, been pretty dull affairs, with the odd high point, such as the Palaeontological Museum at Tøyen and the scary dinosaur skeleton on the stairway up to the Reptile Hall. One museum did, however, stand out: the Museum of Technology—the old one, that is, south of the city at Etterstad. And not so much because of the planes suspended from the roof, or the enormous model-railway layouts, which put even Wolfgang Michaelsen's in the shade; the real fun lay in all the buttons you could push: on the model of a windmill, say, to set water flowing and the millwheel turning. You placed your finger on a button and a fire engine emerged and put out a fire. Amazing! One push and you saw how a turbine drove a dynamo and the light came on—an entire industrial process activated. When Jonas stood in front of those glass cases, pushing buttons, he was never as impressed by the actual demonstration—of how Norway's power grid functioned, for example—as he was by how much was set in motion at the touch of a switch. It was the button itself, the inherent potential of the button that fascinated him.

The journey to Bygdøy was, in itself, a milestone in Jonas's life, since this was the end of the line for the bus from Grorud, so he had seen that name on the front of buses ever since he was tiny. It was only natural, therefore, that something big was bound to happen on the lovely summer's day when he went all the way, so to speak; a feeling which was confirmed as soon as he found himself standing, clad in shorts and a new, gaily-patterned Hawaiian shirt like any other tourist, outside Arnstein Arneberg's pure-white building, bathed in sunlight and surrounded by bright greenery. A cathedral and a chief's castle in one, thought Jonas solemnly.

Inside the stark, vaulted chamber, with the smell of rotten wood in the air, he was not so sure. Before him lay the Oseberg ship—it wasn't all that hot really. Pretty ordinary, if you asked him. Boring even. And it was actually a lot smaller than he had expected. He pressed on, feeling let down, spotted the Gokstad ship over to the left. More boring still. Miles away from his mother's colorful stories from the sagas. And to the right, nothing but an old wreck. What sort of thing was this to show tourists? Overgrown rowboats. How could these blackened, dried-out boards possibly have anything to do with Olav Tryggvason's proud warship, *Long Worm*?

The room straight ahead of them looked more promising, with glass cases in the center and lining the walls. Aunt Laura had nipped off to the section where works by the Viking smiths were displayed, so Jonas wandered aimlessly around until all at once he found himself face to face with a horrific-looking creature. A thing with a fearsome, gaping maw, poised to strike. And yet it had a compelling beauty. He is rooted to the spot, stands there staring. Just as at the Museum of Technology, he feels that he has pushed a button, that some great and intricate industrial process has been set in motion, that water is gushing out, turbines kicking in—only now all this is going on inside his own body. It would not be going too far to say that Jonas Wergeland was granted his vision of life while standing before that glass case—which was not altogether unlike a television screen—that the seeds of his career, his creativity, were sown here.

It was one of the animal-head posts from the Oseberg Ship. Jonas immediately took it to be the head of a dragon. By coincidence, of the four posts in their four separate glass cases, the one he had noticed first was the head attributed to an artist known as the Academic, and this would always be Jonas's favorite. Because it was not so much the shape of the creature that drew the eye, as the woodcarvings: the designs covering the head itself. Jonas had seen this before. It was just like the worm ball, and the two snakes in the quarry. And not only that: he knew now where Aunt Laura had found the pattern for his mother's lovely brooch. Jonas Wergeland stood looking at a dragon's head in the Viking Ship Museum on the island of Bygdøy feeling that he had come home. If, that is, he was not—although he did not know it—in Samarkand.

At first he thought the carvings were purely for decoration, but he soon began to make out figures amid the coils and swirls, and suddenly it dawned on him that a whole story was harbored within these lines; animals—or no: birds—stretched out into bands that were swept into curves and kinks and loops, at the same time intertwining and criss-crossing in such a way that they covered the whole surface. He could not have said how long he stood there with his nose pressed up against the glass, had no idea where he was, just looked, stared, tried to drink it in. It's like being inside a piece by Bach, he thought.

Besides which, he had been right! For years Daniel had teased him because once when he was little he had insisted that the animal on the Norwegian coat of arms had to be a dragon because of its long, jagged tail, reptilian head and flickering tongue. "It's a lion, dummy," Daniel had hooted. But now, confronted with the Academic's animal-head post, Jonas knew he was right: there's no such thing as the Norwegian Lion, but there is a Norwegian Dragon.

By concentrating hard, running his eyes along curves and lines, he managed to detect four birds in the network, two on either side of the head—possibly because of the long necks he assumed that they were swans. Jonas took his time, separating each figure from the maze, seeing how they split and looped, interwove, interlocked, a tangle of wings, legs and bits of bodies. It was delightful, unbelievable: a dragon made up of four swans, of other creatures, that is. Like looking into the dragon's brain, he thought.

Jonas stands transfixed in front of the glass case, a boy with slicked-back hair, wearing shorts and a new Hawaiian shirt, a tourist in his own country, oblivious to the sounds of feet round about him, the murmuring voices, guides speaking all sorts of different languages. What were the Viking ships, compared to this! Instinctively he understands that one could sail much further with the aid of these patterns—their significance—than on the ship itself. That they are more than just a tracery of ribbons, they are a way of thinking, something terribly concentrated. Looking at the carvings on the dragon's head Jonas felt rather like he had done the first time he saw a microchip.

Aunt Laura had noticed how taken he had been with the head, so the next time Jonas came to see her she brought out a book, not from the bookcase containing her art books, but from the exquisitely carved chest—and placed it in front of him. "Maybe you should try to copy some of the drawings in this," she said, not knowing what forces she was awakening. Because this book happened to be the third volume in the Norwegian state's magnificent series on the Oseberg ship, and when Jonas asked why these books were kept in the chest normally reserved for rare travel journals, she replied: "Because these too are about a journey. The most important journey of them all. To the kingdom of the dead."

There were two Haakons in Jonas Wergeland's life. His father and Haakon Shetelig. The one worked with traceries of notes, the other with traceries in wood. Haakon Shetelig was an archaeologist and next to Gabriel Gustafson the most important person involved in the unearthing of the Oseberg ship. He was also co-editor of the work describing this national treasure and author of the third volume, which presented a detailed study of the woodcarvings. And while Jonas was sitting drawing, trying to reproduce the designs pictured in this book, Aunt Laura recounted, in simple terms, some of what Shetelig had written, about the animal ornamentation generally and about how it had been developed into a distinctive Nordic style, most strikingly perhaps in the earlier posts, carved with the so-called gripping beasts. Even though Jonas did not understand all of it, he would always remember one statement: "This style of carving," his aunt said, "is one of Scandinavia's few contributions to art history."

Jonas sat amid all the brass and the Oriental rugs, patiently copying the inimitable illustrations in Shetelig's book, mainly those of the figures from the Academic's dragon head, including some fold-out spreads which gave a clearer idea of the composition—in other pictures individual figures from an animal pattern had been separated, or rather disentangled, from one another. What an edifying experience. Jonas felt as though he were drawing the dream that had haunted him for so many years. That he was turning something abstract into something concrete. Sometimes he had to color in the different creatures to make them easier to see, much as his big brother Daniel would later do with the interwoven source texts in the Old Testament. And it was these studies, this painstaking copying, which taught Jonas one of his most crucial lessons, one which was to have a bearing, not least, on his work with television: that Norwegians do in fact have something to contribute to world civilization. Even if imitation seems to be the mark of Norwegian art, it may be that if one goes on copying and recopying these copies, in the end it will suddenly give birth to something unique and original—something new. As if one's appendix had unexpectedly turned into a womb, to anticipate an idea with which Jonas would later become acquainted.

That summer's day on Bygdøy also endowed him with a passion for woodcarving—which fitted very well since, after the rather namby-pamby handwork of fifth grade they were now to have proper woodwork classes. And it is no exaggeration to say that Jonas displayed the most extraordinary aptitude for and, above all, delight in only one subject: woodwork. It seemed that even at this point he knew what his life's work would be, no matter which profession he chose: just once to carve a figure like the Academic's, the perfect dragon head.

As early as the autumn of sixth grade he made a start on his first head, with the woodwork teacher's blessing, since Jonas had completed the obligatory chopping boards and bowls, shelves and bats in double-quick time. The teacher, a keen fiddle-maker, even allowed Jonas to stay behind after school on those afternoons when he was working on his instruments.

Sometimes, especially at the start when he often made a wrong cut or wasn't sure how best to proceed, Jonas also took the bus out to Bygdøy alone, to see Sverre G. Sundbye, the Museum of Antiquities' resident woodcarver: which is to say, not only did he have his workshop there, round the back of the Viking Ship Museum, he did actually live there. Luckily for Jonas, just at that time Sundbye was working on a copy of an animal-head post, the one known as "the Carolingian post"—the finished result is, by the way, on display in the depository of the Antiquities collection at the Museum of History. Jonas and Sundbye became firm friends. The elderly woodcarver, who was otherwise known to be a bit of a loner, had nothing against having a little disciple and gladly taught him some tricks of the trade, as well as giving Jonas tips on tools and types of wood—and, above all else, on the greatest challenge of woodcarving: "The hardest part," Sundbye said, "is the actual composition of the design, to be able to visualize the lines, the links between one part and another, the hidden connections, if you like." In other words, it was here at the woodcarver's bench in the basement of the Viking Ship Museum that Jonas Wergeland began his apprenticeship as a television producer.

As a grown man, when he moved in to the Villa Wergeland, taking over the house from his mother, one of the first things he did was to install a woodwork bench in one of the smaller rooms and put up a cupboard in which to keep his tools, including a collection of almost fifty different wood gouges—as well as some old "Acorn" iron chisels which Sundbye had given him. This became his most fruitful pastime, to stand in this workshop with a piece of birch-wood or—when he became adept enough—maple or pear-wood in his hand, holding it up to the light, like another Michelangelo with a chunk of stone, to see whether it might contain the perfect dragon head: to stand there hour after hour, cutting away at the wood; for the fifth or sixth or seventh time in his life trying to reproduce the Academic's masterpiece, to bring it still closer to perfection. And as he was carving, following a pattern which he now knew almost by heart, it was as if he were pulling back the skin from the dragon's head to disclose the structure underneath, the veins, the nerves; and he could make believe that these interlacing bands constituted the very essence of the dragon. Inside that hideous, snarling creature there dwells something beautiful, he always thought. The swans betray the fact that the dragon's thoughts are soaring.

Although Jonas Wergeland never completed any university or college course, and although he was an artist within his own field, he thought of himself as an academic—an academic in the special sense of the word as it pertained to the Oseberg ship. Jonas Wergeland had no wish to give lectures; he wished to carve his pictures into people's heads.

The Empress

On the Friday evening when, as part of its celebrated venture *Thinking Big*, NRK screened the program on Gro Harlem Brundtland, Norway's and Scandinavia's first female prime minister, Jonas Wergeland was strolling along Bygdøy Allé, unconsciously humming the chorus of Jens Book Jenssen's old favorite "When the Chestnuts Blossom on Bygdøy Allé" because it happened to be just that time, and the chestnuts were in full bloom. Jonas had been to the Gimle Cinema to see a film starring Diane Keaton, had almost had the cinema to himself, and it was only as he was cutting across Solli plass that it occurred to him how few cars there were on the road, how few people at all: as if, while he had been sitting, all-unsuspecting, in the cinema, the city had been struck by some terrible catastrophe and only he and a handful of others had survived. Jonas Wergeland carried on down Drammensveien, then pulled up short, sensing that he was being watched; he turned and almost jumped out of his skin. He was staring straight into the face of another person. Or at least he thought it was that of another person. It took him several seconds to realize that he was standing face to face with himself. It always took him a while to recognize his own features on the television; it was as if the medium changed him, gave him a new identity. Jonas stood there watching close-ups of himself, the one constant in the series, alternating with close-ups of the prime minister, Gro Harlem Brundtland—as she was played, with great authority and uncanny accuracy, by Ella Strand, that is. It was a weird moment: Jonas Wergeland stopped in his tracks and held captive—or even, why not: seduced—by his own gaze. Suddenly he understood why the city seemed deserted: just at that moment the large majority of Norwegians were sitting at home in front of their TV screens, watching his program.

Jonas went on standing in front of that shop window on Solli plass, could not tear himself away from his own opus on Gro Harlem Brundtland, in which the key scene—to many people's surprise—took place in a Chinese home. Jonas had racked his brains for months before, with the deadline approaching for this, the last program in the series, he figured out how to present a personage as overexposed as Gro Harlem Brundtland; everything fell into place when he got wind of an incident in China which, more or less indirectly, said more than anything else about this exceptionally strong-willed and ambitious Norwegian woman and her standing, one might almost say her clout and her reputation; the name Harlem Brundtland which, in the world at large had some of the same ring of quality and dynamism to it as Harley-Davidson.

In January 1988, in her capacity as Prime Minister of Norway, Gro Harlem Brundtland visited China, land of the dragon, where she was received with full honors: a point underscored by the meeting she had with Deng Xiaoping himself—a signal which did not go unnoticed in diplomatic circles, since Deng was still the most powerful figure in the world's most populous country. The Chinese deliberately lionized Harlem Brundtland, a socialist and a woman who, by the standards of this country was, at just forty-eight years of age, very young to be a government leader. To Norwegian eyes, Gro Harlem Brundtland's trip to China must have seemed like a modern-day Viking raid, a kind of peaceful conquest.

During her visit, Chinese television did a feature on the Norwegian politician, and it was around this event that Jonas built his program: which is to say, the fact that the Chinese television station totally misread the material they had obtained. Some time earlier the prime minister's office had produced a so-called Video Press Kit on Gro Harlem Brundtland for the use of foreign television stations, to save her from constantly having to attend film shoots. This video contained footage of Gro—the first politician to become known to Norwegians by her first name—in a variety of situations, so-called stock shots, together with an information sheet, so that the stations could choose for themselves which shots they wanted to run, either to illustrate some news item on Harlem Brundtland or to use as the background to some relevant commentary.

But the Chinese broadcast the entire video, with no commentary, to every home in China which owned a television, with the result that the viewers were treated to a total of eight different episodes in which the Norwegian prime minister played the lead, separated only by some blurb and a short title in English. For Jonas, this said everything there was to be said about communication, the divide, between Norway and China. Because to an ordinary Chinese this stream of images must have seemed nigh-on incomprehensible—a bit like a silent film about head-hunters in Borneo being screened in an igloo in Greenland. So Jonas reconstructed a typical Chinese room in the studio, and in this he showed a Chinese family sitting watching this television program—he had been granted permission to use the actual video in this section of his dramatized documentary.

Thanks to some authentic exteriors—footage which Jonas had had taken of the *hutongs*, the narrow lanes and alleyways of Beijing—and thanks to the excellent Chinese extras he found among the citizens of Oslo, mainly in the restaurant trade, it looked to the viewers as though the whole sequence had been filmed in Beijing, that the scene they were witnessing here truly was taking place in one of the little houses in one of Beijing's countless, labyrinthine *hutongs* in January 1988.

It was a sight which few viewers ever forgot: a Chinese family sitting round the table eating dinner and watching the *Evening News* on CCTV1, when suddenly a twenty-minute long video about Gro Harlem Brundtland starts to roll across the screen; the Chinese family are told only that this is a film about the Norwegian prime minister, no more than that, there is no voice-over: nothing, just one sequence after another, with a blank screen in between—like a series in which none of the episodes seems to follow on logically from the one before—and in which the only language spoken is Norwegian, except for the last shot, filmed at the UN Headquarters, although that doesn't make any sense either since none of the family speaks English. Jonas showed the family chattering animatedly about the program and occasionally laughing heartily and pointing at the TV screen with their chopsticks; the father and grandfather were particularly vocal, making loud comments in a form of Chinese few, if any, Norwegians would understand.

There they sat, all well wrapped up in a room in which, in winter, the temperature never rose above 59 degrees, over their frugal meal, stewed celeriac with sweet soy sauce and boiled rice, in a room dotted with those characteristic lace cloths; with portraits of their ancestors hanging on the walls next to a landscape of Guillin—a place which Harlem Brundtland also visited on her trip; a calendar on a red cord by the door, a sideboard holding thermos flasks for boiling water as well as some small statuettes of the Eight Immortals and, beside it, in the place of honor, a television, a Peon or possibly a Panda with the plush cloth pulled back, and on the screen: Gro Harlem Brundtland, as if she too were one of the immortals—making, as she did, a succession of ghostly appearances in such widely disparate situations: on the rostrum in Parliament, standing outside the palace with her new Cabinet—and here the female members of the family noted that eight of the government ministers were women—in her office, at her home on the island of Bygdøy and so on, in all sorts of roles, evincing the same dynamism in each, maintaining the same breakneck pace, as career woman and housewife, as grandmother and government leader, party chief, electioneer and, not least, European: as Margaret Thatcher's hostess in Tromsø and as a visitor to Downing Street, this sequence clearly demonstrating Harlem Brundtland's awareness of how these days foreign policy is also a crucial factor on the domestic front.

Here Jonas killed two birds with one stone. On the one hand he managed to show what an honor, what a compliment, what an invaluable advertisement for Norway this was: Gro Harlem Brundtland and her life shown in brief sequences interspersed with bits of blurb on—potentially at least—the 150 million televisions which were already to be found in China at that time. How proud that ought to make any Norwegian feel! How symbolic: the world's most heavily populated country, now in the process of becoming a Great Power, of opening up—also via television—and there was Norway, and its prime minister, right in the thick of things.

And on the other hand, Jonas managed to show how fantastic the Norwegian premier must have seemed to Chinese eyes, what a bafflingly Utopian place Norway must seem; a country where half of the government ministers were women and where the country's leaders walked the streets and talked to ordinary people, lived in perfectly normal houses—it was almost an insult to a nation that had only just put behind it a modern-day reign of tyranny which had cost possibly as many as fifty—some said eighty—million lives, in the name of a fanatical and mistaken political strategy, in a country where you still could not criticize anyone at all openly without being ruthlessly consigned to long-term imprisonment. And after the final shot on the video, in which Harlem Brundtland was seen speaking at the United Nations General Assembly, authoritatively and in her faultless English, in her capacity as chairman of the World Commission on Environment and Development, which is to say: as the world's ambassador for the environment, the role which forged her eminent international standing and won her awards and distinctions left, right and center, Jonas had cut to footage of heavily polluted Beijing exteriors, close-ups of gunge clinging to walls, the smoke from briquette fires hanging heavily over the *hutongs* in the cold January air, as if to say that from the viewpoint of the Beijing *hutong*, all of this, an awareness of the environment, this video, Norway in general—a small society wrestling with the luxury problem of how to shift the balance from prosperity to preservation—did not matter; the Norwegian social-democracy, its queen, or empress, included, would never be anything other than an exotic postcard passing across the television screen, an almost non-existent, picture-book idyll—a fact which is confirmed by a look at a Chinese map of the world, in which Norway appears as a bracket the size of a fly dropping tucked way up in the left-hand corner, or Chinese history or geography schoolbooks, in which Norway is barely mentioned and only then in the greater context of Scandinavia or Europe in general.

In a way all of this was rendered doubly strange for Jonas as he stood outside that shop window on Solli plass, gazing through it at his own program, because he could not hear a single sound. He felt totally distanced from it, or as baffled as any Chinese viewer. It also seemed to him that she, the Mother of her Country, was trying to tell him something, although he did not know what, because no words reached his ears even though she was moving her lips.

The hypnotic effect of this was further enhanced by the fact that there was not just one television in the window; the program was being run simultaneously on twelve different TVs set close together. Fabulous, thought Jonas. He could not help thinking of synchronized swimming: Gro Harlem Brundtland and eleven clones all mimicking her actions. Or that this duplication created a kind of pattern, a broadcasting network which also led to an accumulation of the program's effect. He remembered that someone had used the words "interwoven strands" when speaking of the programs shown so far. And it truly was as if this, the screens in front of him, enabled him to see the big picture, the one formed by the twelve small ones, as something else—and, most importantly, as something more complex, the sum of the individual, identical images. The figurative aspect, the pictures of Gro Harlem Brundtland, dissolved and something ornamental, abstract took its place. Like looking into a brain, he thought, seeing a way of thinking laid bare.

Where are the dark holes in Jonas Wergeland's life?

Jonas Wergeland stood in the middle of an all but deserted Oslo, outside a shop window and saw again, on television, how he himself stepped onto the scene, into the room with the Chinese, in his regular spot, saw himself in a matrix of screens, divided into twelve, stood and stared, utterly captivated, at himself, twelve identical figures. I'm possessed by demons, he thought, unconsciously leaning so far forwards towards the window that he ended up bumping his forehead on the glass.

In Transylvania

To be a spectator. The trauma of traumas, the one thing he feared most of all: that he wished, at all costs, to avoid. Once more I shall tell the story of the radio theater.

East of the flats lay a wooded hill, a triangle wedged between the cliff face, Bergensveien and Trondheimsveien about which, for many years Jonas and his chums had mixed feelings. Because through this lonely spot ran the short cut to the People's Palace, better known as Grorud Cinema. The cinema was, in fact, a trade union concern, and so from an early age Jonas was brought up to regard films, illusions, as a natural part of working-class life. You hack out stone during the day and lose yourself in dreams in the evening. Every place has its Cinema Paradiso.

The room in which the films were shown was the same one in which Jonas had attended his first Christmas parties: a hall, in other words, reserved for boisterous festivities, and though Jonas would later be bowled over by the decor of such gems as the Klingenberg, the Sentrum and the Eldorado, in terms of atmosphere no cinema could match the stark surroundings of Grorud Cinema, with interlocking steel-framed chairs ranged in front of a grimy, battered screen upon which fantastic pictures could be discerned even before the picture had started. At Grorud Cinema children also got in to see adult films—far too often, in fact. Pretty much the only criterion for being allowed in was that you could reach up to the ticket window with your money, a window which was, as it happens, not unlike the ones at the Eastern Railway Station, so you felt you were asking for: "A ticket to Hollywood, please." Thanks to this very liberal regime, Jonas not only saw a heap of harmless films about Lassie and the sons of Lassie, but also a lot of hair-raising pictures which he definitely should not have seen, among them at least two Dracula movies in which a fearsome, bloodthirsty Christopher Lee was repeatedly seen standing silhouetted against the full moon, baring his needle-sharp fangs at some quaking woman. It was after the latest of these, *Dracula Prince of Darkness*, as a bunch of boys were walking back to Solhaug through the wood in a huddle, not unlike what the Romans called a "square formation"—faint with terror, eyes flicking this way and that—that one lad with a rather macabre sense of humour came up with the idea that they were in the middle of Transylvania. To crown it all, the moon chose that moment to go behind a cloud, and it didn't take too much imagination to hear the eerie flapping of bat wings and the howling of wolves echoing off the granite face of Ravnkollen, on top of which the outlines of Dracula's black castle could clearly be discerned. From then on the wood was never referred to as anything but Transylvania. It was a mystery to Jonas how they could have whipped themselves up en masse into such a state of hysteria over something they knew to be so silly, but it just went from bad to worse. It got to the point where they were even pinching their mothers' gold crucifixes and wearing them tucked inside their shirts when they had to walk home from the cinema in the evening. Even during the day the boys avoided crossing this spot. In Transylvania anything could happen.

At Solhaug there were not too many years between the different "generations," which is to say the groups of children who played together. Jonas belonged to the second generation. The first batch of kids were all three or four years older, and their undisputed leader was Petter, or Sgt. Petter as he was known after the new Beatles album came out and, by some enviable means, he managed to get hold of a silk military-style coat—from London's Carnaby Street itself, no less—just like the ones the Beatles were wearing on the cover of said album. Not only that, but under his nose he sported some wisps of hair which he called a moustache.

None of the girls really stood out. Apart from Mamma Banana. Mamma Banana was what was known as "easy." The sort of girl who, if she didn't exist, every boy would have to invent. There were the wildest rumors going around about how insatiable she was and the things she found to console herself with on hot summer nights if there was no boy around. "Nothing can satisfy her," Guggen whispered to Jonas and rolled his eyes. "Not even a magnum bottle of beer." Mamma Banana just couldn't get enough of it. Hence the name.

Her real name was Laila, and she lived farther up Bergensveien in a tumbledown Swiss-style villa with colored glass screening the veranda. If Jonas were honest with himself, she seemed more quiet than randy. But she was pretty; and they also had proof, of course, that those demure, downcast eyes were just a cover. One autumn, the smaller kids had been running around telling everybody that Karl's Beetle was alive, that it rocked and rolled after dark. Jonas and his chums almost laughed their heads off at such daft notions. The Beetle in question was an ancient Volkswagen, an old banger really, which everybody called Charlie's Chariot—an allusion to their name for what is also known, depending where one comes from, as the Plough, the Big Dipper or Charles's Wain. It had been sitting outside Number Four for ages, covered by a tarpaulin. But the kids kept going on and on about it, so one night Jonas and a couple of the others stole down to the courtyard and hid behind some bushes. And it was true enough: Charlie's Chariot had to be a creature of the night, because it did indeed come to life. It shook, rocked back and forth, like a giant tortoise, except that it never left the spot. Five minutes later they had their explanation. From under the tarpaulin crept Laffen and Mamma Banana. They must have managed to unlock the door and were using the car as a love-nest. But even this was not enough to convince Jonas—Laffen was an okay guy, he actually moved away soon after this, and no one knew what had really gone on under that tarpaulin. Jonas still found it hard to bridge the gap between the vulgar rumors about Mamma Banana and the happy face he had seen in the light of the street lamp when Laila clambered out of Charlie's Chariot, as if she really had been on a trip around the stars.

This sight did, however, fire his erotic imaginings, much in the same way as the show on the flag green in the summertime, when the older girls armed themselves with plaid traveling rugs, Bambi record-players and piles of well-worn singles and Laila danced the twist along with the others, while Jonas and the younger lads lay on the slope a little way off, pretending to be playing on grass-blade whistles. And I tell you it was some sight: sixteen year-old Laila twisting her body this way and that in a sort of trance-like dance, with hips and a polka-dot bikini top that produced such inexplicable collisions in their thoughts that the boys had to fix their eyes on the pennant outstretched in the breeze for a second or so, before again daring to scan the green sward filled with girlish bodies wriggling out of the sheer, youthful joy of being alive.

Laila seemed to like Jonas; or at least she spoke to him. She had even been known to walk home from the shopping center with him if they happened to bump into one another there—despite the fact that he was younger than her. Maybe it was because he didn't tease her or shout rude remarks after her like the other boys. Some people said she wasn't all there, but Jonas realized—even more so after Buddha came along—that there could be well be some other reason; that she had understood, seen, something which caused her somehow to shut herself off from the world a bit. And after Aunt Laura told him that the Arabian name for the *One Thousand and One Nights* was *Alf Layla wa-Layla*, Jonas always thought of Laila as being a princess of sorts, an initiator of tales.

What sort of sound does a dragon make?

One evening—in the spring of the year when he was in his first year at junior high—Jonas had gone to Grorud Cinema and happened to sit down next to Laila. No Dracula film that night but a romantic affair with lots of kissing and a couple of nail-biting scenes which moved Laila to grip his hand—whether consciously or unconsciously he could not have said. Sgt. Petter also betrayed his presence in the hall with demonstrative hoots of phoney laughter at unlikely moments. Outside, after the film, he drew Jonas aside and asked if he could talk Laila into walking home through the wood. Sgt. Petter was with three other boys of his own age, a trio known to some as The Lonely Hearts Club Band. "What for?" Jonas asked.

"Just for a laugh," said Sgt. Petter. "We're just going to give her a bit of a fright." More laughter. The other three laughed too.

Jonas wasn't sure. He utterly despised Sgt. Petter, but the older boy did possess certain talents Jonas wished that he too possessed: Sgt. Petter had a creative streak. He could create things. All Grorud knew, for example, that he was the originator of the following joke, which at one point was being told all over Norway and beyond: "What did the Beatles say when they were caught in an avalanche? Watch out for those Rolling Stones!" Sgt. Petter was, in short, a trendsetter; he was, among other things, the first person back then to sport a pair of the fabulous new Romika football boots, which looked just like proper football boots and hence easily outclassed the more old-fashioned Vikings. All in all, Professor, I think that the difference between Romika and Viking football boots would prove a worthwhile peg on which to hang a local cultural analysis—the difference, as it were, between the elegant and the clodhopperish: a comparison elevated to a global scale by anthropologist Claude Levi-Strauss when he writes about the raw and the cooked. Boys who favored the Romika boot tended to be fleet-footed forwards who quite often went on to play for top clubs like Frigg or Lyn, while the heavier and more robust Viking boots with their red laces were the preferred choice of backs who walloped or dunted the ball, characters like Frankenstein who usually wound up playing for deadly company teams. That Sgt. Petter was the first person in Grorud with Romika boots basically says all there is to say about him.

"Okay," Jonas said. He had defied Petter once, years before, and he was still smarting from that encounter. And yet: why did he do it? Because he knew what would happen. Or was that why: that he wanted to see whether what he knew would happen really would happen? As if he wanted to tempt fate. Press a strange, new button.

"Great stuff," said Sgt. Petter. "You're a right tough nut, Jonas you've proved that before."

Laila was glad to have someone to walk through the wood with—they'd get home faster that way, she said. Jonas felt his testicles constrict as they entered the path between the trees. It was dark, but Laila did not appear to be at all frightened, in fact she seemed very cheerful, was more chatty than usual, wanted to know what Jonas thought about some of the scenes in the film as they were walking past sheds with a graveyard air about them, blocks of stone just waiting to be turned into gravestones.

When she took his hand, halfway through Transylvania, he had second thoughts and was about to turn back. Too late. Just level with the quarry's gaping amphitheater they ran into the wolf pack, Sgt. Petter and the other three crashing out of the bushes, not with a "Boo!" but with dangerously set faces. They grabbed Laila by the arms. "You keep watch here," they ordered Jonas. "Give a howl if anyone comes."

They disappeared, dragging Laila between them. Jonas knew no one would come. He heard Laila say something, the boys laughing. "Take it easy, we know you want to." Sgt. Petter's voice. Then that laugh. An innocent laugh and yet steely. Out of place. Beyond creepy.

Jonas heard what it sounded like. Dragon laughter. The sound they had created in their radio play.

He stood there, in the middle of Transylvania, a prince of darkness, staring at the ground, heard Laila moaning. She liked it. Well, why not? With his own eyes he had seen her slipping out of Charlie's Chariot with her hair all mussed up. *Alf Layla wa-Layla.*

He stands there, in the middle of Transylvania, in the amphitheater of the quarry as it were, staring at the ground, hears fabric being ripped, a stifled cry of ecstasy, or was it a muffled scream, a scream for . . . He can't help it, has to look up, spies them in among the trees, sees them clearly even in the dark, sees how three hold her down while the fourth lies on top of her. He looks up just as two of them swap places. And seeing it with his own eyes it is impossible to misinterpret those sounds: it is not moaning, it is sobbing, a human being wailing in pain.

He knows what he ought to do now. Hold up a cross. Be a Saint George. Anything. But he is paralyzed. Stands in the middle of Transylvania, in the amphitheater, and just watches. A spectator.

And at the same time, appalled, he realizes that what he is feeling, what he thinks is horror, is not horror. It is a breathless awareness, a tremendous opening up, a receptivity, to impressions. The scene before him, everything around him, seems to become a lever, dislodging a rock inside him, uncovering a dark hole, a treasure, a ball of snakes, he doesn't know. He stands there and feels himself almost being torn apart with despair, even while wishing that this moment would last. For everything, even the smell of damp granite, permeates him and he is transformed into one enormous overview, an explosion of ideas, a kind of chord which sums up everything, which is both grating and divine, as is the rhythm—"That I'll have to try out on the piano," was the thought that flashed through his mind—a beat, a whole lot of beats at once, thudding, pounding, right through him, a wild, primitive, compelling pulse.

The four boys staggered out. Sgt. Petter had an ugly scratch on his cheek, he was bleeding. "Great stuff, Dickie. I knew you were a tough nut." He gave Jonas a quick thump on the back before they all ran off toward Solhaug. On their own: innocent lads. Together: a mob. The mystery of the mass. Four swans forming a dragon.

Jonas followed the sounds of weeping. Laila was sitting on the ground, her trousers still round her ankles, her sweater rucked up above her waist. There were scratches under one breast, blood on the back of her hand. Jonas noticed some pine needles on her white thigh, wanted to brush them off, but didn't. "Laila?" he said.

No answer. Nothing but heartrending sobs.

"Was it horrible?" he asks.

She looked at him. Despite the darkness he saw it. Despite the tears. A hate he had only seen once before. In Ørn's eyes that time when they fought and Jonas held him down.

She got up, clearly in pain. Crying soundlessly. He tried to help her, but she turned away, it took her a while to straighten her clothes, then she started making her way back through the trees, so unsteady on her feet that she had to stop every so often and prop herself up against a tree trunk. He heard her throw up. He followed slowly after her. Only once did she turn round, and though she didn't say anything, from the look in her eyes he knew what she was thinking. The most horrible thing about it, those eyes said, was him.

Jonas stayed right behind her the rest of the way home, benumbed by conflicting emotions. Guilt turned his legs to lead. A rhythm galloped around in his head. He could not rid himself of it. Then: Dickie, he thought. Why did Sgt. Petter call me Dickie?

He knew it. It was bound to happen. He had known it all along.

From the Annals of the Potato Monarchy

"What was the name of the marshal in command of Napoleon's I Corps at the battle of Austerlitz?"

The idea, usually, was to come up with the best strategy for life in general: or rather, to achieve immortality, but on this particular evening the matter in hand was the more prosaic one—in both senses of the word—of the tactics for getting the best possible mark for the mock Norwegian exam held just before Christmas, a rehearsal for the actual university Prelim, an essay which tested not only one's command of the finer points of the Norwegian language, but the whole of one's shaky way of thinking. The Prelim essay was simply one of those trials that had to be undergone, like the BCG vaccination or the army's long-distance endurance march.

Viktor and Axel had just finished playing a duet: "Someone To Watch Over Me," meant as a kind of time-out. Viktor played the piano—no one played the piano like Viktor Harlem, the king of melancholy; he could elevate the blandest tune into a melodic heaven or make any tired old standard sound like you'd never heard it before—set free somehow, brand new. His left hand in particular spoke of a true gift, playing around with triads and switching about the notes in the chords as though the possibilities were endless. Axel's double-bass playing was not up to the same standard, but it was impressive enough. Axel had always sought out the bass line in life anyway—Jonas regarded his fervent interest in the DNA molecule as a variation on this same theme.

Speaking of bass lines in life, I ought perhaps to intimate my doubts regarding the previous story. Because, knowing you, Professor, you will automatically assume that such an apparently shocking incident must have a decisive effect on a person's development. But what if that were wishful thinking? The episode can, of course, provide some clue as to how Jonas Wergeland sowed the seeds of an acknowledgement that the spectator is the guiltiest of all criminals, but such an insight could also spring from other experiences. At this juncture I am tempted to ask you to forget all about the story from the wood, for the moment at least. I am afraid that it may distract your attention. For what if the really dark holes in Jonas Wergeland's life lay in the bright stories, or in perfectly ordinary days, or in an incident akin to the one I am about to describe, one that revolves, not around Laila but around the love of Beate?

The Three Wise Men were at Viktor's place, in Seilduksgata in Grünerløkka, in a cinnabar-red room known as "The Bamboo Grove." Every Friday evening they gathered here—and often stayed all night—to talk and toast his illustrious patron, in the form of an icon on the wall. It was actually Viktor's mother's flat, but she had moved in with a new man, so he had the place to himself. At the end of the street stood a proud, old building that had once been a sailcloth factory. Appropriately enough, since they often felt that they were setting sail up there in Viktor's flat, that they were weaving the fabric for great intellectual voyages.

The living room resembled a combination of bar, travel agency, and joiner's workshop. On the only wall not painted cinnabar red—but instead covered in wallpaper with a bamboo design—hung an enormous map of the world marked with a distinctly meandering line which looked as if it were following the round-the-world voyage of another Captain Cook, and the floor was covered in tools, off-cuts of timber, and wood shavings. Aside from the table—two still pungent halves of an old oak sherry cask—Viktor had made all his own furniture, not least the bookshelves he was constantly having to extend to accommodate new books bought to provide more insight into Ezra Pound's *The Cantos*. Viktor claimed that everything, absolutely everything, he had ever learned—right down to the fact that he could, at the drop of hat, sum up the ins and outs of phenomenological, hermeneutic, and analytical philosophy—derived from his tussles with Ezra Pound's poetic conglomerate. It is also worth noting here that there was no television in the room. "The salvation of the world is bound to come from a corner other than the one in which the TV stands," said Viktor.

There was also another, less philosophical, explanation for the absence of a television. Having first entered the gates of the Cathedral School and instantly homed in on one another—rather like ants, by dint of chemical secretions—Viktor and Axel eventually discovered that they had a common bond in their fathers. It was hard for Jonas to see how a director with the Akers Mek shipyard in Oslo and a manager at the Løiten Distillery in Hedemarken could have anything in common, but the key here was the Wilhelmsen shipping line. "If it weren't for our fathers," the two said, arms wrapped round one another, "Norway would never have had its most famous product: Line Aquavit."

Furthermore, both Axel and Viktor loathed television—again because of their sires. Axel's father had had a brief, but hectic political career and in connection with this had once had to take part in an edition of *Open to Question*, in its day an extremely popular discussion program on NRK. On this he was given such a lambasting by the program's aggressive chairman that he never got over it.

Viktor's father worked, as I say, at the Løiten Distillery but cherished a distilled passion for another subject—Napoleon. In the very early sixties he took part in the quiz show *Double Your Money*, answering questions on this multifaceted topic. It went like a dream until they got to the 10,000-kroner question—a hairsbreadth away from winning a fortune, and he gave the wrong answer, or rather his mind went a complete blank when it came to one part of a multiple question, namely: "What was the name of the marshal in command of Napoleon's I Corps at the battle of Austerlitz?" He could remember both Soult and Davout and even Lannes but not the last one. And of course it was Jean-Baptiste-Jules Bernadotte, no less, the future Karl Johan, with a street in the center of Oslo named after him and all. Viktor's father lapsed into such a deep fit of depression after this that eventually his mother could not take it any more; she divorced him and moved to the capital, leaving her husband on his St. Helena. Viktor soon followed his mother: in the long run it wore you down to be reminded every other day that you were the son of "the man who got the 10,000-kroner question wrong" and on Karl Johan of all people. He developed a complex about it. If you said one word about Napoleon to Viktor, if you so much as hummed the *Double Your Money* theme tune or that old favorite, "Do You Still Care for Me, Karl Johan?," you risked being strangled on the spot. They never went anywhere near the royal palace and the equestrian statue of the marshal, and walked down the street named after him only if absolutely necessary. Jonas had a suspicion that Viktor had sworn to avenge his father some day, and that it was Napoleon who would be on the receiving end.

Not surprisingly, the Three Wise Men's favorite tipple was aquavit, procured through Viktor's incredible network of contacts. To them, aquavit was a sacred beverage, primarily because, according to Viktor, they ought to follow the example of The Seven Wise Men, seven famed Taoists of Ancient China—a group of poets and rebels who represented the very essence of Taoism's "action through non-action," who did indeed spend all day in a bamboo grove, where they drank and saluted everything that was against the establishment. Viktor believed that this *wu-wei*, non-action, was an excellent ideal, since it was exactly the Norwegian way. Do things without doing anything. Everything would sort itself out anyway. Norwegians had been living like that for centuries. The Three Wise Men were simply trying to perfect, to refine, this mentality. So, while other pupils at the Cath became Maoists, the three friends became Taoists; they sat in the Bamboo Grove and paid tribute to China in their own way—they had even been known to write poems, quite spontaneously and in their finest calligraphy, which they pinned up next to the wall newspaper in the schoolyard.

Viktor drank for another reason too: he had a fanatical obsession with immortality and believed that aquavit—perhaps because of its name—could help him. Inspired by the old Taoists who had used alchemy in order to achieve immortality, Viktor tried first of all to get his hands on the secret recipes for aquavit which were kept in the Wine Monopoly safe and, when he had no luck here, experimented with combinations of different Norwegian aquavits, in much the same way as whisky is blended in Scotland, and with drinking various brands in the perfect sequence. "The Taoists concentrated on the minerals cinnabar and gold," said Viktor. "I'm going for cumin and alcohol."

They enjoyed the aquavit for its own sake too, naturally, and had many a heated argument as to which one was the best. While Jonas was a fan of Gammel Opland and was wont to launch into lengthy panegyrics to a flavour so full and rich, and at the same time so smooth and complex, that one had a sense of two forces colliding, or as he put it: coiling towards one another, and rising onto a higher plane—Axel and Viktor were almost programed to give pride of place to Løiten Line Aquavit. Hence the reason for the map on the opposite wall—a world suspended between bamboo canes—showing the route taken by the ships of the Wilhelmsen line. "Like all good Norwegians, the aquavit has to leave the country in order to become refined," said Axel, raising his glass to the meandering line denoting the aquavit's 135-day voyage across the seven seas, a mandala upon which they could meditate while they drank, to truly see the miracle of the passage from potato to golden liquor: a metamorphosis which began with cooling coils and ended with the ocean waves. "Cheers," said Viktor. "Here's to the potato, grape of the North!"

The room was filled with a glorious aroma—of new wood and alcohol, combined with the promising smells emanating from the oven in the kitchen—as in an exotic forest or, why not, a bamboo grove. Other than that it was the need to discuss things, "a yen for upsetting the universe"—Viktor's words—which brought the Three Wise Men together in Seilduksgata, and there's no getting away from it: seldom, if ever, has so much absolute tripe been served up in a Norwegian living room. As if they were well aware of this themselves, the three had developed an ironic method for classifying their arguments, a sort of Richter scale designed to measure their greater or lesser shock effect: by the number of glasses drunk. And if the truth be told, their discussions were usually at their best, and certainly their most entertaining, towards the end of the evening, when they had reached the "ten-aquavit arguments."

On this particular evening, since the main topic of discussion was the strategy for the mock exam in Norwegian, Viktor began with a pretty well considered theory to the effect that *Pet Sounds* by the American group the Beach Boys was a far more important album, in terms of musical history, than *Sergeant Pepper* by the British group the Beatles. "It was here, with Brian Wilson's bass harmonica playing, that it all began," said Viktor. "The rest was easy." This, particularly because of the comparison with Picasso's *Les demoiselles d'Avignon* was a typical two-aquavit argument. The same could be said of Jonas's later assertion, based on outrageously tenuous grounds, that Kierkegaard's engagement to Regine Olsen was broken off because he had syphilis. Whereupon Viktor introduced a three-aquavit argument for a new ideology: Merckxism—inspired by the racing cyclist Eddie Merckx—which involved keeping the masses down by showing sport on television, before Axel launched into a tirade about Tojo: "How come we know so flaming little about Tojo, when we know such a helluvalot about Hitler and Mussolini? That crook Tojo was the Second World War's real *éminence grise*!"

What fascinated Jonas most was the sum of opinions formed, those leaps from topic to topic, or the points that flew thick and fast—as, for instance, in the poems by Ezra Pound which Viktor sometimes recited while standing by the ever-expanding bookcases. Something new seemed to come into being, not out of the substance of their arguments, but in the gaps between *Pet Sounds* and Kierkegaard, Eddie Merckx and Hideki Tojo.

Then it was time to eat. All three harbored the same fondness for Beate, a yen which, as the evening wore on could also set the mouth watering. Because the Three Wise Men ate just one thing in the Bamboo Grove: potatoes, and Beate—a relatively new variety—numbered among their absolute favorites, for its appearance too: the delicate contrast between red skin and white flesh. The Three Wise Men were "enologists" on the potato front. Not since the so-called "potato preachers" of the eighteenth century has anyone taken so much interest in the potato—especially in combination with its liquid by-product: "We have to use Mr. Potato Head!" was Viktor's constant refrain.

It was not the first strawberries that the Three Wise Men looked forward to but the first potatoes; they knew when all the different varieties were due in the shops, that Ostara was an early, Kerr's Pink a late crop; they sampled every sort, from the Dutch Bintje with its rather mild flavour to the powerful potato taste of the floury, yellow Pimpernels. They would go to any lengths to get hold of Saturna, a much underrated potato, and stuffed themselves silly when an extra tasty almond potato came on the market, a potato normally only grown in the mountains. "And I'd pay anything for those little Ringerike potatoes," Axel told his greengrocer.

Although they tried cooking potatoes in all manner of ways, from mashed to au gratin, for the most part they stuck to baked potatoes—not least because they were so wonderfully easy. The only other ingredient they added was garlic, in the form of garlic butter. Because it so happens that around 1970 Norway was invaded by an armada—a fleet of garlic boats, and despite the fact that these met with fierce resistance, as did everything from the outside world, and despite the fact that most people reacted with disgust and would even change their seat in the bus if someone smelled of garlic, in the end they succumbed. For the Three Wise Men, baked potatoes with garlic butter, presented in their silver-foil wrappings like some precious gift, represented the perfect blend of the Norwegian and the international. "To Wilhelmsen's ships and garlic boats!" they cried.

From time to time they would raise their glasses to the icon, to the portrait of Viktor's illustrious patron, the notorious picture of the then prime minister, Per Borten, clad in nothing but his underpants, with what looked like a potato stuck down them. "The premier, deep in thought," the marvellous caption proclaimed. Jonas took much the same pride in this photograph of Per Borten, clipped from the newspaper *Dagbladet*, as Daniel did in the picture of Ingeborg Sørensen in *Playboy*. Per Borten was a true Taoist, so ambiguous in his replies that no one knew what he meant, and he saw things from so many sides that he would later be described as a poor prime minister. "Every Norwegian is at heart a member of the Farming Party!" Viktor whooped at the picture. This icon always filled them with a profound gratitude that, in a country where such a person had been the head of government for six years, nothing bad could possibly happen. If anyone asked "What is Norway?," one only had to bring out this photograph and say: "This man was our Prime Minister"—and that said it all.

But by now the discussion had risen onto a higher plane. Axel put forward the theory, based on Dr. Christian Barnard's recent magnificent achievement, that one could in all likelihood fix a broken heart simply by having a heart transplant—a typical five-aquavit argument. Jonas considered the time was right to insist that the Norwegian film *Vagabond* really deserved to rate as highly as *The Battleship Potemkin* and *Citizen Kane*, after which Viktor proceeded to enlarge upon the reckless notion that human thought was possibly just one of Mother Nature's many whims, much like the spiral-shaped horns with which she had equipped certain long-extinct creatures, excrescences which were, in fact, of more harm than good to the creature—an assertion which I think can safely be counted as a seven-aquavit argument.

As the evening drew towards its close, with the table strewn with potato skins wrapped in crumpled silver foil and Axel revealing that he had at long last deciphered the meaning of the lyrics of Procol Harum's celebrated hit "A Whiter Shade of Pale" and, just to make sure they got the point, bawling out the words "We skipped the light fandango, turned cartwheels 'cross the floor . . . ," Jonas, who was still at the lowest aquavit level, began once again to give loud vent to his worries about their Norwegian mock, the essay, which was only a week away. Viktor had no fears, he had worked out a strategy ages ago—a strategy which he would go on fine-tuning until the Prelim. He swore by the creativity of the afterglow of alcohol—or as he put it: its *te*, an inner force—particularly in evidence during the couple of hours when the brain came to life and lay there, razor-sharp, like a sparkling, freshly polished optical instrument. The only problem was how to get this limbo-like state between death and new life to coincide with the first hours of essay writing. Viktor planned to turn up for the mock exam suffused with a perfectly calculated afterglow, arrived at by drinking a variety of aquavits in a particular order, thus assuring himself of a dazzling overview of the subject matter. But it was risky—just one shot too many the night before could take him from the heights of the afterglow's Capitol to the Tarpeian cliffs of the hangover the morning after.

"So what's your problem?" Axel asks.

"I could do with a dose of originality," Jonas says. And well he might. Up to this point, mediocrity had paid off; Jonas received his best marks ever for bland essays consisting of material copied from one source or another and totally devoid of individuality. "So how," he asked, "am I supposed to write an essay containing any trace of independent reasoning and still get a good mark?"

This question remained unresolved. Jonas left Seilduksgata as Viktor was getting to his feet, glass in hand: "I've finally discovered the deeper reason for why you and I are friends, Axel," he said. "It's because I'm a Taoist and you're a biochemist. There's a parallel, you see, between the sixty-four possible hexagrams in the *I Ching* and the sixty-four possible combinations of base triplets in the genetic code!" The last Jonas heard before he closed the door of the cinnabar-red room was Axel embarking on a long harangue on which of Ibsen's totally crazy and unlikely endings was the most totally crazy and unlikely and announcing that he was going to call Agnar Mykle to ask what he thought—by this stage he was always ready to call Agnar Mykle—while Viktor had sat down at the piano and put everything he had into a rendering of "Bye, Bye Blackbird" featuring some hitherto unheard-of harmonies—a ten-aquavit argument if ever there was one.

Jonas really did take this Norwegian mock exam seriously: so seriously that he took himself off to the extensive archives of *The Worker*, which were housed high up in the People's Theater building on Youngstorget; he had sought refuge here before when he had a tricky subject to write on for homework, lying as it did on the way from school to the subway. Here he sat, working his way systematically through folders containing cuttings on subjects which he thought might come up, so that he would be able, within a couple of hours, to resolve international questions presented to him under such ghastly, imperative headings as "Give an account of . . ." or "Describe and discuss . . ." But he was afraid that it was no use: that the result would still depend on how he felt on the day and on the sheer luck of the draw.

It was at that point that Einar Gerhardsen—I almost said God—walked through the room. And bear in mind—this came to pass in the days when only the King was more popular than the old prime minister, or "Man of our Times" as he was dubbed a few years later. He had an office on the ninth floor, he was writing his memoirs, writing, you might say the essay of his life.

Gerhardsen gives Jonas a friendly nod, possibly remembers meeting him on the stairs with Aunt Laura at home in Sofienberggata, although he may of course nod and smile at all goggle-eyed high-school students. It is a big moment all the same: Gerhardsen standing there tall and straight in a chequered shirt and knitted waistcoat: a road worker who truly had paved the Way. A symbol of security on a par with Mount Dovre, large as life in front of him. And actually talking to him, making Jonas feel he has to tell him how nervous he is about the essay, whereupon Gerhardsen smiles, and this in turn encourages Jonas to ask about NATO. "Because the fact is," says Jonas, "that a lot of the radical pupils at the school keep agitating for Norway to pull out."

Maybe it was the complexity of the question that prompted Gerhardsen to invite Jonas into his office where, once they were settled on a sofa, he told Jonas in simple—I almost said "folksy"—terms his opinion on this subject. Jonas listened intently, with his eyes on the long, wiry hands before him, which were constantly in motion, seeming to conduct the old premier's words about what a difficult process it had been, a thumbnail sketch, and yet detailed, surprisingly detailed, so much so that Jonas almost felt guilty for taking up this man's doubtless very valuable time. "The Norwegian ideal was of course impossible," Gerhardsen said in a slightly tremulous voice. "The idea of wanting to feel secure, but without being under any obligation." Initially, Gerhardsen told him, he had been in favor of a joint Nordic defense program, and then, when this proved impossible to implement, of a Western alliance, although he was skeptical of American foreign policy. "That was a very hard time for me," he said, wringing his hands in mild embarrassment. "You could say that I doubted my way to saying yes." Jonas gazed with something approaching adoration at the monumental features across from him; the thought of the enigmatic stone figures on Easter Island flashed through his mind. Before he left, Jonas was given the second volume of Gerhardsen's memoirs, the one which appeared in the bookshops that autumn and in which he had actually described Norway's path to membership of NATO.

Came the day of the exam. Viktor showed up looking deathly pale and with a thumping headache. No cause for concern, he assured them; he was in perfect form, felt sharp as a razor. Jonas had been more strung-out than usual as he sat there waiting, freshly sharpened pencil at the ready, in the gym hall—normally a place for physical exercises, but now dedicated to mental gymnastics. He was not really surprised when he was handed the exam paper; it all had to do, as Viktor would have said, with alchemy: "Assess the importance of Einar Gerhardsen in Norwegian post-war politics" read one option.

Jonas dashed off a rough draft, scribbling like mad, wrote down all he had read, all the conclusions he had reached, so pleased that he almost wept after he had made his fair copy and handed it in. He knew he could simply have presented the generally accepted view, that of a man who had spearheaded the rebuilding of the country and worked for social levelling and equality, of an era epitomized by unprecedented economic growth and a rise in prosperity which, perhaps more than in any other country, benefited all the people—he could have written about all of that and got good marks for it. As a reward for delivering exactly what was expected, the conventional response. But Jonas wanted, for once, to think for himself, to be provocative, and so instead he wrote—wrote so hard that his pencil snapped several times while he was still on the rough draft: the most important factor was that of international solidarity, he wrote, Gerhardsen understood that if there was one country in the world that could no longer act as if it were living in splendid isolation, that country was Norway, he wrote. Only through painful collaboration could one hope to contribute to détente and have a positive influence, he wrote. "Gerhardsen—possibly because he was a socialist first, last, and always—embodied the will to see beyond the bounds of his own country," Jonas wrote. "Gerhardsen simply took up the fight for a political agenda which led Norway from being a spectator to being an active participant."

Jonas took his departure in the long peacetime, stated that the nigh-on unnatural, 125-year long period of peace up to the outbreak of the Second World War had left Norwegians pampered and blind. And even during the war—in the minds of most people the greatest national catastrophe of the twentieth century—the number of Norwegians killed was no greater than the number killed on Norwegian roads in a couple of decades. This had given birth to a kind of collective illusion, Jonas wrote, that it was possible to stay out of the turmoil of international affairs. The Norwegian people were used to having bounty flowing into their laps, despite the fact that they kept themselves apart from the world. The Gulf Stream factor, Jonas called it, came up with the name then and there, was all at once a fount of inspiration and ideas. The way he saw it, the Norwegian people seemed to have been in a prolonged state of shock ever since gaining their freedom and independence in 1905; they were absolutely terrified to open their mouths at all in case something went wrong and they found themselves entangled in a web of ties and obligations. They seemed to be hanging on to the notion of themselves as a nation of free peasants and had closed their minds to the fact that Norway was an industrial nation, dependent on a global market. Jonas's heart sang in his breast, he felt as though the graphite of his pencil was being transformed into diamond. In conclusion he unabashedly wrote that joining NATO represented the most crucial change of the post-war years, namely the internationalisation of Norway. This was also Gerhardsen's greatest claim to fame. He had recognized—albeit reluctantly—that it was international politics, rather than the labor movement, which had shaped and would go on shaping the development of Norwegian society in our century. Gerhardsen understood, in short, that the prosperity of Norway—and indeed the potential for creating a welfare state—depended on conditions existing beyond the borders of Norway. "Einar Gerhardsen saw," the Norwegian teacher read in Jonas Wergeland's essay, "that what we today call 'autonomy' had in fact been lost long before."

What Jonas did not realize then, although he did later, was that Gerhardsen, by taking Norway into NATO, also laid the foundations for a "No" to the EU. In reality, the two Norwegian referendums on whether to join the European Union were decided back then, in 1949, by Einar Gerhardsen alone, because, no matter how you look at it, he was the key player, both in the government and in the party. Had it not been for Gerhardsen's stance on a Western defense treaty, the famous national congress in February 1949 would never have passed a resolution supporting negotiations on membership of such an alliance. And had Norway not become a member of NATO, it would, due to the uncertainties surrounding national security, in all probability have gone on to join the EEC or, later, the EU. To Jonas's mind, there was no one to whom the Norwegian anti-EU movement owed a greater debt than Einar Gerhardsen.

Jonas sat in that gym hall, tired but happy, as if he had just finished a hard training session: feeling, for once, that he had written something with a bit of bite, a dash of originality.

And I ask you, Professor: can this person—can this faltering, naïve, vulnerable individual really be a murderer?

Axel got good marks, as always, for a gift of an essay question. He wrote about Henrik Ibsen—a glib, sycophantic, coolly calculated essay, totally at odds with everything he believed. Viktor, for his part, got top marks, a six, for an essay which "assessed the role played by heroes in the lives of ordinary people"—top marks in melancholy, alcoholic afterglow. He wrote about Napoleon, he tore Napoleon to shreds. Four Løiten aquavits, two Gammel Oplands and Five Gilde Taffels. His words were hammered in like nails in a coffin. Napoleon didn't stand a chance.

Jonas, on the other hand, got a two for his essay, subtitled "From Spectator to Player." He didn't know what to think. His Norwegian teacher made some remark about it being all very well to show a bit of involvement, but God knows there were limits. It should probably be borne in mind that this was at a time, during the build-up to the EU referendum, when feelings ran high, among schoolteachers too. Nevertheless, Jonas Wergeland's first attempt to realize his dream of becoming the Father of his Country—if, that is, it was not a covert experiment aimed at bringing him immortality—was almost a total failure.

$$

Now we are taking a leap—or rather, this is not a leap, it is a continuation—to Jonas sitting in the lavishly appointed kitchen of Ambassador Boeck's residence in Ullevål Garden City; it is less than a year since Margrete moved back to Norway and Jonas was reunited with the great love of his boyhood. He has just finished a late breakfast when she arrives home from Stavanger and dumps her bag down in the hall. "How did it go?" he asks, without looking up from his newspaper. "Fine," she says, no more than that, only that it went fine. "I need to lie down for a bit," she says and disappears into the bedroom.

It may be—I would not rule out the possibility—that after this brief exchange Jonas Wergeland packed his few belongings into a suitcase and left the solid brick house among the apple trees in Ullevål Garden City, because there were people who swore that they had run into Jonas Wergeland in the transit lounge at Copenhagen's Kastrup Airport that same afternoon—and the date is easy to remember, because it was the very day on which banner headlines were proclaiming the return to Iran of the Ayatollah Khomeini, a political and religious event that was to have historical consequences—on his way, by all accounts, to California, to Los Angeles "to make a fresh start, to live in the light." He was even supposed to have said something about resuming a former course of study and was therefore planning to visit the Hale observatory with the express purpose of seeing the new solar telescope at Big Bear Lake. Or as he said, or was purported to have said: "It's high time I put my pointless, eclipsed life in perspective."

But according to my information, Jonas followed Margrete into the bedroom where, despite the fact she was tired, she embraced him passionately, hungrily, then made love to him with a tenderness and an ardor, not to say impatience, that surprised him, almost wore him out; so he lay and dozed for a long time with Margrete snuggled up against him fast asleep, pondering her erotic mystery, what it could be, because it wasn't really as if sex with her was any different from sex with women he had known before her, and yet with her it felt unique, because the pleasure she gave him was of a totally different order—even when performing the same actions. Jonas lay in his future in-laws' bed, staring at the golden statuette from Thailand which stood against the end wall and thinking to himself that her secret must lie in a kind of orchestration, the ability to coax something fresh and new out of a tired old tune. And he could not stop his mind from running on, starting to mull over the newly accomplished act, because there had been something about it, an almost diversionary intensity which worried him, which caused, yes, a suspicion to well up inside him; and no matter how much he told himself that what he feared couldn't be true, he knew that it was true, or if not true, then perfectly possible. And however much he tried to fight it, these little stabs at his heart made his temper rise and forced him in the end, against his will, to tug at her, not gently, but roughly; and when she woke up, appearing more bewildered than surprised, he looked, or gazed, searchingly into her eyes, remembering as he did so, for a split-second, the sense of awe he had felt the first time he looked through a telescope, and then he said: "You didn't?" He heard himself all but begging. "Did you?"

And yet there is still a chance that he wasn't there at all, that instead of following her into the bedroom he wrote her a loving note to say that he would be away for a day, then walked out the door, because there was one person, Professor, one of our most famous architects no less, who doggedly maintained—I have this from a reliable source—that on that very day—the same, that is, on which Khomeini returned in triumph to Iran—he had bumped into Jonas Wergeland in Trondheim, in the afternoon that is, outside Nidaros Cathedral, where Jonas was doing some sketches for a project which, with all the hesitancy of the novice, he immediately began to describe: ideas for a new kind of church, "a space formed by light," part of an assignment at the College of Architecture, while at the same time sounding out this well-established architect on the possibility of a job in his office when he had completed his studies, because as he said, or is supposed to have said, he was going all out for this and only wanted to work with the best.

But all the signs are that Jonas Wergeland spent the rest of that day indoors, in Ambassador Boeck's museum-like flat in Ullevål Garden City, more specifically in the white bedroom where, after having asked or begged or threatened Margrete and received no reply and after having contemplated her face at length, with some of the same mind-reeling wonder, or dread, as when he had stood looking at a cathedral, he pulled back and dealt her a searing slap in the face, causing her to roll her head on the pillow in pain. "Tell me it's not true," he said.

"Shall I tell you the truth or the truth you want to hear?" she said.

Jonas could tell that this was bound to end badly, that something was already starting to collapse, as relentlessly as a fragile structure of ice hit by a little puck, and at that moment, as he was lifting his hand to strike her again, even though he didn't want to, he wished he could turn the clock back almost two years, to an early summer before he met Margrete again, but long after he had entered the College of Architecture and, at last, begun on what he believed to be the right course of study. His only problem was money; his money had run out. He feared that there would be no more traveling for him. He could have borrowed money, of course, but he hated being in debt. Then one day in late May he meets his cousin, Veronika Røed, in the street, quite by chance—to the extent that anything happens by chance—and she, being in a good mood, invites him to the nearest café where, because it's a very long time since they last saw one another, they sit for some hours. And the odd thing is—if one can regard it as odd—that on this day of all days Veronika is bursting with excitement about a plan she has, a plan based on information she has picked up in the circles in which she is currently moving, working as she is—as the final part of her course at the Norwegian College of Journalism—on a dissertation on certain captains of the business world, a topic of her own choosing. "Information is the most valuable of all commodities today, Jonas!"

He could not help admiring her: dark and sultry, face framed by black hair that flowed down over a striking and doubtless very expensive silk scarf. Her suit too was exceptionally smart, her work as a financial journalist seemed to have had an unconscious effect on her choice of dress. She came to the point. Since they were related, she was going to give him a really hot tip; she placed a hand over his, as if insisting: "This is your big chance to make some money," she said. "A lot of money, and fast," she said. "How?" he asked, when she paused. "Buy shares in Tandberg," she said or almost whispered, rummaging around in her briefcase and producing a chart which showed movements in the price of Tandberg shares over the past four years. "Look at this," she said, or whispered, "look how low the share price is now, the lowest it's ever been, down to thirty kroner." The factory was in trouble, but Veronika had it from a reliable source that it would be receiving an injection of fresh capital in the very near future, which meant that the share price was soon going to rise sharply. "But don't tell anyone," she said, in a voice which reminded Jonas of summers when they were children playing in the attic of his grandfather's house. "It'll be our secret."

Jonas took the sheet of paper from her. It was a risky proposition, that he could see; temptation was being put in his way, but it was a serious temptation, that much he understood: the prospect of making some easy money, a lot of it—without moving a muscle. And his cousin couldn't possibly know that he was short of cash. "Why bother playing about with those buildings, Jonas, all those drawings that hardly ever come to anything?" Again the slender hand, the long fingers, the beautifully manicured nails, on his hand. "Why not make some money, get rich quick?"

He heard her. Heard her all too well. For a second he saw himself from the outside, or felt it with every bit of his being: how the pupils and irises of his eyes were replaced by dollar signs, like Uncle Scrooge's in the American comic books. And although he did not know it, in this he was embodying the spirit of the times. Because the people of Norway were standing on the threshold of an era marked by market liberalism and a swing to the right, by free play in so many areas. In parenthesis I must be permitted to say that at this point they were also in the process of letting an historic opportunity go to waste, since the existence of a welfare state presupposed two things: national solidarity and economic know-how. In the fifties they had had the first, but not the second. Now, on the other hand, they had at long last acquired the latter, only suddenly to throw the former overboard. As Denmark had its Legoland, so Norway was transformed into an Egoland.

"What about you?" Jonas said.

"I'm buying 100,000 kroners' worth," she said. "I've never been so sure of making a real killing." As she spoke she had unwittingly tied a knot in her scarf, one of the fine knots that their grandfather had taught them.

I ought perhaps to point out that in those days buying shares in Tandberg could be a somewhat hazardous business. Things were not going well for Tandberg Radios Ltd. Veronika certainly did her bit to persuade him, but there was something else which did just as much to sway him: the name of Tandberg was rich in nostalgia. For Jonas, to buy shares in Tandberg was to invest in a beautiful dream, something he believed in, a grand vision. To put money into Tandberg was to put money into the motherland. Jonas knew that for far too long Norwegian exports had consisted solely of raw materials and semi-fabricated products, as was the norm for an industrially underdeveloped country. If, however, one wished to build a modern industrial society—and this was one of Vebjørn Tandberg's big dreams—one had to be properly geared up for the production of finished goods; the electronics industry in Norway, not least, was in need of a boost. The more Jonas thought about it, the more confident he felt. Absolutely nothing bad could happen to a cornerstone company like Tandberg. Everybody, a whole nation, would come to its aid.

There was only one snag: "I don't have any money," he said, feeling perhaps slightly relieved.

"That's the trouble with you," she said. "You don't dare take chances. You don't dare to risk more than you've got." And then, quick as a flash: "You could borrow the money." Then: "You could borrow it from someone who won't charge any interest." And then, as if it were the final phase of a three-stage rocket launch: "I'm sure my Dad would lend you the money."

The mere thought of borrowing money from Sir William tied Jonas's stomach in knots. And yet. This could be his big chance, maybe his only chance, to make a staggering amount of money very quickly, salt away funds for many a worry-free year.

The next day he plucked up the courage to call his uncle, Sir William, who was now working for Statoil and had long since forsaken Gråkammen in Oslo for Stokka in Stavanger, where he had 4,000 gilt-edged square feet all to himself. When the family moved to Africa in the sixties as part of a development aid program, Sir William's wife had taken leave from her job with Norges Bank. In Kenya, however, she met an American working with the World Bank and allowed him to break into her vault on numerous occasions while she was lying around, bored stiff in Nairobi; it ended, you might say, with a merger between Norges Bank and the World Bank—in other words, she left Sir William. Jonas had always had the feeling that his uncle's fantastic commitment to Statoil sprang from bitter thoughts of revenge: fewer Norwegians should be dependent on American oil companies.

It was easier to speak to Sir William on the phone than to meet him face to face, although Jonas shuddered at the thought of his uncle's appearance: he looked not unlike Count Dracula with his hair brushed back and canines that spoke of a man who, after his spell in Africa at any rate, had acquired the taste for sucking up commodities. Jonas outlined the situation, more or less in Veronika's inviting terms, and his uncle sounded very positive, in fact he almost seemed pleasantly surprised that his ne'er-do-well nephew was finally beginning to take things seriously. Jonas was promptly granted a short-term loan. "Of course I'll help you, you're family, after all!" There was only one condition: his uncle wanted it in writing. Jonas agreed; he'd be able to pay the money back as soon as the share price rose and he had sold his shares at a massive profit. He had made up his mind that this would be a short-lived adventure, a one-off.

The contract came by post. Jonas signed it, and the agreed sum was duly credited to an account in Jonas's name with a well-known brokerage firm in Oslo. Jonas called the stockbrokers and asked them to put all of the money forthwith into Tandberg shares. Later, when he received the share certificate and regarded this visual proof that he owned 3,000 shares in Tandberg Radios he felt much the same pleasure as when they had played Monopoly as kids and he had picked up the title deed to see what astronomical sum the person who had landed on his street now owed him. The thought of possibly losing money may well have crossed Jonas's mind, but the prospect of making a fabulous profit eclipsed all else. Only a few years earlier Tandberg shares had been worth over two hundred kroner. Jonas was doing sums in his sleep and dreaming of becoming a rich man. Behind his eyelids, irises and pupils had once more been supplanted by dollar signs.

His dream of a big killing was short-lived. The shares did not rise in value. At the end of August trading on them was suspended, and in December Tandberg was removed from the Oslo stock exchange. Still Jonas did not give up hope. But then, in March of the following year, the shares were written down to nil. Everything was lost. Vebjørn Tandberg, the company's idealistic founder, committed suicide. Later that same year Tandberg Radios was declared bankrupt.

With hindsight it is, as always, easy to see what went wrong. Tandberg was a victim of over-expansion, lack of capital and poor long-term planning. Above all else they underestimated how vulnerable the company was to competition from commercial electronics products from Asia. It was right what I wrote in that mock Norwegian essay, Jonas thought. "Autonomy" is a bloody illusion.

Nevertheless, Jonas—typical Norwegian that he was—had fallen prey to nostalgia and unrealistic notions about the world: which is to say, the state of the market. But for Jonas there was also another side to this tragedy: an entire childhood had gone bankrupt, all those radio plays, all those happy radio days, an infatuation with wood nymphs. He felt that he had lost, and lost big-time, because—like a naïve child—he had had too much faith in Norway.

As for Veronika, in case anyone was wondering, she did not buy one single share in Tandberg.

The bitterest pill of all was that he was now in debt to a detested uncle. Jonas managed, nonetheless, to push the problem to the back of his mind, almost blocked it out completely, until the cold January day when he was sitting in his own flat in Hegdehaugveien, and Sir William called from Stokka in Stavanger, from the desolate reaches of his 4,000 square-foot stronghold, and said that he wanted his money back, now: made this demand with a curt brutality that wounded Jonas deeply, as if his uncle were some monstrous Shylock, calling for a pound of his actual flesh. For Jonas, this was a matter of pride. He muttered something about taking out a bank loan to free himself from Sir William's contemptuous clutches.

It was at this point, after Jonas had spent several evenings at the flat in Ullevål Garden City, surrounded by brass Indian gods and jade Chinese dragons, sitting gazing into the fire, with something obviously weighing on his mind, that Margrete put down a book on Istanbul and persuaded him to tell her what was bothering him. And when he told her how he had gambled away his kingdom, just like that, with one throw of the dice, she suggested, with typical assertiveness that she should go down to Stavanger and speak to Sir William: she, who did not know his uncle, who was not one of the family. "Maybe I can fix it somehow." She had looked at him for a long time. He had looked at her for a long time. He heard what she was saying. He knew what she was saying. Or at least he thought he knew what she was saying.

A couple of days after this she went off, and twenty-four hours later she returned. "It went fine," she said the minute she walked into the kitchen where he was sitting over a late breakfast. And then, on her way to the bedroom: "The debt's cancelled."

"How did you manage it?" he asked.

"I talked to him," she said.

He asked no more questions.

It could be, as I say, that not long after this brief confrontation, which left him in a state of quivering uncertainty, Jonas Wergeland walked out of the house, because on that afternoon, the very day, that is, on which the Ayatollah Khomeini landed in Iran, a former friend of Jonas Wergeland appears to have met him in the basement of Grøndahl's in

Øvre Slottsgate, where he had been busily intent on trying out a number of pianos—the friend remembered how a couple of radically beautiful fragments of "Someone To Watch Over Me" had sounded pensively on everything from a Bechstein to a Schimmel. Jonas had said he was going to take up music again, that from now on he was going to devote himself solely to this, to "harmonies like shining constellations," and thereafter, still according to this other person, he asked, or supposedly asked, a sales assistant whether it would be possible to pay in installments and to have a piano delivered to his bedsit in Hegdehaugsveien.

But as far as I can tell, this has to be a pack of lies, Professor, at any rate if it is true that instead, on that afternoon, Jonas followed Margrete into the bedroom where they made love, briefly, but with extraordinary passion, and where afterwards Jonas lay on the bed thinking about how she had been aflame with desire when he came to her, as if she wished to hide something or ease some hurt. And the more he thought—not least about her capacity for acting impulsively and improperly, like the time when she was dared into stripping for some mutual friends, almost taking his breath away with her shameless behaviour, and afterwards simply shrugged it off, said it was no big deal—the more he thought about that and about other things, the more he found himself picturing what must have happened in Stavanger, somewhere in Sir William's lonely labyrinth of a mansion. He was also painfully aware of what a temptation it must have been for his uncle, a man without a wife, a man of temperamental longings and no scruples, and then there she is—Margrete, that dazzling creature, right in front of him, in his own barren home, a woman who politely asks a favor of him, with a look in her eye that says she is willing to do anything in return. Jonas lay there, tossing and turning, thinking, conscious that he did not know Margrete, only knew that there was so much he did not know, she was full of secrets; he could not lie still, shook her, woke her up, began to probe, to ask what had really happened down there in Stavanger, "Are you telling me that he actually waived the debt, just like that?"

"Why are you so worried?"

"Because . . ." He chopped the air helplessly with one hand, listening as he did so to her voice, as if it were complex chord, on the very edge of dissonance.

"No more questions," Margrete said, getting up.

Jonas was suddenly seized by a pain in his stomach, his back, his shoulders. He stood up, grabbed hold of her arms and swung her round, slapped her face hard with the flat of his hand. The crack resounded around the room. "Say it, I want to hear it," he said through clenched teeth. "Did you?" He looked, he glared at her. "You really did it?"

"What if I did?" Margrete said defiantly, running her fingers over her cheek. "You certainly wanted me to. I could see it in your face."

He hit her again, so hard that she fell back onto the bed. He hadn't wanted to do it, but he did it anyway. She could have stood up, walked out, but she lay where she was.

"I want to know what happened," he said. "I want to know everything."

"I remember once . . ."

He hit her again, hated how she always told stories instead of answering.

I do not know if it is true—I have to express my doubts—because there are, there's no hiding it, people who this selfsame afternoon, which is to say while Jonas was, as I have explained, standing in that bedroom, hitting Margrete again and again in his desperation and trying to worm out of her something he really did not want to hear—there are those who believe that, at exactly the same time, they met Jonas Wergeland on the Sognsvann line with all his skiing gear, on his way up to Nordmarka, and who maintain that he remarked, a mite flippantly, that one might just as well ski off the track a way and plonk oneself down in the snow. "Then you have to decide what to believe in," he said, or supposedly said. "The cold or the light?"

I ought perhaps to allow for the possibility that this really did happen, I mean that Jonas Wergeland actually was in several places at once, although—and I hate having to admit my own limitations—I only know about the one strand: the goings-on in the bedroom in Ullevål Garden City, where he went on torturing Margrete.

"What was he like?"

"You know him better than I do," Margrete said.

"Was he good?"

"For God's sake, Jonas, what do you want me to say? No matter what answer I give you, it'll be the wrong one. You'll only see what you want to see anyway. The debt's cancelled. That's what you wanted, wasn't it?"

"Did you?" he repeated.

Margrete waited a long time before answering, lay gazing at the golden idol against the end wall. "Whatever I did, I did it for you," she said.

"I'll kill you," he said and struck her again, only just managing to overcome the urge to clench his fist. He was seething inside, and yet somehow distanced from it all, so he could see that he still had those dollar signs in his eyes, not a sign of avarice, but of blindness: a serpent in each eye. He struck and struck again, feeling that he was punishing himself, that this was a form of suicide, but he could not stop himself; it was like the sexual encounters of youth when the ecstasy of the moment outweighs any possible consequences that could last a lifetime. She could have put up a fight, but she did not. She lay there and allowed herself to be beaten, lay there and allowed Jonas Wergeland's suspicions to grow and grow, curling herself up into a ball, tighter and tighter, as if practicing for a future situation, or kept hoping that this would be the last time he would hit her, that this had to be done, to ensure that it never happened again; which is why, she was already willing to forgive him, even while the blows were raining down on her.

It may well be that the path from one point to another; from—say—a kitchen table in Ullevål Garden City to an office in Marienlyst, has to be understood as being the sum of all the possible paths one could take from that table to that office; if, that is, it is not the case that of all the likely routes only one becomes a reality, for one fact which a great many people can corroborate—indeed it is pretty much common knowledge—is that, no matter what happened on the day in question and wherever else he might have been, not long afterwards, during a quite unseasonal shower of rain, and after having had lunch with Margrete at the university, a lunch which was rounded off with a Napoleon cake, Jonas Wergeland presented himself at the Marienlyst office of NRK's head of programming, to ask whether they were looking for new announcers, and thereafter—according to later rumors—not only did he come out with a story which made the normally rather reserved TV director burst out laughing, but to the latter's question he replied that he was fed up studying architecture, fed up with the whole bloody business and felt like starting on something totally different, like television, for instance.

"Up to now I've just been wrestling with shadows, now I want to work with light." And when he stepped out onto the street, his head buzzing with undreamed-of possibilities, he unconsciously made a kind of discus-throwing movement with his body: a pirouette combined with a leap in the air—rather like the triumphant gesture with which an exultant footballer expresses his delight at scoring an almost staggeringly unexpected, yet quite magnificent goal.

I—the professor—sat for a long time, thinking things over, after she had gone that evening. If the last thing she had told me proved to be true, then perhaps it was not so surprising for someone to ask themselves how such a person could have become the object of an entire nation's abject adoration. This set me thinking once again about Jonas Wergeland's description of Norwegian people—myself included—and I had to agree with him: we are a nation of laid back viewers, laid out in our Stressless chairs.

During the night, as I was frantically working to transcribe my pages and pages of notes in shorthand while her words were still fresh in my mind, I was struck by a twinge of doubt. What should I call the pages I was covering with writing: a biography or a novel? It worried me, from a professional point of view almost, that I so often—much more than usual—slid over into fiction, gave myself up so unreservedly to the narrative. Now and again I glanced around at the piles of information on Jonas Wergeland: everything from family trees, family photographs, copies of report cards and of the speech he had made on his thirty-fifth birthday, to the list of all the addresses at which he had stayed and statements of earnings and assets for every year, as well as that mountain of other notes and clippings which I had fleetingly imagined would illuminate a whole culture. It galled me to think that I had not managed to use more of all that meticulously gathered material, that almost without noticing it I had acceded to another, very different set of terms, had in some way not stayed true to an original plan. Not infrequently I had the feeling that I had been well and truly seduced by this woman's stream of stories. Or perhaps I should say conquered.

And when the book was published—would it be her story or mine? I comforted myself with the thought that she had forbidden the use of a tape recorder, had left the final selection up to me. At the end of the day it was my memory and my associations that counted; even as her audience I was the real narrator. She told these stories so that I would understand—there were actually times when it struck me that she told them so that I could form the understanding she herself lacked.

For a long time the trial looked like being an affair which hinged upon forensic evidence—with the focus on strands of hair, fingerprints and times of day—and a prosecutor who put all of his energy into building up a viable chain of circumstantial evidence. So people went on hoping that Jonas Wergeland was innocent, as if they realized that if he were to be convicted, they too, their blindness, would be exposed. And as I say—more and more people had the feeling that somewhere along the line something was scandalously wrong, that an appalling injustice was being committed, a suspicion which seemed to be borne out by Jonas Wergeland's inexplicable silence. Folk stubbornly refused to believe, for example, one of the witnesses for the prosecution who, in the midst of explaining something else, had launched an attack on Jonas Wergeland's credibility, his "amazing fund of knowledge" by telling the court about a red notebook in which Jonas Wergeland had apparently copied down twenty-odd extracts from books written in the nineteenth century. Even when the press followed up this assertion and showed how one saying, variations on which Jonas Wergeland had employed in countless different situations and which was even attributed to him in a Norwegian edition of *Modern Quotations*—"The essence of lying is in deception, not in words"—that this maxim had actually been coined by John Ruskin, people refused to believe it. The more Jonas Wergeland was exposed to view, the more mud was slung at him, the more the mood seemed to turn in his favor.

And then—yet again—the media spotlight was turned full-force on Jonas Wergeland: at the point when the defense had only a couple of witnesses left to call, just before the summing up, just before the jury retired to decide the verdict, he broke his silence and asked to be allowed to make a statement; and within half an hour, once the defense counsel had had a word with the counsel for the prosecution and the judge in the latter's chamber, everything was turned on its head. Jonas Wergeland took the stand and described in horrific detail how he had murdered Margrete Boeck—in other words, he confessed.

For a society that had for so long suppressed all knowledge of tragedy, it was like suddenly being ambushed by irrationality. I remember how surprised I was myself and how at the time, drawing on information from various sources, I tried to form a coherent, if sketchy, picture of the actual course of events on that evening when Jonas Wergeland returned home from the World's Fair in Seville. By all accounts, it was the staggering announcement by Margrete that she wanted a divorce which had started it all; she had apparently told him this as soon as he walked in the door, almost before he had managed to put down his suitcase; she wanted out, this latest trip of his had been the last straw, the fact that he had gone even though she had begged him to stay home; she was sick and tired of him putting his career, that blasted job in television, before everything else, and she did not want to discuss it, she had given the matter—their marriage, the future—careful thought; she should have done it long ago; all of this, or words to that effect, she had supposedly said, trembling all the while with a fury that had been allowed to build up to breaking point due to the fact that he had gone so far as to delay his return by several days. Jonas, for his part, was in no way chastened by this, instead he had flown off the handle—it was the shock, really—and had said some terrible, deeply hurtful things to her. They had been drawn into a spiral of spiteful remarks which, at one point, "in a haze of resentment," had moved him to fetch the Luger from the cupboard in his workshop, a pistol he had had in his possession for many years—as his conscience-stricken brother, Daniel W. Hansen, had informed the police—and which, being perhaps a little overwrought, what with all the threatening letters after his program on foreign immigrants, he had kept loaded in case he suddenly needed to defend himself. And when he came back with the pistol in his pocket, "only to give her a fright," according to his own testimony, she had carried on berating him, pouring scorn on him, and Margrete had a sharp tongue in her head, she could be devastatingly waspish, everybody knew that, and he had been astonished, horrified, to find how much he hated her; and when she laughed, yes, laughed in his face, he had shot her, which is to say, he had overcome his first murderous impulse and gone to her to ask for forgiveness, ask for time, ask that they wait a few days before deciding anything, maybe he would even hug her, but then, when she laughed—"a laugh I couldn't bear to hear"—he changed his mind, or rather: he lost control and banged her head off the wall, overcome by rage, and perhaps by fear, before shooting her at close range, in a split-second of boundless hatred. "I loved her, I wouldn't have killed her for anything in the world, and yet I did it." One journalist encapsulated the case thus: "In the final analysis it comes down to the oldest of all questions: why do people do things against their will?"

After the adjournment necessitated by Jonas Wergeland's confession—the place was in uproar—the counsel for the defense finished examining the last witnesses; then came the presentation of documentary evidence and statements from expert witnesses. Thereafter, the prosecuting counsel could make his final remarks, now revised and much abbreviated. The newspapers were, however, all agreed that the lawyer appointed to defend Wergeland came more into her own now, after his confession, even though all the signs were that Jonas Wergeland would be found guilty as charged. In her summation she claimed with impressive eloquence that at the moment when the crime was committed the balance of her client's mind had been disturbed, that he had been driven into a black rage by a fickle woman's sudden and unreasonable demand for a divorce. Fortunately, as her last witness before the final remarks, she was able to call the writer Axel Stranger—Jonas's high-school classmate and a close friend of the couple—who, in answering the defense counsel's questions, coolly and astutely built up a reasoned argument to the effect that the murder was totally inexplicable, that it had to be the result of a terrible fit of temper, sudden and irrational. This testimony was the defense counsel's one strong card, and she made the most of it: she pleaded that this was not a premeditated crime, but that it was the product of a sudden impulse; she attempted in other words to have the prosecution's charge changed from willful murder to involuntary manslaughter. And in this she succeeded. Jonas Wergeland got off, as I'm sure everyone knows, with seven years' imprisonment.

"It takes imagination to understand evil," the dark-robed woman said when she called on me on Maundy Thursday. "No rational theory can explain why Jonas Wergeland did what he did," she said and then, after gazing for some time at the tops of the fir trees outside, she added: "But a story can. Or several stories. If only we can put them in the right order." She was still gazing out of the window, as if seeking inspiration from the night, or the comings and goings at Fornebu. I also had the impression that her stories followed one another as much according to plan as the planes, that the slightest deviation could spell disaster.

I had started looking forward to it getting dark, because I knew she would appear then. In my mind I had begun to call her "my muse." I lit the fire well in advance, got everything organized, the jug of water, the glass, the chair, knew by now what would please her. She also seemed to feel at home here, she roamed soundlessly around the room while I pretended to be getting ready, so that I could eye her surreptitiously—not a little fascinated—saw how she picked up a sheet of paper here and there, flicked through a book, smiled briefly to herself. I had never seen anyone like her, dressed in such black garments, with such black-lined eyes, such a white face, such blood-red lips. And enveloped in that strange, somehow smoky, scent: a scent I had never come across before, but which as time went on I found intriguing, attractive even.

"Shall we begin?" she said, though without her usual brusqueness.

"Why are you doing this?" I ventured to ask, yet again.

"I told you: to save a life."

"From punishment?"

"Of course not. Something far more difficult. From pointlessness."

It occurred to me that she had also come to save me, save me from the chaos in that room. Because each time she started to tell one of her stories, she seemed to cast a net over all the mounds of paper, the piles of books, and gather them up, making them hang together. And yet I was not sure. Sometimes I felt that the stream of words that fell from her lips swept me up into a spiral, and I found myself asking whether we were working away from or towards a center. Occasionally I would think that the story she was telling lay at the heart of it all, only then to realize that it was more peripheral—other times the opposite was the case. And my understanding of Jonas Wergeland's life grew or dwindled accordingly.

As if sensing my frustration, every so often she would resort to the idea of the jigsaw puzzle as a metaphor for our endeavor. "This is an important piece of the puzzle," she might say out of the blue, in the midst of a story. I knew that she was referring not to one of those degenerate, modern jigsaw puzzles consisting of machine-produced, almost identical pieces, but a real jigsaw puzzle in which every piece has a shape all of its own, means something in itself, independent of the whole. The sort of jigsaw puzzle that only a master can design. Full of traps, where two pieces that may fit together do not actually belong together, or where details on one piece mislead you into thinking that it should go somewhere else. Or where you fit a piece into place and find that it changes everything, the whole picture. "Imagine if you were to find a box full of jigsaw-puzzle pieces in an old attic," she had said on our very first evening, "but you don't know what the picture should look like, you don't even know if you have all the pieces . . ."

Well, that was true enough. It felt more as if several jigsaw puzzles had been tipped into the same box. So far I had not discerned any overall picture. And I missed all the identical pieces of sky or grass, the everyday bits or whatever you want to call them. And she did not present the stories, the pieces, as if they were meant to form something two-dimensional, a picture, a rectangle, but rather as though the pieces fitted into different places in a long chain, a chain that coiled around the room, striving to take on three dimensions.

I regarded her as she stood by a desk that was close to collapsing under all that material. Despite her pallor, she had an Oriental look about her. She was reading a copy of a newspaper article published just after the verdict was announced—yet another jigsaw piece—a survey in which the majority of those asked condemned Jonas Wergeland in the strongest terms. Because the people of Norway were outraged by his confession. They had believed in him right to the bitter end, and now they felt let down. He had woven a colorful magic carpet under their TV chairs, and when he pulled it from under them they lost their balance. "If you ask me, I think that trial was more like a sacrificial rite in which Jonas Wergeland was made the scapegoat for the embarrassing naïvety of a whole nation," my guest said.

I did not altogether agree. Because although after the verdict was announced some people did take part in demonstrations of the sort seen in fundamentalist countries in which protesters burn dummies, portraits or flags to show their deep contempt—in this case it was videotapes which were thrown onto the flames or down the rubbish chute—there were others, women in particular, a remarkable number of women, who wrote to Jonas Wergeland in prison to say that they understood him, that he had deserved a better wife, a woman who realized that when you lived with a genius you had to make sacrifices. Several of these women, intelligent women, made proposals of marriage to him.

I have sometimes wondered what it must have been like for Jonas Wergeland to be imprisoned—a man used to traveling, to constantly changing his outlook, and then the same slice of the world day in day out, year in year out, broken only by day release, the odd outing: a life in which everything was done according to a strict timetable, so that you felt you were perpetually waiting for a tram. To the best of my knowledge, Jonas Wergeland has never complained. And Norwegian prisons are, of course, among the best in the world. I don't know much about his day-to-day routine, although some information does slip out, a drop here and there in the papers at yearly intervals. A number of these have, for example, remarked on the lacquer casket—displayed in his cell like some sort of sacred relic—in which, word had it, he kept an ice-hockey puck, a round silver brooch and a slightly imperfect pearl. He allegedly spends his free time—under supervision—in the woodwork room, hard at work on a fresh copy of the Academic's dragon head. On a couple of occasions, while out on day-release, he appears to have visited sports grounds where—and this may surprise a few people—he has practiced throwing the discus.

Apart from his mother and his Aunt Laura, for a long while only his little brother Buddha and his daughter Kristin visited him regularly. As far as I know, Buddha's conversations with his brother in the visiting room concerned such things as the archery in Kurosawa's films or the new kites he had made, which could fly higher than ever, or the round twelve-man tent he had put up in the garden out at Hvaler, a perfect *ger* which he planned to live in, even during winter. With Kristin, who would soon be a teenager, Jonas did not talk much; for the most part they spent their time drawing—trees mainly, but other things too, or possibly the trees simply evolved into other images.

Other than that, Jonas Wergeland refused to see anyone. Even Axel Stranger, one of the few people to speak up for Jonas in court was apparently denied access.

During the week in which the woman filled the turret room with her almost unsettlingly powerful presence, I spent my days reading through the stories I had scribbled down the evening before. Sometimes I also hooked my own little tales onto the bigger ones, adapting them to her style. In the beginning I did all of this with mixed feelings, like someone relaxing their initial insistence on originality, but after a while it dawned on me that something unique can also be created out of other peoples' thoughts and ideas. I was gradually beginning to look upon us as a team: two individuals narrating with one voice.

As I say, it was evening, Maundy Thursday. There was less air traffic than usual. Only now and again did a plane take off or land, lights in the darkness that we both followed with our eyes while she drank water, I coffee. "How idyllic," she said every time, at the sight of the landscape beyond the window, the heights of Holmenkollen glittering in the distance. "You should see where I come from, the want and the torment." For once she helped herself to something from the refreshments I had put out, a couple of grapes from the fruit bowl.

"I'm sorry," she said. "I just have to remind myself that I am back in paradise."

I have to admit that more and more often I caught myself wondering about her, about who she was. She was of indeterminate age; she could have been anything from thirty to fifty. Yes, that was the word: indeterminate. Dark. And I kept asking myself: how did she know all this? What powers was she in league with? Had she learned these things from other people or had she been there herself? There was something about this blend of seemingly objective observer and eager participant that both confused me and made me immensely curious. On the one hand, she related her tales with lofty detachment, dreamily, as if she had suddenly forgotten that she was talking about a real, live person. On the other hand, I sensed a reluctant, but deep, involvement, as if she knew Jonas Wergeland as well as Boswell had known Johnson or Eckermann Goethe.

I dimmed the lights, conscious of how she was gathering herself. She shifted round in her chair so that she could see out of the window overlooking the fjord, where a ship was slowly disappearing in the direction of Drøbak, lights twinkling, the shimmer of a starry constellation on a frosty night. It struck me that that ship, visible as it was only as strings of lamps, could prove deceptive, that in daylight it could turn out to be a rusting hulk. I had an idea that the same could be said of her stories, that they were not how they seemed to me at first glance.

Maybe it was time for me to reassess the myth of "the complex Jonas Wergeland," she said, extending a hand to the surrounding room, in which every piece of furniture was spilling over with material about this man. And then—taking me completely unawares—she declared that Jonas Wergeland's life was extremely straightforward, that it was his incredible simplicity that was so difficult to fathom. Just as life itself seems complicated—even though strictly speaking it amounts to no more than twenty amino acids in different constellations—so Jonas Wergeland had succeeded in creating the illusion of being a complex character by coiling his simplicity into spirals. "That is why you got bogged down, Professor. I know it sounds strange, but the way I see it, it is this very ordinariness that is the key to his rise to stardom. His genius, if that is the word, lay in turning this into a strength. As when a minus and a minus give a plus." She took some more grapes from the bowl, absentmindedly, not really aware of what she was doing. "Hindsight's a great thing," she went on, "in the wake of his conviction there was no shortage of people coming forward to point out that there obviously had to be something suspect about a man who could bring an entire nation to its knees; that no one could be surprised if such a person had an inherent demonic streak. But I ask you, Professor: what if the reason for his success as a seducer lay not so much in evil as in emptiness? In the tendency which all people have for filling the emptiness with substance. And the greater the emptiness, the greater the substance."

The Interpreters' Kaiser

This leads me on quite naturally to the next tale—because I have not yet spoken of the most important person in Jonas Wergeland's life. Not that I have unconsciously been wishing to put it off, since it is so dark, overshadowing all else, but simply because only now does this part slot into place, even though everything is in fact interwoven with everything else, just as in the Academic's carvings. Each story can only really be told by telling the lot.

It was night, and Jonas Wergeland was standing with a power saw in his hands. With one part of his mind he could see the inordinacy of the situation, saw himself from the outside, like a character in a low-budget melodrama. And one that dealt with the most primitive of all impulses: revenge. An eye for an eye. So bloody theatrical, he thought. Gabriel was asleep in a bunk down below, helped along by a half-bottle of whisky. Jonas could hear him snoring all the way up here on the deck. He was on board the lifeboat *Norge*, a weather-beaten circumnavigator riding at anchor in Vindfanger Bay, just north of Drøbak, at the head of Oslo fjord. And he was not standing just anywhere; he was standing at the boat's heart, before the mainmast.

He almost jumped out of his skin when the power saw started up. It sounded hellish in the darkness, as if the ghost of the *Blücher* itself had risen again from the deep. Jonas has already cut the lanyards of the shroud on the one side, and it won't take him long to fell the mast, he knows what to do, cuts into the wood between the mast step and the fife rail; stands there in a cloud of exhaust fumes, watching the saw blade slice through the mast. No sign of Gabriel, although by the racket you would have thought someone was driving a motorbike around the deck. Jonas watched the mast slowly topple over. Not the tearing apocalyptic crash he had expected, had possibly been hoping for, something akin to a lightning strike, ropes flying in all directions with furious whiplash cracks; instead it was all very quiet, like an echo from that time when a pine tree fell somewhere deep in a Norwegian forest, in a snow-covered landscape perhaps. The boat didn't even tilt as the mast hit the manrope and the rail; it was more like a great soft bump. What cracked so loud? Jonas thought, nevertheless, as he stared at the damage he had wrought. Norway from your hand, a voice sniggered somewhere inside him.

Jonas was in the dinghy and some distance away from the boat by the time he saw a white figure come stumbling through the hatchway and heard this person grunting into the darkness, asking whether Hell's Angels were on the go or what. It was Gabriel—Gabriel in anachronistic long johns and long-sleeved undershirt, eccentric to the bone, you might say.

"You bastard," Jonas hisses. "You fucking bastard. I should have sunk her, but you don't get off that easy."

Jonas didn't know if the elderly man on the deck could see him, knew what was going on, or whether he was too drunk. As he became more and more mired in the rigging now lying on the deck Gabriel began to declaim, as if he were on a stage, as if this too was a drama, though one more rooted in reality. "A knife! I am blunt," he ranted in a voice hoarse with sleep and booze, "mend me and slit me! The world will go to ruin if they don't mend my point for me."

Jonas realized that Gabriel had some idea of what was going on, because he remembered where he had heard those words for the first time, the ones which were now being roared out into the night.

It had all begun, as so often before, with a conversation down below in the saloon on board the *Norge*, not—according to Gabriel—a decommissioned lifeboat, but a true-blue royal yacht. From the minute Jonas first met Gabriel the two had been firm friends, but back then he had known nothing about this man's profession. In his manner Gabriel was rather like a distinguished old major-domo. It was only when Jonas came aboard the boat, Gabriel's domicile, that he discovered the man had been an actor. On one of the bulkheads, next to a sea chart of Western Samoa, he noticed some photographs which made him smile: stills from an earlier era showing Gabriel in the oddest rig-outs, wearing crowns and ridiculous-looking tights, pictures in which the faces looked like masks and the figures cast sinister shadows.

Also in the saloon was a bookshelf containing nothing but plays; Gabriel called it "Nemo's library." It held no more than about twenty volumes. "That's enough," he said. "And I could probably chuck ten of them."

Sometimes, when he was in a good mood, Gabriel would treat Jonas to a one-man show on board the *Norge*, in a crossfire of unfamiliar odors—tar and paraffin, birch logs and whisky—which lulled Jonas into lounging back contentedly on the bench seat. Amid the creaking of the rigging and the gaff, in a floating proscenium of fir, pine, oak, and teak and with the minimum of props—possibly no more than a walking stick and a handkerchief—Gabriel acted out, and played all the parts in, scenes from some of the world's great dramatic works, from *Oedipus Rex* by Sophocles and *Phaedra* by Racine to Pirandello's *Henry IV* and Beckett's *Krapp's Last Tape*—masterpieces in which he had also performed, so Jonas was given to understand, in his formerly so renowned, now legendary, one-man theater, "The Tower Company," in its moldering premises on Storgata. Jonas sat in the dimly lit saloon, as enthralled as a child at a pantomime, all but falling off its tip-up seat. He could well believe the story that stated Gabriel had once played an Iago so vicious that he had been beaten up after the show by an incensed member of the audience.

Every time he was on the boat Jonas would also hear Gabriel reciting a brief monologue—it might be while he was in the galley, spreading marmalade on toast, or stoking the stove, while he was winding up his fine gold pocket watch or rowing Jonas ashore; he hollered it, sang it, whispered it. "I recite it every day, for practice," he said. It was, moreover, a woman's monologue, Ophelia's speech after Hamlet has humiliated and tricked her, making her believe that he is mad: "Oh, what a noble mind is here o'erthrown," and so on: lines which Jonas eventually knew by heart and hence was even more impressed by the fact that Gabriel was forever bringing out fresh nuances in them, thus presenting a different picture of Ophelia, or of Hamlet, each time—perhaps simply by dint of a pause, a cheery grin at the wrong moment, or with those hands of his, a tiny gesture which suddenly made everything clear, words redundant. But Gabriel was never satisfied, he altered the tone of every word, the set of the head, every aspect that was open to variation, year after year, as if it was of the utmost importance to come up with the perfect rendering of these particular lines. "Oh, what a noble mind is here . . . o'erthrown."

On several occasions it was evident that Gabriel found Jonas's open admiration irksome. One day when they were each sitting with a somewhat tardy ploughman's lunch in front of them in the penumbra of the saloon, Gabriel broached this subject: "I am not—and you'll never hear me admit this again—a great actor." He pointed to an ugly scar under one eyebrow, as if this were proof of his statement. "Why am I good? Because of you. It's your generosity that turns my acting into more than empty gestures, cheap effects created by the contrast between words and expression. The roles lie within you, I merely bring them to life. Do you want some pickle? More whisky? Help yourself. Now listen: how much stuff do you have to put onto a stage in order to create a forest?" His gold tooth gleamed. "One stick is enough. The audience'll see to the rest. The audience is the real creative element in a play." He got to his feet, picked up a log, opened the stove door: "And this, my friend, is all it takes to give a glimpse of hell." He tossed the log into the stove. "Thanks to the audiences, people like you, I learned early on to what heights even a second-rate actor can rise." He crossed the room and tapped the barometer, which did not budge, however, from its perpetual "Fair Weather." Then he added: "I'm telling you: it's a temptation worthy of Lucifer himself."

As the daylight waned and Gabriel lit the paraffin lamp—lending the place the air of an English pub, he turned—and Jonas saw this as a natural progression of their conversation—to the subject of no less a person than Adolf Hitler. Gabriel maintained, and I will confine myself to a potted version of what was a lengthy discourse, that it was not in fact Hitler's uncommon gifts which had dazzled people, but his fabulous ordinariness. Hitler had hardly any talent to speak of, but he had spied the potential of the theater, succeeded in employing these dramatic devices on a larger scale, on society itself; he had understood how easy it was to hold a mass spellbound, that simplicity was the key, that in the depths of their souls people, everyone, especially those who felt confused—and who, in our day and age, did not feel confused?—longed for drama and ritual. "You have no idea how very, very easily people allow themselves to be seduced," Gabriel said. "Christ, boy, you're not drinking anything."

Maybe it was his very sobriety that brought out the skeptic in Jonas: "If you'll excuse me for saying so, that is the biggest load of codswallop I've ever heard."

Gabriel looked at him with his mismatched eyes, the one with a weary cast to it because of the scar, the other gimlet-sharp: "Listen here, my young friend: I'll bet you that I, the simplest person in the world, a failed artist, could seduce folk anywhere, anytime—on Karl Johan tomorrow, if you like; I'll prove to you that I can draw a crowd the like of which you've never seen, and single-handed at that." Then, after a pause during which they both sat listening to the roar of the stove, he added in a quieter voice: "Only to help you understand the forces which are contained within every human being. But which we repress. And that includes you."

"I bet you can't," Jonas said.

"What d'you bet?" retorted Gabriel, quick as a flash.

"My soul!" said Jonas, quite carried away, as if he were on a stage.

The following day after school Jonas was walking along Universitetsgata. He was just passing the point where the Studenten ice cream parlor cast its tantalizingly aromatic Banana Split lasso across the street, when he caught sight of Gabriel outside the National Theater, standing between the statues of Ibsen and Bjørnson, as if the old thespian had no qualms about setting himself up against these verdigris-coated intellectual giants. With all the finesse of a major-domo he had rigged up a small puppet theater, not much more than a board with a square hole cut in it, no bigger than a television screen, and this he had placed on a folding table with a little Oriental rug draped over it, behind which he could sit on his suitcase, invisible to people directly in front of the stage. He's mad, Jonas thought. They'll laugh in his face. But no one laughed when Gabriel Sand took up his stand in that heavily symbolic corner of the city—between parliament and palace, university and theater. He was ready for combat; a failed actor in his ancient, dark, chalk-striped suit, with waistcoat and watch-chain and all, and on his head a bowler hat which endowed him with a look of bygone nobility. Or Charlie Chaplin.

To begin with Gabriel did nothing. He stood stock-still beside the tiny stage, and still he attracted attention. There was something about his stance, his face, his eyes that made passers-by stop and stare expectantly at the man standing to attention there between Ibsen and Bjørnson.

Jonas reaches the square just as Gabriel begins upon a scene from the fourth Act of *Peer Gynt*, the high point of the play, in which Peer arrives in Egypt. Gabriel, or Gabriel's hand, makes the puppet playing Peer look up at the statue of Ibsen as if it were the Sphinx outside of Cairo: "Now where in the world have I met before something half-forgotten that's like this hobgoblin? Because met it I have—in the north or the south. Was it a person? And if so who?" And immediately thereafter: "Ho! I remember the fellow! Why of course it's the Bøyg that I smote on the skull." From that moment on Gabriel had the audience in the palm of his hand.

Unlike the people who crowded around the little stage, Jonas stood back a little, in order to keep an eye on Gabriel where he sat on a suitcase plastered with scuffed labels, with a puppet on each hand, acting out the meeting between Peer Gynt and Begriffenfeldt, which ended with Begriffenfeldt saying that the interpreters' kaiser had been found, before leading Peer into the madhouse.

It was as with all great theater: something invisible was made real. By some magical means Gabriel transformed Oslo, the surrounding streets and buildings into Cairo, and the spectators—Bjørnson and Ibsen included—into the inmates of an insane asylum. More and more people stopped to watch, even though they really didn't have the time; they were caught and held by Begriffenfeldt, which is to say the puppet on Gabriel's hand proclaiming to the insane, which is to say the audience: "Come forth all! The time that shall be is proclaimed! Reason is dead and gone. Long live Peer Gynt!" For a moment, because of the two hands inside the puppets, Jonas was reminded of another drama: the spectacle of two snakes twining themselves around one another.

A small crowd now filled the square in front of the National Theater, forming a semicircle that spread far out onto the street, all eyes fixed on a puppet theater no bigger than a television screen; people jostled one another to get a better look, as if the oriental rug underneath the stage was a magic carpet that could carry them anywhere. Gabriel would later say again: "It wasn't me, it was them. Everyone has this longing inside them for something that's a bit different."

Jonas stood there thinking. Above all he was struck by how simple it seemed, with what uncanny ease Gabriel had hypnotized this host. Jonas found himself despising the general public, the folk round about him, not only because they had caused him to lose the bet—or rather, make a mistake—but because they could fall for something so transparently false: puppets with hands stuck inside them. Then he remembered how quickly he had allowed himself to be taken in by Gabriel. If I'm honest with myself, I'd probably be the first to stop in front of something like this, he thought, incredulously witnessing the way in which Gabriel Sand held more and more passers-by spellbound, it was quite a crowd for a normal weekday.

Later, Jonas himself would enjoy the goodwill of the public at large. Right at the start of his television career, when he was working as a television announcer, he discovered how the public could credit him with qualities he did not have. Just before he was due to announce a harrowing program produced by the NRK foreign affairs department, he had got something in his eye and had to blink more often than normal. Viewers thought the program had moved him to tears. Which meant he must be a sensible, soft-hearted person. Big splash in newspapers and magazines: "The announcer who dared to show his feelings." People showered him with sympathy. It was brought home to him then: you don't win your uncommonness, you have it bestowed on you as a gift.

As he watched, Gabriel showed Peer meeting and listening in turn to Huhu the language reformer, the fellah with the royal mummy on his back and the Minister Hussein—Gabriel swiftly slipping one puppet after another onto his one hand; really beautiful puppets which Jonas realized he must have made himself—with Peer's words of advice having increasingly bloody consequences, though in the end he is, nevertheless, wreathed by Begriffenfeldt with the words: "Long life to Self-hood's Kaiser!" Just at that moment the police appeared, as if they were guards in a madhouse, an asylum in total uproar.

It was a memorable sight. The little theater and the crowd of people. That was all it took: a piece of wood with a square hole cut in it, two arms and a voice. And to top it all off: the police. As if a dangerous crime were being committed.

The policemen ask Gabriel—very politely, it must be said—to pack up and leave because he is causing an obstruction. Gabriel, for his part, starts winding them up, making fun of them, doing a sort of Charlie Chaplin turn, imitating the way the policemen are standing, crawling between their legs, miming a plea for help to the statues of Bjørnson and Ibsen. When, as the police see it, he refuses to comply with their request, he is driven off in the patrol car to Møllergata police station—amid a chorus of booing from the crowd. People have forgotten that they ought to be getting home, that they have to catch the bus or the train or the Nesodden ferry. They want to see more playacting.

Jonas sat in a dinghy in a bay just north of Drøbak, rowing slowly towards the shore. Without its mainmast, the old lifeboat looked like a floating chest, or a bin, a real loony bin. He saw how Gabriel, this man who had once stood on Karl Johan's gate and seduced a crowd of people with nothing but his voice and a bit of hand-waving, had been caught in his own net, become entangled in the ropes of the sabotaged rigging. Jonas remembered his grandfather's lovely model of the *Colin Archer* lifeboat, and with that thought came the realization that this too resembled a puppet theater. And Gabriel's sleep-sodden cries reinforced this illusion: "I am all that you will,—a Turk, a sinner,—a hill-troll—; but help; there was something that burst! I cannot just hit on your name at the moment;—help me, oh you—all madmen's protector!"

Jonas knew he would never see him again. "You bastard," he hissed. "I'll never forget you. More's the pity."

Gabriel was standing stock-still on the deck now, looking like the ghost from Hamlet in his white underwear. What a noble mind is here o'erthrown, Jonas thought. Gabriel Sand. An impostor. And yet: how long had it taken for Jonas to see through him? A man who ate his meals on board a boat every day, at a table fitted with a fiddle rail, with a bookshelf constructed in such a way that the books would not fall off in heavy weather—and who had never put to sea in his boat. Who kept a logbook for the lifeboat *Norge*, even though he had never tethered up to a buoy, had never been south of Drøbak, had never been to any of the places or done any of the things he had described so vividly: killer whales off the Canadian coast, Princess Aroari of the Marquesa Islands, the plums of the Azores, storms around Cape Horn. It was all a bluff. The stupid idiot couldn't even swim. Jonas rowed away, still annoyed with himself. How could he have been fooled, and for so long, by such a character?

Gabriel's white form grew smaller and smaller. This was the final scene. Jonas had the impression that he was acting now, too. That he wasn't really hopping mad. That Gabriel appreciated this stunt, this act of rebellion, this parting. That he had actually been waiting for something like this to happen for three years. That he was pleased, regarded this as a worthy ending, a test-piece that proved that Jonas had completed his apprenticeship.

For Jonas it was, nonetheless, a relief to see the boat's rigging destroyed. He felt as if a net had ripped apart and he was, at long last, free.

Due East

Perhaps once, perhaps twice in their lives, most people will find themselves undergoing a radical transformation. You could walk out onto a plain and leave that plain as someone else entirely. You have a sudden urge to start anew, with a different set of values, quite different ideals. A war can have that effect on a person. For Jonas Wergeland, who had never been to war, it was a spell in what he was inclined to call a loony bin that did it.

I am talking, in other words, about the year he spent doing his national service, with N Brigade, and more specifically about an incident which took place just after they had completed their ABC survival course at Skjold, up north in the Indre Troms region, a course geared not towards anything as innocent as mastering the alphabet but to learning how to survive under extreme circumstances: in the case, that is, that Norway were to be attacked by atomic, biological or chemical weapons. For two weeks Jonas Wergland dealt, in theory and in simulated practice, with the sort of possible scenarios which few people dare think about; he had, for example, to plot out on a sheet of paper those zones which would be affected by radioactive fallout; he learned how lethal bacteria and viruses could be spread most effectively over the widest possible area, and he tramped about in protective clothing and a mask like a spaceman, pretending to establish the presence of such fiendish inventions as sarin or mustard gas.

Maybe it was the ridiculous skills he learned on that ABC course, this illusion of being able to survive even if the world went due west, that drove Jonas to go off into the wild; as if, after all those staggering, hypothetical possibilities, he sorely needed to scrape about in a piece of concrete Norwegian reality, the soil he was in fact supposed to defend—or maybe he simply wanted to confront the foe that was forever being waved in their faces and at whom they had for so many months been haphazardly firing blanks: an adversary they never saw but who, according to high command, was out there somewhere and might at any minute start making life hell for them. No one could be surprised if a man—frustrated at being charged with an important task, but one which is never clearly defined—suddenly goes off willy-nilly, in hopes of meeting this mysterious foe. In case you have not yet guessed it, Professor, I am once more about to relate the story of the radio theater.

Jonas had a weekend's leave. He took advantage of an army recreation scheme and the fact that he was friendly with the officer in charge of transport to borrow a jeep on the excuse that he and another soldier were going to camp out for the night in Dividalen National Park, a little way to the southeast. His mate hopped off, however, a couple of miles down the road, outside his girlfriend's house in Andselv, with instructions on what to say to the company commander on the Sunday evening. Jonas then headed towards a much more remote destination than Dividalen, namely Alta in the far north which, despite the long drive, he passed right through before cutting south again and arriving, after driving for a couple of hours through mountain birch and rosebay willowherb, at Kautokeino where, on a whim, he made a sharp swing to the left, onto a narrower road which he followed for about six or seven miles, until he came to Av'zi. Jonas parked the jeep, got out, shouldered his rucksack and struck off resolutely into the wild, bearing eastward, as if intent on doing the exact opposite of going due west.

He made his way up onto the bare, open plain at the foot of Muv'ravarri, skirted round Gar'gatoai'vi and eventually, after an unexpectedly tough march over rocks and moss, bogs and streams, reached the eastern side of Stuora Oaivusvarri, where he pitched camp 1,600 feet above sea level. The most incredible thing so far was that he had not encountered the notorious Finnmarksvidda mosquito. All he could hear was a vague humming; there was something there, all the time, but hidden from view.

Having dined on combat rations from his Readiness Support Package, also known as "dead-man-in-a-tin," and boiled coffee, Jonas settled himself outside his tent and gazed at the sun, which was slowly sinking, but which, here in the third week of July, would still stay above the horizon all night. He felt limp. Drained. As if the radiation he had been dealing with in theory had in fact permeated his body. Although he had actually been feeling like this for some time. Ever since Viktor's accident. That chunk of ice falling out of the blue. Jonas sat there, gazing at the landscape, struck by how remarkably desolate it was. This must be the closest one came in Norway to a desert. And how still it was.

Like finding oneself in a world after a nuclear war, he thought. Was this really his country? All of a sudden it seemed so totally alien that Jonas's interest perked up again. He knew he would encounter something of crucial importance out here, but not what form it would take. It merely lay there, latent, like a hum, behind everything else. In his heart of hearts he may have been hoping to stumble upon some inconceivably massive diamond find. Or better still: a chunk of ice with a pearl ear-stud inside it.

The next morning he wended his way further eastward, through unfamiliar terrain where the ground was covered mainly by moss and heather, dwarf birch and greenish-grey willow, with a scattering of rotting reindeer antlers. He soon mastered the technique of planting his army boots on the tangled roots of the willow trees when crossing streams. Although the landscape seemed monotonous it was not flat, but constantly rose and fell, a fact that made it hard to get his bearings. The soggy peat sapped his strength, and the walk was not made any easier by the heat, with the temperature in the mid-eighties. And yet you're actually inside the Arctic Circle, Jonas told himself. If you were to follow this same line of longitude you'd be walking across the ice on Greenland, so help me. And that is absolutely true: anyone wanting to see how much Norway owes to the warm embrace of the Gulf Stream need only go for a hike across Finnmarksvidda.

At long last he reached the top of Lavvoai'vi and sat there surveying the view all the way across to the snow-covered peaks on the coast, feeling that he had much the same perspective on things as the rough-legged buzzard swooping over his head. But it was not an outlook he was after: it was insight. He scanned the surrounding scene, feeling that he was at the very center of the country, that to be sitting here on this hilltop on Finnmarksvidda must be the equivalent of being on Ayer's Rock, the red mountain in the heart of Australia, a place where it was so forcibly impressed on one that every landscape has a story to tell. Sitting there, staring out across the boundless plain, he realized that it was true what some people said: Norway was one big, protected national park. And it is not a bad idea to pause for a moment here to consider Finnmarksvidda, Professor, because what can you know about Norway unless you have visited Finnmarksvidda? Not Jotunheimen, but Finnmarksvidda is Norway's primeval home, as well as an outer limit of the imagination, a sort of Timbuktu within the country's borders. Not until he was sitting on the top of Lavvoai'vi, with a view that ran full-circle, did Jonas really appreciate a fact which he had come across so often in school textbooks: that an incredible ninety-six per cent of Norway was virgin territory. Only now did he see how desolate, how wild Norway actually was, how uncivilized, how fundamentally uninhabited. He surveyed the landscape, feeling for a moment that it exuded an emptiness that his imagination could never hope to fill. "Holy shit," he muttered to himself. "You could dump a small European country here, just on this deserted plain round about me, and all the millions of people in it."

Jonas sat on the top of Lavvoai'vi, next to a trigonometric point, a pole, rather like a seamark in a sea of moss, lichen and stone and almost had to hang on to it, so mind-reeling were the prospects. Because there was something about this vast, untamed wilderness which also helped him to see the reason for the golden age which his country was living through: the gift granted to Norway was that of remaining untouched. Just as Europe had been thrown into chaos during the age of the great migration, while Norway was enjoying a time of plenty and prosperity when it could relax and consolidate its glorious Viking Age—so it was now, too. They had entered upon a new era of great migrations, and once more Norway had succeeded—again thanks to its strict legislation—in remaining untouched, if you didn't count the handful of poor refugees who slipped through the needle's eye, and a few thousand immigrant workers. It could, in fact, be on the threshold of a new golden age, while the rest of the world lay bleeding.

But—he could not rid himself of this thought—this was also his chance. The country was wide open to conquest. The whole of Norway lay spread before him like an enormous blank page.

This was also why he had, perhaps unwittingly, made for this spot. He did not want, like Nansen, to cross anything, or to reach some far frontier; he wanted to work his way inwards, into something, in towards a vital center: the riddle that is Norway. If there was one place where he had a chance of finding an unknown—nay, unlikely—Norwegian reality, a vital source of inspiration, it had to be here. In the emptiness. He took another compass bearing, still due east, towards Urdutoai'vi, and tramped off, first down, then straight ahead, alongside lakes and over marshes dotted with reddish-orange cloudberry maps. Still no mosquitoes. He kept a sharp lookout in all directions, with the monotonous call of the golden plover in his ears. He was brimful of optimism, knew that there was a part of Norway that could not be pinned down on a map.

Here, right here, at any minute, he might run into what he sought—a lion or, if nothing else, a diamond the size of a pinhead.

It was still abnormally hot. Plump white clouds, nigh-on identical to one another, glided across the sky at regular intervals, their bottom edges flattened out as if they were being pushed across a glass surface. Jonas felt an incipient tightening of his balls. Late in the afternoon the humming sound grew ominously louder, so much so that the whole plain suddenly sounded like a camouflaged generator. Jonas kept looking round about as he pitched camp on a knoll in a little hollow between Lavvoai'vi and Urdutoai'vi, right next to a stream. The sun was hovering low on the horizon, and he was on his way into the tent to unroll his sleeping bag when the ground began to shake, and at that same moment he heard the rumbling, it sounded as if a tank was driving straight for him.

He spun round. He had known, and yet not known. It was a dragon. At first he was disappointed. The next instant, delighted. Delighted because it confirmed that all his ingrained ideas about the world, everything he had learned in his twelve years of schooling, was wrong, or at any rate not the whole story. He also had time to think that Daniel ought to have been there, to see that Jonas was right: the Norwegian lion was not a lion. The creature in the national coat of arms, the creature that lived at the heart of Norway, was a dragon.

How did this dragon look? It was transparent. By which I mean, the dragon was made up of mosquitoes, millions of mosquitoes. It was formed, quite simply, out of the most common of all things. That was the secret: at the heart of Norway lived a dragon, a monster composed of small fry. And it emitted a shimmering glow, like the Northern Lights, or like something electrified. And here—at last—Jonas found the answer to the question of what sound a dragon makes. It hums. Like a transformer. He should have known it, because the dragon is a creature that has mastered the art of transformation.

For this reason he only saw the dragon clearly, in all its unnerving gruesomeness, at the second when he turned around—the next moment it was transparent, a dense swarm of glistening mosquitoes. Only when he had had his back to it had the dragon assumed its real form. Consequently there is only one way to slay a dragon, and Jonas instinctively knew how, had learned this skill long before, was not even surprised to find hidden strands in his life suddenly revealing themselves in this way, a little like the secret writing they used to do as children, which only became visible when you held the paper over the cooker ring. A dragon could only be killed by a discus throw, a swift, surprising pivotal action. Jonas stood with his back to it, picked up a flat, almost circular stone, a good two pounds in weight, stood with his back to it and gathered himself, hefted the stone disc in his hand, made a couple of swings, heard the hum turn into a roar, whirled round and threw the stone with all his might, like a discus, so that it struck the dragon right between the eyes, with a noise like that of a vase smashing, before it had time to become transparent. The dragon fell down dead, lay revealed as a true dragon in all its banality, as seen in countless pictures. It reminds me of something I've seen before, Jonas thought to himself, only it's bigger.

And what did he do then? This too he knew by instinct. He took out his knife and cut the brain out of the dragon's head. As he did so, the body crumbled into dust, leaving only the horns behind; they looked exactly like any old set of reindeer antlers. Jonas stood with the brain in his hand, surprised by how small it was, like a black-lacquer puck with a silvery pattern shining through when he turned it to the light. It smelled sweetish, like fruit. It should come as no shock to anyone that a dragon brain is prepared in the same way as one of Norway's national dishes. Jonas boiled up water in a pan and gently laid the brain into it, just as one would do with slices of cod, and let it steep for a little while. The sight he beheld did not really surprise him: the black-lacquer appearance of the clump gradually changed, as if the dragon's ability to metamorphose did not stop even when it was dead. Within a few minutes its dark aspect gave way to a dull white hue, like that of a lichee inside its shell or—why not?—a pearl. Jonas lifted out the brain and placed it on a pot-lid. He saw how it gave off a faint white glow, a glow that came from within.

He sliced off a piece and ate it, just as hunters eat a piece of the lion's heart in order to steal the animal's strength or, in Jonas's case: its way of thinking. How did it taste? Warm. Like when you popped a torch into your mouth as a child. He took several bites, realizing as he did so what lay stored within the dragon's brain, what that silvery pattern denoted: light. I wouldn't be surprised if this turned out to be as valuable as any diamond, he thought.

Jonas sat there, somewhere between the two ridges on the vast expanse of Finnmarksvidda and suddenly he saw it all so clearly: all his life he had wanted to be a conqueror. Not so that he could lord it over other people, but to find someone who could lord it over him. As he consumed the last piece, he felt himself being lit up from within. He knew that light was bound to play some part in his future and when, after his national service, he began his studies at the Institute of Astrophysics and turned all his attention to the stars, this represented his first attempt to pursue that presentiment. From a certain point of view, it still involved hunting dragons.

The trek back to Av'zi went surprisingly smoothly, he seemed to be filled with a new kind of energy or enthusiasm. It should be added that, safe back at camp, Jonas Wergeland was given a dressing-down that is still talked about today, in front of the whole company. When he did not show up on the Sunday evening, only his mate's story prevented the launching of a wide-scale search, complete with missing person announcements on the police wavebands. No civil charges were brought against Jonas, but he was given the maximum disciplinary penalty: twenty days' detention under guard, or in the glasshouse, as it was called. As far as Jonas was concerned it was a small price to pay. He had not merely seen the light; he had swallowed the light.

Monopoly Capital

We are often fooled into believing that life progresses in a straight line. But it would be truer to say that life forms a spiral; it is full of repetition, events which all but touch, even though they are far apart in time. I'm assuming that you too have made spirals in the snow, Professor, at least as a child and that you have, therefore, experienced the fun of being able to shift, with just one short step, to an outer turn or an inner one.

The first time that Jonas Wergeland encountered the unknown Norway was on an expedition masterminded by Little Eagle, because there were times, as I mentioned earlier, when his otherwise so puny little friend could reveal unexpected sides of his character. And the fact that he normally walked one step behind, like a humble slave meant that these occasional aberrations made an even more lasting impression on Jonas.

They were playing Monopoly, a popular board game then as now, and the following story could, in a way, be regarded as a footnote to the story of Jonas Wergeland's disastrous speculation in Tandberg shares—or vice versa. Jonas had just raked in almost all of Ørn's money when his friend, after whooping and cheering because he'd managed to avoid the square that said "Go To Jail," had seen his red plastic VW Beetle come inexorably to land on Trosterudveien's green square—on which Jonas had four houses. And it was at that point, as he was flicking through a pile of thousand-kroner notes, that Jonas said, more to make Ørn feel better: "You know, there isn't any difference in Norway now between the rich and the poor. Gerhardsen has distributed the wealth more evenly, everyone's becoming more and more equal." Jonas had heard the chairman of the residents' association say this when the men were standing around a newly planted tree, drinking brown ale on one of the communal work days.

What was Ørn's reaction? He was angry, really offended: "Yeah, well, some are more equal than others, mate," he said, tossing his little Beetle into the box to indicate that the fun was over.

This was in the early afternoon on a lovely, if slightly chilly, May day. "Get your jacket," came the order from Ørn, this lad who was normally so meek and mild. Jonas thought the little shrimp was going to kick him out, but after a few reassuring—but, as Jonas was later to discover, mendacious—words with his mother, his chum more or less took Jonas in tow and marched off to the baker's on Trondheimsveien, where they stocked up on provisions in the form of a bag of day-old cakes before catching a bus into town and thereafter climbing into one of the exotic carriages on the Holmenkollen line, with a sense of boarding a sweet-smelling schooner bound for undiscovered lands.

"Where are we going?" Jonas asked.

"Due west," Ørn said.

Until now, the most daring expeditions they had made had been up the banks of the stream to find the source of the Alna—equipped with airgun and packed lunches, and usually accompanied by Colonel Eriksen the old elkhound. I should just add here that they discovered no less than three branches of the river, which they dubbed the Red, White and Blue Alna respectively. So their journeys of discovery actually had something in common, since the trip up the hillside on the rails of the Holmenkollen line would also bring them to a secret source.

"I thought we were going to see your Dad at The Grand," Jonas says, a mite disappointed at the thought of the Napoleon cake that might have been.

"No, we're going to take a look at the cannibals who eat there," Ørn said.

By the time they passed the sign for Slemdal station, Jonas had figured out that all this had something to do with Monopoly—Slemdal was one of the classy red properties on the board—and he felt a sudden surge of expectation when they got off at the next station, Gråkammen, and found themselves in the middle of Hemingland, the self-same district to which, in a few years' time, Sir William, his uncle, would lay claim as if it were the most natural thing in the world, after the lucrative African campaign, masquerading as an altruistic endeavor, which he had conducted under the auspices of the Norwegian state's foreign aid program. But this was the first time Jonas had ever got off at Gråkammen. Burning with curiosity, he followed Ørn across the road, munching as he went on one of the rather dry cakes that the boys had been able to buy for a few øre, although it actually tasted not too bad, what with the pink icing and the thin layer of jam in the middle. They passed some fine yellow-painted villas on the right-hand side. But Ørn was making for a building at the end of the road, on the opposite side, with a garden which Jonas had first taken to be a park, due to the glimpses they caught of bronze sculptures and duck ponds, not to mention ornate pavilions. "Look at that," Ørn said, his hands on his hips. "That house used to belong to Ringdal the ship-owner. What do you think Einar Gerhardsen would say to that? Is that what you call more and more equal?"

Ørn could be pretty sarcastic when he liked.

The building before them could hardly be described as a house, it was more like a fortress, only a little smaller than the block of flats in which Jonas lived, which was home to twelve families, all of them content with the space they had. This villa had been built out of natural stone and had a huge balcony extending over the front entrance, its teak balustrade seeming to speak of links with distant climes. Ørn pointed and talked, going on about the massive wall that had apparently been built in the thirties by the unemployed. Jonas couldn't think how he knew all this. "It's a lie to say that there aren't any dukes or counts in Norway," he said. "Because there are, and this is where they live, hidden away inside their castles."

They turned right onto the next side road, strolled down a street lined by houses which left Jonas feeling that all the people who lived up here must be ship-owners. Pennants fluttered over acres and acres of grounds, as if the flagpoles were masts on grass-covered tanker decks. Beyond the fences, statues of deer stood among blossoming fruit trees, and now and again they caught a glimpse of a servant or a chauffeur who—even now, in a Norway with a Labor government—lived in their own wing, or in the lodge. "Look up there," Ørn said, pointing to a towering redbrick mansion on the hillside, as if they were on a guided tour. "There's Herlofson the shipping magnate's humble but and ben."

More than once in his life Jonas would be reminded of that walk around Hemingland with Ørn: when he himself was in Africa and saw Africans wandering around white residential areas, staring through heavily guarded gates at lush gardens and swimming pools fronting fabulous bungalows—this sight made him think of his tour of Oslo's west side with Ørn, that it was the same thing, that they, Ørn and Jonas were almost like wide-eyed blacks in surroundings they found it hard to believe could exist in the same country as their own Grorud.

They carried on along the road, gaping in disbelief at gardens graced by red tennis courts, or driveways in which Mercedes-Benzes and Jaguars sat behind cast-iron gates, like rare beasts in their cages. Jonas could almost hear that dry voice on the radio: "Oslo stock exchange, stocks and shares, government bonds . . ."

"Know where we are?" Ørn asked, clearly looking as if he was about to play his trump card. Jonas shook his head; he hadn't noticed any street sign.

"Trosterudveien," said Ørn.

So there they were, at the source of the Monopoly board, on the self-same desirable green property on which Jonas, only a few hours earlier, had built his costly and, for Ørn, ruinous houses. The board was suddenly a reality. And there was no talk of play money here; even Jonas knew that.

Ørn cut down to the left, and a moment later they were standing outside the gates of a building that made Jonas think that there must, after all, be more than one palace in Oslo. Before them lay an enormous brick edifice, three storys tall with a black glazed tile roof and Virginia creeper climbing picturesquely over the walls. At either end was what looked like a sort of kiosk. But the most impressive feature of all was the doorway onto the garden: four massive pillars supporting a balcony topped by a curving copper roof, and a semi-circular flight of steps leading down to the lawn and the pond with its fountain. Fifteen years later, at the College of Architecture, Jonas would discover that this wonder was the work of the famous architect Henrik Bull, who had also designed the National Theater and the Museum of History, but even now, as a child, Jonas sensed that he was looking at something complex, which had to do with both history and the theater. "Soria Moria Castle?" he said.

"Wilhelmsen," said Ørn. "Wilhelmsen the ship-owner's, or rather, his widow's, residence. Standing on ten acres of ground. That ought to do it, even in a country with Gerhardsen as prime minister."

This made Jonas think. Not so much about the distance from here to Grorud as about that from his grandfather's cottage, the home of one of Wilhelmsen's employees, to this palace on Trosterudveien. Could it be, Jonas wondered, that the network of sailing routes depicted on the cardboard backing of an old calendar in his grandfather's outdoor privy, a sight he had contemplated while answering nature's call through all the summers of his childhood—that these lines actually ended here. In the spider's nest, as it were.

"So I suppose you could say there is still some small difference," Ørn said. "Everyone has more, that's true, but only because the cake is bigger. You still have people who are poor and people who are rich." He took the bag that Jonas was holding, only to discover that Jonas had eaten the lot. "And some get nothing but the crumbs," he added.

"But why?"

"It's all a game," Ørn said. "And some people cheat."

The term "monopoly capital," which became so popular in the seventies, had a very special connotation for Jonas. But at this particular moment he had to turn to look at Ørn, and suddenly it seemed to him that his friend was surrounded by a great aura of dignity. Or courage.

To be honest, Professor, in this case my sympathies are with Little Eagle, that Red Indian in the palefaces' hostile territory. Maybe all those people who are feeling oh, so pleased with the way things are, and like to parade fine words about equality, should take such a walk around their own city now and again, and visit unknown corners where the very grandest residences lie hidden, where the really wealthy live behind tall hedges, as if they would prefer to keep their fortunes a secret, almost as if they feel guilty. Because it is not done to flaunt one's wealth in Norway, a country where feudalism never took root and where any sort of disparity is still regarded with deep mistrust. And that is why, as he was walking there among these houses—or, not houses, but properties, several of them as big as the whole estate at home—it became clear to Little Eagle that he was a Norwegian. For what does it mean to be a Norwegian? To be a Norwegian is to express indignation at an unfair distribution of the assets that a society has created collectively. Ørn understood, despite his tender years and despite his precocious, didactic oversimplifications, that he was a true child of the Gerdhardsen era, and indeed of five hundred years of history in which so much emphasis had been placed on equality, an idea guarded so zealously that it would have to be described as a passion.

Jonas's thoughts ran along very different lines: "You see?" he said. "It's all a matter of throwing your dice the right way." He felt no sense of moral outrage, nor of envy; his response was more one of wonder or excitement at having come upon a slice of unknown Norway, and one which was connected, at root level, to his own life. Their walk had, moreover, sown a vital seed: he fancied becoming an architect, designing houses, when he grew up. You could say that the idea for the Villa Wergeland, and particularly the extension in natural stone, was conceived that day on Trosterudveien.

As if reading Jonas's mind, Ørn said: "I'm going to be a socialist."

"What's a socialist?" Jonas asked.

Ørn blew up the empty paper bag and hit it hard with the palm of his hand, making a loud bang.

Whether socialism was responsible or not, in the years to come a number of those vast gardens would be divided up into plots not unlike Jonas's green squares on the Monopoly board, and houses built on them. Times change. Many of the proud names from the Monopoly board have long since lost their original ring.

While they were waiting for the tram, Jonas stood looking at Ris Church, thinking that it couldn't be easy for a vicar in these parts to preach a sermon based on a text that says one should not lay up treasures on earth. "What's that on the top of the spire?" he asked. "St. George?"

"St. Olaf," said Ørn, suddenly a mine of information. "With his cross and a lance to run through the foul enemy, the dragon."

"That reminds me," said Jonas. "We still haven't found out what sound a dragon makes."

"Why don't we just flap a big fat bundle of banknotes," said Ørn. "That ought to sound spooky enough."

4'33"

(Suddenly she falls silent. She has never done that before. Stayed quiet for so long. I think she is crying. No, she is not crying. Just looking out into the darkness, staring. As if at an aeroplane, a craft, with no lights, no sound. Angels. All stories deal with what cannot be said, cannot be written. Time for stillness. Time to feel the weight of one's own body. Time to listen to the beating of the heart. This miracle. To live. To be granted another second. And another. Another. Another.)

And I Beheld Another Beast Coming up out of the Earth; and He Had Two Horns Like a Lamb, and He Spake As a Dragon

In my capacious head I set this next piece in the wrong position several times before finding its rightful place: before the dangerous sabotage mission, after the boys' expedition to Trosterudveien. Because Jonas had just realized his old dream of studying at the College of Architecture when he was witness to a very strange scene in Vestre Aker Church. Daniel's church practicum group was holding a service there, and Daniel—half in jest—had invited his brother to come along. Jonas had the huge church pretty much to himself; he felt like an observer at a military exercise.

The idea of these meetings in the church every Monday morning was to give the students in the Faculty of Theology a chance to practice holding a church service, in authentic surroundings as it were. The students split up the various duties among themselves and on this day it was Daniel's turn to give the sermon—which was, of course, why he had invited Jonas to attend—so now Jonas was sitting there with a smile on his lips listening to his brother, the boy who had with ruthless consistency beaten him black and blue throughout their childhood, delivering a sermon based on the words from Matthew 5 about turning the other cheek. Jonas had to admit that he had never heard the like of that sermon, it wasn't like any of the rants to which he had lent half an ear while nodding off in the balcony of Grorud church; it really was a most original sermon—at that moment Jonas felt genuine, warm affection for his brother. Come down here afterwards and apologize for all the trouble you've caused, and I'll be blowed if I don't forgive you, he thought.

But Jonas was, if he was honest, far more interested in the student who led the actual liturgy before and after the sermon, a girl in an ankle-length white surplice, a beauty who held him enthralled even with her back to him; he could not take his eyes off the dark tendrils that had broken free from the hair pulled up into a topknot and curled, little-girl fashion, over the nape of her neck. She moved in a solemn, almost trancelike manner behind the altar rail, looking so lovely against the backdrop of church silver and stained glass: embodying a kind of consummate innocence. She reminds me of a nun, Jonas thought, wishing it were communion, so he could sneak up and have a wafer placed on his tongue by her hand.

During the break before the students were to discuss each other's performance and hear the voice coach's comments, he mentioned her to Daniel. His brother didn't know much about her, only that her name was Anne S., that she came from Fåberg in Gudbrandsdalen, from a strict Evangelical family, and that she was a wizard at Latin, Greek and Hebrew; she adored grammar, there was no one to beat her when it came to detailed exegeses. "She chose witches as her topic for her ecclesiastical history project, you know," Daniel said with a sly grin. "She wrote with particular insight on those witches who were accused of having sexual intercourse with an incubus—the devil—while asleep."

"She should have a go at you, then?" Jonas said.

Daniel didn't laugh: "I'd watch out for her if I were you," was all he said.

Jonas took this last remark as a joke. As he walked down Kirkeveien he could still see her in his mind, Anne S. behind the altar rail, those ethereal features, the rather timid eyes.

Jonas was not at all surprised to meet her again, later that autumn, at a wild party thrown by one of Axel's many friends, a medical student—Anne S. had been invited because she lived in the same bedsit complex. While the others found escape from the daily round of lectures and cramming by letting their hair down in all manner of ways, she sat in a corner all by herself; she was wearing a white, embroidered blouse; her eyes were an almost uncanny blue. She seemed a little anaemic and rather out of place, like a Sunday-School girl among a crowd of hooligans, not to say bedevilled souls. When almost everybody else had collapsed on the floor in a state of hedonistic exhaustion and lay there surrounded by lighted candles, holding hands and listening to Keith Jarrett's endless, introspective improvisations on the piano, Jonas went over to speak to her. As they talked he noticed how she searched him with those blue eyes, how she filled him with substance, qualities of which he knew nothing, but which—having learned from experience—he allowed her to pour into him, after which she asked him, with eyes demurely downcast, if he would like to come up to her place. And when Jonas said yes it was by no means simply because he felt sorry for her.

He thought the party had been too noisy for her taste, but it must have had more to do with the choice of music, or the quasi-religious mood, because once inside her bedsit she put on an album called *Horses* by the pretty innovative poet and rock musician Patti Smith—she played it quite loud, even though the music was raw and intense, with Smith's rather nasal, singsong vocals. There was something primitive, shamanistic about the whole thing that seemed to fit Anne S., his memory of her silhouetted against the fragile glass altarpiece in Vestre Aker Church, that is.

He was no less surprised when she suddenly appeared carrying a tray of caviar and thin slices of toasted white bread. She then produced two small, fogged glasses containing what Jonas took to be iced water. She passed a hand over them: "It was water, but now it's vodka," she said with a smile. "I just got off the boat from Denmark," she added, almost apologetically. Jonas eyed the wedges of toast heaped with black pearls, the goblets of ice-cold vodka. I managed to celebrate communion with her after all, he thought.

While they chatted, and the vodka was making his brain lighter, he drank her in with his eyes, the combination of blue eyes and hair blacker than ebony, aware as he did so that the button had been activated, felt an insistent pressure spreading from his spine out into the rest of his body, a pressure which told him in no uncertain terms that he was faced here with a woman who could help to steer his life in an unexpected direction. On her desk lay some books that aroused his interest. "I'm learning Chinese," she said.

"What are you going to do with that?"

"I want to become a missionary," she said. "I've applied to the Missionary College. Why stay here, casting pearls before swine, when China poses such a big challenge? A billion animists hiding behind a nonreligious façade."

"They'll never let you in there to do missionary work," he said.

"Patience," she said. "It's only a matter of biding my time. It won't be long before China starts opening up again. And until it does, there's always Taiwan."

Once again Jonas was taken by surprise. There was something about her that he couldn't quite make out, the clash between her delicate appearance and the vodka, which she was really knocking back, although without getting as drunk as he was. Her eyes were veiled with sensuality, but at the same time full of innocence, or no, not innocence, but a lack of experience, an ignorance of young men's lust. More records by Patti Smith were placed on the turntable, *Radio Ethiopia* he read on one sleeve, as if this too had to do with missionary work.

She began to sway slowly around the floor, dancing to "Ask the Angels," looked at him as he sat there, befuddled by drink and with the taste of roe and raw onion in his mouth, looked at him with blue eyes, blue eyes and black, black hair, as she raised her arms over her hair, disclosing dark tufts under her arms and filling the room with a faint odor of perspiration. He got up and danced with her, they said nothing, merely glided around to the intense music, husky vocals, lyrics Jonas couldn't quite catch, only a mystifying phrase here and there: "pissing in a river." He put his arms around her, felt the pressure rise, felt both sure and unsure, wanted to conquer, or be conquered, was never certain which was which; there came a point, at any rate, when, by his reading of the situation, all he had to do was to lead her over to the bed, she would lie back unresistingly, surrender to a boy with experience, she was desperate for it, had been desperate for it for ages, but at that moment she suddenly stopped dancing, said something to the effect that she was tired, that she had things to do the next day, Sunday, those blue eyes once more apologetic, troubled. "Kiss me just once," she said before he left. He did so, greedily, pressing her up against the wall. "I said kiss," she whispered, "not crucify."

Poor girl, he thought to himself on the way home, as confused as he was exasperated; all that vodka, and she was still terrified of her own sexuality.

Some weeks later he received a letter. Anne S. asked him to meet her in the Grand Hall. Jonas Wergeland knew that this was an offer he could not refuse, so on the Saturday evening he walked up Staffeldts gate to the Inner Mission Hotel—a building he had always admired for its clean lines—where a youth club meeting was under way in the Grand Hall. The mood in the lobby was lively; he had to hang about until the people in the hall broke into exultant song, and when she eventually appeared, dressed in a neat pleated skirt and a black leather biker jacket, she surprised him by leading him outside and round to the hotel side of the building, on the upper floors. Everything is happening much too fast for Jonas, but it seems to him—he would swear to it—that she doesn't have a key, that she actually picks the lock on one of the doors. All of a sudden he finds himself alone in a hotel room with Anne S., black hair and blue eyes, with a look in them that speaks to him of a colossal hunger, either that or sheer, evangelical zeal. As if she were somehow out to convert him. And speaking of conversion: Anne S. never did become a missionary; in later years she was appointed to a top post with the World Council of Churches in Geneva, became a leading figure in the fight for the furtherance of women—not before time—in ultraconservative religious circles, and as such a missionary of sorts for her sex in a field full of inveterate heathens.

The way Jonas construed it—or as he realized as soon as he received her letter—she had made up her mind to say goodbye to her virginal existence. She had opted for the Inner Mission Hotel, he thought, its safe, familiar surroundings, so that the transition would not be too abrupt. For once he was nervous, felt almost as if he were the instrument of higher powers. To a certain extent he had been chosen to take her virtue. He had a responsibility. He had to see to it that that an untouched girl received a gentle introduction into the intoxicating mysteries of sex. This was not like other adventures—not an outer, but an inner mission.

She undresses quickly, clearly embarrassed and yet at the same time impatient, climbs into bed and pulls the quilt up to her chin. Only one thing is worrying Jonas: that she will change her mind. But a moment later she lifts up the quilt for him—as if welcoming him into a tent—or perhaps I should say a tabernacle.

The faint sound of singing reached their ears from somewhere down below. It occurred to Jonas that he might have misunderstood. Maybe she wanted their encounter, the sex, to be a sin: a sin she committed with her eyes open, well aware of what she was doing, as if it were an act of blasphemy.

He felt her tremble and regretted this thought, felt a rush of tenderness, ran his hands gently, soothingly over her body, her skin, which was strangely cool. He was very aroused, possibly because she lay there so passively, so still, as if she did not know how to respond, or did not dare respond as her body was telling her to do. Only when, after many a long detour, his fingers reached her crotch, and he felt how moist, how wet she was, how ready as it said in the passages Daniel had read aloud to him when they were boys, only when he could not hold back any longer, but twisted round to the bedside table, where he had with the greatest discretion left out a condom which he now rolled onto his cock, deftly, with none of the clumsy fumbling of the first-timer, although the ring felt tighter than usual, his cock bigger; the condom sheathed it like a sausage skin as he rolled on top of her with a primitive pounding in his veins, placed his forearms against the inner sides of her thighs and spread them apart, a little roughly perhaps, and just for a moment there he thought she offered some resistance, tried to push him away, as if to say that he was taking her against her will, he could never be sure, because it only lasted a few seconds, then she relaxed and he slid as deep inside her as he could, but with such lack of control that he could not help seeing how her brow creased in pain. There might even have been tears in her eyes.

He managed to restrain himself, lay still, as if to give her time to get used to being filled for the first time, come to terms with the thought of having lost the seal upon her virgin status, it may have come as a shock, something over which one ought really to shed a tear. Jonas, for his part, had more than enough to do just enduring that warmth, as blissful as always, that almost stupefyingly good feeling, and when he began to move he was pleasantly surprised to find how well she clenched the muscles of her vagina together, so hard that the friction instantly gave rise to an itching sensation, an exceptionally powerful illuminating force, along with a fear that he was going to come right away, so turned on was he by being inside a nervous, naïve virgin.

All this time she lay with her eyes closed, unmoving, just crossing her arms over his back, her palms on his shoulder-blades, lightly pressing him down onto her, as if she were getting used to it, beginning to enjoy it, learning that sex was not only a part of God's creation, but also a foretaste of the splendors of the world to come—something which the Islamic religion had long understood, of course, with its paradise pervaded with erotic dreams.

Then she turned away, and Jonas, worked-up to bursting point, felt sick with disappointment. He thought she'd had enough. But she simply turned around, onto all fours, inviting him to take her from behind, maybe because she didn't want to be reminded of the word "missionary" he mused and gazed hungrily at the long cleft, the swollen lips surrounding it, the damp, black tufts of pubic hair, before driving into her, panting with impatience; he watched his whole length disappear, right up to the ring of the condom and was again amazed by the way in which she gripped him with her muscles, how beautifully she pushed back against him, almost without moving; he took in the sight of her breasts swaying, dare one say, titillatingly, back and forth, a tiny gold cross dangling in the air in front of them, helpless-looking, forgotten;

and when she twisted her head to the side, he noted with triumph the moment when her mouth dropped open, though no sound came out, as if a mask had fallen from her face, and she could no longer conceal from herself how wonderful this was, how absolutely heavenly, how divinely Jonas made love to her.

The rhythm, the movements grew more and more frantic, hers too, she appeared to have lost all her inhibitions, willingly gave herself up to a long pent-up lust, as if, having once become a sinner she could not get enough of sinning—like a missionary suddenly throwing herself, stark naked, into the ritual dances of the natives. He was growing more and more inflamed—yes, just that: inflamed, he felt his penis swelling to a size that astonished him, he could see it clearly from this position, and yet she was gripping him so tightly, despite his long, deep thrusts, that he was put in mind of a stallion he had once seen covering a mare, how the mare visibly held the stallion in place with her powerful internal muscles. He could not help groaning, growling, out of sheer, raw, ruttishness; he could see why Taoists gave sexual positions names such as "wild horse rearing," "white tiger leaping," or "the dragon's claws"; half in a fog he saw that the condom was sliding off, or not sliding, being pulled off, the friction was simply too great, she was sucking it off him and he had to toss the rubber sheath to the floor before thrusting his cock inside her again, he could not stop, was working in a narcotic haze of pleasure, or in a sphere where powerful, dangerous, forces prevailed, out of the blue he remembered something about a transformer, and this should come as no surprise since all memories are stored away and can be recalled, as it were, at the turn of a key, but for some, perhaps the most important ones, a password is required, and that was what his women gave Jonas, which is to say a handful of them, whom—thanks to a gift, an extra vertebra of dragon horn in his spine, a gift of grace—he was able to recognize; if, that is, it was not the other way round: that that was how they recognized him. Be that as it may, their lovemaking had a special effect on him: something unfolded, or rose up from the dark recesses of his memory, like a genie from a lamp. Which explains why, as he hunched over Anne S. in that bed in the Inner Mission Hotel, his mind was split between the pleasure and a memory which was more or less pumped up to the surface, a not exactly happy memory, something to do with a switch, a lethal button; and even as he was struggling to assemble these fragments, from somewhere far off he caught what at first he took to be a stream of gibberish, like the glossolalic outbursts from the tent meetings of his childhood, then he realized that it was her, Anne S., that she was screaming dick, dick, crying out for more dick; again he was astonished, astonished by this word, dick, only common girls said dick, but here she was, yelling it out, what a lovely dick, she cried, he heard it quite clearly with one part of his mind but was too busy trying to remember, or to come, come in a way that was so gloriously, breathtakingly out of this world, somewhere deep inside among her powerful, blood-red, sucking muscles. You've just got to say fuck it, was the thought at the very back of his mind; you've just got to press a button and go for it, even if it kills you.

He slumped down, rolled over onto his back, thought he was going to pass out. She got up; Jonas lay with his eyes shut, going over his climax again in his mind, the convulsions of his orgasm which had also enabled him to complete a leap, bring to life a memory. She had been miraculously good. He felt like doing it again, as soon as she returned from the bathroom. He dozed off, started at the sound of the outer door slamming. When he looked up her clothes were gone—she had simply vanished into thin air. Jonas lay where he was, mind working, heard muffled sounds from the meeting in the Grand Hall. He got dressed, checked to see if she had forgotten anything but found nothing. She had, however, left her mark in the form of some good-going gonococci that, less than a week later forced him to make the trip to the fifth floor of the Oslo Health Center. That really is so typical of Jonas Wergeland, Professor: to contract gonorrhoea after going to bed with a girl he was sure had to be the safest in the world.

Final Episode

Is it possible, as a twenty-four-year-old, to experience one day of your life as a nine-year-old, and in such a way that it affects the rest of your life?

The memory Anne S. gave him—a story which is a result of all the stories I have told so far, and a prerequisite for all of those still to come—goes something like this: it is a Saturday, and Jonas and Ørn have just been home to dump their schoolbags when something exciting happens, one of those welcome breaks in the humdrum routine of the housing estate, on a par with the tarmacking of footpaths or the emptying of cess-pits: funny little steamrollers and sewage trucks with hoses which gave off a stench that seemed to come from the nethermost regions of hell itself. A van pulled up beside the electricity substation, or "transformer" as they called it, at the foot of the hill known as Egiltomta—which was, by the way, a spot as central to boyhood games of Cowboys and Indians as Monument Valley was to the westerns of John Ford—and out stepped a man in a smart, grey-blue uniform with shiny buttons and the letters "O" and "L" on a badge on his cap, though these initials had nothing to do with *de Olympiske Leker*—that is, the Olympic Games—they stood, instead, for *Oslo Lysverker*—the Oslo Electricity Board; this man was a technician, doing a routine check. You see we're talking here about a springtime in the days when children went to school on Saturday morning and when, for most people, though they've forgotten it now, the working week did not end until early Saturday afternoon.

Jonas spied a golden opportunity and acted fast; that the Oslo Electricity Board should have come along just at this moment fitted so perfectly that his heart skipped a beat. He ran back into the building, having first given instructions to Ørn, who stayed where he was and watched, as enthralled as Ali Baba himself, as the man opened the door on the low-voltage side of the substation, positioned himself in front of what looked like a row of porcelain door handles—in fact these were the so-called "knives" used to break the circuit—and checked something with an instrument that hung on a cord around his neck, then he took a reading from something else with what looked rather like a square pair of pliers—it was all a mystery to Little Eagle. The technician had just stepped from behind the double-doors in the middle, where he had been inspecting the actual transformer, when Jonas emerged from the entry carrying a torch and a packet of Gjende biscuits; by sneaking round the foot of Egiltomta in a wide arc he managed to reach the back of the little brick building without being seen. Once the man had opened the third heavy, metal door to carefully examine whatever lay behind it, even making some notes in a little book, and was about to lock up—he had swung the door to again—Ørn attracted his attention, as arranged, by shouting: "Hey, there's some kids fiddling with your wing-mirror!" The man ran to his van, and at that moment Jonas darted inside the door of the transformer station and pulled it to, as it had been before.

Over by the van, the man shook his head in exasperation at Ørn, who was thumbing his nose at him from a safe distance. He walked back to the substation, where the door in the side was still standing slightly ajar, shut and locked it. Then he drove away, shaking his fist at Ørn.

But inside the transformer sat Jonas Wergeland, and Jonas Wergeland was both lucky and unlucky. Lucky, because only on this side of the sub-station could he do what he had in mind. Unlucky because he was in the most hazardous part of it, a highly dangerous area, to put it mildly, for anyone who didn't know what they were doing, a fact which he instinctively knew, as he sat there with his back against the metal door, as if perched on a mountain ledge with a sheer drop in front of him. He had all the time in the world now. He was waiting for the evening, and he waited with the patience of an avenger, because this was not just any Saturday, it was an evening on which everyone was thinking about just one thing: the radio. Or to be more exact, the eleventh and final episode of the radio series *Dickie Dick Dickens*, which is to say, the first of three series which had been made, a golden moment in the history of Radio Theater, with an unforgettable Frank Robert in the leading role—not to mention the score, composed by Gunnar Sønstevold, the man who had once heard a piano crash to the ground from a fifth-floor window.

How does one become a murderer?

If you knew how hard I have hunted, Professor, hunted for this story, this incident which, like one gene among thirty thousand, could be the cause of something out of the ordinary happening to a life.

Jonas had always been a little afraid of the electricity substation which lay between the blocks of flats: a building of the old type, a little house which hummed faintly, but tantalizingly, so that children often felt an irresistible urge to put their ears to the vents in the solid doors, as if faced here with a giant shell. Generally, though, the metal sign, the red lightning bolt and the legend "Danger—High Voltage" were as good a deterrent as the Phantom's skull. Any mention of the words "high-voltage" tended to touch Jonas on the raw. It was not that long since his Uncle Lauritz, that cologne-scented man of the world, the SAS pilot who had sent his nephews postcards from every corner of the globe, had been killed when his private plane flew into a power cable: an occurrence which was rendered no less nightmarish by the fact that Jonas himself had once sat, rigid with terror, in that same, flimsy little Piper Cub. No one could see how the accident could have happened; his uncle was an experienced pilot. The way Jonas saw it, it must have been the forces contained within the high-voltage cable that had, in some mysterious way, lured his uncle into steering straight into it.

And now Jonas himself was only inches away from death. He sat listening to the hum, much louder in here than outside. Powers beyond his understanding, like in the Pentecostalists' tent. After a while Ørn came over and talked to him through the air vents in the door, as if he were a prisoner in a condemned cell. "Everything's fine," Jonas assured him, "but run up to my mum and tell her I'm spending the evening at your place." Nobody must know that he was hiding in here. Least of all Petter, that dirty louse Petter, later to become better known, not to say notorious, as Sgt. Petter.

Jonas sat with his back against the door in the gloom and waited, ate some Gjende biscuits, ran his fingers over the raised shape of the reindeer on them as if it were Braille, telling the tale of a breathtaking ride on a reindeer's back. He must have dozed off, because all at once it was pitch dark. He switched on the torch. Right in front of him was a baffling-looking device, and behind it sat the transformer itself—that he knew—he could also hear the humming of the copper coils inside it. The beam of the torch fell on thick cables covered in some sort of insulating tape that made them look like bloated anacondas. For some reason they reminded him of a constantly recurring dream. Or perhaps they aroused his curiosity, in the same way as the pipes of an organ. It had something to do with hidden connections. He had always been interested in cables, in where they went, the whole hydroelectric network; he could hardly put a plug into a socket without thinking of one the detested Petter's many jokes. What's real power? To blow into an electric socket and make the current flow backwards!

Recently he had also seen something that had made him even more curious about cables. Here—and apropos of all the speculations regarding Jonas Wergeland's penchant for round-the-world voyages—it should perhaps be mentioned that a journey need not be very long in order to be of crucial importance. A journey of five yards can be enough.

Jonas was a bit scared of Samson Berg, their neighbor right across the hall, a burly widower with a bushy beard and a cigar butt almost invariably wedged in the corner of his mouth, not unlike Mickey Mouse's archenemy Black Pete, in fact. One day when Jonas was outside, struggling ineffectually with a cable, Berg came along and offered to help. "Do you want to come up and see a real cable?" he asked once the new Bosch lamp was wired up to the bike. Jonas wasn't altogether sure; on the other hand, he liked the idea of seeing inside another house, because although the flats at Solhaug all had the same number of rooms, stepping inside any one of them, even those flats belonging to the most boring people, was like entering an alien universe, an absolute jungle—especially because of the smell which, in Samson Berg's case, was predominantly that of Brylcreem and cigars. The central feature in Berg's living room was a luminous green aquarium which stood next to the radiogram, like a sort of forerunner to color television, but that was not what Samson wanted to show him: "Look at this," he said and led Jonas over to a table on which sat a circular thing with a sort of pyramid rising out of it. At first Jonas thought this was what he had heard referred to and ridiculed as "modern art." But Samson Berg worked for the Standard Telefon og Kabel factory down in the Grorud Valley, and this was nothing less than a cross-section of a cable, a circle full of smaller circles, sliced through in such a way that the circles climbed higher and higher the closer you got to the center: a brilliant teaching aid, for use in showing the different layers of the power cable: the copper conductor, the insulating lining of oil-impregnated paper, the lead sheath and so on—all of which Berg eagerly explained to him. "It looks like a brooch," Jonas said reverently, thinking of Aunt Laura's gem. Berg was so pleased with this remark that he brought Jonas a bottle of Solo orangeade as a reward, and while he sipped on this he was regaled with a mass of information about electricity, about the "lighting-up celebrations" of the old days, when electricity came to a country village, and about the cables that lay buried in the ground, like wormballs. Above all, though, he was treated to a whole lecture on the project Samson was most proud to have been a part of: the laying of the huge undersea cables across Oslo Fjord at Filtvet three years earlier. "You know what, Jonas, they used to talk about going around the world in eighty days—now all it takes is eight seconds," he said, then added: "There are people who think that power lies in guns, but these days it's all about having control of the cables, the arteries of society. And d'you know something else? Soon we'll be laying them—invisibly!—across the heavens."

Thanks to Berg's teachings, Jonas also knew a bit about transformers; in particular he remembered what Samson had told him about the windings, those copper coils: how, with something akin to a miraculous, electrical discus throw, they converted 5,000 volts—the standard high-voltage level in those days—to 230 volts. And even more importantly: that there was a switch somewhere inside the substation, a switch that could cut off the power to all six blocks of flats in Solhaug. I bet you can't wait to hear what's going to happen to *Dickie Dick Dickens*, Petter, you rotten devil—well, too bad, Jonas thought.

He flashed the torch over his surroundings. The big grey box right in front of him was the switch for an oil-immersed transformer, although he found it hard to believe—that a switch could be that big. Jonas had pictured it as being just an ordinary switch, something like the mains switch in a fuse box; this bulked as large as the engine compartment of a car. Cables carrying 5,000 volts, which might, in fact, have been supplied by Standard Telefon og Kabel, ran from the electricity pylons into the bottom of the switch, these first had to pass through "knives" and fuses, then down into the relays and the white bushing insulators at the top of the switch. Jonas's heart sank. He came to the conclusion that the switch must be worked by the cast-iron wheel fixed to the front of the box, because he could see the word "On" printed on a red semicircle in the middle of it, and below an arrow pointing anticlockwise: "Off." He tried turning the wheel in the direction indicated but couldn't budge it an inch; he was conscious that he was now dangerously close to the cables running into the switch, 5,000 deadly volts. Although he did not know how much danger he was in: had he put his hand close enough to the connection points of any of the cables running into the switch, the current would have flashed over and he would have been killed on the spot.

Jonas sits with his back against the door. It is twenty-five minutes past eight. Up and down the blocks people were settling themselves next to the radio to listen to *Dickie Dick Dickens*, eager to know whether Dickie would win through to become king of the Chicago underworld, and no one was more keen to know the outcome than Petter. Hence the reason Jonas was sitting there—despite being afraid of the dark, despite the high-voltage sign. At long last he was going to have his revenge on the dirtiest, rottenest pig of them all. And if this surprises you, Professor, if you are wondering what act of villainy could possibly drive a child to plunge a whole housing estate into darkness to get at just one person, then you will have to wait, because this is not the place for the answer to that question.

Jonas sat inside something big, dark, dangerous, perhaps sensing even now that this was the fundamental situation in his life: to sit inside something totally unfamiliar, looking for the point from which one could, nonetheless, make an impact, set something in motion. If, that is, this was not a desperate attempt to fill the emptiness inside him. To become someone else, become something. He shone the torch this way and that and finally caught sight of a little red button on the side of the metal box with the wheel on the front. He edged over to it. One last chance. He knew it was foolhardy. Thought of all that tremendous power. What if he was wrong, and he dropped down dead the minute he touched that button? Or perished in a shower of sparks as the whole thing short-circuited. Jonas pictured how they would find him lying there, all charred and shrivelled, like the potatoes they wrapped in tin-foil and then forgot to take off the bonfire. He looks at his watch. At eight-thirty on the dot he presses the button. He registers the fact that he is still alive. And that something is happening with a chain and a cog, that the wheel is turning, that the word "Off" is now showing on a green semicircle. I did it, he thinks. There is dead silence, the hum has stopped: it's as if the electricity supply to life itself had been shut off. I hope you're pissing yourself, he thought, with Petter in mind.

He could not see the result of his handiwork himself, but Ørn told him what a magnificent sight, or anti-sight, it had been; he had stood at the window watching the area served by the substation, the whole of Solhaug, being blacked out, and, far more importantly as far as Jonas was concerned, the green cat's-eyes of the wireless sets being extinguished, at the same time as the voices died away. Fortunately very few people had portable radios, Petter certainly didn't, and neither did any of the neighbors in his building who happened to be at home. In any case, all thoughts of Radio Theater were forgotten in the general confusion caused by a power cut, a minor catastrophe, when people had more than enough to do just trying to find out what had happened and remembering where they had put the candles. It wasn't until the next day that Petter was heard complaining loudly over the fact that he had missed *Dickie Dick Dickens*: "Aw, bugger it, and it was the last episode, too!"

In just a little under half an hour two men from the Oslo Electricity Board turned up outside the substation on Hagelundveien. They went into the low-voltage side first. Jonas could see the light from their torches, heard them talking to one another, muttering something about a possible overload. When they eventually unlocked the door on the high-voltage side they got such a shock, such a fright, that Jonas managed to nip between them and run up Egiltomta, which he knew like the back of his hand, before they could get a good look at him.

Word that somebody had been inside the transformer soon spread and was the subject of much comment among the residents of Solhaug—there was some talk of communists—but no one ever found out who it was. Jonas did, however, have the feeling that Petter regarded him with some surprise, as if he had discovered that Jonas was charged in a totally different way, had become a different person. In years to come Jonas would be plagued by the fear that this sweet revenge would have grim consequences—a fear which was borne out six years later when he took that walk through Transylvania with Laila. Deep down, and despite the time gap, Jonas always felt that the assault on Laila was prompted by something he had done, that it came as a consequence of Petter's missing the final episode of a radio detective series.

But his immediate feeling was one of pleasure. He caressed the thought of how pressing such a little button could do so much, how easy it was to make an impact on so many people at once in the society in which he lived. This was the first time on which Jonas Wergeland synchronized people's attention. Later he would do so again, on a much bigger scale, the only difference being that then people, the inhabitants of an entire country, would voluntarily put off lights so that they could sit in semi-darkness and switch off from everything else in order to concentrate on the light which his television programs bestowed on them.

Brain Power

I have the suspicion, after having told such a story, that I have changed Jonas Wergeland's life completely—and that I ought, therefore, to tell all the stories I have told so far over again. However that may be, this brings us to a new beginning:

There are various conflicting accounts as to how Jonas Wergeland got the idea for his great television series, but all confusion on this score is dispelled if one goes back to an incident in the mid-eighties when Wergeland, frustrated by his respected—but rather isolated—position within NRK, granted himself a "thinking trip"—if, that is, this was not an instance of sheer escapism, a sudden and desperate urge to get away, seeing that he felt totally flat and longed, in a metaphorical sense, to touch a high-voltage cable. Having completed a feature in New York on Arnstein Arneberg's and Per Krogh's work on the Security Council Chamber at the United Nations building, he embarked, hopefully—or as tremulously as someone making their first parachute jump—on this quest, traveling almost in a loop around the earth; but not until he was flying in over Tokyo was he struck by the sense that something big was about to happen, as if it was because of him that they landed—as if he had been sitting dozing, then suddenly shouted to the pilot: "For God's sake, go down here!" It might also have had something to do with the fact that they were put into a holding pattern, that they had to circle over Narita airport several times, and as they were coming in to land Jonas felt a fluttery, sinking feeling in the pit of his stomach, as if he were being dragged down by an airy maelstrom towards a center, a gravitational point for which he had always been searching.

How does one become a conqueror?

The sight of all those cables and wires hanging in midair, so unlike Oslo—like being inside an enormous transformer—confirmed his feeling that it must be possible to change one's way of thinking in such a metropolis; Jonas walked around, rejoicing in the fact that, as always in a new place, he had to be guided by his nose, ears, mouth, eyes; that for a few days he would need to recapture the sensual intelligence he had relied on as a child. And so he wandered, at all times strangely on the alert, into the abundantly-stocked stores, with sales assistants bowing and murmuring "*Irasshaimase*?" at every turn; he breathed in the aroma of noodle soup behind black curtains in little bars, peeked inside garishly lit parlors where hundreds of pachinko machines filled the air with their ear-splitting din, watched people on the underground standing totally engrossed in erotic comics, gazed expectantly at tempting displays of wax food in restaurant windows before stepping inside and letting his taste-buds decide for themselves, put his fingertips to those flimsy walls of rice paper which reminded him of the model gliders of his childhood, stood outside in the evening gawking in disbelief at streets where shops rigged out like pure *son et lumière* extravaganzas sat right across from tiny, moss-grown temples that might have been portals to unknown regions. And all the while he was instinctively looking for a center, with no success, because Tokyo was the most bewildering city he had ever visited, it had no obvious center to it, or rather: it had so many centers, below ground too—Shinjuku station, for example, or the underground Yaesu arcades. Jonas had the feeling that forces were sweeping him round in a spiral and that the center was everywhere and nowhere.

That he should wind up in a shop selling electronic goods was inevitable, and of all the astonishing new products he found there, nothing astonished him more than how much smaller things had become. He had had a Sony Walkman for ages, but on sale here—he could hardly believe his eyes—was a Sony Watchman, a tiny, flat television set, not much bigger than a pocket calculator and in Jonas's eyes as much of a masterpiece as a Renaissance miniature. He just had to have one of these, and it was as he was standing with the box in his hand that he was struck by an irresistible impulse: he would speak to—no, not merely speak to—he would interview Akio Morita, the founder of Sony. Not for television—that would be too complicated—but for a newspaper. "It's probably impossible," he said to himself as he stood there eyeing the Sony logo, the best-known trademark in the world after Coca Cola, "but I will, I must, do it."

And thanks to his impressive business card and a few carefully considered words written with a calligraphy pen purchased in the Kyukyodo stationery shop in Ginza on the NRK notepaper which he had had the foresight to bring with him, and thanks, not least, to the fact that Morita chanced to be in Tokyo just then—a stroke of luck to which Jonas

Wergeland turned a blind eye—two days later, with a newly acquired dictaphone in his pocket, he was bowed into Morita's office in Sony's flamboyant headquarters on Gotenyama Hills in Shinagawa on the south side of the city. Jonas knows that this is a huge scoop, and he has already made a deal with an editor back home in Norway; he can just picture how people's eyes will pop when they open their Saturday paper and turn to the sensational double-page spread: a Norwegian having an exclusive tête-à-tête with Akio Morita, one of those men whom some would say exercised more power over the lives of ordinary people around the world than any national assembly.

One might well ask what possessed Jonas Wergeland to do this, Professor. Because, even though he did have genuine admiration for the Japanese gentleman across from him, who seemed—perhaps because of his mane of white hair—to be surrounded by a nimbus of wisdom, the deeper reason lay, of course, in that old, niggling suspicion that he was a middle-of-the-roader—something which, so far, his television career, despite all the respect, despite all the attention, tended to suggest. So yet again it was his extraordinary caliber that Jonas Wergeland was endeavoring to summon up, or have confirmed, as he sat there conducting his carefully prepared interview with Akio Morita, an individual who had helped to change the world in which Jonas lived and even shaped the medium from which he earned his living: television. For a second Jonas felt as though he were talking to God, his creator.

Such a thought would surely have been far from the mind of Morita himself, with his steel-rimmed glasses, his white shirt and dark tie, as he sat there describing the history of Sony, from its early beginnings just after the war right up to the present day. "Our aim was always to break new ground," he said, "and we knew that we had to export in order to survive." Morita had lived in New York in the sixties and spoke very good English. Jonas was struck by his charming manner, his un-Japanese candor and, not least, the honesty with which he answered questions about management techniques and the difference between the American and the Japanese styles. This is going to look great in print, he thought exultantly as Morita was rounding off with some pearls of wisdom about business management and the world economy. Before he left, and after they had duly posed together for the photographer whom Jonas had hired, he thanked Sony's founder heartily.

Not until he was in the lift did it occur to Jonas that he had just met the man who had been the ruin of Vebjørn Tandberg and as such was, in a way, the reason why his own little flutter on the stock market had come to such a sorry end.

Some hours later he was sitting in the café at the top of the Akasaka Prince Hotel, an extraordinary half moon-shaped skyscraper designed by Kenzo Tange, the architect responsible for the ultramodern sports stadiums which, as a boy, Jonas had seen in television broadcasts from the 1964 Olympic Games. And it really was like being on the moon. Far below him spread the whole of the center-less city of Tokyo, looking as though it were floating, was in motion, and in that chaotic mass down there Jonas actually thought he could make out a spiral formation, like a galaxy. On the marble-topped table in front of him lay a postcard he had written to Kristin, a card with a picture of the cherry trees in blossom, because his daughter collected pictures of trees. He had also bought a pretty lacquer casket in which he hoped she would keep her sacred things, as he had once put the puck and the silver brooch in his casket. Jonas returned his attention to the enormous slice of Queen Elizabeth chocolate cake, sat there congratulating himself, hundreds of feet above the ground in a shimmering blue and white room. And then, in the midst of his triumph, while he was sitting there patting himself on the back as it were, an enormous wave of despondency—not to say, nausea—washed over him.

Suddenly it was all so clear—and not simply because he was so high up, with such a stunning panoramic view: he was nothing but a spectator. He could travel halfway around the world, but he would always be a spectator. He was a Norwegian, and as such born to be a spectator. Here, in Tokyo, he had the ghastly feeling that Norway was not represented at all, not as an active participant. No, wait—there were a few products: in one shop he had seen a toothbrush manufactured by Jordan, and if he visited a bookshop he might find a book by Thorbjørn Egner about two little dental demons called Carius and Bactus—as if all Norway had to offer to the Far East—to the whole world, for that matter—was a moralistic injunction to keep one's teeth clean. While the Japanese had permeated everyday life, even in Norway, with technology, from the cars on the roads to the sounds and images in living rooms, the Norwegian contribution to the world was stuck at the level of goats' cheese and woollen mittens. Looking at it from here, from the top of the crescent-shaped Akasaka Prince Hotel, in this magnificent Asian amphitheater, Jonas Wergeland realized that Norway was but a part of an obscure and totally inconsequential periphery.

The blue interior no longer shimmered. Jonas sat there surrounded by marble and mirrors and looked out over Tokyo. "It was as if a scream ran through me," he said later. The Morita interview was not a triumph. It was a sham. An adolescent fancy, a bit like collecting autographs—or having one's dream of kissing Brigitte Bardot come true. Jonas could not help thinking of ordinary people who had their pictures taken with celebrities, as if securing themselves lifelong proof that they were not, after all, invisible or insignificant: "I interviewed Akio Morita!" The truth slid over him like an unseen roller of lead: he had never been anything but a walking tape recorder, it seemed that he was forever doomed to copy others, to merely be someone who repeated or reproduced the thoughts and ideas of great people. And although up to now he had proved to be a master copyist, a true virtuoso in his field, he would have given a lot—everything—for the ability to create something with a dash of originality. All at once he felt completely flat, as if he had been just about to reach a finishing line but now found himself back at the start.

It was in this frame of mind that he took the underground further down the line and got off at Tokyo station, a little, redbrick Renaissance castle; from there he made his way across the moat, through the Otemon Gate in the steep wall encircling the Imperial Palace, and into the palace gardens, perhaps because he felt that he had to be out in the open, otherwise he might suffocate. He plodded glumly along paved paths and eventually found himself in the middle of the Imperial Palace's East Garden where he sank down onto a bench, surrounded by flower beds, small coniferous trees and rhododendron bushes and by office workers armed with handy cardboard cases containing chopsticks and a little marvel of a lunch: minuscule dishes arranged as neatly and delicately as chocolates in a box.

Jonas sat gazing at the man-made landscape before him—a miniature mountain, a stream running into a pond, stone lanterns and a bridge—all forming a harmonious whole, true to the Japanese ideal. Across from him stood a brown, wooden tea pavilion with a green copper roof. The sounds of birdsong and running water mingled with the faint rumble of the surrounding city. Jonas took out his dictaphone and removed the cassette, began to pull the tape out, slowly hauled out the cassette's innards, until the entire tape lay in a tangled mass in his lap. He did the same with the camera film, the pictures of himself and Morita and, without thinking about it, tied a knot in the whole lot. Right next to him a gardener was clipping a bush; it gave off a pungent odor, a mixture of spice and perfume. Beyond the trees Jonas glimpsed one of the white corner towers on the wall, a sight that reminded him of something he had once heard: that a Norwegian marble quarry had supplied stone for the new Imperial Palace here in Tokyo. That was always something, he thought, reminded also of how he and Ørn—on one of the few, but memorable, expeditions instigated by Ørn—had made a tour of Oslo to look at buildings constructed out of Grorud granite. With pride, true pride, they had paced round the foundation walls of the Palace and the Historical Museum and stood outside the University Library, admiring the plinth of the building. Even the writer Bjørnstjerne Bjørnson's gravestone had come from Grorud. It was really the same story with the marble from Fauske, the only difference being that this stone now sat outside of Norway.

Feeling a little more cheerful, Jonas lifted his eyes to the soaring buildings of the banks and big corporations in the Marunouchi district on the other side of the wall and the moat; he was dazzled for a moment by the sun reflecting off their façades—and, perhaps, by the thought of the vast power which, like Sony, these multinational concerns represented—companies each one of which boasted a greater turnover than the GNP of some countries in Europe. A new, almost invisible, capitalist power was in the process of conquering the world, including little Norway, without anyone noticing.

The thought of Sony reminded him of something: towards the end of their conversation, Morita himself had brought up the subject of Norway, or more precisely, of Edvard Munch, mentioning something to the effect that he was a great admirer of Munch's work, particularly *The Scream. The Scream*, Morita felt, had to be Norway's answer to the *Mona Lisa*. Was it for sale? Jonas just smiled, it never occurred to him that Morita might be serious; how could he know that Japanese buyers would later be prepared to shell out nigh-on a billion Norwegian kroner for a single European painting without so much as a murmur. "And do you know?" Morita had said as Jonas was leaving. "When I tried out the first Walkman on a friend of mine, I used a tape of Edvard Grieg's piano concerto. It gave the perfect demonstration." Jonas had smiled at this too, taking it as no more than polite chitchat. But now, only hours later, he spied another, very different, dimension to these snippets of conversation.

It is not entirely true that the city of Tokyo has no center to it. Jonas Wergeland was sitting not far from the new Imperial Palace, built on the ruins of the Tokugawa Shogun's residence, Edo Castle, which, for the

Japanese in ancient times, represented the hub of the world. But now all power had been removed, also from the Emperor. Jonas Wergeland was sitting, in other words, at a center that was devoid of meaning. And he also felt that he was at the center of—nothing. As if he had been sucked into Nothingness. All of a sudden he understood why he traveled so much. He was a pilgrim, a man on an eternal quest for a sacred spot. And he had found it here, all the world's altar, the empty center. Here, right here, anything could happen.

And perhaps it was this very emptiness, this sense of a vacuum, which generated the extraordinary pressure necessary to prove to Jonas Wergeland that human beings are also polymorphous, that they too can assume different forms, as carbon can crystallize into something other than graphite. Here, in Tokyo, he finally found his other possible, maybe even optimum, form: a form which he had, in a way, possessed for a long time, though he had never acted upon it: his diamond form. Jonas Wergeland felt, in other words, an original idea working its way through, like a shoot rising out of the sludge of run-of-the-mill thinking: no more would he content himself with bringing ideas home, he—the perception made his head spin—was going to be someone who took ideas out, for others to copy. Thanks to what Morita had said about Munch and Grieg, he realized that instead of simply exporting stone—or G-MAN saws for that matter—Norway would have to concentrate much more on producing concepts, yes, fictions, pure products of the imagination. Norway sold energy, after all, so why not sell people's ideas too? The last time Norway had made a great leap forward it had been on the back of hydroelectric power—now everything was going to depend on brainpower. People were willing to pay for that too, and pay a lot—a powerful man like Akio Morita was proof of that. Jonas Wergeland sits in the middle of Tokyo, surrounded by the clamor of one of the biggest cities in the world, in an empty center, and has a vision—a few seconds of clear-sightedness which will determine the course of his life for many years to come: the great hope, for him, for Norway, lay in being able to offer knowledge, a different kind of knowledge. Because of all products, knowledge had become the most valuable. The future lay not in hardware—white goods—but in software—grey matter.

Jonas Wergeland knew in a flash what he was going to do, he was going to make a television series about just such people as Munch and Grieg, and he would do it so well that it would become a piece of merchandise, a program in two senses of the word, and one so attractive that it could be exported. On the threshold of the millennium, the Japanese would not just be asking for marble, or toothbrushes, or smoked salmon from Norway; they would be asking, they would be begging for, television programs about enterprising Norwegian men and women, programs whose worth rested not on a material but on a symbolic foundation. As with the Grorud granite, this too was all about spreading the local Norwegian bedrock, only in this case on a much larger, international, scale. That was his, Jonas Wergeland's, future, not creeping around the offices of foreign demigods like a copycat, a spectator, a parrot with a tape recorder in his hand.

He had been in possession of this clue for a while, but only now did he see that the Japanese lacquer casket he had been given by his grandfather when he was a boy was a precursor to the television set. TV too was a black box just waiting to be filled. With symbols. At home he had even placed one of the dragons he had finished, a head covered in carvings, on top of the television, as if he had always known.

Jonas Wergeland got up from the bench. Before he left the gardens he threw, he hurled, the ruined cassette and film into a wastepaper bin, coils of tape on which Akio Morita's words and image had left invisible traces. In his mind he could already see the Grieg program, saw how fantastic it would be, he jogged through Tokyo—in a spiral, it seemed to him—back to the hotel, in order to scribble down some of the ideas that were simply pouring out of a brain under pressure.

It is not so surprising, when one considers Jonas Wergeland's traumatic fear of the dark, that he should have had his momentous vision in the Land of the Rising Sun.

Norway's Gold Reserve

There were a few of the programs in the *Thinking Big* series the symbolism of which was known only to Jonas Wergeland. He derived an almost childish pleasure from this: to know that despite all the bouquets and brickbats no one really knew what he had had in mind. These film sequences harbored a secret meaning.

After the episode on Edvard Grieg was shown—a program that also caused quite a stir in Japan—Jonas Wergeland was much complimented on the fabulous scenes from Karlsbad. People who had been to the old spa town were even moved to ask whether it had been filmed at this or that hotel. Jonas merely smiled and kept his eyes on the ground. Others actually went to Karlsbad because of what they had seen in this program. To Jonas Wergeland, such responses proved better than anything else just how little it took to hypnotize people—sometimes he felt he could have got away with presenting his programs as puppet shows.

The film crew had never been near Karlsbad. The sequences showing Edvard Grieg at the spa were shot in the Bank of Norway. Yes, that's what I said, Professor: the Bank of Norway.

Jonas Wergeland had originally planned to build the program on Grieg around his Concerto in A Minor, since that had been conceived abroad and thus illustrated perfectly the liberating effect which going out into the world had had on the talents of Norwegian artists. Jonas even made an unofficial reconnaissance trip to Denmark, to Søllerød on Zealand, where Grieg had written the piano part for the concerto, but he changed his mind about this, which is to say: he could milk no original ideas from this first flash of inspiration. There was also something about the predictability and opportunism of this approach which he did not feel happy with.

In the end, after giving more thought to the question of how to reveal Grieg's essential dilemma, Jonas decided to set the key scene in Karlsbad, now Karlovy Vary, in the west of the Czech Republic, the famous spa where Grieg stayed, on doctor's orders, on several occasions, the first of these in the summer of 1881. There was one snag, however: the budget wasn't looking too healthy. There was no way they could go to Karlovy Vary. It was at this point that Jonas had the idea of looking around Oslo, to see if they could find a building, or even just a room, which would present some semblance of Karlsbad, or at any rate some aspect of Karlsbad; and it was while conducting this search that he was fortunate enough to come across the majestic, almost rocklike, old building on Bankplassen, which happened to be standing empty right then: the Bank of Norway having moved into its superb new premises next door—a jewel in Norway's crown, if I may say so, and well worth the controversial price paid for it—and the work of converting the old building into the Museum of Contemporary Art not yet begun. All the pieces fell into place. As it happens, this also supported one of Jonas Wergeland's theories: you can find any place in the world in Norway if you look hard enough.

The program opened with some stills of Karlsbad in its heyday in the nineteenth century: exteriors of the fine buildings along the banks of the River Teplá, of the Mill Colonnade and a couple of hotels, and of the most famous spring, the Strudel, shooting geyser-like over thirty feet into the air; then the camera panned across a façade of roughly hewn stone before passing through massive and imposing bronze doors flanked by lions' heads and into a magnificent entrance hall, and no one, absolutely no one suspected that this too was not an authentic shot from Karlsbad, from one of the luxurious sanatoriums which were still in operation.

The year, then, is 1881. Grieg is thirty-eight years old and seriously run down. For some time he has had to conduct and give concerts in order to make ends meet. He has had no chance to concentrate on what he wants to do more than anything else: to compose. Not only that, but his marriage is in difficulties. All of which leaves him, as he himself writes in a letter, with "chronic gastritis, enlarged intestines, a swollen liver and the devil knows what else besides." Add to this that he has only one good lung. Edvard Grieg is not just in Karlsbad, he is also at a crucial turning-point in his life. What will he do now? Although of course it's easy to guess what he does: he drinks the curative mineral waters, takes different types of bath, follows a strict diet, is given massages, goes for walks. But what is he thinking?

In the first scene Grieg was seen walking slowly along corridors, past highly-polished walls of different types of stone: inside the Bank of

Norway—or rather, inside one of Karlsbad's elegant sanatoriums, a place of gleaming mirrors and brass, with ornate stucco ceilings and doors and furniture in dark-stained pine with bronze fittings. At one point Grieg, frail looking and bent, as if carrying a load of questions on his back, turned into the vaulted central corridor. Here, at the foot of the labradorite sweep of the main staircase, a large orchestra was entertaining the residents. And the musicians were not playing just anything. No, Jonas had them perform a piece from the Viennese classical repertoire, the thorn in Grieg's side. And the accompanying shots of the other residents made it excessively clear that they belonged to Europe's wealthy upper classes, that they were members of German high society, a kind of overblown symphonic culture. One saw Grieg's despair, his unhappiness, saw how the music tormented him, how it hurt him almost physically, like a painful bout of indigestion. Jonas Wergeland wanted to give viewers the impression that Greig, this little man weighing hardly more than eight stone, was in the Hall of the Mountain King, surrounded by trolls; that he was filled with a constant temptation—embodied by the orchestra—to make a Peer Gynt slash in his eye. Or his ear.

In the next scene, the program's hub—in stark contrast to the previous turbulent sequence—Grieg is seen lying in a solitary bathtub in an enormous chamber. In actual fact he was in the very vault of the old Bank of Norway, in the basement, where the bars of gold had once been kept. But to the viewers, this was a room in a sanatorium in Karlsbad—an illusion underpinned by the pillars and the mosaic floor. One saw Grieg inside the Troll Mountain, Grieg held spellbound, imprisoned in Europe, in a health resort, where symphonic music, the musical idiom of German Romanticism, reverberated indoctrinatingly off the stone walls. Grieg lay as if dead, eyes closed, in the bathtub, only one hand moving, rubbing his lucky charm, a frog which he always rubbed when stepping up to the podium, to calm his nerves. Close-ups of his fingers around the frog, a creature of fairy tale, bore witness to Grieg's fervent desire, or prayer, for change. One could positively feel the pressure to which Jonas Wergeland subjected his hero, how he got Grieg to assume a character other than the usual stereotype.

I don't know whether you remember it, Professor, that memorable shot: Edvard Grieg up to his neck in water in a room that seems far, far too big, Grieg at the blackest moment in his life, knowing that he only has one good lung when he has need of two. It is several years since he created a work on the so-called grand scale. A few vehement voices had accused him of being totally wanting in compositional technique, of having no mastery of the classical forms. The introductions to a number of ambitious works are just lying there, like torsos. Grieg is afraid that he has lost the power to create music of a true dramatic dimension, that something in him has stagnated; his confidence is at a low ebb; he is worried that he will never be more than a small-town genius.

Grieg lies listlessly in that bathtub—the Japanese loved this scene—encircled by pillars in a vast, vaulted chamber. By editing in a succession of different images, Jonas Wergeland made it clear to the viewer that Grieg was thinking about the vital early inspiration he had received, not least from Rikard Nordraak in Copenhagen. Had he betrayed that vision of writing Norwegian music that was not an imitation of the German romantic style? Grieg lies in a bathtub in a sanatorium, mentally depressed, in two minds. Because although he felt tempted to write symphonies, he was still moved, more strongly than ever in fact, by a desire to explore the musical style of his native land; he had not abandoned the idea of giving expression to the "hidden harmonies" in Norwegian folk music. Grieg lies in the middle of Europe, feeling torn, you might say, between the sonata and the cattle call.

The sound of the swelling orchestral music died away, and the camera cut from the lonesome-looking figure of Grieg in a pressure chamber, to brief shots of scenery, Norwegian scenery, mostly that of the "great, melancholy landscape of the west country," as Grieg himself called it; and viewers heard, faintly at first, then louder and louder, evocative piano music, fragments of pieces which Grieg had already written or would later write, snatches from such gems as "The Goat-Boy," "Evening in the Mountains," and "To Spring," as well as his amazing "Chiming Bells"—a clear demonstration of Grieg's unique and inimitable talent.

Edvard Grieg lay in a bathtub deep in the heart of Europe, longing for his home; he rubbed the frog as if it were a pipeline to the natural world, or to inspiration from it, and on the screen it actually seemed as if, with the frog, he were rubbing into existence the sounds of mountain streams and birdsong, along with parts of the Norwegian landscape, as he wished to do with harmonies and distinctive modulations in his music. Grieg lay there dreaming of how he could paint with music, depict the countryside, nay, the whole of Norway, with a sound that had never been heard before.

As if to suggest that the longed-for change had taken place, that the bout of mental constipation was at an end, Jonas Wergeland had the passage played at Karlsbad flow into a little concert in which Grieg was seen playing compositions of his own in a lovely room with a domed glass roof and an arched marble colonnade, once the banking hall of the old Bank of Norway: in the program—so everyone thought—a salon at Karlsbad. And he was not playing pieces in the sonata form, but something that had begun as Norwegian folk music and was now something quite different, something new. Jonas Wergeland wanted to tell the story of a man who, while he could doubtless have gone on writing monumental works full of pathos and bravura, had rejected this option—not necessarily because he recognized his limitations as a symphonist, but because he realized that his personal style could no longer be pressed into the old molds. It was within this other area, the exploration of harmonies, that he would be able to develop and—though he did not know it—become a trailblazer for the new musical styles of the next century. Seldom has an inner dilemma been filmed, dramatized, with such verve, and yet very few detected the personal pulse behind it, saw that these excerpts from a life could only have been produced by someone who had once had their own bold and ambitious dreams of working with music.

So there sat Edvard Grieg, in the Bank of Norway's—which is to say Karlsbad's—sumptuous salon, playing something strange, hitherto unheard-of, something that had once been Hardanger fiddle tunes. The whole scene was so paradoxical: this magnificent chamber in the heart of Europe, filled with a blasé, conservative audience, and then this shocking, foreign music on a so-called small scale, it was an insult. But at the same time this tableau captured the essence of Grieg: playing Norwegian music in an international setting. The great artistic conflict of his life was actually resolved here, a fact underlined by the light filtering down on the little man at the grand piano. Jonas Wergeland let Grieg anticipate what he would later do in his opus 72, that epoch-making piece for piano inspired by the folk melodies of the Norwegian fiddlers, so simple and so subtle that it was regarded by many as Grieg's finest work. And the audacious harmonies that poured from the piano were not Norwegian; there was a sound inside him that, to future generations, to audiences, to the viewers, sounded Norwegian. The harmonies were all his own, Griegian; this was his original contribution to musical history—a slice of Norway that did not exist until he created it.

In the barrage of criticism unleashed by his conviction, Jonas Wergeland was accused of having stripped the lives of his celebrated subjects of their greatness, their very coherence. Some even said that he had murdered them. In Grieg's case, they charged Jonas with having accentuated the "small scale" at the expense of the big works. As one well-known musical expert wrote: "The program on Grieg is valueless, in both senses of the word."

Jonas Wergeland may have had a presentiment about such future fault-finding, because right from the very start he took a singular delight in knowing that no one, apart from the film crew, knew the mint of values which lay behind the program on Grieg: which is to say, where the Karlsbad scenes were filmed. It was a pleasure, a feeling he had no wish to share with anyone: to picture Grieg in the vault of the Bank of Norway, where the bars of gold had once been kept, and understand that Grieg represented something similar, a national gold reserve, capital in the form of a creative human being, a man who exploited his talent to the full. That was Norway's most important resource: the intellectual and artistic values. So it was only right and proper that Grieg's portrait would one day grace Norway's 500-kroner notes. Grieg had, Jonas knew, brought home vast sums of money to his native land, not just through his musical works, but also indirectly, in helping to promote Norwegian trade and industry.

And as he sat there playing, not in Karlsbad, but in the banking hall, in what is now the main hall of the Museum of Contemporary Art, Grieg was himself a modern work of art. The sound produced by his daring, innovative harmonies was so extraordinary and so modern that a hundred years on it still defies belief; this was music of the future, a sound which paved the way for such composers as Debussy, Ravel and Delius, as well as Bartók and Stravinsky. The episode on Edvard Grieg was Jonas Wergeland's personal favorite; it stood for everything in which he believed, everything he hoped for, it was the most honest and open, but at the same time the most enigmatic of them all.

Trio

It is in the spaces in between that things happen. Sometimes I have the urge to stop, linger, by these black holes created at the crossover point between two stories. Though it is my aim to describe all of the significant moments in Jonas Wergeland's life, I cannot rid myself of the suspicion that the really crucial stories, or keys, lie hidden here.

Judge for yourself, Professor, as I turn now to the episode in which Jonas Wergeland is in the car, on his way home from Hvaler, where he has been getting the house ready for the summer. It is the middle of the day, and traffic is light; Jonas is driving a black Ford Sierra estate, heading north on the E6 at a good speed. His head is buzzing with ideas for new projects, something with a Nordic slant, something entertaining, but intelligent that will beat everything ever shown on TV before into a cocked hat. At another level his thoughts are just drifting, as always when he is driving.

How does one become a murderer?

The radio was on, some arts program, something about literature; he wasn't really listening, he wasn't interested in books. He did prick up his ears, however, when someone or other started talking about Axel Stranger's new novel in rather high-flown but flattering, terms. The way it was presented, the book's subject matter sounded, to Jonas, like sheer lunacy, but to the speaker on the radio it was "that blend of modernism and dark eroticism which has become Axel Stranger's trademark." Jonas could not help smiling. He found it impossible to think of Axel as a writer. Axel was a friend. Jonas didn't know how he would have managed without him the year before, during the distressing public debate sparked off by Veronika Røed's full-frontal attack, in her newspaper, on his television series. Jonas recalled with gratitude all the conferences, all those keen discussions, at home in the Villa Wergeland: Axel, Margrete, and him—an unbeatable trio.

He had reached the top of a gentle dip, one of those miles-long, dead-straight stretches of motorway just north of Moss. A couple of hundred yards ahead of him was a trailer-truck. No cars in front of them or behind them. Suddenly he noticed something odd. The opposite lane was also completely empty, apart from a trailer-truck at the other end of the straight stretch, this too with a car about two hundred yards behind it. Jonas realized that he and "his" truck would pass the other two vehicles pretty much at the very bottom of the dip. The symmetry of this intrigued him, though he did not know why; he watched as they slowly closed on one another. There was something magical, almost awe-inspiring, about the balance that was at all times maintained. To his surprise he saw that the oncoming car, the one behind the trailer-truck, was also a Ford Sierra estate, a white one, a fact which made him even more keyed-up, as if he understood that something was about to happen, that such a correspondence was too weird, too perfect—like yin and yang—to be a coincidence. And as the two cars neared one another, Margrete came into his mind, possibly prompted by Axel's name, since both were bookworms, ready at the drop of the hat to put their heads together in long, intimate conversations; and yet there was something deeper, more ominous, which had nudged her to the forefront of his thoughts, something associated with these four vehicles, two traveling in either direction, something to do with a dangerous symmetry, or rather: a symmetry close to breaking point, a niggling suspicion; and he had no idea why he should have thought of this right now, but he was thinking about it right now, about her anarchic, not to say destructive, impulses, like the time when she had smashed one of her father's, the ambassador's, valuable Chinese vases, one with a blue dragon spiralling around it—on purpose, Jonas believed; she just sort of elbowed it, quite casually, and said "Oops!"—an incident which had left him with the worry that she might one day do something similar to him, since promises, morals, apparently did not mean the same to her as they did to other people; and without knowing why, and even though he tried to concentrate on his driving, he found himself connecting that memory with her tendency to lie, possibly inspired by the novels she read, lie for no reason whatsoever, and not only to him, but to everybody, as if this lent her an air of mystery. Or maybe simply because it amused her: to see whether she could manage to keep track of the web of lies she spun around herself; there was something about all of this, Jonas feared, that he had not taken seriously enough, that he had underestimated, just as he had underestimated the situation in which he now found himself on the motorway, in a car, driving at high speed.

The two trucks passed one another, and Jonas knew he ought to have taken note of what it said on the sides of them: a slogan or sign, the name of the company, as if knowing what they carried would have given him some kind of warning; on the other hand he already knew something was up, even before the twinge in his balls, before the white Ford in the opposite lane, which was sitting a couple of hundred yards behind the trailer-truck, shattered the mirror image and veered across the white line into his lane, then came racing towards him at sixty miles per hour. It all happened so quickly, of course—banally so—but for Jonas each tenth of a second seemed like minutes—as I say: it is in the spaces in between that things happen—he had plenty of time to think about all sorts of things: from the time, as a boy, when he used to amuse himself by smashing toy cars into one another head-on, to something that had happened only the other day, when he had been searching through Margrete's pocket for the garage key and found a strange key, a Trio key—for some unknown reason his first thought was that this was the key to her secret, that there was danger here. And in the second or two that it took his subconscious, working at lightning speed, to convert years of driving experience into muscle action in feet and arms, Jonas had all the time in the world to reflect on such things as where Buddha might be right now, or consider the car radio on which Axel's name was being mentioned again, which in turn reminded him that he often wondered how Margrete could know so much about Axel: not just about his books, which came to her inscribed with highly personal dedications, and in which she totally engrossed herself, but about where he was, what he was doing, and at the same time there was a different light, a new color almost, in her eyes, even the smell of her had changed, it reminded him of how she smelled during their first happy years together; she actually walked differently, briskly, with more of a spring in her step; and meanwhile, at an even deeper level, he was frantically trying to recall what sort of lock Axel had on his door—all these reflections were flying around inside his head as the two cars, two identical cars, one black and one white, sped towards one another; all these thoughts, and chaotic though they were, nonetheless they formed a whole of sorts, an explosive conviction that the symmetry had been broken, that it had been broken for a long time, that something did not fit; a puck was skimming towards a fragile construction, only this time he was the puck.

The collision left no memory of a bang in Jonas's mind. It was more of a soft pop, like the sound when you squash a tin can, accompanied by a sickly smell, as of tainted meat—he had no idea where that came from—and when he at last looked out of the window, the car was sitting nowhere near where he would have expected it to be. Only later did he realize that his body had, of its own accord, braked sharply—he remembered catching a glimpse of Kristin's cuddly toy flying through the space between the seats—and that, almost simultaneously, he had managed to swerve out of the way, to the left, because his car had been hit in the rear end and sent flying, spiralling, round to the right, though without being spun off the road. Some guardian angel must also have been watching over the other driver, who escaped with nothing worse than an injured knee. It transpired that he had dozed off for a few seconds, but that he too, when he woke up, had managed to decelerate enough, although he did lose control of the car. Naturally the incident made the headlines in several newspapers. There was no way Jonas Wergeland could be involved in a crash on the E6 without it being duly reported by the media; it was even believed that he had saved the other man's life, thanks to his admirable driving skills. But none of this is of any relevance to our undertaking, Professor.

What is really interesting here is the space in between: what happened when Jonas Wergeland's car had come to a halt after the crash, before other cars arrived on the scene and help was called. Jonas has been out cold for a few seconds, and the first thing he registers, before he opens his eyes, is that his fingers are touching glass; he instinctively thinks that he has gone blind, that he is unhurt, but blind, that he is going to spend the rest of his life in the dark, the one thing he dreads most of all. And as he opens his eyes and realizes that he is not blind after all, it strikes him, with the force of a blow that he has been blind. That Margrete is seeing another man. And that man is Axel.

He was unhurt, but his world had changed. The dramatic occurrence here was not the collision between the two cars, but the collision inside his head, the thoughts which, by dint of chemistry, by dint of physics, had been released only in order to become all tangled together in a shower of sparks. This was his gift, to be able to take two unrelated elements and make a story out of them, a story that was greater than the sum of its parts—and now, as if there were a curse attached to it, a price he had to pay, he had been forced to use this gift on himself, his own life; the realization ran round and round inside his head in a merciless loop, as if spelled out by 9,000 light bulbs on an electronic headlines sign: It was not just him and Margrete; it was not just the two of them, there were three of them. Margrete was cheating on him; she was having an affair with Axel. And he knew something else, too: it had been going on for some time. They had had every possible opportunity, for years. The conditions had been perfect. So perfect that there could be no doubt. It was this, the fact of Margrete's infidelity—together with the recognition of his own inadequacy—that crashed into him, made him feel like dropping down dead, even though he had sustained no physical injury. In his own eyes he had been a past master when it came to fooling people. And all the time it was he who was being made a fool of, betrayed. This must be what they call being hoist with one's own petard, he thought to himself later.

Jonas felt queasy, sick to the marrow, managed to open the car door and crawl out. "I'm not hurt," he said when the ambulance men came running over to him, "I've just been taken for a ride."

I—the professor—worked long into the night after my unknown guest had gone, writing like a soul possessed. It would not be going too far to say that I too was involved in a collision of sorts—her tales crashing into mine. I saw, at any rate, and quite suddenly, a wealth of unexpected cross connections in my own material: details, aspects which I had to weave in before they slipped my mind. I flitted purposefully to and fro in my turret room, stopping at one table only the next moment to dash over to another, possibly not altogether unlike a cook in a hotel kitchen, who has to keep an eye on a whole lot of things at once: sampling a little here and there, lifting food from all the pots and pans to make up one large and mouth-watering platter; I leafed through papers, looked things up in books, flicked through filing cards, listened to tapes of interviews I had forgotten I had. And I wrote, scribbling things down as fast as I could, as if the notes I had made while listening to her—which covered what she had actually said—were nonetheless only half the story. After one of her visits I rarely got to sleep much before dawn, and when I did finally tumble into bed in order to be reasonably fresh for our evening meeting, I was filled, exhausted though I was, with a strange kind of happiness.

Nonetheless—for all that I was thankful, or perhaps simply because of the congruities which I was discovering in my own material—her way of telling things was starting to annoy me: there were, for example, many things which she had hinted at, whole stories, which she had never mentioned again. She had given rise to expectations within me that were not being fulfilled. I began, quite simply, to suspect that she did not have the overview she claimed to have, that she frequently lost track of threads in the loom she was setting up. That her semblance of omniscience, in fact, masked her ignorance.

The same went for the sequence of the tales, which had confused me so much to begin with because of the daring leaps from one stage to another in Jonas Wergeland's life. Now all at once I found myself getting exasperated because her leaps were not radical enough; more and more it seemed to me that the "links" she used to hook one story up to another were completely arbitrary, that they were by no means as carefully considered as she maintained. Sometimes I almost became quite angry with her when, having finished one story, she would move on to some pretty predictable tale rather than the one I was expecting, or one which—on the basis of my own knowledge—I might have suggested, a far more exciting leap. It struck me that I could almost have made a better job of it myself. I had the urge to alter her sequence but decided to keep my part of the bargain. There was also something else which prevented me from making any objections; it was becoming increasingly clear to me, from her ardor and her agitation, that she had something—a great deal—at stake here. I was actually afraid to distract her. She could be knocked totally off balance. On a couple of occasions the evening before I had had the distinct impression that, underneath the apparent composure, behind the supposedly so carefully formulated stream of words, she had long since lost control.

It also surprised me that she had not mentioned the book about Jonas Wergeland which had excited more interest than anything else so far: the award-winning biographical novel *The Seducer*—a book considered to be not much more than a starry-eyed hagiography—which had really put the cat among the pigeons, both because it went totally against the stream of broadsides being levelled at Jonas Wergeland around the time of its publication, and because its author remained anonymous—for a while at least.

Naturally, thanks to the unscrupulous, stop-at-nothing tactics employed in journalism today, it was not many weeks before the author was exposed—I almost said stripped bare—with headlines on the front page of some of the tabloids so big you'd have thought Martin Bormann had been tracked down in Norway. She turned out, in fact, to be Kamala Varma, a woman of Indian extraction, an anthropologist who had eventually become a Norwegian citizen and who wrote and spoke Norwegian as well as anyone in the country. Despite all the media coverage, even now very little is known about her. No one, as far as I know, can, for example, say to which caste she belongs. Although this probably didn't matter so much, since she came from a prosperous, westernized family in Delhi and had taken her degree in anthropology at Columbia University in the United States. Kamala Varma undoubtedly saw herself as a citizen of the world. It was said that she came to Norway because she had seen *Song of Norway*, of all things, on one of the TV channels in

New York. And despite the fact that this is—it's only fair to say—the most awful film, it did leave her wanting to see Norway, especially the Norwegian countryside, so when she got there the first thing she did was to visit all of the exotic locations from the film: Bergen, Geiranger and, not least, Ulvik in Hardanger, where Toralv Maurstad and Christina ride up the sides of the valley on a Norwegian pony. This may have been Kamala Varma's first impression of the country, one which would always color her view of it: that in Norway she was walking, or should one say riding, into an idyllic fiction that would never end.

The interesting fact, for our purposes, is how she came to meet Jonas Wergeland; and even though this is still a little unclear, I have been able to establish that during the latter half of the eighties Kamala Varma was conducting an anthropological field study at the very prison to which Jonas Wergeland would later be committed—an achievement in itself, testifying to a nigh-on diplomatic shrewdness, when one considers how difficult it was to gain permission to observe such a closed society. While working there she became friendly with the prison chaplain and later, long after her anthropological study had been completed, she became a prison visitor under the auspices of the Norwegian Red Cross; as such she was paired up with an inmate of the prison, to whom she would make regular visits, outside normal visiting hours. Kamal Varma became a very popular visitor. She had an exceptional gift for listening and for establishing a rapport with the prisoners—not so much because she was a woman, but because she too was an outsider.

It so happened that the prisoner whom Kamala Varma had been visiting for some years completed his sentence just as Jonas Wergeland arrived at the prison, and because Jonas was something of a special case and kept himself very much to himself—he adamantly refused to speak to anyone—the chaplain asked Kamala Varma whether she would consider being Jonas Wergeland's prison visitor. She said she would. And it was as the chaplain had hoped: when the suggestion was put to Jonas, his curiosity was aroused—if nothing else, a woman of Indian origin would make a change from Norwegians of whom, not surprisingly, he was pretty sick after the trial and everything that had been written about him. He agreed, and their very first meeting marked a turning point for him. They had talked about Indian architecture. And thus it came about that Kamala Varma and Jonas Wergeland spent several hours together every week for almost two years, and not in the visiting room but in his cell: a privilege granted to prison visitors. Wergeland must have told her a good deal during these visits, must really have opened his heart to her. Then suddenly, for no apparent reason, he refused to see her any more. Apparently she took it very hard. There were also rumors that Wergeland had attempted to take his own life. Then, to everyone's surprise, her book appeared. Her motives in writing it, what induced her to break the prison visitor's oath of confidentiality, can only be guessed at. In any case the book sold like hot cakes, even better than my own new biography that year, on Johan Sverdrup.

It was not just the circumstances which I have outlined above which caused such an extraordinary furor when her anonymity was destroyed, the real problem was that Kamal Varma was also the detested and lambasted author of *Norway: An Appendix*, a book regarded by many as the most scurrilous attack on Norway and Norwegians ever penned.

Soon after Kamala Varma came to the country in the mid-seventies she obtained a post at the University of Oslo, and after years of work, studies in the field you might say, her sensational socio-anthropological treatise was published by the Oxford University Press: a work which has gone on—many would say, unfortunately—to win wide popularity and acclaim in international anthropological circles. To what extent this has harmed Norway is not something we will go into here. The title: *Norway: An Appendix* does, however, say a lot about its main standpoint: that a book on Norway can never be more than an appendix to a book about the world. To Kamala Varma, Norway is, as its contours on the map suggest, an appendix, an inconsequential adjunct, nourished by the body, but making no appreciable contribution to it, or—if it does—only in some obscure way. Certain chapters even give one the impression that there is talk here of an inflamed appendix, an area which could easily be removed without this having any effect on the rest of the world.

Right at the start, in the foreword, "Report from a Parenthesis," the tone is set for a book in which each chapter looks at a different aspect of the Norwegian people and their culture: the survival of old Norse pagan rites ("The Christmas Dinner"), the inhabitants' relationship with the forests and mountains ("The Rucksack"), the fear of making a stand ("The Ash Lad"), oil as an economic sheet anchor ("Blinkers"), gambling fever ("Lottery Land"), the annual exercise in absolution ("Collecting-Tin Nation"), the mania for encyclopaedias ("Great Norwegian"), and, not least, the powerful faith that prevailed in Norway, faith so strong that there is even a church for those who have no faith ("The Heathen Church"). Earlier I touched upon the question of Kamala Varma's caste—it is no exaggeration to say that after this book was published, in Norway at least, she became a pariah, a person who did well not to show their face in public. For a lot of people, her biographical novel, *The Seducer*—which is to say, the combination of this woman, author of *Norway: An Appendix*, and Jonas Wergeland, viewed by many as a traitor to his country, no better than Quisling—was too much to take. A flood of letters to the press called for Kamala Varma to be stripped of her Norwegian citizenship and expelled from the country—an attitude that only served to confirm everything she had said in a chapter on the Norwegian's latent hatred of foreigners ("Norwegian Front").

Not until the last evening but one did my black-clad visitor see fit to bring up the subject of the Indian woman. Her arrival—that of my unknown helper, I mean—happened, by the way, to coincide with a mysterious occurrence. Just before the doorbell rang I heard a boom, sounding right over the house, like a roll of thunder or a plane that had flown off course. It gave me quite a fright. I went to the window but saw nothing. Nor could I see anything when I opened the door for her. And yet there was something about the look in her eyes: it seemed even more intense than usual, as if she had taken some sort of stimulant, or perhaps rather, had just had a very exhilarating experience.

Up in the turret room her eye immediately fell on Kamala Varma's biographical novel, which was lying on my desk. She ran her fingers over the jacket illustration of a Persian rug. "She did what she could to save him," she said. "No one can take that away from her." Right next to it, like an antipodean, lay the Norwegian translation of *Norway: An Appendix*. She picked it up, weighed it in her hand. "The question is whether this anthropological study does not provide a better key to some understanding of Jonas Wergeland than her faction," she said, taking her seat in her usual chair by the fire.

From where I sat I could see her profile silhouetted against the window, overlooking Fornebu, and beyond: the proud outline of Kolsåstoppen, like the back of a stranded whale. Again I asked myself who the regal figure before me could be, to what she owed her incredible memory, what motives she might have, behind those motives which she had declared to me—and for the first time I may have had a faint, a very vague, inkling. Be that as it may: what I had first construed as hate seemed more like concern, a sense of desperation almost, on Jonas Wergeland's behalf. That evening her eyes were lined with an even deeper black than before, if that were possible, and this too conjured up thoughts of the Near East or possibly Arabia. I had also been wondering about the expressions she sometimes used, mostly when she wanted to underline a point: "inscribe it on the nail of your little finger," for example, or: "lift my words like an earring to your ear"—phrases which reinforced my suspicion that she had her roots in another culture.

As she browsed through Kamala Varma's book on Norway she stretched her legs out to the fire, shivering visibly—she was always cold. "Listen to this," she said, "from the foreword: 'I have set myself the fine goal of bringing to life an entire small civilization of which we know next to nothing.' Good, eh? As if Norwegians were an overlooked minority in Outer Mongolia." She turned a few more pages at random: "'What does it mean to be Norwegian?'" she read. "'To be Norwegian is to watch a rape being committed and imagine that one is innocent.' Sounds familiar, wouldn't you say, Professor?"

She put down the book, held her hands out to the flames in the hearth, looked out at the day which was fast fading outside, thus reducing our view to a band of darkness dotted with points of light, some of which moved and flashed. "I've said it before: part of the key to understanding Jonas Wergeland lies in the fact that he was Norwegian. It was the Norway within him that made him what he was—for good and ill. Some people say, you know, that every biography is everyone's biography. Hence it must be possible to regard the biography of Jonas Wergeland as that of every Norwegian. In many ways I would agree with that. Let me begin, therefore, with a story in which Norway itself plays the lead. Hurry now, Professor, we're running out of time."

I had been ready for some time, sitting with my spiral notebook in my lap. I noticed that look of concentration come over her face, as if she were juggling things about in her head, already composing subsequent stories while wrestling with the opening of the first. And at the same moment I saw again, quite clearly, although she tried to hide it from me: she was in the depths of despair—like someone who had no idea what she was doing.

The Snow Planet

Is it possible to change a life by recounting it? If so, then we will have to begin with a February day in the early seventies, with three lads in holiday mood, standing at Tretten station in Gudbrandsdalen complete with skis and rucksacks. Like all good Taoists, the Three Wise Men often went wandering, but this was more than just a wander: this was a pilgrimage. They were about to head off into the Norwegian countryside. To be perfectly frank, the Three Wise Men had come to Gudbrandsdalen to follow in the tracks of Scandinavia's greatest cross-country skier.

Before I go on, I ought probably to say something about the Norwegian countryside, because the question is whether the Norway countryside is not more famous than the people inhabiting it, whether the landscape of Norway has not made a greater contribution to the world, not to mention the history of ideas, than the Norwegians themselves. Because we are talking here about Norway as a place or, as they say in the movie business, a location.

To many children in the world, or at any rate to those who grew up in the fifties, Norway was synonymous with a country overrun by lemmings. The mere mention of the word "Norway" conjured up in their minds images of hordes of these little rodents, millions of lemmings all marching in the same direction across a rugged, fjord-side landscape. This can be put down, not to a common intuitive sense of the Norwegians' innate urge to act as one, but to the influence of a comic strip by the aforementioned Carl Barks, a story about Norwegian cheese and a lemming which, because of a medallion hanging round its neck, was of vital importance to Uncle Scrooge. It later came to light that Carl Barks got the idea for the lemmings and Norway from an issue of *National Geographic*, although we won't hold that against him; whatever Norwegians may think, this is how the majority of foreigners have always seen and always will see Norway. As a gaudy color spread in *National Geographic*.

One of Barks's most avid readers in the fifties was George Lucas, soon to become a successful film director. He and another movie giant, Steven Spielberg, were the men behind the *Star Wars* epic. And now we're getting to the crux of the matter, because in the second film in the first *Star Wars* trilogy, which bore the famous subtitle, *The Empire Strikes Back*, Norway plays a starring role. It was, in fact, in Norway that George Lucas and his team shot the part of the film which takes place on the inhospitable snow planet of Hoth, where the heroes and their rebel forces have sought refuge after the dark side's temporary victory. Many cinemagoers will never forget those spectacular scenes with the bounding Tauntauns and fearsome battle droids. No, don't laugh, Professor. This may well be Norway's most valuable contribution to the world to date: to have fired the imaginations of almost a billion people, given them the illusion of a distant ice age. And when you think about it, it isn't really such a far cry from fantasy to reality, or vice versa, because no matter how you look at it, this image was only further consolidated by the 1994 Winter Olympics, when Norway provided collective proof of a modified version of Andy Warhol's theory, by showing that every country gets its fifteen days of fame. Not because of the citizens of Norway—although, with their massive turn-out and energetic use of sheep bells, they yet again proved themselves worthy of the epithet: "world's best spectators"—but because of the picture-postcard shots depicting Norway as a chilly, sun-spangled snow planet, which were beamed irretrievably around the world by satellite and would remain fixed in the world consciousness, no matter what Norwegians might say or do to try to change that image—for two or three generations at least.

Don't worry, I haven't lost my thread: you see it was this same snow planet Norway that the Three Wise Men were going in search of when they got off the train at Tretten station and, after hitchhiking a short distance, found themselves outside the remains of what had, in times gone by, been known as Winge Sanatorium, situated roughly halfway between Tretten and Skeikampen. For it was here, at Winge, that the greatest cross-country skier in Scandinavia had once stayed. And the greatest cross-country skier in Scandinavia is not, of course, either Fridtjof Nansen or Johan Grøttumsbråten, but Niels Bohr.

Now to some people such an assertion—that the Dane Niels Bohr should be the foremost cross-country skier in Scandinavia—probably seems as shocking as proclaiming Denmark's Kurt Stille to be Scandinavia's greatest speed skater, but when it comes to the consequences of cross-country skiing, its significance for posterity, this postulate is sound enough. Because there was no talk here of skiing as fast as possible, or of crossing a geographical continent, but of conquering an ideational pole. Niels Bohr's skiing expeditions in Gudbrandsdalen changed the world. It is as simple as that.

"I already know all this," Axel said as they were standing on the steps outside the Winge. "Bohr saw the trees as particles and the landscape as waves."

"Rubbish," said Jonas. "They've got trees and a landscape in Denmark too, you know."

"Yes, but to talk about something more important," said Viktor, turning anxiously to Axel. "I sincerely hope you remembered the elixir?" He was referring, of course, to the aquavit.

Winge Sanatorium had had a checkered history, from its modest beginnings around the turn of the century to its time as one of Norway's more fashionable hotels; a palatial white building, patronized by royalty, with tennis courts and a golf course, open fires and an indoor swimming pool. Then, in 1957, the main building burned down. A new, less ostentatious building was built; the Winge was sold and converted into a rest home. The Three Wise Men had, however, been in luck, because although the Winge Convalescent Home, as it was now called, was not normally open to the general public, the proprietress did allow them to stay there for a few days, partly because the home was not very busy that week and partly because she was won over by Viktor's irresistible charm and powers of persuasion. After all you don't turn away pilgrims.

Not many people, not many Danes or other Bohr scholars even, have taken much interest in physicist Niels Bohr's four-week trip to Norway in 1927, although it has long been known that it was during this skiing holiday that Bohr gained his momentous insight into the concept of complementarity: a discovery which he presented later that year at the conference in Como in Italy, in a lecture entitled "The Quantum Postulate and the Recent Development of Atomic Theory." Bohr's theory endeavored to resolve a conflict, inasmuch as some experiments showed that light behaved like particles, and others that light seemed to be waves. According to Bohr—Bohr after those skiing expeditions, that is—it has to be acknowledged that these two possibilities are mutually exclusive, and yet both are essential to a complete understanding of the phenomenon—a most provocative philosophical and scientific contention, to put it mildly. Bohr's "complementarity" is history's greatest argument for having it both ways. A massive expansion.

But why was no one, not even the Norwegians, interested in where this idea had come to him? The Three Wise Men saw it as only natural, not to say their patriotic duty, to find out more about Bohr's skiing holiday, about the inspiration that Norway must have given the Danish genius. I believe Viktor Harlem should be regarded as a pioneer, for the zeal with which he threw himself into this undertaking, even visiting the Niels Bohr Institute in Copenhagen, in whose archive he at last unearthed the location of Bohr's "base camp" on this expedition to those intellectual peaks. Viktor was not only able to differentiate, at the drop of a hat, between such complex concepts as analytical, phenomenological, and hermeneutical philosophy, he also managed to lay his hands on a copy of a letter which Bohr wrote from Norway, dated February 25, 1927, with a letterhead which quite clearly gave his place of residence as Winge Sanatorium, near Tretten Station: ". . . my staying at present here in Norway on a short recreation tour of a few weeks." In Bohr's day—this was another fact thrown up by Viktor's research—the Winge had been run by Agnes Berle; at that time the place had consisted of one large manor house, built on two storys.

"To Agnes Berle!" said Axel.

"A credit to Norwegian hospitality!"

"A woman who did more for Gudbrandsdalen and Norway than Prillar Guri!" Viktor declared after pouring generous measures for everyone from the aquavit bottle. And in case you still haven't got the point, Professor, you should know that Viktor Harlem was by far the most important person in Jonas Wergeland's life; no other person had anything like such a fundamental effect on Jonas. Once, when Jonas was a little boy staying on Hvaler, his grandfather had been in the blue kitchen sharpening a knife with a practiced hand, drawing it up and down the steel. "That's the sort of friend you ought to choose for yourself," he told Jonas, holding up the knife sharpener, "a friend who can hone you." Such a friend was Viktor Harlem.

The very next day the Three Wise Men were outside the Winge waxing their skis: because if there was one thing they were sure of it was that Bohr's vision somehow had to be connected with skiing. Norway was skiing. "Ski" is one of the few words that Norway has given to the world. Even the Norwegians' most traumatic national experiences are ski-related. In the United States they ask you where you were when

Kennedy was shot; in Norway they ask where you were when Oddvar Brå broke his ski pole.

They followed the most commonly used track—a track which Bohr must also have taken—from the Winge, through the forest up to Musdal Saeter. It was a steep climb. And already here Viktor was propounding his first hypothesis: could it simply have been sheer exhaustion, or light-headedness, that had brought the idea of complementarity to the surface.

This suggestion was withdrawn, however, when, puffing and panting after all the uphill stretches, they reached the snow fences below Musdal Saeter—or rather, the tops of the fence posts marking out their course like channel markers in a sea of snow—and then, a little further up, found the splendor of the mountains spreading out before them, with Bjørga's almost bald summit in the west and in the distance, over by Valdres, Synnfjell shimmering like a pearly mirage. Could it have been this, they whispered in unison, something about this suddenly expanding vista that appealed to Bohr? Or something to do with those vast expanses unmarked by skis making him think of white sheets of paper, a blank page? "Or maybe Bohr's *ch'i* was actually changed by the mere fact of his breathing this air," said Viktor.

They pressed on, much heartened; cutting between the saeter buildings, using their eyes like detectives, fine-combing the terrain for clues, signs. They climbed so high that they could see the imposing profile of Skeikampen on the other side of the valley. The sky was cobalt blue and the snow-laden trees were like something straight out of a postcard entitled "Winter in Norway." But what—what in all of this scene before them—could have acted as a springboard for Bohl's mental, championship-winning jump? They squinted up at the sun, asking themselves, as the Danish physicist himself might have done, whether the light was hitting them as waves or particles? They imagined Bohr, standing where they were now: how he might even have made some neat drawings with his pole, symbolic attempts, as porous as the snow itself. "One thing we don't know, but which may have been of vital significance," said Axel gravely, "is whether Niels Bohr also smoked his pipe when he was out skiing."

They turned north and headed across the marshes beyond Musdal Saeter and before too long had Killiknappen and its marginally smaller counterpart, Roåkerknappen, straight ahead of them. "Like Great Ararat and Little Ararat," Viktor murmured. Taoists could never get enough of mountains. They rested on their poles and feasted their eyes on the twin peaks, which looked not unlike a pair of white breasts. "Who wouldn't be able to dream up a notion of complementarity when faced with such a sight?" Jonas said, his thoughts going to his brother Daniel. Viktor broke into an impromptu rendering in faultless English of some lines from Bohr's speech at Como: "In fact, here again we are not dealing with contradictory, but with complementary pictures of the phenomenon, which only together offer a natural generalization of the classical mode of description."

"Amen," said Axel and Jonas.

Back at the Winge they pursued their speculations in their room, fortified by an excellent trout dinner. Their hostess had put them in the west wing, so they could at least have the experience of living on the site of the old, burned-out Winge. And even if the walls were orange and fitted with green sconce lamps, to them this was a shrine—like one of those garish little Hindu temples—a place over whose lakes the spirit of Niels Bohr hovered. Nevertheless, and despite the festive mood: they were stuck. "Things are moving too slowly," Axel said, digging a bottle of Linie Aquavit out of his rucksack. "It's time to set sail."

The next morning they put on their skis again, determined to look under every bush on the slopes above Musdal Saeter. "If you think about it, cross-country skiing is in itself a form of complementarity: gliding and walking," said Axel, this thought striking him as they were sitting with their backs against the wall of one of the rickety saeter outbuildings, eating oranges. "And if you look back you'll see the continuous line of our tracks and the dots made by our poles, waves and particles! Can there be any doubt?"

"No, I think Bohr must have set off a harmless little avalanche," Viktor said. "Experienced an instance of non-locality, seen how with one innocent step he affected something in an entirely different spot."

They racked their brains incessantly, for three days they racked their brains. On their last evening they stayed in their room, firing off suggestions that got wilder and wilder as the stock of aquavit in Axel's rucksack dwindled. What if he ran into a tree, and this made him see double? Viktor ventured. Could it have been something to do with his skiing gear? Axel wondered. His poles would have been of bamboo and of a thicker sort than today's. Axel made a long, impassioned speech on the bamboo as a possible source of inspiration—a typical five-aquavit argument.

They were growing more and more desperate. "Say it was misty," Jonas said, already in a fog of his own. "Just think: all that whiteness. Like walking through nothingness. Or being on another planet."

"That's it! Another planet," said Viktor. "It's an image you often find in the work of revolutionary artists. Arnold Schönberg said something similar when he devised the dodecaphonic technique. One feels the air of another planet. Maybe that's how it was for Bohr."

Axel suddenly remembered the tracks of a hare seen down by Abbot Tarn, at the foot of Killiknappen. "It made me think of formulae written in the Sirian alphabet."

Deep down inside they were all afraid that the whole thing was just a coincidence, that the idea could have come to Bohr anywhere, but they refused to accept this. It had to have something to do with Norway.

They drank on and had reached the stage where Axel was dead set on having a contest to see who could sing "I Love You Because" in the deepest voice, when Viktor started flicking through a book he had borrowed at random from the bookcase in the smoking room, which also functioned as the "library." The minute he saw the blessed Christian Winge's name written neatly in ink on the flyleaf he guessed that in his hand he held a key, and when he realized that the book was Aasmund Olavsson Vinje's *Memoir of a Journey*, or at least the second volume of his *Selected Writings* from 1884, he felt even surer. This book must have been rather like the baton in a relay, passed from owner to owner, a cornerstone which had survived the Luftwaffe's presence here during the war and subsequent fires: a true memoir of a journey, the perfect travel account.

Viktor leafed through it and came to the part where Vinje writes about "Capital People." "Listen to this," he cried, jumping to his feet with his glass in his hand in his excitement: "'Were I to name some differences between we people from the capital and other city folk, then the greatest would have to be that we are more liable to see everything with a kind of double vision, at one glance we seem to see both the right side and the wrong of life's tapestry . . .'" Viktor stopped, went on reading to himself and then as this same thought crystallized inside his head into a single word: "That's it!" he cried. "Duality!"

And as if that weren't enough, they then found something scribbled in the margin in pencil next to Vinje's paragraph on "duality." Viktor promptly dug out the copy of Bohr's letter, a treasured relic, and compared the writing. With a bit of good will one could see a resemblance. And with a little more good will one could swear that the letters formed the following words: "complementary but mutually exclusively characteristics"—a phrase which Viktor immediately recognized as coming from a key passage in the Como lecture.

The Three Wise Men were able to crawl into bed, very drunk, but with clear consciences. They had proved that Norway, the Snow Planet, was at least good for something. Although it was never uttered out loud, all three fell asleep with a ten-aquavit argument on their lips: the concept of complementarity was Norwegian! In fact the whole of quantum theory could be said to be Norwegian! Bohr's epoch-making concept was nothing other than Vinje's duality, transcribed into cosmopolitan and scientific terms.

"Well, the holiday's not over yet, so while we're here why don't we stop off in Lillehammer for a day or two," said Axel the following morning, when they were standing at Tretten station, all feeling slightly hung-over. Jonas was all for it. Viktor wasn't so sure—it was almost as if he sensed that this would be pushing his luck, that the Snow Planet might have a chunk of ice all ready and waiting: that the Snow Planet not only imparted ideas, it also snuffed them out.

Branching Out

Is it possible to change a life by recounting it? If so, then it is Sunday, a holiday—holy day—in the true sense of the word, and Jonas is reverently at work in a room that smells of wood-shavings and beeswax. He is standing at a bench in the little workshop in the Villa Wergeland, working on his seventh dragon's head—a new version but still inspired by the old prototype in the Viking Ship Museum, those sinuous coils which posed the eternal challenge. For Jonas, the Academic's masterpiece was testimony to duality: a head capable of embodying both a fearful dragon and four beautiful swans—and only when you could see it as both did it look right, did it look good. At a desk next to him Kristin is sitting drawing, as he had once sat drawing in Aunt Laura's rug-clad living room. It is summer, afternoon, and outside the window the trees shine brightly in the grove of trees, the spot that, as a boy, Jonas had called Transylvania.

You might accuse me of leaving out all the ordinary days, Professor. But no occurrence, no day in a person's life is so trivial that it might not be crucial. Important things happen all the time. And so this day too, like the others I have described, can be regarded as being the center of Jonas Wergeland's life. All days are, in a way, holy days.

So it is very appropriate that it should be a Sunday, that Jonas should be in the workshop that is his sanctuary, his temple. As Margrete took refuge in the kitchen and ransacked the well-stocked spice rack when she wanted to relax, Jonas came here, to his bits of wood and the cupboard containing all his carving tools. It was in here, while he was sawing the wood, a crude three-dimensional form, while he was wielding knife, file or rasp in an effort to get closer to the form of the creature's head, while he was drawing the design and while he was making a start on the actual carving—that he did his best thinking, was aware of how his head simply teemed with ideas, like echoes of, or parallels to, the patterns he was coaxing out of the wood which, no matter how stylized they might be, took on the appearance of a living thing. It often struck Jonas that his pleasure in this was the same as he had felt in nursery school, the first time he was allowed to work with a fretsaw and some plywood, and cut out a big heart, a heart that beat in his hand.

He went over to Kristin, stood and watched her. She was drawing a tree, sat there in a world of her own, drawing with a stick of charcoal on a large sheet of paper—there was charcoal on her cheek, too. Her hair glinted in the light falling through the window. It came to Jonas: she, his daughter, was a diamond; she was him, metamorphosed into diamond. Kristin almost always drew trees. He did not know why, but he liked it. They were both working with trees, with wood. He stood for a long time just watching her, a little girl with branches growing under her hand, charcoal, dust, coming alive. He noticed how big she was getting, it didn't seem any time since she had been lying in her cradle while he played "I Have a Little Lass with Eyes of Blue," lay there in her cradle smelling of milk and encouraging him to search out new harmonies on the piano, create a tree of notes in each chord, while at the same time varying the melody, playing it in every key, endeavoring to make the verses stretch out, each in its own direction. She always inspired him; he never worked better than when she was with him in the workshop. And in the living room Margrete would be lying on the sofa, reading, trees turned into books. From one kind of leaf to another. Sunday was a holy day.

Jonas stood behind Kristin, studying the sheets of paper covered in finished or half-finished drawings spread in a semicircle round about her. Some showed rows of bare trees, networks of branches converging on a vanishing point. On the sheet in front of her the contours of a strange tree were taking shape, roots and all. Jonas thought of the many times they had sat in the living room talking about trees. Sometimes they had music playing in the background. "Listen to this one, it's about willow trees," he might say, putting on Billie Holiday's "Willow Weep For Me." Or it might be Bach—Bach was perfect for looking at pictures of trees. Jonas brought out art books and showed his daughter how the Chinese painted the leaves of bamboo trees, or how the Japanese drew the branches on the cherry tree. "It looks so easy, and yet awfully difficult," Kristin said.

They could sit for hours, with the piles of art books growing up around them like a hedge and the music of Bach encircling them with a fretwork of notes. They pored over Caspar David Friedrich's spiky, romantic trees and I. C. Dahl's weeping birch; they compared Edvard

Munch's majestic oak with Lars Hertervig's gnarled pines. Kristin was particularly fond of Claude Monet's poplar trees painted in different lights and of Piet Mondrian's apple tree, progressing in stages from a recognizable tree to a totally abstract shape. "It's like a magic trick," she crowed, running her eyes over the pictures again and again—but, unlike Jonas as a child, she never tried to copy what she saw, she came up with her own ideas.

"Have you ever chopped down any trees?" she asked him once.

"Only one," he said. "It was on a boat."

Kristin seemed almost bewitched by trees. Jonas always envied her that childish knack of picking a maple leaf off the ground and becoming genuinely lost in wonder: staring at her hand, her fingers, then back at the leaf, placing them against one another. Or the gift for stopping short and standing rooted to the spot, nostrils vibrating, when she passed a lilac bush in bloom. She was a great climber too. Now and again, when she was big enough, she would go off with Hans Christian Andersen's *Fairy Tales* under her arm to sit up among the branches and read about the hollow tree in "The Tinder Box" or "The Old Oak Tree's Last Dream." "She has to be a distant descendent of the druids," Margrete always said. "Those Celtic priests who held certain groves of trees to be sacred. "Hm," said Jonas. "Either that or she's living proof of what it says in Norse mythology: that mankind was born out of the trees, like Ask and Embla."

Sometimes he and Kristin would sit together in the old apple tree in the garden, a hardy Sävstaholm which had been growing there when Jonas's parents bought the ground. It was like entering another dimension, another element, like water—he could see why the Chinese called trees "the fifth element." And as they sat there listening to the sighing of the leaves, he would tell Kristin stories about how important trees were to people; he told her about the bodhi tree under which Buddha was sitting when he finally achieved enlightenment, or about the apple tree which prompted Isaac Newton's contemplations on gravity. Jonas suddenly discovered—as if their botanical surroundings were also having an effect on him—that he knew a whole lot of stuff about trees, that he must have been picking up bits and pieces all through his life: that sitting here in a fork in the tree trunk seemed to call them to mind, and he found that he was able to weave these snippets of knowledge together again. He told Kristin about trees in North America which were thousands of years old, or about the cedar trees of Lebanon King Solomon had ordered for the temple in Jerusalem; about the baobab trees of Africa which were used as houses, and the two trees whose branches entwined over the grave of Tristan and Isolde. "Old trees are like dragons," he said, after describing the Nine Dragon Tree, an ancient cypress he and Margrete had stumbled upon in Beijing, or the dragon's blood trees they had seen on Tenerife. Kristin, for her part, might make some comment about the sounds trees made, they breathed, she said, or about their bark, that it smelled better than perfume, as well as asking questions which he could not answer: "What does 'achieve enlightenment' mean?" she would say. Or: "Are there trees inside our heads?"

Jonas turned away from the drawing child and crossed to the high bench where the piece of wood sat ready and waiting in the vice. He would spend a couple of years working on a dragon's head; with this one he was past the first, roughing-out, stage and had shaped and smoothed the surface with one of the bigger U-gouges. The face was also completed—eyes, nose, jaws—and he had long since begun on the actual decoration, first of all by "grounding out," which is to say: cutting down to the deepest points in the relief—a painstaking process calling for lots of different gouges. He was now faced, in other words, with the demanding task of carving the fine detail; he carefully examined the tracing paper on which, once and for all, he had copied the Academic's exquisite design on a scale of 1:1, the patterns formed by the stylized swans. He had to take care of the contours first, get the main lines right. That done, he could move on to the outermost edges of the bands, then the ornamented surfaces. He studied it at length, knew that an understanding of the motif as a whole, its lines, was half the battle. He could hardly wait, took down a big No. 2 gouge, whetted and polished it, needed to get it as sharp as possible, felt a thrill of apprehension run through him as he put the steel to the wood and cut away the first sliver, like an archaeologist setting his spade in the ground, about to unearth sensational discoveries.

How does one become a murderer? Or, to put it another way: in that "sacred" room, in the selfsame cupboard in which he kept his precious woodcarving tools, could Jonas Wergeland also have hidden an old Luger? I refuse to believe it. That is why I am sitting here, Professor: I refuse to believe it.

Jonas makes a rhomboid cut, a tricky device, then an oblique hatch; he has to strain his eyes to the utmost, it is the eyes that tire first; he is working on a small patch, but using a large gouge—"Always try to work with as big a gouge as possible, to get the cleanest cut," old Sundbye had told him—Jonas loves the resistance offered by the wood, loves the smell, loves the thought of how good it will be, better than the last head anyway, always a little better, bands running under and over one another, four birds and yet something else entirely. He knows, he has always known, that woodcarving is not merely a hobby: that it has something to do with the world, with all of his problems. That this might even be his purpose in life: in the end, not only to master the craft itself, but also the thought behind this intricate tracery. There were times, even at the height of his television series' success, when Jonas Wergeland had the feeling that nothing mattered but this: to carve the perfect dragon's head. "I don't make programs," he said, "I make dragons."

After an intense bout of carving, he looked up, became aware that Kristin was still sitting at the desk next to the window, drawing with colored pencils now. It was very quiet—the quiet of a forest. The light slanting through the window formed a halo around her. He was filled with love at the sight of this child with her head bowed over the paper, her face rapt with concentration, her whole mind focused on just one thing: the drawing of a tree. Jonas stood there with his gouge in his hand, looking at her, a child drawing, a perfectly normal sight, but at the same time, what a sight, an everyday situation which shone with a timeless beauty, a kind of blinding revelation of the miracle of existence, akin to the ineffable light of mysticism. Why do we give up drawing? Why do we do all those drawings as children, as if it were the most natural thing in the world, covering sheet after sheet of paper, revelling in it, and then all of a sudden one day it stops?

He crosses to the desk, glances down at her paper, notes how she too has created something that coils and twines, a large tree, a tree unlike any he has ever seen before. She has done something odd with the branches, sort of plaited them together, and the tree is half fire, glittering, and half green—it looked, more than anything else, like a piece of jewelry. "It's a tree with leaves that are wet with dew, in the sunshine," she said, without turning, knew that he was standing behind her.

He was filled with a sudden sense of dread. A fear that something might happen to her. Or to him. He placed a hand on her head. "How lovely," he said. "You've drawn . . . lots of things at once."

He knew she was practicing for something—this thing with the trees, all these sheets of papered covered in networks of branches—but he didn't know what.

"What was he called, that painter who cut off his ear?" Kristin asked as she was getting out a fresh sheet.

"Van Gogh."

"Why did he cut off his ear?"

"Nobody knows," Jonas said. "Some people say he was in love, but I think maybe he was afraid of the dark."

"Or maybe he thought he was a tree," Kristin said.

They had devoted a whole day to the Dutch painter the Christmas when Aunt Laura gave them the book on him. He had shown Kristin Van Gogh's chestnut trees and bluish-green conifers, the twisted olive trees and, not least, the cypress trees like green flames against the sky. They had studied the pink and white gardens of Arles with their pear and peach trees and, best of all, the little almond tree in bloom—and afterwards Jonas had taught Kristin the verse by Nikos Kazantzakis which Margrete had once taught him: "I said to the almond tree, / 'Sister, speak to me of God.' / And the almond tree blossomed."

It is Sunday, holy day. Jonas returns to his bench, sets to work on the dragon's head again, on the piece of wood into which he means to carve life, cover it in an intricate play of lines. He glances out of the window, towards Ravnkollen's granite wall, spies a crack in the middle of the cliff face, a black hole that can still make him shiver in horror. He turns to where Kristin sits with her head bowed, still drawing—drawing with wax crayons now, possibly inspired by Van Gogh's thick daubs of paint. He knows that some day this child will be the saving of him. That this is why he had her, to be the saving of him.

Living Death

Is it possible to change a life by recounting it? If so, then we must focus on the challenge facing Jonas Wergeland. Because, while his woodcarving concerned seeing swans on a dragon's head, Jonas Wergeland's problem was rather the opposite: whether you could be a swan even if you were carved with dragons. Can you be composed of dragons and still be good?

As a little boy, Jonas had thought that the cave in Ravnkollen's sheer face was a dragon's lair. As time went on it was reduced to being the big boys' secret den—which was daunting enough, in its own way. It wasn't actually a cave as such, but a deep fissure directly above the bomb shelter. It may well have been this last which had given Petter and his gang the idea, because the Civil Defense Corps's exercises were such a mystery: days when the massive steel doors in the hillside were opened, and the kids got to peek inside that hidden labyrinth, an enormous tunnel with narrow passageways running off it; trucks and jeeps driving in and out, fathers suddenly appearing in grey uniforms and yellow helmets, as if all at once real life had been turned into science fiction.

How does one become a conqueror?

It was of course absolutely forbidden for anyone else to go in there: into the big boys' secret den, that is. Getting up to it was also a tricky business and not a little risky. No one of Jonas's age knew what the cave looked like inside; some nurtured fantasies of a temple of sorts, with an array of ghastly objects at the very back; others whispered of crossbones on the floor and signs written in blood on the walls.

Jonas had wondered just as much about the cave and what it contained as he had about the canvas bag which he and Daniel had found in the safe on Hvaler, but which their grandfather had snatched away from them before they had a chance to lift it out of the lacquer casket. They often lay in bed at night trying to guess what was in it. "Pearls, for sure!" said Daniel. "No, I think it was probably a bundle of love letters," said Jonas. Because, of course, they hadn't been able to weigh the bag in their hands. It could have contained anything.

One autumn afternoon, Jonas braved his fear of heights and stole up to the den. He simply had to find out what lay beyond that black cave mouth, even if it turned out to be something indescribably nasty. But as so often happens in such cases, it was a disappointment: apart from a primitive cave painting on one wall—not of an elk or a wolf, I grant you, but of what Jonas took to be a girl with no clothes on—the den was totally bare. A couple of bits of plank served as a table. On a natural shelf in the granite lay a box of matches. Jonas looked about, but all he could find was the paper off a bar of chocolate, some orange peel, a few stumps of candle and four sparkplugs. Nothing really exciting. Not even a Swedish porn mag.

Down on Bergensveien once more, he did not know whether to feel let down or relieved. At any rate he was glad that no one had seen him. But someone had seen him, in such situations someone always sees you, and this "someone" tattled. So Jonas discovered the very next day, during the lunch break; he could tell by the looks they sent him, Petter and his chums. They were three or four years older than him, and three or four years is an awfully big gap at that age, like the difference between Goliath and David—at least.

Jonas was going to get his hair cut that afternoon, and Little Eagle accompanied him to the shop down by the bend in the road, to a hairdresser who bore a striking resemblance to David Niven, with his pencil moustache and hair slicked back like a South American bandit. Although, of course, they didn't say "hairdresser," they said "barber," possibly because they liked the word's manly connotations, the associations with facial hair. I ought perhaps to say something here about boys and their hair, since the history of the sixties could probably also be written as the saga of parents' constantly nagging at their sons to get a haircut. But these events took place in the time before the Beatles, when the length of a boy's hair had not yet become a source of domestic conflict; the barber employed his clippers as much as his scissors in order to produce such drastic works of art as the "buzz-cut" and the "flat-top." In those days a mother's main concern was for the need for thrift, a virtue that also led to the buying of clothes and shoes that were invariably too big. The aim, therefore, when going to the hairdresser, was plain: that haircut had to last as long as possible.

Nonetheless there was something special about these visits; even before you stepped inside, the sign flashing in the salon window conjured up thoughts of ritual acts, of guilds or the Freemasons; the brass basin was actually a leftover from the days when the barber did far more than cut hair and shave faces, when he was, in fact, a "barber-surgeon." The barber's emblem was actually a bleeding bowl, and from this the boys knew, right from the start, that a visit to the hairdresser was a deadly serious matter.

Jonas particularly liked the moment when the sweet-smelling proprietor pumped the barber's chair, that miracle of hydraulics, high into the air and began the treatment by placing a collar made of stretchy paper around his neck—as if initiating Jonas into a brotherhood. Glee and horror mingled inside Jonas at the thought of putting his appearance for some weeks ahead into the hands of this slick-haired man, but he eased his mind by running his eyes expectantly over the posters hung above the mirror, depicting men with perfectly groomed hair—the Arab stallions of the hairdressing world; at the same time he could not help admiring the barber's professional talent for making small talk, even with children: remembering certain things about you, asking after your dad, your mum, your sister and brother, your sporting activities, how you were getting on at school, and for the fact that he told the same joke every time: a man pops his head round the door of a barbershop and asks: "Doc Willis here?" The barber says: "No, we only cut hair." And through it all, Jonas stared and stared at the carton of condoms on the counter, which seemed to say that a haircut also boosted your virility, necessitating, as it were, that one's next call should be on one's fancy woman; and this brings me to the most mysterious part of all, namely the wordless sign used to ask for a "packet of three." The boys had taken it into their heads that this consisted of holding up a fifty-øre between the index and middle fingers—a V-sign, possibly anticipating a sexual victory—while dropping the other hand sharply to the thigh. Where did they get that idea, the boys? And what becomes of this marvellous imagination, the ability to read signs in everything: the way a watch sitting squint on a wrist was code for "just got screwed," for instance? I'm simply trying to say something here, Professor, about boys and their love of mysteries, to tie this up with the secret cave, because even if that black crevice really wasn't all that exciting, woe betide you if you crawled inside it. Such mysteries were no joke.

Jonas left the barber's looking like a crew-cut Elvis all set to do his military service, with Little Eagle like a shadow right on his heels, to find Petter and the gang waiting outside, arms crossed, gum-chewing in top gear—and Petter looking more like St. Peter the Reckoner than a future Sgt. Petter. And as if the hour of reckoning truly had come—it was starting to get dark—Jonas was grabbed by the arm and half-carried across Grorudveien and into the Memorial Grove, downhill from the church.

"So you've been up in our den, have you?" Petter says

Jonas keeps his eyes on the ground. Knows he ought to tell them something, a story so good that it will get him out of this situation, but he can't think of anything.

"So you've been up in our den?"

Jonas feels everything go black. In his memory this incident would always seem like an eclipse. He could have admitted it, apologized, been given a belt round the ear and that would have been that. But there is nothing but blackness. Jonas discovers that he has a dark cave inside himself, a dragon carved into his head. He says nothing. This is what it comes down to: the art of saying nothing. He has no chance of beating Petter in a fight. But he can keep his mouth shut. A partial victory. Or a partial defeat.

Petter doesn't punch Jonas. That's not how boys fight. Petter wrestles Jonas roughly to the ground, just beside the stone monument to the fallen of the Second World War, where a wreath was laid every May 17. Jones sprawls on the grass, nonchalantly, or hopefully even, knows that this is what he wanted, to lie here and see whether what he thought would happen actually would happen, whether life is that predictable. He gazes at the broad, empty steps up to the square in front of the church, where the girls' choir used to stand and sing like an angelic chorus.

Petter kicks him, not very hard, more as an indication that worse is to come: "Admit you were in our den."

Jonas lies still, playing dead the way you're told to do if attacked by a bear—something that all boys regard as a not-so-remote possibility. There is something about Jonas's stubborn silence that makes Petter madder than he had planned to be. He throws himself down onto Jonas's chest, pins his arms down with his knees and hits him in the face, quite hard. "Admit it, you snotty little twerp," Petter says, louder now.

Jonas is admitting nothing. This is his only weapon: to keep his mouth shut, deprive them of that pleasure. Although he knows it would be smartest to own up, since this would entail a symbolic and not too unbearable punishment: Chinese burns, maybe, or something of the sort. But now the big boys are losing face, and big boys don't like to lose face: still less do they like being defied by brats three years their junior. Such things get out. Besides which, Jonas senses that something he has not foreseen may be about to happen, a possibility that almost gives him hope. Petter is capable of anything; on one occasion he locked some poor sod in the cold-storage room at the shopping center for so long that the guy almost snuffed it.

"D'you give in?" Petter grunts. "Just say you give in." Jonas understands that Petter is holding out his hand, offering the chance of a compromise. Jonas does not even meet his eye.

Jonas lies on his back in the church grounds. The grass is cold and damp. Just across from him is Trygve Lie's tombstone. Petter punches him in the face. Jonas says nothing. Petter punches him again, harder this time, Jonas says nothing, Petter punches him again and again, harder and harder, Jonas says nothing, Petter hits him so hard that Jonas begins to bleed, first from a split lip, then from his nose, but he does not open his mouth. "For Christ's sake, Jonas, can't you just say you were in there?" Petter all but begs, staying a final, dangerously hard blow.

Last chance. Jonas is admitting nothing. They know he's been there, but he's not going to admit it, so he hasn't been there. That's the way of it. That's the law.

Petter crouches over him, his fist clenched. Jonas can taste blood, but he's not so much frightened as curious.

There is something unresolved about the situation. Ørn is standing there. The other big boys are standing there. The expression "lost honor" hangs in the air. Petter gets up. They know they'll have to come up with something else, something dreadful, something that will show the world, show all the other brats, that it did not pay, it most certainly did not pay, to climb up and sniff around in the secret dens of big boys.

"Let's chuck 'im into a grave," somebody volunteered. Not really meaning it seriously. More as a threat, a terrible threat. A hair-raising threat. An impossibility. The very thought made Jonas go rigid. Suddenly this was no longer fun. He longed for a return to predictability.

Petter noted Jonas's reaction, seized his chance: "Yeah, let's dump him in a grave. I know where there's one."

They trailed Jonas across the ground, which was strewn with chestnuts—Ørn and he always made believe that the green shells were oysters and the nuts were pearls—dragged him between them to an area roughly in the middle of the graveyard, where it sloped downwards. One of the other boys chased Ørn off home, forcibly, much as one would shoo away a crow. They reached a spot where a fresh grave had been dug for a funeral the following day. The pile of earth was covered with a tarpaulin; the grave was framed by wooden boards, the hole itself covered by planks. The day was growing steadily darker, the headstones cut adrift from the ground, swam menacingly towards them. Jonas didn't really think they would go through with it, but he was scared all the same, more scared than he had ever been in his life.

One of the boys stepped up and pulled away a plank, shrank back from the black hole. "Maybe this isn't such a good idea," he said. "Come on," said Petter. Jonas felt like pleading with them, was suddenly willing to lick the soles of their shoes, eat worms, anything. But his willpower had a life of its own, refused to let him open his mouth. His body on the other hand, his body reacted. From somewhere he found incredible strength, wriggled like mad, while the tears gushed uncontrollably and little whimpers issued from his throat. They managed to hold onto him, shoved him down into the grave, may even have been a little surprised themselves at how deep it was, at least six feet—and only three feet wide. Jonas hurt himself as he hit the bottom, thought he might have twisted his ankle. They dropped the plank into place. Jonas heard them dragging something heavy on top of it, a park bench.

The boys went off. Jonas could not move. Not because of his foot, but because he was numb—his whole body was numb, numb from sheer terror. He had never actually been afraid of the dark, he liked the autumn, games of hide and seek, cones of light cutting through the gloom like lighthouse beams, but this impenetrable blackness, the association with death and the total absence of anything for the eye to fix on, scared the shit out of him. And his fear seemed to make the darkness even blacker. He was sitting in a chamber that was closing in around him. Or stretching out into infinity. It was so dark that his scream was strangled at birth. Then, all at once, time and space were no more. He could not tell up from down, was plunged into a kind of vertigo, he was weightless, floating around, or maybe he was just falling so slowly that he thought he was floating, falling down into a black hole, down through a fissure leading to an unknown physical space, maybe he was in another galaxy, maybe he . . . yes, maybe he was actually already dead.

There was a raw smell, like clay, the thought of pottery, modeling, flashed through his mind. He felt that he was fighting: that he was sitting motionless, benumbed, or floating free, but that he was fighting,

fighting something evil, the Devil, and they were battling for command of his wits. He got it into his head that at any minute skeletal hands would come squirming out of the sides of the hole and fasten on him, skulls would be grinning at him. He remembered all those horror stories about being buried alive, films the bigger boys had talked about, scenes in which people were dug out with their fingertips in tatters and the coffin lids covered in scratches from their attempts to claw their way out.

He was terrified. To be perfectly straight—and this should come as no surprise—Jonas Wergeland was afraid of the dark from that day onwards. Down in the grave, the darkness crept over him, usurped him, left a black mark on his cerebral cortex, a hole he would never quite be rid of.

But in the midst of his terror, a terror which was like a physical pain, like having a needle stuck into the spinal cord itself, he learned something, just as Dante's character in *The Divine Comedy* learns something from his visit to Hell: the darkness showed him that it was not the eyes, but the brain which was the wellspring of all the images that really count. And in the depths of that awful terror he had caught an inkling—I say an inkling because it was the merest glimpse of something which he would later have confirmed—that in some cases the darkness is necessary if one is to experience, or perceive, something important.

Later he was to link this experience to one of the stories his grandfather had told again and again, although Jonas had no idea why—unless it was because this story was the key to the tale, the Story of Stories, which underlay everything; the story which his grandfather was constantly feeling his way towards. Once, when he was sailing the seas, Omar Hansen had witnessed a total eclipse of the sun. At first, as he stood on the deck, in some far-off harbor, gazing through soot-blackened glass at the moon slowly slipping across the sun, like a lid, he felt afraid, as people in ancient times were horror-struck when the sun's light was extinguished. But then he noticed something else, something that completely took his mind off the black hole which, for some minutes, took the place of the sun: all of a sudden he could see the stars. He saw something else, something he normally didn't see during the day. His grandfather told Jonas that he did not remember that day for the solar eclipse, but for the fact that, in the middle of the day, he saw the stars twinkling. The momentous thing was not that one light went out, but that thousands of others came on.

This association lay, however, some years in the future. Right now, Jonas was sitting in a grave, shivering, with cold and with fear. The thought of rats came into his mind, the thought that there had been several sightings of rats in the graveyard. They fed off the bodies, it was said. What if they picked up his scent, suddenly started digging their way through the walls, a whole pack of them, hundreds of eyes in the darkness.

He was very close to losing his mind. But he knew it was up to him, to his powers of imagination. He could make this black hole into a heaven or a hell. He felt something in his pocket: the box of matches he had taken from the big boys' den. As proof that he had been there. He fumbled with the box, hands trembling, managed to strike a match, flinched at the sound and was taken by surprise at what good light a single match could give, it was as though he had come out of an endless swoop through endless space to find that he was sitting in a narrow grave with damp, clay sides. The light brought him a moment's comfort—warmth too, in fact. He gazed into the flame, seemed to see visions within it, distinct images, a film. Then the match went out, he burned his fingers.

Darkness again. Deeper than before. Vertigo. Once more that vast, black space which knew no bounds. Swooping. Falling, even as he sat there motionless.

He lit another match. Wanted to wait, but couldn't. How many did he have? Twenty-odd? How long was he going to be here? He shuddered at the thought of having to stay in the grave until midnight, when the dead rose up.

He sat in the dark until his nerves were so frayed that his limbs shook with pain before he lit another match.

How long did he sit there? An hour? Two? He did not know.

He had used up all the matches.

The darkness. A darkness that wormed its way inside him and became a part of him. A darkness that never left him.

He was surrounded by screaming. So loud that it sounded like silence. Or like a hum, a transformer. And in the midst of all this, in the midst of the terror—as the cold pinched his pee-soaked groin—he thought about revenge.

He heard a light footfall. And something that sounded like sluggish, scrabbling claws on the wood above his head. Someone was struggling with the bench. A plank was lifted away. Jonas saw the sky, a night sky studded with stars, and the outline of an animal's head.

"Are you there? Are you alive?" It was Ørn. And Colonel Eriksen.

Jonas was overjoyed, felt like laughing. But instead he said: "What took you so long?"

Ørn merely slid the bench down into the grave until it wedged fast, giving Jonas something to climb up. "They followed me all the way home," Ørn said. "And I didn't dare come back to the graveyard on my own in the dark. Then I had the idea of bringing the dog. It took a bit of time."

Jonas finally managed to clamber out. Colonel Eriksen the old elkhound stood there wagging his tail. "Flippin' heck, Ørn, I could've been a goner," Jonas said.

"Thought you were Houdini," said Ørn. Jonas looked at him. Little Eagle had a sly, lopsided grin on his face, clearly he thought humour would be good medicine right now. Jonas gave him a clout round the ear, harder than he intended, but didn't succeed in wiping the smile off his friend's face.

There was something about the expression on Ørn's face that Jonas couldn't quite fathom. A look that said he thought Jonas had deserved this punishment, that he saw nothing wrong with it. As if Ørn, without saying a word, was openly admitting that he had deliberately waited as long as possible.

Jonas won a certain respect from Petter and the big boys after this incident. Simply for having survived perhaps. Or because he didn't tell on them. Petter even stopped tormenting Jonas, became almost friendly towards him.

Jonas, for his part, thought of only one thing: revenge. For over six months he puzzled over how to get his own back. Just you wait, Petter, he thought. I'll put out your light, so I will, you slimy, rotten, low-down sadist.

Little did he know that he would, in fact, manage to do just that on the Saturday evening when the Radio Theater broadcast the final episode of *Dickie Dick Dickens.*

And if you think his time in that grave made a murderer of Jonas Wergeland, Professor, then you're wrong. It would be truer to say that this was what made a television producer of him.

The Loop

Is it possible to change a life by recounting it? If so, then I must ask yet again: why did Jonas Wergeland travel? I know it sounds strange, but this does actually tie in with his fear of the dark. There was a period, after his hours in that grave, when Jonas suffered real torments, dreading the moment each evening when the light had to be put out, because Daniel—merciless as always—refused point blank to have a lamp burning all night. But one Christmas Aunt Laura gave the boys a globe—a rarity at that time—a glass sphere on which a wonder of topographical details, mountain ranges and wide plains, the various depths of the ocean, stood revealed in rich, warm colors when the light inside was switched on. In a fit of compassion Daniel agreed that this could be kept on at night. "What did you get for Christmas?" the teacher asked after the holidays. "The whole world," Jonas replied.

After that the nights were not so bad. Seen from his bed at night, the globe must have been as beautiful and comforting to Jonas as this blue planet seemed to the first astronauts viewing it from space. Jonas might wake with a start in the middle of the night, and when he sat up in fright he saw the world shining at him. Sometimes after a particularly upsetting nightmare, in which rats' eyes stared at him from the cold, damp clay walls, he would get out of the bottom bunk and hug the luminous globe, hold the warm sphere to his breast. It gave him what a certain Norwegian musician would later teach all the people of Norway to experience: "lots of light and lots of warmth."

So when Jonas Wergeland became a globetrotter, he was in fact only doing the same thing on a larger scale: he embraced the world. Jonas Wergeland did not travel to distant lands in search of thrills and excitement like so many others; he set off in search of security. Which is why he never felt anxious, but dared to let things happen. When he landed in Bombay and, as usual, thought to himself "Where will chance take me this time?" he could never have guessed that his trip to India would lead him into a living loop, a loop capable of squeezing the life out of him in a single second.

But it was Ahmadabad, not Bombay, which was the first stop, for Jonas and his traveling companion had not come to India to see starving children sleeping on pavements with garish film posters plastered, like dreamscapes, on the walls above their heads. This was not to be yet another tour from which one returns with a head full of images of the ceaseless, claustrophobic crowds mixed with memories of one's own painful attack of diarrhoea. They did not block out the noise and the stench and the shocking sights of Indian city life, but they wanted to see more than people doing their business in full view of everyone, more than the flies and the dirt, the funeral pyres and black exhaust fumes, the ragged beggars sheltering under temple roofs bedecked with a Disney-hued growth of obscure gods and swarming with monkeys. This was to be a visit that would leave some edifying imprint on them, preferably indelible impressions of buildings. Because they were both attending the College of Architecture, and this was in the nature of a study trip. While others went to Rome, Jonas and Inga V. went to India, but it was the modern India they had come to see, the new temples. And just as Benares was a holy place for Hindus, so Ahmadabad was a Mecca for architects, inasmuch as the city was home to masterpieces by both Le Corbusier and Louis Kahn—not for nothing did those two names call to mind a conjuror and a conqueror.

Inga V. and Jonas Wergeland had never really been close friends, even though they were in the same class and had known one another for some years. In fact Jonas would probably have said that he didn't like her, particularly disliked her penchant for cigarillos and the way she meticulously noted down all her observations in work journals, as if knowing she would one day be famous. And he knew she had her reservations about him: more than once when they were talking he had caught her glancing at her watch. So he was surprised when she—the last person he had asked—said she would come with him. "On one condition," she said. "That you don't go getting any ideas." Jonas found it hard not to laugh. As if it would ever have occurred to him to think of Inga V. in that way.

Now, as two colleagues with nothing in common but a professional interest, they explored Ahmadabad, armed with sketchbooks and cameras. And their focus was most definitely not on the dusty splendor of the old city, nor on the countless, ultra-picturesque drying racks hung with freshly dyed cottons from the local textile mills; instead they went to see—or rather, basically made a pilgrimage to—the Indian Institute of Management, designed by Louis Kahn: a college complex on the outskirts of the city, a campus where it was the overall picture which impressed the two students most of all, the way in which Kahn had juggled with the basic forms—circles, squares, diagonals, arcs. While Jonas—and this I hope you will now understand, Professor—extolled the sacral quality of light and shade in the shady walkways, Inga V. was more interested in the building materials and the sculptural attributes of the buildings. She loved stone, everything that had to do with stone, natural or fired, was almost brought to her knees by Kahn's use of the local brick. "Not since the Romans, not since the master builders of the Caracallas, has anyone understood the nature of brick and its potential as Louis Kahn does," she said.

The following day, on the north side of the city, they took in Le Corbusier's lovely—from a landscape-architecture point of view—Villa Sarabhai, as well as the three buildings by him which lay alongside one another on the left bank of the river: a museum, a private house and, possibly the most interesting, despite the weathered aspect of its concrete, the Mill-owners' Association Building where the use, not least, of an open but deep and slanting *brise-soleil* drew cries of delight from them. After a look round the inside of the building, a space notable for the bold interplay of curves and lines, Jonas exclaimed blissfully: "It's an absolute revelation! Those shadows are downright tangible!" They revelled in the place, felt how the encounter with this piece of architecture, which was also a work of art, sparked off masses of ideas inside their own heads. It all boiled down to one thing: light and shade. This was the enigma of architecture, as it was in life.

In Udaipur, their next stop, they celebrated the success of their trip so far, by checking in to the Lake Palace Hotel—a couple of days with fountains and marble floors, rooms with chairs like thrones and peacock feathers in vases; so when they got to Jaipur, lying rose-colored, almost cliché-like, between the mountain ridges, they opted for a somewhat cheaper hotel to save overstretching their budget. It didn't worry them that they had to share a double room, but they soon realized they were going to miss the air conditioning. India quivered at its hottest, you could positively feel the pressure of the monsoon which was just around the corner. Jonas thought longingly of his first attempt at being an architect, the ice monument on Steinbruvannet.

Inga V. was more enamored with actual Indian culture than Jonas, so on the day after their arrival they split up: she wanted to find a place to see classical Indian dancing. Jonas chose instead to take a walk through the old town's network of broad, straight streets and visit the Hawa Mahal; on the way home from this Palace of the Winds—which had made him feel as if he were standing before an organ façade of pink sandstone—outside the city wall, he decided to take a shortcut between two streets and for a moment escaped the traffic, the sea of beeping scooters and overloaded lorries decorated like temples. He crossed a piece of open ground flanked by two tumbledown buildings, their walls blazoned with illegible inscriptions, and came suddenly face to face with a man and an elephant. Jonas was so taken aback that he just stood there gaping, simply staring at these two creatures, both of them chewing: the man on *pan* and the elephant on twigs. Again Jonas was struck by the intrinsic sense he had wherever he went in India: that he was in a zoo, or that he was a voyeur. The two were standing in a sort of stall, between an old Ambassador and a cart, as if the elephant was the third possible mode of transport. And as the Palace of the Winds had made Jonas think of the organ in the church, so the animal put him in mind of Grorud and his childhood, because of the exquisite patterns painted on the elephant's forehead and trunk. They reminded him of the red letter day at school when the teacher brought out the wonderful, but seldom used, box of colored chalks and they were allowed to cover the whole board with a Christmas picture, after which the teacher wrote "Do not remove!" in the bottom corner, also perhaps as an order to the children's memories not to forget this. If I stood here long enough, Jonas thought, I bet I could relive the whole of my life so far. As I say: for Jonas Wergeland all journeys, no matter how exotic, were journeys home.

Although warned by a faint contraction of his testicles, he could not bring himself to move on. Jonas had the definite impression that the elephant, not the man, was the central character in this tableau: that he was looking at a wise god and his dwarf. The man, a little older than himself, was clad in a grubby dhoti, the sort of loincloth with which Ghandi caused such a stir at Buckingham Palace, and on his head he wore one of the gaily colored turbans seen everywhere in those parts. He smiled happily, didn't mind Jonas stopping to look. "Isn't he grand?" he said, patting the elephant. A penetrating, sickly stench rose from the enormous droppings on the ground. "His name is Mohan, he has been in the circus, and now he is going to be a temple elephant, we have just taken part in a wedding." The elephant seemed, to Jonas, to be observing him, assessing him with eyes that nestled within whorls of wrinkles. "I too have worked in a circus," the man went on, motioning to Jonas to come closer. Jonas did not dare, branches crunched and snapped between the elephant's jaws. "When I was a young man I had a chimpanzee," the man said. Jonas thought the Indian was pulling his leg, then he saw that there were tears in the man's eyes. "Did you know that a chimpanzee costs more than a tiger? Li-Li was its name, you know. Called after Trygve Lie, the Secretary-General of the United Nations. I saw a picture of Mr. Lie during the conflict in Kashmir; they looked like one another, those two—the ears. And he was a man who changed history. You know Hanuman the monkey god was a great warrior, he helped Rama . . . you know our epic story?" Jonas had not said where he came from, but he liked this comparison between Trygve Lie and the monkey god, suddenly he found himself taking a new, more relaxed, attitude to Grorud's famous son.

The Indian shifted a bale of hay. Would Jonas like to see some tricks? Was Jonas a brave man? Come! Follow your dharma! The man drew Jonas over to the elephant; it really was huge, much taller than he remembered elephants as being. He mustn't be afraid, the man said. Jonas felt its trunk nuzzling him; he stiffened. The man said something to the animal, then Jonas felt the trunk wrap itself round his waist, like a belt, before he was lifted up to dangle flat out in midair, face down, as if he were a log. At first Jonas was panic-stricken, abruptly reminded of something else, an encounter with another, a more malignant trunk, but then the fear left him; this was different, and bigger, bigger in all ways, truly an experience second to none. He was caught in a knot, the sort of knot his grandfather had taught him and Veronika when they were children. The scent of wild beasts filled his nostrils. The elephant could have shaken him to bits, but it didn't, Jonas felt more as if it was caressing him, and he heard strange sounds coming from the creature, from its throat, a kind of thrum, almost like a cat purring, only deeper, stronger; he was encircled by a living force, one which endowed him with a crystal-clear insight, something to do with at long last being an active participant, not just a spectator, a voyeur; and then, when he was least expecting it, he was lifted through the air—no, not lifted: swung and somehow or other, by dint of mighty forces, he found himself sitting on the elephant's back. Jonas always felt, later, that in that split-second when he was flying through the air, he was lifted out of himself—which is, by the way, the aim of Hindu meditation. When he dropped down onto the broad shoulders, it was as if he embraced the world anew, the way he had done with the globe of his boyhood; and although he could not explain it, he knew that his landing on that solid back, with his hands planted on skin rough as sandpaper, also marked a new beginning, that this sudden shift brought about a transformation, pure and simple. Because, and in case anyone should be in doubt: Jonas Wergeland did not travel in search of himself or his soul, as they said where he came from—Jonas Wergeland traveled in search of a different self. Jonas sat on the elephant's back, stroking the coarse hide, the short, sparse hairs feeling more like pins pricking the palm of his hand. He wasn't dreaming. He was wide-awake. He was alive. The animal knelt down, and he slid off. I am an enlightened one, he thought. I am a Buddha.

The thrill of this was still singing in his limbs when he got back to the hotel room. Inga V. was not there, but she had obviously been in at some point and left behind a newly-purchased book on Indian sculpture. Jonas got himself a drink in a plastic bottle, his mouth and throat were thick with dust; he was forever thinking about ice and water here in Jaipur. He settled himself on the bed with some chapatis, got out his sketchbook and looked at the drawings he had done the day before. Just before dusk—the loveliest time of the day, when the colors were so limpid and luminous—nigh-on transparent—he had gone to Jantar Mantar, the largest of Jai Singh's astronomical observatories. He had strolled around among those abstract, dreamlike, stone structures, thinking of Meccano sets or gigantic building blocks. There were tilting sundials, strange holes in the ground, ramps resembling truncated stairways to the sky, gangways to ships that had already sailed. Jonas sensed that he was standing at a personal crossroads, that he was particularly well equipped to understand this, since both his areas of study, astronomy and architecture, met and melded here, in Jai Singh's observatory. He had always wanted to make a conquest, create something new, something no one would have thought possible. Maybe that was why he had stopped studying astrophysics—because he realized he was never going to discover a new celestial body, and nothing less could satisfy his ambitions: a totally new planet, called after him or a god of his choosing. But here, in these weird grounds, he walked about in a daze, making sketches, feeling promising ideas welling up, possibly because these two areas apparently so remote from one another—the firmament and the observatory buildings—cross-pollinated one another in his imagination.

Maybe I can discover a new planet after all, he had thought—in the architectural universe.

But a day later when, sitting in a cheap hotel room onto the walls of which a rapidly sinking sun was casting shadow pictures, he examined the forms in his sketchbook, considered these rough ideas for a new type of building, he realized that they were as uninspired as the musical vision he had once had. He would always be a monkey, an imitator, at best a monkey god. His schemes would never be anything but pie in the sky. Like the monument of ice he had built as a boy, fragile and transparent, doomed to be short-lived. Sitting there, in Jaipur, in India, Jonas knew—perhaps because he had just been hurled through the air by an elephant—that he would never be an architect, that before too long he would have to give up this course of study too, because he would, as it were, be slung over into something else. I am tempted to go further, Professor: maybe even at this point, on his visit to Jantar Mantar, he had a suspicion that television represented a possible combination of the heavens and building styles, or an extension of same. That television was a kind of projection of architecture into space. That it was in this his talent lay. His only talent.

He had lost all notion of traveling on to Chandigarh in the Punjab, Le Corbusier's great city. He ate some more chapatis, drank some water, flicked through the book Inga V. had bought, with its pictures of erotic sculptures from the temples of Khajuraho: bodies twining around one another or captured in the act of fellatio. The heat was almost unbearable. A fan on the ceiling spun ineffectually. It would soon be evening. Through the window drifted the reek of vegetable refuse mingled with the smell of fires and spices. The monsoon was in the offing. I'm sitting inside a transformer, he thought, at the moment before someone flicks a switch off, or on. He wriggled out of his damp clothes and took a shower, and when he came out of the bathroom, wearing nothing but a towel wrapped round his waist, Inga V. was sitting on the bed, glistening with perspiration and enveloped in the smoke from a cigarillo. She was trying on some slender bracelets she had bought in a market, loads of them, a whole orchestra. She kept them on, smiled at him, an odd smile, a different kind of smile, he thought. She wore her hair in a ponytail. Her neck was moist. Little wisps of hair coiled damply against her skin. She picked up her book, a mite distractedly, leafed through it, put it down, Jonas caught a glimpse of naked bodies in unusual positions. Darkness was falling fast outside. They chatted a little about their respective days. There was going to be dancing the following evening, she told him with a flourish of her arm. Jonas sensed that something had changed between them, felt something seize hold of his body, like a trunk wrapping itself around him, groping its way toward a point on his back, pressing. He told her about the elephant, tried to describe the feeling of being swung through the air. She laughed, told him about a little temple, described it in a way which perhaps revealed that, to the surprise of all her fellow students, she would one day be a world-class architect, with a host of awards to her name, best-known for her views on the setting of a building within its surroundings—some people actually compared them to sculptures in a landscape.

She gets up. It is dark in the room. Her bracelets smolder, the brass and copper. The odor of tobacco and sweat comes at him in waves from her. Without thinking about it he too gets up, stands motionless in the center of the room. They crash into one another, collide in a fierce embrace, as if each means to press their body through the other. For a long time they stand there, kissing as though each kiss provokes a still more ardent kiss. The way Jonas saw it—this, at least, is how he rationalized it later—it may have been the danger he had been in, or thought he had been in, which had heightened his libido, the way war was said to do.

Jonas let the towel fall to the floor as she pulled off her clothes. They plunged straight into mad, passionate lovemaking, clinging to one another, Jonas did not know if he was standing or sitting or lying, felt like part of a giant knot of erect flesh and soft muscle, that together they became something greater, mirroring the ornamentation they saw all around them. The little flashes of light from her bracelets accentuated her nakedness, made her seem seductively foreign. And there was something about the combination of the street smells filtering through the open window and the pungent scent of her body, not least from her crotch, which made him think of the oracle at Delphi, imagine that he too was sitting above a deep cleft, breathing in fumes which put him into a trance, induced visions. Suddenly they were on the bed, where she threw herself on top of him, but she didn't bounce up and down, she slid back and forth on him, so damp, so oily, that it could hardly be called friction, just warmth, a warmth which generated light; she rolled about on top of him, crumpling the sheets, pulled him down onto the floor where they wrapped themselves around one another, wrestling, while the sweat poured off them—not that they noticed; they tore at one another, almost coming to blows, to the music of jingling metal and the moist slap of limb on limb. They were like two irreconcilable ideas, unexpectedly juxtaposed, like a silver brooch and a puck, a union that set sparks flying; Jonas felt his thoughts crackling, flowing along unwonted lines, and he concentrated, with one part of his mind, on following them, giving them room, believed that he noticed a difference in the images in his head, depending on whether he thrust deep inside her or only a little way in, began to feel his way forward, alternating between slow and rapid strokes, growing more and more urgent, as if this was a search of some sort, as if he was rummaging frantically in a drawer, until all at once the thought of athletics came into his mind, perhaps prompted by their strenuous exertions, the heat, the sweat: either that or the fact that a few of the brickwork circles at Jantar Mantar—the memory simply floated to the surface—had reminded him of something for throwing: a reflection which led him to think of the elephant, something about the way in which the trunk had hurled him through the air, a recollection which, as he lay there, whipped up to bursting point by Inga V.'s movements, set him thinking about rotation and not only that, but feeling that something lay at the end of this, a story, an extremely important perception which held the key to some future event, a story about a device, an instrument; an occurrence which would say something about who he could be, someone he had not yet become—a persona which had nothing to do with astronomy, nothing to do with architecture. Underlying the pleasure he was now conscious of anger, or a desire to use the powers he felt inside him in some way; he would suddenly grab her by the hair, throw her over his shoulder or lift her up, hold her over his head, and it may have been these urges that caused something to happen to her, because she seemed to lift off, they both appeared to be floating in the air, and all at once she looked at him with eyes which did not really seem to see him; from the pit of her stomach there came a moan, stop, she said, stop, stop, I can't take any more, she said, stop stop stop, she said, struck him, lashing out into thin air, oh, god, she said, grrr, the rest was drowned in gurgles that culminated in a little scream, a howl almost, as if she really had crossed over to the other side, propelled by a violent physical reaction, a surge spreading from her vagina outwards, and this made him feel proud, proud that together, through the combination of their inner fantasies and a few simple movements, two people could experience such pleasure, take themselves to such heights of ecstasy; and at the same time, this he knew, she might have been faking it, and he could never have told the difference, he would still have believed it to be an orgasm, and this did not depress him, on the contrary, he had always liked the thought of how little it took to persuade someone to make up their version of things, their own story, turn something small into something great.

The Great Bear

Is it possible to change a life by recounting it? If so, then it must be emphasized that later in life when Jonas Wergeland closed his eyes and thought of the women he had been with, he did not remember them as lovers but as storytellers. Through his encounters with these exceptional representatives of Norwegian womanhood he finally came to understand what Rakel, his sister, had been trying to drum into him for years: that sex and storytelling went hand in hand. And Eros came first, then the stories—not the other way round. Such was the doctrine of the *Arabian Nights*, according to Rakel. So Jonas Wergeland's women did not just make love to him, they activated, they transformed the stories within him. A story that had been lying there for ages, like boring black graphite, suddenly stood revealed as a scintillating diamond—as here:

While Daniel's promising athletics career was brought to a halt only by a serious case of tenosynovitis, a strained calf muscle which caused even Kjell Kaspersen—the former Skeid goalkeeper who was now treating sports injuries in a room at Bislett Stadium—to raise his eyebrows, Jonas's career was relatively short and painless. In any case, he did not have his brother's self-destructive determination, still less his motivation, because, as with everything else, when you got right down to it, Daniel's sporting endeavors were just a way of showing off in front of the girls, a kind of strenuous foreplay before the foreplay. If Jonas was mad about athletics, then it was for the sport's sake, for its inherent beauty.

For the last time I shall tell the story of the Radio Theater.

Jonas tended to take up sports in which the competition in his age group was not too stiff. He went in for high-jumping for a while but soon switched to a discipline for which he had some small aptitude and which did not appeal to very many other people: throwing, more specifically discus throwing. There were things that Jonas did for spells in his life, without quite knowing why he did them. Like this thing with the throwing. Maybe it was the discus itself that attracted him. He had stumbled upon it on the playing field down by the stream, a makeshift arena the big boys had made with their own hands. The discus had been lying on the ground next to the equipment shed, and when Jonas came by, on his way to catch minnows, this circular object seemed to catch his gaze—the metal core, the laminated wood body and the steel rim—no, not just his gaze, his whole being. Like an eye. A magical thing. Something which might have had its place in the lacquer casket along with the puck and the brooch—if it hadn't been so big. In any case he simply had to pick it up, just as you pick up lovely round, polished stones on the beach. And not only that—he had to throw it, or at least try to throw it. It was asking for it. And although Jonas did not pivot, he had an intuitive understanding—possibly derived from the picture of a Greek statue in his history book—of how he should hold the thing and how he should swing from side to side a bit before throwing it; and although the discus did not go far there was something about the sight of this object's glide through the air—because it really did glide, albeit with a bit of a wobble—which won over Jonas completely. Perhaps also because he realized straight away that it was not a matter of throwing but of whirling. And once he had thrown it once, he had to try again, to see whether he could whirl it a little further. From that day onwards, for a couple of years, he devoted a lot of time to the mysteries of discus throwing, indeed you might even say that Jonas Wergeland remained a discus thrower for the rest of his life, that this was his only real talent. For a second, when he spotted the disc lying there in the grass, he had actually perceived something that only later, during a heated discussion with Viktor, would he manage to put into words: "The discus is akin to the vertebrae of the spine," Jonas declared. "This disc is also in some way related to the central nervous system."

Jonas was just old enough to be able to start competing, so he bought a juvenile discus weighing 1 kilo and a junior discus weighing 1.5 kilos, both made by Karhu, which means "bear" in Finnish—this was before the marvellous French Obol brand came on the market—so he called them the Little Bear and the Great Bear. Jonas practiced on his own at Grorud sports ground when there weren't too many people around and took part in a few meets, including the Tyrving Games no less, although he didn't do very well. But he watched the others closely, picked up a few training tips by keeping his ears open, learned a few pointers, to the stage where he could at least get the discus to spin in the right direction by delivering it from his index finger and not, as he had done to begin with, by releasing the steel rim with his pinkie. "Remember to let the discus be friends with time," he heard somebody say. "It has to spin clockwise."

Is it possible to fight a dragon and win?

The pleasure he got out of the throwing simply grew and grew. If truth be told, this was his favorite pastime in those days: to nip over to Grorud sports ground at dusk and practice a few discus throws, chasing that magic moment, the seconds when everything fell into place—the moment when even the aerodynamic forces were on his side. He would spend hours there, working on the rhythm and balance that had to be developed; strove to be as keyed-up but at the same time as relaxed as possible, jumped for joy when he got it right, threw it in such a way that he felt the torque in every fiber of his body—because that is what it was like: a good throw always felt like such a tremendous release. To Jonas, these sessions at Grorud sports ground, the monomaniacal repetition of the same throw, were like a battle against gravity itself—if, that is, he was not endeavoring to defy another powerful, natural law: that of ordinariness. Whatever the case, he always came home purged.

It was on just such an evening that it happened. Jonas was alone on the field, poised on the concrete circle and throwing towards the fence in the top corner of the ground to save having to walk so far to retrieve the discus. In his head he was the young Alfred Oerter. Al Oerter who had already won three Olympic Golds in succession and would go on to take a fourth, an unbelievable sporting achievement. Jonas Wergeland was Al Oerter, up in the corner, hurling the discus with such force that it sang triumphantly off the wire fence. He also did a lot of "dry" throws, practiced his coordination, his torsion, his footwork and the drive forward; it was almost like ballet. With the legs, the challenge lay not just in getting the balance right but in achieving one smooth, continuous movement. "You mustn't stop, not even when you're driving forward," he had overheard one experienced thrower tell a younger pupil. "You have to keep your feet pivoting so that you don't lose speed, remember, speed is essential!" And so Jonas spent a lot of time just practicing the pivot, it was a bit like a pirouette; even in the schoolyard he would catch himself doing it, to the great amusement of the other kids. "Look at Jonas, he thinks he's Sonja Henie!"

At one meet he got talking to an old trainer who taught him a number of secrets: which is to say, the way he, the old trainer, saw the challenges of discus throwing at that time. Above all, what Jonas learned from him was a lesson in technique; he realized that he had to start his turn low down, begin his pivot with the right knee and not with his arms and upper body as a novice would automatically do. An accelerating tempo was also vital. "You have to start gently," the trainer told him. "Most folk uncoil too fast and that makes it harder to accelerate." The actual delivery had to be made at maximum speed. The thrust had to be like a spark, giving the disc a final, crucial boost.

So there he was, on this lovely, mild afternoon in late summer, trying out these new theories; enjoying every throw, feeling that it was going better and better, the spiralling turn and the outward trajectory; soon, any minute now, he was going to beat his own record of close on thirty meters. Because that was his goal: to outdo himself. That was reward enough; he didn't need an audience.

That, however, was just what he was about to get. Oddvar Kvalheim—no relation, it should be said, to the Kvalheim Brothers, the idols of every boy runner—but the chairman, nonetheless, of the Grorud Sports Club's athletics division, was approaching. Not on foot either, but driving in his spanking new Mercedes—"I've got myself a Spanish fancy woman," he would joke—a well-deserved reward for many years of hard slog, building up his own small business. Anyway, there was Kvalheim, no mean triple-jumper himself in his day, bowling along Trondheimsveien, and just about to turn in at Sigvartsen's Bakery and Rygge's hardware store, the stalwart local distributor of G-MAN saws, and drive through the gate closest to the ski-jump hill, right next to the corner where Jonas was throwing.

Jonas stood in the concrete circle, swaying loosely from side to side, with the pleasant weight of the discus, wood and metal, in his right hand: stood there swinging, trying to find his rhythm, thinking as he did so that he had melded the best of his mother and his father, ironmongery and music, then he set about preparing himself mentally for the throw, because he knew he had to become one with the discus, that a good throw was effortless—every Taoist knows that, Viktor would tell him later—it never worked if he gripped the discus too hard, he had to "ram it" perfectly, this was the time when he was going to do it, he thought, there was something about the air, the light, the tingling inside him; he spat on the discus, passed it from hand to hand before switching to an easy swing of his discus arm, and as he was starting on the actual rotation, engrossed in the hypnotic process of twisting himself into another dimension, Chairman Kvalheim—in the dimension of the real world—was only a second outside his field of vision, but Jonas did not hear the purr of the Mercedes engine; all his concentration was focused on spinning his body round in a circle, one and half turns, at the same time driving forwards in the ring and sending the discus into a skyward trajectory; and maybe it was because he did, after all, hear an unfamiliar sound, the Mercedes' wheels on gravel, that he threw "out," as often happens, and to the right of the planned throwing sector—as is quite natural if one is right-handed—but it was still a magnificent throw, he got a tremendous momentum on the disc—all at once the wind was very much in his favor—Jonas saw the discus skimming away, farther than he had ever thrown it before, because that's always the way with a good throw, they travel so very, very slowly, you can follow the course of the disc all the way, you fly through the air with the disc, as if it also carries with it a hope, the longing to break away completely.

And just at that moment Chairman Kvalheim turned the corner and drove his new Mercedes into the ditch, no real damage done, but nonetheless he was in the ditch, because Oddvar Kvalheim had not been watching Jonas Wergeland, he had been running an eye over the ski-jump hill, thinking to himself, a mite tetchily, that somebody jolly well ought to get that tidied up before the winter, when he spotted something which made him forget all about the winter and the ski-jump hill and, for a second, lose control of the car, because there, straight ahead of him, clear as could be, even with the sun in his eyes, was a flying saucer, hovering there, low on the horizon; he saw it quite plainly, for a long time, it seemed to him, although it was, in fact, only a couple of seconds, it swooped gracefully through the air, and then it was gone. "No flaming wonder I drove into the ditch," he said later in concluding a story he would tell again and again for years, not least because for a few minutes it made him the center of attention.

Jonas, for his part, did not see what happened, to the car that is; all he saw was that the discus appeared to be on a collision course with the Mercedes, as if the badge on the car's bonnet was a gun-sight and the discus a projectile shooting backwards—Aunt Laura had of course told him years before about how, in their ancient epic, the Indians regarded the disc as a weapon, a weapon capable of creating illusions, very much in the way of a diversion, stunning one's foes. Jonas was therefore, not unwisely, well away from the throwing circle by the time Kvalheim climbed out of the foundered car; Jonas jogged lightly down the side of the pitch, pretended to be warming down after some hard tempo training, but when he cast an anxious glance over his shoulder Chairman Kvalheim was standing with his back to him, rooted to the spot, staring, as if he had just witnessed a revelation or something of the sort. Jonas jogged on at a brisk pace, out of the other gate, onto Grorudveien and home.

Late that evening he ran back to the playing fields; he searched for his discus in the grass bordering the ditch, on the road side of the fence, about thirty to forty yards beyond the throwing circle. He didn't find it; it was gone. The fact was that he had never seen the discus land, and in his heart of hearts he began to think that it never had landed, that it had carried on out into space, that he had done the impossible, defeated gravity, that a Karhu was now winging its way to its proper home, in the constellation of the Great Bear.

A couple of days later there was the headline, emblazoned across the front page of *Akers Avis* (besides getting a small mention in the evening edition of *Aftenposten*): "UFO over Grorud," with a picture showing Chairman Kvalheim pointing almost proudly to the point in the sky above Ammerud Woods where he had seen the flying saucer, an elliptical object, disappear. "It seemed to be made of some shimmering alloy, and the bit in the center glittered like a block of ice filled with gems," said Oddvar Kvalheim. And Oddvar Kvalheim was a down-to-earth man, the sort you could trust. But one should not laugh because this was at a time when otters were constantly being taken for torpedoes and a swan seen in the right light could very quickly become a sea-monster. Even in Nidaros Cathedral—this really takes the biscuit—supposedly sensible people saw ghosts: monks wandering about at night. So why not a UFO over Grorud?

But not even then, on the day the UFO story broke, could Jonas have said what made him throw. It remained a mystery, seemingly meaningless. The only thing he sensed, very faintly, was that his discus training was a preparation for something else. That there would come a time when he would need to use this pivotal action. That one day—possibly when confronted with something inconceivable—he would have to make the discus throw of his life.

Jonas confined himself to cutting out the piece in *Akers Avis* as a sort of trophy, a reminder of how much can be set in motion by a perfect, whirling throw. And perhaps one should not entirely rule out the possibility that this incident had some part to play in his decision—in the eyes of many an incomprehensible one—some years later, after taking his high-school diploma and sitting the university Prelim, to study the movements of the heavenly bodies, to begin reading astrophysics.

Finally—dare I suggest it?—there is always a chance that Jonas Wergeland may also have been mistaken: that there actually was a UFO over Grorud that day. Because as you well know, Professor, we are living in an age when reality is as fantastic as fantasy is real.

Pyrrhus

Is it possible to change a life by recounting it? If so, then we must look at the question of what can have lain at the root of the enmity that existed between Jonas Wergeland and Veronika Røed, these two cousins. The relationship between them need not have been of an incestuous nature, as some have hinted, although I don't think this rumor was plucked entirely out of thin air either. To some extent they were, as their grandfather said when they were small, "spliced" together. Their hate of one another was of the type that is only a hairsbreadth away from love, a demented kind of love.

The truth is that Veronika had been more or less in love with Jonas since she was very small, but not until the age of seventeen did she make a serious attempt to conquer him, really lay him low, quite literally. Sir William's family, or what was left of it, had just returned from Africa after years of camouflaged exploitation of the natives—or, depending on how you look at it, of the Norwegian taxpayers—and even before the summer holidays that first year Veronika had made several expeditions from the new mansion on Gråkammen—built, you might say, with development funding—to her relatives in Grorud: visited them with remarkable frequency, although this sudden beleaguering of his person made no great impression on Jonas. Which is to say: he liked Veronika, had always been captivated by her—and at this particular time she also happened to be brimful of Blixenesque stories from Nairobi and the surrounding region. And yet there was something about Veronika that made him feel uneasy—no, not merely uneasy: afraid. She was too pretty, he always thought.

And his fears were not unfounded, as he discovered on Hvaler that summer, one weekend when the air was heady with the scent of the honeysuckle growing up the side of the house and they were alone out there at the mouth of the fjord, he and Veronika. Jonas still slept away from everyone else as he had done as a child, up in the little room in the attic. He slept soundly as always, and he slept in the raw, as always. On this Sunday morning he was woken by a faint clenching of his testicles, it felt as though someone had just clasped a firm hand around his balls. His duvet was gone. Veronika was standing over him, dark and smoldering, gazing down at his naked body. She smiled. Jonas had no idea what she was smiling at. Not until he tried to get up did he realize that his hands and feet were tied to the bars of the iron bedstead, bound with soft scarves, four knots. "Bowlines," said Veronika. "I could have chosen one of the trickier knots Grandpa taught us, but I like to keep things simple." She smiled again, teasingly, or was it desirously as she ran her eye over his body, as if he were a prize catch she had snared, rather like a unicorn. He tugged tentatively with one arm. "You'll never be able to undo them," she said.

She kneeled on the bed. She smelled of sun cream. Jonas cursed the fact that he was a sound sleeper, as she brushed his belly with her long dark hair. Jonas didn't know whether to lie back and enjoy it or put up a fight. Put up a fight? He was helpless, bound to the bed by colorful silks and soft knots; in one way he felt like an ornament of sorts, a bit of decoration, in another like a victim of torture, like you saw in pictures. But torture? Who could possibly regard this as torture? Veronika Røed sweeping her long, black hair across his stomach and chest, stroking a finger along his thigh, slowly, upwards.

Where are the dark holes in Jonas Wergeland's life, the tales that are hidden deep down, like a ball of hibernating snakes, all potent and intertwined?

She got to her feet and planted herself in front of him, gleaming black eyes and gleaming black hair, looked down at him lying there with arms and legs spread, like a big unknown "X." She pulled off the baggy T-shirt that covered her to mid-thigh, stood there before him in just her panties: ninety-five per cent summer-bronzed skin, five per cent white silk. From a purely objective point of view—this much Jonas knew—this ought to have been one of the sexiest bodies one could ever imagine, an almost timelessly perfect figure in terms of breasts and curves—classical beauty, as they say. Something told him he would never see a more consummately lovely body. And yet he said no. By which I mean, he said no with his eyes. And with his undercarriage. It was not fear alone that prevented Jonas from rising to the occasion but also, and to as great an extent, contempt. "You'll never get it up," he said.

The sighing of the wind in the tops of the pines reached them through the open window. Veronika stood perfectly still in front of him, gleaming black eyes and gleaming black hair, and yet Jonas realized that she was offering herself to him. And he realized something else, too: that this was the peach all over again—temptation on a silver platter—only this time it was more serious, would have even greater consequences. Veronika stood on the wooden floorboards in a loft where the dust danced in the lovely morning light streaming in through the old lace curtains, stood there tattooed by light, a sight to take a man's breath away, pure feminine beauty, pure sensuality; she let her panties slide to the floor then flipped them up to her hand with her foot before, with a light flick of the fingers, slinging, yes slinging them, with such perfect precision that they landed smack on his face, and he could not avoid inhaling that most distinct and possibly most arousing of all female smells, that blend of body odor, vaginal fluids and perfume. The very alchemy of this ought to have induced a solid erection. But Jonas's nether regions remained unmoved.

Veronika eyed him defiantly, picked up the wisp of silk and drew it slowly down over his belly, swished it around his groin, as though tickling him with a feather. When this did not produce any visible effect either, she bent down and proceeded to kiss him, grazing the inside of his thigh with her lips, her long tongue caressing that incredibly sensitive spot between the balls and the anus, a spot which, theoretically, ought to house the spring-release for an erection, but not in Jonas Wergeland, not now at any rate. And here, in a way, Jonas Wergeland showed the first sign of his genius: his inclination for viewing the penis not as hardware, but primarily as software. And, I may add, Jonas did not perceive this as the fulfilment of a vague piece of erotic wishful thinking, a kind of male fantasy, but quite simply as a most unpleasant experience—his main worry, his main fear, throughout all this was of what she might take it into her head to do.

Veronika looked at him with gleaming black eyes. He caught a look of surprise, but also one of warning, in her eyes, a threat almost, before she lowered her head once more and took his penis into her mouth. I do not know, Professor—many people have, of course, spoken of Jonas Wergeland's alarming stubbornness—but one has to wonder whether he ever gave a more convincing demonstration of his almost supernatural strength of will than at this moment: there was Veronika Røed, working the head of his penis into her warm, soft mouth, following all the instinctive rules, and still he managed, God knows how, not to get the world's most eagerly throbbing hard-on. So I do not rule out the possibility that there could have been more to this; that in refusing Veronika—this gorgeous girl who had stripped off and offered herself to him—Jonas Wergeland also humiliated her: that behind that demonstration of will there lay a not inconsiderable dose of malice.

So it is perhaps understandable that Veronika saw red, and something about Jonas's immunity to her advances, or apparent impotence, infuriated her still further, moved her to climb on top of him, making Jonas think for a second, with something approaching horror, that she was about to start masturbating, in a last attempt to turn him on: fondle herself, make it glisten with moisture, right there in front of him, but after taking a deep breath through her nose, as if coming to a decision, she began instead to kiss his stomach, then worked her way up across his chest until she came to his shoulder where, quite unexpectedly, she bit down, hard, so hard that Jonas cried out in pain. At that she jumped off the bed in exasperation. When she looked down at him, looked down at the shoulder where the blood was welling up, her eyes were still black and gleaming—and perhaps bewildered—as if they reflected her thoughts: the knowledge that this was a critical situation, possibly the most baffling experience she had ever had: a situation in which everything had gone "right" but which, nevertheless, had turned out "all wrong."

The problem with Veronika was, though, that she simply could not lose, she had a knack for doing something at the very moment of defeat that cancelled out the whole game, just as you could tilt the old pinball machines or knock over a chessboard when you got yourself into a tight corner. That was Veronika Røed's strategy for life.

And now she was standing in an attic on an island at the mouth of a fjord, aged seventeen, looking at Jonas stretched out on the bed, tied down with soft knots, looking the picture of defeat. For some unknown reason Jonas felt more afraid now than when she had been bending over him with her black eyes and moist lips, or when she had bitten down, cutting through his skin with her flawless teeth.

"What do you think he had in that safe?" Veronika said. Her voice was low, but Jonas could tell that she was struggling to control herself. Her tone, those words, aroused in him something of the same panic as the sound of a horsefly could do; he knew that what was coming had nothing to do with memories of kittens or red currants with custard. He refused to listen, felt like humming loudly, the way they used to do as boys when they didn't want to hear the result of a sporting event before it was shown on TV.

"What do you think Grandpa had in that canvas bag he kept in the safe?" she said, standing there naked on the wooden floor, a perfect body, a remorseless body tattooed by light in the lacy patterns of the curtains.

Jonas knew that something terrible was lying in wait. Worse than a dragon. "He's dead," he gasped. "Can't you just let him rest in peace?"

"A Luger," said Veronika. "Fancy that, Jonas, a Luger." Veronika edged right up close to him; Jonas was looking up at her already full breasts. "How on earth could that pistol, that detested pistol, so bound up with the Germans, have landed in Grandpa's safe?" she said, oozing ruthlessness.

"Please don't," Jonas said. The minute she mentioned the Luger he had known that this was a piece that would change everything. Possibly even the future. Intuitively he understood that his life too could be altered by the mention of this Luger.

"Too late," Veronika retorted smartly, as if she knew that Jonas might go to very great lengths to be spared having to hear the rest. But this was another of Veronika's talents—once she had started something there was no stopping her, no matter how fateful the consequences.

So she told him, stood there naked in the morning light, in the very loft where Daniel and Jonas had once succeeded in opening the safe, and where their grandfather had snatched the canvas bag out of the lacquer casket before they had a chance to touch it. And for the first time Jonas heard, from Veronika's lips, the story of their grandfather's treachery during the war, of the day when two men dressed as islanders and carrying forged border resident papers, stepped off the ferry. Omar Hansen had seen at a glance that behind their disguise they were really fearful city folk on their way to Sweden; all they had to do was wait for nightfall and a rowboat that lay waiting, but they never got that far, because when their grandfather spotted the German border police's patrol boat out in the fjord he wasted no time in rowing out and hailing it; and then, out of a sadly misplaced sense of duty, he actually reported them, those two fugitives, and hence gave the Germans no choice, even though they were amazingly tolerant out here, turning a blind eye to this, that and the other. Thanks to this zealous and enterprising action on the part of Jonas Wergeland's grandfather, the two men, who also turned out to be Jewish, were found and arrested. Fortunately, for Omar Hansen that is, no one had witnessed the brief meeting out in the sound except his two mortified sons, William and Haakon, who knew better than to say anything, not least because in May 1945 other informers had already been jailed and given a very hard time of it. It was just after this incident with the Jews that Omar Hansen secretly acquired a gun from the Germans. Maybe he felt threatened, or maybe he wanted to be prepared in case any more fugitives showed up and he had to escort them back to the German garrison at Gravningsund.

"And what do you think happened to those two Jews?" Veronika said when she was finished. "D'you think they came back to Hvaler for their summer holidays after the war?"

In his mind Jonas saw a boat sinking, slowly and softly into the deep. At this point he had no idea how Veronika knew all this, whether there were other people besides their fathers who remembered it, or whether it was simply something she had dug up herself, evidence of the talent which had shown itself in her at an early age and would one day make her a top-notch reporter. But, knowing the Veronika who stood before him as he did, he also knew that it was the naked truth.

He lay there, tied to the bed, involuntary tears streaming down his cheeks—cursing those tears, that Veronika should see them—and all at once he understood that this—this—was the Story behind the stories, the tale his grandfather had been searching for as he rocked back and forth in his chair, flanked by the dark, carved sideboards in the parlor, like a knight fighting shadowy monsters. His grandfather did not only have a dragon tattooed on his arm, he also had an invisible tattoo on his heart. And the reason he screwed up his eyes when he told a story was that he always had his sights on that one story, as if he were frantically trying to alter it by telling all those other stories. That was also why he always backed when he was rowing, because he so desperately wanted to turn back time, travel backwards and maybe one day reach the point, that total eclipse of the sun, when he had made his terrible mistake.

Veronika had scored a bull's-eye. If she hated Jonas for spurning her she could not have found a better way of taking her revenge—not even the pleasure she derived later from seeing Jonas gamble away a whole bundle of money on worthless shares could compare to the triumph she felt at the sight of Jonas's stricken face on that pillow. His grandfather was as good as a god to him; she knew this must hurt him dreadfully.

"Christ, you're mean Veronika, you're so mean," was all Jonas managed to blurt out.

"And you, Jonas, you're such a loser," retorted Veronika, as if alluding to the pleasure that could have been his but which he had lost all chance of now. “In fact you’re worse than that: you’re a mediocrity. Even your cock gives you away.” She picked up her panties and T-shirt, disappeared down the stairs. By the time Jonas had worked himself free, two hours later, she was gone.

But there was one thing Veronika had not reckoned on. She thought she had dealt Jonas’s image of Omar a mortal blow. But Jonas would only grow to love his grandfather even more after this disclosure, because now he understood his grandfather’s air of vulnerability, his desperate bent for telling stories, the effort it took to go on living in spite of his act of treachery: an occurrence which no amount of remorse could atone for. In time Jonas came to see that this was his story too, since it had to do with his roots. Hence the reason he kept returning to the question of whether a story about evil could, by some strange metamorphosis, some day become a beautiful story, whether Hitler could even become Homer or, as he thought of it when working at his carving bench, whether a dragon could become a swan.

Jonas Wergeland never really rid himself of the fatal suspicion that you had to be a criminal to be a good storyteller. Or that behind the best stories there was always a hurt, a wound, much in the same way as a foreign body will, in the course of time, cause an oyster to make a pearl; which, when you get right down to it, means that a pearl is disease transformed into beauty.

The Battle of Thermopylae

Is it possible to change a life by recounting it? If so, then we must start with words: *Tenerife, Tortugas, Tancred, Touraine.* All through the program this catalogue of names was recited, like beautiful alliterations, stanzas from a patriotic poem everyone used to know and which Jonas Wergeland meant to bring to life once more—lines as memorable as "You must not take so much to heart, that injustice which touches not your own part."

Many have remarked on Jonas Wergeland's ability to keep the viewers' eyes glued to the screen from the first flicker, to stop them from zapping to another channel within those first, critical thirty seconds. The opening sequence of the program on Wilhelm Wilhelmsen was no exception: it is the Second World War; a German submarine is seen firing a torpedo at a merchant ship. Thanks to an absolutely brilliant montage of clips from old documentaries, seen partly through the periscope, partly from the surface, Jonas created an almost unbearable cliff-hanger of a scene, rendered doubly effective by a shot in which the camera actually seemed to be following the torpedo through the water to its target, to the accompaniment of a spine-chilling soundtrack not unlike the theme from *Jaws.* The whole thing culminated in a grim, long drawn-out explosion and a dreamlike sequence in which the ship slipped down into the deep—a brilliant illusion created by an underwater camera filming a sinking model ship in the clear water of a swimming pool.

More than once during the shooting of this episode Jonas was reminded of what a thrill, what a boost he had got from making his first ever program. Because, although Wergeland's colleagues have insisted that he was a natural for television, that he had a sixth sense for where a camera ought to be placed, which passages were good and which were bad, this was not the case. When NRK, with some reservations, offered Jonas Wergeland, the increasingly popular television announcer, the chance to make programs, he just about panicked, his mind went blank.

The story is that he went to London and stayed there for a month, and that when he came home there was nothing he didn't know about TV. No one knows what he got up to in London, not even I—whether, as some people maintain, he sat through Alfred Hitchcock's *Vertigo* fifty times, or whether, as others say, he spent every single day and night at the BBC's Broadcasting House—but I am pretty sure that there, in his mysterious fashion, he found a key to the secret of television broadcasting. However that may be, he returned to Norway possessed of a self-confidence worthy of a television Einstein. And in the first program he made for NRK, about the Norwegian elkhound—yes, that's right, the Norwegian elkhound—he discovered, to his heartfelt delight, or relief, what a perfect medium television was for a person like him, one with such limited abilities; he gave thanks for the fabulous stroke of luck that had led him to such an enormously suggestive medium: a single twirl of the camera and people saw a UFO, their eyes just about starting out of their heads. Jonas Wergeland had found his arena, a field in which he could become a conqueror. Despite the fact that he created a series of what were—objectively speaking—outstanding programs, definite milestones in television history, Jonas knew something which he never told to a living soul: making television programs was the easiest job in the world—the TV studio the perfect refuge of the mediocre. Television was the salvation of Mr. Average.

What he really needed in his new career was staying power. And, as you know, Professor, if there was one thing Jonas Wergeland had plenty of, it was staying power. How many times have we had to listen to the same old stories of how thorough he was, of the time he spent touching up his programs, eternally cutting and editing: how he was never satisfied—with the sound, the lighting, his commentary, the tempo, the very pulse. He would sit on his own, going over the drafts of programs again and again, making notes for improvements. "He sat in his office long into the night," it was said, as if this were something remarkable, because this was NRK, and at NRK no one worked overtime, least of all if it was unpaid. But Jonas Wergeland worked on long into the night, of his own free will, because he wanted to make programs that people would never forget.

There was another factor—unknown to most people—which lent the program on Wilhelmsen an added personal touch. In many ways this was Jonas's tribute to Omar Hansen: a covert attempt to clear a man's name—a salute to a grandfather who had, after all, been a seaman for half his life and "sailed Wilhelmsen" to boot. The scenes had a personal feel to them because they were colored by his grandfather's countless stories about the Wilhelm Wilhelmsen shipping line, all those repeated boyhood references to "Speed and Service" and "The Wilhelmsen Style." And whenever his grandfather made Jonas a promise he always sealed it by saying: "You may rely upon Wilhelmsen."

This program was, therefore, in large part a declaration of love for the ship, for all the names beginning with "T" which were read out like an incantation in the background, like symbols from a deep-sea poem—*Talleyrand, Tudor, Triton, Taurus*—because even though the Norwegians never designed a Model-T, they did have their T-ships, a whole succession of them, a genuine glossary in which each "T" evoked its own universe, a snippet of geography or history, and it was these potent words which Jonas Wergeland wished to remind the viewers of. Here, it was the ships which played the lead in a program which took a loving look at the lines and the profiles of those great vessels: "a real Boy's Own program," people said, and everyone who has ever strolled along a quayside, taking an unadulterated, lordly delight in inspecting the boats and dreaming of faraway places, knows what they were talking about. "Never has a ship been captured on film with such empathy and invention, such beauty and grace," as one critic wrote.

Jonas made use of everything from old film footage of the ships to postcards commissioned by the company, showing those Wilhelmsen vessels which had also carried passengers: prestigious cards which Jonas himself had been given as a child by a first mate, a relative from Hvaler, and had stuck up on the wall so he could look at them and dream that he was a ship-owner and this was his proud fleet. More than anything else, though, he used model ships, the kind that are normally kept in glass cases, yard-long copies in which every detail has been conscientiously recreated, a mouth-watering sight for anyone with a liking for ships, exquisite miniatures which left one wide-eyed and wondering, like Gulliver in the land of the Lilliputians. With the theme tune for *Postbox*, the shipping channel's most popular program, playing in the background, Jonas panned the camera lingeringly over these elegant ships, following their curves and caressing individual details, as if this were a program about the erotic arts, not the art of engineering. And the viewers' response, their bedazzled eyes, proved beyond a shadow of a doubt that Henrik Ibsen was right: Norwegians are under the spell of the sea. The ship has been Norway's great achievement, from Viking times onwards. As the program progressed, Jonas filled the screen with a map of the world on which the famous Wilhelmsen Lines were gradually traced across the seven seas, giving the impression of a colossal and almost incomprehensible conquest, a web, a veritable internet, a global embrace. And throughout it all, those names like points on a line—*Talabot, Tabor, Tarifa, Trafalgar*—as if the entire world consisted of nothing but "T"s. It was possibly a rather nostalgic program, meant as a reminder of how shipping was one of the cornerstones upon which Norway's affluent society had been built: of a quite inconceivable time when this nation had boasted the fourth largest merchant fleet in the world, but a fine reminder all the same: images that could not fail to touch the hearts of every Norwegian. These lines across the oceans were as beautiful a sight, as great a national treasure, as the Academic's woodcarvings; the Wilhelmsen Lines were testament to the fact that a piece of artistic decoration could be carried out into the world.

Which was what made the contrast so striking. Because at the program's center was a ship-owner who had lost half his fleet, seen one after another of his precious ships go down without being able to lift a finger. Jonas Wergeland was never in any doubt about which situation said most about Wilhelm Wilhelmsen, popularly referred to as the Captain. For Wilhelm Wilhelmsen was not the sort of ship-owner who loves only money, Wilhelm Wilhelmsen was a ship-owner who loved boats above all else, to whom the seafaring side—the ship, the men on board—meant as much as the commercial side. His older brother may well have been a more distinguished and far-sighted ship-owner, but in Jonas Wergeland's eyes Wilhelm was the obvious choice, epitomizing as he did the Norwegian's relationship with the sea: a ship-owner who, like most Norwegians, put safety first—there is even a story of how once, when a mouse had nibbled a hole in a chart, Wilhelm plotted a course round the hole, just to be on the safe side. And for those same reasons of safety he decided to put his faith in something sound, on lines, to take no chances, to bank on oil; Wilhelm was a ship-owner and a seaman, an owner with fifteen years service at sea, an owner who knew the bars of Saigon and Shanghai, a man who joined the company offices as a captain, with a roll in his walk and malaria in his blood. Wilhelm Wilhelmsen's most treasured possession was not the stable of horses he would later own nor the palatial mansion with a Chinese pagoda in the pool in the grounds but a battered, camphor-wood ship's chest from his years at sea as a young man.

For such a ship-owner, the war was not merely a source of patriotic indignation, but to as great, or a greater, extent, a source of real pain. There was nothing Wilhelmsen did not know about his ships, nothing; he had been involved in discussions about new vessels with the shipbuilders, he inspected the ships himself as soon as they docked at Oslo's Filipstad Wharf, he knew every captain, every chief engineer on board the boats that were now being bombed, torpedoed, sunk on the high seas. Which is why Jonas Wergeland depicted Wilhelm Wilhelmsen on the bridge of a sinking ship, and replayed this shot again and again, to denote the twenty-six times during the war when Wilhelmsen was lost at sea in his thoughts. The filming of this scene had been a tough enough job in itself, involving a gruelling shoot down at a place called Verdens Ende, Norway's very own World's End on the tip of the Tjøme peninsula, not far from Wilhelmsen's hometown of Tønsberg. Despite the NRK management's worries about the expense, Jonas had organized the building of a set representing the last visible part of a sinking ship, the bridge upon which Wilhelmsen stood—although of course ships seldom sunk in such a way that the bridge was the last thing to be seen, but it was meant to be symbolic, and not one viewer complained. Actor Normann Vaage said later that he almost drowned during the shoot, because Jonas was never satisfied and Vaage had to put up with being sunk into the waves again and again. "Stop moaning, Vaage," Wergeland had shouted at him. "We're at World's End, remember!"

There is nothing so terrible, so ghastly, so disillusioning, so tragic, as a sinking ship. During the war the Wilhelm Wilhelmsen shipping line lost twenty-six ships, a whole string of "T"s which disappeared into the deep, and it was not only boats that were wiped out, it was words: *Tenerife*, *Tortugas*, *Tancred*, *Touraine*—and, not least, *Thermopylae*—they were legends that went to the bottom, whole epics: an Argos with all of its tales. And the main point of the program was that Wilhelm Wilhelmsen took the tragedy of all this as personally as if he himself had been on board and gone down with each ship. Which is why Wilhelm Wilhelmsen was shown in that recurring shot, standing stiffly to attention in his captain's uniform while the water slowly engulfed him; sequences with a primitive, almost brutal rhythm to them, accompanied by the discordant strains of an organ; sailors who had survived had described how the most infernal noise was heard as the air was squeezed out of the different sized valves when the boat went under—several times Jonas was put in mind of his first composition, the piano piece "Dragon Sacrifice." By dint of such devices he created an effect that had viewers hanging on for dear life to their Stressless chairs, to save being sucked down into the deep themselves. Jonas Wergeland was in his element on this shoot, chasing the suggestion that only pictures can create, ships sinking again and again, and at the same time drawing on all his images of the war, that sore point in Norwegian history—an era in which the people of Norway took such an insatiable interest. Jonas Wergeland did not wish to manipulate but merely to underpin the viewers' imaginations, and in so doing he helped them to see more than pictures on a screen; instead it was as if they sat in darkened rooms dreaming the whole thing up for themselves. "To be honest, I've never really done anything but Radio Theater," Jonas Wergeland remarked on more than one occasion.

They say that during the war, when the Wilhelmsen fleet was being run from London, Wilhelm Wilhelmsen went to the office as usual, had his black Cadillac sent to collect him every day from the mansion on Trosterudveien, a house which Jonas and Ørn were to take stock of a good twenty years later, and was driven to No. 20 Tollbodgaten, where he stepped through the heavy oak doors and said good morning to the caretaker before hurrying up to the first floor, past "The Three Graces," and letting himself in to his office. What he did up there, in a room lined with old paintings of sailing ships, no one knows. But Jonas Wergeland knew what went on in there. Because during the war Wilhelm Wilhelmsen was neither in Trosterudveien nor in Tollbodgaten, he was at sea, he was on board all of his ships, every single one of them; he was in several places at once and every time he heard that a ship had gone down, Wilhelm Wilhelmsen went down too. Why? Because he was still the Captain. When the *Tudor* was torpedoed, Wilhelmsen was not in Norway; he was somewhere northwest of Cape Finisterre, on board the *Tudor*. Wilhelmsen went down with his ship. When the *Triton* was torpedoed northeast of the Azores, Wilhelmsen was on board; when the *Taurus* was bombed off Montrose in Scotland, Wilhelmsen sank along with it, and when the *Talabot*—a name which aroused even stronger feelings in the Captain, because not only had the *Talabot* been the first of the T-boats, but Wilhelm Wilhelmsen had actually served as an ordinary seaman on that ship—so when, after a heroic crossing from Alexandria, this second *Talabot* was set ablaze by bombs in the harbor at Valletta on Malta and thereafter partially sunk in order to prevent its cargo of munitions from exploding, Wilhelm Wilhelmsen went down with the ship. It is not true to say that Wilhelmsen spent the war sitting behind a desk; in his thoughts he spent every day, his whole life in fact, on the bridge. WW, a quadruple V-sign: We Will Win. This was what Jonas wanted to show, and showed in such a way that even the most hard-bitten Norwegian could not help but be moved.

After this program—which, to Jonas's surprise, was never criticized for its pathos—NRK received masses of thank-you letters from seamen, surviving war veterans. They thanked Jonas Wergeland for so clearly illustrating a fact which people in Norway had, for over half a century, blocked out: what a debt not only the nation, but the whole world, owed to those seamen. In Norway it was the sailors who made the biggest sacrifice during the war. Almost half of all Norwegian casualties were seamen. They were like Leonidas's soldiers at the battle of Thermopylae, they helped to thwart a far superior force. No one can overestimate the contribution made by the Norwegian merchant fleet to the defeat of the Axis powers, and it is easy to see why the lines tracing the routes followed by the Wilhelmsen fleet and other shipping companies reminded some people of the diagrams of battles in historical atlases. What Churchill said about the RAF is equally true of the Norwegian seamen: Never was so much owed by so many to so few.

Talleyrand, Tabor, Tarifa, Trafalgar—a heroic poem, an epos. Those words beginning with "T"—recited as scene followed scene—were the names of boats, all of which sank, went down, during the war. Jonas closed the program with a clip from a documentary that showed the launching, four years after the end of the war, of the *Thermopylae II*, which was actually built at the Akers Mek yard in Oslo. "What a triumph," wrote one old wartime seaman. "Like witnessing a resurrection."

Axel, on the other hand, was scathing in his criticism of this program. Three quarters of an hour on Wilhelmsen and not one word about aquavit. Outrageous.

And if I might add my three ha'pence worth, in retrospect I cannot help thinking of the resemblance between the shots of Wilhelmsen on the bridge of a sinking ship and the photographs taken of Jonas Wergeland just after the murder of Margrete Boeck, and indeed as he looked in the courtroom, standing there with an air of defiance mixed with quiet grief and cool dignity, as if he, Jonas Wergeland, were also in the midst of a terrible shipwreck.

Penalty Kick

Is it possible to change a life by recounting it? If so, then we must concentrate once again on a thread which winds to the surface so often that it may well lie under everything. I am referring, in other words, to the story of the great shipwreck in Jonas Wergeland's own life. And as in the war, here too a villain stood behind the torpedoing.

Although Jonas escaped miraculously unscathed from the crash on the E6, it left him walking about like a wounded man. He considered kicking up a fuss, making one hell of a scene, but decided in the end not to say anything to Margrete, not even in the way of veiled accusations regarding what had finally dawned on him, something so obvious that he ought to have tumbled to it long before. In any case, Margrete was not the crux of the problem. Somewhere in his mind Jonas had always harbored a fear, prompted by her inherent unreliability, or by something he could not put into words, that there would come a time when she would betray him. Even though he wished he did not love her half so much, there were times when he saw a witch in her, a supernatural side which was most evident in her constant insistence on freedom, a freedom which also included the right to behave unpredictably, or respond to motives he could not fathom. He had caught a glimpse of this way back in seventh grade, before she left Norway, in the ruthless way in which she had broken up with him. I never want to see her again, he had thought, with something close to relief.

The problem, as far as Jonas was concerned—the shock—was Axel.

He went around in a daze, went to work as usual—although he didn't do anything there except sit and brood—but was always on the lookout for clues, signs that might give them away, lead him to a place where he would, as it were, catch them red-handed. It was here that the underside side of his creative genius was revealed: one and one made three—here, in his private life, as in his programs. He rummaged through Margrete's closet, disgusted with himself for doing so; rooted around in a wardrobe drawn from all over the world: colorful kangas for the beach, black Thai silk for evening; even Margrete's soiled panties were turned inside out and examined for suspicious stains; he went through her diary, looking for coded appointments, hunted through her handbag for a letter, a note, some item that ought not to be there, if only a strand of hair. And incessantly, a wormball in his head: one and one makes three, had to make three. He found himself admiring them, the whole affair, how clever they were, this web of lies which they had spun and arranged so brilliantly, this triangle which they had constructed, as perfect and intricate and yet as jaw-droppingly simple as Pythagoras's theorem about the square of the hypotenuse. What annoyed him most of all was his helplessness. He stood there shamefaced amid a heap of dirty washing with a metallic taste in his mouth, born of fear, or spite, a psychosomatic secretion from the organs of jealousy, and when he pulled off his shirt that night a sour, unfamiliar smell wafted up to him from his armpits, as if his body were trying to tell him that—if not physically, then mentally—he had been infected. He could understand, and even agree with, those who said that jealousy was a sickness, a chemical reaction in the brain; he didn't give a toss, he knew he was sick, wanted to be that way, he nursed this state of green madness, viewing it, through the fog, with a certain curiosity even, as if he had just discovered new sides to himself, had sniffed out the darkest springs in the human heart. He peered, fascinated, into this hallucinatory chasm, astonished, almost impressed by the monster of hate which he saw taking shape, growing more and more terrible, day by day.

Until the evening in June when he stood outside the door of Axel's apartment, unannounced and a lot more breathless than the several flights of stairs could warrant. He notes the Trio lock, rings the bell. Axel opens the door, opening also onto muted jazz and a faint whiff of garlic. Jonas had expected Margrete to be standing there, had been coiled and ready to spring, lithe as a wild beast, push the door wide open, squash the louse, before storming through every room, but he could tell straight away that she was not there. Axel let him in, looking surprised, pleased, expectant. And perhaps—in the suspicious eyes of Jonas Wergeland at least—a shade nonplussed.

"Can you hear what that is?" Axel asked once they were standing in the living room. "The Oscar Pettiford Trio, 'Bohemia After Dark'—just like in the old days at Seilduksgata," he said, answering his own question, pleased by this coincidence: this music, and Jonas suddenly turning up on his doorstep. He is already on his way over to the drinks cabinet, across a pinewood floor strewn with little rugs, laid out like a jigsaw puzzle, studiedly asymmetric. He could bake some potatoes, he joked, but he was all out of aquavit. Instead he returned with glasses and a rare malt whisky, a name Jonas had never heard before, a name that was hard to memorize, get one's tongue round.

It was a bright summer evening, not a cloud in the sky, and yet standing in that room Jonas felt an ominous darkness stealing in. Three of the walls in the room were filled, floor to ceiling, by bookshelves; the fourth was dominated by windows and some paintings that looked like windows. Filmy white curtains fluttered gently over the deep window embrasures, casting shifting patterns over the rugs in a sort of double-exposure. In one corner stood the double bass. Jonas had a painful, recurring fantasy, in which Axel was making love to Margrete in the same way that he played the double bass, standing behind her, with his hands on her breasts, passionately intent on turning her into an unusual bass line under those probing fingers of his: Oscar Pettiford, "Bohemia After Dark." Jonas had always wondered why Axel, such an attractive man, had never married. Now he knew. There was nothing Axel needed: he had Margrete. And any man who had Margrete had no cause to ask for more.

"Aren't you going to sit down?" Axel says, pouring some whisky. "Water? Ice?"

"No, nothing," Jonas mumbled, knowing he ought to have asked for ice, take something to cool him down. There was a tinkle as Axel dropped ice cubes into his own glass. Jonas observed his friend's clothes, the same old "uniform": the tweed jacket draped over a chair, the white cotton shirt, baggy trousers and thick-soled shoes, as if he were still a boy who walked the streets at night, a nomad as in his student days—a person who had never grown up, a man who still lived in a world of fanciful chatter and airy-fairy dreams of being able to rock the Milky Way on its axis. Irresponsible bastard.

"Sit down, please," Axel pointed to an armchair, a Stressless Royal identical to the one that Viktor used to sit in, staring at a blank television screen, there and yet not there.

Jonas put out a hand, as if to ward off such a fate, or as if realizing that for a very long time he had been as insensible and distant as Viktor.

"Something struck me the other day when I was watching a repeat of your program on Nansen," Axel said in his usual quick, intense fashion. "D'you remember the time after that mock exam when Viktor gave

Napoleon what for, when we were sitting talking? I said there were no heroes any more, and you quoted something by Carlyle, from that rag of his which you'd probably never read, *Heroes and Hero Worship* or whatever it was called; something to the effect that history was simply the biographies of great men—I think maybe that was more or less what you were trying to say with your television series. Or am I wrong?"

"Axel stop it, please," was all Jonas could say, he had a momentary urge to laugh, barely managed to stifle a hoarse and pathetic "*Etiam tu, mi fili Brute.*"

It was light outside, and yet it was growing dark, very dark. Jonas stood in the center of the room, trying to make time stand still, looking at the shelves, all those book spines. Behind glass doors. As if they were treasures. Or as if this were some sort of hall of mirrors. A den of narcissism. When did Jonas first begin to have doubts about Axel? It must have been when he dropped out of university and started writing. Jonas could not understand it. Laughed at his friend, teased him, sneered at him even. What a waste. Axel, with his matchless gifts, his flair for combining biology and chemistry. Jonas had been baffled by his decision. His flight from DNA to fiction, from the genetic to the grammatical. "You, who would rather uncover a chain of cause and effect than be the King of Persia," Jonas had sneered. "Yes, that's just why I did it," Axel said.

Jonas had never got more than halfway through any of Axel's books; they did nothing for him. Axel himself claimed that his novels were inspired by DNA, that the search for a structure, a bass line in life played a part in his stories too. But Jonas could make nothing of them, was not even turned on by the rather pernicious, raw eroticism that pervaded some of the stories, this element which a number of critics found so intriguing and which they called "perversion as innovation." In recent weeks Jonas had, however, nurtured a reluctant interest in—almost a fear of—this darker aspect; at home he had leafed with trembling fingers through some of Axel's novels, hardly daring to read for fear of coming upon something he recognized. He remembered only too well what Axel had once said about writing: "Being a writer comes of being a liar," he said. "Books are the paths where deceit, lies and truth intersect. When two lies meet a truth is born, and when two truths meet, a lie is generated."

Jonas is still standing in the center of the room, rocking back and forth as though teetering on the brink of a precipice. The faint tang of malt whisky invades his nostrils, the music of the Oscar Pettiford Trio streaming from concealed loudspeakers coils itself around him. "Are you just going to stand there gawping all evening?" Axel says. "Come on, sit down." Again the hand motioning towards the chair, as if he were offering Jonas a vacant throne.

Axel was wearing a pair of old, black-rimmed glasses, with tape wrapped round one arm. All of a sudden his friend, this former friend of his, seemed such a tragic figure to Jonas. "I can't believe it," Jonas said. "It's just too fucking awful, it's just too . . ."

He could not look Axel in the eye. He still had his gaze fixed on the bookshelves. He had always been suspicious of people who had a lot of books, who spent such a large part of their lives reading. From the very start he had disliked Margrete's reading. She read whenever she had the chance, read with an avidity, an ardor that was written all over her face. And in all sorts of positions, often more or less on the spot where she came across the book: standing, sitting, lying down, as if the book immediately hypnotized her body into a state of immobility, total concentration. Sometimes, when she had hunted for and found a novel on the bottom shelf of the bookcase at home, Jonas would find her kneeling on the floor, bent over the book, her behind in the air, as if she were performing a devout act, praying. Or maybe it was an invitation, an expression of a secret longing to be taken from behind. Lately, with the jealous man's amazing gift for visualizing, sticking certain images onto the mind's eye so that they overshadow everything else, he had pictured Axel finding her like that, here, on one of those little rugs.

"Where do you do it?" Jonas said, finally fixing his eyes on Axel, skewering him. "Here?" He waves his arms in the direction of the chequerboard of rugs. It was the perfect place. Axel's flat. A man living alone, working at home. "Or have you been going along on all these weekend trips she's been taking over the past few years—to London, Paris, Amsterdam?"

He could have sworn there was fear in the look Axel sent him: "Sit down, Jonas. Let's talk about this."

This was the proverbial last straw, this partial admission, because it may be—let us be honest, Professor, and give Jonas Wergeland the benefit of the doubt—it may be that deep down he had hoped that Axel would deny the whole thing, obdurately, even if it was true, refute everything, and then end it with Margrete, pretend it had never happened, so that they could still be friends; or at the very least that he would go down on his knees and ask forgiveness, burst into tears, beg Jonas not to think too harshly of him, but now, after what he had already taken to be a confession, Jonas lost control completely, gave vent to two weeks of accumulated wrath, hailed accusations down on Axel's head, peppered him with all of the worst expletives he had been storing up, vitriol and gall, while Axel stood there quietly, taking it, knew that he had to stand quietly and take it, stood there wearing those old glasses with the taped arm, like one who was already wounded, a pathetic figure in Jonas's eyes, a man who, in between Jonas's volleys of abuse, still managed to break in to say that this, this whole performance, was unworthy of a man of Jonas's intelligence, of such a brilliant doyen of the arts, couldn't Jonas see that he was reducing himself to the oldest cliché of them all; and after Jonas, maddened still further by such an ill-timed reproof, ducked his head and knocked back all of his whisky in one gulp, to slake his parched throat as much as anything; and after Axel had nodded approvingly, as if he thought Jonas had at last come to his senses, and after Jonas had set his glass down neatly, almost gently, on the table, and after Axel had promptly lifted the bottle and refilled it, and after Jonas had straightened up and just stared at Axel, and after Oscar Pettiford's music, the bass lines which had accompanied the whole carry-on, had come to an end, and after Axel had said something funny, and after Jonas had smiled, yes, laughed, and after Axel had walked over to Jonas, possibly meaning to get him finally to sit down, or to hug him, Jonas kicked Axel in the groin—in his mind, in the nuts—as hard as he could, with a power and precision comparable only to that of a kicker in American football, and his thoughts went to an incident in a basement in his childhood when he had experienced on his own person the full force of such an unspeakably painful mode of attack, learned that the sac containing his precious testicles was a button which, when subjected to remarkably little pressure, could put the whole body out of action: a trick which he had, therefore, memorized carefully, although he had never had need of it till now, the perfect opportunity, a swinging boot to the balls, to the very solar plexus of sex, unexpected and hence supremely effective—and Jonas savors, truly savors, the moment when Axel, that unspeakable son of a bitch, first doubles up then sinks to the floor like an empty sack, a felled mast, with a long-drawn groan of pain.

Axel lay writhing on the floor. But Jonas couldn't stop there, he was working in a red haze, he kicked him, heard something crunch, was suddenly reminded of the collision on the E6, the feeling that it was not just a matter of a crash, but of squeezing a pliant tin can; he kicked and kicked at Axel as he lay curled up on the floor in a sort of foetal position, moaning, kicked him as hard as he could, in the chest, in the back, the thighs, the head, till the glasses broke and the blood ran from Axel's nose. And even as he showered Axel with the foulest curses he could think of, went totally, verbally, berserk, while kicking away at what, as far as he was concerned, was a miserable worm—once his friend, now a traitorous worm—he was filled with a strange sense of release which made him stop.

When he left, Axel was lying lifelessly amid a tangle of rugs, as if buried in a broken up jigsaw puzzle. Jonas considered smashing the double bass but managed to restrain himself. Don't go too far, he told himself, well aware that he couldn't possibly go any further than he already had. He staggered out of the flat, out into Oslo, wandered around aimlessly, found a restaurant where he gorged himself like a Roman emperor, out again, on to a bar; he felt like celebrating, got as sloshed as it is possible for a man to get, before he was all but thrown out, politely, but firmly, and as good luck would have it managed to flag down a taxi right outside, a taxi with an inexperienced woman driver. "Bergensveien," he said, hearing how he slurred the word. And then, muttering to himself: "Or to hell. I've just killed a man."

I—the Professor—had long suspected that there was something odd about the confession Jonas Wergeland made in court. That he should have killed his wife in a fit of uncontrolled aggression brought on purely by her unexpected request for a divorce did not fit, or fitted only in part, with the red—or rather, green—thread of jealousy that wound its way through so many of the stories, a thread which was bound, in the end, to be drawn tight, like the noose on a gallows.

Modern physics is right: observation alters the thing being observed. I was confused. On the one hand, I had—there was no denying it—a bundle of exceedingly unpleasant stories; on the other hand, I had all the positive things I myself had experienced—learned, in fact—thanks to Jonas Wergeland. Could I—I mean during that year when I, like most Norwegians, let everything else go hang in order to catch every single program in the *Thinking Big* series—really have been wrong about Jonas Wergeland's talent for television? Would his programs too have evinced other, very different, qualities, maybe even fallen completely flat, if viewed in the light of what I now knew? I unearthed the folder containing comments on Jonas Wergeland's television work, flicked through the bundles of cuttings and copies of articles. Superlatives all the way: "He has created a new National Portrait Gallery inside our head," wrote one critic. Despite the controversies that were sure to be sparked off by such programs, there was no doubt that, prior to his arrest at any rate, Jonas Wergeland was regarded by expert media researchers as a television genius—not because he had gathered an entire nation around the TV, but because he had produced original programs, films which broke with the usual, tired old fare. "A born natural," as several commentators put it. He was proclaimed television's Copernicus because he upset prevailing ideas of what should lie at the center of a program. "Jonas Wergeland did not just transform the media," one writer concluded, "he reinvented it."

But still I was not sure. I got out one of his programs—I have them all on video, ranged on the shelf next to my own biographies; picked one at random: "The Dipper," the program on Sam Eyde, and slotted it into the video machine. I felt tense, afraid almost, as I sat in my Stressless chair, eyes riveted on the opening sequence, the close-up of a stylized form, a Viking ship, a logo on a plastic bag, before the camera pulled back to reveal a factory and then, from above, the surrounding countryside, a foreign landscape—the viewer would automatically place it in the Middle East—and right enough, it was Qatar, a fertilizer plant in Umm Said, part-owned by Norsk Hydro: a Viking ship in the desert, a strange conquest, like a fantasy, not to say a mirage. One could not help asking what was the connection here? And as if in reply the camera homed in once more on the drawing of the Viking ship, which gradually began to change, clearly working backwards through various graphic incarnations until it ended up at the original, far more figurative Viking ship logo, now on a barrel containing Hydro's first major product: what was known as Norwegian saltpeter.

I had been thinking of getting myself a cup of coffee, but I couldn't get out of my chair nor stop the video; I went on watching, had to see the next scene and the next and the next, felt almost as though I had become Sam Eyde in those last years before the turn of the century, first as a student and then working as an engineer in Germany, in metropolises such as Berlin and Hamburg, Dortmund and Lübeck. I meant to get myself a cup of coffee, but I went on watching, losing myself in the shots of the massive constructions which Eyde tackled: stations, docks, bridges—I even took his great idea about communication for my own. Without knowing how I got there, I found myself standing, so it seemed, beside Sam Eyde in Germany, in a highly developed society with lots of heavy industry. I identified with Eyde, living and working in a country experiencing explosive growth and thinking of Norway, a dirt-poor, underdeveloped country. But, Eyde thought—or we thought, Eyde and I—Norway had one enormous resource: its waterfalls. The question was: how to use all this potential? One would have to create a major industry—founded on what, though? And this is where Eyde mobilizes his powers of imagination, his bridge-building skills, by connecting two separate ideas. In Lübeck, two years before the start of the twentieth century, he reads a lecture on the catastrophic shortage in nitrogen with which the world will soon be faced. This is just the spark that is needed; a bridge is formed between two synapses in the brain. What, besides water, does Norway have in abundance? Answer: air. Eyde—or rather, we: Eyde and I—see a way of generating wealth in Norway from two things as elementary as air and water. He—we—will quite simply pluck assets out of thin air! An electrochemical industry! I sat there watching, staring, oblivious to all else, I was there, in the scenes depicting his collaboration with Kristian Birkeland, the development of the electric reverberatory furnace which drew nitrogen from the air; an invention which, once they had secured the capital and formed the company which would one day become Norsk Hydro, paved the way for the quite incredible development—by Norwegian standards—of the hydroelectric stations and factories at Skienvassdraget and Rjukan, while the people of Norway shook their heads: until, that, is, they were presented with the aforementioned Norwegian saltpeter—Norwegian air packed into barrels, nitrogen fertilizer for the soil—and what a success it was, a Viking ship which conquered the world. Thus the whole program revolved, in an almost imperceptible but exceedingly elegant fashion, around the four elements: air, fire, water and earth.

As I say, I went on sitting there, had thought of getting up to fetch something to drink but went on sitting there, delighting in the way my senses became so involved; I spotted delectable details which I had not noticed before, even though I must have seen this program at least four times. And it was not only the actual substance of it, those uplifting trains of thought, which enthralled me. I saw, or felt inside myself, with the whole of my subconscious, how important the sound was; I understood this better now, of course, after the story of Jonas Wergeland's love of the radio and radio plays. Like its theme, the soundtrack to the program on Sam Eyde was inspired by the four elements; the camerawork almost took second place to the sighing of the wind, the crackling of fire and electricity, the scrunch of shovels delving into earth—this last alluding both to the groundbreaking work done by the company's founders and the relevance of the fertilizer. But the predominant sound—the essence of the program—was that of water: waterfalls, of course, but also rain and murmuring brooks, conjuring up associations of something close to paradise, of Norway as an oasis of opportunity.

As I pressed the stop button on the remote control, I realized—as if this were a criterion of excellence—that not for one moment had I sat back in my Stressless chair, I had remained bolt upright through the whole thing, my wits somehow sharpened. There was no doubt: this program, this grand conception, this bubbling, sparkling program, would surely act as a counterweight to some of the dark tales my guest had told me.

Seeing that portrait of Sam Eyde again helped me to get over the worst of my frustration. It also reinforced my suspicion that this woman was not out to discredit Jonas Wergeland, a feeling which—to my relief—she confirmed the following evening by making what might almost be called a heartfelt plea. I could tell that I was ready for just such a clarification. For some time she had slowly and imperceptibly been turning what, to begin with, I had felt to be a negative picture of the man, into what I would call a defense of Jonas Wergeland. "Nothing, Professor, nothing is easier these days than to expose someone," she said, holding my gaze with eyes that seemed even more penetrating because of the black eyeliner. "You think, perhaps, that I am going to show you—and others—Jonas Wergeland's treachery," she said. "Strip him bare and make fun of him for being a despicable charlatan," she said. "Not at all." She looked as if she was about to grasp my hands in her vehemence. "In my eyes, Jonas Wergeland is the embodiment of a heroic project, a project of the type that will always be in danger of coming to a tragic end."

"And what does this project involve?" I was afraid I might offend her, but I was too curious not to ask.

"Jonas Wergeland's aim was nothing less than to do the impossible, even though he really did not have what it took. And he almost succeeded." She said all of this, embarking upon an argument from which I am only quoting fragments, while gazing out at the planes taking off from Fornebu, as if they could take her to a place that did not exist.

Jonas Wergeland's story, she said, was the story of a man who refused to accept his lot in life. Unlike a character in a classic epic, she said, Jonas Wergeland had rebelled against his fate. He managed, she said, to become someone other than who he was destined to be. Instead of being a single-cell creature, she said, he became a two-celled creature. And thus, she said, he played a part in mankind's development into something better. Her face glowed as she talked—and not merely with the reflection of the flames in the hearth. There was something about her eyes too, a look of entreaty that stripped her words of any pomposity; they were not so much statements as expressions of an almost traumatic, personal concern. Because this was not the story of a man who hoodwinked a nation, she said, but that of an individual who succeeded, with the help of others, in discovering the best in himself, she said, or begged me to believe. Jonas Wergeland was—could just as easily have been—a hero for our times, she said, or implored, me to consider, as if she knew I was just about to think something else, something damning.

We sat for a long time saying nothing, with only the crackling of the fire disturbing the silence, but she kept her eyes fixed on me. She did not wish, her eyes said, to do as so many others had been working very hard to do lately: reduce the genius to a banal, ordinary person. She wished, her eyes said, to lift the ordinary person up to the level of the genius, show that a man who considered himself talentless might in fact be in possession of tremendous riches, a wealth of possibilities. "We are all Sauls," she finished by saying. "Ordinary people who might at any minute be anointed king."

I did not want to disagree with her, despite the inescapable reality which cast a disquieting shadow over this beautiful monument of a rationale, I almost said testimony: Jonas Wergeland was a murderer. I could not bring myself to repeat this painful fact—not because I was unwilling to, but because there was an insistence bordering on desperation in her argument which made me think she had some other explanation, that she had a card up her sleeve which could still make this impossible game of patience come out right. Or as she had said during our first session together: "There is only one reason for telling stories: to save someone who has already been condemned. Tell the story against all odds."

This, our last evening, was Easter Saturday, and again her arrival was heralded by a distant rumble and the feeling that the whole house was shaking. I knew this would be our last meeting. I could tell it also by the way she glided slowly around the room, as if taking her leave of everything, before sinking into her chair and closing her eyes, as though gathering herself for a final, mighty push. It was with some sadness that I scribbled down notes in shorthand as she spoke, telling stories in a sequence, and with a conclusion, that made me gasp at the thought of a hitherto unimagined possibility.

No sooner was she done than she got to her feet, clearly exhausted. "I have to go now," she said, stopping by the window. "You'll have to excuse me, but I have a long journey ahead of me." She looked out across the fjord, where it lay shimmering in the darkness, as if wishing to brand that view into her memory. Or—this occurred to me later—as if she were weighing up something important, something she was about to say, but didn't.

Before she left I signed the contract she had drawn up. She waived her claim to any royalties—she didn't want the publicity, she said—but I undertook to transfer part of my fee to a certain person. I was both surprised and not surprised when I saw the name. A girl.

I had known it all along, really, I thought to myself. She swathed herself in her black cloak, like a magician about to make his exit, and moved towards the spiral staircase, then turned, with almost surprising abruptness, and clasped my hand—as if she knew that I guessed who she was and with this gesture was begging me never to divulge it. But I think she also took my hand in order to thank me. She confirmed my sense of having been her muse, as much as she had been mine. That for some reason she needed me in order to tell this story. "Several times you've asked me why I was doing this," she said at the last. "And I could just as easily have said: out of love. And sheer desperation. Because I do not understand it. I have also told it for my own sake. Not just for yours, or Jonas Wergeland's."

For the first time I remained standing by the window, watching her leave, the black figure walking down the driveway and through the gate. I could sense that I was more than fascinated: I was close to falling in love. Amazed and yet not so, I saw her climb into the cab of a semi-trailer, the biggest I'd ever seen: or rather, it was just the truck part, without the trailer. I couldn't see what color it was, but I would bet anything that it was black. The enormous cab, and the naked, little rear section made the vehicle look very alien, oddly empty. At first I thought someone was collecting her, but then I saw her slide behind the wheel herself, heard the mighty roar as the engine started up, and a sea of lights came on. She must have spotted me, because she beeped the horn, loud as the siren on a massive boat, and drove off. I watched the truck fade from view, gleaming and formidable, as though she were lifting off in a spaceship. I stood there, feeling that a great obligation had been placed on me, feeling as though she had uncoupled her trailer and dumped a heavy load in the garden: in my study, as it were.

And while all this was going on, or had gone on, late on an Easter Saturday, my thoughts went to the central character, a man sitting in his cell a couple of miles away—once the emperor of Norway, now emperor of a hundred square feet, whose final, curt comment to the press had been: "I got off too lightly." But if he really did have the creative powers which I had discerned in his programs—and plenty of breathing space—it could be that a few square feet was enough. I stood in my "control tower" wondering who he was. Could be. I gazed at a plane, possibly the last one of the evening, coming in to land; a plane which Jonas Wergeland might also have followed with his eyes if his window was facing in the right direction, and I reflected upon another possibility which my visitor had chanced to mention: that the real Jonas Wergeland was to be found somewhere in between all these stories. Maybe—in reality—he wasn't even in a cell at all.

Or, as she said when she began upon the last story of the evening: "There has to be another way." And after a long pause: "There is another way."

In Seventh Heaven

So it is with pounding heart, Professor, that I now continue. For, as Jonas Wergeland was standing with his finger on the trigger, aiming at Margrete Boeck's heart, his mind went back to the moment when he had stepped through the door of the villa, only half an hour earlier, thinking that everything was going to be fine, even though he had just got back from the World's Fair in Seville and was still recovering from a rough flight home. He was upset, certainly, furious in fact, but when he rang the bell and no one answered the door, he calmed down. Everything's going to be fine, he told himself, I just need to get some sleep, have some time to myself. He felt relieved, unspeakably relieved, the way you do when you've got out of doing something you've been dreading for ages. He let himself in, flicked the switch for the outside light, but the bulb wasn't working, he didn't like that, never liked it when a switch was turned on and nothing happened, everything would be fine, he was alone, he would sit down in the living room, he would put his feet up, sift through his mail and listen to a CD of Bach fugues, he would ride it out, he would take a shower, stand under the hot water for a long, long time, he would be alright, he just needed a little time. He left his suitcase and his duty-free bag in the hall and wandered into the office he shared with Margrete, looked away sharply on seeing her textbooks on the shelf, a number of them on dealing with venereal diseases, far too many of them, didn't want to think about that now, didn't want to think about that, or about Margrete at all, instead lifted the bundle of letters lying on the desk and took a quick look through them, then on the way into the living room he stops at one, the only one which comes as a surprise, an envelope stamped "Oslo University," from which he can tell that the sender is a woman, a well-known name in academic circles.

It would be untrue to say that Jonas Wergeland was totally unprepared for the bleakness of prison life. Once—one winter—he had spent hours listening to details from the *Inferno*, to the description, for example, of how Brutus, Cassius and Judas were chewed for all eternity in the three mouths of Satan. Or how those who had accepted bribes wound up in a bath of seething pitch, a molten mass like the tar they used to boil up in the old shipyards, with little demons holding them down in the mire with the help of forks, like a cook would prod bits of meat bobbing to the surface of a stew. Jonas knew what happened to murderers too—though he had no idea, of course, what the future held in store: they were doomed to boil forever in a river of blood. Jonas had sat in a blue auditorium, in the front row, with his ears pinned back, while next to him Axel was busy taking notes—when, that is, he wasn't leafing frantically through a book in order to score yet another exclamation mark in the already overcrowded margin. Round about them, solemn-faced souls were writing as if their lives depended on it. They were all students, attending a series of lectures on *The Divine Comedy* by Dante Alighieri.

The mid-seventies was not exactly a time when students flocked, of their own free will, to lectures on Dante and the medieval worldview—not if it wasn't on the syllabus, at any rate. The university was draped and hung, inside and out, with banners screaming out demands and declarations of support to all points of the compass. To some extent, the Norwegian version of the Cultural Revolution could, I'm sure, be characterized as a divine comedy, although as far as the students were concerned, modern-day Albania was a great deal closer to the ideal than Dante's Italy. In Norway it was the imaginary Vømmøl Valley that set the standard for both paradise and poetry. So it goes without saying that it was Axel—Axel, who had for some time known that he would never be a biochemist and who had secretly sent his first clumsy, literary efforts to several publishers—who had sniffed out the Dante lectures in their students' course list and managed to lure Jonas into making the leap, so to speak, from the revolutionary university routine to the Middle Ages—or was it, perhaps, the other way round? But the bait which Axel used to snare Jonas was not the content of the lectures, it was the lecturer—none other than Suzanne I., who is now known to everyone in Norway but who at that time, despite the fact that she had by then turned forty, had not yet found her calling and was recognized only within a very narrow circle. Axel had, however, heard of her through some literary friends and saw right away that she was one of those women who fulfilled all the strict criteria required to merit the distinguished epithet "sophisticated" which he and Jonas had thrashed out while wandering aimlessly through the city late at night.

And from the word go, Jonas, who had really just come along for the fun of it, was hooked, in spite of the fact that he was the only person in that auditorium who had not read a word of Dante—he had never been any closer to a classical text than his big brother's *Illustrated Classics.* He wasn't entirely ignorant, though. As a little boy at Aunt Laura's he had—speaking of picture books—found a volume containing Gustav Doré's engravings for Dante's *Inferno,* and these illustrations were still clear in his mind; indeed they enabled him, perhaps to a greater extent than the others, to follow Suzanne I.'s increasingly complex constructions and tempestuous zigzagging between the allegorical and the literal planes, which, by the way, showed him that hell, like the eroticism in Agnar Mykle's books, was on the whole a matter of metaphor.

That said, there is no concealing the fact that for Jonas the most fascinating part of it all was Suzanne I. herself; she fascinated him as only very few women did, more specifically: those who could lift him up onto a higher level—to stick to the Dantean imagery. While Suzanne I. was talking about the hideous torments of hell and the striking correlation between crime and punishment, while she was explaining Dante's overall plan and the conflict between Aristotelian philosophy and the teachings of the Church, Jonas, sitting in the front row, felt a button in his spine being pressed, felt his entire nervous system being put on red alert. While the rest were reading Dante, he was studying her, not least the austere face in which one eye seemed to look inward while the other gazed outward. There was something oddly anachronistic, not to say aristocratic, about her, partly also because of the way in which her hair was pinned up, like an elaborate snail's shell, and her rather old-fashioned, though stylish, taste in clothes, which made her look like a wealthy, conservative, middle-class lady. It was winter, and exceptionally cold, with ice everywhere—a fitting climatic backdrop to the lectures, inspired by the nethermost circle of the *Inferno*—and usually, when she stepped out of the lift, always bang on time, so punctual that you could have set your watch by her, she was clad in an almost demonstratively voluminous fur, making no attempt to hide her vanity. Axel said she was reckoned to be something of an eccentric and that she had only recently come home to live in Norway after many years abroad, in Italy among other places—hence the reason that she was liable, every now and again, to recite a few stanzas in vibrant Italian, making Jonas feel that behind her mask she concealed many more passionate sides to her character.

The lectures were hard going, and student and after student dropped out—including, fortunately, those Pharisaic pains in the neck who found it necessary to argue about everything from improbabilities in the chronology of the work to impossibilities in the topography. Only a fraction of the students were still sticking with it by the time the colorful and relatively entertaining *Inferno* section had been completed and they moved on to the much greyer *Purgatorio*, in which Suzanne I.'s long-winded expositions and scholastic leanings came more into their own—and had a soporific effect on quite a few listeners. But Jonas—who was not all that impressed with the *Inferno*—he had, after all, spent several hours in a pitch-black grave—was growing more and more interested and looked forward—I was about to say: like a sinner—to Tuesdays, to Suzanne I.'s monologues about free will and the nature of the soul, not to mention her interpretations of Dante's three dreams and Virgil's discourses on love; he half-ran down the hill from the university—not to the Student Union at Chateau Neuf, where Axel and he occasionally attended one of the riotous gatherings in the amphitheater-style auditorium and had no trouble imagining that they had been consigned to some wailing circle in the *Inferno*—but to the building next door, the old Divinity School, the top floor of which was home to the Institute for General Literary Studies, as if it had by some divine irony been set on a higher ledge on the Mountain of Purgatory than the theologians themselves.

By the time they got to the *Paradise* section, that pretty rarefied and by no means readily accessible ascension, fraught with transparent faces, indistinct souls and star-like spirits capable of choreographing their points of light into all manner of forms, only Jonas and three others were still sticking it out in the blue auditorium—even Axel the bookworm had opted out, muttering some sheepish excuse about a tough end-of-term exam. But Jonas sat there, still in the front row, and let himself be held transfixed, let the pressure build up inside him; he did not merely listen to what Suzanne I. was saying, but paid as much attention to the way she said it, her gestures, the look on her face, especially when she was talking about light, about how Dante used light—as a kind of visual music—and even more so when she got onto the subject of Beatrice's strange and problematic part in the whole thing, all while Suzanne I.'s amber necklace smoldered like embers at her throat. There was also something in what she said that tied in, in some strange way, with his own area of study, astrophysics, the exploration of the heavens, of the cosmos, those vast entities which were just about driving him round the bend with their staggering, nebulous dimensions, their billions upon billions of galaxies. You could say that in some ways Jonas found Dante's text just as enlightening, even if it was six hundred years old. It seemed to him that Dante's observations on the celestial spheres, based on Ptolemy's theories, were at least as right or wrong as the theories about the universe with which he was confronted in his astrophysical studies. In six hundred years, today's hypotheses would seem every bit as arbitrary as Dante's, he thought. And I ought perhaps to mention here that it may have been Suzanne I., with her highlighting of the architectonic and symmetrical aspects of Dante's work, who led Jonas Wergeland to cut short his astronomy studies and begin, instead, on a course which revolved around architecture.

Meanwhile, the days were growing longer and lighter, although the weather was still cold. At the last lecture, held appropriately enough just before Easter—which, of course, also plays a part in the *Comedy*—only Jonas and one other student turned up. Suzanne I. did not seem the least put out, although she had long been intrigued by Jonas Wergeland, a student who had sat steadfastly through all her lectures, without making a single note, it's true, but apparently hanging on every word she said about the progress from darkness to light, as if it really mattered to him, gazing at her the whole time, gazing at her with something close to rapture, a look which could not fail to make an impression. Jonas, for his part, felt that during that last lecture she lifted him from one heaven to the next with her eyes alone, much as Beatrice's radiant and loving eyes had done for Dante: felt also, again like Beatrice, that she looked much lovelier now than she had the first time he took his seat in the auditorium. So after this concluding lecture, in which she quite surpassed herself with her interpretation of the medieval view of woman as a possible channel to knowledge about the hereafter, not least in her discussion of the huge revelation in the last canto, the stream of effulgent images designed to help the mind reach out to a point beyond time and space—and after these expositions, which ought to have accorded any interested listener an insight into the whole of the *Comedy*, as the vault doors of national banks are occasionally opened to allow the man in the street a peek at the unforgettable splendor of the gold reserves, after all this she asks Jonas what he is going to do next.

And Jonas, who understood right away why he had sat through nine long lectures, and who had in fact also seen what she was getting at, that *The Divine Comedy* was actually a gigantic love poem, said that he was going take a walk into town. He knew what was coming. And it came: she suggested that they could walk down together. Jonas realized that he had made an impression, though of what sort he did not know; but we, Professor, acquainted as we are with the inexplicable frailties of the female of the species, know that simply by holding out through nine separate sessions, sitting up straight with his eyes aglow, by giving her his steadfast attention, he had won her in much the same way as a woman, no matter what she may say, is always bowled over by a man who gives her nine bouquets of red roses in quick succession.

It was the last really cold day of the year. She walked beside him wrapped in her black fur—mink, as far as he could tell. In the sunlight, however, it had a kind of golden sheen to it. Jonas caught her checking her reflection in a number of shop windows with undisguised self-absorption. He tried to bring up various topics of conversation as they walked down Bogstadsveien but was surprised to find that she appeared to be ignorant of most subjects: seemed, in fact, rather prickly, disagreeable. Only when he came out with one of his quotations did she show any interest. It was a thought lifted from Friedrich Nietzsche, taken from the only book by Nietzsche that Jonas had dipped into—or rather, from the only passage by Nietzsche which he had ever read: "Someone once said," said Jonas, "that anyone who fights with monsters must take care that he or she does not become a monster themselves." Suzanne I. looked at him in some amazement. "I was thinking of Dante and the *Inferno*," Jonas went on. "But what about the *Paradiso*? Would it also be the case that, when wrestling with angels, you would have to be careful not to become an angel?" Suzanne I. had a wise answer to this. A very wise answer, Professor. And when they get to Homansbyen, where she lives, she invites him in for a cup of tea—typical: a cup of tea, what else?

Where are the dark holes in Jonas Wergeland's life?

The decor of the attic flat was surprisingly impersonal, almost as if she were just passing through. The paintings on the walls were pretty pedestrian efforts, more like pseudo-art. A window was open. It was cold in the room. She made tea. They sat facing one another in two old-fashioned armchairs. Light poured strong and intense through a skylight. Jonas thought she was waiting for him to say something about her lectures, the last one in particular perhaps—or maybe he should tell her that he had been to Ravenna—but when he made to speak she raised her hand. "Don't talk," she says, sounding weary, as if outside the auditorium she wanted to stay silent—and preferably alone. She holds both hands around her cup; her fingers are plainly ice-cold.

Jonas got up to look at a well-thumbed Bible lying on the table behind her chair. As he walked past her she suddenly put down her cup and drew him to her, drew him down to her, firmly, commandingly almost, and kissed him fiercely, and awkwardly, he thought to himself, yes: awkwardly, as if she had never kissed anyone before, or not in a very long time; it was the kiss of someone who has been starved, he thought. She pressed his head down to her breast, to the silky fabric of her blouse, panting heavily, tugging at the buttons herself, fingers shaking; she swore when a couple of buttons popped off and landed on the floor; she swore, he told himself again, surprised, as she pulled up her bra and ground his face against her skin with greedy determination, as if, after all those lectures, she had finally got to the heart of the matter, to what lay behind all that talk of sin and redemption. There was nothing banal about all of this though, what happened next is as difficult to describe as the abstract concept of paradise; Jonas himself had the impression that this was a unique and very special occasion, that she had possibly never done this before, had never wanted to do it before, had been too inhibited, maybe too proud, but now, at long last, had decided that the time had come, because she pushed him further down, impatiently, down to her crotch, as if it were an order, all shyness gone now; she swiftly undid her skirt, tore off her tights and panties and pressed his face against her vulva as if this was a gateway to salvation, inviting him to browse his way to her innermost secrets, and as she did so she grabbed the fur coat, which was hanging over the chair right behind her and spread it over herself and Jonas: it was still cold in the room.

He began to kiss her, fired by a potpourri of scents, not unlike a blend of perfume and ammonia, or—the thought flashed through his mind—heaven and hell; and he instinctively knew, perhaps because of the way she held his head, that Suzanne I. had never been kissed like this before. He remembered Daniel, how Daniel had given a lecture, an actual lecture, on the art of what in scientific parlance is referred to as "cunnilingus." That too had been in an attic, on Hvaler, in his grandfather's house, one rainy summer's day when they were sitting reading—it might even have been the *Illustrated Classics*. Daniel had pointed to the safe where they had once found the lacquer casket containing a canvas bag which they had thought might hold pearls but which had in fact concealed a pistol, a Luger. Daniel had walked over to the safe, and as he was struggling yet again to open it, turning the dial in the center as gingerly as if he were attempting to locate "Lux" on the radio's chaotic medium wave, he described to an inexperienced Jonas the challenges which that place between a girl's legs held in store for him. Because, according to Daniel, there was a certain similarity between the manipulation of such a combination lock and the licking of a girl's pussy. Every woman had her own code; no two were exactly the same. "There's nothing more complex than a woman's privates," he said. "And yet you can give any girl, even the hardest nut, an orgasm just by using your tongue—if you've had enough practice, that is." It was like a robber being faced with a safe and saying to himself "Aha, a Diebolt from the thirties" or "Great, a Chubb from England," instantly calling to mind all the technical subtleties and special features of the make in question and how to open it—that, said Daniel was exactly what it was like for him when he ran a tentative finger over a girl's delights; he knew right away exactly what was needed, how many licks in one direction, how many in another, the requisite number of light or penetrating flicks of the tongue, when to take a break, when to up the tempo. That evening, out in the yard, Daniel had pointed to the cat, which was lapping milk from a bowl: "There," he said, "that's how to do it."

And now Jonas was lying between a woman's legs, and not just any woman, but Suzanne I. who, only a few years later, would publish her first major critical work, the fruits of learning accumulated and allowed to ripen over years of silence, as if she had suddenly found release, as if the pieces had suddenly fallen into place for her, enabling her to publish several books one after the other in rapid succession, most of them in English. Thus Suzanne I. in fact became the first ever Norwegian critic of true international standing: a scholar who won worldwide acclaim for her original approach to her subject matter and a distinctive style bordering on fiction.

Lying there, Jonas saw how the light coming through the skylight fell, like a spotlight, on the area between her legs, in such a way that her clitoris seemed almost to glow, like the chunks of amber around her neck. And he accepted the challenge with pleasure, accepted the privilege and set to his task with a resolve and, not least, patience, that Daniel would have applauded; it also seemed as if she was now expecting him to make up for the fact that he not spoken, asked a question, used his tongue at all, during her lectures; and he loved the feeling of being able to drive her wild with nothing but these simple oral exercises, causing her to shed the role of prim and proper middle-class lady—so much so that she began to mutter what sounded like gibberish, obscenities and taboo words mixed with phrases from other languages; she's speaking in tongues, he thought groggily, either that or these were utterly elementary words and sounds, the whistling of air through her teeth and visceral grunts that issued from her as she tore at the fur with her fingers, pulling it further and further down over him, so that for a moment he felt as if he was making love to a black beast. I admit it is tempting to draw comparisons with Dante: the idea of making a circular descent into a dark hole, to finally wind up in paradise, but images were, nonetheless, beginning to take shape in Jonas's head, like a vision almost, if I may be allowed to pursue this same thread. As he lay there in a kind of stupor, weird thoughts came into his mind, words which, by means of metaphorical leaps, or—why not—an erotic discus throw, transported him to that other attic, to the house on Hvaler, even as those thighs turned into sinuous creatures and his tongue into a line plunging into a vast deep, an ocean containing things of which he knew nothing, objects that gleamed dully in the darkness, and when she came, when at long last she reached a climax, and Jonas had placed his hands on her breasts, thinking perhaps that there was a connection between her nipples and her clitoris, or that her whole body was a complex locking mechanism, like the ones in the ancient pyramids, where you had to press several spots at the same time in order to make the heavy stone doors pivot on their axis—when the culmination came, when her body began to signal that she was about to come, Jonas felt more words and images inside his own head coiling themselves together to form something bigger, turning into a story, a story that he understood even more clearly perhaps because—the darkness between her legs notwithstanding—his head was closer to a light source than normal; and as she, after an assiduous oral onslaught on Jonas's part, spread her legs even further apart, tipped up her pelvis and stiffened—soundlessly, but as if it took tremendous effort—a corresponding convulsion, or mental release, occurred inside him and left him, for the first few moments thereafter lying, damp-faced and as lifeless as she. He did not come to his senses until he heard her whisper: "Go—please go." She regarded him with eyes so heavy that she might have been drugged. And with a flash of resentment, he would think later. "Get out," she said. On his way out, as he was closing the outer door, with the scent of vaginal juices still in his nostrils, Jonas heard her swear, a couple of times, swear loudly and clearly, almost infernally.

Norwegian Baroque

I do not know where all this is leading, Professor, for when Jonas Wergeland was standing with his finger on the trigger, aiming at Margrete Boeck's heart, his thoughts returned to the minutes just before when, after arriving home from Seville, he had sat on the sofa and told himself that everything was going to be fine; sat and read a letter, an inconsequential inquiry, while Bach's organ music filled the room as in a church, seeming to soothe his frayed nerves and once again give him hope; until, that is, Margrete suddenly walked out of the bedroom, wearing a dressing-gown, his dressing-gown, and this really upset him, the fact that she was wearing his dressing-gown, as if she were saying that she was him, that she was his self; so he turned off the music—she had shattered the cocoon of music in which he had been endeavoring to wrap himself, the one that was meant to shield him from the wrath which was once more starting to stir inside him, terrible and unstoppable; and he turns beseechingly to the portrait of Buddha, as if to elicit from it another angle on his troubles, but it does no good, and he looks at the coltsfoot in an egg-cup on the coffee table, but it does no good, and she looks at him as if she is the one who is surprised and not the other way round, as if she were accusing him, and not the other way round, as if she were about to come out with a sarcastic "A-ha, so you thought you might pop home, did you?" but she doesn't; instead she tells him, very quietly—demonstratively so, he thinks—that Kirsten is spending the long weekend with her grandmother, on Hvaler, and that she, Margrete that is, had been lying down reading but must have dropped off; all of this said with such bloody control, as if she can see that she is dealing with somebody who is close to cracking, a man struggling to curb his uncontrollable aggression. "Did you have a good trip?" she asks. "Good to be home," he says, and feels himself falling into the dark abyss between these two trivial and completely inane remarks, but still he believes that he can do it, cool down, all he needs is a hot shower, a brandy, a big brandy, more Bach fugues, everything was going to be fine, and as a means of distracting himself he picks up his suitcase and carries it through to the bedroom, looking and looking all the time, looking, round about him, as if searching for something, some object, some clue, something that will give her away, give them away: this book on her bedside table, for example, which is probably not hers, probably his, and he looks round about, confused, as if he is also searching for something else, anything at all, something that will help him, anything at all, which could give him back his hope.

How does one become a conqueror?

Jonas knew that he had been searching for something all his life. Everyone is searching for something. Life is a search. As children, they had rooted around in the rubbish tip at home, a landfill lying right behind Solhaug that was owned by a local entrepreneur and market gardener. Every time the trucks drove up and tipped all sorts of rubbish onto the edges of the tip, the kids had swarmed down the sloping sides like beggar children in Rio to hunt through it, because someone had once—no one remembered when—found a big box full of enormous film posters, a forgotten treasure hidden among discarded fixtures and fittings from an office building in town. So for years they had hunted diligently, combing every inch. But it probably didn't matter so much whether they found anything—although there was always the chance of stumbling over an unexposed film or a brilliant tin of paint—what mattered most was the search.

That was how it had been that time out on Hvaler. At first he hadn't wanted to go on the trip to Berby. It was more fun to play on the island and cat bread and syrup at old Arnt's place, to sit there surrounded by the most fantastic model ships and listen to his yarns than to lie in the bow of the peter boat, peering down into the water all the way there. But when his grandfather asked him again on the morning when he was going over there, Jonas said yes. He knew something would happen. I'm going to find something, he thought. And thanks to a woman, Suzanne I. to be exact, he would one day understand what it was that he found: a story. His own story. Late in life, but not too late, Jonas realized that he was not only doomed to uncover the reasons for who he was—he could actually invent them, make up his own reasons.

On the sail across to Halden, Jonas was sunk in an expectant stupor, didn't even look up when they slipped under the stunning Svinesund Bridge, hardly heard the stories his grandfather was telling him as he pointed up to the white bell tower at Fredriksten Fort or over at the granite quarries which they passed. Something's going to happen, Jonas thought. His hopes were high; he was in stonemason country, just like in Grorud.

His hopes rose even further when they reached the head of Idde Fjord, and the face of the landscape somehow changed, acquired a somehow magical cast, possibly because of the light. A storm was brewing, black clouds towered up around them. Jonas felt as if they had entered a secret valley, a sort of hidden paradise, because only here was the sun shining. Many people think that Norway stops at Svinesund and Halden, but to the east and south of Idde Fjord there is an enclave—an appendix, you might say—jutting right into Sweden. It would be only natural for him to find something completely out of the ordinary here, in such an out-of-the-way part of Norway, Jonas thought. At the very top of the fjord the water was so shallow that they had to follow the marker posts to the mouth of the River Berby, then sail some way up a channel in the river before tying up at a little jetty attached to the sawmill. His grandfather had to deliver an old sewing machine to a relative who worked at Berby sawmill, and once that was done he asked Jonas if he wanted to come with him up to the manor house, to pick up a lilac bush at the nursery there.

"Is it okay if I just stay here and have a look around?" Jonas asked.

"Alright," his grandfather said. "But promise me you'll be careful."

As Omar Hansen fell into step with somebody further up the road, Jonas turned back to the broad, quietly flowing river. He followed it upstream, under a bridge and up to the first, shallow rapids and stood there staring into the dark waters. He could see the bottom, stones which looked golden in the strong sunlight. Here, he thought, it has to be here. It was like walking with a dowsing stick in your hands, and suddenly it dips. The weather had turned bad, black clouds all around; only the spot on which he stood was bathed in a glorious light. If I dive in here, I'll find treasure, he thought. He knew.

The day before, the afternoon had been close and thundery too. When it thundered, Jonas sat on a pouf in the house's open-sided porch. Thunder and lighting held a magnetic attraction for him, that meteorological drama; he thought about radio plays, how on earth to create that sound? It would be even more of a challenge because of the stereo effect: the thunder rolling like a landslide from skyline to skyline, followed by ear-splitting bangs. Jonas particularly liked those wonderful moments before the storm broke, the silence and the tension in the air.

The pressure. Blue-grey clouds building up menacingly one behind the other. The colors of the landscape pulsating, as if they were under attack from some hidden darkness. Then came the rain, and the lightning. He sat on his pouf—sheltered from the showers but outside all the same—and counted the seconds between the lightning flash and the thunder. He was never scared, not even when the crash came almost immediately after the lightning and it sounded as if someone was ripping up a sheet right next to his ear, while at the same time hammering on the bottom of a zinc tub. Jonas thought it might even be a vague dream of his: to be struck by lightning—and survive, of course. He had the idea that this must surely leave you charged up for the rest of your life; you'd be able to stick a light bulb in your mouth and make it light up, the way they did in the comics. He sat on the soft pouf on the stone step and gazed almost yearningly at the lightning flashes. Two dragons playing with a pearl, that—so his grandfather had told him—was what people in China believed caused thunder and lightning and rain in general. Jonas had never swallowed the story about Thor and his hammer. "The lightning is the glittering beams from an enormous pearl, tossed across the sky by dragons playing among the clouds," he had once told wide-eyed classmates at Grorud School.

Afterwards, when the rainbow hung over the neighboring island and the landscape was looking all fresh and new, as if it had just been run through a gigantic, electric washing machine, Jonas usually went fishing. The day before, too, he had taken out his rod and gone down to the boathouse, walked barefoot along the path through a meadow that smelled like a spice market after the thunderstorm. He had taken the little rowboat: Jonas was good at rowing, he could row for hours without tiring, flicked the oars like an old seadog; he rowed all the way out to Flaket and beyond, through the farthermost inlet at Svanetangen point, to sit bobbing on the waves on the outer side of the island, with the sea—the ocean, he thought to himself—stretching out before him.

Here, after taking a cross-bearing, he let out his line, a good solid construction of his own devising: a combination of weighted line and gig; not spoon bait, but hooks baited with mussels, a sinker, thick nylon, sound knots. Jonas always dreamed of the Big One, had heard that there were supposed to be Greenland shark out here—in his mind's eye he saw the little shark from the book on fishing, shuddered. It would be something to show off, though, and take photographs of, the way they did in tropical waters. He had fantasies of one day sitting with his children on his lap: "And here's a picture of me standing next to the biggest shark ever caught off the coast of Norway."

The truth is that Jonas seldom got a bite. But he liked fishing anyway, liked raking up the mussels, liked drifting in the rowboat, listening to the water lapping at its sides. Sometimes he simply tied the line to a tholepin and left the swell to keep the gig dancing while he opened more mussels, he liked that too, found it exciting to open them with his stumpy-bladed knife, erotic even—the sight of the soft, aromatic innards, at any rate. "Did you know there's a sort of pearl that's found in mussels?" his grandfather had once said.

He has just decided to turn for home when he feels the boat beginning to drift out to sea, even though there is a light onshore breeze and no current to speak of. He has been sitting no more than twenty yards from the headland, directly off a break in the rocks, a small pebble beach. The water isn't all that deep here, either, nine or ten fathoms maybe. But his line is sitting at an angle that fits with the direction in which he is drifting. Jonas feels the nylon cord. Taut as Einar Tambarskjelve's bowstring, he thinks, and straight away he knows: it's a fish—the Big One itself. "A whale!" he thinks at first, overjoyed, then terror-stricken. He puts out his oars and rows for shore but doesn't budge an inch: in fact, he is actually drawn further out. He doesn't know what's going on, is growing frightened, pulls for all he is worth, churning up the water but goes on drifting slowly but surely away from the shore, out onto the open sea, out into the deep.

He could, of course, have cut the line, but that would have been too bad. He rowed and rowed with all his might and finally succeeded in keeping the boat still. The line was running straight down. Jonas thought the fish must have got away from him, he rowed almost all the way to shore before pulling in his oars and putting a finger to the line. There was still something there. He managed to haul the fish in a bit, then put another half-hitch around the tholepin, repeated this process several times, until he glimpsed a shape down in the depths, a huge shape, something that gave him a jolt before the line again shot away from the boat and the—creature—that was on his hook broke the surface. Jonas all but fell over the side. He saw humps. Actual humps! About ten yards away he could see several humps sticking up out of the water. The first thing he thought of was an anaconda. Then he decided it must be a sea serpent. Time and again his grandfather had told him the story of the Hvaler sea serpent, told it so vividly that Jonas had huddled up against him in fright. "The beast has been sighted off both Torbjørnskjær and Akerøya and later on out between Tisler and Heia," he said. "Even a dean of the church, the soul of reliability, once wrote about the sea serpent, and wait till you hear this, Jonas, it was forty feet long and as big round the middle as a potbellied stove." Jonas stared at the spot in the waves where the incredible creature had appeared. Whatever it was, it was too big. And this close to land? It could have been sunning itself, Jonas thought. It had been a chilly start to the summer, cold in the water.

After a fierce tussle—Jonas could not have said whether it went on for minutes or hours—he managed to reach the beach, where he tied up the boat, grabbed the line and hopped ashore. Thanks to a combination of luck and skill Jonas succeeded—despite its weight—in dragging the monster up onto the shingle. It writhed and squirmed so ferociously that it wriggled right off the hook. Before the fish, or the serpent, could get to the water, though, it worried its way down among some large stones and got stuck, lay there helplessly.

Jonas regarded this fearsome creature from a safe distance. It had to be at least six feet long and weigh a good sixty or seventy pounds. The jaws were the scariest part. For ages Jonas stood there, spellbound, staring at those teeth.

What was he to do? How was he going to get it home? He could just see the pictures in *Fredrikstad Blad*. The sensation of the summer. He picked up a heavy stone, meaning to throw it at the beast.

Then something happened. What it was Jonas would never say. But he put the stone down, jumped into the rowboat to fetch an oar, and using this as a lever he managed, a bit at a time, to nudge, or help, the creature down to the water's edge and out among the clumps of seaweed, where it revived and disappeared with a splash.

Jonas knew no one would believe him, so he never told a soul. Except me, Professor. Likewise I am the only one, apart from Margrete, to have heard what happened up at the top of Idde Fjord.

Because, as I say, the next day, with a sense of crossing a boundary, Jonas had padded—like a Red Indian, so he thought—up the bank of the River Berby, in this somehow alien Norwegian landscape, until something made him stop, a feeling that here, right here, he would find something precious. It was oppressively hot. He stood on the riverbank and watched dark clouds swelling up on all sides, saw the sun breaking through here and there, the apocalyptic radiance you see depicted on altarpieces, with the sun's rays falling like lighthouse beams on the earth. He stepped into the river, just next to the first stretch of rapids, waded out a bit before taking a header into a deep pool. Jonas was a good diver, and he was diving now, looking for unusual stones. Instead he spied something else, he didn't know what they were, but they looked like shells. He had had no idea that shells could be found in freshwater, too. He picked one up at random and carried it ashore.

Jonas sat on the bank examining his find. Almost four inches wide. And heavy. Like a piece of slate. He sat by a dark, gently flowing river and knew, with solemn conviction, that this thing could decide his fate.

He met up with his grandfather as the latter was coming down the road with the lilac bush, and once they were back in the rowboat and heading for home, Jonas took out the shell and showed it to his grandfather. "What is it?" he asked.

Omar Hansen only needed to take one glance at it. "A freshwater pearl oyster," he said.

Jonas almost dropped it into the water he was so taken aback. Really? His grandfather nodded. Jonas studied the shell. Never in all his wildest dreams had he imagined that it was possible to find something like this in Norway. A pearl oyster. Something so—he searched for the word—un-Norwegian. And he, Jonas, had found one. His whole conception of what Norway had to offer in the way of new frontiers instantly changed. It was as though Norway had expanded with a jolt round about him, as he sat there in the peter boat, sailing down Idde Fjord. And who knows, perhaps it was here, in a secret corner of Norway, that Jonas Wergeland laid the foundations of his career, a career that was rooted in the belief that the impossible was possible. Because, as I am sure most people will understand, no one who has found a pearl oyster in Norway can ever have any doubts about this country.

Jonas sat with both hands round the oyster, as if he were holding a thing of great potency. Alive. A heart. He pulled out a pocket knife, so excited he could hardly breathe. He had no problem seeing how this situation could branch out into two totally different lives. Depending on what was inside.

As if he read Jonas's mind, his grandfather said: "There's maybe one pearl for every hundred shells. And maybe a perfect pearl in every hundred pearls."

Jonas gazed at the gnarled oyster. But if it was one of those shells . . . It was one of those shells. He just knew it, could already picture the fabulous dull-sheened sphere embedded in the soft flesh, was already wondering what he should do with it, whether he should have it made into a pearl earring to give to somebody he loved, or what. This was not just a question of a pearl. It was a button. Something that could trigger unimaginable processes.

He sat with the oyster in one hand, the knife in the other. Then, all of a sudden, he stretched his fist out over the rail, uncurled his fingers and let the oyster slip into the water. It floated for a moment before it sank.

His grandfather eyed him. Said nothing. Not until they were level with Halden did he point to the shore: "Look, Jonas, over there's the quarry that supplied the granite block for the Monolith in Vigeland Park."

Jonas nodded. Proudly. As proudly as if they were towing the stone for the Monolith behind them. Or the stone for something much bigger than the Monolith.

The Ark of the Covenant

I still do not know, Professor, whether I shall succeed in this ambitious undertaking of mine, because when Jonas Wergeland stood with his finger on the trigger, aiming at Margrete Bøeck's heart, so excited he could hardly breathe, just as he had felt as a boy that time when he found a pearl oyster, he thought of what had taken place only minutes earlier, when he was in the bedroom, trying to collect himself, determined that everything was going to be fine; and yet, even while he was struggling to calm down, he could not help himself: he picked up the novel lying on her bedside table, and he opened it, and he saw the handwriting, and he read the owner's name, and he saw that the book belonged to the very person he least wanted it to belong to, and this provided him with a kind of final proof, proof which he did not need, because it was true, it had always been true, only he, in his hopeless naïvety had not realized that it was true; and it must have been then that he conceived the idea which propelled his feet from the bedroom to the little workshop where he dug out the pistol tucked well away in the cupboard, behind all the gouges, a pistol which Jonas's father, Haakon Hansen, had found among Omar Hansen's possessions when they were going through the house on Hvaler after his grandfather's death and which Jonas and Daniel had, in their turn, found hidden away, still in its thick wrappings, in the Villa Wergeland, when their father, Haakon, died and which, that day, with trembling fingers they unwound from the oilcloth, to at long last lay eyes on the weapon, a Luger P-08, the unequivocal proof of their grandfather's, their family's, crime, long hidden in a safe, and this they immediately wrapped up again, almost shaking in their shoes, a pistol which they obviously should have handed over to the authorities but which Jonas, with Daniel's blessing, kept safe for many years, like a shameful relic, and which, in an overreaction to some threatening letters only a few weeks before he went to Seville, he had taken out and wiped the grease off, a skill he had learned while doing his national service, from a gunsmith who could never have known why Jonas was so keen to see a Luger, never mind learn how to take it apart and clean it; and this was before he actually saw his grandfather's pistol at a time when all of his curiosity and interest—not to say, anxiety—was founded on intelligence supplied by Veronika; but Jonas had learned everything there was to know about this gun, applied himself so single-mindedly to it, you would have thought that by taking that pistol apart and cleaning it he was also dismantling an act of treachery, in order, if possible, to understand some inner logic, and as if that weren't enough: he had also committed these skills to memory so well that later, even ten years after completing his stint with N Brigade, at any given time he was not only able to clean the old grease off a similar weapon but could also coat all of the Luger's movable parts with a thin, thin layer of oil, and slot seven bullets, from an ammunition box which had also been kept perfectly dry all those years, into the magazine and push it into place, so that suddenly the gun was ready for use again, a fact which makes it possible for him now, newly returned from Seville, to walk into the workshop and slip the pistol into the pocket of his roomy trouser pocket, before trying once again to stop everything, stop time, stop the green pictures in his head, pull himself together and ride it out; he looks at a half-finished dragon head sitting on the bench, and he looks at the ornamentation on which he has barely begun, the dragon not yet come to life, and he shuts his eyes, and breathes in the powerful odors in the room, wood and beeswax, not unlike the smell on board a boat; and he asks himself, as I have asked myself, whether there was a safe in his own life too, or rather: a secret that was locked away? In other words: what could possess a boy to cut down the mast of an old lifeboat?

The following incident took place during one of the first years after Jonas started hanging out with Gabriel Sand, and please note, Professor, that I am still not sure whether this is a dark story or a light one. Whatever the case, the evening had begun as usual. It was autumn and the miserable weather outside only made it seem all the more cosy on board the *Norge*, where they were sitting in the saloon, amid the rumblings of the stove, talking about everything under the sun. There were few places where Jonas felt freer than on that ancient vessel, a place as crammed with oddities as Strömstad market and the attic on Hvaler put together. "This is my ark," Gabriel often said. "Here I've got everything I need to survive the deluge." After a game of chess, which Jonas won with the help of his knights, Gabriel had gone through to the galley and cut some thick slices of bacon, which he fried and served up, with the grease, on slabs of bread—with tomatoes and diverse obscure relishes on the side. They had a good laugh, while they were eating, at a picture that Jonas had found of Gabriel standing at a microphone next to Frank Roberts during a recording of *Dickie Dick Dickens*, a photograph which prompted Gabriel to trot out some of the most outrageous stories from his time with Radio Theater. Jonas had had his first taste of whisky that evening, and although he didn't drink much, he could feel his head getting fuzzy. From somewhere far off he heard Gabriel say: "We even had one guy there who could imitate any kind of animal—right down to different breeds of dog!"

Maybe it was his own fault, for collapsing into the starboard bunk, the skipper's bunk, as leading seaman Jonas's place was, according to Gabriel, in the port bunk. But Jonas had been so worn out that he had had no idea where his feet were taking him. He was already drifting into a dream when he became aware, even though half-asleep, even in his drunken stupor, that Gabriel was climbing into his bunk; something bristly, a mouth that reeked of spicy relish was breathing on the back of his neck. All at once the bunk seemed claustrophobically small, he felt himself being pressed up against the wall, against the inner shell of the hull. It was pitch-black too, and Jonas didn't like the dark, he was scared of disappearing, falling into a black hole. The amazing thing, he managed to think to himself, was that it hadn't happened before, because he had known it all along, really: that it would come to this, to Gabriel's groping paws. I'm dead, he thought. I'm in a coffin, I've been buried alive.

Jonas was conscious of Gabriel pulling down his trousers. He half expected a hand to close over his balls and squeeze, but instead felt the touch of lips on him; even in his befuddled state he could tell that his penis was in somebody's mouth, that he was being sucked off and that, in the state he was in, it was not as horrible as it might have been. He felt relieved, hoped it would stop there, things could maybe go on as before if it would just stop there, but it didn't stop there; a remarkably muscular, hairy arm flipped him over onto his stomach. "Like an elephant's trunk," Jonas thought wildly, not knowing what made him think of that.

He wanted to scream, but no sound came out. He tried to roll out of the bunk, or shove Gabriel off him, but the old man was strong, gripped him tight. Jonas felt totally helpless. Or was that how he wanted to be? And did he, nonetheless, hear a cry for help? Did it escape his lips, or did it only sound inside his head, like an echo of the scream he had heard in a grove of trees only a few months earlier, a scream that still resounded inside him? He relaxed. Let it happen. Knew, as Gabriel penetrated him from behind, that he would never fathom that sensation, say whether it hurt like hell or felt like heaven, whether he was being punctured or pumped full of something, whether he would die or live when it was over. For a moment it felt as if something long and thick was being pushed inside him, a baseball bat, a beer bottle, any one of the things with which, in their fantasies, Laila, Mamma Banana, had pleasured herself, something which made him think his body was going to rip apart, be pulverized. It was not just a feeling in his bowels; it was like having something stabbing into his brain. Like being given a lobotomy, the thought shot through his mind.

Say it did hurt—how did he endure it? Jonas Wergeland endured it because in a split-second of clarity he saw what this was: it was something he had to go through. It was a sacrifice. It was something he had to do because of Laila, in order to live down the shame, the fact that he had watched her suffer in Transylvania and had not intervened. And yet that was only half the truth, because he also knew that his lack of resistance now would be to his advantage later. It was part of a tacit agreement. If I had managed to get out of there before it happened, I'd have been Mr. Average, nothing but a dilettante, for the rest of my life, he thought later.

Earlier that evening, in a moment of weakness possibly induced by his first glass of whisky, Jonas expressed a certain doubt as to his abilities. He really wanted to make his mark in some field or other, he had to, he told Gabriel—rather bumptiously perhaps—but he wasn't sure whether he had what it took. I feel it's worth pausing here for a moment, because Jonas Wergeland made this admission even though he was actually in the midst of composing his "Dragon Sacrifice," the musical work which, with remarkable self-confidence, he assumed would cause a sensation or at least a scandal. As I say, it may have been said in a moment of weakness, but it does indicate that behind the cocky façade, Jonas Wergeland was not blind to the fact that he tended to overestimate himself.

It was then that Gabriel pointed out to him that he had a rare gift. He straightened his bowtie as he was speaking—in addition to his usual, outmoded, chalk-striped suit he was wearing a bowtie, perhaps to mark the fact that this was a big day. Gabriel reminded him of the first time they had met, at the Torggata Baths. Did Jonas know why Gabriel became interested in him?

"Because I didn't dare to dive off the five-meter platform?"

"No, because I peeked into your cubicle and saw the pictures you had drawn on your schoolbag. They were fantastic. Where did you get the idea for them?"

"From a dragon head I saw once." Jonas had drawn the Academic's designs on the flap of his leather satchel with a black Magic Marker.

Gabriel looked as though he was turning something over in his head, an impression reinforced by the creaking of the rigging. He took a hefty swig of his whisky before saying: "Now listen carefully, Jonas, because what I'm going to say now you have to write down on a piece of paper and put it in a casket and guard it well because it is worth more than pearls. Write: 'You have to put a twist on everything you do.'" Gabriel took another mighty swig from his ship's tumbler. "D'you follow me?" he asked urgently. "You have to let yourself be inspired by those criss-cross patterns of yours."

"Carvings," Jonas said.

"I don't give a bugger what they are, as long as you put your money on those lines. Metaphorically speaking, if you know what I mean. You've no idea how much difference a little twist can make. You're a Napoleon, lad. Wake up!"

Beyond the skylight it was pitch black, but the paraffin lamp cast a warm, if dim, light on the table. Jonas noticed how Gabriel's gold tooth glinted as he talked; it seemed to him that it was glinting more than usual, as if to underline the importance of his words.

These figures, Gabriel went on, these figures which Jonas had mastered, were more than enough. Jonas had to get it into his head that he could be ordinary and brilliant at one and the same time. It was like good, old Bohr's theory of complimentarity: there were two explanations which, while they might well be mutually exclusive, were both essential in order to arrive at a full description of him. Most "great" individuals were also perfectly ordinary people in many ways, exceptional only in a few, crucial areas. That was what it came down to: excelling within a narrow field.

Jonas sat there shaking his head, shaking his head in an effort to ward of this temptation or offer; but this only added fuel to Gabriel's fire. Had Jonas forgotten what country he was living in, dammit? The most egalitarian society on earth, a land with an almost pathological bent for equality. And what did that mean? It meant that any talent that was the slightest bit above the average stood out like a red fox among a pack of grey lemmings. Had Jonas truly never noticed that? Norway was a paradise for charlatans. In no other country in the world did it take so little to catch the attention of a whole nation.

"In the land of the blind the one-eyed man is king," Jonas said, repeating a saying that Gabriel was fond of quoting.

"Exactly," Gabriel said, gratified. "Everybody makes the same mistake. They think they have to be Leonardo da Vinci in order to do great things. But you don't need to strive for brilliance; an ounce of originality will do the trick. At the moment, anyway. Because you should think yourself lucky: we're living in an era when the most heroic thing you can do is to appear on the telly! Here, take the bottle—it's time you grew up. That's it: fill it up. You have to have an eye for the main chance, Jonas, see how far you can get even with very limited resources. A nose for how to weave a few commonplace elements into something greater is all it takes."

"But wouldn't it still be commonplace?" Jonas asked, sitting back on the bench, his head growing more and more befuddled, from the whisky, from the smells of the boat: smoke, tar, paraffin—and from Gabriel's words.

"Wrong again. Put a number of ordinary things together and you can get something pretty phenomenal. Not to say, terrifying. Take a dragon, for instance. What is it, except a dog with a twist? A dog with wings. Or four or five animals put together to form something extraordinary."

His gold tooth glinted, flashed. Jonas liked what he was hearing, liked it a lot. But he felt scared too.

"It doesn't take much," Gabriel said. "Look at me." He stood up, pulled out a key and wound up the ship's clock before going out to slice more bacon. "I'm an actor, remember," he called from the galley. "I know what I'm talking about."

Jonas could not know that he was, at that moment, living proof of this statement. Because although Gabriel could not, in fact, tell a foresail from a mainsail, for a year and a half he had led Jonas to believe that he was an old salt, simply by learning the jargon—"after leech" and "gaff end" and "barber hauler"—in the same way that an actor memorizes his lines. And Jonas had allowed himself to be taken in. "Are you mad!" Gabriel had roared, looking genuinely appalled, once when Jonas was trying to coil a rope. "Don't you know that all ropes have to be wound sun-wise, you landlubber." And this from a man who had never been to sea.

And now, only a couple of hours after listening to Gabriel's urgings, Jonas was lying with his nose pressed into the mattress of one of the bunks, with Gabriel on top of him, puffing and panting. He was drunk but lucid enough to feel like a puppet, with a big hand stuck up inside him.

He turned his head to the side, to scream, to say something, but still could not utter a sound, nor did he want to; instead his eye fell on a glass standing on a small table next to the bunk, he saw the false teeth lying in it, caught the glint of a gold tooth, but still it took a few seconds for him to connect this with Gabriel, for him to realize that even the man's teeth were false. And as Gabriel took him harder and harder, driving into him, uncontrollably, groaning, Jonas saw the gnashers cackling at him from the glass, as if they were laughing at his naïvety, at how easily he had allowed himself to be hoodwinked.

And yet, in the midst of this humiliation, or act of atonement, or pleasure, or reparation, or liberation, or whatever it was—maybe he was quite simply being put to the test—the glass reminded Jonas that Gabriel had also stressed the importance of willpower, the need for reckless defiance. Because even if you could only tie one knot, through perseverance something great could be created: by tying that same knot again and again—until at last you had a magnificent rug. "You've got the stubbornness that's needed," Gabriel said. "I know. I've seen it."

Yes, it was true. He lay with the sour smell of the mattress in his nose, proving it now. Unless it was Gabriel who was demonstrating it to him now. Showing him that he could stand it, this penetration that went beyond the tentacles of words. Jonas recalled how even as a little boy he had been capable of summoning up reserves of stubbornness from some unknown source. Like the time when they were playing down by the stream and they found a swarm of tadpoles. They caught as many as they could in a jam jar, gazed at them wide-eyed, those tiny pucks with tails. Then somebody bet Jonas that he didn't dare drink them. Bet him a flick-knife—a novel and dangerously cool item at that time. Jonas drank the whole jar of tadpoles down without so much as blinking, he could still remember the feeling and the taste as they slipped down his throat. "They're gonna turn into toads in your stomach," the boy who had bet him said in an attempt to save his flick-knife. "If you throw up, it doesn't count." Jonas could veritably feel the tadpoles crawling up his gullet, but he did not throw up. He exercised his willpower.

And as if to illustrate the link between that memory of the tadpoles and the situation on board the lifeboat, Gabriel was shaken by some violent spasms and Jonas felt something running down between his legs. At that same moment, Gabriel jerked him roughly backwards, as if he were pressing, trying to squeeze the breath out of him, or doing something to his back, snapping something into place, the way a chiropractor would do, causing an agonizing stab of pain to run right through him, accompanied by a flash of light. Gabriel rolled off him, grunted and slapped his backside. "Sorry," he said. "It'll never happen again. I promise." He got up and fell in to the other bunk.

Jonas was left lying there, feeling sure that he was going to die; but gradually he felt the pain give way to a pleasant warmth and a realization that, for some minutes, he had been bounded in a nutshell but was now a king of infinite space, to paraphrase another of Gabriel's favorite sayings. Almost against his will he was dragged down into a deep, peaceful sleep, into a dream of sailing through a long, unnavigable passage.

Coming up through the hatchway the next morning was, nonetheless, like climbing out of the belly of a whale. Jonas felt sticky, smelly. He stood on the deck, gazing into white space. It was misty and perfectly still. Some large seabirds came gliding towards him, skimming the waves. Other than that, everything round about had disappeared, like the images on an overexposed picture.

Gabriel rowed him ashore straight away, knew there could be no talk of breakfast. The bowtie was gone, but the false teeth were in place—and on his head he wore an idiosyncratically molded Borsalino. He sat there looking like the eternal cosmopolitan, wearing a dark coat over a chalk-striped suit, out of place in a little rowboat, sitting hunched on a thwart, handling the oars. The dinghy slid slowly through the white light. Just before they reached the beach, Gabriel broke his silence, quoted yet again from Ophelia's monologue, whispering it, so it seemed, to the mist: "Oh, what a noble mind is here o'erthrown . . ."

Jonas stepped ashore and began to walk towards Drøbak. "Will I see you again?" Gabriel called after him.

Jonas turned. "Yes," he said.

Three years were to go by before the reaction came: in the form of a power saw.

Back home in Grorud he went to bed. He felt sick in every cell of his body; he sank into a white mist, a luminous nothingness. He lay more or less in a daze the whole weekend, with a terrible ache in his back, an ache that gradually became more in the nature of a pressure.

It was almost as if he was pregnant, carrying a foetus in the marrow of his spine. Or as if he was about to sprout wings. Jonas both knew and did not know that something was happening to the button, the button of dragon's horn that he had swallowed as a little boy, and which he had persuaded himself had lodged in his spine like an extra vertebra.

On the Monday morning, when he got out of bed and took his first faltering steps across the room, he felt, in some strange way, "switched on."

Master of the Art of Survival

Speaking of that white light over the water, the mist—speaking of the lifeboat: I have not given up hope of being able to do it, to save him, save her, because Jonas Wergeland is still standing with his finger on the trigger, aiming at Margrete's heart, has got no further than this, because he is thinking about the seconds it took him to walk from the workshop with the pistol in his pocket, a pistol he really did not want to use, into the living room, where he stood and watched the light fading outside the window, a dark-blue sky with a band of yellow on the horizon, before he noticed that Margrete was now sitting on the sofa with an orange in her hand, staring at the television which she had switched on; he stood there watching how she shifted the orange fruit, absentmindedly, from hand to hand, how she seemed to be suspended in a vacuum between the glare from the television and the unspeakably beautiful, fading light outside the window, in a place where he cannot reach her, and he remembers her way of peeling an orange, slowly and deftly, in such a way that the fruit itself becomes a ball of light with a spiral-shaped tail hanging below it, like a big, pearly spermatozoon, a symbol of life, "Axel," she says out of the blue, and he starts. "Axel popped by the other day to borrow the program on Amundsen," she says and nods at the screen as if to explain what brought it into her mind, "but I couldn't find the cassette," she says, cupping both hands protectively around the orange.

The program on Amundsen opened with a scene from a lecture tour of America in 1907, a hall full of people and Roald Amundsen speaking and presenting a magic lantern show, as it was then known: a Roald Amundsen who clearly did not like doing this but was forced to go on these lucrative tours in order to pay off some of his debts. Jonas Wergeland had endeavored to capture the atmosphere and the audience's air of expectancy, remind people of a time when there were still—quite literally—white spots on the map; he shared with the viewers those faded, hand-tinted pictures of Amundsen and his men during their ordeals in that frozen wasteland: excellent photographs by the standards of the day but which, to Jonas Wergeland's eyes, only made it clear that all they had left of those heroes now were some colorless snaps, and with one of the palest of these he let the light take over completely, turning the picture into dancing "snow," a swirl of dots out of which the outline of a figure gradually emerged—like the picture used to do, back in television's infancy, when you adjusted the aerial—until eventually the real live Amundsen stood revealed, standing in the polar light at Gjoa Haven in the far north of Canada. The washed-out photograph had been transformed into bright, colorful reality. Amundsen was seen from the side, but it was easy to tell just from that strong profile that his face was glowing with happiness; it was a true magic lantern picture: a magical, light-suffused picture of a man in his own personal paradise.

I must say something about this light; it was of crucial significance to Jonas Wergeland. Not for nothing had he worked so hard on the lighting in his programs. A lot of people have remarked on Jonas Wergeland's inventiveness, his technical brilliance and, more than anything, his uniquely charismatic face, but for Jonas himself it all came down to light, to darkness and light. From the moment he started in television he knew that here, in the flickering of the TV screen, he had found, as Amundsen had done in the radiance of the ice, the golden fleece he had always been endeavoring to win: unsuccessfully at first, through music, then the study of the stars, then architecture. To Jonas Wergeland, television was primarily light. He was at all times conscious of the TV screen's dual function, as a projector of visual images and as a lamp: it often amazed him, when a television was switched on, to see how well it lit up a dark room. Making television programs was storytelling with light. It was no coincidence that NRK celebrated the screening of the last program in the series—in December, no less, on the darkest day of the year—with a little, internal, torchlight procession or that one, possibly rather overexcited, individual referred to Jonas Wergeland in a speech of congratulation as a Prometheus, an enlightener, the one who brought fire to mankind. Jonas himself was more modest: "All I've done is to strike twenty-odd matches in a dark grave," he said.

Hence the reason that Jonas dwelled for so long on that picture of Roald Amundsen standing in the glaring light of the frozen wasteland, like a worshipper before a crucifix. Needless to say, Jonas Wergeland never came close to choosing the trek to the South Pole as the central element in his program. He wanted to focus on another Amundsen, on the skills that were the secret behind the success of the South Pole expedition. Because, the way Jonas saw it, Amundsen was a collector. He did not simply collect artefacts from a foreign culture, though. Above all else, what he collected was knowledge, about everything that could help him to survive the cold. Jonas concentrated, therefore, on Amundsen's first major expedition, the *Gjøa*'s voyage through the North-West Passage, that barrier of ice, and the program placed little emphasis on the formidable fact that Amundsen and his six men were the first to sail all the way through this passage in one ship; instead it centered on the daily life of the team during the two years they spent in the country around Gjoa Haven, a little bay on King William Island, as they charted hitherto unknown areas and made scientific measurements close to the magnetic North Pole—activities which were as nothing compared to their encounter with the nomadic hunters of the region, an Eskimo tribe called the Netsilik: "people of the seal." In the old days men had dreamed of a shortcut to the East, a hidden passage, possibly up here in the north, and like Columbus discovering America in his attempt to find another route to the East, Amundsen, too, found his New World, namely the world of the Inuit. Amundsen liked it here. He perceived that the Arctic was an enigma, that it harbored mysteries of which we knew little but which presented a challenge to our technological presumption, as an Arctic iceberg would take the *Titanic* itself by such grimly symbolic surprise.

The Amundsen program proved to be the most expensive in Jonas Wergeland's series. For one thing, it was filmed on location, near today's Gjoa Haven, and late in the winter at that, both in order to film scenes of the harsh winter conditions—they were lucky enough to catch one of the season's last storms—and to get some shots of the hunting. And for another, Jonas used a lot of the locals as extras and did not stint when it came to props: teams of dogs, Eskimo suits made from reindeer skin and so on. They even built a rough facsimile of the old Gjoa Haven in a bay, with the Villa Magnet, the Uranienborg astronomical observatory, igloos and all—the boat alone was a set: all they needed was the rigging jutting out of the snow like an antenna. It seemed that Jonas Wergeland did not want to spare any expense when it came to the depiction of a Norwegian who had displayed those rare qualities: curiosity, a willingness to learn—and respect for another people.

The program revolved, in other words, around Amundsen the ethnographer, a man who patiently observed the way of thinking and the way of life in an icebound region: an image which broke with most people's view of Amundsen as nothing but an adventurer on skis, a ruthless egotist who would walk over anybody to get where he wanted. In Jonas Wergeland's program, Amundsen came over as a man who took an enormous interest in his fellow men and had a knack for getting on with people. In scene after scene one was shown how keen Amundsen was to learn tricks which could save a life in extreme weather conditions, how he studied the products of the Eskimos' inventiveness, everything from the five different items which went to make up their footwear to the technique for checking the quality of the snow; from the difficult art of building an igloo to the way in which, when traveling across hard-packed snow, one should allow a thin layer of ice to form on the runners of the dogsled. These scenes must be among the finest ever shown on a television screen when it comes to depicting life amid the snow and ice, something every Norwegian is certainly in a position to appreciate. But above all else, viewers were shown how Amundsen learned the two lessons which would bring him victory in the race to the South Pole: firstly, how to dress in trousers and anoraks of animal pelts, from the skin out—in other words: no woollen underwear—and leave both the inner and the outer anoraks hanging loosely outside his trousers, to create an insulating layer of air between them and prevent a build-up of sweat; and—secondly—how Amundsen and his men, especially Helmer Hanssen, picked up a lot of new and important tips regarding equipment and techniques for handling dogsleds. They learned one particularly vital lesson: in extreme cold and snow the only thing you could depend on was the dogs. "On this expedition Amundsen not only conquered the North-West Passage," Jonas Wergeland said, addressing the camera during his regular spot in the program. "He also won an insight into the art of survival. When all is said and done, it was here in the north that he conquered the South Pole."

The Amundsen program was full of scenes that caused viewers to avert their eyes. During the last hectic days of shooting outside today's Gjoa Haven, just before the advent of spring, Jonas Wergeland had been granted permission to reconstruct an old-style hunt for the first wild reindeer of the year, which were felled on land with bows and arrows. Jonas got in plenty of close-ups from the slaughtering, showed the slashing of the knives—most of them pretty primitive—showed the blood, the entrails, the meat being warmed, people gobbling it down, people cracking bones and slurping up the marrow, people scooping up the contents of the reindeer's stomach and drinking them down; there were pictures of raw meat, dripping grease, bloodstained fingers and lips, dogs baring their teeth: a glimpse of life pared down, quite literally, to the bare bones. And in the midst of this steaming tableau: Roald Amundsen, looking exactly like an Eskimo.

Here and there Jonas had inserted shots from the collection of Netsilik weapons and artefacts which Amundsen had brought home with him and which was now on exhibit in the Ethnographic Museum in Oslo. With this montage he managed to say something about the gap between the dusty, neatly-arranged glass cases—Jonas himself had found this place deadly boring as a child—and the bloody, ice-cold reality, what a far cry it was from that incredible hunting aid, the *kiviutchjervi*, as it looked hanging on the wall of the museum, to an actual seal hunt. In one long sequence, filmed in total silence, Jonas Wergeland showed how the Netsilik caught the little fur seals found in that area; how first, with the dogs' help, and often through a layer of snow several feet deep on top of the ice, they located a breathing hole and how they then, by dint of a number of remarkable devices, chief among them the aforementioned *kiviutchjervi*, which consisted of a length of reindeer sinew and some tiny bits of wood with a piece of swansdown stretched between them—in actual fact an ingenious sensor which told them when a seal was approaching—were finally able to drive the three-pronged harpoon into the seal, even through a thick layer of snow, just as it was coming up for air. This was the high point of the program, and Jonas did not stint when it came to detailed shots of the seal lying at last on the ice and the hunters ripping out the liver and kidneys and eating them right there and then, raw. He followed this with a scene inside an igloo, where the animal was being skinned and quartered with the *ulo* and its entrails dropped into a pot for heating up. As people watched white teeth munching on such delicacies as the seal's eyes and brains they could almost smell the whale oil burning in the lamps, hear the dogs howling and feel the bite of the icy polar air. Some viewers claimed that they sat there shivering in front of the screen. And afterwards they got themselves something to eat. "I've never been as hungry," was the comment from NRK's own director.

Amundsen was no hunter, he didn't like hunting, but you had to take life if you wanted to survive, kill with your bare hands if necessary. Even so, there was something terribly barbaric about this program; it was just a little too raw and primitive. There were some who felt that Jonas

Wergeland had used unnecessarily shocking effects, as if he were out to break some taboo. I don't suppose anyone would have been surprised to find that just such a program, containing so much bloody harpooning of seals, so many red-stained patches of ice, would be studied carefully by forensic psychiatrists, when the man who had made it turned out to be a murderer.

Jonas Wergeland was also accused more than once of being a con artist. Certain experts maintained that he had chosen the less well known, or at any rate, less well documented aspects of the series' heroes for obvious reasons: he didn't know the first thing about them. By highlighting a less well-recognized facet of a character he ensured that fewer people could check the accuracy of the scenes he presented—and the fact that he focused on just one aspect of his heroes' lives meant that the majority of viewers also believed Jonas Wergeland knew everything about them, that he was just as well informed about the rest of their lives. That is not for me to decide, Professor, I will simply say that if Jonas did not know almost all there was to know about Amundsen, then he hid it well.

More serious was the assertion that he used the same key to an understanding of all his subjects. He presented them as mediocrities or, to be more precise, mediocrities in every area except one. One could, therefore, be tempted to say that he modelled them on himself. Every one of them had a unique gift for which they found a special use. In Amundsen's case it was his stubborn, obsessive efforts to learn by experiment—even to the extent of wearing in a new pair of expedition boots by walking up and down Karl Johans gate in them; an almost alarming determination when it came to acquiring as much knowledge as possible about how to survive in snow and ice, in extreme cold. As I say: Roald Amundsen was a champion when it came to doing his homework. Without this, no Norwegian flag at the South Pole.

For what it is worth, I think it would be truer to say that Jonas Wergeland did not create these people in his image, but that he did try to give himself some hope, by depicting his heroes in the way that he did. If there was any truth in his portraits of Amundsen and the others—well, then there was hope for him, too. Jonas Wergeland wished, in other words, albeit latently perhaps, to create, or attempt to recreate, himself through the images of his subjects. In any case, he saw no point in celebrating a person who had everything going for him and achieved his goal. There was, however, good reason to salute someone who, despite their limited abilities, succeeded in conquering a corner of an unknown world. The message Jonas Wergeland wished to convey was a hopeful one: one, just one, great thought can be enough. One single, unusual thought—and you can do something that no one has done before.

In the short run, though, no one was thinking along such lines. Since the Amundsen program was sent out during the winter, people were too busy rushing out into the snowdrifts. All over Norway courses in igloo building were suddenly being arranged. The *Evening News* did a piece on a hardy family with young children who had lived in a snow-hole for a full week. Jonas Wergeland himself could confirm that there had never been so many ice-fishers on the lakes around Oslo—it was, as he said in an interview, as if the Norwegians had suddenly discovered that they were Eskimos at heart.

Midpoint of the World

I still refuse to accept that this cannot be done, Professor, for when Jonas Wergeland stood there with his finger on the trigger, aiming straight at Margrete's heart, he was still thinking, upset though he was, about the minutes immediately prior to this, when he had seen her sitting with a golden orange in the vacuum between the flickering light of the television and the fading light outside the window, dark-blue with a yellow band at the bottom; he stood there watching the way she contemplated the orange, as if she got more out of the thought of the wonder that it represented, than he got out of a whole World's Fair; and it is then that he plucks up his courage and says he has to talk to her, and he tries not to say it but says it anyway: "Are you still having an affair with Axel?"—and he thinks she hasn't heard him, thinks she is too busy watching the television, and "Thank heavens" he thinks, but then she gently puts down the orange and she gets up, and she stands there in his dressing-gown, his dressing-gown, and she looks deep into his eyes before saying: "What do you mean?"—a question so arrogant that he starts yelling, and although she is obviously trying to control herself, she is unable to bite back the short laugh he heard for the first time when the ice palace came tumbling down on Steinbruvannet, and he has to scream at her, don't stand there and deny it, don't you bloody dare, you whore, because somebody had told him, she'd been caught in the act, don't fucking stand there and think you can fool me, because he knows, dammit, he had met someone who knew the whole story, he says and feels the pistol burning a hole in his pocket, a pistol he had had absolutely no intention of using but which all at once is burning a hole in his pocket, suddenly telling him that he might end up pulling it out anyway, at any moment, in fact—a possibility he could never in all his life have conceived of when he packed his case and left for Seville.

Why did Jonas Wergeland travel? He traveled in order to find the midpoint of the world: an anachronistic objective, of course, since a search for such a midpoint presupposes a belief that the world is flat.

Nonetheless—when he reached Seville he was tempted to declare that he had found it, for here, on an island in the middle of a river, the whole world truly had converged.

And it was not only a midpoint; it was also a personal crossroads. As he sat high in the air in the little monorail—a touch of science fiction there—which carried visitors to the different parts of the exhibition site, he saw how the three pieces from his somewhat wide-ranging education finally slotted together to form a whole, because here the astronomical and the architectural aspects came together—more strikingly than in Jaipur—in a cluster of buildings of every conceivable style, many of them futuristic, standing shoulder to shoulder and making the whole island look like some alien planet. As for television, his third pursuit: the most notable feature of this planet were the screens, everywhere you looked there were screens; one could have been forgiven for thinking that life itself, all communication had been transferred onto gigantic video screens. The theme of Expo '92, invoking the very spirit of Columbus, was nothing less than "The Age of Discovery." And how apt that was, because Jonas Wergeland had at long last found his *terra incognita* and was now about to conquer it.

To anyone who knows Jonas Wergeland's merits, it may seem obvious that everything in his life was bound to lead him here; Jonas Wergeland was made to visit—or no, not visit: understand, enjoy—a World's Fair. He darted about like a child at the biggest funfair on earth, stood spellbound before the massive, thousands of years-old block of ice from Antarctica on display in the Chilean house, took the elevator to the top of Japan's massive wooden building to gaze in wonder at a man demonstrating the art of origami, followed the stream past the tableau depicting a Bedouin tent in the Saudi Arabian pavilion, sat in the dark, feeling very small, watching a laser show at the bottom of a square well in the French cube—and all the time he was on the lookout for inspiration, something that would help him to move on, the way that the Asian music which Debussy heard at the World's Fair in 1889 had shunted him onto another track.

Jonas was genuinely proud of the Norwegian pavilion, the main section of which was shaped like a pipe; inside this pipe a stunning multimedia show was presented: sounds and images, all based on the theme of water—the element from which all of Norway's riches derived: fish, waterfalls, shipping, oil. Downstairs, on a screen set up at the crossover point between the shop and the restaurant, highlights from Wergeland's own series on Norwegian heroes, including Roald Amundsen, were run non-stop. A foreign magazine compared the Norwegian pavilion to a jewelry box, and in this box, the journalist wrote, the television art of Jonas Wergeland was unquestionably the pearl.

But Jonas was actually here to work. He was doing a program on the public's reaction to the Norwegian exhibit—already in the can, for example, he had an impassioned interview with a French lady, found looking at sweaters in the souvenir shop, who was very disappointed, truly shocked in fact, to find no sign of anything by Per Spook: "Norway's greatest living artist" as she said. Jonas was also working on a framework for the program and found it only natural to take water as his theme here, too; to look at the way in which water was used throughout the exhibit: from enormous globes cloaked in a mist of droplets and water running in cascades down the walls, to man-made lakes and canals and fountains of every description—possibly the most memorable feature of the entire Expo, certainly for a Norwegian, a "dipper"—a bird of the falls.

The program pretty much made itself, so Jonas had plenty of time to look around, had never felt so good; he was filled with an exhilarating feeling of being in command, of really ruling the world, embracing the earth as if it were his boyhood globe. He saw absolutely nothing of Seville itself, not even the cathedral; he spent all of his time, when not asleep, on La Cartuja, the island in the middle of the river, an artificial, optimistic universe where he could flit from pavilion to pavilion, from gallery to gallery, from café to café, take in a spectacular show every evening—without his feet, as it were, ever touching the ground. At one point he woke up—out of a trance almost—to discover that the film crew had left Seville, that he was on his own, that for several days he had been roaming around, so busy just trying to see and experience a mere fraction of all the things there were to see and experience; he ate in the pavilions of the various countries, in restaurants serving national dishes, drank in the bars, was in the process of turning into a doped-up Ulysses in the land of the Lotophagi. My old neighbor Samson was right, he thought, one evening when he was sitting with a dry martini in front of him, scanning the scene outside the windows of the Belgium pavilion's stylish bar, as if surveying continents: nowadays you really can travel round the world in a matter of seconds.

Then, one day, right outside the hall housing the Age of the Future exhibit, he was stopped by a tall, majestic figure with an almost unsettlingly keen gaze—the word that automatically popped into Jonas's head was "chief." "Jonas," this person said. "I don't believe it, it really is you, Jonas Wergeland Hansen," said the man standing right in front of him. Jonas was totally at a loss, did not even try to hide it. And who should it be but Ørn, Ørn-Henrik Larsen. Not Little Eagle now but Big Eagle and a company director, head of a well-known firm, Jonas immediately recognized the name, a company dealing with satellite telecommunications, a pioneering concern, constantly cited as one of the leading lights of Norwegian industry. Ørn had, in the end, lived up to his name; it struck Jonas that he was looking at Norway's answer to Akio Morita, the founder of Sony. "We're in the same boat, you and I," Ørn said jokingly or perhaps more in an effort to be pleasant. "We are today what Norsk Hydro was at the beginning of the century, with its nitrogen production. We both create assets out of thin air: out of nothing, so to speak." He stood there smiling, though with no great warmth. "We've become the lords of the airwaves," he said, giving Jonas a friendly pat on the shoulder, or not so much a friendly pat as a nice way of saying that he had to be getting on, he had a lot to do, they were taking part in the exhibition.

What he did not say—having had his fingers burned before—was that he had built up a new stamp collection, an assemblage of Norvegiana so fine it could have been put on display in the Norwegian pavilion. The pride of the collection was a stamp from Chad, depicting Jan Egil Storholt, gold medallist at the 1976 winter Olympics. From Chad. And there may have been a connection here. For surely it is no less logical for the poverty-stricken inhabitants of Chad to be treated to the sight of Jan Egil Storholt's mysteriously crouching figure on their envelopes—a skier, in the heart of hottest Africa—than for a company in Norway to become world-leaders in satellite communication.

His meeting with Ørn-Henrik shook Jonas awake. It was time to head for home, but first he had to go to Cordoba, because Margrete had been adamant that he should not leave that part of Spain without having seen La Mezquita, the magnificent mosque in that city. So the very next day he took the train to Cordoba. I could do with a couple of hours in some quiet backwater, he thought to himself, a bit of peace after all the hurly-burly.

There wasn't to be much peace or quiet, though. Even as he was strolling through the arcade, alongside a garden thick with orange trees, he had the feeling that something was going to happen, that the time of reckoning, as they say, had come. A debt was about to be called in. He walked through one of the doors and promptly found himself in the vast expanse of the mosque's prayer hall. It was dim inside, with surprisingly few people around. Slowly he ventured further in, fascinated, the very sight taking his breath away. No two pillars were the same, but from a distance, in the half-light, they looked identical. And they were all linked to one another by double horseshoe arches decorated with light and dark rectangles, as if to illustrate that everything is connected, in at least two ways. This is the midpoint, he instantly thought. This is the midpoint inside me. He was surrounded by invisible mirrors, an endless succession of possible duplications stretching in all directions. He knew right away that he was going to go astray in here—not in the sense of losing his way but of losing himself. Or, as it is written: losing his soul.

And yet he went on, proceeding step by step into something which seemed more and more like a subterranean chamber, an enormous basement, as if Expo '92, that megalomaniacal manifestation of the five hundred years of civilization since Columbus, was the surface and this was the bottomless pit below it, an empty grave, a black hole, a place fraught with mirages, illusions, temptations, things beyond understanding, things no invention could ever encompass or put a name to, a place which forced one to see that in the course of a life a person merely conquered air, wind and nothing, that all the things one thought represented expansion, in fact constituted contraction.

He had the constant feeling that he was not alone, that a shadow was following close on his heels, lurking behind the pillars. He reached a point where the sense of gazing into infinity became overwhelming, where the symmetry of the pillars made his head spin, and the light threatened to go out altogether. I've been here before, he thought, it's the bomb shelter all over again. At that same moment he felt an unseen hand squeeze his testicles. He turned and saw a figure standing facing him, just a step away, strangely familiar and yet indistinct. "Who are you?" Jonas asked, thinking for a moment that he recognized this person, caught the glint of a gold tooth, but then the face changed to that of someone else he knew and then to yet another face, which again changed, and so it went on until the figure had once again merged into the shadows and Jonas relaxed, sure that he had been seeing things. Just then a voice sounded from the darkness, like the hiss of a reptile—if, that is, it was not simply some incidental noise, something to do with the acoustics which led him to hear what he wanted to hear, just like a radio play: "I know something you ought to know," the voice said, or what he thought was a voice.

Standing there, in what had once been a mosque, a massive Moorish edifice, Jonas had a vision, not of light this time, but of darkness, as if a stream of black ink had come surging towards him and eventually engulfed him. He was overcome by the very opposite of what he had always striven for, felt something radiant and adamantine inside himself, his diamond, turning into graphite, black and terribly friable. Looking back on it, he would not be able to recall what language they spoke or how long the conversation lasted, nor indeed whether he had actually spoken, whether there had been a conversation at all, not that it mattered, as long as he got the message, and in a nutshell the message was that Margrete was still having an affair with Axel Stranger, that no matter what Jonas thought, they had not broken it off.

He was stunned. Thought of Axel whom he had knocked senseless a year before, or tried to knock senseless at any rate. In spite of that, thanks to Axel's bigheartedness, or what Jonas saw as bigheartedness, they had managed to reach a sort of reconciliation, become friends again—to the point, at least, where they would call one another now and again. But the moment those words were spoken, whispered, hissed, among the pillars, inside his head, Jonas knew that they were true and that he had suspected it all along; he would never be able to keep them apart and not only that: Axel was more worthy of Margrete than he was, they made a good pair, they were, as they say, made for each other; the whole Expo, all of the world's advances and civilization were nothing but a joke compared to that brutal fact and no magnificent cultural achievements could rid him of the primitive feelings that raged inside him, there, in the gloom, among those rows of pillars in Cordoba. He had had to come all this way, to the midpoint of his flat world, before the penny finally dropped: Margrete preferred someone else. He could accept that, as others might do. But he did not accept it. Would not accept it. He stood in the shadows, surrounded by a stupefying, neurosis-inducing array of pillars, as if he had gone astray in a forest of mirror-images, had got lost inside himself, and he noticed that he was seething inside—was not even surprised to find that he welcomed back this state of demented fury like a long-lost friend. He looked round about him; saw the rows of pillars extending in all directions. These, he thought, these are not pillars, they are bars, this is my dwelling-place from now on.

And here I too have reached a point, Professor, where it pains me—more than you could ever know—to have to admit defeat, because until now, till this very second indeed, I have hoped against hope that Jonas

Wergeland's stories, when told in this carefully worked out sequence, would lead somewhere else—rather as if, by taking a different path through the labyrinth, one could avoid coming face to face with the monster at its heart. Or as if, by allowing a child to find a pearl in an oyster, you could prevent a lump of ice from falling off a roof years later. I have always believed that it must be possible to tell the same stories in a different order and thus arrive at a different ending, just as evolution would produce quite different beings were it to start all over again, from the beginning, even when working with the exactly the same raw material. I still think it is possible—but it is beyond my powers. Forgive me. I have done what I could to prevent a murder.

So it is with anything but a light heart that I force myself to continue, to say that the flight home was a nightmare, that even a few drinks on the plane could not dampen Jonas Wergeland's inner turmoil. His head was not a head; it was a ball of snakes, or a tangle of high-voltage cables, more like. In his mind's eye all he could see was Margrete and Axel, Axel and Margrete, not only locked in steamy sexual embraces but also deep in intimate conversations, yes, that more than anything else, their well balanced discussions, their laughter, their total identification with each other's thoughts, their mutual admiration. He could not stop shaking in the taxi from Fornebu to Grorud, asked to be set down at the station so that he could collect his thoughts, collect himself, while walking the last couple of hundred yards up Bergensveien. With his suitcase in tow he strolls slowly through the landscape of his childhood, with a memory at every step, and the air smells of spring, the evening is mild and coltsfoot glows on the grassy banks, and he walks more and more slowly, and when he catches sight of the Villa Wergeland sitting under Ravnkollen's brooding granite face, he has no sense of coming home, only of facing another long journey—because, he thinks or fears, all journeys begin with a death. But still, despite the terrible clenching of his testicles, he rings the bell with that same old feeling that a cable is about to snap, that he is about to plummet into the abyss, that the dream he had in Cape Town all those years ago is about to come true after all.

And when no one answers the door he feels relieved, steps inside, reads a letter, listens to a bit of a CD of Bach fugues before Margrete comes in and all hell breaks loose, inside him I mean, and he goes into the bedroom, then into the workshop, where he picks up the pistol, then back to the living room where she is sitting watching TV, and Jonas Wergeland stands there and looks at her hefting an orange in her hand, while his life falls apart, and that is why he has to spit out that accusation about Axel, that he knows about them, and what makes him snap, the thing that is to have such fatal consequences is that, instead of admitting it, or swearing it isn't true for that matter or dissolving into floods of tears, she gets to her feet and asks him a question, and then he has to bawl her out because she pretends not to know what he's talking about, but still he does not become really mad, his brain doesn't really cloud over, until she is standing right in front of him, in his dressing-gown, his dressing-gown, giving him that look, and naturally she doesn't say anything about being tired of his being away so much, tired of his selfish lack of consideration, or that she wants a divorce, she just stands there looking at him, her eyes bore into him, and he has no trouble reading the message in them: "You are not worthy of me," they say, "You don't deserve me," they say; she casts a swift glance at the television screen then fixes her eyes on him again, eyes which tell him, which have always told him, that he might be able to fool the whole of Norway but not her, because she knows, has always known, who he is, that only a couple of simple dodges, a couple of twists, separate his conquest from his mediocrity. But she says nothing. Merely stands there looking at him, and this makes him even more furious or bewildered or downright sad. And suddenly Jonas knows what it is, why he has to kill her, it's got nothing to do with jealousy, not jealousy at all, it's something else; he has simply tricked himself into thinking it was jealousy, because underneath that there lay something dreadful, something appalling that he hadn't thought of, or certainly never been plagued by since that day, at the age of fifteen, when he was "converted" in Grorud Church; it's not the idea of losing Margrete to another man that is driving him insane, it is the loss of his own illusion of being extraordinary, an illusion which—he sees this now—does not rest on his success in television but on one thing and one thing only: her. Because any man with whom Margrete Boeck chose to share her life was, by definition, special; he was bound to be different. Without her he stood revealed as something other than what he imagined himself to be. He could not stand it: first to seduce, to conquer, an entire nation and then nonetheless to see himself stripped bare, to stand naked in all his vacuity before his wife, the woman he loved, the only person he really wished to conquer; he was a conquistador who had won everything, then suddenly found himself confronted with a culture which he did not understand and which he therefore had to destroy, and so he had to disguise his rage, his terror, as something more probable—like jealousy.

And as the light died outside the window, he was overcome, or blessed, he thought, by the necessary seconds of black hate. Seconds when a switch was turned off and everything went dark, seconds when anything could happen. With a hate so fierce that it shocked him, he grabbed her by the arm and pushed, almost threw her to the floor, causing her head to crash into the brick wall with a dull, metallic thud, like the sound of a tin can being squeezed; she had been totally unprepared, lay in a heap on the floor with a bloody graze on her forehead, lay for a long time with her eyes closed before at last she got up, stood facing him with an air of defiance, stood with her eyes closed, stood there swaying, only semiconscious, and he was glad she kept her eyes closed, he knew he couldn't shoot her if her eyes were open; and he pulled out the pistol, cocked it and took aim and seeing her standing there in his dressing-gown it was like pointing the gun at himself, and he curled his finger round the trigger, feeling that all the threads of his life came together here, in the sickle of the trigger, and that they were pulling it back, and he knew that whatever his motive in doing it, this act, firing this gun, would be the last, irrevocable proof of his abortive originality: taking the easiest way out, a pistol, killing his wife, one of the eternal clichés in life and in crime; and yet one cannot rule out the possibility of a little method in his madness, because he may have guessed, at that moment, that while everything else he had conquered, his status as a television genius, would eventually be torn to pieces, this, this monstrous act and the circumstances surrounding it would assure him, his name, a place, at least as a footnote, in the history of Norway for all time.

And I, Professor, I feel no urge to gloat, I feel only sorrow because I have failed, and because Jonas Wergeland did not understand that a man could embody elements which seemed to be mutually exclusive: did not understand that his own achievement, the fact that he had stretched his own meager abilities, done something brilliant with them, lifted himself up by his bootstraps, and by so doing had given hope to a lot of people, to all of us who would like to do great things with our ordinariness; I can only apologize for the fact that it should end here—a whole life spent in becoming a conqueror, and all he wants to conquer is a dead body, the corpse of the person whom he has fought hardest to hold onto: Jonas Wergeland pulls back the trigger and out of the corner of his eye he searches for the light outside the window, that band on the horizon, that unspeakably beautiful, last gleam of light before everything goes dark.

Purpose

And as he readies himself for the recoil, the bang, the big bang, it occurs to him that this trigger is not necessarily the consequence of a whole life, a hunt for the buttons, the switches, that set things in motion—that, if he pulls it back far enough, it might instead be the starting-point for a new world, another life. This is where it all began, he thinks, this is the cause of everything that has gone before. He was standing not at the end, but at the beginning.

He had found himself in a similar situation, though he did not know it, that day when he stumbled out of the last piano lesson before Christmas, convinced that his life was over, even though time went on passing and his body was dragged along a road by what seemed like a chain of seconds. His shoulders were hunched, he felt as though he was running the gauntlet between trees full of mocking great tits; lowered his head against the snow that was falling softly and heavily, flakes that felt like lead. He had spoken to Fru Brøgger about the Pupils' Evening, when he had played "Dragon Sacrifice," and she had given him a little lecture in which she had very gently, but nonetheless ruthlessly, exposed him: showed him that his new ideas were actually pretty old. He was beaten before he could even begin. So now he was plodding home, fifteen years old but feeling burned out, and yet—to challenge the standard conceptions yet again—the following story need not result from an event in the immediate past, that Pupils' Evening when he had "failed", it could just as easily be the outcome of the account you have just heard, Professor, of the return from Seville or, if you will, of the whole network of stories I have told so far.

Jonas had the urge to go up to the granite quarry where once, at the sight of two stupid snakes, he had been tempted to believe that he had it in him to do something extraordinary—as though he had suddenly pulled a king's sword out of a stone; he would sit up there and let himself be covered by the falling snow, lose himself in all that whiteness. He was a dwarf. Just before his confirmation he had inherited a very smart suit from his cousin, one of the Brothers Grimm, but when he tried it on it almost drowned him—everyone had just about died laughing. That was how he felt now: he did not have the stature to fit his ambitions. He might discover gunpowder anew. Or reinvent the paperclip. Or the cheese-slicer. That was about all a Norwegian could manage. That or poor imitations. On the Norwegian border sits a huge, invisible transformer, he thought: a transformer that converts great, high-voltage concepts into small, manageable ideas, the sort we can cope with. He walked along with his head bowed, through the flock of great tits, kicked a chunk of ice so hard that he hurt his toes. Wrong, he thought, or a voice inside him screamed: if there's a transformer then it's inside me.

Only one thing could save him: if this longing to create something unique were to die inside him, if his aspirations sank to the level of his abilities. Then the problem would be solved and he could live a happy life, a normal life, just a face in the crowd.

The snow came tumbling down as if to order: it was almost Christmas Eve. Enormous white crystals transformed the whole of Grorud into a pretty Advent calendar. Jonas trudged up to the church to see if his father was there, he needed a bit of comforting. Or to hear some Bach—it came to the same thing. But his father wasn't there, and the parish clerk was on his way out. Jonas decided to wait. "My dad's bound to be here soon," he said. "Otherwise I'll just shut the door after me." But his father didn't come. Jonas plodded upstairs to the balcony, stopped in front of the organ, eyed the instrument. As a little boy he had had the idea that the organ was a dragon, that the ornamental pipes were metal wings that might start flapping at any minute and fly off with the whole lot. A dead dragon, he thought now. Somebody killed it before I could get there.

Almost inadvertently he lifted some sheet music off his father's pile: Rikard Nordraak's "Purpose" from Mary Stuart. They played it at weddings, he knew, so why not at a funeral too. He sat down on the bench and set the music up in front of him. He switched on the organ and heard the air rushing into the pipes. There was something invigorating about this. As if the organ meant to revive him. Fill him with oxygen. His father had explained to him how the organ was really a huge wind instrument. The sound was made by air vibrating. "Playing the organ is like steering a full-rigger," his father always said—then he would place his hands on the keys: "Listen, Jonas! Can you feel the wind filling the sails?" To Jonas, it seemed more like making contact with a mighty spirit. When Daniel told him, after he started studying theology, that the Hebrew word for "spirit" was the same as the word for "wind," Jonas was not surprised, he had known it all along.

He started to play; played Nordraak's beautiful "Purpose" from the sheet music and felt something happen. As he played, as he changed the registration, allowing more and more voices to chime in with the surging music, as he got to grips, what is more, with the booming bass notes, working the pedals—it was easy using the pedals in this piece—he could hear how grand it sounded, how impressive. It reminded him of an experience he had had in the attic on Hvaler, with the harmonium, when the octave couplers had been engaged, and the keys had been pressed down without him touching them. It had been like having a spirit playing alongside him. For a while, sitting at the organ in Grorud Church, his feeling of transparency left him. Something about this instrument, the exultant *tutti* effect, the tremendous cascades of sound created at the touch of a finger, convinced him that he was better, greater, than he was. And he knew that this had to be the solution: to find a niche in life, a job, a business, in which he would have access to something similar to the organ, an instrument which could, as it were, inflate his ideas, in such a way that his thoughts, simple though they might be, would seem astounding, would touch people's hearts like the sea of notes now encircling him, making the hair on the back of his neck stand on end.

I do not know whether I need to say this, Professor, but there is at least a chance that it was here, on this organ bench, that Jonas Wergeland laid the foundations of the career you have seen unfold on the television screen. If, for Haakon Hansen, the organ was a full-rigger, for Jonas Wergeland, it was more like a lifeboat. Because, in the same way as the organ, television presented the most wonderful demagogic opportunities—for manipulation, for trickery even. Although he would never have said so, and although he was genuinely proud of his programs, this thought did sometimes occur to Jonas, particularly when he was sitting at the main control desk in the NRK studios—he found it ominously reminiscent of sitting at the console of an organ.

But as he sat there, a fifteen-year-old, at the organ in Grorud Church, still bursting with the loftiest ambitions of his life, he would not—could not—accept it: the possibility of another strategy, that is. The longer he played, the more the granite crystals of the church seemed to oscillate with the music, the walls positively vibrating, the less the thought appealed to him. It's all a big sham, he thought grumpily. He could well see why the organ had been called the Devil's Instrument. To sit here playing "Purpose" as if he were a whole orchestra wasn't true originality. He was still a performer, not a creator.

With a discordant crash he stopped playing and switched off the organ, in panic almost, as if wishing to strangle at birth the monster he had been coaxing into existence. He got up from the bench and pulled out the puck—the puck he sometimes removed from the lacquer casket and carried in his pocket, especially in wintertime. He was standing contemplating it, staring at the scratches on it, those illegible hieroglyphics, when he felt eyes on the back of his neck. He turned to look down the church but could see nothing but the eye of God on the large fresco behind the altar at the far end. The eye of God inside a triangle. Jonas looked at the puck; it crossed his mind that it was a pupil. That the puck was this black thing that he could see through.

Just then he noticed a figure breaking free of the altarpiece, the painting entitled "The Great White Flock," gliding out of the crowd and perching on the window-ledge overlooking one of the side-aisles, under the church's magnificent, new stained-glass window, its pride and joy—anyone who has read Martin Luther may well recognize the phenomenon: a wee devil sat there laughing at him, leering and thumbing its nose. Jonas knew what it was: a little Hansen devil. A monkey. A gnome who was telling Jonas that there was only one path open to him in life: to imitate others. To be a sham.

Jonas acted instinctively. And in fury. He hurled the puck at the figure with all his might—and remember, Jonas Wergeland really could throw, so the puck hit the tiny devil smack in the face, and not only that, it also hit the stained-glass window. The sound of tinkling glass went on for ages. Who would have thought one small puck could do so much damage; it looked as though the whole window had spilled out, like water, to make patterns in the snow, like the glitter they sprinkled on plaster Christmas ornaments. And it occurred to Jonas—horror-stricken though he was, conscious though he was of what a dreadful scandal, what sacrilege this was—that the tinkling of the glass had sounded like his ice palace when it came crashing down, that there was some connection here, a connection between everything that fell and everything that was created in the moment of that fall.

For at that same moment he hears the main door opening, hears someone enter the church beneath him, shocked voices, he peeps over the edge of the balcony, sees the vicar and the chairman of the parish council, with snow on their shoulders and the hats they hold in their hands. They look up, spot him. "Who's there?" they shout.

A second passes. A whole life is shaped in that moment. You always think you have years in which to plan your path in life, and then, in the time it takes to snap your fingers, the choice is made.

Because it is now, for the first time and with unmistakeable clarity, that Jonas feels that pressure on his spine, that pressure which was to have such a determining influence on him later in life—not least where women were concerned. And all at once he understands the reason for this: it was Gabriel who had activated it, the button Jonas once swallowed, made of dragon horn, when he had squeezed his back earlier in the autumn; or at least that could be the reason, but whatever the case, Jonas realized that it was a gift, that he had discovered an uncommonly sensitive spot within himself. Something which would alert him to crucial situations, moments when a distinctive pressure, a great potential, made itself felt: episodes which, when considered as a whole, over time, might show him how, and in which fields, he could, with his endowments, become a conqueror.

Jonas leans over the balcony, looks back and forth between the vandalized stained-glass window and the two adults standing in the central aisle down below. He knows he has to come up with a story. And not just any story. When he sneaked up to the big boys' den he got beaten up for not being a good enough liar. He knows he's going to be in trouble now too, if he doesn't think of something quick. That he will be thrown into a black pit, only this time he'll have to stay there for ever, for the rest of his life.

He had a couple of things to work with: he had a shattered window and a puck lying outside in the snow, and he had—he ran his eye around the church—the church silver on the altar, set out for the evening service. He remembered the year when Daniel had a chapter accepted for the *Children's Hour* Storybook. The idea was that you had to carry on the story from where the last chapter left off. Daniel had concocted the next part of what was a pretty corny story; he really laid it on thick. Jonas almost killed himself laughing at all the hilarious, over-the-top descriptions, the unbelievable coincidences, when Daniel read it aloud to him in their room. But on the radio, as the latest instalment of the *Children's Hour* Saturday Serial, with sound effects and good actors, it sounded great, almost feasible.

Jonas raced down the stairs and along the scarlet runner in the center aisle, as if he were treading the red carpet to a new career. He came to a breathless halt in front of the men—two powerful individuals who could have cause to suspect him of all sorts of misdemeanors.

"Who's this?" the chairman of the parish council whispered.

"Jonas Hansen, the organist's son," the vicar said.

"Jonas Wergeland," Jonas corrected him, taking his new name, his mother's, right then and there. The "W" he had inserted in fifth grade had now ripened into a whole name. A word. A future.

"Can you tell us what happened?" the vicar asked, pointing to the wall where the remaining stained-glass windows shone with an added, almost accusing, glow.

"I saw a man over there, a stranger. He was sneaking up to the chancel," Jonas said, nodding in the direction of the corner off the side-aisle, under the windows. "He looked like a burglar, and I shouted at him, but he didn't stop, he was heading for the candlesticks, so I threw the only thing I had handy at him, a puck, but it kind of went the wrong way and smashed the window instead, I'm sorry, I didn't mean to do it, but it did make the burglar turn and run, I'm really, really sorry . . ."

Pause. Rather a long pause. Both adults looked him in the eye. "Which way did he go?" the vicar asked.

That put him on the spot; he hadn't got this far in his thinking. "That way," he said, pointing to a door onto a corridor leading to one of the church's side entrances.

"But that door's locked," the chairman said.

"No, he ran through there," Jonas said, for some reason convinced that this was true. A pressure on his spine.

The vicar had already walked across to the door and out into the corridor. He came back.

The moment of truth.

"It's right enough, the door was open," he said. "And there are tracks in the snow."

Jonas could have fallen to his knees and given thanks to the person who must have forgotten to lock the door. And who had only just left. On the other hand, he had known it would be that way.

"It's a shame about the window, but I realize you must have been scared, I don't think anyone could blame you for doing as you did, although it's going to cost a fortune to have it repaired," the vicar said, gently running a hand through his hair.

Jonas stood on the red carpet, feeling the warmth spread from the top of his head right down to his toes, as if something, a leaden destiny, had melted and now offered the possibility of another form. Here before him were these two powerful men, pillars of the community, and they believed him: he had laid it on really thick, but they believed him. You do not conquer your uncommonness, it is granted you as a gift, he thought. At that moment, and even more in the days that followed—when, despite the breaking of the window, he was made out to be the savior of the day, a minor hero—Jonas perceived the chances that now lay before him. That this—rather than the sham of the organ playing—might be an alternative path, a way to survive. He had discovered the generosity of people's imaginations. Their willingness to believe him. And furthermore: that lying was not a sin, but a talent. In principle, at least. He gazed up at the organ in gratitude, as if it were a laboratory. He felt like a scientist who had drawn a blank but who, in the course of his experiment, or thanks to a by-product of it, had nonetheless spied a new, and perhaps even more revolutionary, possibility.

Because that is how it was: very simple elements, boldly interwoven, could open doors—in two ways. Inside people's heads. In the real world. Who was to say that somebody had forgotten to lock the side door? The way Jonas saw it, it could just as easily be the story that had opened it. Left its tracks in the snow. In fact, it really wouldn't have surprised him if the vicar had come back and announced that he had seen an angel, a real live angel.

Jonas went out to look for his puck in the fresh snow. Hunted for it as if it was an irreplaceable pearl. He found it at last, was so happy that he kissed it. He had known it all along: this puck was not a puck at all, it was a button, something he could press, mightier than the biggest organ. From now on he would be able to get away with just about anything. All he needed was a simple melody and the right instrument. It felt as though God was dead and anything went. He could conquer a whole world.

The Silk Road

The final, the ultimate, proof was granted him with his conquest of Margrete Boeck. Although, conquest is absolutely the wrong word. And as he lowers the pistol, not knowing whether he has shot or not, he thinks of life with Margrete.

What was it like, life with Margrete?

For a long, long time, life with Margrete consisted simply of lying in a big bed, in a nest of duvets and pillows and sheets which reminded Jonas of the atmosphere in his Aunt Laura's exotic flat in Tøyen, where her goldsmith's bench smoldered in the far corner of the living room. He would lie in this big bed, having his body stroked by Margrete's warm hands—when it wasn't the other way round and he was trying to stroke her skin, cover it with caresses, a skin that was never the same twice, a body whose rises and hollows were always changing, changing with different times of day, different times of the year, of life. Whenever he lay like this, running his fingers and the palm of his hand over Margrete's limbs, he thought of travels, of riches. One time when he was lying there, fondling her ankle, that exquisite spot, she asked him if he knew how many bones there were in the foot, and when he shook his head she answered herself: twenty-six. "That says something about how complex we are," she said. "And how vulnerable."

If there was one thing Jonas learned, or ought to have learned, from his very first second with Margrete, it was that love is not blind, but seeing. That love gives you fresh eyes.

It never ceased to amaze Jonas how Margrete could make him forget old habits, and hence memories too, so that each time they made love it seemed to him—no matter how unlikely this may sound—like the first time, or rather, like something new. And, perhaps an even greater miracle: she taught him, a man, to set greater store by those long interludes when they explored each other's skins than by the act itself. She helped him to see, or learn, that sometimes it can be better to touch a shoulder than a breast. And although Margrete could also wrap her arms around him, make love to him with a passion which almost frightened him, this gentle stroking of the skin was a pleasure above all others, a thrill which transmitted itself to the very smallest of cells. When Margrete laid her hand on his body and ran it over his skin from the sole of his foot to his crown, he understood what life was about: intensity, a heightened awareness of the moment, of his own breathing even, as if by placing her hands on his skin she put him into an unknown gear. It was a kind of education. "Be a vessel," she whispered to him again and again. "Be a vessel, not a sword; learn to take, Jonas."

And did he? Is it at all possible to sum up a life such as Jonas Wergeland's? Whatever the case, I hope that any assessment of this man will depend upon which story we place last, Professor. And might it not be—I ask you at least to consider the possibility—that there are other branches to this story, that what I am describing here forms the real starting point for Jonas Wergeland's future life?

So let us end, or begin again, with the years when they were living together in the ambassador's lavishly appointed apartment in Ullevål Garden City, in rooms painted in different colors, terracotta, ochre, cobalt: rooms as different from each other as the continents themselves, not least because, taken as a whole, they constituted a proper little museum of ethnography, filled as they were with objects from a goodly number of the earth's more far-flung cultures—even in the garden, moss-covered statues sat half-concealed among the shrubbery, as if the ambassador had attempted to recreate a corner of some overgrown temple. The bedroom was all white, right down to the sheets and duvet covers—a white broken only by a gold statuette from Thailand. Particularly during those first weeks after they—a student of architecture and a medical student—met one another again and entered into a new relationship, the bed in this room was their domain. In his mind Jonas called it the Silk Road. It was Aunt Laura who had first told him about the miracle of silk—about the silk worms and the way the silk was turned into soft, smooth, shining fabrics—and about the Silk Road, the name given to the trade route, the historic link, between Asia and Europe. And once when he was sitting in his aunt's flat in Tøyen, lolling back against soft cushions, surrounded by oriental rugs and the glimmer of gold and silver from her workbench, she had suddenly said: "The road that runs from a woman to a man, that too could be called a Silk Road."

And only now, years later, as they lay there in a white room, blessed by a golden idol, lay stretched out alongside one another in a big bed, like two continents, like west and east, did he see what she meant—for with them too, it was as much a matter of exchanging gifts, just as cultures swap inventions, ideas, historical knowledge. This was what Margrete meant when she whispered to him: "Be a vessel, learn to take." And he took. For many weeks he lay beside her in bed and took from her the equivalent of fine porcelain, peaches, rich fabrics and strange spices, while he gazed at her eyebrows, which looked as though they had been brushed with black ink by a Japanese master of calligraphy. And in the same way he tried as best he could to give, to shower her with the equivalent, from his world, of grapes, walnuts, metals and fragile glass. Because what they were doing as they lay there side by side, with their fingers wandering like caravans over the landscapes of their bodies, was telling stories; for hour upon hour they took it in turns, as all lovers do, to tell each other stories from their lives. A good many of Jonas's were about Buddha, about how clever he was at imitating people on the television, not to mention his repertoire of ABBA songs, and there was a lot about Daniel: the account, for example, of the bizarre incident which had converted him to Christianity; and Margrete told him about her parents, about her mother's unhappy life, or about the time when she, Margrete, supported herself for a whole year in Paris by doing street theater: stood on an upturned rubbish bin outside Saint Germain des Prés, dressed as Buster Keaton and doing a doleful but hilarious imitation of him which elicited both roars of laughter and money from passers-by; or about the walking tour she made, not in the mountains of Norway, but of China, not from hut to hut, but from temple to temple. She told him, not least, about all that she had read, all the books, and when Jonas asked her why she read so much she replied: "Because I'm lonely, and reading helps me learn to live with my loneliness."

On one such evening, when Margrete had just finished a long story about the International School in Bangkok, Jonas leaned back, his body heavy with contentment: "Do you think that one day's happiness could save a whole life?" he asked.

"Yes," said Margrete. And a moment later: "Just as a second's hate can destroy it."

He didn't understand what she meant, that she may have been trying to forestall something, make him see that any fruitful transaction can be ruined the minute one of the parties starts to feel dissatisfied and decides they would prefer to be in charge, become a conqueror, have the upper hand.

One evening, one bright evening when the scent of spring was drifting through the open bedroom window, after he had told her about the strange fish and the oyster he hadn't opened, she got out of bed and disappeared for a couple of minutes. When she returned she held out a clenched fist to him. "Open it," she said. "Pretend it's an oyster."

Jonas prised open her fingers, one by one, really had to work at it, because she truly seemed to be trying to make her fist as hard to open as an oyster shell. In the palm of her hand lay a pearl, a small, slightly irregular, natural pearl. She had found it in Japan when she was a little girl. "Here take it, it's yours," she said. Jonas looked at it, noted the way in which the light was both absorbed and reflected by it, sat gazing at it for ages, with his throat constricting and his lips tightening. "It may not be perfect, but it is a real pearl," she said.

Jonas looked and looked. The pearl seemed to be made of white silk. But to Jonas, the incredible thing was not the pearl itself but the thought of the steady, painstaking process by which the oyster converts the foreign body—strokes it, if you like—into a pearl.

"It takes a long time," Margrete said, as if reading his mind. "It takes a long time to become a person."

The next day, back at his bedsit, Jonas unearthed his old lacquer casket, the casket which he had once found in a safe and which had been carted along with him every time he moved, like a portable altar. It contained just two things: a silver brooch and a puck. Two sacred relics. When he placed the pearl between them, luminous and clear, but at the same time impenetrable, it became a multiplication sign between two unknown quantities, an "x" and a "y," but somehow this tiny white sphere brought about a massive increase in their combined import. He shifted the pearl around, tried every possible combination. When he placed it after the brooch and the puck it made him think of a full stop, a sign that his search was at an end; and when he set the pearl on top of the puck he observed how the white dot seemed to fertilize all the black, turning it into a totally different object. Jonas felt as though an entire past, a string of stories, had suddenly acquired a new and brighter character.

And it is on this same day, on his return to Ullevål Garden City, that it happens, as he is lying quietly, on a perfectly ordinary evening, it happens quite undramatically, the thing which on several occasions he thought he was on the track of, but which he now knows he was never on the track of, because it is now that it happens, while Margrete is stroking him, endlessly, reading his body intently and single-mindedly, the way she would read a book, running her hands all over him, caressing every single inch of his skin with her fingertips; it is at this moment that he experiences something so all-pervading that it would not be unreasonable to associate it with what, in his diary, Søren Kierkegaard described as an upheaval "which suddenly pressed upon me a new and infallible Interpretation of all Phenomena . . ."

And that night, on his way to the bathroom, naked, he passed the large mirror in the dim hallway and gave a start. He did not recognize himself. He met his reflection in the dark surface of the mirror and saw that his face had changed. And not only that: his face, the whole of his naked body shone with a kind of inner light. He knew what it was. An afterglow. A product of her love. It was something her hands had stroked into being in him. Because even when they made love he was more conscious of her hands than her vagina: the feeling when they had sex was that of being stroked, caressed, rather than a physical sensation of sliding in and out. He stared at his reflection, at his body, which seemed almost luminous, surrounded by a halo. Jonas stood in the dark hallway studying his own face in the mirror, smiled to himself, she had made him glow; and although he could not know that what he was actually witnessing here was the dawning of his career as a charismatic television personality, he did feel that the pressure, or the sum of all the instances of pressure, had at long last turned the carbon within him into diamond, that he was finally ready, and had the ability, to do something extraordinary.

Up to this point in my life, he thought, I've always been a hairsbreadth away from being a loser. Now I'm sure. I'm going to be a winner.

For a whole week Jonas puzzled over what he could give her in return, or no: not in return, in reply—something precious, beyond compare. He could not stop thinking about it, even when they were lying in the white room, running their hands over each other's skin. Then one morning she was lying there telling him about a secret place she had had as a child, down by the seashore among a cluster of solid, little pine trees, where she could lie surrounded by a confusion of scents, with the sound of the waves in her ears, looking at the way in which the pine-branches formed a fretwork screen against the sky—and as she was telling him this, it came to him what she should have, and that evening he went to fetch it and gave it to her, like Marco Polo presenting a gift to Kublai Khan: the latest dragon head he had carved, a copy of the Academic's fine head, his best attempt so far.

"What is it?" she asked with a smile that said she liked it.

"It's the start of a ship," he said. "I haven't got any further."

"Where do you mean to go on this ship?"

"To a new land," he said. "Somewhere no one else has ever been."

For a long time she lay saying nothing, stroked his back, working her way slowly upwards, over every vertebra, sending waves of well-being right through him.

"Do you know what I like best about you?" she said.

He didn't know what to say.

"Your weakness," she said. "You're so weak that you could seduce a whole nation."

Jonas both understood and did not understand what she meant. He was lying with his back to her, just about falling asleep. All of a sudden she wrote something on the tablet of his back with her finger, a swift, intricate flourish that induced a quite unique thrill of pleasure, a ripple that ran from the roots of his hair to the tips of his toes. "What was that?"

"The Chinese character for dragon," she said.

So the days passed. They lay closely entwined in bed, stroking each other and telling stories. And while they lay there, while she was talking, Jonas was considering her skin, and all at once he knew what it reminded him of—it reminded him of the layers of lacquer on his grandfather's old casket; he had the same sense of peering into something unfathomable, incomprehensible and yet infinitely beautiful; and as she went on talking, telling him about her life abroad, about university, about books, a realization gradually welled up inside him: Margrete was the golden fleece for which he had always been searching, she was what stood at the end of the longing that had taken vague form that time in the granite quarry. Everything else would only be stopping-off places on the way to this goal, even eventual celebrity, even international celebrity.

"I want to have a baby," Margrete said one day.

"Why?"

"So there'll be someone to be the saving of you when I'm gone."

"Were you thinking of going somewhere?"

"That's up to you."

This, these weeks, these years, were the fullest in Jonas Wergeland's life. He lay there clinging to that body, stroking that skin again and again, in circles, in spirals, happy because he realized that through her he had found a way which also led to possibilities so fundamentally different from any that had gone before; but still there was this hollow dread, a fear that it would not last, as if, for all their happiness, he could not help thinking that even Silk Roads can become overgrown.

Nevertheless, Jonas Wergeland gave up the chance of a completely different life, a different destiny when, on one of those quiet evenings, he placed both hands gently on her skin and said: "I've always thought that I would kill you if you left me. But now I know I would never do that. From this moment on my life begins anew."

About the Wergeland Trilogy

The Conqueror is the second book in Jan Kjærstad's "Jonas Wergeland Trilogy," a collection of novels that can be read independently of one another, each detailing the life of Jonas Wergeland and the tragic death of his wife Margrete from a different perspective. Individually each book is an accomplishment; taken as a whole, the trilogy is a masterpiece.

The other two books in the series are:

The Seducer: The first title in the series, this novel leads up to the moment that Jonas finds Margrete's body, and it tells the story of Jonas's ascent to fame. The identity of the narrator of this volume is revealed in *The Conqueror.*

The Discoverer: The final book in the trilogy, this novel takes place after Jonas has been released from jail, and it is narrated by Jonas and his daughter. In this novel, readers discover who assisted the professor in writing *The Conqueror.*

Jan Kjærstad made his debut as a writer in 1980 with a short story collection, *The Earth Turns Quietly*. The three books in the Wergeland trilogy—*The Seducer, The Conqueror,* and *The Discoverer* (also from Open Letter)—have achieved huge international success, and led to Kjærstad receiving the Nordic Prize for Literature in 2001. He has also received Germany's Henrik Steffen Prize for Scandinavians who have significantly enriched Europe's artistic and intellectual life.

Barbara Haveland was born in Scotland, and now lives in Denmark with her Norwegian husband and teenage son. She has translated works by several leading Danish and Norwegian authors, including Peter Høeg, Linn Ullmann, and Leif Davidsen.

Open Letter—the University of Rochester's nonprofit, literary translation press—is one of only a handful of publishing houses dedicated to increasing access to world literature for English readers. Publishing twelve titles in translation each year, Open Letter searches for works that are extraordinary and influential, works that we hope will become the classics of tomorrow.

Making world literature available in English is crucial to opening our cultural borders, and its availability plays a vital role in maintaining a healthy and vibrant book culture. Open Letter strives to cultivate an audience for these works by helping readers discover imaginative, stunning works of fiction and by creating a constellation of international writing that is engaging, stimulating, and enduring.

Current and forthcoming titles from Open Letter include works from Argentina, Austria, Brazil, France, Iceland, Lithuania, Spain, and numerous other countries.

www.openletterbooks.org